# Everyone
## wants to . . .
# BLESS
# THE
# CHILD

"A stolen child . . . an ancient curse . . . a cop, a priest, and a grandma for heroes. What a walloping good story!"

**—Gerald A. Browne, author of *18mm Blues***

"This book has really touched my heartstrings as both a mother and grandmother. And Cathy Cash Spellman is one hell of a writer!"

**—Maureen Stapleton**

"The windup rescue . . . is a wow . . . will probably materialize on the bestseller lists."

**—*Kirkus Reviews***

✻

"Horrifying. . . . As usual, Spellman's thorough research and her broad view of supernatural matters adds a distinct and impressive integrity to the story."

**—*San Diego County Preview***

*more . . .*

## Other Books by Cathy Cash Spellman

*Nonfiction*

NOTES TO MY DAUGHTERS

*Fiction*

SO MANY PARTINGS
AN EXCESS OF LOVE
PAINT THE WIND

# CATHY CASH SPELLMAN

# BLESS THE CHILD

## WARNER BOOKS

A Time Warner Company

We gratefully acknowledge the following sources:

"And life goes on forever like the gnawing of a mouse" from "Lament" by Edna St. Vincent Millay. Copyright 1921, 1948 by Edna St. Vincent Millay. "Life goes on; I forget just why" from "Ashes of Life" by Edna St. Vincent Millay. Copyright 1917, 1945 by Edna St. Vincent Millay. Both from *Collected Poems*, HarperCollins. Reprinted by permission of Elizabeth Barnett, literary executor.

Excerpt from "The Marrow" from *Collected Poems of Theodore Roethke*. Copyright © 1962 by Beatrice Roethke, Administratrix of the Estate of Theodore Roethke. Used by permission of Doubleday, a division of Bantam Doubleday Dell Publishing Group, Inc. By permission also of Faber & Faber Ltd.

The lines from "my father moved through dooms of love" are reprinted from *Complete Poems, 1913–1962*, by e. e. cummings, by permission of Liveright Publishing Corporation. Copyright © 1923, 1925, 1931, 1935, 1938, 1939, 1940, 1944, 1945, 1947, 1948, 1949, 1950, 1951, 1952, 1953, 1954, 1955, 1956, 1957, 1958, 1959, 1960, 1961, 1962 by the Trustees for the e. e. cummings Trust. Copyright © 1961, 1963, 1968 by Marion Morehouse Cummings. Reprinted also by permission of HarperCollins Publishers.

Excerpt from *Cults That Kill* by Larry Kahaner. Copyright © 1988 by Larry Kahaner. Reprinted by permission of Warner Books, Inc.

Excerpts from *Kabbalah* translated by Gershom Scholem. Copyright © 1974 by Kater Publishing House Jerusalem Ltd., P.O. Box 7145, Jerusalem, Israel.

WARNER BOOKS EDITION

Cover illustration by Michael Racz

Warner Books, Inc.
1271 Avenue of the Americas
New York, NY 10020

 A Time Warner Company

Printed in the United States of America

Originally published in hardcover by Warner Books.

First Printed in Paperback: April, 1994

10 9 8 7 6 5 4 3 2 1

*For all the poems read*
*Hurts comforted*
*Wisdom freely shared.*
*For all I know of courage, honor,*
*strength and generosity.*

*This book is for my wise and gentle father*
*Harry Cash*
*With more love and gratitude than mere words*
*could possibly express.*

# ACKNOWLEDGMENTS

Writing novels tends to be a labor of love, and not only on the part of the author. Remarkable people give of their expertise—very often with profound generosity. I sincerely hope that each who contributed so munificently to *Bless the Child* will understand both my gratitude, and my pleasure at having shared the journey with them.

Raphael and Linda Benaroya, whose loving and bountiful sharing of knowledge about Judaism, Israel, and many other intriguing subjects helped me enormously in the creation of both Abraham's and the Rebbe's characters.

Robin Beningson, who allowed me to glimpse the remarkable world of Antiquarians, and the treasures they know so much about.

Valerie and Joel Brodsky, whose photographic magic always makes my pictures so much better than reality.

Reverend Dudney Breeze, who enthusiastically discussed theology and the war between Good and Evil, while we practiced Wing Chun at 7:00 A.M.

Calasanz, my remarkable martial arts teacher, who made me realize how few limits there are on the human spirit.

Detective Sergeant William J. Cavanaugh, who not only advised me on police procedure, but showed me so clearly the complexity, tough-mindedness, code of honor, and all-round good-heartedness that would be the component parts of Malachy Devlin's character.

Earlyne Chaney, of Astara, whose extraordinary story of initiation in Ancient Egypt was both informative and inspiring, and helped greatly in my understanding of Maggie's esoteric training.

Jessica Gordon, who has done such a splendid job typing this very complex manuscript.

Robert Gottlieb, the first to believe in Maggie, Cody, and me—whose great talents have made everything happen for me and my work, in so special a way.

K. T. Maclay, whose great and loving knowledge of all things Brazilian gave Maria Aparecida both her name and her lovely spirit.

Mary Muryn, magical friend and mystic, whose extraordinary knowledge of, and connection to, the unseen world added so much to the creation and protection of *Bless the Child*.

Nanscy Neiman, my brilliant editor and friend, whose insights and contributions to both the word and the spirit of *Bless the Child* were made with grace, and genius, and love. I'm so very grateful.

Dr. Jeffrey Pascal, whose generous sharing of Chinese philosophy put many wonderful words in the mouth of Mr. Wong.

Josseph and Alice Rynear, dear friends and spiritual mentors, whose encyclopedic knowledge of both esoteric doctrine and Universal Truth, and whose personal loving kindness contributed far more than simple information to my tale. Their spirits shine in Ellie.

Dr. Francis Virgulak, whose firsthand knowledge of both the Catholic priesthood and exorcism were seminal to the creation of Father Peter's character. And whose generous sharing of experience and wisdom added a dimension and insight that was rare and beautiful.

Rabbi Mordecai Weiss, whose fascinating and enlightening conversations on both the letter and the spirit of Judaism and Kabbalah contributed greatly to my spiritual education.

Dr. Jeffrey Zimmerman, who not only advised on Maggie's Chinese treatment plan in my story, but kept my own energy in balance, as I worked.

I sometimes think my family lives my books as much as I—they give so much of love and help along the way.

Connacht Cash, my sister and mainstay, who is always the one to be counted on, the one who understands without words, the one who comes through with magic in the clinches. No loving thanks could possibly be enough.

Roe Callahan, who kept the architecture straight, as well as graciously reading and rereading manuscripts, until she could probably recite them.

Dakota, my granddaughter, without whom I never would have known just how much a grandmother could love a wondrous little girl.

This is a work of fiction. No individual
or organization in it is meant to be
confused with real life.

There is no Isis Amulet or Sekhmet Stone.

As far as I know.

# PART I
# THE
# WOMEN

In the beginning was Isis. Oldest of the Old,
She was the Goddess from whom all Becoming
Arose. She was the Great Lady, Mistress of the
House of Life. Mistress of the Word of God.
She was unique. In all her great and wonderful
works, She was a wiser magician and more
excellent than any other God.

**Thebes, Egypt**
*Fourteenth Century* B.C.

# CHAPTER 1

Maggie O'Connor set the burglar alarm with trembling hands and pounding heart. She turned the key in the lock of the little antiquities shop on Sixty-eighth and Madison that provided her livelihood and tried to regain control. But the memory of the voice on the phone had undone her completely.

Jenna, her daughter, had called. Jenna, rebellious, head-strong, hostile, and *missing* for the better part of two years. The urgent voice, not-quite familiar . . . the pain of memory seared in its almost childlike cadence . . . the brutal question marks of where she'd been, a punishing enigma. A fearsome kaleidoscope of visions had flooded Maggie at the sound. Jenna, the precious child she'd loved more than life—Jenna, defiant and unforgiving at one futile drug rehab after another—Jenna, the heroin addict, who'd cut your heart out for the price of her next fix. Maggie shook her head forcefully to clear it of unwanted images and flagged a taxi in the driving rain.

"I have to see you *tonight*, Mother," Jenna had demanded, a disembodied voice from nowhere. Was it fury or frenzy or desperation in the tone? "At the house. Six-thirty. For Christ's sake *be there!*" Then only the hum of the dial tone to evidence that a call had ever happened.

3

Where had it gone so wrong between them? Maggie pillaged her soul for the millionth time in search of answers. Where had all the love gone? Surely the exquisite little girl she remembered so vividly had loved her once upon a time. The child with the flashing mane of silver-blond hair and eyes like the Irish Sea, who'd held her hand and lisped out stories over cupcakes, had loved her.

Fourteen had been the incomprehensible year when the silver child had disappeared forever, and a sullen, defiant teenage changeling took her place. Fourteen, the year her beloved daughter had metamorphosed into something unlovely and unreachable. How many times after that had Maggie reached out to touch, only to have her hand bitten back by reproachful words and hostile accusations? "Her ears aren't attuned to your frequency, sweetheart," Jack, her husband, used to say, shaking his head in consternation. "It's the damnedest thing to watch, Maggie, but it's like she can't comprehend a word you say. It's probably just some stupid Freudian mother thing she'll grow out of. You'll see. We'll all laugh about it when we're old and gray."

Maggie caught her breath at the pain those words evoked. Jack's voice still vibrant in her ears . . . Jack's face still inviolate in her memory. Wasn't time supposed to heal all wounds? Wasn't the loneliness supposed to lessen?

Tears welled up and she bit them back. Now, they would never laugh together, never grow old, never understand why life had thrown them such an unconscionable curve. Jack was dead. Even if she still reached for him on the pillow in the long dark hours before dawn . . . even if she still held conversations with him in her head when she needed advice. Even if she sometimes fantasized that he gave it. Jack was gone.

At least he hadn't lived to see his little girl with track marks on her arm, selling her body on Eighth Street to get money for heroin. Maggie had borne that alone.

She tried to force her heart to a bearable staccato,

paid the driver, and turned her collar up against the steady slate-gray downpour. Maggie needed the comfort of home.

Jenna was slouched in the doorway with a bundle of clothing in her arms. Or that was what Maggie thought, until it cried.

"It's cold out here!" Jenna's voice was accusatory, as if Maggie made the weather. No greeting. No "I missed you, Mom. How have you been?"

"I came as fast as I could, sweetheart. I couldn't believe it was really you on the phone. I've missed you so damned much!" Maggie threw her arms around the soaking figure, and tried to control her hurt when Jenna wriggled free of the embrace.

Maggie managed the lock with unsteady fingers and reached inside for the light switch; tears were choking back all the words she knew she should be saying. She stared at the tiny being in Jenna's arms, struck dumb by the magnitude of so small a creature and all it presumed about the past and future.

"Aren't you going to say anything else, Mom! I thought you'd be glad to see us." Jenna, spare as a Communion wafer, stood in the foyer, shedding water like a drainpipe. Still angry, still unforgiving.

"I would have been glad to see you two years ago!" Maggie blurted as she shrugged off her dripping coat, then instantly regretted her outburst. *She's home*, she chided herself. That's all that matters. *She's alive*. Anything else we can fix.

"Of course, I'm glad to see you, sweetheart, I'm just overwhelmed by your really being here. I've dreamed of this moment so long! Oh, Jenna, I didn't know if you were alive or dead . . . I tried so hard to find you—a private detective, the police. But they said there wasn't a trace . . ." The words were only fragments, tiny abbreviations of the anguish suffered, the heartache stored forever in some private compartment of the heart.

Jenna wasn't listening anymore. Her eyes were darting around the room, casing the possibilities. A survivalist assessing the terrain.

"I'm hungry," she said, laying the baby on a chair, casually as a box from Bloomingdale's.

Maggie shook herself to dispel the sense of unreality, of unreasoned fear.

"The baby, Jenna. Is it yours?" Stupid question. *No, Mother, I found it on the subway.*

Maggie picked up the bundle tentatively, as if it were made of fairy wings. She moved the wet receiving blanket away from the fragile, wriggly lifeform and was startled by its breathtaking perfection.

"My God, Jenna. This baby is brand-new!"

"She's ten days old. The birth certificate is pinned inside the blanket. I figured you might need it for something."

Maggie looked up quickly, searching her daughter's face.

"I might need it? Why on earth would *I* need it?"

Jenna looked away, uninterested in the question.

"Is it okay if I get something to eat? I haven't eaten in a while. She's hungry too." Non sequiturs were the speech pattern of addicts, Maggie remembered, her stomach tightening at the thought. As if the brain only focused at random selections, like a CD player.

Maggie tried to quell her anxiety. She unwrapped the soggy blanket and gingerly extricated the tiny infant, pressing it to her heart. "Funny, but you never forget how to hold a baby, no matter how long it's been," she whispered, lost in the small warmth. "Fifty million years of biology, I guess." Jenna blinked at her mother, uncomprehending as a lizard on a rock.

Not certain what to do next, Maggie started toward the kitchen, tears dangerously close. "We can figure things out better on a full stomach . . ." she said quietly. Anything was better than standing there, stared at by wraithlike, unseeing eyes.

"What's your daughter's name, sweetheart?" she called over her shoulder, forcing cheer into the sound.

"Cody. I call her Cody."

Maggie smiled down at the infant, trying the name on her for size. "That's a beautiful name . . . I think it suits her. Is it from her father's family?"

The bedraggled girl spat her reply. "Look! I'm only here because I have nowhere else to go." The voice was strung out, on the verge of something.

Maggie took a sharp breath and tried again.

"I didn't mean to hurt your feelings, Jenna . . . it's just that I'm way out of my depth here. All I know is that I love you and whatever trouble you're in, we can fix it . . ."

The girl silenced her mother with an impatient gesture.

"*Listen* to me, Mom. I've got this baby. I can't take care of her. I have to leave her somewhere. She's your granddaughter for Christ's sake!"

Aghast, Maggie turned from the refrigerator, words spilling against her will. "You can't be serious, Jenna! You just *appear* after two years without a single word, and you mean to tell me you're only here to deposit your baby on my doorstep? That's absolutely outrageous! Where have you been? Why didn't you let me know you were all right? Where did this baby come from? If you need help, you know I'll help you . . ."

"I *need* a place to leave this baby," the voice insisted, relentless as sleet and twice as cold.

*This is really happening*, Maggie thought; the blood pounded so hard inside her, she felt dizzy. Instinctively, she clutched the baby tighter to her body and it began to whimper, an infinitesimal sound. *Oh, Jack, where are you when I need you?*

"She's soaking wet, Jenna," Maggie said softly, not knowing what else to say, wanting to calm the lunacy with something commonplace. "Do you have any diapers for her? I didn't mean to shout at you. Let's just stay calm and try to figure this out, okay?"

Jenna searched her mother's face, alert for nuance.

"On the sideboard in the foyer," she answered quickly, "there's a bag with diapers. I'll get them."

Maggie heard the wet sneakers squeak down the parqueted hall, and thought of other, better times. Then she heard the front door slam and knew that Jenna was gone.

Maggie sat in the old nursing rockèr she'd dragged up from the basement, and crooned to the infant in her arms. Irish Revolutionary ballads . . . the kind with twenty-seven verses, all of them emotional. She'd been singing softly, for over an hour, remembering, remembering . . . *And life goes on forever like the gnawing of a mouse*, Millay had said. A woman would know.

But, just looking at the baby was balm for the heart. The translucent eyes were closed in sleep, the tiny lips still wet with the formula she'd gotten at the corner drugstore. One tiny fist was wrapped around Maggie's finger in a grip that seemed permanent.

Only an hour ago, she'd felt wrung out by anger and the inexorable sense of failure that had flooded her in the wake of Jenna's departure. She'd sobbed out her frustration silently, as she rocked the baby—feeling as she had when Jack died, ravaged by forces outside her control. But none of that seemed remotely important now. The baby made it all curiously irrelevant. Cody was perfection. Cody was love. She deserved laughter, not tears. How could anyone not be grateful she existed in the world?

Maggie rose painstakingly and placed the sleeping bundle in the middle of her big bed, then turned out the light and climbed in beside her granddaughter, careful not to disturb. A crib would be needed tomorrow, and about a million other things . . . Lights zigzagged across the ceiling in an artful pattern and she watched them, grateful for the many quiet hours before morning.

She needed to think, not sleep.

And she needed to pray.

# CHAPTER 2

Maggie rapped sharply on the glass door of the shop she'd owned for ten years, and waited anxiously for Amanda Bradshaw to let her in. There was no traffic on Madison Avenue at 8:00 A.M., the usually bustling street seemed surreal in its serenity.

"Tell me that's *not* a baby in your arms!" Amanda's drawl was startled, concerned; she'd caught the haggard, sleepless look in Maggie's eyes. She was Maggie's store manager, but that didn't preclude the genuine friendship that had grown up between the two women over the years.

"You think *you're* surprised?" Maggie answered nervously, shrugging off her coat while juggling Cody. "Jenna materialized out of the rain, handed me this baby and vanished again. I've been up all night . . ."

"The baby was fussy?"

"No. *I* was fussy! My brain's on circuitry overload, Amanda. Where has Jenna been all this time? Is she still on drugs? Is she planning to come back? I feel like I've fallen down the rabbit hole, and found a baby at the bottom!"

Amanda's tall, lanky body always seemed to Maggie to move in a fluid medium of some indeterminate kind; a secret grace, born of generations of privilege, she supposed. The beautifully manicured hands now reached inside the receiving blanket gingerly, to uncover the baby within.

"Oh my, she's precious, Maggie. There's something almost luminous about her, isn't there? How on earth could anyone on drugs ever produce such an exquisite little peach?"

Maggie gazed at the tiny life in her arms and sighed. "I'm hooked on her already, Amanda. It doesn't take more than ten minutes to fall in love with her."

"And the charming Jenna?" Amanda probed, her lips tight with disdain. "What's her story?" She'd watched Maggie's desperate and relentless efforts to rehabilitate Jenna fall on barren ground too often to have illusions about the girl. One heroin addict in thirty-six is ever cured, the doctors said; she didn't think Jenna would be the one.

"Whatever it is, or was, I may never know. She's gone again."

"As in disappeared?"

Maggie nodded, drained. "She said she needed a place to leave the baby."

"And you're it?"

"I'm it."

"Well, now, that's a fine fish fry. And you're just supposed to leap into the breach, change your whole life around, and become Mother Cabrini?"

"I think that's the general idea."

Amanda's well-defined eyebrow lifted eloquently. "And that selfish little twit just reproduces like a hound dog and hits the high road? That must frost your petunias for fair, Maggie."

"Amanda!" Maggie answered, aghast. "I love Jenna! All I want to do is try to help her, but she keeps slipping away from me . . . She seemed really strung out last night. Desperate and all alone. I'm afraid even if we found her, she's not in any shape to take care of this little cupcake."

"And you are?"

Maggie stared at the baby for a long moment before answering. "I think so," she said hesitantly. "Isn't that crazy? I really think I could do it."

Maggie looked younger than her forty-two years, Amanda thought, despite the sleepless night. Her face was pretty, not beautiful, but the features had aged with charm, so that the youthful firmness of jaw had mellowed into simple strength, and the laughter in her eyes had somehow survived hardship and remained, so there seemed always to be a smile, trying to spring free. But there was sorrow, too, mostly veiled. It was a face that hid its private vulnerability and let the world see only generosity of intent.

Maggie searched her friend's eyes for understanding. "It's been so long since I had anyone who needed me, Amanda . . . anyone to truly love. It's hard to explain, but this little one and I already know each other in some special way."

The South Carolinian smiled indulgently. "But of course you do, darlin'. Why, you've been together at least twelve hours now."

Maggie groaned. "Oh God, I sound like a grandmother, don't I?"

"What a ghastly notion. We'll have to come up with another name for your condition. Why, you look young enough to be her mama, darlin' . . . lots of women have babies at your age."

Maggie smiled fondly at her friend's blarney. She'd hired Amanda because of her spectacular knowledge of antiquities and for her impeccable social connections that brought the crème de la crème of purchasers into the shop. But it hadn't taken long to discover the deeper, rarer qualities. The genuine good-heartedness, the bawdy sense of humor beneath the well-bred surface, the piercing intellect that could skewer a bogus thought, or object, with the same rapier skill.

"I've been thinking all night about how Fate makes you really lay it on the line sometimes, Amanda. No molly-coddling, no equivocation, just Who the hell are you, Maggie? It asks. My mother used to say, 'Character is who you are in the dark' and I'm beginning to understand what she meant."

Amanda leaned against the edge of a nineteenth-century table and smiled. "Well, darlin', we've had an acute excitement shortage around here for the past few months. I guess we're up to a little lunacy."

"I'm forty-two years old," Maggie went on earnestly. "That's far too old to raise a child. Jack's gone, and it isn't right not to provide a daddy for this baby. So there are big question marks here . . ." She hesitated, then plunged on.

"Since Jack died, and Jenna ran away . . . I've felt hollowed out by their loss, Amanda. By grief . . . by guilt . . . even by expiation, I suppose. And by a million emotions that have reworked me, so I'm not who I was before."

"You're really wrestling this one to the mat, aren't you, darlin'?" Amanda said, quietly. "But you'd like to try . . . am I right? Against all odds, and common sense, and the will of the majority . . . and the devil take the hindmost . . ." Her soft laughter was throaty and well intentioned. "It's no wonder I love you, Maggie. You look so straight and sensible on the outside, but underneath you're as soft as a bowl of corn mush. How, might I ask, are you going to mind a baby and work all day? As far as I know, Jack didn't leave you in real high cotton. Besides, you need this place to keep you in touch with people. Left to your own devices you'd become a hermit for sure."

Maggie didn't reply.

"And, maybe more importantly, have you brooked the wrath of Maria Aparecida, yet?" Amanda persisted, as if that might be a formidable bridge to cross.

Maggie winced and shook her head. "You know she's an old softie, really. It isn't her fault she's built like Pilar in *The Sun Also Rises*."

"And with a temper to match, if I recall."

"Only when justified . . . and maybe on alternate Thursdays . . . besides, she's been a godsend, since I've been alone, Amanda. Having Maria as my housekeeper is the only continuity I have from the old days."

"You don't need continuity from the old days, Maggie. You need a new life in the *now*."

The baby in her arms opened its eyes and mouth simultaneously, and cooed; Maggie shifted her gently to a shoulder. "Looks to me like that's just what the Fates have provided," she said with a soft smile.

"You're insane, of course," Amanda replied pleasantly. "But an awfully good person."

She shooed Maggie and the baby out the door and stood watching them walk down Madison toward a cab. It was probably just the silvered light of early morning in New York, or maybe a little too much Courvoisier after dinner last night, but she could have sworn they both shimmered softly in the morning sun.

"*Nossa Senhora!* You could have told me we were expecting," Maria announced wryly. Maggie laughed as the powerfully built woman swooped the baby from her arms and plopped it onto her mighty bosom like a landing pad. Cody gurgled responsively.

"I would have, if I'd known," Maggie replied, as she shook her rebellious curls out from under the hat she'd donned against the chilly morning. Her hair was brown with golden highlights and the soft curls had a mind of their own. She'd taken pains in her youth to beat them into submission; now she was grateful they asked so little of her.

"Jenna?" Maria muttered, with the intimacy of a longtime servant who knows all the family secrets.

"She came and went last night."

"And the drugs? She is still hooked?"

"That would be my guess."

"So this little sparrow is at least of our blood," the woman pronounced with satisfaction. "This is good. When we adopt, there is no surety of the blood."

Maggie nearly laughed aloud. You never knew what to expect from Maria. A generous heart and a volatile temperament, but honorable to the bone. She couldn't remember how many years the woman had kept house for her. Twenty-something. She must even have been young once, although she'd never seemed anything but the same indeterminate age to Maggie.

"If we raise her, there will be a lot of extra work, Maria, I can't ask you to—"

"What you mean, dona Maggie, *if* we raise her?" Maria interrupted. "She is our *family*. What else would we do, give her to the 'SPCA?"

The large woman cuddled the tiny baby with the expertise of the genuinely gifted. Without asking Maggie's leave, she padded toward the kitchen, the baby still perched on her pouter-pigeon bosom. "*Coitadinha, Coitadinha!*" she murmured as she walked. *Poor little thing.* Maggie didn't speak Portuguese, but after all the years with Maria Aparecida she'd picked up a few dozen phrases. She stared after them, thinking maybe the Lord knew what He was doing after all.

Maggie kicked off her shoes and sat down on her bed with a sigh, determined to think things through. Since Jack's death, the silver-framed nest of photographs next to her bed had become the haven she went to for tough decisions. She lifted a favorite photo from its hallowed place and her husband's face stared back at her with laughing eyes, crinkled just a little at the corners. Funny how she'd never noticed the silver in his hair when he was alive . . . such robust, abundant hair, he'd had, for running fingers through . . . Tears suddenly blurred her vision of the man she'd loved so long, and she swiped at them, annoyed they were still so near the surface. "Oh, your bladder's very near your eye, child," her Irish father had said often, when she was small . . . She missed him, too. How many of those she'd truly loved were gone? Jenna was lost now, too . . . perhaps forever.

What was it the doctor at the last rehab had told her? "You didn't *cause* your daughter's addiction, Mrs. O'Connor. You can't *control* it, and you can't possibly *cure* it. Until you get that into your head you'll never find any peace."

Didn't he understand that getting it into your head was easy, it was your heart that refused to cooperate? And your soul that longed to save her. That's why she hadn't given up . . . that's why she would never give up.

"My sweet, sweet Jenna," Maggie whispered to the tall fair-haired girl in the suspended animation of the silver frame. "I miss you so. I love you so."

*Not my will, but Thine, Lord.* She tried to mean it as she breathed the old childhood prayer. You must learn to accept the Will of God, Maggie, Mother Superior had chided her years before, when she'd questioned why God didn't cure her mother's terminal illness, no matter how hard she prayed. "You think that God had better pay attention to your demands. That's the sin of pride, Maggie! You have no right to interfere with God's Plan. You can't see far enough or wide enough to know what it is He has in mind."

"But it would take so little effort for Him to cure her, Mother. Why doesn't He take better care of His friends?"

She'd been sent to the convent to do extra chores for that bit of irreverence. So she'd scrubbed the sisters' kitchen until she repented her outburst, but that didn't mean she'd changed her mind.

With a sigh, Maggie pressed the beloved picture to her lips, before replacing it on the nightstand.

"Tell you what, God," she said fervently, the old habit of holding conversations with Him as ingrained as breathing. "I'll take care of this baby, and you take care of Jenna for me."

# CHAPTER 3

Maggie paced the floor with Cody in her arms. She strove not to think about the escalating ache in her back, arms and shoulders, from the weight of the hefty fourteen-month-old. *She ain't heavy, father, she's my granddaughter* . . . The thought almost made her laugh aloud.

Cody was teething. And she had the flu. Maggie could feel each rattling breath through the child's back, with frightening intensity. "You mustn't worry so much about her breathing, Mrs. O'Connor," the pediatrician had said yesterday. "The antibiotics will do the trick." But Cody wasn't *his* baby, and what kind of grandmother wouldn't worry about so major an enterprise as breathing? For two nights, Maggie had awakened every half hour to listen for Cody's labored breath in the darkness. Tonight she hadn't had to worry about waking up.

The cold from the floor crept up under her nightgown and her feet were icy, but she couldn't stop the walking now. Cody was nearly asleep, the fitful kind, of sick babies, where the slightest deviation from your strolling, crooning, soothing pattern sets them off again. She held the child tighter in her arms, as if to ward off danger and illness with sheer strength of will.

I *can* do this! Maggie pulled herself up sharply as she began to buckle toward fatigue. No wonder God gives babies to twenty-three-year-olds. The clock read 3:38 and she was bone-weary. I can live without sleep, she told herself sternly. Saint Simon sat on top of a flagpole for thirty years. He couldn't have slept much.

But then Saint Simon didn't have to get up in the

morning and earn a living, did he? a little voice inside her nagged.

She sighed and kept on walking. Raising this baby alone was the toughest task she'd ever attempted, and tough tasks always looked scarier at night. Teething and flu were a snap compared to what lay ahead, she thought dispiritedly. Measles and multiplication tables, play days and PTA meetings with women half her age, were yet to be faced. To say nothing of college tuition and calculus and trying to do everything right in the meantime. Get a *grip*, Maggie! she chided herself, as she gingerly placed the now sleeping Cody into her eyelet-trimmed crib. You're just daffy from exhaustion—everything will look fine in the morning.

She pulled up the covers, then stood a moment staring down at the cherubic face of the child she loved so much. "I don't care how hard it is, or how tired I am," she whispered to the sleeping baby. "You're worth it all."

MAGGIE yawned, picked up her third cup of coffee of the morning and struggled to keep the paperwork on the London acquisition in correct order. The little bronze statuette of the God Ptah was one a favorite client had lusted after for a decade; it had been a great stroke of luck that the man who owned it had decided to thin his collection.

"I've finally figured out one of the great riddles of life," she said wryly to Amanda, who sat on the other side of the small office area of the shop. "The components of success in business are: talent, humor, quick wit, endurance, dedication, ambition, salesmanship, intuition, flamboyance, wardrobe, hard labor, and getting enough sleep. The latter being the most important."

Amanda looked up from her notes with an amused expression, and added, "It doesn't hurt if you're born into the right family, go to the proper schools, belong to the best clubs, and are male, or seriously oversexed with bodacious ta-tas.''

Maggie laughed out loud. It was hard to ever get the last word in with Amanda.

# CHAPTER 4

Maggie pushed the swing and breathed in the pleasure of the splendid day. The sound of Cody's laughter always thrilled her. How fast three years can flit by, she thought, as she saw the confident way the little legs pumped to keep the swing moving between pushes. Three years of reinventing a life, and letting joy back in. Of loving and laughter, of unselfishness and kissing boo-boos, of teaching little competencies, and a million other "mother" things that had given her life real purpose once again.

The crisp, clear weather was exhilarating, the sky bluer than it had been all winter. She buttoned up the old Irish fisherman's sweater that had been Jack's favorite, and listened to the gleeful sounds of Cody's happiness ringing like Soleri bells against the late January wind.

"She loves you, dona Maggie," Maria Aparecida had said judiciously over breakfast. "Beyond the ordinary, this child loves you. I am her friend, but her heartstrings are woven into yours with cords of steel. You will see. My words are true."

Maggie knew it was true. She and Cody intuited each other's moves like dancers . . . ebbing and flowing with each other's rhythms. When they were together, all was right with the world. "How different life is from our perfectly sensible expectations," Jack had said wistfully, as he lay dying . . . he was right, of course . . . but sometimes the surprises were good ones. Like the gift of this laughing, loving child who had come so unexpectedly into her leftover world.

"Higher, Mim. Higher!" the little voice piped between giggles. But, on impulse, Maggie stopped the swing instead, and lifted her granddaughter into a sudden bear hug. She stood there clasping Cody tightly for a long moment, needing to hold and be held.

"Do you have a boo-boo, Mim?" Cody asked, concerned over the tears in Maggie's eyes. She wiped one away with small chubby fingers.

"No, sweetheart," the grandmother lied, forcing a smile. "I think the sun got in my eye."

"I'll kiss it," the little girl offered, relieved she knew how to heal the pain. She pressed her sweet lips to Maggie's face and kissed away the hurt with confidence.

"Let's go home and see what goodies Maria has baked for us today," Maggie responded, restored by the child's love. "I hope it's brownies."

She buttoned up Cody's jacket and kissed her lightly on the perfect velvet cheek.

"I love you, pumpkin," she said, meaning it with every fiber of her being.

"I love you, too," the child replied happily, and they set off toward St. Luke's Place hand in hand.

"SHE is too smart for her own good, dona Maggie. This little one could mind rats at a crossroad." Maria shook her great head, a profound gesture halfway between annoyance and admiration. Her hair was gray as a battleship, and captured in a vast braid that bounced down a back that was straight enough for West Point. She had grown to love Cody fiercely in the years she'd contributed to her upbringing.

"She told the butcher today to give the slice of bologna he offered her, to the poor children at the orphanage.

Can you imagine? Like she was forty years old, and a benefactress to the poor.''

Maggie laughed, envisioning the scene. "She's such an odd little duck, Maria," she said lovingly. "Her nursery school teacher told me Cody always tries to be the peacemaker in disputes among the children. 'You'd think she was sitting on the Supreme Court, Mrs. O'Connor,' " she mimicked the teacher's voice. " 'The other little ones always turn to her with their troubles. I've never seen anything like it.' "

Maria swiftly blessed herself. "She has the magic this one. You will see, dona Maggie. She has the Gift. There was one in my village who had it . . . born with the caul over his face, he was. It is the sign of the Gifted Ones."

Maggie sighed. "Only Jenna would know if this little munchkin had a caul or not, Maria. And after so many years, I doubt she'll ever come home to tell us."

"My lady goes to bed each night in sorrow," Maria murmured, caring genuinely. "Not knowing if her daughter lives or dies."

"No, Maria," Maggie said hastily, "she's still alive, *somewhere*." That was the only thing she was sure of. "I'd know if anything terrible had happened." Death would have severed the psychic cord that bound her to Jenna and the cord still tugged at her, keeping the memory vibrant, keeping the hope alive.

The housekeeper crossed herself and made a swift sign against the evil eye. I'll have to keep a weather eye on Maria's superstitions when Cody grows old enough to understand them, Maggie thought absently. She had no quarrel with the woman's peasant religious devotions, even if they were a little extreme, but she didn't want Cody frightened by eerie stories of the Unknown.

"Do you know Cody gave her lunch yesterday to that homeless man on University Place, Maria," Maggie said, suddenly remembering. "The one who lives in the cardboard box. We were on our way to the playground with peanut butter and jelly sandwiches when she spotted him and decided he looked hungry. So she scooted over and dropped her little bag into his hat so fast I barely knew what was happening.''

"The heart is big and there is softness in the soul, dona Maggie,'' Maria intoned reverently. "It is the best gift, the generous heart.''

The housekeeper's words surfaced another recent memory, and Maggie laughed as she recounted the story. "There's a little blond boy in the playground, Maria. And every day, for the last few weeks, he's been coming up to me and climbing onto my lap. He plays with my hair, and nuzzles his little face into my breasts, then he climbs down, says, '*Fank you*,' to Cody, and goes away. So I finally asked her what it was all about, and she said very sweetly, 'His mommy has short hair and a hard chest, so I lent you to him to make him feel nice.' ''

Both women laughed at that; they'd made a habit of sharing anecdotes about this beloved child. Their little family, odd though it might seem by ordinary standards, was an exceptionally happy one.

CODY held the broken bird tenderly in chubby, cupped hands, almost too small for the task. The damaged sparrow didn't struggle in her grip, so Maggie thought it must be dead.

"I can fix it,'' Cody said, more to herself than to Maggie.

"I'm afraid that little bird may be dying, or he wouldn't let you hold him like that, sweetheart,'' Maggie said sadly. "We may not be able to save him.''

Cody looked up at her grandmother, thoughtfully, like an adult trying to decide how much to tell a slow child. "I know how to do it, Mim,'' she said softly, but with absolute confidence. "Don't worry. I can fix sick things.''

Maggie frowned, puzzled, not knowing what to say. "You can, cupcake?" she asked, surprised. "How did you learn to do that?"

Cody smiled, still holding the bird in one small hand and petting it gently with the other.

"I didn't *learn*, Mim," Cody said patiently. "I just knew how."

Without further discussion, she proceeded into the house in search of Maria. When Maggie had helped the child ensconce the bird in a shoebox, she took her housekeeper aside.

"Do you know anything about this business of fixing sick things, Maria?"

"Oh yes, dona Maggie. She has the healing hands, this little chicken. Did you not know this? When my rheumatism makes the great pain in my leg, the little one, she puts her tiny hands around it and soon the pain is nothing. You will see, tomorrow the little bird will fly."

After Maria went back to her work Maggie stood a moment, pondering what to do about this lovely healing fantasy, but since it didn't seem harmful, she simply went about her business.

# CHAPTER 5

The school-bus yellow of her new coat made Maggie feel cheery. She tossed a black-and-white houndstooth silk scarf around her neck, tied it jauntily, and took one last look at herself in the hall mirror. Not bad for a middle-aged granny, she thought with a grin. The fact that the couple in the park had mistaken her for Cody's mother, yesterday, had made her feel young again. In truth, Cody made her feel young again, full of possibilities.

Maggie heard the gleeful contrapuntal laughter of Cody and Maria Aparecida coming from the kitchen—the child's voice, trilling giggles into the air, the older woman's, deep and merry. They were great pals, which made it feasible for Maggie to work half days at the shop without worry. And as Amanda had taken up the slack in hours without a whimper, Maggie could be surrogate mommy for part of every day, as well as nights and weekends.

She checked her handbag for all necessities, and let herself out the front door, glad to be alive.

The black stretch limo glided to a halt, just as Maggie reached the bottom step. She watched with mild surprise that such a splendid car should be in her neighborhood. Somebody's son must have become a rock star while she wasn't looking.

A uniformed driver alighted, opening the rear door, so a handsome forty-year-old man could emerge. Maggie's curiosity was piqued by the impeccably cut Italian clothes, and the air of polished confidence that made him look so European. He moved like a polo player, self-assured, used to commanding notice. His glance met Maggie's with a small smile of acknowledgment, then he reached inside the darkened car to help a young woman make a graceful, leggy exit.

Tall, slender as a reed, blond hair swinging freely at shoulder length . . . Maggie caught her breath in shock. The girl was Jenna.

"Permit me to introduce myself, Mrs. O'Connor," the man said in a faintly European accent that Maggie couldn't place. "My name is Eric Vannier. Your daughter has told me so much about you, I'd have recognized you even without the photograph she carries." He extended a manicured hand, which Maggie took automatically in her own. She could not tear her eyes away from her daughter. Armani suit, Hermès bag, hair and makeup culled from the cover of *Vogue*—but Jenna, nonetheless. The gray-green eyes with their fringe of dark lashes . . . the pale oval face and full pouty lips, all heartbreakingly familiar.

Without thinking, Maggie reached out to touch the girl tentatively. Jenna didn't reach back.

"It's good to see you, Mother," she said blandly, pushing back her hair, with the nervous flick of a colt in fly season. "Eric and I have just gotten back from our honeymoon in Europe, and we're anxious to pick up Cody."

*Pick up Cody* . . . The words hit Maggie's brain like buckshot. *Pick up Cody!* As if she were a package left behind on the subway, now to be retrieved from Lost and Found. She tried to calm herself enough to make an appropriate response, whatever that might be. Sensing the tension, Eric took control.

"We've moved into a family estate in Greenwich, Mrs. O'Connor, less than an hour away from here. We were certain you'd want to continue to see Cody, so we've decided to live here in the States for a time, to make the transition easier on all of us. Jenna told me what an angel you've been, caring for her daughter while she was unwell."

*To see Cody . . . transition . . . for a time . . .* His words tumbled over and over each other inside Maggie like a silent scream. Who are these people? How can they even *think* of taking Cody away?

"This is quite a shock," she stammered. "I haven't even heard from my daughter in years. I had no way of knowing if she were alive . . . if she would ever return . . ." She let the words dwindle, unable to imagine how to say all she meant.

Eric's smile was dazzling. Perfect teeth, perfect jaw, perfect aplomb . . . but there was something imperfect beyond it. Maggie's mind, on overdrive, reached out to grasp the flaw, but Jenna interrupted.

"Not return? How could you even think such a thing, Mother? I've simply been unwell. You do remember that I had a drug problem, don't you?"

*"Remember that you had a drug problem?"* Maggie gasped out the words. "Are you demented? Of course, I know you had a drug problem! Why on earth else would you have left me with a ten-day-old baby and not come back for three years?" She was suddenly furious; at their unruffled cool, at the blatant manipulation of her life.

"You act as if I'm a post office box where you can just drop things off and pick them up when the spirit moves you. Do you think your daughter is an *object* for retrieval at your convenience? Where the hell have you been, Jenna? What have you been doing with your damned life? Why did you never send so much as a postcard? It doesn't look to me like you couldn't afford a stamp. I think I deserve a few answers here, before we talk about picking up anything other than a blunt object!"

Jenna turned to Eric, all tranquillity replaced by anger.

"I told you she'd be like this, Eric. Selfish and hostile."

The commotion of voices had roused Maria from inside the house; she stood in the doorway with Cody tagging close behind.

Eric leaped on the diversion. "What a breathtaking little beauty you are," he announced to Cody with seeming sincerity. "You have your grandmother's exquisite eyes and your mother's glorious hair." The dazzling smile beamed its way to Cody and she took it in, without returning the greeting. She peered out, instead, from behind Maria's bulk, to investigate the smile's owner.

Maggie moved up the steps, in a daze, motioning them to follow her into the house.

"Mim?" Cody whispered urgently, tugging at her grandmother's sleeve. "Who's that lady?"

Maggie bent down to the child's level, struggling for words; her heart pounded so hard she could barely breathe. "I have a wonderful surprise for you, sweetheart," she managed, forcing her voice to steadiness.

"Remember all the stories I've told you about your

beautiful mommy? The lady in the picture by my bed?''
She waited for Cody to nod her head yes before continuing.

"Remember, I told you about how much she loves
you, and how she would come back one day to tell you
so herself?" Reluctantly, the little girl nodded; some
note in Mim's voice was making her nervous.

"My dear love," Maggie said gently, trying to keep
the tears from her inflection. "This beautiful lady is your
mommy."

Cody's head turned slowly at this startling revelation,
and she looked at Jenna, with intense concentration.
The gaze was clearly one of appraisal. And something
else, indefinable.

Jenna stared at the child, entranced. She moved forward
with outstretched arms, but Cody turned her head
away and buried it for safety, in Maggie's breasts. Rebuffed
but determined, Jenna tried to pluck her out of
Maggie's arms. Cody cried "No!" and clung to Maggie
with a death grip.

Maggie, distraught, clung, too. She saw Eric assess
the situation.

"It's only natural for her to be a bit unfamiliar with
you, darling," he interjected in a voice of warm oil.
He was very handsome, she noted; a Spanish dancer's
sensuality, the hauteur of a grandee. "She'll get over it
as soon as we're home."

"Home?" Maggie blurted. "You can't possibly mean
you intend to take her with you, *today?* That's absurd!
This is the only home Cody's ever known!"

"She's *my* child, Mother, not yours," Jenna cut in.
"I left her with you while I was ill, not forever. I'm back
now and I *want* my daughter."

Maggie straightened, still holding the clinging three-
year-old child tight against her pounding heart. "You
may *want* to do that, Jenna, but that doesn't mean it's
the *right* thing to do. This is entirely too sudden for me
to cope with, how can you expect a little child to adjust?

You'll have to give us some time to take this all in."
She took a deep breath, fighting for calm.

"You say you have a house in Greenwich? And you're married? Are there any other surprises you're saving for me? Like that you're president of General Motors, or you're planning to take over a Third World country later on today? . . ." Maggie's Irish temper was slow to engage, but once it did . . .

Eric moved to defuse the escalating anger. "Mrs. O'Connor, I assure you, both Jenna and I totally understand your surprise, and your reluctance to part with the child, whom you've obviously become attached to. Perhaps I can set your mind at rest by telling you a bit about myself, so I don't seem so much the mysterious stranger."

Maggie nodded, thwarted by his civility. She motioned vaguely toward the couch, and both visitors sat.

"My family's an old and respected one in Europe, Mrs. O'Connor—"

"Where exactly in Europe?"

Eric smiled. "Originally, we were from the Middle East. But many generations ago, the Vanniers moved to Paris and, although we have banking offices and philanthropies throughout Europe, you might safely think of us as Parisians." Something about Eric's unctuousness, covering the raw animal power she sensed in him, was unnerving.

"If you'll permit me to continue, I promise to give you enough of my *curriculum vitae* to assuage at least a few of your fears, Mrs. O'Connor. Although our family fortune is primarily engaged in international banking, my own particular area of endeavor is that of running the Vannier Foundation, a rather large philanthropic enterprise, which distributes a great deal of money to worthy causes. The nature of my work forces me to travel quite a bit, although as I said earlier, in deference to your obvious devotion to my wife's child, I have taken residence in one of my family homes, near enough to you so that your transition from surrogate motherhood to grandmotherhood . . ." He smiled ingratiatingly again. "No matter how absurd a title 'grandmother' seems when one sees you, Mrs. O'Connor . . . will be less traumatic."

Maggie acknowledged the compliment with a small nod and tried to force herself to fairness. He was certainly civilized; perhaps he could be reasoned with.

"May I ask how you met my daughter, Mr. Vannier?" she countered. "When last I saw Jenna she didn't appear to be moving in the circles you describe."

"Do call me Eric, Mrs. O'Connor. I am, after all, your son-in-law," the man responded, the dark eyes alight with charm. "And perhaps I might call you Maggie?" He didn't wait for a reply.

"It's really quite serendipitous that Jenna and I ever met at all. You see, I had a slight injury to my spine, sustained in a riding accident in Central Park, and I was taken to Roosevelt Hospital, where, as fate would have it, Jenna happened to be recovering from her addiction. Part of her therapy entailed doing volunteer work within the hospital complex, caring for other hospitalized patients in a variety of ways—rather like a candy striper, if you will. She was particularly kind to me, as I lay restless as a caged tiger." Eric smiled at Jenna suggestively.

"I'm afraid I was smitten by her, rather intensely, and when I found I was able to escape the hospital, I asked Jenna to return with me to our château in Lucerne, to help me through my recuperation. Jenna said she had no ties that would preclude this . . . and the rest, as they say, is history. We recovered together . . . and much to my delight, we have been together ever since."

During this extraordinary soliloquy, Cody had relaxed her grip on Maggie and was now sitting quietly in her lap, watching the others in the room with studied curiosity. Jenna was trying to gain the child's attention, and Cody was watching her mother judiciously, but making no move in her direction.

"I love my daughter, Mother," Jenna suddenly interjected, a pleading note in her voice. "Very much. And I have missed her dreadfully. I know you don't have much reason to trust me, but you must see that I'm well now. I'm happily married to a wonderful man who'll take good care of both of us. I finally have the chance to make Cody's life perfect. Please, *please* help me put our life together the way it should have been from the start . . . for my sake and for Cody's." Her large eyes glistened with a hint of tears and Maggie felt torn between loyalties. What if Jenna really was recovered from her addiction? What if she really *could* care for Cody, and wanted to? What if Cody could finally have, not only a real mother and father, but all the privileges this obviously wealthy man could provide? She owed it to everyone concerned to try very hard to be fair and unselfish.

Maggie encouraged Cody to slide to the floor, in hopes that she would show Jenna some sign of affection, but the child's reluctance was unyielding.

"I feel I need a cup of tea rather badly, just now," Maggie said finally, needing an excuse to escape them and think this through. "If you'll excuse me for a moment, I'll have Maria put the kettle on." There was a phone in the kitchen, Maggie thought desperately. She'd call John McCarthy, the family lawyer, and ask his advice. She put the kettle on and whispered hastily to Maria, "Jenna's married. They've come to take the baby."

"*O meu Deus!* Senhora . . ." Maggie couldn't follow the rapid-fire Portuguese, but the tone left no doubt about its intent. "You cannot permit such a sinful thing, dona Maggie. It is the work of the Devil!"

"Maria!" Maggie said sharply, the strain evident in her voice. "Let's try to keep this rational, at least. Please." She was dialing as she spoke.

"John, thank God, you're there!" she breathed when the lawyer answered; he'd been a good friend over the years. "I'm afraid I need some sage advice, rather quickly. Jenna's come back, out of the blue, and she wants to take Cody away. She's married to a wealthy European and they've got a place in Greenwich, and . . . Oh my God, John, they want to take the baby *today* . . . now! What should I do?''

"First of all you should slow down enough so I can understand what you're telling me, Maggie. Let's just take it from the top. Jenna's back, and off drugs, I presume? Okay. And married. That complicates things considerably, especially if he's rich. The law's pretty clear on this kind of case, Maggie, the child is Jenna's. She's only been with you because of the mother's incapacity, but if Jenna's well, now . . . capable of caring for Cody . . . I'd say you'll have to hand her over."

Maggie's heart sank. "Oh, John, I'm so unclear about what's *right* here. If Jenna's really healthy and straight, of course, she should have Cody . . . no matter how much it breaks my heart to let her go. I know *that's* right. But they're both strangers to her. Cody doesn't know them from Adam's house cat! She's terrified. I can't just let them walk out the door with her. How do I *know* Jenna's straight . . . how do I *know* he's not an axe murderer? What's right here, John? Screw the law, I'm talking *right*!''

She heard the low whistling breath let out slowly at the other end of the phone. "If you're asking me as a father, and one who's observed your daughter's conduct over the past few years, Maggie, I'd say *right* is to tell them to go fuck themselves. If you're asking my legal counsel, I'd have to tell you, they have the law squarely on their side. Christ, Maggie, you've practically got to prove somebody dips a kid in boiling oil, twice a day, to get custody away from its birth mother . . . and, in the abstract, that's a good law. In the real world . . . in this case . . . who the hell knows what right is? Certainly not lawyers, I assure you. All I can tell you is this: If she calls the police and tells them she wants Cody, you'll have to hand the child over."

Maggie replaced the receiver and wiped the frustrated

moisture from her eyes. She saw Maria standing in the living room doorway eyeing Eric with calculation. His urbane charm did not seem to extend to household help.

"Get the child's coat," he snapped at the woman autocratically. *Oh God, they're leaving!* Maria Aparecida crossed her arms in front of her mighty chest, raised a Frida Kahlo eyebrow and stood her ground awaiting a signal from her mistress.

"I implore you, Jenna," Maggie said, facing her daughter. "Think first of Cody in this! She's a sensitive little girl and you're complete strangers to her. Can't we figure out some kind of gentle transition that will give her time to get to know you both? I could bring her to you on weekends, or you could come here to visit . . . I'll cooperate in any way that helps you learn to love each other."

"I'm afraid you Americans coddle your children to an outrageous degree, Maggie," Eric rebuked. "In Europe, we find that the more definitively we set rules and regulations for our young, the easier it is for them to comply. Standards of behavior, discipline . . . from what I've seen here, you have little regard for these things in America."

"But we have a great deal of regard for love and compassion," Maggie snapped. "Perhaps that makes up for our other deficiencies." Eric's smile faded.

"Be that as it may, Maggie," he persisted, his voice several degrees cooler than before, "my first doctorate was in the law, and I assure you, however our attitudes may differ about child rearing, the law will see to it that Jenna and I raise Cody . . . according to our own standards. You appear to have been a perfectly acceptable substitute mother for a period of time, but that substitution is no longer required. The *real* mother exists and she wants her child. For your own sake, and Cody's, do not attempt to stand in our way, or you will simply force us to remove her from your sphere of influence, permanently." Eric let the threat hang so ominously Maggie bit back a sharp retort and quelled an urge to kick him in the knee. She stared at Eric, then at Jenna, but it was apparent she would get no support from that quarter. "I'll get her ready," she murmured hoarsely, the words rebelling. "Maria will pack her things."

Maria muttered a stream of expletives as she packed the little suitcase. Maggie caught only the "illiterate of father and mother" and "thieving ox" parts, as she stood clutching Cody's hand, feeling the child's fear electrify her own. *Oh God, I can't do this!* I can't let them take her into *nowhere*. Can't not share her laughter anymore, or heal her hurts. Oh Sweet Jesus, how will they know she has a scrunched-up pillow she can't sleep without? Will they care that oatmeal makes her skin itch, or that Yehudi Cat sleeps on her bed?

"I don't like that lady," Cody said softly. "That man has mean eyes." Maggie fought back tears and forced herself, for Cody's sake, to be brave.

"Listen to me, love," she pleaded. "You've got to listen to me, now! Your mommy left you with me to mind, a long, long time ago . . ." She felt her throat fill up with tears and beat them back. "She was very sick then, and she couldn't take care of you, so she asked me to keep you here where you'd be safe and loved. And I did that because I love you with all my heart. Now she's well again, angel, and she's been missing you all this time, and now she needs you to come home."

*"Home is here!"* Cody said emphatically; Maggie's stomach lurched.

"Yes, sweetheart, this will always be your home, but your mommy has a nice new home that she wants to share with you."

"Can you come live there, too?"

"No, love. I have to stay here with Maria."

"I want to stay, too!" Maggie could see the rejection cloud the child's eyes.

"Please don't send Cody away, Mim," she pleaded, tears running down her cheeks. "Please don't make me go with those bad people. *I love you!* I'll be good!" She began to sob and Maggie shot a glance at Maria, whose stern face was already bathed in tears, and made up her mind. She'd make a fight of it if need be, but she wouldn't let them take the child. At least not today.

Maggie held Cody close as she descended the staircase. She could feel the beating of the little girl's heart against her own.

"Jenna, Eric . . ." she began, holding Cody tight. "Please try to understand what I'm going to say, because it's very, very important. I believe Cody *belongs* with her mother, if Jenna is able to care for her—but this isn't the proper way to accomplish that. You must see how shockingly difficult this is for me and for Cody . . . she's never known any home but this, any family but me and Maria . . ."

"That is precisely what we're here to remedy," Eric cut in, smoothly. "Prolonging the *good byes* is not going to make them easier, Maggie."

"Why must there be good-byes?" Maggie demanded. "Why can't you just let her learn to love you, before you take her away from all that makes her secure?"

Everything that happened next occurred so fast it was just a ghastly blur. Cody wrapped her arms and legs around Maggie and began to shriek, as Jenna tried to pry her free from Maggie's grip. Cody, terrified and defiant, hit Jenna squarely in the jaw, and Eric, who'd been waiting a chance to pounce, roughly yanked the baby away from the two women.

"No!" Maggie screamed. "Don't do this!" But Eric was already heading out the door. "She's only three years old. She doesn't understand why you're doing this!"

"She will, Maggie," he called over his shoulder, sprinting down the steps, Cody flailing pitifully in his arms.

Maggie ran after them, grappling for the child, but Eric and Jenna were too fast for her; in a screech of tires the huge car pulled away from the curb. Maggie could see Cody's stricken face pressed against the rear window, screaming soundlessly.

Feeling as if her heart had been torn from her breast, Maggie clutched the porch railing, stunned, tear-blind and heedless of the cold or the stares of passersby. She sank to the steps, put her head in her hands, and wept.

# CHAPTER 6

It had been thirty days since the Tiffany card arrived from Jenna, with an address in Greenwich, and the admonition to stay away for a month "so Cody could adjust to her new surroundings."

Maggie checked the directions Scotch-taped to the dashboard of her Volvo, and turned off I-95 onto Roundhill Road, pushing the trip odometer back to 000 so she could monitor the 2.8 miles to her next turn. *Left at the stop light, left again after the church* brought her into horse country. Tiny buds were trying to force back the gray-brown barrenness of winter, with minimal success, but the cold wind had lost some of its bite. Under ordinary circumstances Maggie would have taken pleasure in the late-winter landscape and the Connecticut air. Today, only one thing mattered; Cody was somewhere around the next bend in the road. Cody, whose beloved voice she hadn't heard in a month, would soon be in her arms again, laughing and chattering; easing the fears that had nagged her night and day since the awful moment of Jenna's return. How tragic it was that what should have been a joyous reunion had gone so awry. There had to be a way to mend the wounds.

*Every child belongs with her mommy*, she'd reminded herself ten thousand times, since the horror of parting.

If Jenna was well, as she seemed to be, she and Cody would love each other, and be good to each other, as God intended. And Maggie would be a grandmother, like other grannies. She would spoil the child with trips to F.A.O. Schwarz and Rumpelmayer's. They would do the zoo together, and the Museum of Natural History. She would teach her, and love her indulgently, as other grandmothers did, with none of the hardship or responsibility of parenting. Maggie recited all these perfectly sensible arguments for the umpteenth time, and didn't feel better in the least. Caring for Cody had been more blessing than obligation; she would miss her till the day she died.

She sighed and rolled down the window, so the cold air could clear her head. *This isn't about you, Maggie*, she reminded herself. This is about Cody living happily ever after.

*Just as long as she's safe*, she said aloud to the lush countryside, in an effort to buoy her own spirits. *That's all that matters*.

The land had changed from side-by-side great houses, to those on huge tracts of elegant real estate. Maggie checked the mileage and realized the immense iron gates straight ahead of her must be the Vannier estate. They appeared to be unlocked and unmanned.

A long winding driveway curved languidly to the right, and disappeared into mature white pines and Acer maples that forested the estate, all the way to the Sound. Maggie steered the Volvo along an endless driveway until a house loomed up ahead of her—although "house" hardly seemed an adequate description for the vast mansion that materialized around the last wooded bend. Beyond a lawn so manicured it looked like the eighteenth green at St. Andrews, a French château of the late Gothic period stood. Elaborate turrets, mansard roof, and stone balustrade balconies gave the place the specter of a fortress from another century. Some besotted robber baron's effort at immortality, she thought. Wouldn't you know!

Maggie parked at the center of the circular drive, shaken by the unexpected grandeur of the estate. The iron gates that preceded the eight-foot double doors at the entrance did nothing to calm her agitation.

Wonderingly, she rang the echoing chimes, then stepped inside the marble-floored foyer, and handed her coat to a uniformed servant. "Madame will receive you in the East Drawing Room," the woman said in a librarian hush, gesturing for Maggie to follow her through one elaborate room to another and another. The ominous quiet filled her with apprehension; there were no signs of life or laughter here. Where were the child-sounds in this mausoleum? Where, the small fingerprints on the walls? A clock chimed, startling her with its intrusion, and she focused more clearly on the room she'd been brought to.

Her educated gaze caught an exquisite collection of New Guinean Cult Hooks and a display of kris knives; over the door arch, a culthouse lintel perched, and she remembered that the Sepik River tribes who carved such images were cannibals. Very unusual collections for Greenwich. An assemblage of queer metal and leather artifacts in a glass case caught her attention; they looked vaguely familiar, but the only thing she could imagine them to be were thumbscrews, and that was absurd.

"Good morning, Mother," Jenna's voice interrupted, sounding as if she'd taken elocution lessons from Katharine Hepburn. Maggie turned to see her daughter enter the room, graceful in a tailored Ungaro. The high-heeled shoes, stockings, jewelry, were all perfectly chosen, but oddly formal for so early an hour.

"You look so . . . grown-up, Jenna," Maggie said, confused by the image before her. "It's hard for me not to think of you as the teenager I remember, and now . . . you're so elegant." She smiled and walked toward her daughter, tentatively; Jenna permitted an embrace, without enthusiasm. Maggie took a deep breath and tried again.

"All these years, I always believed you'd come home someday, sweetheart, but I suppose I never imagined you'd come home so full of surprises."

"I have a wonderful life now, Mother," Jenna responded, but Maggie heard no joy in the words.

"This is quite a house, darling. You and Eric and Cody must have to leave a trail of bread crumbs to find your way back to your room at night."

Jenna relaxed a little. "There are fifty-some rooms here . . . I haven't seen all of them yet. Eric's grandfather built the place before the turn of the century, to duplicate one they own in the Loire Valley."

"And these collections are astounding," Maggie prompted, wondering if humor might lessen the strain. "Who's their decorator . . . Torquemada? Not everyone collects thumbscrews, you know."

Jenna blinked, not sure how to respond. "Eric's grandfather and father were sportsmen who hunted all over the world, Mother. They brought back artifacts from everywhere. I'll get Eric to take you on a tour."

"And how is Cody coping with all this splendor?"

*She sounds straight and lucid*, Maggie thought uncomfortably. *Why are my hackles up?*

"Tell me about Eric, Jenna. Are you happy with him?"

"Eric is brilliant and charming, Mother. He's involved in extraordinary projects. He's a wonderful husband and father. Cody adores him."

*Spoken like a true Stepford Wife*, Maggie thought, disturbed. Like a windup toy. Where were the simple girlish protestations of love and adoration? *Oh Mom, he's so gorgeous! And did you see those adorable dimples when he laughs?* And it wasn't her imagination that Jenna's pupils were slightly dilated.

"I'll take you to the nursery, Mother. You can see for yourself how well Cody's doing." Jenna glided off, a spectral presence in the silent rooms.

"The nursery's in the West Wing," she explained, as

she led the way. "Eric's family has a very specific code of conduct for children, and all sorts of rules and regulations about raising them. They have to, of course—in their world, children are expected to behave perfectly from the earliest age."

Maggie swallowed the reply that leaped to mind, and followed Jenna through a succession of lavishly decorated rooms, each containing art and artifacts of incalculable value. What appeared to be a Raphael graced one hallway, a Titian and a Goya were in another. All the paintings were remarkable, but Maggie found their themes oppressive.

"You'll like the library, Mother," Jenna offered as she passed a cavernous two-story room, lined floor to ceiling with leather-bound books. Maggie walked wonderingly into the dazzling library, her eye drawn to an ancient-looking volume in a glass case. She paused to study it.

"That couldn't be a *Clavicule of Solomon*, Jenna, surely?" she asked, genuinely startled by the possibility. The only one she knew to exist had been owned by the Borgias. "I mean, it must be a copy . . . the original would be beyond price! I think they're scarcer than Gutenberg Bibles."

"You'll have to ask Eric about specifics, Mother, but I doubt they'd have anything other than an original, here. My husband doesn't like counterfeits."

*Then what on earth must he think of you*, crossed Maggie's mind, but she was annoyed at herself for such an unworthy thought, and said nothing.

They ascended a staircase at the end of the wing, and entered an immense nursery.

"This isn't a nursery, Jenna," she said, startled. "It's a world."

"Yes, it is, isn't it? There's the nursery proper, the nanny's quarters, Cody's bedroom, her sitting room, a schoolroom, and a small library. Even a kitchen and dining room. It's all very self-contained."

"And very far from the rest of the house."

"Eric doesn't like to be disturbed when he works."

"I see. So when does Cody get to see you and Eric? At mealtime . . . during the day?"

"Cody eats her meals here, of course. She's far too little to be invited to the dining room."

They turned a corner and suddenly Maggie saw Cody, sitting in a puddle of pale sunlight on the nursery floor, coloring diligently in a book.

"Sweetheart!" she called excitedly, holding out her arms for the little girl to run into.

Cody looked up; an expression of joy and relief flooded her small features, then diminished like a receding tide. The child rose and walked toward them solemnly; there was tension in every movement.

Maggie ran forward and swooped her up into loving arms. "I've missed you *so much*, munchkin!" she breathed into her hair, as she hugged. "I've thought about you every minute, and missed you *all* the time! Let me look at you, angel. You must tell me every single thing that's happened in your new life . . ."

Maggie felt the little body stiffen in her arms. The head came up sharply, as the child's gaze was drawn to the far doorway.

A formidable black woman had entered the nursery. She was well over six feet tall and seemed taller still because of the native headdress she wore. She had an imperial mien and searing black eyes that were fixed on the child in Maggie's arms. At her side were two massive rottweilers, silent and menacing. Cody wriggled out of Maggie's embrace and stood facing the woman, at a sort of quiet attention, as if awaiting orders.

"Mother, this is Ghania, Cody's Amah," Jenna said in a rush. "She's from Madagascar, and she's been with Eric's family for years and years. As a matter of fact, she was Eric's Amah, too. She raised him from infancy. We're so lucky to have her for Cody."

What age could the woman possibly be? Maggie wondered automatically. If she raised Eric, who must be forty . . . Ghania looked ageless as a North Atlantic cliff. And just about as tractable.

"How do you do, Ghania?" Maggie asked politely, but she thought with distress, *Oh my poor, dear baby, what will become of you in that woman's care?*

"I give you greetings, Madame," Ghania answered, her voice resonantly flavored by the Malagasy French of her island home.

"I've missed my granddaughter so very much," Maggie said. "Has she been well?" What on earth was there to say to such a creature?

"She has. Had she not been, I would have restored her."

"Like a Queen Anne chair?" Maggie responded, annoyed. But the Amah had no sense of humor; she made a gesture and Cody walked obediently to her side, a dog trained to hand signals. *This is definitely not Mary Poppins*, Maggie thought with a sinking heart.

The child turned, hesitantly. Without waiting for permission, Maggie crossed the room and picked her up, before Ghania could intervene. "Let's go play outside for a while, my love," she said.

"The child should rest now," the Amah interjected.

"The child should play with her grandmother," Maggie answered sweetly, heading for the door. She was relieved to see that her daughter followed.

Maggie tried a dozen ways to get through to Jenna on some human level, as the day progressed, but all doors and windows of the heart seemed closed. The facade was so beautiful, but who was home inside? *What did life consist of here?* Maggie asked. *Did she have a therapist or counselor to help her stay straight? What did Jenna do all day? Did she see her old friends?* Maggie asked the questions and Jenna parried them noncommittally. There seemed only a perfunctory connection between mother and child, and Jenna's conversation about Eric sounded like a recorded message.

Maggie and Ghania were at odds over nearly every aspect of Cody's day. She was not permitted to play with other children, the grandmother was told. Nursery school was not an option. The Amah was to be her only teacher and companion. Jenna kept a disinterested distance, deferring to Ghania on all points.

*Do you ever just hold your baby in your arms and thank God she exists in the world?* Maggie wanted to ask her daughter, but didn't. *Do you play with her and laugh with her and help her learn what she'll need to know to be happy? Or does Ghania hold sway over every nuance of Cody's small life, now.* The thought chilled her.

"Don't you find Ghania a trifle heavy-handed?" she finally asked.

"She's a superb nanny, Mother," Jenna said dismissively. "Why, Cody's manners are impeccable now, after only a month. And she's not so spoiled anymore."

Maggie accepted the slap without comment; if she lost access to Cody altogether, the little girl would be swallowed up by this cloistered, laughterless world, of mothers who dress up to go nowhere, fathers who are disturbed by child sounds, and nannies who look like they should be minding the Addams family children.

All afternoon, Maggie struggled to break through the strange new reserve she saw in Cody; she played all their old games and sang the songs from Gymboree . . . like a therapist luring back an amnesia victim with familiar scenes. By late in the day, the child seemed a bit more like the Cody she remembered. Then it was time to go.

Maggie lingered with her leavetaking; far from feeling relieved by what she'd seen, she was more troubled than when she'd arrived.

Cody stood obediently at Ghania's side, staring at Maggie's preparation for departure; the distress in the child's eyes mirrored her own. Maggie bent to kiss her good-bye, holding her longer than need be, breathing her own strength into every cell of the little body. She felt it was a criminal act to leave her behind in this frightening place, but could see no alternative.

"I love you, little bug," she said, lifting Cody into her arms once more and hugging her close. "I guess I have to go home now, but I promise I'll come back very, *very* soon." Maggie felt the small arms tighten around her in a resolute grip.

"Take me with you, Mim!" the child whispered urgently, into her grandmother's ear. "*Please* take me home. They hurt the baby." Maggie's stomach clutched; those were the words she and Maria always used when Cody banged her head or skinned her knee. "*Did something bad hurt the baby? Don't worry, we'll kiss it and make it better.*"

"You really should try to beat the rush hour traffic, Mother," Jenna prodded, glancing significantly at the Patek-Philippe on her wrist. She reached out to take the child from her mother's arms; both Maggie and Cody let go with equal reluctance, and the grandmother got only as far as the door when it happened.

"Mim!" Cody screamed, with sudden desperation, wrenching herself free of Jenna's grip. She ran after Maggie, grabbing her legs in an iron hold.

"Don't leave me here!" she shrieked. "*They hurt the baby!*"

Ghania moved with incredible swiftness for one so large. She crossed the floor in a stride and twisted Cody from Maggie's arms in a wrench so fierce, the grandmother had to let go to keep the child from being torn apart.

"Help me, Mim! *Help me!*" Cody screamed, pounding at Ghania with her little fists and feet, as the woman carried her away.

"*Please*, Jenna! Don't do this!" Maggie begged, tears welling. "Let her come back to New York with me for a little while. I miss her so badly. I'll bring her back to you in a day or so. Please, Jenna. She's so upset!"

The sound of Cody's screams made her words nearly unintelligible.

"I think you'd best go now, Mother," Jenna replied icily.

"Jenna, please! She needs to be comforted," Maggie pleaded. "At least let me try to calm her down."

"Mim! Help me!" Cody's cries were echoing now, down the long corridors. She sounded far away.

"Dear God, Jenna!" Maggie breathed, furious, frightened. "Is this really necessary?"

"If your visits will cause the child such distress, Mrs. O'Connor," a male voice interrupted, and Maggie turned to see Eric had entered the room. He was bigger than she remembered, more rugged of feature. "I'm afraid we won't be able to ask you to visit, if you have so unsettling an effect on her."

"How dare you threaten me," Maggie snapped, sick to death of the whole macabre situation. "It wasn't *I* who upset her. She simply misses me! I'm the only family she's ever had . . . surely you can understand that she misses me, as I miss her."

"And surely you can understand that such a disturbance isn't good for the child's constitution. I wasn't threatening you, Mrs. O'Connor, I was merely seeing to Cody's welfare."

"And what about her emotional welfare? What about the loss she feels at having her world turned upside down?"

"She will get over it."

There was nothing left to say, and no reason to stay a minute longer.

CODY sat on her bed, in the austere nursery, after Maggie left, looking fearful, but defiant. She could see Ghania and the man Mommy said she was supposed to call Daddy talking in the doorway; but she didn't care. *She*

*wanted Mim!* No matter what they said, or what they did to her, she wanted Mim. Two big tears welled in her eyes and trickled down her plump cheeks. She wasn't supposed to cry, they said. If she cried again, they would never let Mim come back. Cody tried hard not to, but there was a big, hurtful lump inside her, and the tears came from there. Mim had made her feel so safe again, for a whole day! Mim's chest was just as soft and warm as she remembered. Her hair and skin smelled like home . . . and all the love in the world was in Mim's eyes. Cody sat on the edge of the bed and tried very hard to know what to do to get Mim back.

The words they were saying drifted toward her. "We must keep the woman away," Ghania stated emphatically. "The child will be contaminated. There is a heart bond between them. Very strong. Very old."

"We have no need for concern," Eric replied, with confidence. "There's so little time left. Even if she finds out, she can do nothing."

Eric stared for a long moment at the little girl on the bed. "At times it is difficult to believe that so small a human can have such importance in the world."

"Do not mistake her for a child, Eric. The envelope is an illusion."

The man nodded and left the room.

Cody saw the Daddy-man shut the nursery door behind him. Ghania smiled malevolently at her. "You will remain here until I return. Then we will determine what your punishment shall be." She didn't sound angry anymore, just mean.

Ghania made her way from Cody's bedroom to her own. She glanced in the mirror as she entered her suite. There were a few stray hairs escaping her turban, so she stopped to reposition it, then, suddenly craving freedom, she shook it off entirely and loosed a long torrent of jet black hair, that fell to her waist. Ghania examined herself again in the glass; it was the self-examination of a woman of great vanity.

Undoing the frog-closures of her djellabah, she let the cloaklike garment drop to the floor heedlessly. Clad only in the elaborate loincloth *ibante* that is the Ju Ju priest's source of power, Ghania stood before the mirror, breathing deeper and deeper, until a trancelike condition had been achieved.

In this altered state, Ghania glided to the huge armoire that dominated the wall opposite her bed. She turned a key in the lock and opened the double doors wide, revealing an altar within.

A severed goat's head dominated the center, its horns stained with blood, its red eyes glistening with an unnatural light. Black candles stood in candle holders made from human skulls; small bones were scattered in seeming patterns near a chalice that was ancient and well used.

A small rag doll protruded from the goat's obscene lips, its little arms and legs flopped past the yellowed teeth and blackened tongue.

The doll had Cody's face.

MAGGIE sat behind the wheel of her car, after leaving the Vannier house, tears streaming. *What in God's name were they doing to Cody in that house?* Those terrified screams . . . the desperation in her sad eyes . . .

The blaring horn of the eighteen-wheeler jarred her attention back to the road; she fought the steering wheel to avoid a head-on collision with a construction site. Thank God the trucker had blasted her with his horn! I-95 was no place to lose your concentration. *Keep your wits about you, damnit!*

Cody's screams still resounded in her ears. What could she do to rescue the child from that hateful world? And what the *hell* was wrong with Jenna, that she didn't see the disastrous changes that had been wrought, in only one month? What kind of creature had she given birth to, who could wrench a child from home and warmth and safety so abruptly, and plunge her into such a cold and heartless place?

Maggie pulled gratefully into her garage. She barely nodded to the attendant with whom she usually shared pleasantries; she needed to get home to think this through.

Her house felt warm and welcoming, but Maggie merely shrugged off coat and shoes, and headed blindly for the living room. As she passed the liquor cabinet she almost stopped to pour herself a drink, an unheard-of move. She had no head for alcohol and seldom drank anything stronger than wine, but tonight she felt chilled to the bone, with an unnatural cold. As if all the warmth of the world had vanished, and what was left was icy and alien.

She passed the liquor cabinet by and dialed the phone. "Amanda? Maggie. I've been to see Cody." Then the whole story tumbled out.

"Ghania doesn't sound like any mammy I ever knew," Amanda responded, disturbed. "She sounds hard as a piece of the nether millstone, as they say back home." Maggie was smart and rational and not in the least given to hyperbole; the situation in Greenwich must be really bizarre to put her into such a state.

"There's something about Madagascar darkies that's niggling at me, though, darlin'," she mused. "I believe Mammy Erline told me something years ago . . . I'll have to think on it." She paused, trying to remember. "Are you sure you shouldn't go to the authorities about this?"

"I'm beginning to think I've got to talk to somebody who could find out about these people. I just don't know who."

"Just be careful, darlin', won't you?" Amanda replied worriedly. "I keep thinking my daddy would say, 'Never let anyone know you're nosing around, until you know what kind of people you're nosing.' With the amount of money this Vannier has, there's bound to be power somewhere in the bushes."

Maggie collapsed into a hot bath, trying to get warm, and to soak the tension from her bones, but every vision that floated into her mind was of a desperate little girl, begging for help.

# CHAPTER 7

Cody stood in front of Ghania, trying hard not to listen to what she was saying. It had been over a week since Mim's visit; the days were long and the nights worse. Ghania was telling her bad stories about Mim, again.

"You think your grandmama loves you?" the Amah sneered. "She doesn't even come to see you, she is so glad you are gone."

Cody felt tears puddling close to her eyes, and she blinked rapidly to keep them in. "Mim loves me," she said resolutely, but it was getting hard to know what was true. It had been eight days since Mim's visit and she hadn't even called once. And every day Ghania said bad things . . . hurtful things. Things that made her wonder . . .

"Did she ever come back to see you?" Ghania demanded. "Did she even call you on the phone?" Sullenly, the little girl shook her head no. She didn't know why Mim hadn't come back to see her—she'd *promised* she would. She didn't know of the dozen phone calls from Maggie that had been rebuffed on Ghania's orders. Every night when she went to bed, she prayed and prayed, but Mim didn't come back.

"Your grandmama so happy you gone, she tell everyone she know, 'That little girl ruin my life for three years. Now I have some fun.' Ghania laughed, but her eyes didn't change. Cody hated Ghania's eyes. They glittered like an animal's and made her scared.

"Mim loves me," she murmured, afraid to say it out loud, and equally afraid not to. If she didn't keep saying it, maybe she would stop believing.

Ghania threw back her head and laughed. "Foolish child! Doesn't even know who her friends are. Ghania is the one you must have for your friend. Ghania is magic. Ghania knows *everything* you do and *everything* you say. Ghania even know what you think! You can have no secrets from Ghania, so you better be careful of every thought in your head, because I look inside and I see them all! Just like you made of glass."

Cody's eyes widened. What if that were true? Ghania would know how much she hated her, and how much she needed Mim.

"Last night, when you were in your bed, Ghania looked inside your brain, child, like it was a crystal ball. Ghania heard you pray to that stupid God who doesn't care about you, one little bit."

"God loves me!" Cody said defiantly. "Mim said so!"

"He loves you?" Ghania sniffed. "*Ridiculous!* Does he answer your prayers? *No!* Does he make your grand-mama love you enough to come get you? *No!* He doesn't even know you exist, this foolish God of yours."

The Amah caught Cody's horrified gaze with her own mesmeric one. "Ghania knows the *friendly* Gods, child . . . the ones who make your wishes come true."

"There's only one God," Cody said stubbornly. "Mim told me."

"What does she know!" Ghania replied vehemently. "My island got Gods your grandmama never heard of. Gods that kill you if you make them mad . . . Gods that make all your dreams come true, if you know how to ask them.

"I heard your prayers last night . . . you ask for Mim to come. But is she here? *No.* Stupid God did not bring her! I will tell you which God to pray to, if you be my friend, child. I will prove to you how powerful my God is. Tonight, you will pray to the God whose name I will whisper in your ear. And whatever you ask for will be given to you.''

Cody looked uncertain. Maybe Ghania's God was scary, like Ghania and the Daddy-man.

''If you ask him to send your grandmama here tomorrow, he will do it,'' Ghania wheedled, playing her trump. She had instructed Jenna to keep Maggie away; now she would rescind the order. ''Do you want to know his name or not?''

Cody hesitated. Ghania raised her great body, lithe as a cougar, and moved toward the door.

''Wait!'' Cody called after her nervously. ''I want Mim!'' Anything to get Mim back. Mim would understand she had to do it.

Ghania smiled in satisfaction and leaned down to whisper a strange sound into the child's ear three times. It didn't sound like a name, just a hissing noise. Cody started to repeat it aloud, but Ghania's hand closed over her mouth before the word escaped.

''Never!'' she spat. ''This is a God of power! Never speak his name except in your thoughts.'' Cody felt the electricity of fear tingle through her. What if this was a bad God?

''Tomorrow he will give you what you want.'' Ghania dangled the carrot, and the promise of Mim's return was too powerful to resist. Cody repeated the name in her head many times after Ghania was gone, to keep from forgetting it.

# CHAPTER 8

"I was a little startled by your urgent invitation this morning, Jenna," Maggie said when she arrived in Greenwich after her daughter's call. "I've tried to reach you for days with no success, and then suddenly, I'm summoned? I've been really worried about Cody since my last visit here. Is she all right?"

"Of course, she's all right, Mother," Jenna replied, bristling. "Why wouldn't she be?"

"Perhaps, because she's been yanked out of a familiar environment and plopped into one that's hardly ordinary. Perhaps, because she was dragged out of my arms by Jabba-the-Nanny, who seems to have all the child-rearing skills of Josef Mengele."

"Really, Mother, don't you think *you're* being just a little melodramatic?"

"No, Jenna, I don't think so. I think you're putting too much power in that Amah's hands. *You're* Cody's mother, not Ghania. You must see there's been a significant personality change in the child in just a month."

"There certainly has been, Mother, and I think it's for the better."

Maggie sighed, and tried again. "Are *you* all right, Jenna?" she asked, quelling her frustration. "You seem so unreachable. Isn't there any way we can talk to each other?"

"Look, I don't want to fight with you, Mom," the girl replied. "So please don't start with me. My life is perfect here, and then you come along trying to change things where Cody is concerned, and it just makes me mad. That's all."

50

"Oh, Jenna. It's so sad that you and I don't seem to know how to talk to each other," Maggie said, unnerved by the continuing failure. "I'm so sorry if I don't say the right things to you—but I'm just as worried about you as I am about Cody. Something is very wrong here, Jenna! This place seems so desolate, so alien. Are you absolutely sure you're happy here?"

Jenna smiled frostily. "I'm perfectly happy, Mother. How could I not be happy—look at everything I've got."

"*Things* are not what make people happy, Jenna. People do. And valuable work does. And—"

"Look, Mom!" Jenna cut her off. "I don't see things the way you do. I never did. I never will. I called you to come here, because I didn't want you worrying about Cody, after the other day. So, why don't we just go see her and forget about analyzing my life, okay?"

Another closed door. Maggie took the rebuff stoically; at least this time it was civil.

"I'm glad you called—I hate it when things go wrong between us. And I would really like to be able to spend a little time alone with Cody, Jenna, if that's possible. You must realize life is very lonesome for me, now that she's gone."

Maggie could read the calculation in Jenna's face . . . *Maybe if I let her see the child alone, she'll go away.* "All right, Mother. If she isn't napping, you can spend an hour with her."

"Without Ghania?"

"If that would make you happy." Jenna had been startled when Ghania told her to see to it Maggie visited today. She still had no idea why the Amah had insisted.

"Oh, Jenna, it would! I promise I won't cause a hassle about going home. If she sees that I've returned so quickly, she won't be so skittish about my leaving again."

Jenna departed and Maggie stood at the window, staring out across the expansive lawn. Jenna's eyes were dilated and hooded—her speech, slightly slurred. She knew there was no point arguing with an addict who was using, but it saddened her to the soul. She didn't intend to leave today, until she had a handle on what was going on in this strange household.

CODY'S face seemed to implode with emotion when she saw her grandmother. There was joy, dismay, relief, and something else Maggie couldn't decipher. Something terrible and haunted. She took the child into her arms and held her to her heart for a long while, without speaking. She could feel the tension drain, and relief fill up the space it had occupied.

"Sweetheart, let's go outside for a walk, shall we?" she said, when she was sure she could control her voice. "The weather is lovely and we'll have a chance to have a good, long talk." Cody nodded her head yes, but looked so apprehensive that Maggie hastened her out the door. She felt better the minute she hit the lawn, but Cody twice looked back fearfully toward the house. Maggie followed the trajectory of her gaze and saw Ghania, standing sentinel-like at an upstairs window.

She hurried Cody along, protecting her from the malevolent stare with her own body. She headed left, off the great lawn, and zigzagged toward the beach. Surely there was some spot on this vast estate where Ghania's presence could be unfelt for an hour.

The beach was March-cold and the water, slate, with occasional specks of foam. Maggie wrapped the child's coat close around her; took the scarf from her own neck and tied it around Cody's ears to protect her from the chill ocean breeze.

"I love you, sweetheart," she began, not quite knowing how to proceed in her mission, without further frightening the child. "You know I love you with all my heart . . ."

"Ghania says you don't," Cody murmured, not looking at Maggie, but down at the sand. "She says if you loved me, you would take me home."

Maggie's heart lurched at the cruelty of the lie.

"Not love you?" she exploded. "How dare she say such a terrible thing? You listen to me, sweetheart, and listen with all your might, understand?" Cody nodded her head yes, but she still didn't look Maggie in the eye. "The reason I haven't taken you home is because your mommy and Eric *won't let me*.

"I love you so much, Cody, that every single day and night, *every single minute* since you left, I have missed you and thought about you and wished we were together! How could you ever believe such a lie, sweetheart, when you've known since you were the size of a mouse how much I love you?"

"Ghania knows a lot of things, Mim," Cody whispered.

"What things, Cody? What does Ghania know?"

"She knows how to look in my head and see what I'm thinking," the child answered guilelessly.

"She does *not* know how to do that, Cody!" Maggie said, horrified. "No one does."

"Ghania knows God, Mim," the little girl said in an awestruck voice that took Maggie aback.

"What do you mean, sweetheart? We all know God, that's why we pray to Him."

Cody shook her head vehemently. "It's not *that* God, Mim. Ghania knows a different one."

"*Cody!*" Maggie said with great seriousness. "There is only one God, and no matter what Ghania says, she does not know Him any better than we do!"

"Yes, she does," the child persisted.

"How do you know that?"

"Because I prayed and prayed for you to save me and you never came. And then Ghania told me about the God who could make you come here. And I prayed to him last night and then you came."

Rage at Ghania's vile manipulation filled Maggie. She

took Cody by the shoulders and turned her around so that the child's eyes couldn't avoid her own.

"Now you listen to me, my little love," she said in a tone that left no room for dissent. "And you listen *very*, very carefully. Here's how you can know for sure that I love you: You just reach inside Cody, and you remember every day and every night we ever spent together. You remember how you *felt*, safe and warm and loved. You remember every happy moment we ever had together since you were a tiny baby. *Nobody* can talk you out of those memories, Cody. They *belong* to you. Forever. And if anybody ever tries to confuse you, or lie to you, or make you believe anything bad about me, you just reach inside your heart and you will know the truth. Do you understand me, Cody? Love *feels* good. It feels safe and warm and happy. When somebody loves you, that's how you feel, understand? You can believe your feelings, sweetheart, even when people try to confuse you with words. Okay?"

Cody hesitantly nodded her head yes.

"Now let's talk about Ghania. She does *not* read minds because *nobody* reads minds. Some people just pretend to. And I didn't come here today because her God sent me, I came because I love you and I miss you. And I wanted to make sure you were safe. I've been calling every single day since my last visit, trying to get to see you, but it wasn't till today that your mommy allowed it."

Another nod.

"Now Cody, this is very, *very* important. The other day when I was here, you said *they hurt the baby*. Can you tell Mim what you meant by that?"

Cody squirmed in Maggie's grasp, again unwilling to meet her eyes.

"I'm afraid," she said finally in a tiny, frightened whisper.

"Of what, sweetheart? What are you afraid of?"

"Somebody's screaming," she quavered, tears blurring the words. "At night. I hear them. Somebody gets hurt really bad and when Ghania hears it, she smiles and I get scared."

Maggie frowned. Could Cody be hearing the TV and misunderstanding? Or Eric and Jenna? It didn't make sense.

"Are you sure, love? This is very important, Cody. Could it be the TV?"

Cody shook her head no emphatically.

"Once," she said, so softly Maggie could hardly hear, "I saw the blood."

"The blood? What blood?"

"From the Screamers."

Maggie's heart thudded in her chest. She tried to sound calm.

"How do you know it was from the Screamers, Cody? How do you know it was blood? Maybe it was ketchup."

Cody looked haunted again, that strange look Maggie had seen earlier.

"Ghania told me," she said, in a voice so small Maggie really had to concentrate. "I was bad and she showed me the blood from the Screamers. She said she could make me a Screamers, too." The child's voice wavered at the last of it, as if she could barely say the words.

Maggie's stomach turned over. She pulled Cody very close, and hugged her to hide the tears in her own eyes. She had to bite her lip to stay in control.

"Is there anything else, Cody? Does anything else hurt you or frighten you?"

"She tries to make me drink the cocktail. But I won't, so she hits me, and she twists my arm so it hurts me."

"Cocktail?" Maggie asked, puzzled. "What kind of cocktail, sweetie, does it have liquor in it?"

Cody shook her head no.

"What then? What's in the cocktail, and why does she want you to drink it?"

"Ghania says it will make me one of them."

"One of them? One of what?"

Cody shrugged her little shoulders. There was a lost and helpless character to the shrug. "I don't know,

Mim. But it makes you really sick. Once she held my nose and made me drink it, but I threw up on her so she stopped.''

"Good for you!" Maggie applauded. What could this mean? Could Cody be having nightmares? None of it made sense, except that it was all ghastly and abusive.

"Could I come home now, Mim?" Cody asked softly. "I promise to be really good if you let me come home." *Dear God, she thinks it's her fault she's here . . .*

Hot tears trickled down Maggie's cheeks as she cast about in her mind for how to explain to the child that she must stay.

"Oh Cody, I want to take you home, so much . . . I love you more than anything in this world. I want you to know that, *in your heart*. That's where you and I are going to keep everything that's between us . . . in our hearts, okay? So if anybody asks you what we talked about, or if anybody says she can read your mind, you'll know our secrets are safe, because they aren't in your mind, they're in your heart. Okay?"

"Okay." Cody bit her lower lip nervously, something she always did when she was frightened.

"Now, here comes the hard part, sweetheart. I can't take you home with me today." Cody's face fell apart and tears squeezed free. "No . . . no . . . listen to me, baby! You must *listen*. I am going to help you, Cody. I give you my word of honor I won't let anyone hurt you, do you understand? I've never ever broken my promise to you, have I? Not once since you were born. Not in anything little and not in anything big. Oh, please baby, tell me you understand that!" Maggie and Cody clung to each other on the beach, their tears turning icy in the cold wind.

"The law says I can't take you today, sweetheart." Cody's arms tightened around Maggie's neck, terror in the gesture. "But I promise you I will find a way to make you safe again. I just need to talk to some people who'll know how to do this, and it might take me a little while."

Cody was crying hard now, the sobs reverberating through Maggie's coat. But it was silent, unnatural crying for a child. Soundless and despairing.

Maggie could see Jenna and Ghania coming toward them on the strand.

"Listen to me, Cody, they're coming, so I have to say this fast. *I will* be back for you. No matter what anyone tells you. I will come back to get you. Because I love you. More than everything else in this world! And you love me. Nothing on earth can change that. Everything we've said, and everything we are, is in our hearts now, and no one—especially Ghania—can see it, or know anything about it. Do you understand that?"

The urgency in Maggie's voice reached the child through her fear. "Now we can't make another scene like the other day or . . ." She didn't want to say they wouldn't let her back in, it gave them too much power in the child's mind. "Or they'll say I upset you when I visit, and we don't want them to think that."

Cody snuffled and nodded.

"We have to be brave now, Cody, for each other. Remember. I love you. All there is. *And I'll be back*. I swear to God, I will."

Maggie scooped up the child and held her in a fierce embrace, deliberately walking past the Amah without a word.

# CHAPTER 9

Maggie drummed her short fingernails on the desk top, at 8:00 A.M. the next morning, and tried to quell her agitation; she'd been up half the night trying to figure out what to do. There had to be someone who could help her get to the bottom of this morass.

Could it be that one of Jenna's friends from years ago might still be in touch with her? Maybe there was somebody from the past Jenna'd want to show off her new life to. Maggie rifled the Rolodex impatiently, searching for she-didn't-know-who. She dialed six phone numbers without a successful response . . . no one had seen Jenna in years, or if they had, they wouldn't say. Discouraged, she tried one final possibility.

Cheri Adams had been with Jenna in the last rehab; they'd gotten pretty close there, and Maggie had liked the girl, enough to enlist her aid in searching for Jenna when she'd first disappeared. She'd even stayed in contact with Cheri for a while, after the search proved futile, but then had lost touch, until one day she and Cody had bumped into the girl in Washington Square Park.

Maggie dialed her number, afraid to hope. Cheri sounded sober when she answered, subdued and straight. Had Cheri seen Jenna recently? she asked. *Yes.* Jenna doesn't seem like herself, Maggie said. Do you know if there's anything wrong? There was a significant pause at the other end of the phone, as Cheri juggled loyalties.

"I've seen her twice, Mrs. O'Connor, since she's living in Greenwich," she said finally. "She wanted to show off that incredible house and that weird guy she's married to." Again the hesitancy.

"I think she's using, Mrs. O'Connor. Big time," Cheri explained, her voice troubled, uncertain. "I tried to get her to do something about it, but she really thinks she's got the world by the tail. I guess she's gotta do what she's gotta do, so I didn't push it. But she said some things that frightened me . . . I mean, maybe drugs aren't the only thing she's into. I'm only telling you this because of the little girl. Jenna's got a right to screw up her own life with that shit if she wants to, but kids are different. They've got rights, too."

"Cheri, what frightened you at Jenna's? Is Cody in danger?"

"I feel like I'm betraying Jenna's trust even talking to you like this, Mrs. O'Connor, but you've always been real nice to me and I remember thinking, when we met that day in the park, how good you were to Jenna's kid. I could see you really loved her and all . . ." She paused again and Maggie heard the in-drawn breath at the other end, the girl getting up her courage.

"Look, Mrs. O'Connor, please don't ask me why I'm saying this, but I think you'd better get that baby out of that house."

"Why, Cheri? What's wrong there?" Maggie's heart beat faster.

"I can't tell you, Mrs. O'Connor. Honest to God, I can't! It's just that I think I know what she's into, through some friends of mine. I'm not really sure, and I don't want to make trouble for her, if I'm wrong . . . but if I'm right, it's real dangerous for Cody."

"Please, Cheri. Please tell me what you mean! I can't just take Cody away from there without some explanation. It's against the law."

"If I'm right, Mrs. O'Connor, Jenna and Eric are into things a lot more against the law than you could ever be. Just please get the kid out of that house . . ." Cheri's voice was strained, agitated now, with the weight of what she wasn't saying.

"Just *listen to me* and get that baby out of there, will you? Even Jenna would want you to, if she were in her right mind. But there's something wrong with her . . . more than just the drugs. She's like somebody else, not Jenna. I don't know how to describe what I mean, but it's spooky. I can't say any more, Mrs. O'Connor. Honest to God, I can't!" The phone clicked off and Maggie stood with the receiver in her hand, the dial tone making its lonely, persistent sound.

Maybe the private detective agency she'd used to trace Jenna could help in some way, she thought frantically, as she dialed. The director, Bill Schmidt, was an ex-FBI man; he listened, occasionally breaking into her hurried explanation, then he responded.

"Look, Mrs. O'Connor, I like you, and I don't want to mislead you. It's not like you see in the movies. We can't go breaking into people's estates, like Magnum on TV. If you want us to check this out for you on a fact-finding mission, we'll do it, but to get the goods on anyone in a place that well protected, we'll need electronic surveillance. Trucks, men, recording equipment . . . it'll cost you at least a thousand bucks a night, and I gotta be honest with you, the courts don't like to accept recorded surveillance from a PI, because they say it could be doctored. And it's not as if we could go storming in there like John Wayne and pull that little girl out for you, either. I'm really sorry, Mrs. O'Connor, that you're in this kind of trouble, but my advice is it would be a big waste of money for you to hire us. Why don't you try Child Welfare or the police."

The Bureau of Child Welfare was just as drab as every other bureaucratic office in the huge municipal complex. Dreary yellow and institutional gray, no Disney characters in evidence. Maggie chided herself for being repelled by the place; it didn't matter what it looked like, only what it could accomplish. Surely, someone here would care about a little child in danger.

A woman dressed in a blue, shapeless suit ushered her into a small cubicle with a metal desk and sat down.

"What can I do for you?" she asked with the weary expectation of one who runs a complaint window.

"My daughter is a heroin addict," Maggie began, cringing internally at the words. "She had a baby three years ago, and left her in my care while she went back to the streets. I didn't hear from her until a month ago when she arrived back, married, and with a house in Greenwich—"

"If she has a house in Greenwich," the woman interrupted, with the first hint of animation, "you're in the wrong place. We have no jurisdiction over Connecticut."

"But *I* live here in the city," Maggie countered. "The baby—Cody's her name—lived her whole life in New York City. She's only been in Connecticut for a month."

"Be that as it may, Mrs. O'Connor, if the parents live in Connecticut, the case is out of our jurisdiction."

"Please . . . if you'll just let me tell you my story . . ." she persisted. "I'm terrified that my granddaughter may be in some kind of danger. I think her mother may be using drugs again . . ."

"Can you prove that allegation? Has she been tested recently?"

"No. I mean, I don't really know. She's twenty-one years old, so I can't force her to be tested against her will."

The woman wagged her head disapprovingly. "Even if she is on drugs, Mrs. O'Connor, the state won't consider heroin addiction alone a reason to interfere in your daughter's child rearing." She looked annoyed that Maggie was wasting her time. "Are there physical signs of abuse? Scars, burns, unexplained bruises?"

Maggie shook her head. "It's not that simple, I'm afraid. The damage seems to be mostly psychological. Cody's frightened . . . withdrawn. She was never, ever like that before. She isn't allowed to play with other children, she's only permitted to play with her nanny, who's like a character out of *Dark Shadows*. She's being threatened and made to drink some kind of concoction—"

"Look, Mrs. O'Connor," the woman broke in impatiently, "let me save us both some time. A lot of grandmothers are coming in here lately, with similar tales. A drug addict kid drops off a baby and comes back to pick it up years later, after the grandmother has become attached. The law is very clear on this issue. You've got no rights whatsoever. The child belongs to your daughter, and the courts are very determined to keep babies with birth mothers, unless there's documented evidence of physical abuse. So, I'm afraid there really isn't anything you can do but stay out of the picture. If you insist on pursuing this, my advice would be to let your daughter keep the child for a while and abuse her, and then bring it to the attention of the authorities. *Then* you'll have a case."

Maggie sat bolt upright in the chair, genuinely shocked. "Let my daughter *abuse* her . . . then I'll have a case? I suppose if I let my daughter *kill* her, I'll have a better case!"

The woman behind the desk sat back a moment and glared at Maggie. When she spoke her voice was under tight control. "Look, Mrs. O'Connor, I'm sure you're under a lot of pressure, so I'll try not to take offense at that last remark. But here's the reality I deal with every day. There are thirty thousand cases in my files, of children who *do* show physical signs of abuse . . . kids who've been burned or tortured or chained in a bathtub. Kids who *are* in my geographic jurisdiction. I do not have the resources, or the investigators, or the available court time, to deal with one third of those children, let alone your granddaughter. By the time the system gets around to most of them it will be too late to help." She took a deep breath and sighed audibly; she had frustrations, too.

"*You* have no case. Even if your suspicions are correct, *you have no case*."

Maggie stood outside the municipal building staring, unseeing, at the pigeons for a while, before she decided to go to the police, first thing in the morning.

THE living room couch where Maggie sat was piled high with papers. She'd been trying hard to concentrate all evening with minimal success. Her once wide world had narrowed to a tiny focus. Cody was gone. Cody was in danger. Those two thoughts blotted out all else.

*"Oh God, baby, how I miss you!"* A sudden flash flood of longing surged through Maggie like an unexpected wave that hits when you're nearing shore, drowning her in loneliness . . . sucking her out past the markers, into fathomless fear.

She fought her way back through the icy torrent, shocked by its magnitude. The taxes won't wait past tonight, she chided herself forcefully. The IRS doesn't give a damn if my heart is broken. *Life goes on; I forget just why.*

Emphatically, she pushed her glasses up on her nose one more time, hating their damnable reminder of middle age. Another vulnerability. "You can see the grass grow, child," her grandmother always said when she was small; she'd thought it would remain so forever. Instead, she was doomed to these wretched little Ben Franklin spectacles, that slalomed down her nose, and were never where she needed them to be.

The telephone was a welcome diversion; Maggie padded barefoot across the carpet to answer the call.

"I know what your daughter is doing, Mrs. O'Connor," an anonymous female voice whispered hoarsely. The speaker sounded scared. "Your daughter's involved with Maa Kheru, God help her." Maggie's brain shifted gears to sudden alert.

"Who are you?" she demanded. "What do you know about my daughter?

"It doesn't matter who I am. What matters is Maa Kheru!"

"What on earth is Maa Kheru?"

"It's a high-priced cult full of powerful people. They control things! The police . . . the newspapers . . . You don't know how dangerous they are. Oh, God . . . I wish I didn't know, either!" The voice sounded semi-hysterical. "They worship Satan, Mrs. O'Connor. They've sold their souls to get success and money."

"Who *are* you?" Maggie shouted, really frightened, now. "How do you know all this?"

"I used to live with Maa Kheru . . . you don't know

what they're capable of . . ." There was a strangled sob, then, "They killed my baby! I'm in hiding . . . they're after me, and they'll get me, too—it's only a matter of time till they kill me. I only called so you could do something to save that child. Please don't let them sacrifice her like they did my Stacy. *They skinned her alive*, Mrs. O'Connor, do you understand? They skinned my baby and *they drank her blood!*" Before Maggie could recover enough to reply, the phone went dead.

She grabbed her coat from the hall closet and ran toward the police station.

# CHAPTER 10

The Sixth Precinct house was located on West Tenth Street between Bleecker and Hudson streets. Maggie raced up the steps trying to stay calm enough to sound coherent.

The desk sergeant was stocky and dark complected, with what looked like five o'clock shadow, long out of control by 7:00 P.M. He cut her off halfway through her explanation, with a practiced gesture.

"No point telling me your whole story, ma'am. What you need is a detective," he pronounced. "I'll see who's available." He motioned to a wooden bench against the wall, but Maggie was too agitated to sit down. The desk sergeant finished his paperwork, before picking up the phone.

Finally, a big, lethargic-looking man beckoned her from the doorway; he was gray all over, hair and eyes, pants and tie—even his sallow skin had the grayish tinge of one who never sees sunlight. Maggie groaned inwardly as she followed him through the rabbit warren offices; he had the look of a man who isn't happy in his work. Detective Hillyer motioned her to a seat, then ignored her for a full five minutes while he took two phone calls and dialed another.

"Okay," he said finally, glancing at the paper the desk sergeant had filled out. "You've got a drug addict kid who's causing you problems, right? Just like everybody else in New York."

Maggie felt herself bristle and tried to stay calm. She began the tangled story, careful not to sound like an overprotective grandma. She referred to her notebook for dates and times. Hillyer leaned back in his chair without comment, took three more telephone calls in a row, forcing Maggie to backtrack in her story each time for continuity. Finally, he held up his hand to stop the rush of words that was becoming progressively more urgent.

"Look, Mrs. . . . . O'Connor," he referred to the paper to refresh his memory of her name. "This isn't a police matter. You've got no crime, no victim. What you've got here is a family that disagrees about how to raise a baby. What you need is maybe a counselor . . ."

"Have you heard a word I've said, Detective?" Maggie asked tautly. "Or were you too busy on the phone to hear me? In the last twenty minutes, you've talked to everyone in New York but your bookie, while I've been trying to tell you there's a three-year-old child in grave danger, who just might need your help, and all you can tell me is to see a counselor?" Her voice had risen loud enough to attract other ears in the immediate vicinity.

"Listen, Mrs. O'Connor, you come in here with a story about a kid, who's living in the lap of luxury in Greenwich, yet—not even in this precinct—and you expect me to pull some kind of rabbit out of a hat . . ."

"What I *expect* you to do is listen to what I have to say, and give me some sensible advice, Detective. I expect you to care that a baby may be in danger. You're a policeman for God's sake! Aren't you supposed to help people in trouble?"

Eyes all over the precinct house were now riveted on Maggie, as if E.F. Hutton had spoken. Hillyer opened his mouth to reply, when a male voice interrupted. "Hank," it said with quiet authority, "how about letting me take this one?" Startled, Maggie looked up at the source of the voice.

A tall, lanky man in shirtsleeves stood behind her in the doorway. He looked tired and Irish. Maggie's temper and frustration level were now running neck and neck; she was in no mood to be pleasant. She took a long controlled breath and said tightly, "I think I can tell this story just *one more time* before I explode. But after that, the first three rows damned well better step back!"

Hillyer pushed his chair aside and exchanged a glance with the newcomer that said, "This one's a real nut case." Then he left, handing over the small folder as he did so. The new arrival looked slightly amused, which further infuriated Maggie.

"Look, Detective . . ."

"Devlin," he said. "Lieutenant Malachy Devlin."

"Lieutenant Devlin, then," she said sharply. "As I have just told the patently uninterested Detective Hillyer, I have a granddaughter who, I think, is in danger." She caught Devlin's obvious surprise at her being a grandmother, but paid it no mind. "I came here hoping somebody, somewhere, might help me find out what I can do to save her." He heard the tears beneath the taut control and any semblance of amusement faded.

"I don't know what to do—and God knows, I'm scared to death that the system doesn't know either, Lieutenant—but unless I can find a way to help her, there's a three-year-old little girl I love, who may not see four . . ."

Devlin reached over and pushed the door shut. He sat on the edge of the desk near Maggie and put the folder down deliberately. She saw that the six-foot-one-inch body moved with a certain confident strength, despite the fatigue she sensed in it.

"Look, I overheard enough of your story to want to help," he said, "but not enough to know how, yet. I hate to ask you to take it from the top, Mrs. O'Connor, but if you're willing to give it one more try, I can at least promise you my undivided attention, and my best shot at advice." He paused, as if willing to wait until she'd reached a decision on the offer, and Maggie saw him clearly for the first time, as he watched her.

There was something about his eyes that inspired confidence. They were gray, flecked with a gold that didn't quite belong in human eyes, but they were an intuitive surprise in an otherwise craggy Irish face that seemed to have weathered it all, the good, the bad, and especially the hard knocks. They looked at you straight on, and straight through.

Maggie's anger receded a little, but she was dismayed to find that when it did, she was very close to tears. She took a deep breath and told her story one more time.

Devlin's interruptions were few, and intelligent; the probing was not to ascertain the state of her mental health, but the facts of her story.

"The world's a sorry place sometimes, isn't it, Mrs. O'Connor?" he said unexpectedly, in a voice that suggested he'd seen too much and been hurt by most of it. "Let me give you an idea of what you're up against here." He took a long eloquent breath, and began.

"What you're telling me is not out of the question in the least. Bad people hurt little children every day of the week in this city. And presumably in Greenwich, too. Sometimes the bad people are rich enough, so nobody does a damned thing about it. I hate to tell you this, but the law is not going to give you a hell of a lot of latitude here. You see, your daughter's rights are going to be protected before your granddaughter's.

"First off, let's take the heroin addiction . . . even if you could prove it—which you probably can't, because your daughter's an adult and you can't force her to take a drug test against her will—but even if you could, heroin addiction by itself doesn't make her an unfit mother in the eyes of the law.''

Maggie started to protest, but he stayed her words with a gesture. "We're talking *law* here, Mrs. O'Connor. Nobody said anything about right or wrong, or justice, for that matter. Just law." His voice was compassionate; she could hear his own anger at the inequities of the system.

"As to satanism . . . I'll bet there isn't a single statute on the books in New York City that would say a satanist can't raise a kid in his own religion. In fact, you'd probably have the ACLU all over you like molasses, if you even tried to get custody on those grounds. Freedom of religion, even if it is satanism, is a cornerstone of our system. For instance, I can tell you for a fact that there's a satanic bible given to the chaplains at West Point, so their constituents in the army can get equal religious counseling. Nutty as that sounds, it's the God's honest truth.

"So, let's just look at what you've got here. First, you'd have to be able to *prove*—not allege, mind you—*prove* that Cody's being neglected or abused. And I just don't see how you're going to do that. This Vannier guy is rich and he's a lawyer, to boot. The kid is cared for by a professional nanny, *and* by her mother, in her own home. There's food, clothes, toys, training—even if the training doesn't ring your bells—so no neglect. As to abuse . . . how are you ever going to prove abuse? Are there marks on the child's body that you've seen? If there are, will they still be there by the time the Bureau of Child Welfare sorts through its paperwork and gets its ass in gear?''

"But what about her mind?" Maggie interjected, exhausted by the unrelenting unfairness. "They're brainwashing her somehow. She's like a zombie around that nanny creature, and she's absolutely terrified."

"Mrs. O'Connor, I have seen the children of drug addicts . . . and I've seen enough child abuse to make Saint Francis of Assisi question God, so believe me, I'm on your side in this. But let's look at it from the court's point of view. Cody's three years old. What psychiatrist, who never saw her when you had her, is going to swear that these people are altering her mind? Altering the behavior of three-year-olds is considered normal parenting.''

Maggie put up her hands in a gesture of defeat; she knew he was right.

"What if I just take her away, Lieutenant Devlin?" she asked desperately. "What if I just leave the city, and take her to somewhere, *anywhere*, to protect her."

"You'll be arrested for kidnapping," he said succinctly. "That's federal, Mrs. O'Connor. FBI. Jail time. Remember the lady who said her husband was molesting her kid and she shipped the child off to God knows where. That lady did *two years* in jail before the President pardoned her. You might not get so lucky . . . then where does that leave Cody, if you're in jail? Then she's got nobody on her side."

Maggie bent her head to her chest, too close to tears to speak. Devlin watched her struggle for control, knowing instinctively she wouldn't give up, no matter what he told her. It touched him.

"How far are you willing to take this, Mrs. O'Connor?" he asked quietly. "This kind of thing could eat up your life, with very little hope of it turning out the way you want."

She looked up at him for a full ten seconds before she said very clearly, "Whatever it takes, Lieutenant."

Devlin stood with his hands in his pockets, watching her closely for a moment. It was apparent the interview was at an end, so Maggie rose to go.

"You're Irish, too, Mrs. O'Connor," he said in a curious non sequitur, and she nodded. "Then you know about the Christophers? Do you remember their motto by any chance?"

Maggie looked at him quizzically, then quoted, " 'It's better to light one candle than to curse the darkness.' "

Devlin smiled. "I can't do anything for you officially, Mrs. O'Connor, but unofficially . . . one Irishman to another . . ." He paused significantly. "I'll see if I can find you some kind of candle, here. Okay? Maybe, I can at least find out whether this Maa Kheru business is real or not. You'll hear from me, one way or the other."

He handed her a card with the precinct number, and scribbled in his direct line beside it.

Maggie thanked him and left. Devlin watched her retreating figure, out the window of the dingy office, thinking this was the last thing he needed right now. He had a caseload up to his ass, and a boss who would think he'd lost his marbles if he even brought up a kid in Greenwich. But there was *something* . . . maybe he'd do a little checking. He sighed. All the nuts in the world lived in the Sixth Precinct.

But instinct said she wasn't that. Devlin admired dignity and courage in the face of the odds, and Maggie O'Connor appeared to have both. He wondered if that had anything at all to do with his wanting to see her again.

THOROUGHLY unnerved, Maggie went home. She couldn't work on the taxes, so she pushed them, disgustedly, into a pile on the couch and sat staring into the fireplace. She had no idea what to do next.

The phone call came close to eleven. It was Lieutenant Devlin; she could tell he was choosing his words very carefully.

"Look, Mrs. O'Connor, I've been checking into this Maa Kheru business for you, and I have some info. The official word is that it's just a crazy fantasy, but I'm not convinced that's true." Maggie took a deep breath.

"If Maa Kheru does exist," he continued, "it's a cartel of power brokers, heavy hitters from every kind of business. Bankers, politicians, lots of theater people, doctors, lawyers, congressmen, senators . . . According to the story—which of course nobody will confirm—they're all practicing Black Magicians—satanists, Voodoo practitioners, Palo Mayombe . . . a sort of ecumenical *Who's Who* in the Devil worship community. They've sold their souls to the Devil in return for fame, fortune, power, whatever. The words 'Maa Kheru' are ancient Words of Power that supposedly open the doorway to Hell. It's all pretty hard to believe in this day and age, of course, but there's a lot of stuff out there that's pretty weird, so maybe we can't discount this entirely, yet. There are plenty of gruesome murders that go uninvestigated every year, just because local law enforcement doesn't want to start a public panic by labeling something satanic, and then not being able to do anything about it. Like I told you earlier, satanism is protected under the Constitution, just like every other religion.''

"I don't know what to do with any of this information, Detective," Maggie said emphatically, "other than be absolutely terrified."

"There's nothing you can do, at the moment, Mrs. O'Connor. But I'd suggest you *stay* terrified until we find out more. If Jenna's really in bed with the Devil, it isn't just your granddaughter who's in danger here. You are, too."

Maggie finished the conversation in a daze, so the next phone ring jarred her; it was Amanda. "I finally remembered what it is that's special about the Malagasy, darlin', and I thought I'd better tell you, even though it won't cheer you up any. Those Madagascar darkies are feared by the other African natives because they practice a very potent type of Black Magic, Maggie. Something real spooky. More atavistic than Candomblé, and all those nasty South American tribal rituals. My informant told me it's the parent of the most evil side of the Voodoo practiced in the Caribbean. You don't think Jenna could be mixed up in anything that grisly do you?"

*Satanism. Black Magic. Evil.* The frightening words kept sizzling in Maggie's head like hot flares. *Sweet Jesus, what am I going to do now?*

# CHAPTER 11

Maggie hit the mat hard and managed a powerful side kick to the ribs, in time to block a lethal blow to her throat. She was sweating profusely, half from exertion, half from the emotions that had brought her to the dojo. She scrambled to her feet, facing her opponent in fighting stance. "I know, Sifu," she panted, "I blinked."

"Blink while you fight and you will close your eyes for eternity," the stocky Chinese master replied amiably. He wasn't even breathing hard. Maggie had seen him best ten young black belts in a demonstration, several months before; breathing hard was not something Mr. Wong ever did, unless he wished to.

Maggie shook her head in sorry agreement.

"I'll work more," she said ruefully. "Another thirty-five years and I'll get to be good at this."

Mr. Wong smiled, his hooded eyes merry and animated, despite the composure of his face. He was not a young man, but his eyes were lively, potent. "So soon you can learn this, Maggie? Very good. Most people take longer."

Maggie smiled at the old man she revered. There were times during Jack's long illness, when she thought she'd go mad—or simply nova like a dying star, from the fear and the sorrow, the exhaustion and the inexorability of watching something so insidious destroy the man she loved. Then she'd started studying karate at the local Y, as an outlet for her frustrations—and after a year of getting in shape, she'd been introduced to Mr. Wong by her instructor, and she'd begun to study serious martial arts with him. The training and discipline had centered her, strengthened her, kept her going, in the worst of times.

She wiped the sweat from her forehead with the back of her hand now, and fought to stay in control of her breathing. As much not to disappoint him, as for herself, Maggie resumed fighting stance and pushed the small failure down where it belonged, into insignificance.

This was her one self-indulgence, this hour or two a day, spent in class, or in her makeshift basement dojo. Six to eight A.M., before anyone was awake; the only hours of the day that were truly hers. Punch, kick, balance, focus. The powered grace of forms, the concentrated discipline of sparring. The wisdom of Mr. Wong. It was more than physical need that brought her back to train each day.

*"Body, mind, spirit, all must be in harmony."* Mr. Wong would remind her, a Taoist monk, disguised as a martial arts teacher. *"The techniques were there before you were born and will be there long after you are gone. Let them flow through you and marvel at their beauty."* He understood the universe and the energies that drove it; he had parables that cleared the way for her when the road was indistinguishable and dark.

People asked her often if she studied martial arts for self-defense, and she always said yes . . . but she didn't mean what they thought she meant. The real self-defense you need in this life is for the spirit.

Maggie glanced at the clock, it was nearly eight; she'd been here since five-thirty. She bowed to Mr. Wong and hurried home to shower. She knew the library opened at nine. Today, she intended to find out all she could about Satan.

# CHAPTER 12

Maggie frowned at the dictionary. No enlightenment there. At least the computerized index was bursting with references. She jotted down the first dozen, secured them from the stacks and settled down to read.

> Originally, Satan was a great angel; Chief of the Seraphim, head of the Order of Virtues and very close to the throne of God.

> He fell from Grace through rebellion against God, thinking himself God's equal. For this sin of Pride he was banished from Heaven, and all his legions with him, by the power of the Arch-angel Michael and his fiery sword.

Maggie thumbed through half a dozen volumes. Very interesting. The Talmud, Revelation, and Thomas Aquinas all spoke of Satan . . . So, the great mystical thinkers all believed in his existence . . . Maggie checked another source and settled in to read.

> Satan is sometimes called Lucifer, the light giver, and Lucifer is sometimes referred to as "The Chief Council of Hell."

She smiled. Wouldn't you know he'd be a lawyer. *Damn!* She wished she could remember more from the-ology class on the Anti-Christ. It seemed clear he pa-raded under a vast array of names: Ahriman in Persian theosophy, Beezlebub in the Gospels, Iblis in the Koran, and Samael in Jewish Scripture. It was really intriguing that every major religion acknowledged the existence of the Devil. And he didn't seem to be alone; there were references to scores of other demons, as well. One hundred and three fallen angels were identifiable by name, and there were hundreds of other infernal names from every culture and every time period. Babylonia, Chaldea, Egypt, Sumeria . . .

Maggie went back to the stacks for another set of books. A large number of groups were practicing Devil worship openly, it seemed, all over America. There were satanic churches as well as various devil cults like Ju Ju, Voodoo, Palo Mayombe, and certain forms of Santería. She saw no mention of Maa Kheru, but one of the sources, *Cults That Kill*, said:

> There are other orthodox Satanic groups that exist whose names we'll never know, because they are not made public. These, in fact, may be the most dangerous of all.

To her astonishment, there was a considerable amount of information about human sacrifice. In magical theory, it seemed, having a freshly slaughtered victim enhanced the Black Magician's chances of performing a successful spell.

Maggie sat back in her chair and tried to quell her revulsion. Cody was in the hands of people who believed in such things. She picked up another book; this one of interviews with law enforcement officers on the subject.

> Capt. Dale Griffis of the Tifflin, Ohio, Police Department, "The use of blood in Satanic rituals is very important. According to the beliefs, blood contains the life force. If you have it, you

have power. That's why they drink it in their rituals and pour it over themselves.

"So is sacrificing people. When you sacrifice someone, for the instant before they die, they supposedly emit their life energy. That power, Satanists believe, can be harnessed for their use. They believe babies are best, because babies are pure; they haven't sinned or been corrupted yet. They possess a higher power than adults. When you sacrifice a baby, you get greater power than if you sacrificed an adult. One of the most prized possessions of a Satanist is a candle made from the fat of an unbaptized baby."

Maggie's attention was riveted to the page.

Det. Sandi Gallant of the Intelligence Division, San Francisco Police Department, "Some Satanists believe that with specific body parts they can use the power contained therein. The head may contain the spirit, and the heart may contain the soul. These are things that would allow them to be in control. It's been said they like to have a finger of the left hand. I don't know exactly which finger. I understand about the left and right paths, but why the finger? Who knows?"

She put down the book and took a deep breath. Satanists really existed . . . they had churches . . . held services . . . celebrated holidays. This was much worse than she'd dreamed.

Maggie returned the books to the front desk and checked the transcript file for any TV news shows that might have explored this topic. She pulled out several talk show transcripts that looked promising and started to read, her heart sinking as she scanned the first terrifying pages.

There were women interviewed on these TV shows, who identified themselves as Breeders. They said they'd given birth to children, specifically for use in ritual sacrifice. Each story Maggie read was more chilling than the last. There were macabre tales of infants sacrificed and eaten in satanic ceremonies . . . of babies skinned alive . . . of children tortured . . . of blood used in Black Masses as an unholy Communion. She read of mothers brainwashed or forced against their will to be accomplices to their own children's murder; grotesque, impossible stories of depravity and perversion. There even seemed to be a self-help group called Overcomers Victorious for women who had managed to escape the covens, and wanted to pull the remnants of their lives back together.

Each TV transcript seemed more implausible than the last. Could there really be whole towns in which everyone worshipped Satan? Could there really be doctors and lawyers and judges who formed a network of terror that even the police had trouble penetrating? And if any of these stories were true, how could it be that the world didn't simply rise up in a body and stop them from doing such terrible things to people?

Maggie read transcripts for the better part of an hour: Geraldo, Donahue, Oprah, Sally Jessy Raphael, *20/20*, *60 Minutes* all had touched on satanism in some way. Incest . . . child pornography . . . ritual murder . . . baby breeders . . . human sacrifice. The visions these words conjured up swirled like toxic sewage in Maggie's brain.

She closed the last transcript and stood up, too agitated to stay still. People actually *worshipped* Satan . . . they tortured and murdered and abused for him. Right now, in 1993! Right here in New York City. And California, and Texas. And everywhere!

*And they had Cody.*

They used little children . . . innocent babies were raped and mutilated and psychologically damaged beyond repair. Babies were bred for no other purpose than to be eaten . . .

*And they had Cody!*

*Suddenly, Maggie couldn't breathe. Couldn't think. Had to move. Get out of there. Into the air . . . felt faint. Dizzy. Dark. Cold. Falling . . .*

"You all right, miss?" the man standing over her was asking urgently. Maggie tried to focus her eyes enough to learn why she was lying on the floor. *Oh God, I fainted.*

She struggled to sit upright. "I'm okay," she murmured, embarrassed and disoriented. "I must have forgotten to eat today." She felt violently nauseous, but fought back the urge to vomit, and rose unsteadily to her feet. The man looked doubtful. Others were staring. Commotions had no business in libraries.

Maggie gathered up the stack of books and tried to make a dignified exit, despite the stares. *Screw the stares!* she thought, suddenly angry, as well as sick. *They hurt babies, and they've got Cody! I've got to get her out of that house.*

Maggie cut across Bleecker, hurriedly; the library had yielded too much ghastly information, and her head was pounding. The cold wind was a welcome relief; there were several volumes left to read, but she intended to do so in the fresh air of Washington Square Park.

A book caught her eye in a shop window, as she hurried by: *Psychic Self-Defense.* God, do I need some of that, she thought with a weary sigh, and on impulse entered the shop. It was a warm, cozy place, full of glittering crystals, from charm size to huge decorator pieces. The late-afternoon sunlight glinted off an immense cluster of quartz at least four feet around, and refracted through dozens of rainbow flashers in the window. They shivered in the breeze and produced a sort of stained-glass light dance, which brightened the interior of the shop considerably.

There were books, and wind chimes that tinkled musically as she shut the door behind her. Posters on esoteric subjects decorated the walls, and a couple of well-worn chintz armchairs filled a corner. On a table in between, a large crystal ball and a silver tea service gleamed.

A woman occupied one of the chairs. At first glance she seemed a young girl, in an updated flower-child ensemble; on second look, Maggie realized she must be close to forty. A spectacular body provided the deception.

The woman looked up from the book she was reading and smiled, a lovely open smile, unexpected in New York. "I'm Ellie," she said in a lilting voice that suggested contentment with life. "If you'd like to put your books down here while you browse, I'd be happy to keep an eye on them for you."

She had unusual eyes, violet-blue and incandescently sparkly. There was an otherworldly quality about her intelligent gaze, as if she weren't quite human, but some sort of hybrid creature. Galadriel, Queen of the Fairies, straight out of Tolkien. Maggie tried to intuit what her ethnic background might be. Slavic, maybe. Or Russian. Masses of dark curly hair fell gypsylike to her shoulders; beads of every conceivable variety jingle-jangled around her neck, along with gold sigils, zodiacal signs, and a silver cartouche. *I've fallen into a time warp to Woodstock*, Maggie thought, smiling back.

"Quite a collection you have here," Ellie mused, checking out the titles of Maggie's books. "Boning up for a doctoral dissertation on occultism?"

"Something like that," Maggie replied. "But I'm a bit out of my depth in all this, I'm afraid. It's like trying to teach myself nuclear physics."

Ellie laughed with genuine mirth. "Maybe I can help you," she offered. "I've been into metaphysics since just before birth. I'd hate to say I'm an expert on anything, but I'll probably do till you find one. What exactly are you looking for?''

"I'm trying to learn all I can about Black Magic; satanism, I guess it's called.''

Ellie's eyes widened, then she frowned. "Surely you're not thinking of dabbling in the Black Arts. I mean, *I* don't even keep any books around on that stuff—only White Magic. Are you sure you know what you're doing? That's like playing around with nuclear fission for fun." She looked genuinely concerned. "Tell you what . . . I was just about to close for a cup of tea. Why don't you join me.''

Maggie smiled wistfully. "My mother always said if you're Irish, a cup of tea can fix anything that ails you.''

"I'm sure she was right. The therapeutic value has probably been stamped into the genetic matrix by now.''

Maggie relaxed a little, there was something lovable about the woman. Ellie poured out two steaming cups of black tea, offered cream and sugar with the skill of a dowager, then settled back in her chair.

"Now, spill the beans. Why the interest in Black Magic? Are you a researcher of some kind? Or just your average satanic thrill seeker?''

Maggie couldn't help but laugh. "It's a bizarre story, actually, all of which sounds crazy. But my grandchild is in a strange, dangerous situation—and somebody suggested to me it might have something to do with satanism. So, I figured I better find out what I'm up against. Before today, I thought it was a subject fit only for those newspapers you look at on the supermarket checkout line. Now I'm really scared.''

"I see," Ellie said judiciously. "Maybe you'd better give me a few specifics, so I can advise you properly. I really do know what I'm talking about.''

Maggie hesitated, then plunged in. She'd always been a decent judge of character, and it would help to talk with an expert.

Ellie listened carefully. "It's a good thing you're talking to me, Maggie," she said with great seriousness. "Satanism is nothing to mess with. It's a lot bigger and better organized than you could possibly imagine. Magic, White or Black, can be a very potent force—one you'd damn well better learn about, if you're going to try to fight it. Believe me, I know a lot about this, and not just from this ditzy little lifetime, either. A Black Magician of High Degree, say a Magister Templi or, God forbid, an Ipsissimmus, could attack you on the Astral Plane while you sleep, Maggie. Or he could pit the energies of the whole Black Coven against you. Even if he didn't kill you, which he might, you'd go mad as a hatter. There are thousands of people in lunatic asylums for no other reason than that they pissed off a Black Magician, with or without knowing it."

Maggie shook her head in disbelief. "I don't know what to say. This is all so far beyond me . . ."

Ellie looked speculatively at Maggie. "Generally speaking, people don't find themselves touched by magic unless they've practiced it in other lifetimes . . . you may find you know more than you think. Your soul is probably trying to remember what you already know, so you can fight off this current danger. Maybe you should try some past-life regressions, to see what it's all about, and where we've met before."

"What do you mean, where we've met before?"

"There are no accidents in the Universe, Maggie. You didn't walk in here today, by chance . . . odds are you were drawn here by your need for something . . . an ally, maybe. Look. Why don't you go home, finish these books, and then let's talk some more.

"I'll need to do some meditating on the story you've told me, too, of course. I mean, I don't go running around looking for ways to put my astral ass in a sling for strangers . . . but, then, what if you turn out not to be one? Tell you what . . . why don't you come back for dinner at my place tonight and we'll see if we can figure things out."

Ellie handed her several more books to read, and

Maggie went home mind-boggled that there could be so much information about a subject she barely knew existed.

ELLIE climbed up the small step stool she used to reach books on the top shelves of her library, and passed two down to Maggie. Her apartment was high-ceilinged and full of prewar, Village charm.

"This is a fabulous apartment, Ellie," Maggie said admiringly. "It's like a sea captain's house . . . full of exotic treasures."

"God bless rent control," Ellie responded. "How could I ever afford a two-bedroom apartment with fireplaces, if it weren't for rent control? As to the treasures, I'm far too attached to things, I'm afraid . . . probably my Leo moon that's responsible. I've lived in a lot of places and brought back keepsakes."

One of the bedrooms had been turned into a library-study; books lined every wall and surface. The excess crystal inventory from the shop was scattered ubiquitously, under chairs, on tables, inside cabinets. In the bedroom, an immense pink rose quartz lived under the bed. "Great for opening the heart chakra," Ellie explained, with a grin. A huge bronze gong was flanked by two exquisite Thanka paintings from Tibet. Maggie's appraising eye noted the sensitivity of taste with which each piece had been chosen.

"I can't figure out how you've got these books arranged," she said, bringing her attention back to the orderly shelves. "How do you find things if they're not alphabetized?"

Ellie handed three more volumes to Maggie and laughed.

"Oh, they're alphabetized all right. By author's first names. Just a little intellectual snobbery on my part. Sometimes I get pissed off knowing people dismiss me as a pea brain because I'm into metaphysics. So, I fight back in little ways to amuse myself. I suppose that's why I've got half a doctoral dissertation in my top desk drawer."

Everything about Ellie was a surprise, Maggie thought, suppressing a smile. The wifty effervescence she affected belied a swift intelligence and an intuition that obviously perceived life through a different set of lenses.

"Where's your master's from?" she asked, liking the woman.

"Berkeley, where else?" Ellie answered, pouring a glass of wine from a cooled bottle. She was cooking something Muscovian, she said, rattling off the name in a superb Russian accent. The pungent aroma filled the apartment tantalizingly, and balalaika music lent its melancholy strains on the stereo.

"I've done the whole nine yards, Mags, since the late sixties." Maggie noticed, amused, that Ellie had given her a new nickname without any ceremony. "Anything an intellectual flower child could do, I did. Lived three years with a guru in India to study Sanskrit . . . lived two years on a Cherokee reservation, to experience Vision Quest . . . lived a year and a half in a Zen monastery, sitting zazen at four A.M. every day and freezing my ass off, while I chanted." She ticked them off on her fingers. "Oh yes, and let's not forget how I wandered around South America for eighteen months, going to crystal digs and studying Capoiera. Then I came home and apprenticed myself to a Chinese doctor for two years, so I could learn acupuncture."

Ellie had a good, strong-boned face, Maggie saw, as she talked so earnestly; pretty, interesting, betraying little about her age.

"I did everything you might expect," Ellie said with a likable grin. "Protested the war, got jailed in Chicago, helped run an abortion referral service during the coat-hanger era . . ." She took a sip of wine and stirred something on the stove, sniffed, added some sort of pungent seasoning, then sat down again on a zafu in the middle of the floor.

"And a few things I wouldn't expect?"

"Yeah. I guess you could say that. My family is half Russian and half Cherokee, so I was doomed from childhood by being psychic . . . visions, out-of-body experiences, past life memories, more vivid than kindergarten ever was. I had it all.

"Fortunately, I was raised mostly by my grandmothers, since my mother worked and my father wandered. I bounced back and forth between their two worlds, and neither side of the family thought it was odd to have my gifts, they more or less expected it. So instead of discouraging me, they taught me—magic from one side, spirit guidance from the other. They were both unbelievable women—tough as leather, female as Moon Maidens. I go to Mother Hale's every Wednesday night to hold AIDS babies, as my way of paying back the Universe for all those two gave me."

"How extraordinary," Maggie said, thinking how conventional her own childhood had been. "Whatever would have happened to your gifts if you'd been plopped into an ordinary family, I wonder?"

"Oh, I don't think the Universe lets mistakes happen, Mags," she said seriously. "They put you exactly where you need to be, in order to work out your karma. I wasn't visiting those two grandmas for the first time—I was completing a cycle with them."

Maggie frowned a little. "I'm still having a hard time with all this, Ellie. It's difficult for me to accept someone as intelligent and educated as you believing in magic."

Ellie straightened up from bending over the table. "Don't get hung up on nomenclature, Maggie. Magic is just a word used to describe forces that aren't understood yet. You're going to have to stop thinking with your twentieth-century education, and start using your intuition . . . *feeling* out truth, rather than accepting what you've been taught as gospel. The world was once thought to be flat. The atom was thought to be unsplittable. If somebody told Isaac Newton that in a few hundred years, pictures would be beamed into living rooms from satellites, he would've thrown the apple at him."

Maggie saw the point. "May I ask you an impertinent question, Ellie?"

"Shoot."

"Why would someone with half a doctoral dissertation in the drawer be content selling crystals and smudge sticks? Didn't you ever want to choose a different track?"

"Good question," she answered, seating them both at the table that served as dining place or workbench, depending on need. The fire blazed behind them and Maggie thought it one of the most charming dining room settings she'd ever been in.

"I knew from my grandmothers, at a very early age, that I had spiritual gifts, and that those gifts carried obligations. It says in Scripture, 'For unto whomsoever much is given, of him shall much be required.' That seems fair to me. It also says, 'You can't serve God and Mammon,' and that's true, too, Mags—you have to choose, in a given lifetime. If I'd been a doctor or lawyer or marketing director, I would have had to devote all my energies to success . . . there's nothing wrong with that, mind you. I've done it myself in many lifetimes. But I needed to study other things, this time around. Kind of tricky to find a fast-track life that would have allowed me time for all the esoteric learning I've done."

They were genuinely compatible, despite their different backgrounds, Maggie thought later, as she helped with the dishes. Character has nothing to do with birth or bank accounts, her father would have said. Ellie was a bona fide character; the kind the Village had once abounded with, before Burger Kings had replaced the coffee houses, and SoHo had become chic and then a tourist trap. Individuality and intellectual questing had been prized then, at least as much as fame or fortune. They'd been better times.

"So what do you suggest I do now, Ellie?" Maggie asked over coffee.

"You read the books I gave you and let me ask my Guides what's up. I have a hunch this passage you're in may have to do with allies. The Universe never pits us poor mortals against the forces of Evil without providing allies, here and on the Inner Planes. Of course, the only allies we have any control over are the ones we can see . . . like me, maybe. If I'm right, you'll be bumping into more."

Maggie nodded, in for a penny in for a pound. "Why are you doing this, Ellie?" she asked. "Why would you consider endangering yourself for a perfect stranger?"

"I don't think we'd be holding this conversation if you and I were perfect strangers, Mags. I'm involved here, somehow . . . we just don't know how, yet."

"But what could you possibly get out of this awful mess that would make it worthwhile for you to become involved?"

"Enlightenment," Ellie replied with a grin. "It's the only prize worth fighting for."

# CHAPTER 13

Cody followed the maid listlessly on her way from the kitchen to the nursery wing. Sometimes Ghania left her with the maid for a little while, and when she did they always went to the kitchen. In the beginning, Cody had tried to talk with the girl, but she didn't know many words in English. Ghania said she was from the Old Country, but Cody didn't know what that meant. And besides, the girl never smiled or tried to be friendly.

The child kept her head down now as she walked,

letting her eyes follow the pattern of the flooring, just for something to occupy her mind. First, the tiles in the kitchen . . . then, the parquet of the hall . . . then, the carpet of the parlor . . . then, the black-and-white checkerboard marble of the foyer . . .

That's how she saw it.

A tiny gold button, halfway under the radiator leg, at the edge of the foyer door.

It was *Mim's* button!

From the jacket she wore on the first day she came to visit. Cody's heart leaped at the tiny token, and suddenly she knew why it was there. *It was to keep her safe!*

Cody's hand darted out and closed on the golden treasure. It jiggled loose from its corner with only a small tug, and was in her palm before the maid even turned to look.

Cody's heart pounded frantically as she slipped the button into her sweater pocket, fingers still tight around it.

She could practically *feel* Mim's love in it, *see* her face, *hear* her voice . . . all *alive* somehow, in the little gold keepsake.

Cody padded along behind the maid, up the nursery steps, into her hated room, but none of that mattered anymore.

*She had a part of Mim in her pocket*. She would find a place to hide it, where Ghania would *never*, ever look. The child's eyes darted around the room with a new sense of purpose. If this precious button was here in the house, maybe there were other things, too. Parts of Mim, that Ghania couldn't take away. *Now* there was hope . . .

Cody waited until the maid was gone, then she went to the small shelf where her books and toys were kept. She pulled down the battered Teddy Bear that had been in the nursery when she arrived. He was the only thing in this terrible place that was nice. He reminded her of the Love Bear, who slept with her in her bed at home.

The bear had a hole in his neck, under the old satin ribbon that circled it. Stealthily, she slipped the button into the hole and quickly readjusted the ribbon, her heart pounding.

Cody put the bear back on the shelf, with careful hands. Tonight when everyone had gone to bed, she would be alone with her secret.

# CHAPTER 14

"Maggie?" the voice on the phone said, and it took her a moment to recognize that it was Malachy Devlin's.

"Lieutenant Devlin?"

"I was wondering if you'd have dinner with me."

"You were?" The invitation was so out of context with everything on her mind, Maggie didn't field it very well.

"Is this about Cody?"

"I do have some information for you, Maggie," he said good-naturedly, "but that's not entirely why I'm asking. Please say yes. It would mean a lot to me."

As she could think of no decent reply to that except an affirmative one, Maggie agreed. That was when she realized he wasn't calling her Mrs. O'Connor anymore.

The restaurant on Minetta Lane was small and cozy. There were tables in a pocket-sized simulated garden and an air of downtown intimacy about the place. Couples laughed or whispered over wine glasses, and everyone seemed pleased to be there. The proprietor obviously knew Devlin and greeted their arrival.

"Put us somewhere out of the traffic pattern, Dominic," the detective asked over the handshake. "We need to talk business."

"Monkey business, I hope for your sake, Malachy," Dominic said with a grin. "Such a lovely signora . . ." He winked at Maggie conspiratorially. The table was in the far corner, a candle flickered and Maggie's chair backed into an explosion of multicolored flowers.

"I've never been here before," she said when they were seated. "It's a sweet place. Dominic's a pal of yours, I take it?"

"We grew up together in the South Bronx," Devlin answered. "You could grow up to be a cop, a restaurateur, a priest, or a gangster. Any choice would get you out of the neighborhood."

Dominic brought a bottle of wine without being asked and Maggie realized Devlin was watching her closely as they spoke; as if memorizing the details of who she was. She wondered if all detectives did that by instinct.

"Why did you come to my rescue at the precinct, when I was with that other detective," she asked, after they'd ordered.

"Hank's a good guy, really," Devlin answered protectively. "You just caught him after three nights with no sleep." He smiled before continuing.

"I recognized something in you, I guess . . . like going through a door and finding an old friend unexpectedly. I don't know exactly. It wasn't just that I thought you were pretty—which I did—and terribly out of place, in the station house. It was something else." He laughed a little. "My mother made her living as a psychic, maybe I inherited her gift. A little of it, anyway."

Maggie was surprised. "What did your father think about that."

"I never got to find out. He died when I was seven, so I don't have too many clear memories of him. We lived in a pretty poor neighborhood, so after he died, Mom had to figure out how to put food on the table. Reader and Advisor is what she called herself. She wore this great turban . . . pretty funny, actually, with her Irish face, and freckles. But she was good at what she did. Not infallible, mind you. Like all psychics, she had days when the antenna was down, but for the most part her gifts were genuine, so I grew up knowing there was more to life than met the eye. The veil between the worlds is thinner for us Celts than for others, I suspect.''

What a surprise he is, Maggie thought, as she watched and listened. All rough and smooth textures; more interesting and more vulnerable than he'd seemed in the station house. He had nice eyes. *Don't be dishonest with me*, they said. *I'll know*. She liked the fact that they never wavered when they looked at you.

''What were you like as a child,'' he asked, evidently interested. ''Were you anything like Cody?'' She could see he was trying to put her at ease.

''Oh, I don't know anymore, really. It's so long ago. I think I was an odd little person, rather bookish and mystical.'' The wine was beginning to take the edge off her constant anxiety; it seemed surreal to feel momentarily safer, in the middle of a nightmare.

''I always had a love affair with empty churches when I was small, and we lived near St. Joseph's,'' she said. ''So, I used to stop by every afternoon on my way home from school, to say hello to God.'' He smiled encouragement; the look said he found her strange and interesting, so Maggie continued.

''I'd kneel there with the candles flickering and the incense making me feel holy, and have some of the most spectacular fantasies . . . or maybe they were visions of some sort. I would transport myself to Saint Teresa's cell and hold very long convoluted conversations with her about God . . . I even helped Saint Francis feed the birds.'' She laughed a little at herself. ''I must have had the knack for slipping into some altered state of consciousness pretty early, because occasionally, time would seem to suspend itself, and I could sense the presence of angels, just on the periphery of my gaze . . .'' Maggie smiled self-deprecatingly. ''I guess we're all mystics of one sort or another . . . we just don't talk about it much.''

Devlin was watching her speculatively. Hers was a

face that didn't keep secrets out of subterfuge, only out of fragility.

"No," he said. "Not all. Just some, like you and me. It's why I write poetry, I suppose—to touch that other sphere where most can't follow."

"You're a poet?"

"It's not something I'd like the guys at the precinct to know . . . but, yeah, I've had a few things published. Surprised?"

"Astonished," she said genuinely. "Or maybe not as astonished now as I would have been an hour ago."

His forearms were resting on the table in front of him, the sleeves of the much-washed sweater pushed up to the elbows, baring arms with latent strength. Muscles trained, but not dwelled on, she thought. Veins made prominent by testing. It was a ruggedly handsome, lived-in face and body; the kind that took itself seriously where competency was concerned, but stopped short of vanity. Devlin pulled out a pocket notebook and brought the conversation back to Cody.

"I've got a little more info for you on Jenna's husband," he said, shaking his head eloquently. "Your daughter seems to be filthy rich, among other things. Or, at least, her husband is. This Vannier is an interesting character, Maggie. His family banking business is a privately held corporation, so there's no public access to its records. All everybody agrees on is that its holdings are enormous. He has a law degree from Harvard, but has never practiced. What he told you is true—he administers the funds of the Vannier Foundation, an international philanthropic institution with megabucks. The Vannier money seems to be old and Middle Eastern, precisely where or how it was accumulated I don't know, yet. He has entrée into top society on several continents. The guy's an accomplished yachtsman, horseman, sportsman, you name it—if it's expensive and dangerous, he excels at it, so don't go trying to punch his lights out, because he's probably in super shape.

"He knows only the greats and near-greats, but—here's weird fact number one . . . he's never married before, and far as I can tell, his name has never been linked romantically with any other woman, and that's very strange in his circles. I can't think of a way in the world he and your daughter could have crossed paths unless he ran over her in his Rolls.

"And weird fact number two might tie in with your problem," he continued, looking troubled. "Eric's best friend, ever since they were at Choate together, is Nicholas Sayles . . . the talk show host."

Maggie blinked, surprised. "A cross between Geraldo and Mike Wallace, yes? But gorgeous."

Devlin nodded. "Nicky's a wild guy . . . very charismatic, very complicated. From a prominent Boston Brahmin family with tons of maybe-not-so-impeccable money. He has a law degree from Harvard, same year as Eric's, and enough brains for a battalion, but he made his fortune in show biz." He paused significantly.

"I probably shouldn't be telling you any of this, Maggie, since it'll only scare the bejesus out of you, but here it is: there have been tightly guarded, but persistent rumors that he's into satanism."

"But how can that possibly be? Doesn't he spend his life exposing cults and other garbage on the air?"

"Yeah, he does, but there are those who say it's just his means of getting some pretty ugly stuff into the public consciousness. You know, promoting evil in the guise of exposing it. Telling the world, 'Hey, it's all out there if you want it, folks. Just write in for a list of vampires, sex offenders, and serial murderers who eat their victims, and we'll provide it.' " Devlin glanced back at the notes and continued.

"Sayles's father is a munitions manufacturer, not necessarily squeaky clean, but rich as Croesus. The company dates back to Revolutionary times. Nicholas was a whiz kid at the best boys' schools in the East, but was always known as a behavioral problem. Because he kept his grades up easily, and because his father's endowments could have fed Afghanistan, he was never unduly harassed by teachers. When he graduated from Harvard, he started to claw his way up in the TV journalism trade, but his real success was behind the cameras, not in front. Like Merv Griffin, Nicky was a behind-the-scenes genius, producing shows with an uncanny instinct for what the public would gobble up, and with enough money to fund production. So, he made another fortune to add to the one he inherited.

"Nicky and Eric were roommates all through boarding school, and have maintained their friendship to a marked degree, ever since. Each is a frequent visitor at the other's home . . . they share common interests, common investments, and common friends, despite the apparent difference in their professions."

Maggie listened attentively. "How could anyone ever connect such a paragon to Black Magic?" she asked, puzzled. "It seems pretty farfetched that such a prominent media figure could escape being found out, if it were true, doesn't it?"

"I don't know, Maggie," Devlin said noncommittally. "Success is a great deodorant. And enough money can cover a pretty big trail. For instance, there was a frat house incident in their last year as undergraduates, in which a kid died in a ritualistic manner. The police said it was hazing. Later it was rumored to have something to do with a group on campus dabbling in Black Magic. A certain amount of money changed hands, and all rumors ceased.

"Then later, after Sayles's rocket ride to the top in TV, rumors trickled out about certain performers in his shows selling their souls to Satan in return for media success, but everyone thought this was just another spectacular PR stunt, masterminded by the brilliant showman. And of course, these allegations seemed so ludicrous, the world simply ignored them."

"So what do you think the truth is?" Maggie asked, frowning. He thought the vertical lines produced in her forehead gave her an added dimension.

"I'd say these guys are probably dabbling in something dark and ugly—what I can't figure out, is why they want Cody. Or Jenna, for that matter. When a man has all the money in the world, women are generally not in short supply. And if they are dabbling in some kind of satanic garbage, it's easy enough for those lunatics to get kids for their rituals—they kidnap them off the streets, or buy babies from cadaver suppliers."

"What?"

"Cadaver companies exist to supply bodies to medical schools, but there are abuses—"

"This is really too much!" Maggie interrupted. The idea of Cody being used in satanic ritual made her physically ill. "I'm so far out of my depth in all this . . ."

"Look, Maggie," Devlin said quietly, "you can't be in my profession long without learning to read people's character. My take is with or without help you're not the type to give up on this kid and go to Bergdorf's. The reason I'm trying to get information for you is that I wouldn't like to see you go unarmed against the Philistines."

"My martial arts teacher would like the way you think," she responded.

It was Devlin's turn to be surprised. "You do martial arts? What style?"

"Goju Ryu and Wing Chun. I've been doing Karate and Kung Fu for five or six years."

"So you're not Bruce Lee, but you could probably defend yourself if you needed to, eh?"

"Provided I choose my opponents skillfully," she said, and they both laughed.

"I did some Goju in the Police Academy. And I had a pal in law school who was really good. Pak and I used to work out together in the park, when things got hot and heavy in class."

"You went to law school?" she asked, now genuinely intrigued by his contradictions.

Devlin grinned good-naturedly. "Now, you're thinking, what's wrong with this guy? He's got a law a degree and he's not even bright enough to use it. Probably graduated two hundredth in a class of one hundred and eighty-six." His eyes were merry and Maggie realized she felt very comfortable with this strange man, who didn't feel at all like a stranger.

"No," she replied, shaking her head emphatically. "I was thinking, you're a big surprise."

Devlin's face was serious again. "You know, I wouldn't have given up, if you'd said no tonight," he said.

Maggie regarded him with amusement. "Why not?"

"Persistence is one of my better qualities. When something is important, you have to run me over with the IRT to keep me from pursuing it."

"Oh, Lord," she said, suddenly stricken. "I hope you don't think I've been leading you on by having dinner with you tonight, Lieutenant Devlin. I didn't think . . . I mean, I'm living in the eye of the hurricane right now, and I can't let anything distract me from helping Cody. Please forgive me if I've given you the wrong impression . . ." She let the words trail off, embarrassed and not knowing what to say, but wanting to be honest.

"Look, Maggie," he said quietly, all merriment extinguished. "I was married to a girl from the neighborhood, as they say in the South Bronx. A nice girl . . . warm, pretty, and too smart to stay in the Bronx for long. We grew up together in a lot of ways. Married nearly nine years . . ." He stopped, and she could sense considerable pain behind the recollection.

"When things went wrong between us in a big way, I went a little crazy, and did a lot of stupid things. I took risks I shouldn't have, dated women with bodies instead of souls . . . but you can't fill up the holes in your heart that way. When I finally came to my senses, I became so damned discriminating, it would have taken the Virgin Mary to get through my guard." He shook his head at his own confusions.

"Then I saw you at the station house the other night, and something happened. I don't mean to make it sound like I was struck by lightning, Maggie, so don't panic on me. But I wanted to talk to you. To get to know you. Not just to get you in the sack, although I can't say the thought didn't cross my mind. But that wasn't my number one priority when I called you." He smiled sadly, and she could see he wanted her to understand. "I thought . . . I'd like that lady to be my friend."

Maggie sat back in her seat and looked carefully at the man. She saw nothing in his eyes but sincerity.

"I could use a friend, too, right now," she answered, thinking that had a comforting sound. "So I guess I'd better start calling you Malachy."

"Actually, pretty much everybody calls me Dev," he responded quietly. "But you, Maggie . . . you can call me whatever you want."

# CHAPTER 15

Malachy Devlin opened the action on the Glock 17, snapped the slide into place, and shoved it unceremoniously into the well-worn gun leather at his belt. He strapped the snub-nosed .38 backup piece to his ankle with such automatic skill it took no conscious effort, both weapons an extension of self. He intended to use his day off for snooping.

Maggie O'Connor was on his mind. Annoyingly so. He'd tried to be sensible and put her out of his head; the last thing he needed was a lot of potential grief and not much hope of a happy ending. All that notwithstanding, the woman and her story had stayed with him, niggling at him, below the surface, where he couldn't scratch.

She wasn't crazy; instinct had told him that, and dinner had confirmed it. But he'd been a cop for fifteen years, and if he'd learned one cardinal rule, it was that few things are what they seem. So, he'd have to resolve the question marks. Talk to people. Nose around. Call a confidential source or two. Then he'd have to make a decision. In or out.

Malachy pulled on his jacket and stuffed the pen and notebook into his pocket. Maybe he'd learn something today that would change his mind about wanting to help Maggie O'Connor and her granddaughter. But he doubted it.

# CHAPTER 16

St. Joseph's Church on Sixth Avenue and West Fourth was empty of worshippers during most of the day. The diehard Catholics, mostly over age fifty, peopled the 6:00 or 7:00 A.M. masses, but after that, except for an occasional curate, nun, or derelict seeking refuge, the two-hundred-year-old Village landmark was generally empty. Maggie had always loved empty churches. No sonorous sermons, no admonishing clergy, no stringent regulations, or sins to sneak up on you . . . just Maggie and God, together in the hallowed dark.

She knelt upright at the altar, back ramrod straight, mind adrift somewhere in her childhood. It was holier if your knees hurt and your back cramped, the nuns always said. It was your preparation for martyrdom. Sister Benedict had told her of the children in China who had their fingernails pulled out and stakes driven into their ears by Communists, who wished them to renounce their faith. Pain is important. Pain makes you holy. Suffering brings you closer to God.

Saint Lawrence was roasted, Saint Arden had his eyeballs plucked out. Maria Goretti was stabbed twelve times protecting her virginity. Then she forgave her attacker before she died, or so the Sisters said. And she was becoming a saint. Not that Maggie'd ever liked the sound of her. What kind of idiot would forgive someone who'd stabbed her twelve times?

The impious thought dragged Maggie back to the present. She was here to pray for guidance.

She sensed the altar rail beneath her arms; she had knelt there a million times, it seemed, since childhood, asking the Blessed Virgin and Saint Joseph to hear her prayers. Now she needed them to save this child she loved; families were their specialty. *What should I do?* she prayed. *Where should I go? Whom can I trust?* The pleas tumbled out in an endless stream, in the comforting candlelit gloom.

*Father Peter Messenguer.* The name slipped into her head as suddenly and clearly as if a neon sign had been switched on. *Father Peter Messenguer.* Of course! He would know, if anyone did. *Thank you, thank you!* she murmured fervently as she left St. Joseph's nearly at a run, and headed for Amanda at the shop.

"I KNOW you've *heard* of him, Amanda," Maggie prompted excitedly.

"Messenguer?" Amanda repeated. "He's the famous theologian, who came a cropper of the Vatican over his heretical ideas, isn't he?"

Maggie nodded her head vigorously. "He's brilliant and wildly iconoclastic . . . the most astonishing mind I ever encountered, Amanda. The kind that leaves you breathless in the dust. I remember he speaks seventeen languages, ten of them ancient. He lectured once at Fordham when I was a senior, and I was given the privilege of being his escort for the weekend, so I shepherded him around campus, to lectures and teas. He was quite unbelievable—and mischievous, too, in a lofty sort of way, so when he got tired of smiling at faculty members relentlessly, he asked me to show him around the city. I was beside myself with delirium."

Amanda laughed softly. Maggie had a capacity for enthusiasm that was ingenuous and contagious. She could look quite like a little girl when she was in the throes of something that excited her, curls bouncing, eyes dancing. Maggie was so many things, Amanda thought, watching her. Strong and fragile, a pushover for a sob story or a beggar on the street; but there was always more to her than met the eye. Like the Phi Beta Kappa key she kept unceremoniously among the house and car keys in her purse; it was only by accident Amanda had found out about that.

"He's a Renaissance Man, Amanda," she was saying. "An authority on comparative theology and ancient religions—I think he has a doctorate in anthropology, too."

"And why, might I inquire, are we discussing him so exuberantly at this particular moment?"

"Because I've read that he's an expert on the arcane . . . Don't you see? If I can find him, he might remember me!" Maggie looked at Amanda's blank expression with exasperation; she had told her about the satanic possibility. "He'll know about the occult! Amanda. I know he will. The catch is I have to find him, to ask him."

"Isn't there a central file of clerics somewhere?" Amanda asked. "1-800-Find Padre, or somesuch."

Maggie shook her head. "Maybe there's some sort of clerical directory, *if* you know where to find it, which I *don't*—but I think he's gone underground, sort of. Whatever the Church's equivalent of being deep-sixed by the powers-that-be."

"But I thought he was their fair-haired boy. Intellectual wunderkind, expected to be cardinal by fifty."

"All that's true. He was front-runner on the ecclesiastical fast track . . . studied at the Pontifical Biblical Institute in Rome, taught at Loyola . . . the intelligentsia's darling. But he was so iconoclastic that the Church hierarchy decided to gag him. They won't even let the laity read his books anymore.''

"You seem to know a great deal about him.''

"I used to follow his career avidly, Amanda. I guess I had an intellectual crush on the man, or whatever you call it when the object of your fascination is utterly unattainable. Anyway, he was the only really famous person I knew back then, so every time there was an article about him anywhere, I gobbled it up. Until he dropped out of sight, a few years back.

"He's a mystic as well as a genius, Amanda . . . and a devout believer. Nobody ever had the temerity to doubt his faith, as far as I know . . . but his visionary view of man's evolution toward God is so breathtaking and mystical it borders on heresy. And, I think he wasn't always willing to knuckle under to authority on the laity issues, either. So, they put him under wraps, out of the public eye. I imagine the Pope probably knows Messenguer's vision is way beyond the Church's ability to control. They did the same thing with Teilhard de Chardin, remember?''

Amanda did.

"Anyway, they've tucked him away somewhere and I need you to find him.''

"Me? But I'm barely even a Baptist, much less a tracer of lost priests. What makes you think I can find him? Besides, he sounds so saintly maybe you should just look him up in your hagiography . . .''

She expected Maggie to laugh, but the face looking back was deadly serious. "I really *need* him,'' Maggie said pleadingly. "At least he's a place to start in this awful maze, and you always know somebody, who knows somebody . . .''

Amanda nodded, already thumbing the card file in her brain for someone who'd done charity work for the Archdiocese of New York. "Give me a couple of hours, and a telephone, darlin','' she said ruminatively. "I'll find your priestly paragon, wherever they've stashed him.''

Three hours later she called Maggie with the news.

"I've run your mystic to ground, Maggie. They've sent him to the Church's equivalent of Siberia. Some book depository, near Rhinebeck, where they keep all those Indexed books the Church used to forbid Catholics to read. They've made him a glorified librarian of naughty books, if you can believe that. They'd probably put Stephen Hawking in charge of first-grade arithmetic, if they had him, too." She paused for indignation. "Although, in all fairness, Harriet McCarthy says it's a job so 'fraught with intellectual seductions, it can only be given to one who is beyond this world's temptations.' Oh my! Doesn't he sound like he hung the moon."

Father Peter said he would see her.

# CHAPTER 17

Peter Messenguer was an unpriestlike presence. He stood six foot two or three in the leather sandals he preferred to shoes, and the lean muscular build he'd inherited from the ancestral gene pool was the kind that ages well. Years spent on archaeological digs in hard countries had given his face the look of fine-tooled leather. Lines and creases intersected at places that suggested he laughed well and often. Yet his eyes turned down a little at the outside corners, just enough to impart a permanent expression of quizzical sadness. As if he had looked upon the world and found it wanting in some unfathomable way.

The aquiline nose was too prominent for handsomeness, but the rugged face was memorable, and far more male than one expected of a prelate. It was a fine, distinguished face, and marked by life. He looked the kind of man to be found in battered tweed and waders, in an Irish trout stream. Or on a Viking ship. But the eyes showed the haunting of one who looks beyond this world to something others cannot see.

His hair had leftover streaks of blond threaded through the white and gray. He wore it long, the habit of a lifetime lived far from barbers, and of a man devoid of physical pretensions.

He smiled at Maggie as he greeted her, and something wistful in his gaze made her wonder if he had expected her still to be nineteen, or, if perhaps her aging had reminded him of his own mortality.

"I remember you," he said fondly. "We spent a weekend at Fordham, a little over a lifetime ago, running the Casuists to ground and probing the Manichaean Heresy. I thought you were the only thing of purity I encountered in New York." He chuckled a little, as if recalling some great secret, and took her elbow firmly, to lead her into a small sitting room. Maggie smiled to herself; "a thing of purity" was not the impression she had wanted to leave with him.

"You'll take tea, won't you?" he asked eagerly. "It's my only addiction, really—the legacy of my Irish grandmother."

How glamorous this priest had seemed to her at nineteen . . . she, the Catholic school girl, he, so brilliant, so kind, so unexpectedly human. Maggie felt a surge of adolescent nervousness at seeing him again, and wondered at herself.

"Now, Maggie, dear," he said, as the tea tray appeared, "you must tell me why you've sought me out in my place of exile. It can't have been an easy quest."

"I don't really know where to begin, Father. Or whether I'm wasting your time. I have reason to believe that my grandchild has become involved with satanism, and I'm way out of my depth in anything occult. So I prayed for guidance, and suddenly remembered reading that you had performed exorcisms. I thought, perhaps . . ." She let the sentence trail off, for she didn't know what it was she was asking.

Father Peter had been sitting back in his chair, teacup casually suspended between open knees. Now, he leaned forward, alert, put the cup on the table and looked at Maggie with a penetrating gaze.

"Why don't you begin wherever the story needs to, Maggie," he said gently. "Middles, endings, beginnings—who among us knows which is which, anyway? Your guidance brought you here, perhaps mine will figure out why."

Maggie took a deep breath and told him what she knew, what she thought she knew, and what she feared. Throughout most of her discourse, he sat silently, chair slightly tilted back, fingertips forming a small pyramid in front of his mouth. She wondered if he thought her mad.

"What a remarkable story, Maggie," he said, thoughtful and serious, when she'd finished. "And surely no wonder you're distraught. The question before us seems to be, what can I do to help unravel this tangled skein." He stood up. "I think better when I walk . . . perhaps we could wander out among the trees, while I dredge up what I know that may be useful to you."

*Fish or cut bait, Peter,* he said to himself, as he put on his coat. *If you hear her out, you're in . . . if you're in, you're in all the way.* It was always the same. You made the choice and suffered the consequences. And the Demon knew you wouldn't say no.

There was a path that led from the book depository toward the Hudson; they walked toward the silver-gray water, glimpsed ephemerally through the trees.

"I can assure you, Maggie," he said, when they'd walked a little way, "that satanic worship is as genuine a reality in the world today as it has been since the Fall of the Angels. Devil-worshipping cults frequently come to the attention of the Church. In the confessional, for example, people sometimes recount crimes so macabre it's hard to imagine what penance could possibly expiate their sins. And, occasionally, churches or cemeteries are desecrated by Satan's followers, but the police ask the bishop to keep that fact under his mitre to prevent panic. The same thing happens even with murders. Sometimes quite gruesome ones take place, in which ritual acts have been performed on the poor victim before his death, but as no one wants to open Pandora's Box, the satanic connection is generally kept from the press and public.

"For example, some of the best law enforcement people I know firmly believe that Son of Sam was a satanist, and that the slayings were ordered by the satanic cult hierarchy. Then, of course, there's Charles Manson . . ."

"And Maa Kheru?" she asked. "Have you ever heard of that?"

Father Peter nodded. "The Church has been collecting data about that unsavory crew for some years now. My bet is that it not only exists, but is a very potent, very hidden tool for evil around the world. It seems to attract a higher level of intellect than many of the other cults—people with potential to be influential in the community. Rumor has it they've infiltrated government, industry, et cetera."

"I don't quite know what to say, Father. This all seems so preposterous to me."

"I daresay it would to most anyone," he replied with a slight smile. "But remember, Maggie, Satan is a fallen Archangel . . . we must presume he lost none of his powers when he fell—he lost only grace and the company of God. We must assume his power to be vast, and his followers ruthless and plentiful."

"At least you don't think I'm tilting at windmills."

"Not in the least," he answered, "but if you're tilting at Maa Kheru, you may need a rather large jousting pole.

"Something does trouble me about your story, though, Maggie. It seems to me there's a significant missing piece to this puzzle. Why do they want this particular child so badly? Surely, there are a million children they could lay hands on without risking exposure. As I understand it, these Devil cults even use women as breeders to *produce* children for their infernal rituals. From what you tell me, the Vanniers appear to have all the money in the world at their disposal—why would they risk your going to the authorities, and muddying the waters around them? Perhaps the real question we need to address here is whether Cody could be special in some way we haven't yet divined?"

He turned a questioning gaze on Maggie. "You don't by any chance know the precise time and place of your granddaughter's birth, do you?" he asked. Maggie answered yes.

"Come back to the library with me, then," he said enthusiastically. "Let us draw up an astrological chart for Cody, and see if we can discover what it is that's so very special about your granddaughter."

"An astrological chart?" Maggie said incredulously. "I didn't think the Church approved of anything that smacked of the occult."

Father Messenguer smiled gently at her concern. "You're right, of course. I'm afraid I'm a terrible embarrassment to my superiors," he said simply. "But you see, Maggie, in my quest to understand the secrets of God's breathtaking creation, I've studied all the great religions, in exquisite detail. In truth, I became a linguist so I might pursue my quest in the original languages of the great teachers. Along the journey, I've picked up a good many esoteric skills that are never taught in seminaries.

"I've lived in strange foreign places, you see, where Spirit is not constrained by our paradigms. A few of the skills I've mastered—like astrology—are quite frowned upon by the Church fathers—in this generation at least. They've forgotten, perhaps, that the Wise Men were themselves astrologers, and that it was a new star that proclaimed the birth of our Savior.

"I was introduced to the science of the stars by an

old Hindu monk, whom I considered a saint. He was very wise and very, very good, so when I learned of the stars from him, I accepted that there might be something to the science . . . and over the long years since, my empirical observations have borne out that most of what he said was true. Frankly, I've found astrology to be a useful enough tool, so I've blessed him for the gift, on more than one occasion. I fully expect its validity will be explained to the satisfaction of science, in the next century."

"Why ever would you think that, Father?" Maggie was very disturbed by the notion.

"You see, my dear, quantum physicists now perceive the Universe to be a gigantic network of interrelated energy fields . . . personal, planetary, and intergalactic. If that is the case, why should not the electromagnetic fields of planets affect us humans, in much the same way they affect the tides, or the sex lives of mollusks, for that matter? I've always found it sensible to remember that one century's magic is often the next century's science."

The priest continued to talk, in a rambling fashion, but with a clarity and breadth of subject matter that astounded her. They entered the great library, which acted as a repository for books the Church had, until the late sixties, forbidden the laity, and he settled in at what looked like a massive refectory table. Over the next hour he pulled books from stacks, punched data into a computer, scribbled notes on a yellow pad—as Maggie watched, entranced. He talked as he worked, bringing an almost boyish enthusiasm to the task, and she listened eagerly, fascinated by the facility of his intellect and the range of his curiosity. She couldn't help but wonder what his age might be. Late fifties, perhaps. She watched the spare angularity of his movements; everything about him suggested strength and vigor.

"An astrological chart is no more than a map of the heavens at the precise moment of one's birth," he explained. "It presumes the interrelatedness of our individual energies, with the greater energies of the cosmos. The ancient Celts likened this relationship to a giant energetic web that enmeshes us all. If anyone trembles the web, they would say, we all vibrate.

"According to astrologers, the map of one's individual birth planets shows one's character most explicitly—strengths, weaknesses, gifts, burdens, and such. I believe it also delineates the baggage we've brought into this life, from that snippet of the time-space continuum we choose to call the past. And it most assuredly shows which great challenges will lie before us, during a given lifetime." He paused in his dissertation, stuck the pen he'd been using between his teeth, and left her, returning minutes later, laden with books that looked old and worn.

"Bear with me a moment, will you?" he mumbled past the pencil. "I may be on to something here."

"May I help?" Maggie asked, feeling like Alice at the White Queen's tea party. Finally, the priest scribbled something on a lined pad, in some unrecognizable language, and replied.

"You could make more tea, if you wouldn't mind. Mrs. O'Leary will allow that one small intrusion into her domain. What I need to find is written in hieroglyph, so it may take me a bit of time to translate adequately. And tea always helps." He smiled, and looked far younger than he could possibly be.

When Maggie returned from the kitchen, she saw he'd laid out a batch of papers for her perusal, and marked passages in several books. The priest looked up at her, and she tried to read the odd expression in his eyes, but it eluded her.

He frowned, as if deciding how to tell her what he'd found. "What we have here may be a bit difficult for you to digest, Maggie . . ." he said judiciously. "There really isn't any way to explain it in Western terms. I'm afraid your granddaughter is what would be called a

*Way-shower*, in certain faraway places, where life is looked at in a vastly different perspective from ours." He seemed troubled.

"You see, my dear, in parts of the globe in which reincarnation is an accepted notion, it is thought that certain very High Souls are incarnating at this moment in time, in order to help humanity save itself during the coming cataclysms. Your Cody appears to be one of these High Souls. And from what I see here, this child has no personal karma in this lifetime, Maggie—no debts left to expiate, if you will. She is here only to serve humanity. It would appear that she has no time frame, either . . . which means she is free to stay in the body, or to leave it, at will. I'm afraid, my dear, if your fears are well grounded, and these people attempt to take her too far into Darkness, she will simply die and be reborn again elsewhere, so she can fulfill her humanitarian destiny."

"Why would God send such a soul, Father—assuming such as you describe exists—only to let it be destroyed by evil people? That doesn't make sense at all." Maggie was shocked by the implications of what he'd said, and equally so by the fact that he seemed to accept the idea of reincarnation so casually.

"Souls are never destroyed, Maggie," the priest replied patiently. "If the theory of reincarnation is correct—and I have tried always to keep an open mind about that possibility, insomuch as many great spiritual teachers have subscribed to such a theory—each one chooses his next lifetime before birth. Or to put it a bit more scientifically, each one is drawn 'energetically' to a place that will provide the right circumstances to fulfill its destiny—its karma—if you will."

"But you said Cody has no karma," Maggie reminded him, fascinated, puzzled.

"I said she has no karmic *debts*," he corrected. "But she does appear to have a mission to accomplish, and I suspect she may have ties to you that are forged of great love . . . ties she accepts of her own free will. It's also possible, Maggie, that Cody could be here to help you unfold your own gifts of the spirit . . . as well as to help humanity.''

Maggie attempted, with great difficulty, to process all he'd said, and Father Peter continued looking through the books he'd pulled out. "Hers is a very difficult chart to interpret, Maggie . . . I'm afraid I'll have to delve into some of the more esoteric sources, before I can come up with the specific information we're looking for.'' Then, as an afterthought, he said, "Perhaps you should give me similar birth information about yourself, Maggie . . . it might provide some clue to your part in this drama.''

Somewhat bewildered, Maggie left the priest late in the day. It was no wonder the Church had a problem with Peter Messenguer.

Early the next morning, Father Peter called her, urgency in his tone. Would it be all right to visit with her at home? he asked. Two hours later he was at her door.

"I think I know what this is all about," he said without preamble. He carried an armload of books and two full shopping bags, which Maria plucked from his hands, muttering something Portuguese under her breath that had to do with a priest in a sweater, instead of a cassock. With a dazzling smile, Father Peter replied in the same idiom and Maria begrudgingly thawed enough to reserve final judgment of the man for later.

Maggie led the priest to her library; it was her favorite room in the old Federal house, and still sported the original satinwood paneling and plaster ceiling cherubs.

"I think your granddaughter is in terrible danger, Maggie," Father Peter said quietly. "Perhaps more than you've even imagined."

Maggie bolted upright in her chair. "You found some answers in her chart?"

Peter leaned forward, visibly disturbed by what he must report. "It's a bit mad," he began. "And I can't even begin to venture an opinion on whether what I'm about to say is fact or pure fantasy . . . but I feel I must let you know what I've unearthed." He paused for a breath.

"There's an ancient legend, Maggie . . . I'm not an authority on Egyptology, mind you—at least not on the dynasty in question—but I do have some knowledge, and I read hieroglyph, so I'm not a neophyte, either." She saw he was skirting what he must tell her. Then, in a voice that suggested a kind of reverence, he said, "Cody could be the Isis Messenger."

The ground shifted under Maggie with the words. Like a double exposure on a film, *something* imposed itself on her vision for a split second. Too fleeting to recognize. *But old.* Jesus, it was ancient! Whatever it was. And that *sound.* Like high-pitched wind bells, barely audible . . . but it sent shivers through her nervous system.

Maggie blinked herself back into focus. "Did you say the Isis Messenger?" She tried to reach out to touch the eerie experience of a moment ago, but it was gone. "What in the world is the Isis Messenger?"

Father Peter put on his glasses, and referred to the notes in his hand, but it was apparent he didn't need coaching.

"There's an ancient legend, Maggie—references to it first appear in Egypt, nearly five thousand years ago— that at some unspecified future time, when humanity is at great peril, a child will be sent who has the correct vibrational frequency to resurrect the Isis Amulet." He raised his hand to stay the torrent of questions he saw forming.

"The precise shape this Amulet takes has been lost in the mists of history, but every single source who has ever referred to it, did so with awe. You see, it was believed to possess unprecedented occult power, invested in it by the great Mother Goddess Isis herself. It is empowered, so the legend goes, to save the world from final destruction, by reinforcing the strength of all that is Good, and undermining all that is Evil."

Maggie tried to interrupt, but he gestured again. "Let me finish, my dear, then I promise I shall do my best to answer all your questions." He glanced again at the page in his hand. "According to Hermes Trismegistus—who was the greatest authority in history on all things magical—if the forces of Evil should ever get hold of the Amulet, they will use it to retrieve its cosmic opposite, the Sekhmet Stone. With the Sekhmet Stone, all powers of annihilation and war can be controlled." He paused.

"You must understand, Maggie, that just as Christians have sought the Grail, and Alchemists have sought the Philosopher's Stone, Magicians, White and Black, throughout the ages, have sought the Isis Amulet and the Sekhmet Stone." Maggie looked somewhat stunned.

He took a deep breath and began again. "The maze that the Universal forces have constructed to keep this unrestricted power out of the wrong hands is, according to Hermes and others, convoluted and fraught with dangers. In order to retrieve the Sekhmet Stone, an occultist of the highest degree must first gain possession of the Isis Amulet . . . and *only* the Isis Messenger can materialize the Amulet. If by evil chance, the Dark Forces come into possession of the two talismans, Sekhmet will help them destroy the Isis Amulet and its potential good, forever. I needn't tell you the results for mankind if all good were nullified."

Father Peter looked directly into Maggie's troubled eyes. "If my suspicion is correct, Maggie dear, Cody is the Messenger and you are the Guardian, sent to defend her."

"Father, this is really too much!" she exploded. "How could such an insane story possibly be true? There are no Amulets that rule the world! No stones that control Evil. *Human beings* control Good and Evil, not inanimate objects. This is just preposterous!"

"But don't you see, Maggie," Peter pressed urgently. "What does it matter if this is all balderdash? If the Vanniers are members of some satanic cult, and if they believe in such a possibility, Cody could be in the gravest danger imaginable . . . It isn't at all farfetched for them to have done the child's chart, just as I've done. If so, they've seen the same confluence of planets I've seen."

Maggie tried to stay calm enough to reply, but her voice shook when she spoke. "What would they do to her, Father, if they believed any of this nonsense?"

"I don't know for certain . . . from what I've gleaned so far, they'd either sacrifice her, as part of the Materialization Ritual, or they'd banish her soul and give her body to Sekhmet."

"And who in the hell is Sekhmet?" Maggie demanded.

"The female equivalent of Set or Satan, Maggie. You might call her the Goddess of Evil—although she's a bit more complex than that. War, famine, pestilence, death, violent weather, geophysical upheaval, all these forces seem to be within her province."

"Oh wonderful! Evil Goddesses . . . Amulets to rule the world . . . this is truly ridiculous! I'm not having this conversation, and I'm sure as hell *not* having it with a priest!"

Father Peter reached out and took Maggie's hands in his, to calm her agitation. His concern for her was obvious.

"Maggie dear, listen to me! For the moment, it seems clear to me that it doesn't matter one whit if we believe this ancient legend, or we do not. What matters is that we may have found the key to Cody's importance to Eric and Jenna.

"I fully understand your terror and your disbelief—I know every word I've told you sounds like the ravings of a lunatic—but you know I am not a lunatic, Maggie. And you must know I wouldn't have come all this way to bring this news to you, except that it seems to me terribly important for you to have it. This information may be an opportunity to unravel the mystery we face. To beat them, we must understand how they think. You do see the rationality in that, Maggie?" He waited until she was calm enough to shake her head yes, before he continued.

"Others will be able to help you, my dear, but if any of this seeming madness is true, you and Cody are the two major players on this board. You must not let your disbelief make you vulnerable."

"How can I ever begin to understand what's happening, Father?" she said despairingly. "And how in the name of God will I ever convince the legal authorities that any of this is real? If I ever told this tale to that bureaucratic automaton I met at the Bureau of Child Welfare, she'd come at me with a net. And I can't say I'd blame her."

"I can offer you no assistance on the secular side, Maggie. But on the spiritual side, I do have certain knowledge that may prove valuable, so I want you to pay strict attention to what I'm about to tell you. I have lived in strange places, and witnessed stranger sights than you could possibly imagine. I've seen ignorant tribal shamans cut out cancer with a filthy stone age knife and cure their patient . . . I've seen headhunters tell the future accurately from the skulls of their victims. I've seen aboriginals die because a witch doctor pointed a bone in their direction. During exorcisms, I've spoken to demons who are fluent in ancient languages, unheard of by the person being exorcised. I implore you to take this seriously, Maggie! There are many more forces afoot in this Universe than science is currently aware of."

He paused for breath and it was easy to see how seriously he took what he was saying. Maggie was suddenly aware of how far out of his way this man was going for her.

"I'm hearing you, Father," she said softly. "I really am."

He let out a long relieved breath. "Do you own any blessed objects, Maggie? A rosary, a crucifix, Holy Water?"

She nodded her head. "I still say my Confirmation

rosary, and I kept the crucifix from my husband's funeral. No Holy Water.''

He reached into the bag he'd brought with him and pulled out two bottles. "It becomes apparent during exorcisms, Maggie, that sacramentals such as Holy Water and Holy Oil make demonic Presences very uncomfortable. Keep these near you. Try, if you can, to get one of them into Cody's possession. I've brought this blessed Miraculous Medal for you to put around her neck, if you can manage it—you'll remember that Mary is shown on it crushing the head of the serpent. This one was blessed by John XXIII years ago in Rome, and he was close to God.'' He paused to think what he'd forgotten to say.

"You must understand, Maggie, I've never performed ritual magic," he said. "I have merely studied it, which is a vastly different thing. I do, however, respect the power of ritual, and would never dream of underestimating its potential. So, I've brought you several prayers for protection.''

He handed her a marked prayer book, then reached into the shopping bag and pulled out an acrid-smelling length of what looked like hay. "I have no idea whatsoever if this will be useful, but I've brought it anyway. It's asafoetida grass from South America, Maggie—I was told by an Apache Medicine Man friend that it has the capacity to repel evil.''

He straightened and Maggie saw the concern in his gaze. "I believe I'm right about the child's value to them. If she is the Isis Messenger, then the forces of Darkness will stop at nothing to get her and use her.''

Maggie stared at him wide-eyed.

"Do you honestly believe, Father, that such a thing could be? Everything I know about the rational Universe rebels at the notion of Amulets that rule Good and Evil, or children who have divine powers. Frankly, I'm shocked out of my shoes that you'd give credence to such possibilities.''

Father Peter stood for a moment, silently considering his reply, then he said, "When I was young, Maggie, I thought I knew everything there was to know about this 'rational Universe.' Now, I know only this . . . that God works mysteriously, in a grand design far beyond our ken. That those He chooses as His instruments are never the ones we would expect. That all I know or think I know is insignificant compared to what is yet to be learned.

"Whether Cody is the Isis Messenger, or whether the Messenger possesses any magical powers, isn't really the point . . . what matters is that some very evil and corrupt people may *think* she has these powers, and because of that fact she is in the gravest danger. And so, most probably, are you."

"Because I love her?"

"Because you are her Guardian—and whether you accept that in a metaphysical sense, or a grandmotherly one, they know you'll fight for her, even at great cost to yourself."

Maggie let Father Peter out the door and stood leaning against it, trying to regain her equilibrium. She felt as if she'd fallen off the edge of the earth.

MAGGIE hurried to Ellie's shop and pounded on the door, despite the CLOSED sign that hung in the window. The lights were on and she heard footsteps coming toward her; she breathed a sigh of relief.

Ellie was wearing a long robe of some sort and very little makeup, but she looked serene and beautiful. Maggie wondered if she might have been meditating.

"I've got to talk to you," she said breathlessly, holding out the astrological charts Father Peter had given her.

"Where'd you get these?" Ellie asked, stepping aside to let her in.

"Father Peter Messenguer brought them to me. Can you read them?"

Ellie smiled enigmatically as she reached for the charts. "Is the Pope Catholic?"

"He told me the craziest story, Ellie. I'm still reeling! It had to do with some ancient Egyptian legend." But, Ellie wasn't listening, she was staring at the astrological charts open-mouthed.

"Sweet Jesus, Maggie!" she gasped. "She's the Messenger!"

Gooseflesh rose on Ellie's arms, and her blood ran faster. *A Lifetime. A thousand lifetimes, waiting for this one moment. The dream of every priestess since time began . . . to be called by the Goddess! But to do what? To battle? To sacrifice? To witness? Her heart beat hard against her breastbone and she forced herself to be calm. You never knew in what strange guise the call would come. Just as you never knew if you were ready. To be challenged by the Immortals was the greatest honor conceivable. And the deadliest.*

"Oh Mags," she breathed, motioning her in from the doorway. "We've got to think this through very clearly . . . you could both be in terrible danger."

Maggie stared at Ellie dumbstruck. If she knew about this, too . . . "I can't believe you know about this Isis business, too!" she said agitatedly. "Is there a newsletter out there that I don't subscribe to, and everybody else does? How did I live to forty-two years of age, thinking the world was a rational place, if it isn't?"

Ellie sat down and motioned Maggie to do the same. "Look, Mags," she said compassionately, "you may have fallen into something very big, and very important. All my life, I've known the legend of the Isis Messenger. I've probably heard sixteen different versions of it from sixteen different traditions, but the bottom line is always the same. Whoever has the Messenger, possesses the Amulets, and whoever gets hold of the Amulets rules the world."

Maggie's hand was at her mouth, her teeth sunk in the flesh of her index finger, as if she were holding back words or a scream. "And you believe this?" she whispered.

"Like I believe in the Grail, or the Philosopher's Stone, Maggie. All the legends that have persisted for millennia have some basis of truth behind them, even if it's been cloaked in metaphor. What that truth is . . . who can say? But if Cody is the Messenger, and you are the Guardian, you are both endangered species . . . because true or not, there are many, many people who will want to control that power."

"What should I do, Ellie?" Maggie asked simply. "And what do I need to know?"

Ellie sat back and stared at her new friend, as if trying to intuit how to answer her question. Finally, she spoke.

"I want you to suspend what you think of as the rational mind, for a little while, and just listen to me with your *intuition* . . . your *inner knowing*. Nothing I am about to tell you would be sanctioned by your priest friend's Church, or by most of humanity—on this continent, anyway. But to those who practice ritual magic, or any variation on that theme, what I'm about to tell you would be accepted wisdom. So, I'm begging you to hear me out."

Both the seriousness and the kindliness in Ellie's manner touched Maggie. "Forgive me my unbelief, Ellie," she said contritely. "It's just that things seemed awful enough to me when I thought we were just dealing with child abuse . . . but this?"

Ellie's demeanor was serious when she responded. "It would be apparent from your chart, Maggie, to anyone who believes in the wisdom of the stars, that you have practiced a high degree of ritual magic in many previous lifetimes." She held out the astrological diagram and pointed to several glyphs at the top of the circle. You have Neptune at the midheaven, trining Saturn, which means you have not only been a practitioner of High Magic, and a seeker far along on the path to Enlightenment, but it means you have the potential *in this lifetime* to be an Adept.''

"Forgive me, Ellie, but I'm about as close to being an Adept as I am to being Pope Margaret the First."

Ellie smiled as you would at a brilliant, but recalcitrant child. "Let's explore that," she said patiently. "You're psychic, aren't you? Maybe you call it by another name . . . intuition? premonition? Maybe you know things before other people do? Or you've had visionary experiences? Think, Maggie! Help me along here, just for the sake of argument. I'm not fucking around about this. You are treading very close to the Great Mysteries here and they are not to be taken lightly."

"I do seem to *know* things that other people don't, Ellie . . ." Maggie said hesitantly, "to pick them up from somewhere inside me . . . as if I'm tapped into a source other people don't have, I suppose. I thought it came from being Irish. You know, like the visions we Celts sometimes have when we pray . . . or the fact that I fell in love with the antiquities business because I understand old objects in some visceral, nonintellectual way. My store manager, Amanda, teases me about it . . . she says I never have to look up the provenance of a piece, I just have to hold it in my hands for a while. Is that the kind of thing you mean?"

Ellie nodded vigorously. "That's exactly what I mean, Mags. And how about Cody? Is what you feel for her *just* grandmotherly devotion? Or could it be *more?* Is there some special element in it that isn't quite ordinary? What does that housekeeper of yours say? From your description of her, she comes from a culture close enough to nature to still be in touch with the Universal truths our more sophisticated cultures have lost."

Maggie frowned in consternation. "Maria says Cody and I are joined by some kind of bond beyond the normal. She thinks Cody is magical, in some way. I think it's just peasant superstition." She looked sheepish and added, "But there is *something*, Ellie, between Cody and me. I don't know how to explain it . . . maybe all grandmothers and grandchildren experience this, but we seem to read each other's mind, as if we live in each other's skin. And Cody's gifts do seem unusual in certain ways. Her articulation, her ability to understand concepts beyond her years . . . Oh, I don't know, Ellie, that could just be my grandmotherly pride talking."

"Look, Mags," Ellie said authoritatively. "You don't have time for false modesty, or any other bullshit weakness right now. If you are her Guardian, in some karmic battle plan we don't quite understand yet, it's going to be necessary for you to *remember* things you've never known in this lifetime. You're not going to be able to waste time on skepticism . . . and you're sure as hell not going to have time for diffidence. I think you're going to have to 'act as if ye had faith,' as they say in theology class. And you're going to have to get tough as nails. For Christ's sake, Maggie, this isn't a Sunday school exercise. You're up against the Prince of fucking Darkness!"

Maggie stared at Ellie in shocked acknowledgment. "Tell me what to do," she said simply. "Tell me what to learn."

# CHAPTER 18

"You sure you know what you're doing on this one, Lieutenant?" Detective Gino Garibaldi asked, handing Devlin a steaming container of coffee from the Greek deli on Hudson Street. He was just above medium height, but so stocky he looked like a weightlifter in a 1912 carnival. Dark shaggy hair framed the kind of face women thought handsome and sexy.

Devlin looked up, annoyed, then reminded himself of how long they'd been friends. "I'm sure."

"So, you're telling me this is a case, and not a case of jock itch, right?"

Devlin grinned, despite himself. Garibaldi knew, like everybody else, you could get hurt if you let your emotions, or your anatomy, cloud your judgment.

"I'm sure."

"Okay. Okay. I had to ask. So, you need my help? On the case part, I mean."

Devlin laughed good-naturedly and took a sip of the scalding coffee, grimacing. "This stuff tastes like battery acid."

"Yeah, that's why there's so many Greeks in New York with coffee shops. Nobody in Greece would drink this shit."

"You could follow up a couple of leads on this for me, Gino, if you've got time." Garibaldi had good instincts and there wasn't much he didn't know about the gamier side of the Village.

"Time? Sure thing, Lieutenant. What New York cop ain't got time on his hands." He reached for the file Devlin proffered.

"This one's unofficial, right, Lieutenant?" he asked dropping his voice.

"For now, yeah. But maybe not forever."

Garibaldi glanced through the notes hastily. "What do you say we down a few at Clancy's after work, and you fill me in?"

"Like there's really such a thing as after work, in this line of business," Devlin replied sarcastically. After work, before work, during work, he thought. If you're a detective and something grabs you, you're never really off the case.

Garibaldi listened. There was an intensity about his capacity to listen that Devlin had always liked a lot. You could almost hear the brain at work, cataloging, cross-checking, sifting the mental files. Gino was a great kidder, and full of the old nick. But not when he listened.

"Son of a bitch," he said, when Devlin was finished. "You know this may come as a shock to you, but there are actually women in New York who are perfectly good in the sack, and where you don't have to fight the Forces of Evil to get them there. Like, Lieutenant, this is not uncomplicated."

Devlin shook his head. "It's not uncomplicated and it could be dirty, Gino, so I'll understand if you'd rather not get involved."

"So who said anything about not helping. I am merely the voice of fucking reason, here. What do you want me to do?"

"I've got two possibilities at the moment. Jenna and the phone call. If you can pull in a marker, to get the phone company to dump the computer records for the night Maggie got the anonymous call, maybe we can put the squeeze on the caller."

Gino grunted judiciously. To get unauthorized MUDS and LUDS from the phone company could cost big bucks, or cost somebody his job. Of course, it wasn't impossible . . .

"What have we got on the kid? You got a picture?"

Devlin handed over a snapshot of a lanky blond sixteen-year-old in jeans.

"What does she look like now?"

"According to Maggie, straight out of *Town and Country*. Long, perfect hair, designer wardrobe bought in Paris, very tony, very well-bred Greenwich."

"Yeah, like I always say, these satanists sure know a lot about good breeding."

"You know as well as I do, addicts leave trails, Gino. They're sloppy, they steal, they get arrested. She's sure to have been boosting while she was on the streets. Maggie says she was hooking for a while. Maybe there are prints somewhere or old friends. Better call in BCI and get a list of associates to run a check on. Get hold of robbery and get them into the CARS computer, then run whatever you get through the safest system.''

"Yeah, yeah, yeah. You gonna teach your grandmother how to suck eggs, next? I'll get the records, then I'll hit the streets.''

He took a long swallow of beer, then added, ''And I guess I don't have to ask if you've checked out this Maggie, Lieutenant? Neighbors, friends, DMV, the works? It's not possible she's a good-looking crackpot, right?''

"I checked her out. No record. No speeding tickets. No stints at Bellevue. She's a very nice lady in a big, ugly mess that nobody will help her with, and I, being a little bit crazy, would like to help her if I can. You'll like her, too, by the way.''

"She's gotta be a good one, if she rings your bells, Lieutenant . . . I didn't mean to suggest you were thinking with your talleywhacker, here. I just hope this doesn't get too hot to handle, unofficially. From what you've told me, she could be playing against the big kids. And nice ladies tend not to know how to do that.''

Devlin looked his friend in the eye. ''Which is why she's got us,'' he said.

# CHAPTER 19

Nicholas Sayles was almost beautiful, if you didn't take his soul into account. The arrogant nose and aristocratic forehead, the sensuous lips and brooding dark eyes were not run-of-the-mill, even for a network media star. The angular cheekbones of a Magyar chieftain and dark masculine brows lent strength to the rest; like fierce male anchors in an otherwise too exquisite environment, they spoke of power that was willful and dangerous. He had black hair that fell below his shoulders, a rebellious fuck-you to convention. Tethered in a long pony tail, it added to the sleek animal essence of the man; hanging loose it made him hybrid lion and panther. Nicky Sayles seemed more than human . . . and less. It was one of the reasons for his television success.

His intellect was the other. Behind a slick, urbane exterior, a first-rate brain resided. And he was entirely without conscience, a fact he had learned to conceal in the presence of those still chained to the illusion of morality and ethics. He won through skill and charm and ruthlessness and the practice of magic, although only a handful of people knew about the latter weapon in his arsenal.

Nicky reclined comfortably, in the Vannier study, on a long leather couch. Eric was the only friend with whom he was ever truly himself.

"How's the kid getting along with Ghania?" he asked with a smirk. "Being in the care of the old witch isn't a fate I'd wish on even my producer." Eric frowned; Nicky's occasional crassness irritated him.

"Ghania is a master at 'awakenings' as you well know, Nicky. She torments the child and delights her, she teaches her terror, but does not break the spirit. As yet. She is the captor on whose benevolence life depends, and the torturer from the nightmares of the damned."

"So much for Sesame Street," Nicky said with a short laugh. "But what she's trying to pull off here goes far beyond brainwashing, Eric. She can't awaken the kid's powers too soon, or we'll never be able to control her."

"True. It is a delicate balance she maintains . . . honing the instrument to the breaking point, then retreating. Honing and restraining. Honing and transforming. But Ghania is the best . . . there isn't another on this planet I'd trust with this task. The child will be ready at the appropriate time."

Sayles nodded, unconvinced, and swung his long legs onto the floor.

"I wish I felt as smug about this ritual shit as you do. I still think it would be easier if we just killed the kid. Virgin lifeforce packs a hell of a wallop. We could use the death throes to make sure the Materialization works."

"Or kill the goose that lays the golden egg," Eric responded.

"You think we have to keep her alive, after we've got the Amulets? I guess she could be a fucking booby trap of some kind—the Goddess always did have a wild sense of humor. That'd be some frigging joke, wouldn't it, Eric? We Materialize the Amulets, kill the kid, and then find out we need her to drive the bus." He laughed mirthlessly at the potential irony.

"I don't think killing the child serves our purpose," Eric said, untroubled by the possibility of murder. "I expect that Sekhmet will want the body for her own purposes, don't you? It must be difficult to be the quintessence of lust, with no means to assuage your hungers. Even the Gods have needs."

Sayles raised an eyebrow.

"So we banish Cody's Ka and hand the body to the demonic Gestapo, until Sekhmet gets horny enough to use it?" he mused. "But what the hell, it's only eternity, right?"

"Cody is merely a pawn in the game of the Gods, Nicky. Her karma makes her vulnerable."

"Yeah, and also gives her power. Don't forget she'll be 'awakened' by then. We've got no way of knowing exactly what kind of power she'll have, once the floodgates are opened. Isis is no slouch as an enemy."

"Nor is Sekhmet. Remember, it was Isis who devised this test. She cannot intervene for a player, without queering her own game."

Sayles pursed his lips judiciously. "You know, Eric, you're really something. Where do you get off being so cocky about all this? As far as I know, we only get one shot at this Materialization, and the spell is a fucking rat's nest of ambiguities and intricate horseshit that nobody's done for a couple of thousand years—at least nobody's done it right . . ."

Eric looked annoyed. "Magic is a science, Nicky. No more, no less. It's bound by laws, natural and unnatural . . . if we invoke them properly, those laws will assure that the Universe complies with our intent. Don't start getting mystical on me, and acting as if we may fail in our efforts because of some fluke of circumstance. We will *control* Fate, and bend it to our will. Remember Crowley's precept: 'Do What Thou Wilt Shall Be the Whole of the Law.' "

"Crowley my ass, Eric. He ended up an impotent old fart, babbling about the power he *used to* have. There *are* laws, I'll grant you that—but we damn well don't know what all of them are. Sure, we can bend nature to our will, but only when we have the proper formulae at our disposal. And there's a piss-pot-ful of magic we still don't know how to work. And with this particular invocation, let me remind you, we are not dealing with mere demons—these fuckers are *Gods*."

Eric rose from behind the desk to look his friend in the eye and said very coolly, "Our Council of Thirteen includes the most powerful magicians on the planet. They represent every major discipline on the Left Hand Path. Let me remind you, Nicky, we, too, are Gods. We have crossed the Abyss . . . we can fuck with whatever we damn well choose."

Sayles put up his hands in a gesture that said *enough*. "A small difference of opinion, kiddo," he replied. "I'm not expecting any hitches . . . I just don't want to get so cocky we get careless. We're six inches from the pot of gold . . . I don't want anybody pissing on the rainbow."

Nicky stood and stretched his lanky body; it was stronger and lither than it had seemed when recumbent.

"The real question we should be thinking about is which of our trusty band should we distrust most? Which of our esteemed colleagues will make a grab for the Amulets the moment they've been Materialized?"

"Nearly everyone of stature, I should think. Ghania has a psychic hit list already in progress. It's a tricky call, of course—anyone proficient enough to attempt a coup is proficient enough to cover his intent. Nonetheless, she'll monitor on the Astral and kill as needed."

"Why don't we just slip them all one of those slow-acting Chinese poisons Ghania's been screwing around with, at the dress rehearsal. Afterward, we'll decide who gets the antidote . . ."

Eric Vannier laughed aloud.

"I told you we were Gods, Nicky . . . life, death, the fate of the planet, all in our hands now. Why, it's even better than being Republican!"

# CHAPTER 20

*The two young priestesses stood facing each other across the vast temple floor. An ephemeral sunshine filtered through panes of semi-precious crystal, bathing the limestone interior in puddles of colored light that undulated like a rich tidal pool.*

It was a dream, yet some part of Maggie's consciousness knew she, herself, was the dark-haired priestess in another time, and Cody was the fair one, walking toward her, arms outstretched in supplication.

*"Don't you remember me, Mim?" the young girl was calling wistfully. "Don't you remember me?" The dream/Maggie reached out to take her hand.*

*Suddenly, a fissure cracked the ground before them, and a demonic creature hissed up from its sulphurous depths. Its grotesque head roared a ghastly sound, not of this sphere—a flowing lava substance belched from its drooling lips. There was something remotely human about the body, yet its hooves were cloven, and its haunches, bovine. A covering of matted hair and feathers stretched to clawlike fingers. It had pendulous female breasts and a huge erection.*

*The demon seized the Cody/priestess with bloody claws and dragged her backward pitilessly toward the gaping pit that descended deep into the earth. The Maggie/priestess could see a staircase sloping down, downward, miles into the Abyss—flames and sulphur roiled at the bottom, and bursts of steam issued forth rhythmically, as if spewed by a giant bellows.*

*Maggie knew she looked into the maw of Hell.*

*Far, far below, at the bottom of the endless passageway, Jenna—entranced—was descending the staircase.*

*The dream/Cody struggled with the demon; smelling its foul breath, feeling its filthy claws caress her purified flesh. Frantically, the dream/Maggie tried to run to the struggling priestess, but her feet were mired in quicksand that sucked at every step. Angry demons surged from the pit in swarms, to beat her back—stinging, flailing, red-hot pincers flayed at her as she fought her way toward . . .*

*Cody!*

Maggie was awake now, bolt upright in bed. But the dream filled her soul with terrible knowing. Cody was in deadly, immediate peril. Jenna was headed for damnation.

All her life she'd had true dreams. Sometimes veiled in allegory, but always accurate enough so she could tell the visionary dreams from the ordinary ones.

Goosebumps covered her sweat-soaked body. She had to clench her teeth to keep them from chattering. This was real. This was immediate.

She had to get Cody out of that house.

*Today.*

MAGGIE grabbed a cup of coffee and hit the road. She reached the Vannier estate before 8:00 A.M., and demanded to see her daughter. Jenna was still in her dressing gown when she greeted her mother; her eyelids were at half mast and her voice seemed to be operating at the wrong turntable speed. Maggie's heart sank when she saw her; there was no mistaking the influence of drugs this morning.

"What are you doing here, Mother?" Jenna slurred. "I wasn't expecting you today."

Still agitated from her nightmare, Maggie moved close enough to Jenna to grasp her by the shoulders. She would have hugged her, if she thought her daughter would permit it.

"Jenna, sweetheart, you've got to listen to me," she said urgently. "You know about my dreams . . . the true ones. I had one last night that showed me, you, and Cody are in horrible danger. That's why I've come to get you.

"You've got to come with me, Jenna! Right now. Today. I'll get you into the best drug hospital—I'll get the best help for you. We'll fight this thing together, sweetheart. Please let me help you before it's too late!"

Jenna seemed to focus with some difficulty. She wrenched herself away from her mother, pushing her backward violently.

"You're so ridiculous! You always think everything has to do with drugs! I'm not on drugs. Can't you see what a perfect life I have here? I'm rich . . . I'm married to a brilliant man . . . my daughter has the best of care." Jenna's voice was shrill, her face ugly with sudden rage. "You just can't stand to see me so happy, that's all it is. You just can't believe I pulled it off, can you?"

Maggie stared at her daughter, shocked and horrified. "How can you imagine such things to be true, Jenna?" she pleaded, wounded by the vitriol of Jenna's anger. "Don't you know how much I love you?" How could she possibly convey the danger she felt congealing all around them? Lapping at them, ready to engulf their world . . .

"I *know* you're on drugs, Jenna. I can see it in your face—your pupils are as dilated as saucers, your speech is slurred. I don't care about any of that! I'm not judging you—I'm trying to help you! Don't you understand, the drugs are keeping you from seeing what's going on around here. Cody's in terrible danger, Jenna. *Right now*. I feel it with every sense I own. She's in mortal danger . . . and you are, too!"

Jenna pulled herself up to her full height and yanked her robe tighter with a fierce gesture. "That's absolutely ridiculous. Cody is just *fine*, Mother. Ghania has taken care of generations of Vannier children, and look how well they've turned out."

"Let me see her, then," Maggie demanded. It was the drugs talking, not Jenna, she reminded herself forcefully. Maybe the Jenna she loved didn't even live in that body anymore. She prayed to God it wasn't too late to save the child.

Maggie watched Jenna calculate her next move. "All right, Mother," she said finally, "if you'll promise to go *immediately after*."

Maggie took a deep breath and agreed. Jenna had made her own choices, hard as that was to accept . . . she had made her own choices and Maggie must abide by them. But that didn't include letting Cody drown with her mother.

Cody sat like a small stone statue, perfectly groomed and mannered at the nursery table. An untouched breakfast sat before her. She seemed nearly catatonic, as if she'd gone inward, to ward off whatever was threatening her. She looked up as Maggie entered the room, quick tears filling her eyes, but she didn't stir from her place.

The grandmother moved swiftly and scooped her up into an embrace. The child leaned her head lethargically against Maggie's shoulder and whispered very softly,

"Cody loves Mim," over and over—in a strangely lifeless litany.

"What in the name of God have you done to this baby?" Maggie demanded, angry, frightened. "She's only been here six weeks, Jenna, and look at the deterioration in her. She's glassy-eyed, lethargic. Like a catatonic rag doll . . . what have you *done* to her?"

"Cody is my child, Mother, and I'm in charge of her life now, whether you approve or not."

"Then *be* in charge of it, for God's sake! Get her to a doctor, Jenna. There's something horribly wrong with this child!"

"She doesn't need a doctor. Ghania can treat her perfectly well."

"If she treats her so well, why is she in this condition?"

"I want you to go now, Mother," Jenna said, reaching firmly for Cody. "I want you to *go, right now!*" Jenna tried to pry the child loose from her mother's arms, but this time Maggie was ready for the assault.

Clutching Cody to her heart, she pushed past her daughter and ran for the stairs. Jenna's screams for Ghania echoed behind her, as she raced through the first floor and fumbled with the front-door lock. *Goddamnit!* The stupid door weighed a thousand pounds! She jerked it open and dashed for her car. Cody clung so tightly, the terrified grandmother was afraid she wouldn't be able to disengage the child enough to fit behind the wheel.

Maggie slammed down the door locks, jammed the key into the ignition with trembling fingers. She gunned the car out of the driveway just as Ghania, Jenna, and two servants the size of bodyguards hit the driveway, running uselessly after them, shouting words she couldn't hear.

They would come after her, that was certain. Maggie forced herself to think clearly, past her racing heart and fiddle-string nerves. She would take the child to Amanda—Jenna wouldn't think to search for her there.

Then, she would get the best child psychologist in New York to examine her. Amanda knew everybody . . . Amanda would know *somebody* who could help.

Cody lay crouched in a fetal position on the seat next to Maggie, her thumb in her mouth. She had never sucked her thumb! . . . Her legs were drawn up protectively and she was very, very still.

"It'll be all right now, sweetheart," Maggie soothed, still watching the rear-view mirror for pursuit. "Everything will be all right now."

Even as she said it, she knew it wasn't true.

Cody's pediatrician was out of town. *Shit!* Maggie tried to explain to the covering doctor what was happening, but he sounded fearful of embroilment in a potentially litigious situation. Amanda phoned back to say she'd made an appointment with a Dr. Engle for the following morning.

The doorbell rang insistently. Maggie knew as she heard the ring, it was Eric. Thank God Cody was safely out of the house.

Maria Aparecida opened the door and Eric attempted to push past her as if she didn't exist, but the large woman blocked his passage, and Maggie saw from the top of the stair that Maria had a large iron skillet in the hand at her side. There was something wonderfully heroic in her aspect.

"Where is the child?" Eric demanded.

"She is not here," Maria said, without moving.

"Get out of my way, peasant," he spat contemptuously, "or I'll go right through you."

"Try it, senhor," Maria answered, her voice low and intense, "and I will spit on your grave!"

"It's all right, Maria," Maggie called hastily, running down the stair toward them. "I'll speak with him."

"As you wish, dona Maggie," Maria murmured, but she retreated only a few steps, the skillet still in evidence.

"Where is she?" he demanded, without pretense at

civility. Maggie stood a few feet from Eric; he looked more formidable than she remembered.

"She's not here."

Eric moved closer, threateningly. His dark eyes narrowed. "You're a fool to think you can keep the child," he said. "I have powerful friends, Maggie, and the adoption proceedings are already under way. I will see to it that Cody is soon out of your reach forever, because of this little blunder."

"Don't threaten me, Eric," she said, her voice under tight control. "I know who you are. I also know *what* you are. And I will never let you use her as you intend."

Eric eyed her speculatively. "You know nothing of what I intend, Maggie, and if you did, no one would believe you. You're a fool if you think you can keep this child away from me. *If* what you *imagine* about me is true, you must realize there are powers at work here that could crush an interfering insect like yourself, and the world would never be any the wiser." He smiled and the true evil of his nature flashed out from behind his eyes.

"Do you understand *pain*, Maggie? I could cause you to die in an agony no doctor could alleviate. Or can you imagine madness? There are creatures in this universe at my beck who would snatch your sanity just for the fun of it, and leave you drooling in an institution for the rest of your pathetic life.

"Don't fight against what you cannot possibly understand," he warned scornfully, all the urbanity and charm now replaced by malice. "You simply cannot win. Now, where is the child?"

"She isn't here."

"I'll find that out for myself," he said, trying to push his way past her. Maggie body-blocked his passage, wordlessly. He tried to move around her, but she dogged his movements.

"Really, Maggie," he said with a contemptuous sneer. "Do you think your puny martial arts will keep you safe from me? Get out of my way!"

Maggie made a conscious effort to hold her temper poised at a controllable level. *"Use your anger, Maggie,"* Mr. Wong's voice was in her head. *"Never let the anger use you."*

"You rotten, child-molesting son of a bitch," she said, in a voice he hadn't heard before. "I may not be able to take you down, but you better believe that I will *hurt* you before we're through. You better believe I will *make you bleed!"*

*The fox fights for his dinner, the rabbit for his life.*

Eric's eyes narrowed; Ghania had told him not to underestimate this one. And there was still the peasant with the frying pan to contend with.

Eric stared hard at Maggie for a long moment, deciding, then turned toward the door. "I'll send you a message tonight," he warned. Then he was gone.

When Maggie turned to look at Maria Aparecida, she saw that the woman was making the sign of the cross in the air, to ward off evil.

# CHAPTER 21

Maggie checked the locks on all the doors and windows, for the second time since dusk. She'd grown increasingly uneasy with encroaching night, and she'd been unable to reach Ellie all afternoon. "I'm like a child who's afraid of the dark!" she chided herself aloud, trying to shame away the insidious fear that was seeping into her bones. Thank God Cody was safely back in her own room now playing Candyland with Maria, like in the old days.

Maggie picked up the phone and tried Ellie's number one last time. No answer, *damnit!* She hesitated for a long moment, then walked decisively to the shelf where she'd left all the books on psychic protection.

"I can't believe I'm doing this," she murmured, as she scanned the index for what she wanted. If she couldn't reach Ellie, she'd just have to do it on her own. The whole thing was probably ridiculous anyway . . . but at least it would give her a psychological prop to help her get through tonight's jitters.

"Okay," she murmured, heartened by the decision, and needing the sound of a voice, even her own. "Here it is. How to build a protective Pentagram . . ." She scanned the list of needed equipment. Clean blankets, pillows, warm clothes . . . all freshly cleaned or new. *"I wonder why?"* She read further.

> Anything dirty or decayed attracts negative energy like a magnet. The person needing protection must not provide the astral attacker with anything containing his or her personal essence. Everyone has heard of Voodoo doctors using hair or nail parings when they make their dolls. This is done because the debris of our bodies contains enough of our individual essence to make an energy *link*. This link forms a sort of etheric homing device the attacker can use to tap into its victim's energy source.

Maggie jotted down the reminder of the items: chalk, string, Holy Water, cups, white candles . . . She was relieved to realize she already had Holy Water and asafoetida grass from Peter. She even had two of the five horseshoes called for, from a long-ago trip to Amish country. But mandrake roots, four female and one male, seemed a little out of the question. Maggie hesitated, then made a decision to proceed without them; maybe even a half-assed Pentagram would be better than nothing.

Feeling inept and foolish, Maggie explained to Maria that she had decided to try to construct a protective space for herself and Cody, where Evil couldn't penetrate, just in case Eric tried to cause some kind of trouble that night.

Maria blessed herself rapidly. "Very wise, dona Maggie," she responded with great seriousness. "*Sai pra là Satanas!* The Evil One must not be allowed to enter. I will keep the child with me until you have done."

Maggie touched her housekeeper's arm, as she turned to go. "Maria, do *you* feel endangered, being here with us, under these circumstances?"

"My lady," the older woman replied with conviction, "I have a shrine to the Virgin in my bedroom . . . and my rosary, blessed by the Holy Father in Rome, hangs upon my bed. The Devil himself could not overpower such defenses." She started to leave, then turned again. "For the little one, dona Maggie, I would fight to the death, anyone of this world, or the next."

"I'm very grateful to you, Maria," Maggie replied, touched by the words. Moisture glistened in her eyes, as she turned to go.

Resolutely, she took a bucket and mop from the pantry and carried all the equipment she'd gathered to the library. The room was her favorite sanctuary, and the old leather furniture there could be moved out of the way more easily than in other rooms. It took some time to clean to the book's specifications; but the scrubbing comforted her, a definitive positive act, in a world of sinister shifting sands. She turned again to the instruction book.

Measure off a seven foot interior circle, and a nine foot exterior circle, in the center of the room. When that's done, construct a five pointed star with its points touching the outer circle, and its valleys sitting on the edge of the inner one. The angles must be perfect, as Geometrical accuracy is essential to the potency of the defense this Pentagram will offer.

"Oh great!" Maggie murmured as she began to measure out the proper amount of string to make the first circle. "Like, geometry is something I've really thought about perfecting over the last thirty years."

Between the two circles in the instructional diagram were lettered glyphs and sigils that looked very ancient. The book said they were Words of Power that could repel Evil. Maggie studied them all carefully in preparation for the lettering effort, then stretched out her hand to copy the words onto the pentagram.

*In nomine Pa + tris et Fi + lii et Spiritus + Sancti! + El Elohum + Sother + Emmanuel + Saboath + Agia + Tetragrammaton + Agyos + Otheos + Ischiros + . . .* She attempted to re-create the elegant script. She recognized an Eye of Horus and other Egyptian symbols she had seen before, but some of the diagrams were utterly strange and alien; it took great concentration to reproduce their complexity. Maggie glanced from book to floor, book to floor, several times before she realized the rings on her fingers *weren't her own.*

In fact, the hand and the arm she was staring at were not her own, although they seemed attached to her. But the long slender fingers holding the chalk were darker, the tapered nails painted blue. A massive sapphire ring covered the knuckle of the index finger; a smaller ruby and amethyst adorned the ring finger and an elaborate gold serpent bracelet curled up her arm . . .

Maggie yanked back her hand as if it had been plunged into fire; the chalk clattered to the floor.

She knelt back, shocked beyond further movement, one hand clutching the offending hand protectively. But it was *her* hand, again, the alien phantom hand had vanished. Maggie shook her head emphatically. *Hallucination.* That's it. *I'm scared to death and I'm seeing things.* Oh God, this is serious . . .

She forced herself to pick up the chalk again. If she didn't have *some* kind of protective device to rely on tonight she might just as well check into Bellevue. She better just finish the damned thing quickly and get to sleep. *Dumbo's white feather!* That's what this Pentagram would be. A magic placebo that would get her through the night.

Maggie hurriedly finished the rest of the diagram. She didn't have all the necessary items, so she improvised with what she did have. Holy Water cups in each of the star's valleys, lighted white tapers at each point. The book called for five horseshoes, horns pointing out, but she only had two, so she put one on either side of the Pentagram.

The book said to make the Sign of the Cross to seal each direction, and she did so gratefully.

" 'Christ was unquestionably the greatest planetary teacher for our epoch,' " she read out loud. " 'His followers for two thousand years have created an immense collective unconscious—a sort of reservoir of prayer and holy intent that's a very powerful bulwark against evil. By invoking the name and protection of a Deity, you place yourself energetically in the jet stream of that Deity's power.' "

Maggie smiled to herself at the thought of what Sister Magdalene would have said about the notion of Christ having a great jet stream.

You can bring blessed water into the circle, but don't drink it unless you must. Remember, you can't leave the circle to use the bathroom. As a matter of fact, if nuclear war breaks out before morning, you can't leave for that, either.

As a final gesture, Maggie built up the fire in the hearth; obviously, there would be no replenishing it before morning. Then, she carried the sleeping Cody to the makeshift bed she'd made at the center of the circle, wondering if the child would be totally traumatized by seeing all this bizarre preparation around her, when she woke up. She'd just have to make a pretend game of it, Maggie thought, to soften the unfamiliar. Cody'd been

so traumatized by their departure from the mansion—
to say nothing of all that had happened to her while
living there—surely one more strange episode wouldn't
do irreparable harm.

Maggie murmured the ceremonial prayers from the
book as best she could, hoping pronunciation didn't matter much, since they were written in a language she did
not recognize.

She pressed the silver rosary her mother had given
her at Confirmation to her lips, then hung it on her
wrist for safekeeping as she pinned the medal of Saint
Benedict to her shirt. *"He holds the cross in one hand,
and the Holy Rule in the other,"* Peter had told her.
*"It's said that Creatures of Darkness fear him."*

Maggie touched the sleeping child gently on her velvet
cheek, buoyed by the normalcy of her sweet, even
breathing. She looked so angelic in sleep that tears
welled up in Maggie's eyes. *Oh dear God, please let me
keep her safe from harm.*

She glanced one last time at the book.

> Whatever you see or hear or smell tonight,
> remain within the circle. Your lives and sanity
> depend on it! Satan himself cannot breach these
> defenses . . . unless you let him in. If you break
> the geometry of the circle, your sanctuary is no
> more.

Maggie's teeth caught her bottom lip, resolutely. She
had never felt more utterly alone.

Shadows flickered on the walls, headlights flashed occasionally by the windows. The wind rattled the shutters
relentlessly, as she settled herself in beside the child she
loved. Taking Cody's small dimpled hand in her own,
Maggie prayed, until she drifted into fretful sleep.

She was awakened by extreme cold, and the sure
sense that *something* had invaded the library.

A book fluttered to the floor from a high shelf; Maggie's head snapped around to see what had caused it.

*Nothing was there.* She sniffed the air; a nauseating stench of putricity was creeping into the room around her, like a backed-up sewer. A lamp in the far corner suddenly exploded, as if struck by a lightning bolt. Maggie snatched up the sleeping Cody and drew her tightly to her body; the child opened her eyes for a moment, startled by the sounds, then settled back into sleep.

A heavy picture frame crashed from the wall, splintering, but Maggie barely noticed it, because the couch had lifted off the floor and was skittering sideways. "This isn't happening. None of this is real," she said out loud; the terror in her own voice shocked her. A hissing sound pulled her gaze toward the fireplace. As if an unseen water source had dowsed it, the flames flared up, sizzled, and died, to the last ember.

That was when she saw it.

Huge, black, reeking of Evil, yellow eyes glinting at her in the semi-darkness. It had no form; like an amorphous sack of malevolence, it pulsed and throbbed at the edge of the Pentagram. *Jesus, it was Evil.* And inhuman. Not of this plane of existence. From somewhere else. Somewhere terrible.

As she watched, it metamorphosed. The sluglike substance transmogrified into a male creature of infernal beauty. Pan. Dionysius. Lucifer. *Christ, it was beautiful.* Its eyes bored into hers, beckoning her, mesmerizing her. The malevolent intelligence that shone from its countenance was breathtaking. Sensual. It oozed sexuality in some alien and unspeakable way, seductive as Hell itself. Maggie could feel a vicious undertow of raw unbridled sex, pulling at her private parts, pushing and throbbing, causing her to *desire* . . . sex, not love. Unnatural acts. Violent, dreadful obscenities she had never dreamed of. *Need* tore at her. *Those eyes*, she couldn't tear her gaze from those evil eyes. They drew her, commanded her, dragged her toward the edge of the circle. *Help me. Sweet Jesus, help me!* she screamed the words in despair . . . and the thing transformed again. Melting into leprous, scabrous rivulets of corruption. The demonic energy it possessed seemed to be growing, pulsing, oozing slime from a thousand hideous wounds.

A mouth, slobbering saliva over yellow fangs, formed itself in the pulsating spineless *thing*, and grinned in an insane way. The mouth opened and the entity cried out to her, soundlessly, as it clawed at the edges of the Pentagram. Cody sat bolt upright and tried to reach the beast. Maggie lunged after her and clutched the child to her breast, but Cody, with far more than three-year-old strength, struggled violently to get out of her grasp. The entity was exerting some kind of powerful pull on the child; Maggie could feel the inexorable wrench of it, as the little body was nearly swept from her grip.

Cody beat at Maggie with frenzied fists, and clawed toward the edge of the Pentagram, only to be dragged back. She tore at Maggie's hair and scratched her face. The child was a wild thing, with eyes glassy as windowpanes; Maggie knew she couldn't hold her much longer inside the circle. The entity was laughing, a hideous mind-bending sound that had never known joy. Its demonic gaze held Cody in its grip and the child's strength was increasing.

"In the name of Jesus Christ. *Help me! Somebody help me!*" Maggie shrieked the words. The creature blurred and shuddered. Was it her imagination that it drew back? Heartened, she shouted, *"Hail Mary full of grace, defend me!"* It retreated with a roar. Cody slumped comatose to the floor. The lines of the Ninety-first Psalm were suddenly in Maggie's head; she hadn't thought of it since childhood:

> *"Whoso dwelleth under the defence of the most High shall abide under the shadow of the Almighty."*

She cried out the words.

> *"I will say unto the Lord, Thou art my hope, and my stronghold: my God, in Him will I trust.*

*For He shall deliver me from the snare of the hunter."*

The entity seemed smaller, less dense.

Maggie recited every prayer she knew, then sang the hymns she remembered from her childhood stint in the church choir. As she finished *Tantum Ergo*, another Psalm, unfamiliar to her, was suddenly in her head, so she cried out its words, wondering where they'd come from:

> *"He shall defend thee under His wings, and thou shalt be safe under His feathers: His faithfulness and truth shall be thy shield and buckler."*

She recited the words aloud, not knowing how she knew them.

> *"Thou shalt not be afraid for any terror by night: nor for the arrow that flieth by day;*
> *For the pestilence that walketh in darkness: nor for the sickness that destroyeth in the noonday."*

As suddenly as it had materialized, the entity vanished. Petrified, shivering in the unbearable cold, Maggie touched Cody's body with trembling hands; the child had lapsed into a stuporous slumber, and seemed barely to be breathing. Sobbing, she lifted the comatose Cody into her arms and crushed her to her own body, staring out into the terrifying void beyond the circle. She prayed and prayed . . . and tried to stay awake.

It was the longest night of her life.

Finally, somewhere near dawn, Maggie felt her eyelids begin to droop inexorably. She fought to stay awake, bit her hands until they bled . . . shook her fist against the awesome cold. This was *not* just exhaustion; she felt drugged, dizzy, disoriented. She tried to fight the creeping numbness, but it seemed beyond her. The light was fading within her like a dwindling flame. In a last desperate effort at protection, she prostrated her own body over Cody's.

Then she slept.

When Maggie awakened, her granddaughter was gone. She stared at the upended Holy Water cups; the garlic wreath and rosary the child had worn were shredded on the floor. Somehow, they had lured her out of the protective circle. The Pentagram had been compromised from within.

Sick with failure and dread, and now ineradicably aware of the power she was up against, Maggie hung her head and cried.

Then she called Peter and Ellie.

# PART II
# TO BEAT
# THE DEVIL

Lord, hear me out and hear me out this day;
The way to Thee's a terrible long way.

**Theodore Roethke**

# CHAPTER 22

Ellie sat cross-legged on the floor, as Father Peter paced the length of the library. Maggie, red-eyed, was in the corner of the couch. She had just finished telling her story.

"It's *not* your fault the defenses were inadequate, Mags," Ellie said with compassion. "You did what you could—you just didn't have the conscious knowledge, or the right tools. It's a miracle you held that thing off as well as you did! They must have dispatched a Saiitii Manifestation against you, and they're tough to cope with, even with experience."

Ellie looked at Peter. "You might know it as a 'Sending.' They're pretty formidable, even if you're trained properly. Maggie must have tapped into some residual knowledge when she made that Pentagram, or it could have killed her."

Father Peter nodded. "I've seen similar demonic attacks in Africa and South America," he said. "You mustn't blame yourself, Maggie. You were up against a powerful foe."

"Eric called up a demonic elemental from Hell to harass you, Mags," Ellie explained. "And because your defenses were flawed, it probably hypnotized you once

145

you were exhausted, and then got to Cody in some fashion. I expect Ghania has blood, hair, and nails from the child, for links. They probably got her to tip over the Holy Water and screw up whatever protective energy grid the Pentagram had to offer . . . I'll bet those sons of bitches were waiting for her right outside the window."

"After what I experienced last night, Ellie, I *know* they wouldn't hesitate to kill her if it served their purpose. That thing feeds on violence."

"Evil always does, Maggie," Father Peter interrupted. "The *mysterium iniquitus* is brutal and elusive, and it feeds on all that is worst in us."

"Tell me if you think I'm right, Peter," Ellie said. "I can call you Peter, can't I? You're entirely too young to be my father."

Peter smiled. "I'd be pleased if you'd both call me Peter."

"There has to be an explanation for why this is all happening *now*," she continued. "There's got to be a reason they waited this long for Jenna to take Cody."

"You think they waited until the time of their ritual was near, don't you, Ellie? And for some reason they couldn't just snatch her and perform their ceremony the next morning . . . so we must presume they needed to prepare her in some way."

*I like this priest*, Ellie thought, as she took up the thread. *He has an open mind.*

"If they really intend to use Cody to get the Amulet and the Stone, Mags, it will require the kind of High Ceremonial Magic that has almost never been performed in this century," she explained patiently. "It's believed that Aleister Crowley attempted the Evocation in 1929, and nearly died because he couldn't control the forces he called up. Someone in Maa Kheru must be a Black Adept. To even attempt such a Materialization they'll need to invoke the aid of something far greater than mere elementals. I'd guess one of the Fallen Angels or Satan himself. The Egyptian equivalent would be Set or Sekhmet, so one or both will surely be called forth.

"You see, Maggie, all ceremonial magic depends on the Adept having made a pact with specific demons, who are then under his command. It's a tricky proposition—there are many dangers to the Magus if the demon can't be controlled and returned to Hell at the end of the ceremony. If you slip up, not only is the demon's evil let loose in the world, but the Magus himself can be driven mad or killed outright, and his soul forfeited to Satan."

"Maggie," Peter said seriously, "I've been giving a great deal of thought to this three-dimensional chess game the Universe has set before us. Hear me out, will you?

"The Isis Amulet and the Sekhmet Stone are metaphors. They represent the eternally warring factions of Good and Evil, in all their varied manifestations. As such, they provide the ultimate test for humanity—are we capable of commanding forces that heretofore were only controlled by God?" He smiled at Ellie indulgently. "Or the *Gods* . . . as others might style it." She smiled back, feeling a distinct simpatico with the man.

"On this cosmic battleground, for reasons beyond our understanding, you, Maggie, seem to have been designated as a warrior for the side of Good. Just as Eric appears to be carrying the colors for Evil."

"What if I don't have the muscle for such a contest?" Maggie asked. "I don't know what I'm *doing* with all this."

"I suspect Peter and I have come to the same conclusions, Mags," Ellie said quickly. "We're your coaches. After last night, I think you'll agree that you need some training. It's up to us to see you develop the muscles."

"How?"

"We teach you, Maggie," the priest answered. "I teach you what I know of God . . . theology . . . Good and Evil. The heresies they've spawned, the saints they've made. Ellie will give you a crash course in metaphysics and magic. We'll combine our efforts on Egyptology. In case you are the one who must enter the arena, we will see to it that you do not face Goliath unprepared.''

Ellie and Peter exchanged a meaningful look. What Peter hadn't said was that each of them had been called to the battlefield, too.

"I don't know what to say," Maggie answered worriedly, "except . . . I'll do my best. I have to believe you're both endangering yourselves terribly by befriending me, yet you're offering your time and wisdom so lovingly, knowing there can never be a proper repayment."

" 'Even in times of darkness, that is the time to love,' " Peter quoted softly, " 'that an act of love may tip the balance.' "

"Aeschylus," Ellie said, "had a lot on the ball."

FATHER Peter pulled his coat collar up against the chill night air as they left Ellie's. The walk to Maggie's house wasn't a long one and he felt need of the cold to clear his mounting confusions.

He glanced at the woman who walked beside him, trying to imagine what she must be feeling about all that had disrupted her orderly life. She looked so vulnerable in the moonlight; troubled and young. What was it about her that touched him in so deep and unrecognizable a place? He'd always thought that if a woman ever breached his defenses, it would be because of sex. But, this was something subtler than that, and therefore a far more dangerous temptation.

"Would you like to stop somewhere, Maggie?" he asked suddenly. "A cup of coffee, perhaps. I assume all the coffee houses in the Village haven't yet been turned into Blimpie Bases."

Maggie looked up startled, her mind a thousand miles away. "Coffee," she murmured, "I'd like that." Then she glanced at her watch, concernedly. "Isn't it awfully late, Peter? If you're driving back to Rhinebeck tonight . . ."

"No. I've borrowed a friend's apartment for a few days, Maggie. I thought to stay in the city until we figure things out a bit."

"Can you do that? Just up and leave, I mean?" She smiled at her own foolishness. "Forgive me, Peter. I suppose I've been thinking of you as a soldier under orders."

He laughed a little. "I have friends at the *Catholic Worker*, who'll welcome another priest to say Mass on the Bowery. And there's an old pal who runs an AIDS hospice on Thirteenth Street who can always use an extra priest, if it comes to that. I'm more or less on my own recognizance these days anyway, Maggie. What duties I have can get along without me for a little while."

She smiled genuinely, unexpectedly. "Figaro's is still wonderful, Peter," she said, switching their direction toward Bleecker Street. "Almost like in the old days."

The landmark coffee house was dimly lit and smelled enticing; *coffee beans and camaraderie*, she thought wistfully, as memories of good times, long gone, were roused by the friendly atmosphere.

They settled at a table in the corner and ordered. The sun-etched lines in Peter's face crinkled as he sipped the dark steaming espresso that arrived minutes later. He had a good, lived-in face, Maggie thought, watching. A complicated face.

"What made you become a priest, Peter?" she asked, settling into the chair and looking around. *God, this place holds dear memories*, she thought fleetingly. *Youth and carelessness are so quickly gone . . . thank the Lord memories don't vanish, too*. It felt good to be indoors and for some reason she couldn't fully define, it felt good to be with Peter.

"I was enchanted by God, Maggie," he responded musingly. "From the time I was very young, I was enraptured by His Universe, His Power, His Majesty.

Later, when I began to stretch my wings intellectually, I was seduced by the endless learning I saw stretched before me on the road to Him. Do you recall the poem 'The Hound of Heaven' by any chance?''

Maggie smiled, and closing her eyes, leaned back just a little in her chair, remembering. " *'I fled Him down the nights, and down the days . . .'* " she recited, with the reverence of one who truly loves poetry. She could almost hear her father's deep baritone inflections resonate within her own; the memory of his poetry readings lived in her so sweetly. " *'I fled Him down the labyrinthine ways of my own mind, and in the mist of tears, I fled from Him . . .'* "

Peter smiled, surprised at her intimate knowledge of the old poem that had such meaning in his life . . . but it was a sad smile, full of lost possibilities. " *'All things betray thee, who betrayest Me . . .'* " he quoted. "Oh, my dear Maggie, that was the fatal line for Peter Messenguer, I think. You see, from that moment on, I wanted never to betray Him, never to disappoint. I wanted to follow Him into the secrets of the Universe . . . unravel with Him all the great Mysteries . . ." He shrugged his shoulders, the enormity of these desires indescribable.

"So yours was an intellectual seduction, then?" she answered, intrigued by this man, trying to fathom him. "Where could one so gifted as you find an adequate sparring partner, but in God?"

Genuinely startled by the unvarnished insight, Peter looked at Maggie with amused intensity. "Others have heard my story and been awestruck . . . you see the only relevant truth. Pride has always been my greatest sin, Maggie. Intellectual arrogance. The knowledge that I could comprehend things that baffled lesser minds. I was like a kid from the ghetto who has a gift for basketball beyond the ordinary. But my gift was of the brain, not the body." He laughed a little at his own metaphor. "It's hard not to be proud, if you're a 'natural' . . . and yet, who has less reason for pride, than one who didn't have to sweat for his achievement?"

"I'm sure you've sweated enough, Peter," she answered thoughtfully. "The gifts are only the beginning. After that comes the work of being worthy of them."

He nodded acquiescence, and she continued, warming to her investigation of the man. "So you chose the biggest Big League of them all, to test your own mettle, didn't you? Politics, the army or the Church—they're the only bastions of true power left in the world, aren't they?"

Peter laughed aloud. Her irreverence toward him was wonderfully freeing. Everyone else treated him like an icon or a pariah . . . but not Maggie. She refreshed him and made him feel young again.

"And did you never fear, Peter, like the man who fled the Hound of Heaven, that 'having Him . . . you might have naught beside'? "

Peter realized he was staring into her eyes over his coffee cup; he wasn't certain what it was he sought.

"Having Him seemed enough to me in those days, Maggie," he answered slowly. "And, to be honest, the life suited me to a tee. The opportunities for intellectual indulgence, the breathtaking education, the company of brilliant confreres, the unfailing aristocracy of the Church in Rome. I was a boy from a poor family, Maggie—I could never have afforded the kind of education and exposure I was given. I exalted in the freedom to travel, to pursue the complexities I'd dreamed of as a small boy, in a gray little town, next to nowhere."

"And what of women? Or children?" she pursued. "Did the loss of family . . . of sexuality, and all its incumbent responsibilities, seem a great sacrifice to you? It's very hard for anyone in the outside world to imagine choosing celibacy, Peter—it seems so self-abnegating, somehow. Forgive me, if that's too personal a question . . ." Maggie wondered at her own audacity. "I'm only asking because I'd really like to understand . . ."

Peter didn't answer her instantly. "It seemed enough to come so close to God, I think. It seemed a higher octave of the love between man and woman . . . a more celestial choice. And the Mass . . . oh Maggie, when I held the Host aloft each morning, I felt more blessed than any man on earth! And more fulfilled. I could not conceive of any human love ever bringing me such transcendent *ecstacy* . . .'' He smiled a little self-deprecatingly. ''I was young then. The liturgy . . . the Church . . . it was all so dazzlingly majestic and full of magic.''

''And when you grew older?''

He took a deep breath before replying. ''I better understood what I had abdicated,'' he answered. ''Life chastens one . . . scrapes the meat from the bone. When you're young, you think celibacy the great sacrifice—as you age, you understand that the companionship of love is by far the greater loss. There are gradations to aloneness, Maggie dear. At first, I was alone with God and with my pursuit of wisdom—and that was fine, elitist aloneness. Then, somewhere along the road, I reached a crisis of limitations. I came to feel isolated. Yet, after a while, even that was acceptable, for it gave me a chance to think, to hypothesize, to pursue my mystic bent . . .''

''And now? Surely your chastisement by the Church must have made you feel abandonment?''

Peter's eyes met hers and she saw a rebellious sorrow there. And a hunger. She wondered what it was he hungered for.

''*Now*, Maggie,'' he said slowly, carefully, ''I fear I may have reached that most ignominious expression of all the alonenesses. I fear I am merely lonely. And growing old, of course, which is so much more fearsome a blight than one imagines in youth.''

Maggie laughed. She had a good laugh, Peter noted. A heartfelt sound.

''I once lamented aging to my father,'' she reminisced. ''I'd turned thirty-five and discovered I was mortal. I told him, 'I haven't found anything good about this stupid aging business, Dad . . . even the wisdom I've gained, I could happily live without.' He just chuckled, and said, 'Wait till you get to be my age, sweetheart. The memory goes, and you can't even remember the wisdom.' ''

They both laughed, but Peter saw there was moisture in her eyes.

"Tell me about him," he prompted.

She thought a moment, before replying. How can you ever adequately describe a love so deep, so formative? '' *'My father moved through dooms of love,'* '' she said finally. '' *'Through sames of am through haves of give, singing each morning out of each night my father moved through depths of height.'* ''

Peter smiled; so much about her was disconcerting. "So e. e. cummings understood best how much you loved and admired him?" he interpreted, and she nodded.

'' *'I say though hate were why men breathe—because my father lived his soul love is the whole and more than all.'* '' She smiled at the remembered love, and sighed.

"So you've been fortunate in your life where men are concerned?" he responded, moved by her odd turn of mind. Wanting to know more of her than he had ever wanted to know of any woman.

Maggie, chin tilted upward, face warm with memory, smiled as she answered, "My father and my husband were both wonderful men, Peter. Very human, very decent, and both quite rare, I think, in their capacity for loving kindness. Living without them, the world is an emptier, colder place."

"And Cody fills that emptiness?"

"With joy and substance and continuity," she replied. "I see them all in her, of course. The quick toss of her head, like a flash of sunlight through the trees . . . a smile, a gesture, can bring them all back to me, alive again for a heartbeat. I see Jenna in her often, even though they're so unlike each other." He saw the shadow of sorrow cloud her face.

"What went wrong?" he asked softly, compassionately. "If that's too personal a question, don't answer."

Her eyes came up sharply, meeting his. "Not too personal, Peter, just too unfathomable. We were very close when she was small. I was unable to have any more children, so I lavished all my love and attention on Jenna. Maybe too much, I've thought, sometimes since—maybe for anyone so doted on, the world can never again measure up to that remembered safety." She shrugged at her confusions. "I've found that such speculation can be a treacherous, bottomless swamp." She sighed eloquently. It was obviously a swamp she'd visited often.

"Then there was teenagerhood—she became terribly rebellious and unreachable. We thought, hoped, it would pass. Jack used to comfort me about the rebuffs . . . I would get so hurt, when she pushed me away . . ." Maggie's gaze left Peter's and seemed to fade into remembered pain. Her voice was less steady as she continued.

"Then Jack got sick, and we were ensnared in the endless downward spiral of cancer. Diagnosis, disbelief, desperate search for a miracle . . . you know how it goes. Then all those ghastly treatments that made life a living hell. Radiation. Chemo. Pain, suffering, terror. Anger at the doctors. Anger at Fate . . ." She looked up at him, needing comfort and, perhaps, absolution. He'd seen the need often enough to understand.

"It took Jack three years to die. Terrible, grim years. Afterward . . . when Jenna left, I tormented myself with the thought that I should have recognized her addiction sooner, should have fixed it *somehow*. If I hadn't been so desperately trying to save Jack . . ." She let the thought drift off.

"Was there a history of addiction in your family?" he asked, wanting to ease her pain, to shield her from the unbearable burden of what might have been.

She nodded. "We were both Irish, Peter. What Irish family doesn't have alcoholics in its closet?"

"There *is* a hereditary component, you know, Maggie. A genetic link that appears to encompass drug addiction, alcoholism, diabetes, depression, and certain kinds of mental illness. Some very substantial scientists are hypothesizing a biochemical imbalance that predisposes some people to addictive substances, perhaps even to addictive behavior.''

Maggie nodded; he could read easily the endless price that Jenna's addiction had exacted of Maggie.

"Do you think you love Cody so much because you feel guilty about her mother, Maggie?"

"I'm sure people imagine that of me, Peter," she answered ruefully. "But, no, I don't think so." She smiled suddenly. "I love Cody for herself . . . if you knew her, you'd understand. For her love, and her laughter. For her goodness. For her responsiveness to every morsel of love I have to give. To think that my love for her is based on guilt would demean us both.''

Peter Messenguer had sat back in his chair as she spoke, listening carefully. Women were the strong ones. He had learned that early on in his priesthood. They endured, suffered, nursed, bore injustice. And somehow prevailed. How men had ever managed to perpetrate the lie that they were the stronger sex, he couldn't imagine. From birth to death, women were the ones shoveling out the muck of the ages, trying to beat the odds of a lopsided game. Pulling the world behind them on the upward climb from the mire. Relentlessly struggling to change things for the better, while they defied the voices telling them they were second-best. Ask any priest what the world's value system would be, if left to men, and you'd hear who was the cook and who the potato, as his Irish mother would have said.

"I've always admired women," he said aloud, more to himself than to Maggie. "They manage still to *feel* through their scar tissue. Still to love. We men mistake their softness for weakness, I suspect. Or perhaps in recognizing their strength, we fear it so much we must lie to ourselves and denigrate what we cannot match. Men are fools more often than not.''

Maggie heard the regret beneath the words, and wondered about its wellspring.

"You're the odd man out, Peter Messenguer," she replied softly. "I knew it all those years ago, when we were young. You fit no patterns."

He laughed. "I think that's what the Pope said when he reprimanded me." It was so easy to talk intimately with this woman, he realized. It was so easy to share vulnerabilities. Tread carefully, Peter, he told himself. Tread very, very carefully.

An hour later, Peter dropped her off at her home on St. Luke's Place.

"Where are you going now?" she asked him, concerned at the lateness of the hour.

"I've been asking myself that very question all evening, Maggie," he replied quietly.

There didn't seem to be anything to say to that, so Maggie bade him good night, and let herself into the darkened house that was her second skin. She stood there for a while, just inside the door, trying to find her center. Why did he unnerve her so, this lovely, lonely, interesting man . . . priest. *Man.* If he were not a priest . . . she said to herself, not knowing where the thought might end, if she let it. Afraid to know.

*But he is a priest.* She said the words aloud. With finality.

Then she went upstairs to bed.

How *strange.* What was Cody's Love Bear doing on the floor in Maggie's bedroom? As if it had just been dropped there moments before by a small hand. Puzzled, Maggie reached for the stuffed creature that was scruffy from so much love, and sat down on the bed, as a wash of memory engulfed her, and she was looking at the bear through a scrim of tears . . . *Oh, my own dear love, where are you now? Who holds you close at night and soothes your fears? How can you close your eyes without Bear to cuddle near your heart?*

Maggie hugged the battered toy to her body, and began to rock with him, back and forth, back and forth, to that eternal rhythm that comes to mothers with their genes. The rhythm that binds and comforts and cures. The rhythm that binds the rocking ones into the endless continuum of love that is the strength of the ages . . . She could almost *feel* the weight of Cody in her arms; the trusting, loving warmth pressed close to her heart. *Oh God, she trusted me! She thought I'd never let her come to harm.*

Maggie lay back on the bed, without undressing, locked in a kind of communion with the Love Bear. She simply couldn't let him go . . . he was the only link. So, she curled herself into a fetal position, the toy still clutched to her chest, and wrapped herself around him, and the memories of the child who loved him.

After a while she slept.

# CHAPTER 23

Maggie stared out her kitchen window; spring was trying to manifest against the odds. God, how she needed to see signs of life. Something . . . anything, to reaffirm hope.

Every morning for the last three days, she had telephoned Cody. And every morning, her call had been rejected. It wasn't that she expected to get through, just that the thought of the child desperate and alone was so wrenching that even the futile act of telephoning was a connection, however slender. *I'm still trying, sweetheart*, it said. *I'll never stop trying*.

Fear, dread, terror . . . how could mere words begin to convey the anxiety that tore at her gut? Fear for Cody. Fear, too, for herself. *I'm too small for this, God! Don't ask this of me, please. I don't know what to do*.

She turned from the window; it was time to get to the

shop; two major collectors were coming in this morning. She couldn't afford not to pay attention to their needs. One large commission from either of these two men could make up for all the time she hadn't spent on business, since this nightmare had begun.

Maggie sat at her desk, after the first of the clients had left, trying to get a grip on herself. It had been a good meeting; she was fairly sure she could produce at least two of the pieces Mr. Cox had his eye on, even if it took a little time to do so. It always warmed her to meet a collector who truly loved the objects he purchased, as did this charming little man. "We, who are blessed by fate with the money to indulge our desires, are curators in our own way, Maggie," he'd told her. "We are stewards of God's bounty, and must use it to preserve and protect that which is rare and beautiful."

Maggie turned her gaze across the room to Amanda, who sat behind her desk, Mont Blanc pen poised imperially, as if ready to sign a treaty. Maggie needed to talk to a friend.

"I have to keep reminding myself that Jenna has an *illness* that causes her to do these terrible things, Amanda," she said suddenly, and her friend looked up, startled, concerned. "But I just get so furious with her when I think of her harming Cody, I forget that addiction is a disease."

"It's a disease all right," Amanda replied, without a trace of her usual good humor. "A disease of the backbone."

Oh, Lord, Amanda's ex-husband was an alcoholic, Maggie remembered too late. Well, it's a disease that certainly leaves scar tissue, she thought. A sudden sharp recollection of Jenna's odyssey of drug rehabs hit her—three of them in one year. They had given her hope at first, then only the realization of how few drug addicts ever recovered.

"No one can change an addict, but the addict herself," the counselor had said authoritatively, and Maggie had lived to learn what a catch-22 that was; the seduction of heroin so intense, most users never cease to want it more than everything else that might replace it.

"You think of dope as snake venom, Mother," Jenna had screamed once in a therapy session, shocking Maggie, "but I think it's the most beautiful ambrosia in the world. There'll never be a day of my life I won't want it!" It was that terrible wanting that sucked them all back. One addict in thirty-six permanently cured. Nothing else on earth offered such ghastly odds.

"Heroin changes you, Mrs. O'Connor," one of the counselors had told her. "It sucks out lifeforce, and replaces it with something else. After a while, you just aren't who you were before at all. You have the same body on the outside. But on the inside, you are someone else."

That had to be what had happened to her daughter, Maggie thought, tears shimmering Amanda into soft focus. Jenna didn't live there anymore.

"You know you never told me, Amanda, how you came to leave your husband," Maggie said softly, needing to share her sorrow with someone who had been there, too. "Was it because of his drinking?"

Amanda settled back against the desk chair and put down her pen. "He'd been an alcoholic for a great many years of our marriage, Maggie," she replied judiciously. "I'd seen him through some pretty grim times—loss of business, money, health, self-esteem, friends, family— the usual downhill ride. Finally, he got back on his feet, due in great measure, to my Herculean labors at keeping him sober. Then, he became as obsessive about making money as he'd been about drinking. That's when he found 'the mistress.'

"I learned about her by fluke, and confronted him, of course. Frederick told me quite seriously that he loved us equally. It took me twenty-four hours to absorb that rather astonishing piece of news . . . trying to keep my dignity intact, while I bled to death." Amanda stopped speaking, her usual composure strained by memory. She looked down at her folded hands for a moment, and then back up at Maggie.

"The following evening was cook's night off. For some bizarre reason, I decided to prepare lamb chops—a little fantasy about domesticity rekindling the flame, I suppose. Anyway . . . while they were broiling, Freddy picked at me about everything . . . my hair, the household budget, my working . . . Finally he focused on the smoke in the kitchen from my lamb chop enterprise. It was really too absurd—after all we'd been through, it was such a trifling snit . . . but it was the last snit.

"I left the broiler on, left the house, and never returned." Amanda shrugged her shoulders and smiled, a little.

"The lamb chop that broke the camel's back, eh?" Maggie said, realizing that nobody goes through life unscathed. *Life breaks everybody. Some get stronger at the broken places.*

Amanda nodded, a mischievous twinkle animating her expressive eyes, once again. "Leaving well is the best revenge," she said.

# CHAPTER 24

Ghania moved powerfully—gracefully for one her size—down the stone steps to the cellar of the Vannier mansion, with deliberate tread. A white Abyssinian cat padded silently behind her, and the two rottweilers, docile as poodles, brought up the rear of the small procession.

She let herself into the dungeonlike chamber at the foot of the long flight of stairs. It was dark and dank, at odds with the tasteful splendor of the house above. The temperature was colder by fifteen or twenty degrees, so she plucked a cloaklike garment, from a hook, and wrapped it around herself.

She threw the switch on a small lamp, illuminating the interior, just enough for rows of large cages to become visible. Ghania motioned for her pets to follow.

Mutilated, but still living prisoners, occupied the prison cells. Some were animals, most were human. It was apparent from the torpor in which they languished, all had suffered hideous tortures. Open wounds festered, legs protruded at unnatural angles. The prisoners' arms had been fastened to wooden boards in a crucifixion-like posture to make movement impossible, so that the needles and tubing attached would go undisturbed. Each of the imprisoned men and boys was a human blood bank. They were the Screamers.

For the most part, the prisoners were far too weak to move or fight—yet one or two of the younger men managed to croak out curses at Ghania as she passed by; some even feebly rattled their cage bars with their feet, in pathetic defiance. The rottweilers flung themselves at the bars, snapping and biting, but their mistress paid the disturbance not the slightest heed, and proceeded with her work.

Ghania checked each bottle carefully, occasionally poking or probing the unwilling blood donor to assess his condition. She ignored all entreaties, curses, or pleas for mercy, as if they hadn't happened. Most victims were too far gone to even moan in pain, but tormented eyes followed her movements, as she traveled down the line of cages. She had been known to open a cage at random and slit the throat of the unfortunate within, if he no longer produced. Some shrank from the possibility, others prayed for such swift release from their agony.

Finally, satisfied by her assessments, she walked to a large refrigeration unit at the far end of the cages and opened the door. Bottles of human blood were stocked in even rows, as if it were a hospital blood bank. She took one out and opened it, sniffing the contents like a connoisseur with a vintage wine. Satisfied by its freshness, Ghania returned the pint bottle to its place. The rottweilers nuzzled her legs and moaned small begging sounds at her, but she ignored them. Feeding familiars on blood was an ancient custom, but few magicians bothered to indulge their pets, in modern times.

Ghania closed the blood storage unit with a sigh. She would have to find a way to get the child to drink the blooded cocktail without vomiting. The ritual libation would lower her vibratory rate, and cement her connection to the coven. None had ever been able to resist her this long. Of course, no other had been the Isis Messenger.

She moved to the vast refrigerator that stood next to the blood storage unit, and removed a small side of meat. She picked up her butchering tools and cut the carcass deftly into pieces for her pets' dinner.

Skinned human babies were always their favorite, she thought, as she placed the small thigh and leg in one bowl, the arms and shoulders in the other. It was a pity the heart and kidneys were so small, they made barely a morsel for the cat. Sometimes it was difficult to get a constant supply of fresh babies; the best of them were always used for Communion. But the breeders had been fecund this season, and the supply was plentiful. Just this once it wouldn't hurt to give her pets an old-fashioned treat to remind them of home.

# CHAPTER 25

Malachy Devlin hung up the phone after talking to Maggie, surprised at his own exhilaration. He hadn't felt this good about anything in longer than he could remember. Why she affected him that way was anybody's guess, but just knowing he was going to see her this evening gave him a lift.

He'd been with her five or six times, now, asking questions or answering them, trying to piece together how someone like her could ever have gotten into a fix like this. He'd thought of a dozen trumped-up reasons to call on her; they were reconnaissance missions of the spirit, really, more than police procedure; chances to get to know her, down below the surface, where people were real and vulnerable and courageous and interesting. There was a gentleness about her that touched him, perhaps because he sensed it overlay genuine strength.

Who could ever quantify attraction, anyway? Why did she refresh him and make him feel hopeful about the world again? As if maybe some of the things he'd stopped looking for might again be possible.

He liked her forthrightness and her willingness to fight the odds, and she had a quirky sense of humor that always caught him slightly by surprise. If they'd met under other circumstances, it would have been easier to figure out how to proceed . . . how to play the age-old game, how to have some fun. On the other hand, under other circumstances they would never have met at all.

He smiled at his own musing, it was a long time since he'd thought about loving someone. What was it he wanted from her? he wondered. A comfort, a warmth, a shared moment? An animal release, a rebellion against the past, an affirmation of life in a tough, unrelenting world? Perhaps all of that. And maybe a hell of a lot more.

He realized he felt a desire to *give* her something. He just didn't yet know what that something should be.

# CHAPTER 26

The Egyptology section of the Metropolitan Museum had always been a favorite place to take Jenna on rainy Sundays, Maggie remembered with a bittersweet twinge, as she walked through the ancient artifacts, on her way to meet Dr. Hazred. She'd called the curator and requested a meeting with an authority on ancient Egyptian religious magic, and he had suggested meeting a Dr. Hazred at 10:00 A.M. Maybe a genuine expert on ancient Egypt could shed some light on the Amulet legend.

She stood in the Temple of Dendur for several minutes, letting the strange magnetism of the place flow through her. She'd come early for her appointment purposely, so she could explore the ruin once again. It had always attracted her on some visceral level far beneath consciousness . . . just as when she was a child, on a trip to the British Isles, she'd experienced strange visionary moments, in which she could "see" the history of the place, in some extrasensory way she hadn't understood. Maggie felt the peculiar sensation wash through her once again in the ancient temple, a kind of psychic undertow that tugged at her consciousness and made her uneasy.

She remained riveted by the queer sensation, in front of a relief of the Nubian Gods Arensnuphis and Mandulis, when she became aware of a presence immediately behind her.

"You are, perhaps, Mrs. O'Connor?" a male voice inquired.

Surprised by the voice, she turned, only to be more

164

startled by the profile. The man who had spoken looked like one of the stone pharaohs that surrounded her, the autocratic features diminished to human scale.

She regained her equilibrium and extended her hand. "Are you Dr. Hazred?"

"At your service."

"You might have posed for some of this statuary."

"Perhaps some of my ancestors did," he replied smoothly, as he directed her toward his office.

"You seemed quite taken by the temple in which I found you, Mrs. O'Connor," he said, as he opened the door for her. "It was dismantled in 1963 and shipped here from Dendur, where it had stood for thousands of years. The Egyptian government gave it as a gift to the United States—many feel, of course, that it was merely one more desecration of Egyptian antiquities for political gain. The West has a long history of pillaging the treasures of my ancestors, I'm afraid."

"Really?" she answered, bristling a little at this political aside. "Surely, the Egyptians themselves had been plunderers of the royal tombs, long before the West ever got a crack at them, Dr. Hazred. I was under the impression that the temple was removed because of the encroachment of Lake Nasser, which threatened to destroy it."

Abdul Hazred raised an approving eyebrow. "You are a closet Egyptologist?" he asked with a more apparent interest.

"I'm an antiquarian by profession, so I have some knowledge of Egyptian antiquities, but unfortunately, not enough to satisfy my current quest—which is why I've come to ask your help."

He bowed ever so slightly. "I will try to be of service."

"I'm interested in magical amulets and talismans, Dr. Hazred," she began. "If you could give me a bit of background information about how they were used by the ancients, it would be most helpful."

"Have you read Petrie on the subject?"

She nodded affirmatively. "His work seems to catalogue, rather than explain. And his connection to anything metaphysical appears meager. I was hoping to garner a more human understanding of their supposed power."

"I see," he said, considering how to couch his reply. "As I'm sure you know, a belief in the magic embodied by inanimate objects is by no means exclusive to the ancient Egyptians. It has always been commonplace to use amulets and talismans as curatives, or as protective devices to ward off evil. They could even be used to put one under the protection of a specific deity, much like the way in which Catholics wear crucifixes or Miraculous Medals today. You might say they are the opiate of the masses in an aesthetically pleasing, transportable form."

Maggie tried not to let this man rub her the wrong way, just in case he had useful knowledge.

"There are many plausible explanations for mankind's stubborn attachment to such charms, of course, Mrs. O'Connor. Post-Freudians might say carrying an object that one believes provides luck or protection gives one confidence. Naturally, the confidence does the trick, but the talisman gets the credit." He smiled, then continued.

"It is also possible in the light of modern psychology to imagine that medical amulets work by directing positive thought energy to the area of disease, thus causing the brain to release endorphins or other curatives into the system. Then, there is also a prevalent concept among primitive peoples that an *object* may empower the wearer by embodying certain desirable characteristics . . . a bear's tooth to impart strength, a serpent's skin to teach guile, a fox's tail for cunning, et cetera, et cetera."

He sat back expansively in his chair, enjoying his subject.

"Are these objects ever thought to be sanctified by a particular deity?" Maggie asked.

"By all means. Horus, Min, Osiris, others were considered potent talismanic protectors. I'm sure you've seen representations of the Eye of Horus, which was worn to look into the heart of all comers and protect the wearer from evil intent."

Maggie shifted in her chair and leaned forward. "Dr. Hazred, I'm particularly interested in learning about two specific amulets I've read of, which seem to be under the aegis of two specific deities—the Isis Amulet and the Sekhmet Stone."

"You Americans do love the notion of ancient curses and other nonsense you know nothing about," Hazred responded, the previous pleasantness turning acid. "I suppose you have some insanely wealthy collector who now wants to add a bauble to his collection that will allow him to rule the world?"

The shift from courtesy took Maggie aback. "It appears I've hit a nerve that I didn't intend, Dr. Hazred. As an antiquarian, I couldn't help but be intrigued by such a magical tale. Someone I love ran across the story in a rather peculiar way, and I felt I should try to learn more."

"Forgive me, Mrs. O'Connor. I am frequently distressed by Americans who have no genuine interest in our history, but merely in the more sensationalist areas of our mythos. As a serious scholar, I'm offended by such perversions . . . but obviously, such is not the case with you." He watched Maggie speculatively, then added, "I will tell you what I know of the legend, Mrs. O'Connor, although I doubt it will enlighten you much.

"According to the ancients, during the reign of Pharaoh Zoser, in the third Dynasty, the Goddess Isis caused an amulet to be constructed, which she endowed with the incalculable power of her own goodness. It holds rulership over both the good in humankind, and the benevolent in nature, so any mortal who possesses this treasure would control all that which is good on the planet."

"Does the legend explain why she would create such an object?"

"The Great Mother has always displayed immense love for humanity, despite our frailties. A time would come, the Goddess said—in the far distant future—when humankind would become embroiled in a contest between Good and Evil, so perilous it would threaten our very existence. We are an experiment on the part of the Gods, Mrs. O'Connor. This is the schoolroom in which we are tested. Presumably, we are quite capable of failure.

"According to the tale, when that precarious moment in earth's destiny would arrive, a Messenger would be sent . . . an emissary of good will from the Great Mother, you might say. This Messenger would have the power to materialize the Isis Amulet. In the hands of the just, the Amulet could turn the tide for humanity, by reinforcing all that is good within our planetary matrix. In short, Good would triumph, and the planet would be saved."

"And the Sekhmet Stone? How does that figure into the allegory?"

"Ah, there's the rub, Mrs. O'Connor, as your poet would have it. If this Isis Amulet were to fall into the hands of wicked men of Adept status, they could conceivably use it to resurrect the Sekhmet Stone."

"Which is . . . ?"

"The embodiment of all Evil . . . the Isis Amulet's cosmic opposite. Yin and Yang, Mrs. O'Connor, Light and Darkness, ecstasy and anguish. It is the way of the Gods to provide the chance for man to choose wrongly."

"And why would man do so, Dr. Hazred, if he were faced with annihilation as a result?"

"For greed, of course! If one has the Sekhmet Stone, one controls all Evil and chaos. Think of the unmitigated power that would provide. Controlling geophysical disasters means you control the world's stock markets . . . controlling armies and weaponry gives you control of whole populations. For lesser stakes than these, men have killed and maimed and trampled whole populations into dust. With such power at one's disposal, there would be no rules and no limits."

"So Isis has set up the ultimate test," Maggie mused. "A real-life metaphor, mirroring the eternal struggle between Good and Evil. One final chance to see which way mankind would go, if all the power in the Universe were suddenly in *our* hands, instead of in those of the Gods."

Hazred smiled. "You speak of this story as if you believed it possible, and not just an allegory."

"Dr. Hazred, I must tell you," Maggie replied with great seriousness, "at this moment, I just might find it possible to believe anything." She paused and smiled; he saw that she was really quite a lovely-looking woman. "Tell me, if it were true . . . which way do you think mankind would go? Which side would triumph?"

"Human nature is corrupt, Mrs. O'Connor," he answered unhesitantly. "I have seen much evidence of absolute power corrupting absolutely and none whatsoever to suggest that the meek inherit the earth. One ruthless man, with vast sums of money at his disposal, can easily best his milder brethren, who turn the other cheek."

"Gandhi might have disagreed with you, Dr. Hazred," Maggie said, "and Christ most assuredly would have. But that's a philosophical debate that would take a good deal more time than we have." She rose from her chair and held out her hand. "If you could recommend any books to me, to further my education, I'd be very grateful. The information you've provided has given me a good deal to think about."

Maggie left the museum with a lot on her mind.

ABDUL HAZRED picked up the telephone and dialed. The phone was answered wordlessly, and Hazred spoke first.

"The game has begun," he said. "An interesting choice for the Guardian." He didn't wait for a reply, but gathered up the papers from the desk in front of him, and the small engraved bronze plaque that had proclaimed his identity; he placed them all in his briefcase, as the door opened, on cue.

A small, nervous-looking man entered, and seeing Hazred preparing to leave, began to speak rapidly. "I trust I've done the right thing in informing our government of her inquiry, Dr. Hazred," he said. As he spoke he reached into the middle desk drawer and removed the plaque with his own name on it, and replaced it on the desk top. He sat down in the leather chair, facing Hazred. "When she spoke of the Isis Amulet on the phone, it seemed imperative, considering the timing—"

Hazred nodded, cutting him off. "Excellent work, Dr. Gerard. You did the right thing, without question."

"Then the woman is the expected one?"

Hazred shook his head. "Regrettably, Dr. Gerard, I am not permitted to discuss this matter, which touches on national security. I can only assure you that your efforts on behalf of Egypt will not go unnoticed or unrewarded." He smiled his most reassuring smile. "You will, of course, speak to no one about this. Not to your wife, or your children, or your mistress, should you have one. You will be contacted, if we have further need of your services."

The curator's mouth was still full of unasked questions, as Hazred abruptly left the office. If Abdul Hazred's credentials as an Egyptologist were not so impeccable, the curator would have rebuked him for his rudeness. As it was, he felt relieved to know the government was not leaving this matter in the hands of some Secret Service cretin, but had chosen a scholar of Hazred's dimension to handle so delicate a matter.

# CHAPTER 27

Gino Garibaldi stuck his head into Devlin's office at 11:00 A.M. "Guess where your anonymous call came from, Lieutenant," he asked with a grin.

"Cheri Adams's place," Devlin replied. The telephoned warning to Maggie had come too soon on the heels of her call to Cheri to be coincidence. "Maybe we should see what she has to tell us about how that happened."

The two men put their notebooks in their pockets and headed for the West Ninth Street address.

After forty minutes of alternate verbal bludgeoning and cajoling, Cheri, reluctantly, gave them a name.

"Allie Roberts," she said, wanting to unburden herself, but afraid. "She was my best friend since we were kids. I told her about Mrs. O'Connor and she called her from here."

"Why did you want Allie to call Mrs. O'Connor, Cheri?" Devlin asked, determined to keep the girl talking. "What made you think she and Jenna were into the same thing?"

"That day in Greenwich," she answered nervously. "Jenna was showing off all the great stuff she had. You know, money, clothes, jewelry. She took me to her bedroom to see her closet, like, it was bigger than this whole apartment. And, she started trying things on for me. That's when I saw this weird tattoo on her shoulder—and it was exactly the same one Allie had on her back, from Maa Kheru. So, I thought, shit, maybe all Jenna's money was coming from the same place Allie's had. I

171

mean, according to Allie, these Maa Kheru guys are all loaded. Rolls-Royces, mansions, the works.

"Then when Mrs. O'Connor called me, and she was so desperate and all—I thought, maybe I could save Jenna's kid from those creeps, if I got Allie to talk with her. I didn't think you could trace a call like you did," she said disgustedly.

"Where's your friend now, Cheri?" Garibaldi interjected.

"I can't tell you that. I promised. She says they're gonna kill her."

"Look, Cheri," Devlin said gently, "if Allie's in as much trouble as you say, she needs us to find her—and fast. She has a better chance of staying alive with us protecting her, than if she's out there on her own."

Cheri considered the wisdom of that thought, then said hesitantly, "She's in this artist's space on Great Jones Street. One of those old loft buildings they cut up into a thousand cheap studios. Oh God! I hope I'm doing the right thing telling you this."

DEVLIN and Garibaldi entered the filthy hallway together. It seemed deserted. The stairwell smelled like 1906 was the last time it had been washed; the once white marble steps were a dismal gray, worn hollow by the shuffling feet of decades.

They knocked at the door number Cheri had provided, but there was no response.

"Cover me," Devlin murmured, Glock in one hand, the other on the knob. The ancient door pushed open creakily—he kicked it wide, then whipped the gun around the corner of the door jamb, in a military-crouch position. Both men's eyes swept the interior with practiced caution. A filthy mattress in one corner, a cockroach swarm in a pizza box, a Woolworth's cardboard chest, with the drawers pulled out and rummaged. Clean, raglike clothing spilling from the drawers.

Garibaldi moved to the right, Devlin to the left into the space. The only appendage to the large open area was a minute water closet, on Devlin's side.

"Over here, Lieutenant," Gino called from beside the bed. It was soaked in blood.

"Cheri said she knew they'd find her," Devlin murmured, surveying the wreckage.

"This doesn't say a lot for Cheri's prospects of a long life, either."

Devlin nodded. "Call in forensics, Gino," he said, "not that it'll do us a helluva lot of good without a body."

Garibaldi shook his head knowingly. "Yeah, but maybe this'll move Cheri into remembering a few more salient facts for us."

"Maybe. And there's still the tattoo to follow up on. Get her to draw us a picture of it, and maybe you can find us the artist."

"You think maybe it's time to make this a little more official, Lieutenant?"

Devlin frowned. "Let's see what we can shake loose from Cheri first. It wouldn't hurt to know what we're really dealing with here, before we spread the word. She may just have reneged on a dealer, or gotten wasted by her pimp. We don't even know if the blood is hers."

BACK at Cheri's apartment Devlin and Garibaldi waited patiently for the girl to reemerge from the bathroom; the sounds of vomiting had been unmistakable. She was not only sickened by Allie's disappearance, but also scared to death for herself, after hearing about the bloodstains on the bed.

"Look, Cheri," Devlin said, when she reentered the room, eyes and nose shiny red from crying, "if Allie trusted you with the story she told Mrs. O'Connor on the phone, I'm pretty sure she told you a lot more than that."

Cheri shook her head negatively. "What Allie knew probably got her killed," she said adamantly. "I don't want to be next on their list."

"We can help keep you alive, Cheri," Devlin said intensely, "but only if you level with us. Look, kid, if you keep all you know to yourself, it'll take us just that much longer to nail the bastards who got your friend. I don't want to scare you, but you could get to be a big red stain on a bed, too—and I'd rather that didn't happen."

He let the gruesome thought settle in; they could almost hear the frightened calculation being rung up in the girl's head. "What do you want to know?" she asked finally, in a desolate whisper.

Devlin and Garibaldi exchanged glances. "Everything she ever told you about Maa Kheru," Garibaldi answered. "How did she get involved with these Maa Kheru guys in the first place?"

Cheri took a deep breath. "Allie was an addict, like me . . . you know how it is when you get high, things happen. She was working in this club on Christopher, the Loopy Jupiter. Allie was a real good dancer, and it didn't matter much whether she went topless or bottomless, she just loved to dance, and she had this to-die-for body . . . she used to mix up some special kind of shit, so she could dance all night."

"Cocaine and heroin?" Garibaldi prompted.

"And something else. I don't know what, exactly. Anyway, one night, some guy came in who didn't look like a bum—you know, suit, tie, the works. Well, he took her aside, and said he was a talent scout for a special group of people who really appreciated her dancing. He told her if she was interested, there'd be plenty of dope, plenty of food, clothes, you name it—and all she had to do was party with his friends, and play along with whatever went down. So she went with him, after she got off work.

"He took her to some uptown apartment, very ritzy and expensive—and it was full of a lot of men and women who looked rich. Allie said it was a pretty weird scene—like an audition, or something. They let her get high on some real good stuff, and then they told her to dance. She said the music was great, and she just danced herself silly. And, then they gave her some more coke, and told her to take off her clothes, and they all gathered around to watch her. She said they all seemed interested in her body, kind of like doctors or something, and they made all kinds of comments about how great it was, how terrific her tits were, and stuff. So I guess she was feeling kind of important.

"Anyway, she hooked up with them, for a while—dancing for parties, sleeping with whoever they said. She was living pretty high on the hog, with designer clothes and a lot of bread. She thought she was on top of the world—she used to talk about the famous men she was sleeping with—really big names from TV and politics . . ."

"Did you believe her?" Devlin asked.

"Yeah, I believed her. Look, Lieutenant, you only have to watch the news on TV to know how much all those big shots are fucking around. And they're not doing it with brain surgeons."

Devlin and Garibaldi suppressed smiles.

"But it was a real weird scene, and some of it made her nervous. Like they made her get this Egyptian tattoo—"

"Could you draw it?" Garibaldi cut in.

"I guess. It had one of those funny Egyptian crosses with the loop on top . . ."

"An Ankh?"

"Yeah, that's it! And it had some ancient writing—you know—hieroglyphics, like on pyramids—she said they were.

"Anyway, Allie lived with these guys for over a year. Then she found out she was pregnant, so she figured she'd blown the whole gig. But a funny thing happened. When she asked the guy who ran the show for money for an abortion, he said he didn't want her to have one. He said the people in his club liked babies, and if she wanted to, she could have the kid, and they'd take care of her while she was pregnant. Allie called me and said, 'Holy shit! Cheri, it's like some kind of welfare program they run for employees who get pregnant. They even have a house where they let you stay. Someplace up-state, near Bear Mountain.' "

Devlin and Garibaldi exchanged glances.

"So she kept on working until she showed, and even after that he didn't want her to stop, he just provided johns who got off on sex with a pregnant woman."

"Jeez," Garibaldi said, "what a prince."

Devlin motioned her to continue. "Finally, when it was almost time for the baby to get born, they sent her to this place. She didn't say exactly where, just that it was near Bear Mountain.

"Now, here's where the whole scene gets even weirder," Cheri said, lost now in her story; happy to unburden herself of the details. "In this kind of board-ing-house place, she was given some kind of disgusting drink every day, which she didn't want to take. They told her she had to drink it for the baby, because it had brewer's yeast and vitamins in it, but Cheri said it tasted metallic, sort of like blood, and it smelled like shit. So she refused to drink it, but they went nuts over the whole issue, and finally two guys forced her to drink it. They said if she gave them any more flak, she'd have to leave. That's when she started to get weirded out, I think . . . you know, suspicious enough to nose around because it didn't feel right. Anyway, there were other girls in the house, and some of them knew bits and pieces of the big picture . . . that's when she first heard the club was called Maa Kheru.

"Then, about two nights before her baby was born, another one of the girls went into labor, and Cheri heard all this screaming going on. It scared the shit out of her. At first she thought it was just labor pains and all, but then she heard them saying they were taking the baby away somewhere, and she heard the mother begging them not to. Then somebody called them all Breeders.

He said, 'You stupid cunt, don't tell me you didn't know the babies here are bred for Satan's table.' "

Devlin's jaw was set in stone; Garibaldi had seen the look often enough to know he was thinking of Maggie's grandchild. "Had she heard anything about satanism before this, Cheri?" he asked, a sharp edge to his voice. It was obvious Cheri didn't want to answer; she averted her eyes.

"Come on, Cheri. It's your life, too."

Cheri ran her fingers through her already disheveled hair, nervously.

"She'd heard some things from the johns and the other girls. About how these guys were part of some exclusive club that worshipped the Devil. She said she thought it was all a crock . . . you know, like those guys who join the Moose Club and dress up in funny hats and think they're hot shit? She thought this was the same kind of thing for rich guys."

Garibaldi saw Devlin's lips twitch a little at the corners. "So what'd she do next?" he asked.

"She tried to run away, but they caught her before she got very far, and dragged her back. She was pretty sure they'd kill her or something, but instead, they told her they could see she'd make a great mother. They said that other girl she'd heard screaming had been a real bitch who wouldn't have loved the kid. Anyway, they said Allie could keep her baby, as long as she did what they said. She was too scared to do anything else."

"How long did that last?"

"Almost a year. I'd gone into Areba—"

"The rehab on Fifty-seventh Street?" Devlin interrupted.

"Yeah," Cheri said, "so I was straight by the time I saw Allie again. Then one night she called, hysterical, and begged me to meet her in SoHo, on the corner of Spring and West Broadway. I hadn't seen her in so long, I'd thought maybe she was dead, so I was glad to get a chance to see her. Only she looked like dead would have been better . . . I mean, I couldn't believe what she looked like. Skinny and crazed. She kept looking right and left, like she was scared out of her mind. She said they'd used Stacy—that was the baby's name—in some kind of sacrifice like a Black Mass. She said they made her watch, while they skinned the kid alive.'' Devlin's eyes met Garibaldi's.

"She showed me a place on her belly, where they pulled her skin off, too, so she'd know what it felt like. It was about four inches square and real grisly.''

"How'd she get away?'' Devlin asked, wondering how much of this could possibly be true. If there was one thing a cop knew, it was that everybody lies.

"Like I told you, Allie was a dancer. She could do all these acrobatic things—practically turn herself inside out—she was double-jointed or something. Anyway, she said they stuck her in this room on the top floor, with only a tiny little window, but she was able to squeeze herself out of it by dislocating her shoulder. So she climbed down some vines and a drainpipe that was at the end of the roof, and hitchhiked into the city.

"She got that place on Great Jones, where you found the blood, from some artist guy she knew. But she was scared to death. She said they'd find her eventually because they were all witches, and they'd told her that skin they pulled off her would keep them in contact with her, no matter what.''

"When did Jenna contact you, Cheri?'' Devlin's voice was dead serious.

"After she moved to Greenwich . . . maybe six weeks ago. She wanted to show off the house and the guy, I guess.''

"And was it only the tattoo that made you think she's involved with Maa Kheru?''

"That was part of it . . . Allie said they all have that. And besides, the whole Jenna scene was too bizarre. I mean, why would a guy like that marry her? Even if she came from a good family, she was still a junkie . . . and then all of a sudden she's rich and going to Europe?

Maybe if she was straight, I could believe a fairy tale could happen—but she's still on dope."

"You're sure."

"Yeah, I'm sure. She offered me some while I was there. She said all her upper-crust friends use."

"Have you got any idea how Jenna's baby could have been saved from being born an addict? Mrs. O'Connor's had the child since she was ten days old, and she says she didn't have to be detoxed."

Cheri frowned. "Yeah, maybe. Allie told me, they take the Breeders off heroin, and put them on meth while they're pregnant. Maybe Jenna did that, too."

"Methadone?" Dev repeated, surprised. "Why would they do that?"

"I don't know. They don't kill all the kids right away, she said. Maybe they'd be more of a problem if they had to withdraw."

"One more thing, Cheri," Dev said, before closing the notebook. "Do you remember any of the names Allie mentioned. The johns who worshipped the Devil."

Cheri smiled crookedly, some of the pressure relieved by letting the story out. "Yeah. I remember some names. How much protection can I get if I give them to you?"

After they'd driven the girl to the home of an aunt for temporary safekeeping, Devlin and Garibaldi sat in the car and looked at the list of prominent names she'd provided, then at each other.

"Couldn't be . . . right, Lieutenant?" Garibaldi said finally. "The kid's an ex-junkie, with an overactive imagination, and she figured she'd better spin us a good one, or we wouldn't protect her. Right?"

"We'll never find out, sitting here," Dev said, throwing the car into gear, and backing out of the parking space. "At least they won't be hard to find. We can just read the *Times* every morning to keep track of their whereabouts."

"You know, Lieutenant, I always figured you had to screw somebody to get that rich and famous," Garibaldi said musingly, "but I didn't think you had to fuck the Devil himself."

# CHAPTER 28

Devlin brooded overnight about how much to tell Maggie of what he'd learned; under ordinary circumstances, he would have kept most of it to himself. But this was not an ordinary departmental matter; he couldn't offer her protection of any kind, other than information. At least, if she knew what she was up against, she could watch her flanks.

He saw the shock register on Maggie's face, saw her struggle to control it. "That poor, poor girl," she whispered. "Dev, do you think she's dead?"

"The lab guys said the amount of blood on the bed would be consistent with a mortal wound, and it's the right type—beyond that we have no proof it was Allie's. But the good news is this may mean I can get some cooperation within the department."

"If any of Cheri's story is true, these people aren't even human," Maggie said, searching Malachy's eyes for confirmation. "And they've got Cody, Dev. She could be dead already for all we know . . . or tortured . . ." He saw she could barely bring herself to say the words.

"And Jenna . . . Oh, God! What about her? I alternate between being scared to death for her safety, and wanting to kill her, for placing Cody in such danger."

Maggie was up and pacing now.

"It tears at me, Dev!" she said, too agitated to sit

still. "How could I have failed my daughter so badly, that she could ever stoop this low? I lie awake nights, going over and over every act of my life. What did I forget to say? What did I forget to do?" She raised her face to his, eyes flooded by grief and self-doubt.

Devlin steeled himself not to put his arms around her. No fair taking advantage of such vulnerability. He'd seen so much of this corrosive guilt that ate away at the souls of parents of drug addicts. In the old days, every family had a relative somewhere in the bushes who was an alcoholic—they were as common as crabgrass, just an ordinary fact of life. Nobody blamed their parents or their spouses; nobody compounded their sorrow by heaping psychiatric hogwash on their long-suffering loved ones. But now it was a new ballgame, full of rehabs that didn't rehabilitate, and theorists who didn't have to live with the selfishness and the emotional holocaust addicts left in their wakes.

"Look, Maggie," he said firmly, "I've got something to say about this, and I want you to hear me out." He pulled a chair close and made her sit in it, so she couldn't avoid his eyes.

"I've seen a lot of drug addicts in my work—enough to entitle me to an opinion on this subject. The way I see it, Maggie, they make their own selfish choices—and their families and society, and the whole frigging country, suffer the consequences of those choices. Sure, there are addicts out there who were damaged by their families—beaten, abused, raped, pillaged, you name it. But that's not the way it was for Jenna, and that's not the way it is in a helluva lot of the cases I see. Sometimes you can chalk it up to weakness, sometimes it's laziness, sometimes it's stupidity. But it's always a *choice*.

"I know, you wish you'd been able to do everything right for your kid. All the time, every minute of her life. But that's an impossible dream. Because to do that you'd have had to be in charge of Fate and luck and heredity, and everything else that ever touched her, for Christ's sake! You'd have to be in charge of what ambitions she was born with, and how many shortcuts she saw her friends take to fulfill their dreams. You'd have to be on top of whether or not a drug war was being fought in the streets of New York, and what deadly temptations her particular century had to offer.

"Don't you *see*, Maggie, you can only do your best. I know you, now. I see evidence of your character every time we meet. You're good, and hardworking, and smart, and loving, and you fucking well did your best for Jenna! For Christ's sake, Maggie, you're willing to go to the mat for your granddaughter, do you really think you would have purposely shortchanged your daughter?"

Maggie looked so uncertain, so sad, it spurred him on.

"So you gave it your best shot," he said, his voice tough and unrelenting, "and it didn't work out. That's the way life is sometimes. Lousy and unfair. End of story. You're not God, Maggie. And she's not the Virgin Mary. If you're so good at cataloging your own faults, why don't we just take a good hard look at Jenna's. So, life wasn't just the way she wanted it—what'd she choose to do about that? Go out and work her ass off to make the world a better place, maybe? Did she combat her dissatisfaction with a sorry world, by bringing meals-on-wheels to some ninety-five-year-old granny who's too old and worn out to cook her own oatmeal? No! She took drugs. She prostituted herself. She blotted out her conscience with a chemical that stole her soul. And then she sold her baby daughter to Satan.

"Give me a fucking break here, Maggie! If you and I are responsible for our actions, then by God so is Jenna. And Eric, and Sayles, and all those other bastards who are willing to cut somebody's heart out just to get another yacht, or a little more power."

Maggie stared into Malachy's face, shocked by the vehemence of the outburst.

"The time to feel guilty is when you *didn't* do your

best," he said, in an emotion-husky voice. "When you could have, and you fucking well didn't." She looked at him sharply; there was more to this than Jenna.

"What is it, Dev?" she whispered. "What are you telling me . . ."

"We had a son, Maggie," he said, finally, his voice taut. "His name was Daniel." The past tense riveted her; Devlin's head was turned away and she couldn't see his face.

"I wasn't home a lot in those days," he said, almost to himself. "I was young . . . I thought I could change the world singlehandedly. Bring all the bad guys to justice, erase corruption . . . The Caped Crusader of the South Bronx . . . I was going to do it all." He shook his head, painful memories needing to be shaken free. "I made a lot of enemies on the streets—"

"You don't have to tell me this, Dev," Maggie interrupted apprehensively. He just shook his head gruffly, and continued.

"My wife Jan and I had a fight one night, about the hours I was keeping—we both had tempers and the pressures were immense. She said I was a hotshot, that I spent more time with the criminals than I did with her and Daniel. She wasn't wrong . . . it just made me mad that she didn't understand how hard I was trying to make a difference.

"Anyway, I pretty much told her to go fuck herself . . ." He stopped, his eyes unfocused, looking backward. He took a deep breath and let it fill his cheeks, then dissipate, before continuing.

"So we had this stupid fight, and I got my Irish up . . . 'You want me to play more with the kid?' I yelled— 'then you gotta have him up when I'm home from the job.' " He looked at Maggie like a sinner seeking absolution. His voice was soft, almost a whisper when he said, "You know the weirdest thing was, I adored him, Maggie. Danny was the greatest little kid in the world. I would have liked to be with him all the time. I mean,

I had these dreams of teaching him to throw a ball, ride a bike, you know how the fantasy goes . . ." His voice trailed off into history.

"Anyway, I was so pissed off, after this donnybrook with Jan, I got Danny up out of bed. He was in his pajamas . . . Christ, I remember those little foot-things were too big, and he was floppy as a clown when he got up, all sleepy-eyed, and so happy to see me." Devlin bit his upper lip, as if to hold the offending words in. "I put a jacket on him and stuck a hat on his head, and I slammed out of that apartment . . ." Terrible apprehension lapped at Maggie watching him.

"We never made it to the street," he said in a relentless monotone. "The brother of a kid I'd put away was standing on the stoop waiting for me, and I was so caught up in my own anger and self-righteousness, I never even saw the piece in his hand. He was high on crack . . . only hit me once. The slug went through my boy before it hit my shoulder. Danny made this little gasping sound like a bird . . . I still hear it sometimes in my head . . . and then there was all this blood . . ." Devlin clenched his fists and then opened them, staring at his hands. "It didn't take him long to die, and there wasn't a fucking thing I could do about it. So I just kept on holding him, and seeing those eyes of his, pleading with me to help him . . . *Christ!* I can still see his eyes. He was so sure I could fix it . . ." He turned his head away from Maggie, but she could see his tears. She handed back the handkerchief he'd given her, and he swiped at them.

"Oh, my dear Dev," she whispered, "forgive me for ever intruding on such sacred ground."

"No!" he said quickly. "Don't say that. I *wanted* to tell you. I've known a lot of women since Jan, Maggie. I tried to use them to fill up all the holes in my life, after she left me. I didn't blame her for never wanting to lay eyes on me again, but I just missed them both so *goddamned* much." His voice broke and he covered his embarrassment with a cough.

So, this was how he would seek to redeem himself,

she thought . . . a child for a child. One lost, one yet to be saved.

Maggie, stricken by the enormity of his grief and guilt, put her arms around him, and they sat wrapped in an embrace of mutual sorrow, like two refugees from a cosmic torrent they could neither hold back, nor understand.

# CHAPTER 29

The large bouquet from Floralies dwarfed the dessert table in the foyer. Maggie read the card wonderingly. Abdul Hazred. The Egyptologist. How odd. "I believe I can be of help to you," it read. Any port in a storm, she thought with a sigh, as she telephoned for an appointment to see him. Then, she hurried outside, hailed an uptown-bound cab and headed to the museum.

Maggie hurried through the Egyptian exhibit to the conference room off Hazred's office. She was startled to see him surrounded by papyri, books, and a computer console; he looked rumpled, frenetic, as if he'd been up all night searching for something specific. She noted that he handled both ancient and space age with equal skill.

"Please sit down, Mrs. O'Connor," he said, gesturing toward the chairs that ringed the table edge. He seemed somewhat more human than he had on first meeting.

"The flowers were lovely, Dr. Hazred," she said. "And quite unexpected."

"A pity they were not more in keeping with our mutual quest," he answered. "Moon daisies, or lotuses, perhaps. Egyptian flowers are extraordinarily beautiful this time of year."

Maggie smiled, wondering where this was headed.

"After you left, Mrs. O'Connor," he began, his manner conciliatory. "I put two and two together . . . Correct me if I'm wrong, but I sensed that the information you sought had great meaning for you." He raised an enquiring eyebrow. "I would like to suggest to you that we strike a bargain here, Mrs. O'Connor. If you will tell me honestly why you are pursuing this matter, perhaps we may be able to help each other fit a large piece into a puzzle that has tantalized seekers for thousands of years."

Maggie tried to read intent on Hazred's face, but his expression was impenetrable; he could be on Eric's side for all she knew, or he could have his own axe to grind. Ever since the night of the Sending, she'd felt paranoid about everything. But he did seem to know something, and at this point any help could be important, so Maggie told him a somewhat expurgated version of her story. Hazred listened carefully, questioning judiciously, probing just enough. He signaled her toward a group of notes he'd been working on.

"You must know, Mrs. O'Connor, that the odds against your granddaughter actually *being* the Isis Messenger are fifty million to one . . ."

"Believe me, Dr. Hazred," she replied with a short laugh, "I'll be thrilled if you can prove to me that she isn't."

"However, what made me reconsider your request, Mrs. O'Connor," he continued with great seriousness, "is that certain very specific conditions must pertain at the exact moment of Materialization. The Great Mother is no fool, Mrs. O'Connor—she has set up an almost insurmountable obstacle course of circumstances necessary to aport the Amulet into being. My investigations convinced me there are forces stirring in the Universe at this very moment, contriving to set the ancient game in play. It would appear you have been drawn into this cosmic contest." He sat back and regarded her with calculation, for a moment.

"I believe your granddaughter is the Messenger, and

you, Mrs. O'Connor, are the Guardian—which prompts me to make my proposition.''

He paused for a moment. ''We must trust each other, Mrs. O'Connor, at least a little—for if you *are* the Guardian, it may be my karma to provide you with the key to the game's strategy. I wasn't quite honest with you the other day . . . you see, I've devoted much of my life to the legend of the Isis Amulet. I've studied both scholarly sources and arcane ones, sometimes at great danger to myself . . .'' He drifted a little, lost in the memory of his own efforts. ''I fully understand your reticence in trusting me with information, yet I must advise you, Mrs. O'Connor, that you run certain substantial risks in not taking advantage of my offer of assistance.''

''In what way?''

''There is far more at stake here than the just the life of this child, I'm afraid. Do you understand the concept of the Ka, Mrs. O'Connor? You might call it soul or spirit . . . in truth it is far more than that. The Ka is the animus that contains the lifeforce, the true being, mental and spiritual—that gives life to the body. It was the Ka the ancients sought to feed and clothe after death, in their elaborate funerary rites.''

Maggie nodded.

''It is said, in the ancient texts, that the Black Forces will seek to capture the Isis Messenger, in order to resurrect the Sekhmet Stone—but that they themselves may be used as the pawns of a far greater player—the Goddess Sekhmet herself may have a hidden agenda. If I interpret these papyri correctly, the Goddess sleeps, and has slept for millennia, like the genie in the bottle. But if a Black Adept is actually able to resurrect the Stone that embodies her power for annihilation, she may choose to inhabit the body of a mortal, in order to experience the pleasures of the flesh she has so long hungered for.

''I fear, Mrs. O'Connor, that your daughter's husband seeks to imprison your granddaughter's Ka, and replace it with that of Sekhmet. If such were to happen, Cody's soul will wander the Underworld for eternity and Sekhmet will free the demons from the inferno. Life as we know it will simply cease to be."

Maggie shook her head. "Goddesses and curses and demons, Dr. Hazred," she said, striving for rationality. "I keep feeling as if I'm an unwilling guest at the Mad Hatter's tea party. What precisely is it you're suggesting to me?"

"I am suggesting that your granddaughter may not be in danger only from those of the Left Hand Path, Mrs. O'Connor. You see, if all else fails, I suspect the other side will be forced to kill her to keep Sekhmet from reincarnating."

"You're telling me she's in danger no matter which side gets hold of her?" Maggie rose from her chair in agitation. Hazred saw she had taken the bait.

"I think you need the counsel of someone who fully understands the intricacies of this situation," he said. "The Universe is a vast electrical energy system, Mrs. O'Connor. Everything in it—including us—vibrates at very specific frequencies. All magic depends on the manipulation of these energetic patterns. Why, the hydrogen bomb is merely one alteration of the pattern.

"If Cody is, indeed, the Isis Messenger, she is the *tuning fork*, Mrs. O'Connor. The *only* tuning fork. It is her frequency, combined with certain magical components of sound and ritual, that will vibrate the Universal web into relinquishing the great prize."

Maggie, unnerved by his insistence on helping, went home wondering what exactly it was Dr. Hazred wished to gain for himself.

# CHAPTER 30

Peter was coming to work with her again today, Maggie thought gratefully, as she glanced at the clock. There were so many things Ellie had told her that she needed to thrash out with someone. To say nothing of Hazred's hypothesis . . .

She threw a semi-remorseful glance at all the phone messages from the shop, which had gone unanswered. *Screw it!* Cody was the priority and that was that.

She heard the doorbell ring, and then the chatter of voices speaking Portuguese. Maria Aparecida had let Father Peter into the small elitist coterie of those she approved of. "In the end of calculations, dona Maggie," she'd announced one evening judiciously, "the priest is to be trust by us."

"Even if he doesn't always wear his collar?" Maggie had teased.

"God sees the heart, not the wardrobe," the woman had replied with Brazilian finality.

"I keep asking myself," Peter said as he entered the library and laid his briefcase on her desk, "if any of what I'm teaching you has practical application at all, Maggie. There's really no syllabus available for this study program, is there?"

"What you've been teaching me is contributing to my sanity," she replied, meaning it. "Does that count?"

Maggie seemed to him a bit worn by the escalating anxiety, yet he sensed that the central core of her was, if anything, stronger than it had been. "Neither your sanity, nor your fortitude are open to question, Maggie, dear," he replied generously. "The kind of stress you're under would destroy most people, yet you seem to grow stronger and more determined, each time I see you. I marvel at you, to be honest.''

"Don't let my surface cheer fool you, Peter. I'm scared to death. But what you teach me does make me feel less helpless . . . like I'm doing *something* besides fiddling while Rome burns.''

"Then let us begin, again," he said, tugging an old leather notebook from the threadbare briefcase.

"Today, Maggie, I thought to tell you of my own encounters with what exorcists call 'The Presence' . . . the great Adversary of man and God." He said the words with immense seriousness. "I have no way of knowing what genuine supernatural power Eric and his cohorts have at their disposal, but the Saiittii manifestation they sent to kidnap Cody suggests they can call forth demonic entities, at will. So perhaps at least a portion of my experience may help you gird your loins.''

Maggie sat on the couch and curled her stockinged feet under her, in an unconscious gesture of self-protectiveness. "I've always wondered what Possession really means," she said curiously, "and how an exorcist combats it.''

Peter leaned forward in his chair, elbows on knees, hands clasped in front of him; she could sense the strain this topic evoked in him. Exorcism was obviously not a topic Peter Messenguer spoke of lightly.

"There appear to be several gradations of demonic interchange with humankind," he began. "The less severe manifestations, in which a man or woman is plagued by one or more demonic entities from whom they cannot seem to escape, are called Harassment or Oppression. Most cases that come before the Church—assuming they are more than merely psychotic episodes, neurotic delusions, or drug-related hallucinations—fall into this category, Maggie. True Possession is as rare as it is deadly.''

Maggie frowned; this was all so unnerving. "How do you quantify the difference?''

"The simplest test is to attempt to place a blessed article onto the afflicted person's body, Maggie. In genuine Possession, the demonic Presence simply will not allow it. I've seen people convulse, vomit, levitate, toss immovable furniture about like toys . . ." He shook his head to convey the inconceivably strange nature of these events.

"What's it like, Peter?" she asked, fascinated, "this Presence? How do you even know it's there?"

The priest leaned back and stretched his long legs out in front of him, a conscious effort at dispelling tension. He took a deep breath before speaking, "The Presence *wants* you to know it's there, Maggie. A terrible, consuming pride seems always to motivate its actions."

"Couldn't it be just the person's own warped psyche talking to you?"

"The Church takes pains to rule out dementia, Tourette's syndrome, and all known types of psychosis, of course. There are stringent psychological and medical criteria that must be met, before they'll allow an exorcist to be called in." He paused. "But after all the psychiatrists and medical doctors have made their investigations, occasionally, a case presents itself, in which there's simply no way to explain the aberrant behavior, except to say it is caused by something other than human."

"Like what?"

"Like a demon, Maggie. Like an adversarial Evil Intelligence from somewhere else. Somewhere we don't understand."

Maggie frowned. "How could you ever be certain of such a bizarre possibility, Peter?"

"The criteria are very specific, Maggie . . . the afflicted person must be able to do things humans ordinarily cannot. Like speaking in unfamiliar tongues, or levitating, or exhibiting superhuman strength, or telekinesis, or reading the thoughts of those around him. Sometimes even knowing the most intimate sins of those in the room, whom it considers the enemy."

"And you've actually seen all this?"

"I once had an itinerant farmworker converse with me in an ancient Sumerian dialect that hasn't been voiced by man in four thousand years. We were able to rule out cryptomnesia—buried recollections from childhood or infancy—because his access to education had been so limited. On other occasions, I've seen demons turn out to be some obscure Chaldean God of Evil, that even scholars have forgotten."

Maggie had her lower lip firmly between her teeth, without knowing it. Peter almost smiled at the childlike response to the terrors he described.

"How on earth does a person become Possessed, Peter? Surely no one really invites the Devil in and says, hi there, I'd like to make a pact with you?"

"Ah, Maggie, don't be so certain of that fact. It isn't unheard of, for man in his greed, to think this world's goods are worth the exchange. And remember, one may invite evil in behind the lines of defense, in many far subtler ways . . . by lying, cheating, stealing, and the like, one can wear away quite effectively at the lines of fortification. Small evils open the door for larger ones."

"Drugs and alcohol also seem to have the capacity to open the channel to a place where evil entities bide their time, waiting for access to humanity. And any trauma—physical or psychological—that jars a person out of control of his own will, can provide access."

Peter paused to think if he'd forgotten any possibilities, then added, "Occasionally, babies are dedicated to Satan at birth by their parents, so their own free will is not engaged."

"Are you telling me," Maggie said aghast, "that someone can have his soul sold out from under him?"

"At Baptism, Maggie, we Christians dedicate our children's souls to Christ, renouncing Satan and 'all his works and pomps.' The child's own free will is not in question. The other side does the same in reverse." Peter smiled a little; the crinkling lines in his face made him look as if he were squinting at the sun.

Maggie's dark hair bounced as she shook her head. "After experiencing Eric's Sending, Peter, I don't doubt what you're telling me in the least, but I sure as hell wonder how a mere human being could ever hope to combat such an Evil Intelligence?"

"Carefully, Maggie," he answered intently. "Oh, so very carefully. You see, it seeks to *engage* you . . . to lure you into debate and controversy, even into the kind of pride that says 'I can win.' A form of madness, of course. But it becomes the ultimate challenge, don't you see?"

What was there to say to that, Maggie wondered. "So, how do you ever best it, Peter?"

The priest chuckled. "You do not, of course. *You* cannot. Christ can. '*In the name of Jesus Christ, I take authority over you,*' is what you say," Peter thundered the words, startling her. " '*In the name of Jesus Christ, I bind, I rebuke, I exorcise . . .*' It is only that exhortation of the Holy Name, which allows you to engage the Great Enemy. Alone you are absolutely powerless."

"How could anyone even dare to try?" she whispered, and he smiled sadly.

"Only with that strange combination of humility and hubris that is the special province of exorcists, Maggie. We blunder in where others fear to tread, because we trust so utterly in the power and goodness of God."

Maggie nodded, beginning to understand. "This Adversarial Intelligence, Peter," she said thoughtfully. "How does it show itself?"

He made a gesture that said there were no adequate words possible. "The Presence is unmistakable . . . powerful, utterly malignant. It uses all your most secret vulnerabilities against you . . . Sometimes it plays hide and seek, clawing at your psyche like a cat with a mouse . . . But you always know when it's there.

"And you must be intensely careful in all your dealings with it, Maggie, because your own faith, sanity, and physical health are on the line, as well as the patient's, and there can be grave danger."

"Then, how can I possibly protect myself and Cody, Peter? Let's say Eric calls up some horrible demonic power from the Pit. I can't live in a Pentagram forever, even if I could build a good one!"

"Prayer, Maggie! You must attach yourself to the whole two thousand years of Christianity and the Collective Unconscious it has created. And you must never engage the creature in debate . . . a wise, old exorcist I know always warned me, *'Never engage the entity, my boy . . . if you do, he'll beat you every time.'* You must never invite it in, never acknowledge its power, never doubt its existence. And you cannot fear . . ."

"How on earth can I control fear, Peter?" she asked despairingly. "If I go into that awful house to try to rescue Cody, I'm going to be scared out of my wits!"

"You *must* control your terror, just as a warrior does at the moment of entering the battlefield. If you cannot, do not even try to save her. Evil doesn't play fair—and it, too, is empowered by a collective lifeforce, thousands of years old. Fear weakens you, and strengthens it. You must place your faith in the power of Goodness, and you must surrender your fate to God. Perfect love casteth out fear, Maggie. Unless it does, you cannot possibly prevail."

She let out an emphatic sigh; you know truth when you hear it, even if you're not certain you can live up to its demands. Mr. Wong had said very much the same thing: *"When you have lost your fear of death, you are invulnerable, Maggie. What, then, can you be threatened with?"*

THE lessons had lasted until late in the day. Stories of demons whirled in Maggie's brain, scrambling with each other for space.

"I need a break, Peter," she said wearily, around four o'clock in the afternoon. "I think I need some fresh air, and a conversation on any topic but this one." They adjourned to the pocket-size backyard that, in summer, was Maggie's joy.

She pulled two out-of-season deck chairs into what was left of the late afternoon sun and they sat down. Peter, too, was grateful for the change of pace; there were so many troubling memories called up by today's conversation. He put his head against the Adirondack chair's angularity, and pulled his collar up. It was too cold yet to be comfortable outdoors, but the air was restorative. The borrowed sweater he wore had belonged to Jack, and it was small for his large frame.

"Tell me what it was like for you, Peter," she prompted, forcing her mind free of the earlier conversation, looking for a neutral topic that would provide a momentary respite. "When you were young and found yourself on the Church's fast track."

"Ah, Maggie," he answered with a tired smile, "that was so very long ago . . . but it was one of the grandest times in my life."

"How did it all begin for you?"

"In those days, if you had intellectual ability beyond the norm, you were noticed by your teachers during undergraduate days, and the word was passed to your bishop. Philosophy was the only major permitted for a young man entering the priesthood, and Rome was the only destination, if you had high aspirations.

"I was sent to the North American College to study . . . I thought Heaven could be no more extraordinary than that Eternal City. You must imagine, Maggie, what it was like for me there . . . I was a poor boy, from a provincial blue-collar world, and this was the Rome of the Caesars and the saints! I was utterly bedazzled— bewitched by the majesty, the ritual, the history. And by the fact that I could cut it at the Greg, when so many others could not."

He turned to face her, eager for her to understand, and his hair fell forward over his forehead. He had romantic hair, she decided; long and shaggy and robust.

"What's the Greg?"

"The Gregorian University—the spawning ground for the intellectual crème de la crème of the Church. If you couldn't cut the mustard there, you were consigned to the Angelica, but the Greg was the place to be."

"What was the Greg like?" she asked, trying to imagine a world entirely made up of ecclesiastical males.

"Heady, intellectual, austere. All teaching was in Latin, of course—all lectures, orals, everything in Latin. Most American students were way out of their depth in ancient languages—so much so, that the best Latin scholars would take notes for the rest. There were even American priests called Repetitors, in residence, who were sent over from the States to tutor the laggards, so the Americans could get through the exams without making asses of themselves and, by extension, their sponsoring bishops. I was lucky—Latin was second nature to me."

"So the pressure was intense?" Maggie prompted.

"Lord, yes. *Everyone* there was gifted, everyone was feverishly competitive, and the stakes were high. And, of course, there were important decisions to be made like whether to pursue canon law or theology."

"Come again?"

Peter grinned. "The main road to a bishopric or better, was, unequivocally, canon law. But if you wanted not to be a bureaucrat but a thinker, you headed for theology. I gambled that if I distinguished myself in academia, I might solve the riddle by finding room in some large diocese, where the bishop was a canon lawyer, and therefore might like to have an auxiliary who was a theologian. I knew that could give me entrée to high places."

Maggie frowned at the calculation of it, and Peter caught the nuance of disappointment.

"Remember now, Maggie, I was still the young innocent lad from outside Pittsburgh, and I was just beginning to see how the great world worked. I was captivated by the splendor of Rome and by the aristocracy of intellect and experience among the clergy there. These were not provincial prelates, they were earls and princes in service to the greatest monarch of all. And, there was such heady romance to the priesthood in that astonishing city—the history, the panoply, the pageantry of Catholicism—nobody does it better than the Romans.

"The name of the game was *Romanita*—it meant that you must be more Roman in spirit and behavior than the Romans themselves. *Romanita* seduced me . . . and beckoned me to play the game."

"So in this austere cerebral environment, there were still high passions?"

"Indeed, there were, Maggie. There are always passions in the human heart. Particularly in very smart, very dynamic humans, and such abounded at the Greg."

"What you're describing to me Peter is a cloistered, elitist male society. The last bastion. So, let's see now . . ." she mused playfully, "if all the criteria for accomplishment were male, then *power* must have been the substitute for sex!" She said it excitedly, as if she'd just ferreted out a great secret.

"You tend always to cut to the chase, don't you, Maggie," Peter said as he set his cup on the table and grinned at her. "Power *was* sex for us . . . the expression of all our passions."

She smiled acceptance of that interesting statement. "And the crux of the priestly dilemma must then have been which uncomfortable choices you were willing to make in order to climb."

Peter nodded. "I began to see that life was meaner and tougher than I'd thought, and that the more ruthless and expedient survived it best. I began to ask myself how on earth I can walk this tightrope and still honor both my intellectual gifts and my need for success, without sacrificing the integrity of my priestly calling. It was an extraordinary crucible, Maggie. A time of refining, sifting; of navigating Scylla and Charybdis."

"Men so often are forced to kill off the good and the gentle in their own natures as the price of success, aren't they, Peter, even within the Church?" Maggie asked.

"You learned about the human failings of the power structure," he answered, nodding affirmation, "at the same time you learned the inescapable grandeur of the *good* that was the basic motivation for the structure—preservation of Christ's doctrine and spirit. You saw that to survive in this less-than-perfect world, the Church *must* live with certain less-than-perfect choices and yet . . . oh Maggie, it was the sacred repository for Christ's teaching, for God's work! A heady conundrum for a boy from the provinces, however bright. Later, when I was in crisis, this very question added to my dilemma, exponentially. You see, I knew they, too, were imperfect . . . but perhaps not as imperfect as I."

Neither spoke for a long moment, until Maggie broke the silence. "I'd like to know what happened, Peter . . . how you fell from favor with the Church authorities. But I don't want to open old wounds."

His gray eyes seemed to unfocus themselves slightly, as if they looked past her to a distant landscape.

"I followed God around a corner," he said softly, enigmatically, "and I never found my way back."

Maggie waited for him to elaborate, but he said no more.

"Have I overstepped the boundaries of friendship, with my question, Peter?" she asked contritely. "Please forgive me if I have . . . I had no right to pry . . . it's just that you now know all the secrets of my life so intimately, I suppose I feel as if I need to know you in the same way." It unnerved her that she felt drawn to him.

Peter looked at her steadily for a significant moment. "I think perhaps there are no boundaries to our friendship, Maggie," he said. "I don't know why that should be so . . . I've sometimes felt with you like a swimmer who's ventured out too far beyond the reef and no longer knows if he has the will to turn back."

Maggie, disturbed, felt the vulnerability and sadness in this man who had once seemed to her so complete.

He was priest and friend and teacher . . . what else was he becoming? There was no denying the entanglement of heartstrings that was growing more complex each time they met. It was unsettling to know he felt it, too.

"Once, when I was in college . . ." she said tentatively, "I was at a mixer with one of the local boys' schools. A young man asked me to dance, and from the moment he put his arms around me, I knew we were born to dance together. Fred and Ginger, Marge and Gower, Pavlova and Nijinsky . . . what can I say, Peter? For one brief shining moment, on a very minor scale, we were the same as they. He knew my moves. I knew his. Everyone else drifted off the floor to watch us, and I was able to perform feats during that dance I'd never done before, and never could again. He disappeared entirely after that night, but for the space of that one dance, Peter, we were *one* . . . and I'll never, ever forget the magic." She took a deep breath and plunged on.

"You and I seem to me like that, somehow, but our bond is of the spirit. You've changed me, lifted me— altered the way I see the world and life, Peter. It's as if I've always known you, always trusted you, always—"

"My very dear, sweet Maggie," Peter interjected, halting the plunge into the unknown. "I fear we may be pieces in a game of God's . . . and neither of us knows yet how this game is played."

"But we do know the rules, Peter," she said mercilessly. "We can't escape the fact that we do both know the rules."

She folded her arms against a sudden internal chill and got up from her chair, needing to move . . . "I think it's turning too cold to sit here. Maybe we'd best go inside."

He was as grateful as she for the diversionary tactic. They reached the French doors at the same moment, and Maggie brushed against Peter as he leaned forward to open the door for her; she knew he wanted to touch her, as much as she wanted to be touched. They let the moment pass, and she walked ahead of him through the door.

Inside the house they were teacher and student once again.

PETER's hands were plunged deep in the pockets of his overcoat. The Bowery was desolate and sad, as always. Humanity's gray wreckage littered the streets, more now than ever. *Homeless.* How much that one small word encompassed. Loss of warmth and comfort. Loss of family. Loss of dignity. Loss of hope. It was a bottomless pit of a word that cried out to Heaven for redress.

He'd said the early Mass, a task that in the old days of rigorous fasting had gone to the eldest priest in residence. It had amused him to realize that the younger priests had automatically given him the job. Volunteers from the *Catholic Worker* had been at Mass of course— good, stalwart souls, trying to do God's work on pennies. But it was the homeless who filled the rows of chairs; shuffling in, with their despair, to share an hour with God. It always both depressed and cheered him, to help out in this place of Good Samaritans.

There was a silent ache that was always with him now, he realized, as he walked. A curious hunger that hadn't before demanded filling. Maggie was in his heart, beating, throbbing, circulating within him, along with his own lifeblood. Maggie's face was in his head—he had only to close his eyes to see her. Long for her company. *Desire her.* He pushed the unwanted, unthinkable thought away.

What was it about her that had breached his defenses so subliminally? There was a joy in her that even the horror she currently faced could not extinguish. Given just the slightest provocation, it bubbled up to the surface. Perhaps it was that implausible affirmation of life he sensed in her, that he longed to bathe in.

*O Lord, we beseech thee, Stir up Thy power and come; that by Thy protection we may deserve to be rescued from the threatening dangers of our sins.*

His mother had been like Maggie. Joyous despite hardship. Kind in the face of poverty and sorrow. Always believing in him, in his gifts, in his devotion to God. His father had been hurt, threatened, by his choice of the priesthood. "That's no place for a man, son. Eunuchs, the whole damned lot of them! Where the hell do they get off giving orders to real men about anything, much less sex and marriage and kids." Jacques Messenguer had been embarrassed to tell his macho friends that his six-foot-three-inch virile son was planning the life of a eunuch.

But she had understood. Not only that it was his way out of a limited world that couldn't cope with his intellect, but that he wasn't rejecting love, only seeking a higher form of it.

Silently, he blessed his mother's memory, as he'd done a thousand times, since her passing. It hadn't occurred to him until this moment how much he'd missed the joy of her, through all these years.

Oh Maggie, *Maggie*. What am I to do with you? Even if I were free, I wouldn't know. And, I do not even know if I *wish* to be free . . .

Peter turned the corner of West Fourth Street and headed toward the river. He needed to clear his head of Maggie, the woman, before he could help Maggie, the student, to learn what she must. He was teaching her daily now, and he was a good teacher, he knew that from his days in academia. Perhaps, even a great teacher, when it came to certain difficult terrain . . .

And Maggie was a wonderful student. She loved to learn, lusted after knowledge—thrilled at the cerebral leaps necessary to understanding the subjects he put forth. And she had a prodigious memory. *She* was not the problem in this interchange.

The problem was what in the world to teach her. He had schooled her in his own experiences of exorcism, that should she meet the Adversary in any guise, she would not be totally unprepared. But even in so doing, he had felt a terrible despair in the inadequacy of his teaching, for no one can prepare another for so unearthly an onslaught. No one can explain the enormity of the negative *energy* it is . . . an energy with its own roots, its own intellect, its own *beingness*.

He would teach her next what the great minds had said of Good and Evil, but they both knew only too well, that Evil is not theoretical. It is insidious, and is skillful in its disguises. The moment of confrontation comes in the street, or office, or marriage bed, where decisions must be made on practical human grounds, not pontifical ones. He had taught her what he thought he knew of man and God. But it was apparent to him that her odyssey in the real world of life, love, work, marriage, family had fitted her as well to teach him, as the other way around.

*Incline Thy ear to our prayers, we beseech Thee, O Lord, and brighten the darkness of our minds by the grace of Thy visitation.*

He'd go back up to Rhinebeck tomorrow, to use the library. There were one or two references that might bring clarity. And James was there. The ear of a friend is the best comfort in troubled times.

The river looked black and dirty. Poor Hudson, he thought. Men have done evil even to you, in their lust for money. Evil abounded. It was everywhere. In expediency, and ambition, and greed, and need, alike. And it almost always cloaked itself in some less recognizable disguise. Even that of simple omission.

"The only thing necessary for the triumph of evil, is that enough good men do nothing," Burke had said. Peter sighed and prayed for guidance.

*"Et clamor meus ad te veniat,"* he murmured. Let my cry come unto thee . . .

He would teach her what he knew, and leave the rest to God.

CODY waited breathlessly for the sound of Ghania's footsteps to fade . . . then she waited a little longer. Sometimes, Ghania appeared when you didn't even hear her coming, so you had to be really careful.

With nervous eyes locked on the door, the child pulled out her bear, and felt around inside his neck, for her treasures. *They were still there.* She breathed again. One gold button, one woolen thread that might have come from Mim's sweater, at least it looked like the same color, so maybe . . . one tiny seashell from the exact spot on the sand where Mim had stood, and told her about the secret place in their hearts. And there was still room for more things, if she could only find them.

Cody took her treasures out, one by one, and rubbed them up against her cheek, lovingly. When she did that, pictures always came into her head. Pictures of Mim. Sometimes they were scenes she remembered from the past. But not always. Lately, there were new pictures, too. She had seen Mim crying, two times. And once she had seen her walking down the street with a tall man. Once, she had even heard her voice . . .

A sound in the hall shocked the child into stuffing the treasures hastily back into the bear. She pushed him down under the covers, listening to the thud of her own heart beating, *ba-boom, ba-boom, ba-boom* inside her chest. It did that when she got really scared. The door opened and Ghania's eyes scanned the scene, then satisfied that all was quiet, she left again.

Cody smiled underneath the blanket. She had her magic treasures now, that let her see Mim. And she had the place inside her where she kept her secrets.

And, Ghania didn't know about any of it.

# CHAPTER 31

Abdul Hazred rang Maggie's doorbell; he had a book in one hand and a bottle of wine in the other.

Maria Aparecida ushered him into the house with a significant lowering of her eyebrow, and padded off to find Maggie. "The Egyptian, I have placed in the parlor, dona Maggie," she said with an air of disdain.

"He doesn't appeal to you, eh?" Maggie replied, amused.

"Moses didn't like his kind, either," she pronounced her curtain line, and Maggie had to suppress her own laughter on the way to meet her guest.

"Good evening, Dr. Hazred," she said, greeting him. "I was surprised by your phone call."

"If you would be so good as to call me Abdul," he responded, "I would feel you have relented toward me, and will accept my help in this matter of the Amulets."

"Abdul, then," she agreed. "But I'm afraid I'm still not certain what help it is you feel you can offer."

He extended the wine. "I regret to say my country does not excel in the making of wine, so I have had to resort, on this count at least, to a grudging truce with the French. This particular vintage is a favorite of mine . . . I thought perhaps we might enjoy a glass of it as we speak of what service I could be."

He was certainly charming, Maggie thought; maybe she should just chalk her antipathy up to chemistry and hear him out.

"Perhaps, if you sit down, Abdul, and tell me what's on your mind, I'll have a better understanding." She motioned him to an armchair and he followed her cue, as she walked to the bar and opened the wine.

"As I told you, Maggie, I have followed the story of the Isis Amulet and Sekhmet Stone for many years. Enough, in fact, so that it has become something of an obsession—albeit, a scholarly one—for me. I have always known the Materialization would come in my lifetime. To that eventuality I have pursued every conceivable avenue of inquiry. When you contacted the museum, my instincts told me the Messenger had come among us. Needless to say, I long to meet her."

"I see. So you simply wish to be introduced to Cody . . . it isn't that you have information you feel might be helpful?"

Hazred looked offended. "Oh no, Maggie. Quite the contrary . . . if your granddaughter is the *one*, she will need to be prepared for her mission. In arcane terms, we speak of an *Awakening*. You see, contrary to popular myth, the chosen ones of the Gods do not arrive on this plane of existence fully in control of their powers. Like Buddha, Krishna, and Christ, they must awaken to their grand vision gradually, and be coached along the way, both by life itself, and by master teachers who are put in their path for this purpose. In the case of your granddaughter, however, there is little time for her to grow into her gifts, inasmuch as the most propitious moment for Materialization will come while she's still a mere child." He paused in the lengthy soliloquy.

"I, therefore, most humbly offer my services to you as a spiritual tutor for the child. My lineage is both royal and priestly. I think you will find I have a good deal to offer Cody."

Maggie frowned. "You obviously don't know, Abdul, that Cody is no longer with me."

"No longer with you? What does that mean?"

"It means that her mother has kidnapped her, for lack of a better term, and I'm afraid that I've been declared *persona non grata* at the Vannier home."

Hazred looked disproportionately distressed. *That*

*damnable Vannier had gone back on his solemn word;
he had promised the opportunity to work on the Awakening of the Messenger before the ritual. How dare he
steal the child and not let his associates know? It was
the witch's doing, most likely. She wanted to perform
the Awakening by her own methods, Goddess help the
poor child.*

"I am most bitterly disappointed by this news, Maggie," he said, trying to force his mind back to the conversation at hand. "To be honest, it makes me fear gravely
for your granddaughter's safety. These are delicate matters . . ."

"No one fears more than I, Dr. Hazred, I assure you.
If I thought there were a way to get her back, believe
me I would do so."

There was obviously little left to say, so Hazred left
the house and Maggie wondered what it was he might
have taught Cody, had she been available.

"You gave me your word!" Hazred snapped at Eric.
"You know as well as I, the Awakening is critical."

Vannier remained calm in the face of the Egyptian's
tirade. "Circumstances changed, Abdul. The O'Connor
woman became too much of a complication, and I decided to remove the child from her influence, altogether."

"How dare you make this judgment without con-
sulting the Council of Thirteen?"

"I dared that in precisely the same way I shall dare
to decide who plays which role for the Materialization,
Abdul," Eric answered, with only the slightest hint of
exasperation. "Democracy is not nearly as efficient as
autocracy, I assure you. For example, I have chosen
*you* to assist me on the altar during the Ceremony, despite the fact there are twelve others who consider themselves equally well qualified."

"So, you throw me a bone?" Hazred replied contemptuously. "It is my *bloodline* and my *talent* that will place me on the altar, that night—not your noblesse oblige."

"As you wish, Abdul, but as the die is already cast where the child is concerned, I expect you'll surely see the wisdom in dropping these quibbling arguments, before you and I end up seriously at odds with each other."

Hazred, infuriated, but seeing the futility of his position, mended this fence as best he could, and left the Vannier estate.

Eric obviously had his own agenda in this matter.

So too, of course, did he.

# CHAPTER 32

Peter had been working in the book depository since early morning, transcribing, writing, cross-checking in diverse languages. There were groups of papers blanketing the entire surface of the large table, and piles of reference materials littered the floor like earthbound satellites. The more he read, the worse he felt. It was impossible to know what to believe anymore. Truth, myth, archetypal fantasy. It all boiled down to Good and Evil. The eternal war. The drowning pool for heresy. The child was the ultimate metaphor, of course. And Maggie . . . Peter put his head in his hands to rest; his shoulders sagged, as if a great weight had been placed upon them.

Finally, painfully, he stood up and stretched. He felt a weariness of spirit, more than of the body; he needed replenishment of a subtle and profound nature, the kind that could only come from God. He made his way down the long corridor to the chapel. It was comfortably small and intimate. Funny, how he'd always felt closest to God in tiny chapels or poor mission churches. God didn't seem comfortable in cathedrals. They spoke too loudly of power and pelf. Christ liked the common people better than the kings. *It is easier for a camel to pass through the eye of a needle than a rich man to enter the Kingdom of Heaven.* That was a mistranslation, of course . . . camel should have been rope, but what matter? the truth was the same truth. Strange, where the mind rambles to, if you didn't keep a weather eye on it. He sighed and knelt down at the altar rail to pray.

To anyone seeing him there it would have been obvious he was deeply troubled . . . the droop of his shoulders, and the head bent low over folded hands, praying for guidance, or forgiveness.

After a long while, Peter rose, blessed himself, and made his way through the labyrinthine corridors to the area of the building that served as residence. He stopped at one of the doors and knocked, a little hesitantly.

"James," he called out, when the knock went unanswered. "Will you hear my confession?"

A tall, quite handsome black priest opened the door and looked out quizzically. He was Father James Kebede, late of Ethiopia; as close to a confidant as Peter had ever had. The price of brilliance and iconoclasm is always loneliness—few minds could keep up enough for friendship; fewer still were apolitical enough to espouse the cause of an almost heretic.

James and Peter had learned their friendship tentatively, over the chess board. Then, they'd stumbled into conversations that rambled through faith, morals, and the human condition, to probe the mysteries of God's astonishing creation. Peter had discovered in the younger man a true believer—a rarity now within the Church to find one with absolute faith. It had refreshed him like a sign from God. James believed in the difference between Good and Evil, in the reality of demons, and in the exquisite, mind-numbing power of God. And not because he was stupid or simple, but rather the reverse. Father Peter liked and admired him very much, and had asked him, on four separate occasions, to aid him in performing exorcisms.

"Are you in need of confession, my friend?" James asked with a gentle smile. "Or of someone with whom to question this great and puzzling Universe God has vouchsafed to us?" He was taller than Peter, and as powerfully built as a Masai warrior. Yet he moved with a sort of tender diffidence, as if he didn't wish to disturb the world as he passed through it.

"Both, perhaps," Peter responded, and James saw that the older man looked weary, troubled. "I could use your good counsel, James."

"How good my counsel is remains in question," James answered with a good-natured laugh. "That I will gladly share it with you is a certainty."

The two men walked toward the large rectory kitchen and Peter sat down at the table, while Father James made an elaborate process of the preparation of tea for them both. He warmed the crockery pot first with hot water, in the English manner, and watched the steeping leaves judiciously, until they reached the proper state for pouring. He had once told Peter he took pains with the preparation of food because it was so scarce in his country, he felt it should always be treated with reverence and gratitude. He had also told him of the jackals who came down from the hills at night to devour the starving children sleeping in the streets of Addis Ababa . . .

"You take joy in the small things of Creation, my friend," Peter said, watching him.

"Ah, but you see how equably God has divided the labors of the Universe, Peter. I shall take care of the small things and you shall take care of the large ones . . . like unraveling God's Plan, perhaps. Is that what troubles you tonight, my friend?"

Peter laughed, as he was meant to, and shook his head. Despite the laugh, there was a pervasive sadness in his every gesture.

"Nothing quite so grand as that, James," he said quietly. "But thorny, nonetheless. There is a child . . . and a woman . . . both in need of help I may be able to give them. And I want to help . . . more than I've wanted anything in a very long while. I feel almost as if it's fated in some way that I do. But . . ." James looked up quizzically from his pouring, and Peter raised his eyes to meet his friend's.

"I am drawn to her, James, in a way I was sure I had long ago overcome. I'd thought by this advanced age, to be freed from the temptations of the flesh, but something in this woman has stirred me."

James raised his eyebrows eloquently. This was not a conversation to be lightly bantered; this was a challenge each man must meet for himself. It was a lonely kind of combat.

"You are man as well as priest, Peter," James said, understanding. "As long as we are in the body, we are of the body. You've chosen a hard road to follow in conscience." He thought for a moment—there was so much to say, and so little of it that could really help. "Do you recall the Devil in the Sixth Circle, my friend?" he asked finally.

Peter nodded. "It is said by the Chinese sages," he responded, with a rueful smile, "that as each man nears enlightenment, the final test he must pass, before attaining the knowledge of God, is the test of the Devil in the Sixth Circle. He is the most cunning of Devils, for he uses our strengths against us, as well as our weaknesses. For him no Marquis of Queensbury rules apply . . . he lies, he cheats, he lures us into compromise . . . and he knows us better than we know ourselves."

"But you must remember, Peter," the younger man said gently, "he is friend as well as foe, for he is the goad which forces us to our greatest feats of spiritual achievement. To defeat him, we must be more than the sum of our parts . . . we must be servant, warrior, teacher, priest, and sage. All that we can be, Peter. For he is the last opponent."

"What are you saying to me, James?" Peter asked, serious as Judgment Day.

"This woman, my friend," James replied. "It occurs to me, she could be for you the Devil in the Sixth Circle. And you could be very near the end of your journey."

Peter stared at the young priest, considering the implications of what he had suggested.

"Stay near me on this one, James," he said finally, his voice strained by confusions. "I feel that the Lord is about to make demands upon me that I'll be hard pressed to fulfill. I may need a friend."

"Of that you are assured, Peter," James said, with quiet finality.

The two men talked long into the night, and Peter unfolded the strange story that now plagued him. Later, when he returned to his own room, he pulled down a book from the bedside shelf and thumbed through it, searching for a remembered passage. When he found it, he sat down on the bed and read:

> The Devil in the Sixth Circle is the most powerful of all Devils. He will possess one's sovereign, parents, wife or children, fellow believers or evil men, and through them will attempt in a friendly manner to divert you from your journey toward Enlightenment. Or he will oppose you outright.
>
> He is the final opponent, and the most deadly.

# PART III
# THE
# CONFLICT

Man is a rope stretched between the animal and the Superman—a rope over an abyss.

**Friedrich Nietzsche**

# PART III

# THE

# CONFLICT

# CHAPTER 33

"I thought I'd just stop by to see how it's going with you, Maggie." Devlin said the words as he stood in her foyer. She smiled a little wanly and led him toward the parlor.

"I'll tell you how it's going, Dev," she said ruefully. "I'm beginning to feel like my life is one of those headlines in the supermarket—you know—'Two-Headed Baby Kills 18, Then Self.' A series of impossible absurdities."

He laughed, shortly.

"If you're a cop long enough, Maggie, you realize everybody's life is like that. Like the man said, life is a tale told by an idiot. Tragedy or triumph, depending on the day . . . but never what you were expecting. Look at my life—it's not exactly right out of *Father Knows Best*."

Maggie smiled at him indulgently; she'd grown to like this man very much in the short time she'd known him.

"What *was* life like for you, when you were a boy, Dev?" she asked, settling cross-legged on the end of the big couch and motioning him to sit down. "You're such a remarkable jumble of ingredients . . . I've fantasized all sorts of interesting beginnings for you."

He smiled. It always seemed to her like sunlight after

rain, when he did; sudden and unexpected. She wondered if there was much in his life to smile about.

"Growing up in the South Bronx," he answered her, "you might say my education consisted of equal parts sex, religion, and the gentlemanly art of self-defense. The religion was compliments of the nuns, the sex was compliments of the sixties, and the pugilism I learned from having to walk eight blocks to school through the Italian and Polish neighborhoods, where Irish charm held little attraction for the natives."

Maggie realized Devlin always made her laugh.

"My family was Democrat, of course, because the Democratic party fed us when times were tough, and got work for all the boys in the family. Democrat isn't a political choice in a poor neighborhood, Maggie, just a fact of life. Nobody ever heard of a Republican coming around with a food basket to a widow, or getting her kid out of the slammer." He laughed good-naturedly. "Come to think of it, nobody ever heard of a Republican."

She liked to hear him talk. His speech was an intriguing amalgam of street smarts, and unexpected poetry . . . the unstudied cadence of a street minstrel.

"I grew up . . . went to Nam because I thought I was supposed to, and because the other guys were going, I suppose. That's when I found out about the wider world." He shook his head as if to say, not even the Bronx could prepare you for that kind of brutality.

"I was just a kid . . . and pretty idealistic back then," he said. "It was a real shock to see man's inhumanity to man on such a visceral level. You know, when you go through a nightmare like Nam, you always question, afterward, why you survived. Why me, God? and not Jimmy, or Fredo, or Petrie? Why did I get out? What do you want from me in return? It was the questioning that led me to the poetry, crazy as that sounds. In that godforsaken swamp, it was the only way to affirm life, I guess, and the possibility that beauty might still exist somewhere." He shook his head again, the pain of memory in his eyes.

"I'd always been a fanatic about reading—and imagining things different from the way they were for us. I got that from my mother, I guess . . . a sense that poverty wasn't all there was to life, and that anything was possible." He was silent for a time.

"Anyway, I went to school when I got back . . . did pretty well, actually. I had this sense of urgency about time, because of all the death I'd seen. I already had a year of law school under my belt, when I married Jan. That's when I joined the force, Maggie. The military training seemed applicable, and it offered security of a certain kind . . . and a chance to do some good in a crummy world." He sighed.

"I kept on with night school, when I could. It took a long time. In some ways, the discipline of it kept me going, when things got bad . . . kept my mind on order, when the chaos settled in."

"Did you ever intend to practice law?" she asked, touched and curious.

He looked at her, before answering; there was an intensity in his eyes, a longing to be understood, without having to explain. *You'll know me, if you're the one, it said. You'll understand what can never be explained.*

"I don't know the answer to that question, Maggie. I loved the law . . . the order, the intelligence, the civilizing force of it. But the expediency of how it's practiced really left me cold. Police work has a gut-level satisfaction to it. I *like* being a detective. I'm good at it. Sometimes, I even get to see justice done. I never got that feeling with the law. Justice always seemed to be up to her ass in the mire."

"So detecting let you make the system work, and lawyering made you feel it didn't?"

"Something like that."

"Is it a good life for you, Dev? From the outside, it looks hard and unrelenting."

He had his hands pushed far down in his pockets, as he leaned back into the couch cushions. His eyes were full of memories. "Sometimes . . ." he said, taking a deep, eloquent, breath.

"There was this one case . . ." he said hesitantly. "Every cop has one that stays with him, Maggie. This one was mine. We got called to this tenement because neighbors heard screams. In the living room we found what was left of a young woman . . . dead, raped, mutilated. I was the first cop into the bedroom." He paused. "There was this big teddy bear—the kind you win at carnivals—sitting on a bed all soaked with blood. It was moving. There was this little kid behind it. A little girl. She was maybe three. Hiding there . . . whimpering, too weak to cry, but still trying to hide herself from 'the bad man.' She'd been stabbed a dozen times and her belly'd been ripped open." It was easy to see how haunted he was by the memory.

"Christ, I remember wanting to take her in my arms, to tell her it was going to be all right . . . but I was afraid to touch her, the wounds were so grim. So, I held her hand, and just wouldn't let it go. You wouldn't believe the strength in those little fingers . . ." There were tears in his eyes. He swiped at them, with the back of his hand.

"I used to go to the hospital every day to see her, after work. She was so little in that hospital bed, all hooked up to a thousand tubes and monitors. She was in a coma the whole time, but I used to talk to her, Maggie, sing to her. I figured the other guys would think I was crazy. But they didn't. It took her a week to die." He sighed. "When it happened, I was grateful to God, because no one could live with what had been done to her. No one should have to."

He leaned his head against the couch, staring at the ceiling. "It took a long, long time to get the guy who did it," he said.

"What a godawful world you live in, Dev," Maggie

breathed, moved and saddened. "And, yet you seem so able to believe in happy endings . . ."

He smiled, suddenly, and looked straight at her. "More importantly, I believe in happy middles."

"What does that mean?"

"That you can't always live for the future. In my job, Maggie, today is all there is. You have to learn to take from it what joy you can."

Maggie stared at Devlin, wondering what it was she felt about him. He niggled at her, in disturbing, unexpected ways, and he made her feel protected, as if someone again cared what happened to her. There was substance to this man, who'd been so tempered by the wisdom hardship brings; deep-down strength and fortitude, of the kind that endures.

She found she always watched him carefully when they were together, now, wanting to learn more, a little afraid of being hurt to the heart, if she ever did. He had that unruly mane of shaggy brown hair, that was somehow lovable, for it made him boyish, beneath the tough exterior. And there was a laser quality to his spirit, that cut away the dross.

She could tell, never having been to bed with him, exactly what he would be like there. A relentless fact of nature, powerful, urgent, beneath the tousled, brooding merriment. There was a rhythm to their talking now; it began each time where it had left off the last. It would be the same in bed.

Maggie was a little shocked by her own thoughts and forcibly pulled herself back from where they were headed. How did ramblings like these square with whatever it was she felt for Peter?

"What do you think I should do, now, Dev?" she asked, pushing the rest away. "How can I find my way out of this maze?" He could hear the need in her voice, the ache, and something else, not quite definable.

"I think you should let me do what I know how to do, Maggie," he said evenly. "The law won't be on your side in this, unless I can prove some of the dirt I'm scooping up about Vannier. When I do, you can make a case for getting Cody back. Without evidence, you don't have a prayer."

"Have you found anything at all yet, that can help us?"

He averted his eyes. "I've found enough to know what I'm looking at . . . not enough to be considered evidence. Police work takes time. Especially if it's not an official investigation. I know how hard this is for you, Maggie, but you have to be patient. It may seem like eternity to you, but Cody's only been gone eight weeks."

Maggie was so still he thought he could hear her heart beat; then she said softly, carefully, "Every day, Dev, I wake up thinking, Is she hurt? Is she dead? Is she a Screamer, now, too? How long must every day seem to that child? How terrifying is every night?"

His eyes locked with hers for a silent moment.

"I hear you, Maggie," he said hoarsely. "I really hear you."

# CHAPTER 34

Jenna was seated at her elaborate dressing table, naked. There was much to admire in what she saw in the antique mirror. A trifle too thin, perhaps, but the full proud breasts seemed adequate compensation for that deficiency. Cody's birth hadn't slackened her belly, and the track marks didn't show nearly as much since she'd started shooting up between her toes and in other creative places. She'd spent the better part of the morning experimenting with hair and makeup. She pursed her lips and admired their glossy pout, then frowned as she noticed an errant eyebrow hair. Jenna plucked the offender and reexamined her brows with the care of a brain surgeon seeking errant ganglia. She had all the time in the world to devote to being beautiful.

Ghania swept into the room without knocking, and crossed to Jenna's dressing room. She appeared to ignore the nakedness of the lady of the house, but, in truth, she cast a practiced eye over the near-perfect form. She had always chosen the bodies for Eric's bed, ever since he'd left her own, and this was one of the finest physical specimens she'd found on this continent.

Ghania deposited Cody on the floor near Jenna's bench and the child ran gratefully to her mother, scrambling up onto her lap to seek comfort. "Hello, my gorgeous little darling!" Jenna cooed, with theatrical enthusiasm. She hugged and kissed the child noisily, and made a great display of delight in her arrival. Ghania stood patiently nearby, watching the game; she knew it was always momentary.

"Shall I leave your daughter with you for the morning, Madame Vannier?" the Amah asked with mock subservience, but Jenna missed the nuance of inflection.

"Oh, I'd love to mind her, Ghania, really I would," Jenna replied with a languid smile, "but I'm awfully busy right now. You know how Eric likes me to look perfect all the time, and my nails are just a mess. Couldn't you keep an eye on her for me?"

Understanding fully that Mommy intended to send her away again, Cody wrapped her arms around Jenna and squeezed hard. She hardly ever saw her mother anymore, but when she did, they had fun. For a minute or two. And, Mommy was infinitely better to be around than Ghania. Mommy never hurt her . . . except that she made her feel sad, sometimes.

"I want to play with you, Mommy," Cody said plaintively. "Please, Mommy. Please let me stay with you!"

Jenna swooped the little girl up in the air and covered her with quick kisses, being careful not to mess her own makeup.

"I love you *so* much, baby," she exclaimed dramatically. "But Mommy is awfully busy right now. Daddy's coming home any minute, and we have a big dinner party tonight, and Mommy has to look just right." As she was talking, Jenna was deftly untangling herself from Cody, one little arm or leg at a time, and pushing her toward the nanny. Ghania reached for the child, and her hand brushed Jenna's nipple in passing. It could have been accidental.

Realizing the futility of further protest, Cody went into Ghania's arms, the hurt of rejection evident on her small face.

Jenna threw kisses as they departed . . . then she breathed a sigh of relief as she heard their footsteps' diminishing sound. She stretched lazily and touched her own nipple lingeringly; Ghania's hand had awakened her to possibilities. Later she would request a massage. No one could give a sensual massage like Ghania. Just the thought of it excited her and she felt herself dampen. But, for now, there were other, more urgent needs.

Jenna opened the drawer to her night table, and all the paraphernalia of her addiction lay before her in pleasing disarray: burnt spoon, white powder, Evian water, and a small kerosene burner. She examined her arms and hands critically, looking for a suitable vein, then remembering that the scar mustn't show or Eric would be livid, she finally settled on a leg vein, mostly hidden from view, and proceeded to inject enough heroin into her body to blot out all that wasn't quite perfect in her new life.

She had heard Cody's screams at Ghania's hands . . . she had visited the cellar . . . she had participated in rituals better left unremembered. But there wasn't really anything she could do about it all today, she thought, as she drifted into a pleasant oblivion. And the compensations of life with Eric were worth the trade-off.

Minutes passed. She was feeling stronger now . . . and freer. And very, very smart. Smart enough to figure the whole thing out.

Perhaps a little later.

# CHAPTER 35

"You will do as I say!" Ghania demanded harshly. Her eyes flashed angrily; she did not like to be defied.

"No," Cody said, shaking her head vehemently. She bit her lip and backed away, trying desperately to link up with Mim in her mind. If she only had the button with her . . .

"You will do as I say, or I will make you sleep with Malikali again tonight. In the dark. All alone."

Cody's mouth was a grim line of resistance, but it quivered at the mention of the great snake. Cold and terrifying, not slimy as she'd thought he'd be, but something much worse . . . cold as death and strong enough to keep you from breathing, when he squeezed you. Even though Ghania had left the snake caged beside her bed, *that* night of punishment had been the worst of all the many punishments. Lying there, too scared to move, or breathe, hearing it slither and stretch itself against the bars . . . Less certainly, she shook her head no again and pressed backward, but the wall was behind her and there was no place left to go. The little girl shrank into the corner as the huge woman held out the horrid drink, one more time.

"Makes me sick," Cody said softly, trying hard not to cry. "Makes me throw up." The smell of blood emanated from the frothy liquid in the cup, blood and something much worse. Cody had known from the first sip that she must never, never drink this concoction.

Ghania cursed audibly, a mean hissing sound. She laid the cup on the table with a disgruntled snort, and grabbed the little girl's arm in a grip of steel. Cody cried out at the shocking pain of the unexpected wrench. Without another word, Ghania dragged her from the room, down the nursery stairs, bumping and thudding hurtfully, as Cody's small body twisted and flailed, trying to get its balance. The little legs scrambled to keep up, but Ghania barreled through the living quarters beyond the nursery, heedless of Cody's plight. Down, down the back cellar steps the child was dragged, into pitch blackness.

There were sounds of suffering, somewhere in the darkness.

Ghania yanked the sobbing, terrified child to a halt, and threw a switch that lit the room. Cody tried to focus through her tears. In front of her eyes there were big cages, like the ones at the zoo. She blinked hard, and gasped in shock. The cages were full of animals in agony. Eyes gouged out of bleeding sockets, limbs cut off, desperate dogs and cats and rabbits strapped to torture devices, too horrible for her mind to take in. The child snapped her eyes shut and squeezed back the awfulness.

"Behold, my willful one," Ghania said triumphantly, pushing her past the animals, to stand before the cages of the naked, suffering men and boys. *"The Screamers!"*

Shock opened Cody's eyes. She saw them hunched and bleeding, in their prison cells. Then, she more than saw, she *felt*. Their agony engulfed her like a river of fire. She had never experienced such naked pain. *Everywhere*, in her arms, in her stomach, in her heart. And there was *more* than pain. Torturous emotions raged through her, ravaging, grown-up emotions, too intense to be borne by a child . . .

"No!" she screamed, flailing out with her hands to push away the unbearable anguish. "No! No! *No! . . .*"

echoed off the stone walls in harrowing staccato . . .
shriek after shriek after tortured shriek. Only Ghania's
laughter mingled with the haunted sound of Cody's sobs.

Ghania dragged the child back to the nursery. The
limp rag doll body that was Cody, let itself be pulled
without protest. The pain, that lingered inside her now,
was too great for sound to express. It wracked her,
crackled inside her, oozing through her meager defenses. She was *one* with it, and it was *everything that
mattered*.

Wordlessly, Ghania tossed the child onto her bed and
left, locking the door behind her.

Cody lay where she'd been thrown, tears running in
rivulets down her cheeks; she was unable to move or
think or breathe past the pain within. It took her a while
to realize that the Treasure-Bear lay beneath her, in the
bed. Feebly, she reached for its familiar form, and feeling it, warm beneath her fingers, she pulled it close to
her heart, and cried herself toward sleep. She felt herself
sliding into a dream . . .

*She was in a strange hot place of sweeping sands and
oddly shaped buildings. And, she wasn't a little girl
anymore. She was a young woman in an ankle-length
white dress with a purple border, hurrying toward a
great building, where another woman beckoned from
the steps. She knew the other woman was Mim.*

*"Hurry!" Mim said. "He's calling for you."*

*The two women were ushered into a great chamber,
past many soldiers. In the center, a man lay on a magnificent bed with curtains all around it. Everyone in the
room was murmuring, but Cody paid no attention to
what they were saying, for she could feel the man's
suffering clearly, and she had to help him.*

*She placed her hands expertly on his head and heart,
and saw that Mim was standing at his feet, holding one
foot in each of her hands, as the flow of lifeforce began
to surge through them both . . . seeking out the agoniz-
ing pain that wracked the man's body, and transmuting*

*it into something bearable. She could feel the energy surging, healing, transforming everything in its path . . . feel the electric warmth . . . feel the reviving life flow.*

*It was her gift . . . and Mim was teaching her how to use it.*

*Mim was . . .*

*Mim was : . .*

Now.

Mim was standing in the bedroom of their house, in a nightgown. She looked very, very scared.

MAGGIE stood disoriented beside her bed. *Something* had forced her to leap up from a sound sleep, not knowing why. She felt electrified with fear. It raced through her veins as if her blood were molten.

She could *feel* Cody, in every cell.

She was sick.

She was terrified.

She was all alone.

# CHAPTER 36

The morning after Cody's ordeal dawned clear and bright, just as if nothing unusual had happened. Eric and Ghania had taken her from her room after breakfast; now they walked in a leisurely manner along the carved stone path of the Shakespeare Maze on the estate. Cody had run on ahead of them, and was wandering tentatively between the hedges. She was absolutely terrified of Ghania, now. And very, very confused. Some days the Amah was almost nice to her, and then, *some-*

*times*—like last night—she was more horrible than the wicked witch in *Snow White*. And there was never any way to know which way she would be . . . never any way to stay safe. Cody's eyes felt scratchy from all the crying, and a residue of the pain she had touched in the cellar still lingered in her body, making it sensitive and hurtful to the touch. She wished there was somebody to talk to who wasn't mean.

The maze was very beautiful, but the high thick hedge felt dangerous; she knew if they left her there, she would never find her way out. In this terrible house, anything bad could happen, and no one would save you.

"Is the woman pleasurable for you, Eric?" Ghania asked casually, in a tone far too intimate for a servant. "Do you require that I train her for you in your special needs?"

"She is a consummate bore in conversation, my Amah," he responded with a sly smile, "but her body is superb and, God knows, she's willing enough, when it comes to the pleasures of the flesh . . . though unschooled, of course, by our standards. Perhaps, it would be amusing to see if she has hidden talents. The clay is lovely, who knows what you could sculpt from it."

He walked on silently for a few more steps, then looked at Ghania, with amusement. "Do you ask this for a purpose, my wise one, or do you merely wish to see to my happiness yourself, as in other days."

Ghania laughed lasciviously. "I am hard to forget, am I not, my young charge?"

"No one ever had a better teacher in the pleasures of the senses, as you well know."

Ghania chuckled. "The pleasure was mine as well, Eric. You have a lovely body and an imagination as creative as any I have ever trained. But, you are astute in assuming that I ask this question for a purpose. Jenna will make an unlovely sacrifice if she is too far gone into drugs to feel true terror, and she has already served the purpose for which we chose her so carefully. The child is perfect, just as I said she would be."

Eric nodded complete agreement. "You have certainly worked skillfully with Jenna's weaknesses, Ghania. Although, I must confess when you told me I must marry her to ensure possession of the child, I had my misgivings."

"Surely, when you saw the body, your pain was somewhat assuaged," Ghania said wryly. She knew Eric to the bone.

"Nonetheless," he answered, ignoring the rebuke, "one cannot help but wonder what the Old Ones had in mind when they chose so leaky a vessel."

"The Old Ones have a notorious sense of humor, Eric," the woman replied. "You know that the mother of the Chosen One must be chosen, too, and with great care. The Prince had to scan the entire planet in his search, and our opponents of the Light sought to keep her potential hidden from him. It is good that he is a sportsman and enjoys the game. How droll to make her an addict and a prostitute. She must have pissed on the Sacred Flame in the Great Mother's Temple to deserve such karma."

Eric smiled acknowledgment; it was apparent he respected Ghania, and just as apparent that he was the master and she, the trusted retainer.

"I will tutor her in the arts of Eros for you, Eric, if you desire . . . in return for your leave to dispose of her at my discretion. Let us use her death to ward off the mother's inquiries, should they come too close to the Work. Jenna is the only link between the child and the grandmama, and when the adoption proceedings are complete, I propose we do away with your *wife*, at the time and in the manner that will allow her to be most useful to us."

"And you perceive that to be what, Mother of Guile?"

"If the grandmama impinges upon our plans in any way, let us devise a death for the girl that will live in her mother's nightmares for eternity. And let us see to it that only she knows precisely how it took place. Let her try to convince the world, and the world will think her mad. We must make her *fearful*, Eric, and then control her fears . . . as you well know, fear will make her vulnerable on the Inner Planes. She has a strong mind and will, this Maggie O'Connor, and power she does not remember how to use. It will be an entertaining match, I think."

"She seems impotent enough at the moment," he said dismissively.

"That can change in an instant. Many a game is lost to overconfidence, Eric. She is the Guardian, do not forget that. She was not chosen for her ineptitude."

"The child seems sullen today, Ghania," Eric said, tiring of the subject; he had never enjoyed being shown his own lapses in logic. "Is there some reason for that?"

"I am teaching her about pain, my lord, as I once taught you. And she rebels against the blooded cocktail. She has a formidable spirit for one so young; she defies me, not out of fear, but out of inner strength. I find her a most challenging student, as, of course, the Messenger must be. I cannot damage the outer layer, needless to say . . . but we must make certain she is capable of exquisite fear by the time of the sacrifice. The energies generated by the terror of a virgin child are matchless for our purposes.

"We cannot fail in our design this time, Eric. The Master would punish us severely for a failure, when we have come so close. To wait for the stars to be propitious enough to create another child could take a century, and I tire of the wait. Crowley failed because he attempted the transubstantiation with a baby whose planets were not precisely those called for in the formula. He lived his remaining years as a powerless fool, because of his blunder."

Eric shook his head. "We will not fail, Ghania. And you have my leave to do as you will with the girl who thinks herself my wife. But before you dispose of so ravishing a specimen, my Amah, do let me see what your tutelage can produce." He reached over casually, and slipped his hand inside Ghania's dress to fondle her breast; Ghania smiled knowingly. His rampant sexuality was his strength and his shortcoming; she had used it for both over the years. She pushed her djellabah aside to allow him easier access.

Cody turned back and stared at the two grown-ups nervously. Why was the Daddy-man touching Ghania, *there?* And why was he being nice to her when she was such a bad person? The Daddy-man beckoned her to come toward them, but she held back, repelled by the tableau. He wasn't a *real* daddy . . . a real daddy would never let somebody do bad, hurtful things to his little girl. Cody turned suddenly and ran down the path as fast as she could . . . but there was no place to run to.

# CHAPTER 37

Jenna lay on the massage table and let the pleasure of Ghania's expert hands wash through her. Long, kneading strokes teased the tensions from her back and shoulders; deep-tissue work unknotted the kinks from the endless exercises Eric insisted she do each day to stay in shape. He was a fanatic about fitness, pushing himself beyond mortal endurance every morning like an Olympian. If it weren't for the coke, she'd never be able to keep up. Running, stair stepping, bicycling, rowing, bench pressing, leg lifting—muscle-wrenching workouts that would have been grueling for a professional athlete. With Ghania as his coach. *Ghania as his everything* . . . Jenna thought with sudden acid. What weird kind of relationship those two had, she couldn't begin to figure out. Servant and master, confidants and cohorts. They shared secrets . . . and something dark and sexual, too.

Ghania massaged Eric every day after his workout and no one was allowed to see what went on, but the sounds suggested more than massage.

The thought titillated Jenna and she wriggled her body a little under Ghania's touch.

"There is a slight pelvic problem," Ghania said with a knowing smile. "We must attend to it." As she spoke she pulled away the small towel that had covered Jenna's buttocks and placed one large hand at the end of the girl's spine. With the other she began to stretch her legs apart in a widening arc. Jenna felt the cool air hit her secret parts and wondered what would come next. Ghania was always inventive.

The masseuse began to rotate the buttocks in firm, confident circles . . . Jenna felt her legs pulled wider and wider apart as firm fingers felt along the inside of her thighs to the pelvic bone and began to press rhythmically along the edge of it. Goose bumps radiated out from the touched places and Jenna felt herself swell in expectation. She turned over on her back at Ghania's command, and waited in a haze of sexual excitement as one hand massaged the pelvic flesh in a relentless, gathering rhythm and the other sought her nipple.

Ghania smiled at the malleable body on the table. It was so easy to control the will-less ones. Drugs and sex could buy even a Star-Child from the likes of this useless flotsam-and-jetsam creature, mind besotted by chemicals. But the body . . . she moved her hand to a place that would give exquisite pleasure—there were few such places unknown to her—and contemplated the figure on the table. It was truly superb. Had she got hold of this one early enough, she could have honed her into a sexual machine of extraordinary quality. Ghania sighed at the lost opportunity . . . bodies like this didn't come along every day. Men could be made to pay anything for the right body, painstakingly conditioned. As it was, there were still possibilities . . .

Eric had entered the room and was watching Jenna

writhe sensuously on the table beneath Ghania's expert hands. Ghania motioned for him to join them and he moved silently to her side.

His hands supplemented hers on Jenna's body, as Ghania let her own garment fall to the floor beneath her feet. She reached for his belt in a practiced gesture, and swiftly freed his risen organ, which she caressed with infinite care until he signaled her to stop. Eric lifted Jenna and carried her to the bed. Perhaps Ghania would teach them both something new today . . .

He had always loved the training program.

# CHAPTER 38

Now, try as Maggie might, there didn't seem to be any way to overcome the sense of chaos that overwhelmed her; Cody's schedule had been the glue for all their lives. Breakfast together at the kitchen table, then work at the shop for Maggie, until three in the afternoon; home again, to take Cody to the park, or the Y, or whatever small pleasures Greenwich Village afforded for children on that particular day . . . then supper together in the dining room, or before the library fire. Evenings spent playing, or reading, or simply being a family, until Cody's bedtime. The great circle of life, on a manageable scale, comforting and secure. Nothing was as it had been for Maggie; she barely even bothered to put in an appearance at the shop, now. It was obvious her attention was not on antiquities.

Peter had taken to dropping by, every afternoon to tutor her. Sometimes, he brought books, sometimes an idea he thought had value, and sometimes he'd unearthed something new about the Isis legend. She knew he labored to pinpoint the elusive timing for the Materialization Ritual to take place. As did Ellie, by other means.

Maggie sighed. She missed Cody so much it was a wonder the wound wasn't bloody. There was an organic ache within her, as if all love and laughter had been physically wrenched from her heart. *I love you sweetheart!* she sent the thought message to the child, a hundred times a day. If only she could reach her, touch her, comfort her. Let her know she was loved, and had not been forgotten . . .

The clock was ticking, pressure building within her like a time bomb. When could she *do* something? When would she *learn* something that would help?

Maggie looked at the pile of books and papers on her desk . . . Peter had left them there yesterday. Part of her said, what's the use of all this absurd study, while the other part said, what if the key is somewhere in these books? At least studying gave her something to occupy her mind. Without Ellie and Peter—and without the hope that Devlin might get the police to help—she wouldn't be able to face getting up in the morning at all. But the clock was ticking, inexorably, and nothing, absolutely nothing, had gotten her one step closer to Cody.

Maggie snatched up the books vengefully and plopped them onto the couch in the parlor. If Peter and Ellie didn't come up with a date for the Materialization soon, she would have to create a deadline for herself. She would give all this damned studying one more week, two at the most. After that, she'd come up with a plan . . . a way to get Cody out of that godforsaken nuthouse. How long could any child last in there? She was so little and so vulnerable . . . A chill ran through her at the awful possibilities.

"Look, *Lord!*" she said suddenly out loud. "*Ask and ye shall receive*, you told us. *Seek and ye shall find.*

*Knock and it shall be opened* . . . Well, I'm *asking* and I'm *seeking* and I'm *knocking*, and You damned well better keep Your promise, because *it's all I've got!"*

Angrily, she swiped at the tears that had welled in her eyes. Then, she picked up the volume closest to her, and forced herself to pay attention to what was on the page. An hour later, her head swimming in probably irrelevant information, she went wearily to bed.

THE dream stole over her, as if it had been awaiting her arrival:

The beautiful young priestess tried to maintain her temple-trained decorum, but the sight of home and family made her want to run and leap for joy. She threw her arms around her old nanny and squeezed her in an indecorous bear hug, laughing and crying as she did so.

"We have illustrious visitors today, little one," her nanny, Kipa, said conspiratorially. "Your parents have been favored by the Goddess."

Mim was curious at this news, but not surprised. Her father, Senuset, was an artist of such stature that even the Ptah priests consulted with him on the designs of amulets, talismans, and all magical instruments. So skilled in magic, in fact, was he, that to be taken on as an apprentice in his workshop was an honor vied for by all in the kingdom who had great talent or aspirations.

Her mother, Niyohma, was a seeress, revered throughout the land of Khemu-Amenti, home of the hidden God. Both her parents were members of an elite branch of the priesthood—and because of their great gifts of artistry, and spirit, her family enjoyed a fine standard of living. The house she had just returned to boasted many amenities, and guests of high degree were frequent visitors.

"Has Pharaoh's vizier come again to commission a bauble for the royal finger?" she bantered with the wizened old nursemaid she had loved since she was a child.

"Nay, child," the nanny replied in an awestruck whisper, "the High Priestess herself graces our abode."

Startled, Mim blurted out, "But the Reverend Mother has never been known to leave the sanctuary!"

The old lady made a clucking sound and shook her head, pointing with her ancient hand toward the door of Senuset's workshop.

"See for yourself, child." She smiled as she went about her business, leaving Mim standing in the middle of the courtyard, uncertain what to do next.

Mim knocked tentatively at the door of her father's workshop and a slave ushered her into the spacious interior. Her father's face transfused with light when he saw her.

"Daughter!" he cried out, unmindful of his revered guest. "How auspicious that you should arrive this day, of all days." Senuset was a large, robust man whose exuberance for his family was near legend. He extended his great arms toward his daughter and embraced her, before leading her to the Reverend Mother's side.

Mim curtseyed gracefully and gave the secret sign that marked her degree of training. "Holy Mother," she murmured, overcome with shyness at the august presence. "Forgive my intrusion, I beg you. I have come home to Mennofer for the festival, and did not realize my visit would intrude upon yours."

The ageless woman nodded acceptance of the apology, and Senuset interjected himself. "It is good that you have arrived at *precisely* this moment, my daughter," he said gently; he was a kind man despite his great gifts. "Reverend Mother has come to pronounce her final blessing on the Amulet I have striven to perfect, through these many years."

Mim knew of the Isis Amulet, of course . . . her father had worked on its complexities for so long she had almost come to believe that it would never be completed, although it was intended to be the crowning achievement of his brilliant life. Senuset lifted an object from his workbench and cradled it reverently in his hand. The sun caught its golden surface and beams radiated out as if it were alive, a power source of some indeterminate kind.

"It was in Atlantis that the secret of this Amulet was first revealed to the High Priestess of Isis," the Reverend Mother said unexpectedly. She was as austere as her title demanded, and had never before spoken directly to Mim, or anyone of her rank. The timbre of the woman's voice filled the girl with terror; she was as spare as a cadaver, yet her voice could surely shatter limestone.

"The High Priestess who brought the Goddess Mysteries to this land of Khemu," she continued, "was entrusted with the secret of the Isis Amulet, but she was instructed that it was never to be commissioned, until one who was both brilliant artisan *and* Melchizedek priest had come into being. Thus, was the instruction, and the secret, passed from Reverend Mother to Reverend Mother, until it came to me. Your father, Senuset, has been chosen by the Goddess for this awesome task."

Senuset smiled indulgently at Mim's obvious confusion and placed his great hand on her arm. "Do not tremble so, my little priestess," he said. "This Amulet is the greatest gift that has ever been bestowed upon humankind."

Startled, the young girl looked to the High Priestess, for confirmation. The old woman nodded acquiescence. "The Isis Amulet has been imbued with the power to control *all* that is Good on this planet, Mim-Atet-Ra," the woman replied. "The forces of Evil are powerless against it."

Mim's eyes widened in wonder; to be taken into the confidence of a Reverend Mother was awe-inspiring enough, but to learn that your father has been entrusted with the fate of the world was overwhelming indeed.

"The greatest priests of every temple have watched over the preparation of the Isis Amulet, to imbue it with their individual magic," Reverend Mother continued. "Each precious stone has been etched with a magical sigil, engraved at the proper astrological moment, under the correct auspices of the moon. If we have done our work with the perfection required, he who possesses this Amulet will have the Power to rule the world. But only for the Good."

"But, to whom could such a prize be entrusted, Reverend Mother?" Mim asked, astonished. "Would not all the kings and princes of this world—and all the greedy and power-mad—vie to take possession? Who could ever be strong enough to protect the Great Mother's treasure?"

Her father and the High Priestess exchanged glances.

"A single priestess will be chosen as the Guardian, Mim. She will keep the vigil throughout her lifetime, to the exclusion of all else. Because this is both the greatest honor conceivable, and the most awesome responsibility, the Great Mother herself will choose the Guardian of the Isis Amulet, once the final magic has been worked."

The unrelenting nature of this responsibility chilled the young priestess even to contemplate; silently, she thanked her stars that she was young and untried, and therefore could not be a candidate for such a terrifying fate.

"What is to prevent evil men from simply killing the Guardian and taking the Amulet?" she asked softly.

"The Guardian will *not* possess the Amulet on this plane of existence, Mim. It will be held on the Inner Planes, in a place of safety, until it has been called forth."

"A second priestess will be chosen as the Mother's Messenger—she alone will know the secret of Materialization. None will know her identity. If, in the course of mankind's struggle, it becomes apparent to the Goddess that the Amulet must be sent, the Messenger will incarnate. It will be the Guardian's responsibility to protect the Messenger and her sacred burden."

Mim stared into the Reverend Mother's relentless gaze, wondering what should be said to all this, which was far beyond mortal ken.

"May I look upon it, Reverend Mother?" she asked

finally, in a near whisper, and the High Priestess nodded in that imperial way that brooked no arguments. Senuset placed the Isis Amulet in the palm of Mim's hand.

It was the most beautiful object she had ever beheld. Twelve great gemstones adorned it—ruby, emerald, diamond, sapphire, carnelian, sardius, topaz, agate, onyx, beryl, amethyst, jasper—each was etched with talismanic sigils. Some she recognized, some were in glyphs she had never dreamed. Each gem pulsed with the power of its own ray, activating the chakras of the body's field, and those which transcended the body. They were tuned to the pulse of the earth's heartbeat, and to something far more vast and inexorable. The object breathed in Mim's palm, like a living organism—but not an organism from this sphere. She looked into her father's eyes, and read there the anguish of creation. The endless struggle to perfect, not a human instrument, but one to contain the essence of a Goddess.

"The Great Mother has not yet consecrated the Amulet," Mim whispered, more to herself than to the other occupants in their room. Artisan and Priestess looked startled by her words.

"How do you know this?" Reverend Mother demanded sharply. Mim looked up, startled that she would ask, when the truth was so obvious.

"Why, no one can mistake her energy who has been touched by it, Reverend Mother," she replied ingenuously. "Her energy activates the pelvic cauldron and connects us to all females in all time/space. There is immense power already inculcated into this wondrous Amulet, but the power of Isis is not here."

The Reverend Mother looked thoughtfully at the young girl. "You converse, then, with the Goddess?" she asked. Mim, assuming that all those training for the Great Mother's mysteries did so, said yes.

"We will speak again," Reverend Mother replied in a sepulchral tone, like that used in ceremony. She shut her eyes to commune with the Inner Planes, and Mim could see the audience was at an end. She turned to ask her father's leave to go, but the High Priestess spoke again.

"You are the friend of Karaden, are you not?" she demanded abruptly.

Mim answered yes.

"*Beware!*" The Priestess warned. And that was all.

Maggie stirred restlessly on the bed. She wasn't quite asleep anymore and the dream lay heavy on the periphery of consciousness. Senuset . . . Karaden . . . Why were these names so redolent of emotion? So familiar, and so full of pain.

She tried to remember the details of the dream, but it was already fading like mist before the sun.

She thrashed about in the covers, seeking comfort, and finally drifted back to fitful sleep.

# CHAPTER 39

Ellie smiled a good-bye to her last customer, and motioned Maggie to sit down. As soon as the woman was gone, Ellie locked the door behind her, and pulled down the shade.

"How are you doing, kiddo?" she asked, as she sat down near Maggie.

"I'm wearing pretty thin," Maggie replied honestly. "I've been having those weird dreams that I can't quite remember. They seem to take place in Egypt, or some other ancient place, I can't be sure. But they're powerful dreams, Ellie. The one I had last night seems to be hovering just beyond my grasp. As if I *need* to remember it, but can't." She shook her head in consternation.

"And I can't get through to Cody . . . I still phone

every day, but that's a waste of time, so I spend my life thinking something awful may happen to her before I get there . . ." She shrugged her shoulders to say it was far too overwhelming for explanation. "And there's something about these dreams that's really bugging me."

"Enlightenment isn't painful," Ellie answered, "but the process of getting there is a real pisser, isn't it?" She looked thoughtfully at Maggie for a moment, then said, "I think we'll know the date of the Materialization within the next day or so, Mags. Peter and I seem to be headed toward the same conclusion. I think he intends to check with that Egyptian at the museum, to see if he agrees with us. Have you figured out what you'll do, once you know?"

"All I've figured out is that no matter what date you two come up with, I can't wait very much longer before I try to get Cody out of hell-house."

Ellie frowned. "I'd really like you to do some kind of past-life regression, before you attempt that, Mags," she said seriously. "There's a great deal happening here that we don't yet fully understand. Every time I meditate on what's what, I'm told that *you* must unravel the scroll, before I can interpret it."

"Look, Ellie, I'm just not ready for that. It's hard enough as it is, to keep my feet planted firmly on the ground, without regressing into never-never land."

"Knowledge is power, Mags," Ellie insisted quietly. "And I'm convinced you'll have to find power you haven't yet imagined, to save Cody. Those dreams of yours are probably your subconscious's effort to give you the information you need. Just promise me you'll think about my suggestion."

Maggie nodded noncommittally.

"And one other thing . . ."

"Yes?"

"Promise me you'll try to have some fun, nutty as that sounds. Or at least a little laughter. It's a question of balance, Mags . . . all negative emotion will weaken you, make you ill. Even in the worst extremity, you have to attempt to find a little joy. Even if it's momentary."

"How on earth could I do that, knowing the danger Cody's in?"

"Sometimes, it's necessary to compartmentalize, when you're besieged by Fate . . . to allow yourself small pockets of laughter or pleasure, despite the tragedy raging around you. Because those little pockets balance the scales some, Mags. Without a bit of joy, the human heart withers . . . and without balance, the whole system goes down. 'The mind lives on the heart, like any parasite,' somebody said. Somebody wise."

Ellie looked pointedly at Maggie. "Have Dev take you out to dinner—or Peter for that matter—and talk about something other than Cody or theology," she added, with a soft smile. "Mr. Wong would give you the same advice, if you asked him. The Chinese understand the body/mind/spirit link better than anyone. Think *balance*, Mags—and don't you dare feel guilty about it, either. Hanging crepe twenty-four hours a day doesn't do a dammed thing for Cody. Remember, if you go down for the count, she has nobody."

Maggie replayed Ellie's advice in her head, for several blocks, then instead of going home, she went to Mr. Wong's house.

THE old man greeted her warmly. It was customary for students to drop by to speak with their Sifu, at random hours, and since his wife's death, he lived alone.

"Your friend is wise, Maggie," he said, when she'd repeated Ellie's words. "A good friend shields you from the storm. You already know from your martial arts training what happens when the harmony of your qi is disturbed. Your spirit weakens and your power dissipates."

"I understand the importance of balance, Sifu," she said earnestly, "but realistically, how can I control my emotions? How can I *not* be afraid for Cody and me? How can I *not* be angry over all that's happened to us? How can I *not* be heartsick in the face of all this?''

He smiled a little; the parchment wrinkling at the eyes and mouth made him look curiously elfin.

"You cannot stop life from happening, Maggie. Trees may prefer calm, but the wind will not subside! And, you cannot change your nature. Rivers and mountains are more easily changed than a man's nature. What you *can* do is to see your pathway clearly, and work with the energies of your life to meet its challenge. *See* your anger . . . find what is useful in it, discard the rest. *See* your fear. It has no value to you. Let it go. *Accept* your sorrow; it is appropriate. Then leave it behind, for it, too, has no value in your plan.

"What you cannot balance in yourself, you must bring to those who can help you . . . I will treat you today, to bring your energy into harmony. But, then you must plan for tomorrow. My master would say to me, 'Do not wait until you are thirsty to dig a well.' ''

Maggie lay down on the small bed Mr. Wong used for his acupuncture treatments. She knew the Chinese believed the body to be a vast electrical system, with intricate circuitry that could be adjusted to bring the body, mind, and spirit into balance and health.

He had taught her a great deal about traditional Chinese medicine over the years, in fact. About its five-thousand-year-old roots, and its sensible philosophy. She knew that the meridian lines and points shown on an acupuncture chart were renderings of the energy grid that carried lifeforce to the organ systems, and that Mr. Wong knew the ancient secrets of how to tinker with the circuitry to heal and to strengthen.

Mr. Wong took Maggie's left wrist in his strong hand and "listened" with his sensitive fingers for the nine pulses that would indicate for him the condition of her heart, liver, and kidneys. She felt his knowing fingers probe her energy at different levels, until satisfied, then she felt him move on to her right wrist, which carried the message of lung, stomach/spleen, and triple burner, a large energy grid that had no counterpart in Western medicine.

Maggie knew that based on what he found, Mr. Wong would select hair-thin disposable needles, and insert them at half a dozen or so points on her body, to drain or tonify, according to the needs he had perceived in his examination. She also knew that the acupuncture would be painless, and so she let herself drift into the relaxation the treatment always produced, as endorphins flooded the system with relief from pain and anxiety, and complex short circuits were rerouted into balance.

As she drifted into reverie, Maggie saw the image of a slender dark-haired child float into sudden sharp focus. The girl was walking in a stately procession of some kind down a long temple aisle; holding tightly to her parents' hands.

The parents, she somehow knew, were priest and priestess as well as father and mother. Maggie felt herself meld with the child in the reverie, feeling her tremulous emotions and exhilaration. It was hard not to be frightened, but it was a great honor to be chosen.

She had been in temple training since she was three, and now she was nearly seven, so, Mim-Atet-Ra well knew the rules of the ceremony. But up to now there had been home and family to rely on; after today she would be left here at Saqqara, in the great Pyramid Complex of the Gods, all alone. Years would pass before she would be allowed to leave, and even then, she would no longer be the child of Senuset, the artisan, and Niyohma, the Seeress of Mennofer. She would be the priestess-designate of Holy Mother Isis, her every thought and action watched and judged for worthiness.

It was not that Mim railed against her fate; she had been born with the sacred caul covering her face and was thus destined for the Goddess from her earliest breath. And she was a docile child who wished to please her parents, whom she loved, and her Gods, whom she both loved and feared. But the training would be increasingly rigorous from tomorrow on.

One could not be accepted as a candidate for the order of Melchizedek, unless the right was earned. Not Pharaoh himself could buy entry to the Greater Mysteries. Many students were accepted for education in the Lesser Mysteries, for every temple needed priests—but the Greater Mysteries were the province of a secret hierarchy that answered only to the Gods. It was acceptable to fear, her father had told her, that would pass with the years of training. But it all stretched before her at this moment, endless as the desert wastes outside the great Step Pyramid's gates; endless and frightening and unutterably lonely.

*Who are these people?* Maggie wondered, as she lay in the half sleep relaxation produced by the needles. *Who are these people and why do they dog my dreams?* She slept for a little and awoke refreshed.

She felt revived by Mr. Wong's acupuncture treatment. He was a skillful doctor, trained in the old ways by his master; medicine and martial arts went hand in hand in China.

It always amazed her that balancing her body's energy could give her clarity of mind as well. He and Ellie were both right, she had become terribly imbalanced because of all that was happening.

# CHAPTER 40

Maggie put down the New Testament she'd been browsing through, with a thud. "This story of Martha and Mary has always made me furious," she said, rubbing her temples to stave off a headache; she and Peter had been working for hours.

He looked over at her, and grinned despite his fatigue. "You're in good company. It annoyed Kipling, too." He was sitting in his favorite chair by the fire, as if he belonged there. It unnerved her somewhat that they'd slipped into such an easy closeness.

"Here, we have Christ dropping in for tea whenever he's in the neighborhood," she pursued, "and there's Martha cooking, cleaning, sewing, sweeping, and God knows what else, while Mary does nothing but sit on the floor and listen to the Master's stories. Then, when Martha asks for a little help with the dishes, the Lord reprimands her for not taking 'the better part.' "

"And that bothers you, eh?"

"Yes, it bothers me! I am unquestionably descended from Martha's side of the family. And, I thought the Lord was supposed to help those who helped themselves. If we just sit back and wait for the Lord to save Cody, will He do it?"

"I think the Arabs have the most practical theology," Peter answered, amused. " 'Trust in Allah . . . but tie your camel to a tree.' "

They both laughed, and Peter realized with a pang of regret, that being with this woman was, now, the great joy of his life. He had come to mark the hours of the day by her presence or absence . . . missed her oddly reverent irreverence, and the camaraderie she seemed to feel with God, that had nothing to do with dogma.

"When you talk to God, Maggie," he asked suddenly, "what do you talk about?"

"Oh, I don't know, exactly. Whatever seems appropriate, I suppose. 'Hello, God, Maggie, here. That's a lovely tree You made,' or, 'Great work on that sunset, thanks for letting me see . . .' I like to check in when I'm not asking Him for anything, so He doesn't think I'm just a fair-weather friend.

"Sometimes I carp, of course," she continued. "I've had a few things to say about all that awful handshaking and kissing strangers at an English-speaking Mass. I loved the Mass in Latin, Peter. It had such stature . . . mystery, drama, high pageant. The English Mass sounds clunky and flatfooted to me. Language exalted as cement. It's like trading in the cathedral of Notre Dame for a cinderblock prefab."

Peter laughed aloud, as Maggie had hoped he would; it was such a good thing to have someone to laugh with. "I can just imagine your conversation with God on that subject, Maggie," he said, mimicking her speech pattern. " 'Listen here, God. You'd better keep an eye on what they're doing to Your Church. I mean, I don't like to tell You Your business or anything, but who could take it seriously anymore?' "

"Peter," Maggie said softly, suddenly needing to know more, to understand this unfathomable man who had become tangled up in her life, in so strange a fashion. "A long while ago, you told me you once turned a corner, and never could find your way back . . ."

He nodded. It was only fair of her to want to know . . . the corner . . . the turning point . . . but did he himself even know the truth of where he'd wandered?

"Such a complex story, Maggie dear," he said with sudden sadness. "I'll try to find a beginning . . ." Peter was quiet for a long moment, then began again. "I was an anthropologist, as well as a linguist, as you know. Both professions gave me the opportunity, not merely to travel to exotic places, but to live with other cultures for extended periods, close to the people and their belief systems.

"In my wanderings, I ran across recurrent information that there were *avatars*—ascended beings of some sort—living in the world at this moment in time, and I determined that I would seek them out. It didn't seem an odd thing to do—just an extension of my comparative theology studies. Would you not seek out Christ, if you knew where to find him? I asked myself. So, I began my search."

"And did you find such remarkable beings?"

"I found two, although I'd been told there were five on the planet, currently. Then, I created a premise that demanded I spend time in their company. I couched it in theological language acceptable to the Church's new leniency toward ecumenism, of course, so that, while my superiors may have been wary, they did not attempt to deter me." He paused, uncertain how to express the magnitude of what this rebellious action had unleashed.

"As I told you when we met, I had lived in places where our paradigms of reality have little validity. For example, there's an Indian tribe in the Amazon, in which only that which is dreamed is deemed to have substance—waking life, they feel, is too absurd to be given credence. My experiences were beginning to alter my perceptions, nearly that radically.

"I met the first of these avowed Avatars, and he became my obsession. I studied him as if he were an anthropological specimen. I was determined to test him, to expose his flaws, to convince myself that he could not be what he seemed." Peter smiled enigmatically.

"Instead, he cheated me of my goal. He challenged me. Humbled me. Changed me. '*You are in the web of God,*' he told me. '*It will end in ecstasy.*' He was the first to bring me flashes of a shift in reasoning that my Church would consider heretical, and I would consider the beginning of wisdom. I thought I had found the Grail."

Maggie said nothing, and Peter continued. "I had always had a mystical bent, Maggie . . . this teacher opened my psyche to the Unseen Universe that I had only glimpsed before. I began to have clear visionary experiences . . . perceptions of the order of God's creation. Lightning illuminates, and I was split asunder by visions of mankind in an upward spiral that led to ultimate communion with the Godhead. One lifetime or one thousand lifetimes . . . however long it takes us to get there, I saw that we were going home. The curtain had been lifted, and I had seen what the ego forgets, but the soul remembers. The Sea of Light of all Mystics, in all

time. *Shunrata* to the Tibetans, *The Face of Glory* to
the Sufis, *The Omega Point* to Teilhard de Chardin . . .
my life had been shattered open by spiritual lightning! I
had seen the great unfurling of Divinity.

"When I returned to the United States, luminescent
with the Light that had been shown me, I published—
or rather, circulated without benefit of Imprimatur—the
book that made me famous and infamous, simultaneously.

"I was lauded by the intellectual secular press, and
vilified by the conservative elements within the Church.
I was reprimanded by the watchdogs of the faith, but
because of the intense secular notoriety I enjoyed at that
point, I was given a second chance to save my soul.

"I was put on a very short leash by my superiors, and
sent to the spiritual Siberia of an impoverished parish,
upstate. The chastening they chose for me was very
wise, although, of course, I didn't know it at the time.
Peter Messenguer, boy genius and proud intellect, became a lowly curate in a redneck church. I was to be
humbled and overworked . . . there would be no time
left for intellectual pretensions. And, I expect they
thought there would be no one in this particular parish
with either an IQ or an education that could provide me
an occasion of sin." He chuckled.

"They were entirely wrong. For six years, I labored
among the poor and illiterate and desperate . . . and they
taught me what it meant to be a priest. That, my dear
Maggie, you cannot learn in theology school, nor in
the Roman corridors of ecclesiastical power. Only the
*people*, God-seeking and long-suffering, can give you
that particular gift. In the beginning, I was angry, humiliated, anxious for release from my purgatory. After a
while, I understood how God had worked his wisdom in
my life *despite*—and even *through*—the small-mind-
edness of my superiors."

He paused and sighed deeply.

"I remember one particular house call—there were
dozens that could illustrate this same point, I suppose,

but there's always one that is the lodestar . . ." Peter's voice had hushed to a kind of reverence. "I called upon a woman with a crippled husband, in a tumbledown shanty—she had asked for confession and Communion to be brought. When I asked if she had children, she showed me her nine-year-old twin daughters, who were afflicted with cystic fibrosis. Oh, Maggie, dear, how I remember their frail beauty . . . that strange luminosity that shimmers in those on the brink of eternity was already upon them. They were gentle and patient and courageous, and I saw in their eyes, the intimacy they shared with death.

"The woman spent her days and nights clearing their lungs of the phlegm that would ultimately strangle them . . . Hercules in the Augean stables labored no harder. They had almost no money, she told me, since her husband's accident . . . she nursed him, too, of course. And with all that she bore, Maggie, still she had asked me to bring the Blessed Sacrament to her and to hear her confession. What sin could touch a soul like hers? I remember thinking, as I looked at her patient courage." He paused again.

"Before I confessed her, she told me sheepishly that the question of birth control plagued her. She loved her husband, she said shyly, and there was so little that gave them joy . . . but they couldn't survive if another damaged child was born to them, and as they wouldn't dream of abortion, they had no choice but to abstain from sex."

Peter's gaze was far away. "The *laity issues*, they are called within the halls of celibate men, Maggie. Responsible birth control . . . allowing homosexuals to receive the sacraments . . . divorce . . . the issues of frail, patient humanity, trying to stay close to God, despite the odds." He sighed.

"She and I both knew that if she confessed to me that she used contraception, and had no firm purpose of amendment, I could not grant her absolution. So, she had chosen to raise the question with me first, to see where I stood. She seemed fragile as glass to me, Maggie. *Do not make me the instrument of adding one more burden to this woman's portion*, I pleaded with God.

"*Would You really damn these struggling souls, for so responsible an act?* I demanded of Him. *Tell me what to tell them! Help me to help your suffering children. Take me where You will and I will follow* . . . I left her house in a daze of question marks of conscience.

"She was the beginning for me. I went home to fast and to pray . . . and it all began to coalesce for me. The revelations in Africa and India, the people's need, my own conviction of the lovingness and justice of God, my intense desire for cosmic understanding—from all these, and from wherever that divine spark of inspiration originates, I evolved a hypothesis about our evolution toward God. Emily Dickinson said, 'The truth must dazzle gradually . . . or all the world would be blind,' but once the truth begins to dazzle, you cannot help but see. The wild journey begins, Maggie, and you are powerless to leave the roller coaster.

"I found myself in the frenzied clutches of a visionary experience beyond anything I had ever deemed possible. I worked for my 'causes' by day, and wrote by night. There were others in the Church who were questioning, too, of course. 'The Burning Brand' they dubbed me in the press, and I was indeed aflame, Maggie, for I truly believed I had been inspired by a vision that would change the course of humanity's yearnings for God. And, I was so young! Oh Maggie, I still had the passion to support my visions. So, I wrote about that passion.

"This time, there were no cautionary rumblings from the diocese. No 'I hear you're teaching some controversial things, Father, don't you think your parishioners' minds need to remain clear of such confusions?'

"This time, my work was not only never approved for publication, it was summarily banned. '*Do not publish. Do not disseminate. Do not breathe this heresy aloud, on pain of excommunication.*'

"I was called before the Holy Inquisition, currently

named the Sacred Congregation for the Doctrine of the Faith. I didn't even know I was being investigated on such august levels. I was warned of my shameful abuse of intellectual pride. *'Theology is the servant of the Church, Father, not a public forum for your arrogance.'*

"There was, of course, no compromise position for me to take. I didn't wish to harm my Church, I simply no longer had any choice but to follow my own conscience. I was hung on a cross of paradox: Am I at one with God because I'm following my own conscience, I asked myself, in anguish . . . or is the sacrifice He demands of me that I surrender myself and my theories to Church discipline? *How do I serve thee?* was my crucifixion. *What is Thy will for me?* I published *The Long Road from Calvary* in the secular press, not in defiance, but in desperate faith. I had to find God or die. I fully anticipated excommunication."

"My God, Peter," Maggie said softly. "You must have been torn to shreds by all this."

"On your moment in time, Maggie, depends your destiny," he answered. "The Pope summoned me to Rome.

"He was kinder, and more fair-minded, than I had any right to expect, after the debacle of the Sacred Congregation. We had met before, when I was still a student—my favorite moralist, Guiseppi Pontinelli—a brilliant Roman of patrician lineage—was a close friend of the then Cardinal, so when my first book had gained fame, the Cardinal who was destined for the papacy had read it and remembered me.

"I found he had read my newest work, too. And had discussed it with Pontinelli, in great depth. The Pope questioned me on every nuance of my theory, traced every footstep that had led me to it . . . probed not my theology, as I expected, but my sincerity and my love of God. It was, without question, the most extraordinary inquiry I was ever party to.

"He made no pronouncement to me, of his findings, but later Pontinelli told me the Pope's appraisal of me, in precise terms. 'This man is not a heretic,' the Holy

Father had told him. 'He is merely a mystic, who has followed God around a corner and has not yet been shown the way home. That path will be made clear to him, I believe, in the Father's own time. We must shelter him, Guiseppi, until God sees fit to relieve us of that responsibility.' '' Peter smiled sadly, and Maggie saw the tears in his eyes.

"I was not excommunicated. Instead, I was sent to the place where you found me, hidden away among the dust of other forbidden thinkers. A wonderfully cruel jest, on the part of the Sacred Congregation, I suspect. When they could not excommunicate me, perhaps they determined to show me the musty obscurity into which such thoughts as mine inevitably decline. Better than being broken on the wheel, of course—I was fortunate to be a heretic in such a benevolent age."

Maggie realized she'd been holding her breath through the last part of the soliloquy. "And was such exile as you describe better than simply leaving the Church entirely, Peter? Surely you could have pursued your quest, and your writing, on the outside? You had an international reputation for both brilliance and integrity."

"I considered doing just that, Maggie," he said honestly. "And then I remembered how I had railed at my first exile to parish work—and how very wrong I had been in my judgment. My superiors had prescribed precisely the right medicine for my troubled soul, however much I, in my ignorance, had rebelled at the bitter taste of it.

"I began to see my newest exile—and my silence— as an appropriate penance to be exacted for my sins . . . those the Sacred Congregation knew of, and those they did not.

"I settled into this new purgatory, Maggie, to wait for illumination about why God had placed me in this particular quagmire. How would He work *through me*, and *in me*? My librarianship became a time of sorting the wheat from the chaff of myself . . . of my theories, of my priesthood, of my humanity. In truth, it was both humbling and enlightening to see how many had faltered before me . . . it helped keep me honest in my self-appraisal. I have continued to write, of course, and to explore my hypothesis. Worst case, they shall have to deal with my theories when I die."

"Or consign them to a vault under the Vatican, never to be heard from again!" she said, angry at the unfairness.

"Whether or not any of my further work sees the light of day is entirely in God's hands, now, Maggie. Just as it should be, I suspect."

Neither of them spoke for a time.

"I have a friend," Peter said suddenly, brightening a little. "His name is Father James Kebede . . . He has a subtle mind and great love of God . . . I'd like to add his perspective to your dilemma. Would you consider meeting him? It would mean a great deal to me."

He was changing the subject, and who could blame him. "I have a few friends I'd like you to meet, too, Peter," she answered slowly. "Maybe it would be a good idea if we all put our heads together."

Peter walked to the desk and picked up a thick sheaf of notes; he seemed to be saying they should get back to work.

He handed her the folio and Maggie groaned inwardly; they were in Latin. She'd taken five years of it in school, but that had been long ago. "Second nature to you, maybe," she said with a grimace, as she took the papers.

Peter smiled and said, "Don't worry, I'll translate. There's something here I want you to see."

After Peter left, Maggie stood at the parlor window watching the empty street where he'd been. He was such a complex combination of evolved intellect and old-fashioned piety. What was it she felt for him, she wondered. Could it be called love? She always felt curiously *complete* with him; as if some unspecified missing molecule had been infused into her structure. Not like a missing piece added to a jigsaw puzzle, but rather like a chemical added to a beaker, that transmutes the original substance from within.

It didn't feel *new*, as falling in love does. It felt *old*, like some long forgotten strain of music that surfaces in your mind and then cannot be banished.

She couldn't even decide if it felt good. That was the weirdest part of all. Their relationship felt necessary, inevitable. Unavoidable.

It unnerved her to realize that she *wanted* him, so she pushed the thought from her head and went to bed.

CODY stood in the white tile bathroom sobbing piteously. The floor all around her feet was covered in vomit. Ghania had held her nose until she couldn't breathe, and then her mouth had opened all by itself, even though she didn't want it to, and Ghania had poured the horrible cocktail down her throat until it choked her, and spilled all over her face, into her nose and eyes, and down her dress. Even her socks were full of it. And then she had started throwing up, and Ghania had slapped her so hard her head hit the bathtub, and everything had turned dark, and Ghania was cursing as she ran down the hall, shouting for a servant to clean up the mess, leaving the dripping and terrified child.

Cody's sobs were convulsive now, gulping in air and trying to breathe. She stood in the midst of the horrid puddle, not knowing what to do, or where to turn.

Ghania had stopped for *now*, but she wouldn't stop forever.

Cody O'Connor crept to the window and stared at the sea through the blur of her tears. Now there was no place left in her world that was safe. Only Mim. And she was gone. She could see the place on the beach where Mim had stood when she said she would save her. The ache of it squeezed her heart because Mim never came back for her. Maybe she never would. Maybe she got hurt in a car crash, or maybe she got sick, or maybe she died. Or maybe she loved some other little girl . . .

Maybe Cody would be alone, in this terrible place, forever.

"I love you, Mim," she whispered to the phantom on the sand.

There was sand in her dreams, sometimes. Not like on the beach. Some other kind of sand. So hot it hurt your feet and your eyes. So hot it burned you, when you breathed. And Mim was in that other sandy place, holding Cody's hand.

And they were running.

And they were very, very afraid.

THE dream crashed in on Maggie as soon as sleep came. She was poised at the edge of a vast desert landscape. A sea of endless shifting sand stretched perilously before her and the little girl who clutched her hand in fear.

They were being pursued.

Somewhere, not far behind, assassins trailed them. Now, the endless desert was their only hope of escape. The two frightened figures hurried forward into the burning vastness . . . and shimmered out of sight, like a mirage.

Maggie thrashed her way toward wakefulness, and sat up, uncertainly. She still carried with her the longings and the terrors of the woman and the child . . . or maybe the child was Cody, and this was just another manifestation of the terrible anxiety that surrounded her.

She turned in the bed and forced her eyes to focus on the room around her.

And then she knew the unthinkable truth.

It was she and Cody who were running, and they were *somewhere else in time*.

# CHAPTER 41

Maggie looked around the room at the small assembage of friends, hoping Amanda had been right when she'd insisted all the allies meet. *What a zany little army for such a big battle*, she thought. *I feel like Frodo.* Peter stood by the fireplace, Amanda sat decorous as ever, in an armchair, Devlin lounged near Maggie on the couch, his jacket hanging over a nearby chair, his tie loosened. He looked as if he'd been up all night.

"Quite a potent gathering, I'd say," Ellie remarked as she passed out a tray of drinks.

"Of which, I expect, I am the least qualified," offered Amanda, rising and taking the tray from Ellie's hands. "So I shall have the least to say and will therefore make myself useful in more mundane ways." She smiled warmly at Ellie, who relinquished the chore, and sat down on the floor. "I will interject a question here or there, though, if that won't be a bother," Amanda finished and everyone murmured assent.

"We all have parts to play here, Amanda," Ellie assured her. "Your qualifications will do just fine."

"Ellie and I are of the opinion," Peter began, "that Maa Kheru will use the night of April 30th for the Amulets' Materialization." Maggie's heart thudded in her chest. Three and a half weeks, it pounded . . . *three and a half weeks*.

"On what do you base such an assumption," Devlin interjected. Maggie and Ellie exchanged glances; it was easy to see the men's wariness of each other was just this side of antagonism. *Damn*, Maggie thought, feeling the tension, *I should have gotten them together in some other way.* How foolish it had been to imagine they would get along.

Peter turned to Devlin. "As best I can piece the ancient writings together—and let me assure you, this is said with very little certitude, because everything in the papyri is couched in riddles. But, it appears two things are necessary in order to Materialize the Amulets . . . the Messenger, born under the correct planetary aspects must be present, of course. And a conjunction of Saturn and Neptune, trining Pluto and Uranus, must take place, in order to produce the electromagnetic frequencies that will favor materialization. Such will be the case on April 30th of this year."

Ellie chimed in. "When you add in that April 30th is Walpurgisnacht, when malevolent energies are their most powerful, it seems a good bet that's their target date."

Devlin frowned at all the mystic jargon, and Ellie picked up on his distaste.

"When in Rome, Dev . . ." she said pointedly, and he chuckled good-naturedly at the chiding.

"Okay. Okay. I stand reproved. Circumstantial evidence is sometimes all you get. Cops just hate approximation."

Ellie smiled mischievously; he was so like Maggie's detailed description. "It's because you're a *poet* that you hate the approximate, Dev, not because you're a cop. At least that's what Rilke would have said."

Devlin had to laugh; Ellie was more than she appeared. "Okay," he allowed, "for the moment, let's focus on April 30th. That gives us less than a month to pull the rabbit out of the hat."

Ellie saw that Devlin seldom took his eyes off Peter. "Just for the record, Father, what exactly will this Materialization consist of?" he asked.

"Everyone here calls me Peter," the priest responded quietly. "I wish you'd do the same."

Devlin shook his head, with a short laugh. "No way, Father, I'm a BIC."

"A BIC?"

"Bronx Irish Catholic," Devlin replied. "We have our own ways where priests are concerned."

Deftly sidestepped, Maggie thought, glancing at Ellie to see if she'd caught the nuance. *You are Maggie's friend, not mine*, it said clearly. *The jury's still out on you*.

"As you wish," Peter replied. "I'll tell you what I've been able to glean so far. But, I caution you to remember, this is speculation based on encoded arcane data, that has suffered many mistranslations, over a nearly five-thousand-year period.

"Even the Bible differs to a marked degree when read in the original Hebrew or Greek, or the Aramaic of Christ's time, or the King James rendition . . ."

Devlin waved his hand in acceptance of the disclaimer. "I'm used to screwed-up evidence, Father. Just give me your best guess."

Peter took a deep breath, considering how to encapsulate what he knew.

"Let us look at this process as a physicist might," he said. "We must remember that what we think of as our *physical self*—and our entire world, for that matter—is not solid matter at all, but rather a collection of billions of molecules, in constant motion. If Cody *is* the Isis Messenger, she is a kind of cosmic tuning fork. We must hypothesize that her unique vibratory rate can—under certain auspicious circumstances—resonate with a preconceived pattern of Universal energies, to cause things to happen. In this case, to bring into material existence another molecular structure, the Isis Amulet. Just as our galaxy was called into being from *non-being*, or at least from the primordial melting pot of molecules, so, too, will the Amulet be called into being.

"Once that Materialization is complete, another electromagnetic resonance will be set up by the newly Materialized Amulet. This second resonance will manifest into matter, the Sekhmet Stone.

"At the moment, you might say these two Amulets

exist only in a *potentiality of being*, as Saint Augustine called the first creation, that predated the Creation set forth in Genesis. After the thirtieth, we must hypothesize that the Amulet and the Stone could actually exist on our material plane."

He looked around to see if everyone was following, so far.

"It would help us, perhaps, to remember that from a physicist's point of view, light is a form of energy that has no electrical charge or mass, yet it can create protons and electrons that are the components of the atom, and thus the building blocks of matter. According to Planck's quantum theory, light is transmitted in 'pockets,' or quanta, of action, which are also called photons. And photons tend to behave like intelligent human beings . . . for example, the photons that form a ray of light always select a path through the atmosphere that will take them most expeditiously to their destination."

"Come again?" Devlin interjected.

"I merely suggest that as farfetched as creation of matter out of nonmatter appears to us . . . it may not be totally implausible from a physicist's point of view."

"Peter's just telling you we may not know everything the ancients knew," Ellie said placatingly.

"So how would they use Cody? What happens to her?" Devlin persisted.

Peter shook his head, a deep frown on his face. "The texts say only that her Ka must leave her body and journey to the place in time/space where the Amulets are being safekept. She must then successfully journey back with them . . ." He gestured toward Ellie.

"Our resident metaphysician, Ellie, tells me, that according to oral tradition, the Messenger will be gravely endangered while making this journey out of the body. Perhaps she would care to explain . . ."

Ellie took up the thread. "When a human being's spirit—let's call it the Ka for the moment—leaves the physical body to wander on the Astral, or Angelic, or Buddhic, or any other Plane of existence, it remains attached to the physical body by what is called the Silver Cord, an etheric umbilicus that seems capable of limitless extension."

"I've heard of that!" Amanda offered enthusiastically. "Shirley MacLaine goes flitting around the world, nights, and finds her way back by way of this silver string. Yes?"

Ellie chuckled. "That's exactly right, Amanda. So, you probably also know that the Astral traveler must take great care not to sever the cord, and not to let anything jarring happen to the body back home, because the physical body is terribly vulnerable while the genie is out of the bottle, so to speak."

Amanda nodded, obviously intrigued. "So assuming any of this astonishing tale is true, we must worry about Cody not just in this world, but in four or five others, as well? God Almighty, we do seem to have our work cut out for us."

"The dangers are severalfold, actually," Ellie continued. "The Black Magicians could destroy Cody's physical body, so she couldn't get back in . . . her Ka could be attacked or imprisoned by demons, while on the Astral . . . or maybe something even worse could happen . . ." Ellie looked worriedly at Peter, who picked up the explanation.

"There's a very obscure papyrus—part of the Mari Recension—it's so abstruse no one has ever paid it much mind. But if you read it in the context of this Isis-Sekhmet Legend—it might be construed to mean that Sekhmet could choose to follow her Stone into the material world, by means of taking over Cody's body. To do that, the child's Ka would have to be kidnapped on the Astral, and held prisoner by some kind of demonic guardians." He put up his hands in a noncommittal gesture, in response to a derisive snort from Devlin.

"I merely *report* what the Recension suggests, Lieutenant," he said, trying not to be angry. "I can offer no scientific verification for such a happenstance." The priest paused, then spoke again. "I have had, however, empirical experience of demonic intelligences . . . as, indeed, did Maggie, the night of the Sending. So I cannot summarily dismiss this possibility, either.''

*Put that in your pipe and smoke it*, Ellie thought with a suppressed grin. It was obvious Devlin intuited Maggie's connection to Peter and resented it. She made a mental note to try to smooth things over—dissension among allies was not in anyone's best interest.

"Could you tell us a little about Isis and Sekhmet, Peter or Ellie?'' Amanda put in quickly, to quell the tension in the room. "I expect Dev and I are not up to speed on our Goddesses.'' She smiled disarmingly at Devlin, as she said it, and saw him decide to opt for civility.

"Amanda's right,'' he agreed. "We were fresh out of Goddesses in the Bronx.''

Peter looked to Ellie, but she deferred to him with a wave of the hand, so he cleared his throat and began. " 'In the beginning was Isis,' '' he said. " 'Oldest of the Old, She was the Goddess from whom all Becoming Arose. She was the Great Lady, Mistress of the House of Life. Mistress of the Word of God. She was unique. In all her great and wondrous works, She was a wiser magician and more excellent than any other God.' '' He smiled and added, "All that is taken from a Theban manuscript written in the fourteenth century before Christ.

"All the old Gods, you'll find, have some sort of allegorical legend attached to the time when they walked the earth and had exchanges with humans.

"Probably the best account of the Isis legend is the one provided by Plutarch, in his treatise *De Iside et Oside*,'' he said. "It was written in Greek about the middle of the first century of our era, and later substantiated by certain Egyptian hieroglyphic texts. Whether you accept it as history or allegory, the tale is an extraordinary one, in its complex understanding of human nature. I won't burden you with all of it, just the salient points.

"Osiris was an Egyptian king of breathtaking wisdom who set himself the task of civilizing the people, and redeeming them from their former states of barbarism. He and his remarkable queen, Isis, taught them the cultivation of the earth, gave them a body of laws, and instructed them in the worship of the Gods.

"Having made his own land prosperous, Osiris set out to teach the other nations of the world, leaving Isis to rule in his stead. She ruled so brilliantly, in fact, that Osiris's nasty brother Set was thwarted in his evil designs on the kingdom. This enraged Set so, that when his brother returned, he persuaded seventy-two malcontents to join him in a conspiracy to kill Osiris. After they'd killed him by treachery, they cut his body into fourteen pieces and scattered them all over Egypt, or Khemu-Amenti, as it was then called."

*Khemu-Amenti!* The name jolted Maggie. That was the name from her dream; the name that had eluded her. And there was that *sound* again . . . that elusive tinkling, like a bell carried away on the wind. *Temple bells* . . . they had something to do with being in a temple . . . She forced her mind to return to what Peter was saying:

"Osiris became the King of the Underworld, while Isis took her rightful place as Queen of Heaven. She was the archetype, of course, of all female attributes; love, duty, fortitude, courage, and devotion to justice."

"I'd like to add something, here, Peter," Ellie interjected. "In Mystery School teaching, Isis is credited with some unique attributes that we might like to keep in mind when we contemplate the importance of her Amulet.

"Isis is the High Priestess who represents the Inner and most often 'hidden' Sanctum Sanctorum. She is lunar, yet receives her power from the sun, and she is the Spiritual Bride of the Just Man. She symbolizes all intellectual, psychic, and spiritual gifts, and she is the keeper of all cosmic secrets . . . Only the pure in heart may ever come to know them, for she conceals them from the profane.

"She is a High Initiate and sits with her left foot resting upon the crescent moon, symbolizing the feminine principle, which demonstrates her mastery over the lunar-emotional aspect of her nature. In the arcane sciences, the feminine intuitive qualities of the mind are honored more highly than the mentalized masculine will-to-power.

"We humans owe her a great deal. It was Isis who ordained that elders would be beloved by children, and that justice would be more powerful than gold and silver. She caused men to love women, and caused truth to be considered beautiful.

"Every part of her story is an encoded mystery, which represents the judgment of the soul by the Lords of Karma. In the Egyptian Mysteries, if the soul was found to be utterly pure, it was allowed to pass onward into immortality; if it had not *'true voice,'* it was delivered over to the monster Amemit, 'the devourer,' and was swallowed up again in the cycle of regeneration, to be reborn on earth in another body."

"I think I need another drink before we move on to Sekhmet," Amanda said wryly. "These ancients play rough." She replenished everyone's glass, including her own, and sat back down.

"Ellie," Peter said, "why don't you tell us what you know of Sekhmet."

She nodded and stood up, as Peter sat down. Ellie paused a moment to gather herself, then in her ceremonial voice cried out,

> " *I am the Mighty One*
> *who rules the Wastelands . . .*
> *Great and Terrible is my Name.'*

"Thus does Sekhmet call herself.

> *'Greater than Isis am I,*
> *and mightier than all the Gods.*
> *Forbidden is my Name.'*

"And that's only a tiny part of her curriculum vitae," she said, with a grin, returning to her normal voice. "She's quite a girl. Her name is taken from the root 'sekhem,' which means 'strong,' 'mighty,' 'violent.' She tends to appear to devotees in the form of a magnificent leopard-sized black cat, wearing a golden collar studded with rubies, and carrying an Ankh-headed ceremonial staff. A massive disc and uraeus crowns her head, and she is nothing, if not regal. With good reason, of course, as Ra, the Sun God, was her father. She was his wild child." Ellie caught Peter's suppressed smile and returned it.

"It's important to note that she isn't all bad, exactly . . . Sekhmet is a destroyer, but destruction is often necessary to make way for a new order. She represents primordial chaos, and she has a definite blood lust, but there are those who would say that without an energy of destructiveness, there would exist only stasis in the world, and nothing could ever improve."

"A fine distinction," quipped Amanda, "but you can only make it if she's not busy destroying you, at the time."

Ellie laughed. "There's the rub. According to her allegorical legend, because she was 'the force against which no other force avails,' Ra once asked her to punish some earthlings who had earned his wrath. She hot-footed it down here, destroyed the perps, as Dev would say, rending and slaughtering, and drinking their blood willy-nilly. She got such a kick out of what she was doing, that she threatened to destroy the whole human race.

"So in desperation, Ra snapped up some plants said to be of the solanaceae family, plus a little opium, and sent it off to the God Sekti at Heliopolis, who quickly brewed them up into seven thousand jugsful of a drink made from human blood and beer. Sekhmet spotted the brew, thought it looked yummy, lapped up the seven thousand jugs and, quote, 'Her heart was filled with joy.' She also fell into a deep stupor, and when she woke up, she forgot to kill the rest of humanity."

"A veritable paean to intoxication!" said Amanda with a laugh. "What a great story."

"And well told," Peter said admiringly. "I can see that most of the Egyptian scholars I know might do well to discuss their deities with you, Ellie."

"That's kind of you, Peter. And you've just reminded me that there is one other scholarly thought to add in here. Gerald Massey, who was a nineteenth-century scholar and trance-medium, identified Sekhmet as the Great Harlot from the Book of Revelation, 'The Mother of Harlots and of abominations of the earth,' I think it reads. So, even though she also has good manifestations, as well as evil ones, Sekhmet is highly unreliable when it comes to humankind. Like the Druid Goddess Morrigan, she might ultimately do good for us, but it will be by means of pain and destruction."

"All very entertaining," Devlin said as he bade Maggie good night a short while later, "but not likely to get Cody back."

"He who closeth his mind, closeth the door to the future," Ellie chided, overhearing.

"I suppose some ancient Egyptian sage said that?" Devlin asked.

Ellie grinned broadly. "Nope," she replied, "I said it."

# CHAPTER 42

Abdul Hazred made obeisance to the altar and prepared to disperse the sacred energies. It was essential that all powers invoked or evoked be dispatched to their normal spheres before ending any ceremony. More than one celebrant had died mad, as a result of inadequate banishing.

Hazred rendered thanks to all the Intelligences that had been kind enough to aid him in that day's magical working. The heady fragrance of sandalwood incense, one of the few acceptable to all the Gods, filled the room around him, and he felt the energies drain and dissipate, wafting away in the scented smoke.

He retreated down the steps, still facing the altar—it was never safe to turn your back on an Immortal—and returned to the study he used as his robing room.

Hazred removed the heavy lion mask with relief, undid the apron of Sekhmet, and pulled the white robes off, over his head. For a moment he stood, head thrown back, arms outstretched, breathing deeply. It took time to come down from the performance of ritual magic; once you opened your aura to the God/Goddess energies, you were helpless in their grasp. There was nothing as stupendous as the power that surged through you, electrifying, exhilarating, making you *more* than human . . . but it was not your power, it was theirs. Only a fool allowed himself to forget that fact, and fools didn't live long in the practice of magic.

He'd followed a long and winding road in the wake of the Goddess. Had there ever been a time in this life when he hadn't known his destiny as her servant? The Universe had provided the intellect, the wealth, the family prominence, the ambition . . . but he, himself, had been called upon to supply the back-breaking work, the years of study, the infinite varieties of personal sacrifice that would make him worthy of such a Divine Mistress. Finally, she would reward his diligence by placing the greatest prize of all in his hands.

Hazred returned to normal posture; he was fully reconnected to the real world, now . . . fully ensconced in his mortal body, fully in charge of himself, once again. He showered briskly, scrubbing himself, as carefully as had the priests of old, who always purified their bodies, before and after ritual. He left the shower and splashed his face and body with fragrant oils. Patchouli for sexuality, jasmine for good fortune, moonflower for intuition, and a few others that were his special secret.

He thought about the woman. Maggie O'Connor. These Anglo names were so lacking in finesse, so grimly unattractive. But she was not an unattractive woman. In fact, that had been a most pleasant surprise when they'd met. He'd given a great deal of thought to how to win her confidence; had she been ugly, several of those possibilities would have had to be eliminated. As it was . . .

Eric thought she was unimportant, but in the final disposition of the matter, Hazred knew he was wrong. No piece could be construed unimportant, in a chess board set up by the deities. Whether she would prove to *know* something, or to *do* something, or to simply set some energy in motion, he did not know. That she bore watching was unequivocal.

Hazred dressed hurriedly, feeling refreshed, and drove to the place where the agent of the Egyptian government would be waiting. He was beyond politics, but he respected power, especially where it could be useful.

The old book shop on West Fourth Street looked shabby, as if time had already passed it by fifty years ago. A few college kids in jeans or chinos circulated among the dusty stacks; middle-aged scholarly types, pasty-faced from infrequent sunlight, spoke in library-hush to the elderly clerks, who seemed nearly as inanimate as the out-of-print books.

Hazred fingered two or three volumes as if interested, and asked a question of the man behind a heavily laden oak desk. Wordlessly, he was waved toward the remote back corner of the cavernous shop. Hazred glanced right, then left, and, satisfied he was unobserved except by those trained to do so, he rounded the last stack, slipped through the door marked STORE PERSONNEL ONLY, and mounted the dark staircase.

ANUBIS IMPORTING, LTD. was painted on the door in ornate lettering. Hazred knocked and waited to be buzzed in. Beyond the door and small reception area, a large modern office existed, startlingly at odds with all that had preceded it. Sleek metal office furniture, computer consoles, and an elaborate telephone system said that Anubis Importing was other than what it seemed. In fact, it was the New York headquarters of a special section of the Egyptian intelligence service, Mohabarat.

Hazred was ushered into the inner office; he greeted the man behind the desk with a restrained cordiality that was responded to in much the same tone. Hazred understood the military mind of the Secret Service colonel—he just didn't like it much. Empower a civil servant, he had always felt, and you breed a potential tyrant.

"You've made contact with the woman," the man said, as his opening gambit. "What have you learned?"

"She is intelligent and educated, but quite out of her depth. She seeks only the child's welfare and, as far as I could tell, has no interest in the Amulets, as she gives no credence to the legend."

The man raised a dark heavy eyebrow skeptically. "I have known few humans who were truly *dis*interested in power," he said.

The man's supercilious tone wasn't lost on Hazred. "And have you known many grandmothers who would trade a child's life for this power?" Hazred replied evenly. "You must move in interesting circles."

The face of the man behind the desk darkened. He had been handed this arrogant academic as a given, in the matter of the Amulets, but he neither liked nor trusted him. He himself placed no credence in the ridiculous legend—he had been in the military far too long to have any illusions about what real power consisted of, and who wielded it. But he could see the PR value of such nonsense, among the ignorant masses. And he had orders that were to be carried out. So he would tolerate this dandified know-it-all; at least until he became an intolerable nuisance. Once his superiors had made the decision about what to do with the child and the woman, Abdul Hazred would become as expendable as he deserved to be. The thought cheered Colonel Hamid enough to become cordial again.

"I have not yet received orders regarding the disposition of the child and her guardian, Mr. Hazred. You are simply to continue your conversations, and to let us know if anything unusual develops. And, of course, you are to let us know when you calculate the precise date of the alleged ritual."

Hazred smiled reassurance. "These matters are complex, Colonel. You must understand that the ancients took elaborate pains with secrecy concerning the Great Mysteries. You may rest assured you will hear from me the moment I am certain of my data."

They said their good-byes, each knowing the other had lied. That was to be expected, of course. Only fools tipped their hands.

Hazred returned to the street, grateful to leave these bureaucrats and their petty pretensions behind. He had far bigger fish to fry.

*Lifetimes*, he thought, as he rounded the corner and flagged a taxi. *I have spent lifetimes in preparation for this moment, and this imbecile thinks I am on his payroll.*

He would never have consented to the government request that he advise on this matter, except for the fact that these military morons could be useful. After the run-in with Eric, it seemed likely that temporal force could prove necessary. If so, Colonel Hamid and his stormtroopers would be called into play.

Hazred had cultivated Vannier and Sayles through his knowledge of magic; he'd been above their suspicion, as only a handful of humans had Crossed the Abyss and no one could purport to have done so, unless it was true. And of all the Thirteen Adepts who would serve the Materialization, only he and Eric were of the proper bloodline.

Hazred paid the cabbie and stood for a moment on the corner of Park and Seventy-third Street; his plans would have been better served if he'd been able to get to the child through Maggie O'Connor, but he would win in the end, anyway. And that fool of a colonel would help him do so.

# PART IV

# THE
# KARMA

The future enters into us, in order to transform itself in us, long before it happens.

Rainer Maria Rilke

# CHAPTER 43

The Institute for Intelligence and Special Operations, or the Ha Mossad, le Modiyn ve le Tafkidim Mayuhadim, does not officially exist in Israel, or anywhere else. Yet, there are few people in any civilized nation who do not know that the Mossad is the best secret service organization in the world. Espionage, antiterrorist activities, clandestine operations, intelligence gathering and a great deal else fall within the province of its expertise. It is an expertise for a less than perfect world.

Occasionally, an Entebbe happens . . . an incident in which highly skilled antiterrorists must pull off an impossible rescue. Sometimes, a Klaus Barbie must be found and brought to justice. Sometimes, an Iraqi nuclear plant is mysteriously sabotaged, or the plans for a Mirage bomber are lifted out from under the nose of a government. At such times, the word Mossad always surfaces. *"By way of deception, thou shalt do war,"* is said to be its motto. To kill only those with blood on their hands, is said to be its credo. All that is really known for certain, is the elitist quality of its workmanship.

In September of 1951, Prime Minister David Ben-Gurion allowed the creation of the Mossad as an intelligence agency that would always remain in shadow. There are no references to it to be found in Israeli budgets, and the name of its head has never been exposed to the public. Yet no one doubts its existence or its efficiency.

Raphael Abraham was one of only thirty to thirty-five case officers, or *katsas*, operating worldwide. When the head of Tsometʹ, the Mossad's recruiting department, had met the young Zionist, in 1961, he had been struck by certain characteristics in him, that he felt had unusual potential. Abraham was of large and sturdy construction, and there was a certain bull-like quality to his physicality, that was echoed in his psyche. He stood his ground implacably, no matter what the stress level he was subjected to; in fact, the greater the stress, the more stalwart he became. And, he was very smart; in academics and in life, he had been blessed with unusual and astute intelligence.

Abraham had a gift for language and a photographic memory for details. Whether it be maps, charts, columns of figures, or the nuances of discussion—he was capable of stockpiling any information he contacted, like a computer. But more useful than this mechanistic gift was his ability to sort the wheat from the chaff. Even as a young recruit, he'd had singular common sense.

Abraham considered himself a soldier, no more, no less. He considered himself a very good soldier. He was not alone in this judgment.

He found this newest operation he had been given, a puzzlement. The head of his section, Uzi Eisenberg, was no man's fool, and he had made it clear to Abraham that he intuited more to this Amulet business than met the eye. In fact, an astonishing conversation had taken place with him during the briefing. Abraham replayed the dialogue in his head, word for word:

"This Isis Amulet, Rafi," Eisenberg had said musingly, "what a fascinating notion, that a *thing* could embody the power of Good or Evil. And, how ironic that the legend places this wonder in the hands of a child, and a gentile girl child, at that. God must surely have a sense of humor." He was far too much of a pragmatist to believe in magic, of course, but it was apparent the story intrigued him.

"We must find out what part the woman plays in all this," he'd said. "Is she acting for any of the other interested parties, or is she an innocent?"

"No one is innocent," Abraham had responded definitively.

"From a philosophical standpoint you are right, of course, but in a practical sense, she may be merely a pawn in someone else's game . . . or she may be playing a game of her own.

"Look, Rafi, I'll be honest with you. When the Prime Minister handed me this mission, I laughed out loud. *Goyisha bullshit!* I told him. *Boubameisa.* Magical Amulets, magical children . . ." He shrugged eloquently.

"Then I read the legend in the dossier, and realized the PR value for the Egyptians, if they could allege to have such a creature and her Amulet on tap. Besides which, we need to know the whole thing isn't just camouflage for something else. So . . . you must find me the truth. And the child. And her Amulet, should there be one. The Prime Minister thinks Tel Aviv would be a better place for it than Cairo."

"What do we know so far?" Abraham had asked, tapping the barely skimmed dossier he'd been handed.

"A lot of hearsay, garbage, legend, innuendo," Eisenberg had replied. "A woman, not bad-looking . . . a three-year-old, currently in Greenwich . . . a lot of money and power. And maybe some gun running and drugs."

"And this Vannier?" he'd asked, flipping through the papers on his lap. "And, Sayles?"

"Both up to their high-profile balls in armaments and heroin. All Cossacks have the same face, Rafi—but as yet, we don't know how all these faces tie together."

They had spoken for the better part of an hour about the intended investigation before the *katsa* rose to leave.

"So, Uzi, I ask you man to man," Abraham had asked as he neared the door. "Do you believe in this Isis Amulet and its mystical powers? Stones that work miracles? Amulets to rule the world?"

"You ask me if I believe in miracles, Rafi?" he'd responded. "I believe in leaving no stone unturned." Both men had chuckled a little, and Eisenberg had added, "Is not all Judaism built on miracles? Moses and the Red Sea . . . the Tablets on Mount Sinai . . . the burning bush. Tell me, Rafi, are there no mystics in your family to make you a believer?"

Rafi had smiled at that, memory surfacing. "My Uncle Schlomo was an impoverished rabbi, Uzi . . . he was also a great scholar and expert on Kabbalah. But he married my Aunt Sarah, the meanest woman ever to draw breath in Israel. I figure if he really knew anything about magic he would have been rich and had a different wife."

Eisenberg had laughed aloud.

"We won't argue this point, my friend," he'd replied easily. "You know what they say—the only thing two Jews can agree on, is how much a third Jew should give to charity."

They had walked toward the door. "Whatever our personal opinions on this subject," Eisenberg had said, as he turned the knob, "our Egyptian friends must not be the ones to retrieve this Amulet. We do not need an Arab government possessing a talisman that people believe has power to rule the world. Psychology is power, too."

"Rule the world?" Rafi had replied with a derisive snort. "They couldn't even hold on to the Sinai."

It had been a good curtain line, but it didn't mean Raphael Abraham would get cocky. Eisenberg hadn't become head of a section of the Mossad because he was stupid.

That was where it had begun a week ago, for him. So, Abraham had set a team to watch and wait. In his work, the ability to do these two tasks well and patiently was the key to all success. His was a job of painstaking attention to details of the kind that drove others to boredom, or insanity; to Abraham it was an endlessly interesting game. Had he been given the Gordian knot to unravel, he would have settled in to do so, with relish and enjoyment.

By now the dossier he'd been given had grown geometrically. He now knew a great deal about Eric Vannier and Nicholas Sayles. The Mossad, like MI5 and the CIA, had used the Vannier Foundation and their banking network for various undercover operations over the years since its establishment. Abraham no longer made moral judgments about the existence of such organizations; they were useful, or they were not. That was all that concerned him and his work. The Black Magic aspects of the two men's backgrounds had been flagged in their files, long ago, but it hadn't interested Mossad overmuch until now. Every man had an Achilles' heel by Abraham's reckoning; some were womanizers, some were homosexuals, some gambled, some drank, some liked to cause pain—all had a secret that could be used to the Mossad's advantage. So, these two liked to dress up like children and call upon long-dead Gods for assistance that would never come. It was interesting information for a dossier, but up until now had little real use to the Mossad. *Now*, he would rethink its possibilities.

Then, there was the Egyptian, Hazred. Another man with a secret. Abraham pulled out the Hazred dossier from the pile, and studied the arrogant, pharaonic face. The sneer of power, the hooded eyes of an aristocracy that never saw farther than the nose on its face . . . such a face as this must Rameses have had, when he tortured the Israelites, and built his pyramids over their broken bodies.

An interesting case, this Abdul Hazred. Rich, brilliant . . . a doctorate at nineteen. The life of a gentleman scholar, until now. Do not underestimate this one, Rafi, he told himself. Behind that face is intellect and cunning; this is a man with a purpose.

He opened the final folder. Inside, were pictures of Maggie, Jenna, and Cody. He stared a long while at the cherubic face of the child on everybody's wish list. She had spirited gray eyes . . . unusual eyes; steady and unchildlike. But beyond that, she looked like any other three-year-old. Chubby-cheeked, with long shining blond hair, caught in twin pony tails. He sighed. His own Leah had looked much like this when she was three, but that had been long ago. She had children of her own now.

Abraham frowned at the picture of Jenna. Such a perfect gentile face and body. Flaxen-haired, blue-eyed, coltish. But what was under the surface was another story. Any woman who would put her own child in danger . . . what difference what she looked like? She was beneath contempt.

He held Maggie's picture in his hand, studying it carefully. There was strength in this face, and womanliness. It bespoke character, of the kind that doesn't give up easily. What would the owner of such a face do to save a beloved child, he wondered? *Something.* Something unexpected, perhaps. The owner of this face would bear watching.

Raphael Abraham put the folders back in the locked cabinet, and left the room.

# CHAPTER 44

Cody looked furtively to right and left; no one was watching. She snatched the three oatmeal cookies from the supper tray, along with the lone apple, and tucked them surreptitiously into her backpack, under the table.

She looked speculatively at the milk, but she could think of no way to transport it without the glass—and that would be missed by the cook or Ghania. So, with a sigh, she drank it herself. Tonight she would try to help the Screamers.

The idea made her afraid, but something inside her was insistent that she try. The plan had been growing and growing within her. The Screamers had been everywhere in her mind, since Ghania had dragged her to the cellar. She saw their faces, heard their sobs, *felt* their hurts . . . She had collapsed, after that awful night, lying in her bed, crying, terrified, trying to forget. Then the face of one of them had drifted back to her, its eyes bright with fever, its hurt so clear, in the clenched mouth and sunken cheeks . . . and suddenly she had remembered her *gift*. Hurt things, sick things—she could make them well again! Maybe if the Screamers felt better, they could run away. And Ghania would not be able to make them scream anymore.

What would Ghania do to her, she wondered, if she caught her? Cody didn't think the Amah would kill her. She'd heard Ghania and the Daddy-man talking about something called the Ceremony. "No harm must come to her before the Ceremony," he had said. And Ghania had replied, "There are only three weeks left." Cody thought that meant they wouldn't make her a Screamer, yet. She wasn't exactly sure how long three weeks would take, but maybe if she helped the Screamers get away, they would help her, too. Maybe they would even take her back to Mim.

The maid took the tray without a word, and Cody waited holding her breath, until the girl had left. Then she transferred her new acquisitions to the small hoard of similar items, under her clothes in the dresser drawer.

Everyone was sleeping, Cody could hear the silence all around her. Not that she was watched closely at night. Ghania's rooms were down the hall, and far past them, the other servants had quarters, but no one expected a small child to go prowling after dark, so no one watched her very carefully.

The house was so still and dark, Cody almost changed her mind, but the fruit she had collected for three days was starting to smell funny, so she knew she'd have to make her move tonight.

She eased the nursery door open and peeked into the hallway. She wasn't afraid of the dark, and had no great trouble seeing in the dim light. She put her small burden of food in her knapsack and zipped it softly, then took the trouble-light from the wall outlet near the door; the one that stayed lit, even when unplugged . . . it wouldn't do to bang into things and make a noise.

Soundlessly, the child crept to the stairs, and holding the banister, carefully made her way to the floor below. No one was around. She sped to the kitchen, and saw with dismay that the bolt on the basement door was too high up to reach. Cody pulled the step stool over to the door, slowly and fearfully, trying not to make a sound, then with trepidation, she let herself into the staircase.

The dark basement was disorienting; there was only a dim yellow light burning somewhere ahead. Cody stood very still at the bottom of the stairs to make sure no one was watching. The soft moans of the Screamers told her which way to go. Her hands had begun to tingle, the funny way they always did in the presence of hurt or sick things. She could feel the fiery energy filling up her fingers and arms, in an almost-ache.

She stopped at the edge of the cages to gather courage, then crept forward on tiptoe.

"Hello, mister," she said softly to the occupant of the first cage, but he didn't answer her. He was very, very sick; she could tell by the increased tingling in her hands. She reached into the cage and touched the man's mangled right arm; it lay useless and crooked on the floor of the cage beside him, swollen and hideously discolored. The other arm was strapped to the blood bottle tube. Cody felt the transfer of energy begin the instant she touched him; like a torrent of water through a drain-pipe, the flood always started when she touched the sick or the hurt ones. She waited patiently for the flood to abate.

The man opened his eyes and stared in disbelief at the small child's face, then at the tiny hand that was pulsating "something" into his arm.

"How did you get here?" he whispered, his voice barely human. "The witch'll kill you if she finds you."

The *witch!* So *that's* what she was. Of course. Cody hadn't even thought of that because Ghania didn't have a witch's outfit on. But witches were the only ones who did horrible things, like put people in cages . . . just like in Hansel and Gretel.

"Her name is Ghania," she whispered back. "I brought you a cookie." The improbability of the whole scene made the man laugh dementedly; he began to cough and choke.

"Shh!" Cody admonished with real fear; she pulled the cookie from her knapsack and pushed it toward him. "I don't want Ghania to come or she'll hurt me. I have an apple, and an orange, and a banana. We could give them to your friends."

Others had awakened and were murmuring.

"Quiet!" the first man reprimanded sharply. "The kid's here on her own. The witch'll kill her if we make any noise."

Cody started to hand out the food she'd hoarded, but she could see it wasn't nearly enough. Some people couldn't move their arms to take the food, so she had to break off a piece of cookie and try to reach their mouths through the bars, but it was hard to do.

"Hey, kid!" the first man whispered. "What was that thing you did with your hand? My arm feels better . . . I haven't been able to move my fingers since they broke it. What'd you do?"

"I can fix hurt things," Cody whispered, not knowing how to explain the gift.

Murmurs of "help me, help . . ." rose all around her,

dizzyingly. The small child moved from cage to cage, letting the energy run through her to the desperate ones. She could feel it come into her body through the top of her head and the soles of her feet, then flow out through her hands. She did it for a long time, until she began to feel woozy and drained.

"Can you get us out of here? Can you get the key?" they asked, over and over.

"I don't have any keys," she said sadly, wondering if she had the strength even to get back upstairs. "I'm really sorry but I have to go now. I'll try to come back again."

She backed away from the cages wearily, and turned toward the stairs.

"God bless you, kid," the first man called after her softly. "God bless you," they all said, over and over. She wished they'd be quiet, so Ghania wouldn't find out.

She made her way stealthily up the stairs, grateful to be going back to bed.

At the top of the cellar stairs, Ghania was waiting.

"So you don't fear the night, my little one?" the Amah said in a syrupy voice that was sinister in its sweetness. "We shall see."

Cody's stomach lurched violently, as she felt Ghania's iron grip close on her arm; she almost vomited with terror. She barely felt the stone stairs abrade her body, as she was dragged back down to the cellar, past the Screamers. She heard them curse at Ghania, but it only made the Amah laugh.

"You will not move from this spot!" Ghania commanded when she reached the far side of the room; and nothing in her voice was syrup now. "I will show you what happens to little girls who defy me."

Ghania reached inside a small animal cage and yanked out a large white rabbit. Its pink nose and ears quivered, and Cody would have reached for its softness, if she hadn't been so scared.

She watched Ghania strap the pretty bunny upside down on a metal table. The creature fluttered its legs in a futile protest and tried desperately to right itself.

The knife that glinted in Ghania's hand had been secreted inside her dress, and seemed to appear by magic. It looked very old and had jewels on the hilt.

"Because of your disobedience, this rabbit will die in agony," she said, her eyes glittering like the knife blade. "You have killed this poor little thing, you bad, *bad* child; you have made him suffer *pain.*" She slit the animal's belly from neck to crotch and blood spurted up and out in every direction.

The rabbit squealed, an ungodly anguished scream, and nearly tore its own legs off straining against the leather straps that held it. Cody screamed, too; her little hands flew up to her own mouth to cover the scream but it got through anyway.

"You are responsible for this animal's suffering, bad, *bad* child!" the Amah intoned brutally. "So you must taste its blood!"

She cupped her hand in the steaming red liquid that poured from the dying rabbit's belly and smeared it over Cody's mouth and face. The child fought like a caged beast, twisting her head away, but Ghania held her fast.

"Now, you must pull out the worms in its belly for your punishment," the witch demanded, pushing Cody's face so close to the still pulsing intestines, she could see them moving.

Ghania forced the child's hand deep into the steaming aperture. Bloody gray things slithered all around her fingers, as she tried to pull her hand free of Ghania's brutal grip.

Screaming, vomiting, fighting, falling backward, back, back, *down, down into icy darkness*. Dying. *I'm dying*, she thought. *It's my fault the bunny died*. Now, I have to die too. Mim! *Help me!*

That was when she saw the strange white Light for the very first time.

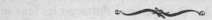

GHANIA sat next to Cody's bed, stroking the feverish little forehead and crooning softly as she rocked. "Little one was bad," she murmured over and over, "and she made the rabbit die. But Ghania understands . . . Ghania is her friend."

Cody lay still as death, very sick and very, very afraid. Ghania was *not* her friend. Ghania was a witch. Ghania killed things and hurt things and made things bleed. But, maybe no one else was her friend, either. No one ever came to help her, no matter how hard she prayed . . . no matter how hard she cried and begged. Maybe nobody else cared anymore, and Ghania was all there would ever be.

*No.* That wasn't true! Mim would care if they made Cody a Screamer. Mim would do *something.* But why didn't she come, ever . . . why didn't she call on the telephone? . . . Cody had tried to call Mim one day, but the operator said she didn't know how to find anybody named Mim.

The child lay very still with terrible, warring thoughts and hideous fears raging through her. She would try to hide out, here in the darkness inside her head, for a while.

At least she wouldn't have to look at Ghania's face.

She would scrunch her eyes shut and lie very still, and think about the Light. There had been comfort in the Light, and courage. And it let her get away from this hateful place. Cody went inward, and Ghania, knowing where she'd gone, smiled.

# CHAPTER 45

Devlin tapped the notebook he held in his hand, absent-mindedly, with a pen. There were the beginnings of patterns here . . . but the implications of the patterns were too big to be plausible.

The names Cheri had given them were a revelation—a senator, the lead singer of a famous rock group, the executive vice president of a TV network, a Superior Court judge, and a big-time fashion designer—and all beginning to show linkages that stretched the limits of simple probability. The more he dug, the more their tendrils intersected. Very interesting.

There was far too much intersecting for coincidence, and on too large a scale. Devlin had divided Cheri's list of names with Garibaldi. If Gino's group of well-knowns showed even a fraction of the coincidences in the notebook he held in his hands, they were on to something big.

Too big, in fact, for the Sixth Precinct detective squad to handle, unless some very specific local tie-in should emerge. And far too rife with important names for the Captain to want to get mixed up in such potential problems. Big names had big lawyers who made their living keeping their clients free from the kinds of taint he was speculating on.

Speculation. *Damnit!* That was the problem. This was all still speculation and April 30th was just around the corner.

Devlin snapped the notebook shut and forced himself to pay attention to the other work on his desk. This Maggie thing was still unofficial, and he had his regular job to do. He'd have to keep this all in perspective

. . . *"Shit!"* he said aloud. "Who do you think you're kidding, Devlin?"

He pushed the other papers on his desk away with an emphatic shove, picked up the notebook with the Maggie notes in it, and left his office in search of Garibaldi.

"What I got, Lieutenant, is a snitch who says he knows where they get the tattoos," Garibaldi said with a grin. "Place on Christopher. The guy's a real *'artiste,'* says my snitch. Specializes in the weird and unusual. You want a peacock tattooed on your pecker, this guy's your man."

Devlin winced. "Don't even say it out loud."

"Yeah, well, it may not ring your bells, but evidently this guy's handiwork is world-renowned in the biker and S&M set. The snitch says he'd be the one Maa Kheru would go to. Wanna see what he has to say for himself?"

Devlin nodded affirmatively. "What've we got to squeeze him with?"

"A couple of old drug busts and some larceny. Typical penny-ante stuff. Nothing major. Nothing recent. Except maybe one thing. It seems he's a closet herbalist. He stocks all kinds of eye-of-newt stuff and prescribes it to his clients—with a few psychedelic mushrooms and other hallucinogenics thrown in. And maybe a little blow on occasion, for special customers."

The tattoo parlor was semi-clean and seedy. The tiny waiting area was littered with magazines with titles like *Wet Teenagers* and *Pussy Galore.*

"This guy could use some *National Geographics,"* Garibaldi observed, leafing through the pile. "Here's a great title, *Love with Little Boys."* He laid it down, like it smelled of week-old fish.

Devlin parted the curtain that partitioned off the inner room. A nearly nude man reclined in a barber chair. Two thirds of his massive body was covered by tattoos of an unimaginable intricacy.

"We'll have to take a break for today, Rudi," the

pencil-thin man, who was holding the tattoo needle, said without looking up at the visitors. He finished the claw of a gorgonlike creature that adorned the man's left thigh, with meticulous precision. Then, he put down the needle and stood up. Rudi beat a hasty retreat.

"Police, I take it?" he said, before they'd identified themselves. "I'm Jake. I don't want any trouble. What do you want?"

"Is this a design of yours?" Devlin asked, handing him Cheri's drawing. The tattoo artist barely glanced at it.

"If I could see the tattoo itself I might remember—I can recognize my own work, after all. But this? Do you know how many tattoos I do in a year, Lieutenant?" He shrugged his bony shoulders dismissively.

"Do you *know* how many jerks I put in the slammer every year because they give me a lot of crap?" Garibaldi said, moving in close. "Let's just see what we got right here in this little emporium of yours. We got dispensing medicine without a license, we got kiddy-porn magazines, we got sanitary code violations, we got suspicion of drug possession—"

"Wait just a goddamn minute!" Jake sputtered. "I got no drugs here. What do you guys want from me?"

"We want to know what you know about this tattoo," Devlin said quietly. His quiet sounded more dangerous than Garibaldi's threats.

"It's part of an ancient symbol," Jake said quickly. "It has to do with eternal life, and the ability to manipulate matter. You know, like magic. There are word glyphs that go with it. The words are in Enochion, a magical language from the Middle Ages. I don't know what they mean."

"So, who gets this tattoo?"

"Different people. Not my regular customers . . ." He seemed about to say more, but didn't.

"If they're not your regulars, who are they?" Devlin pressed. "Do they just walk in off the street? What do they look like? Do they pay with credit cards?"

"Look," Jake said agitatedly. "I don't want any trouble here, understand? All I know is, they send a limo for me, and it takes me somewhere. I don't know where."

"Why not?"

"Because they put this blindfold thing—like a black hood—over my head, till we get there. All's I know is, it's a big house, kinda spooky, in the country, near the water. They take me to a room. I do whoever they want, sometimes one, sometimes half a dozen. They pay cash, twice my regular fee, and then they drop me off again."

"And you never asked who they are, or why they do it that way?" Devlin pressed skeptically.

"Why should I want to know what they're into? Look, there's a lot goes on in this world, you don't need to know. Right? Like, I got this dominatrix broad, uptown, who sends all her johns to me. You wouldn't want to know what she wants tattooed where, on those guys. And there's cults, and clubs, and bikers, and who knows what . . . like, in this line of work you don't usually get to practice on the mayor and the City Council, you know what I mean?"

Devlin and Garibaldi exchanged looks.

"Why do they come to you?"

"Hey, fellas! Like Michelangelo was to ceilings, Jake is to the human torso. You wanna see my portfolio?"

"Are any of these symbols in there?"

Jake shook his head. "They wouldn't let me bring my camera. I asked. It's intricate work doing all that ancient lettering."

"Okay," Garibaldi said, handing him a calling card. "You get another request from the guys with the limo, you call me at this number. Got it?"

"Why should I? I haven't committed any crime! I wouldn't want to lose their business . . . these guys are good customers."

Devlin's eyebrows rose inquisitively. "How good? How many of these things do you do a year?"

"Maybe a hundred or more of the regular ones, and another twenty-five of the specials."

"What do you mean specials?"

"The ones with the Tree of Life imposed on the Ankh."

"What does that mean, do you know?"

Jake shrugged. "I don't know what it means, but the ones who get it seem real proud of themselves. And they're always the ones who look rich and relaxed. You know, like they run the show."

"And the other hundred—what do they look like?"

Jake's rodentlike face wrinkled in concentration. "Ordinary, I'd say. Like you and me."

Devlin smiled inwardly at Garibaldi's look of distaste at the suggestion that he bore any resemblance to Jake.

"Listen," Devlin said, with authority. "You call me, when they call you, and I'll make it worth your while."

"How?"

"I'll stay up nights thinking of ways to keep you out of jail," Devlin said. "Trust me." He smiled as he said it.

"Tell me we don't look like that little rat-faced fucker," Garibaldi said as they hit the street.

"That little rat-faced fucker could identify every member of Maa Kheru if he got squeezed hard enough."

"He'd have to live long enough, first, Lieutenant. They'll stick his tattoo needle where the sun don't shine, if they find out we're on his case."

# CHAPTER 46

James and Peter walked beneath the canopy of budding trees that flanked the river. Peter's hands were plunged deep in his overcoat pockets, his shoulders hunched against the early spring wind, and against the adversity that buffeted him. The walk afforded privacy. And he needed that. He needed James's council badly; his clarity and good-heartedness. He was beginning to feel shredded by the what-ifs of his relationship with Maggie, and the what-ifs of his priesthood. There was nowhere else to turn.

"All my life, James," he said with great seriousness, "I've been possessed by a desperate need to know God. A kind of Augustinian restlessness . . ."

" 'Our hearts are restless until they rest in thee, O Lord,' " the large man quoted, his eyes merry. "I'd call that an excellent credential for your chosen field of endeavor."

Peter smiled wanly. "You know my history, James. You've always understood the complexity of my dilemma. I'd seen Christ outside the Church as well as in. I'd seen Him in the laboring laity, and in Eastern mystics, in the exquisite mind-numbing beauty of the world! And there I was head to head with Christ's Church—surely, we could not both be right.

"But I couldn't *know*, for certain, could I, James? Because there's a Christ within a Christ within a Christ, and He's a goddamn onion of a Christ! And which part of the onion owns me? And why are the layers never in sync? Was I losing my faith, or making a greater act of faith than any I had ever known?" Peter shook his head, the momentum of remembered passions, momentarily obscuring the present dilemma.

"But now I find myself in an entirely new crisis of faith . . . and I'm struggling to square it with all I've been forced to learn."

"And this Maggie of yours . . . is she the crisis?" James prompted.

Peter nodded, avoiding the other priest's eyes. "You know, if I'm honest with myself, she touched me, even years ago, when first we met. For years after that weekend at Fordham, I remembered her exuberance and her goodness . . . she was the only clear, true wind-bell, I think.

"But now . . . she's taken on other dimensions for me, James, that I keep trying to quantify. She's smart, and she's real. I admire her courage. She's been tempered by life and has come burnished from the flames. I suppose I could come up with half a hundred reasons to parade before you, and none of them would have anything to do with how I *feel*." He shrugged, unable to explain. "In some inexplicable way, I believe she and I are comrades on our spiritual journey, but I can conceive no way for that to be other than rationalization on my part."

"I, too, am aware of the spirit-link between you, Peter; it is apparent in everything you tell me of her," James said, surprising Peter with his acquiescence. "In my country, civilization is but a thin veneer—the inner grain is primitive, visceral. There are magnetic attractions sometimes . . . hard to understand, harder to escape." There was no judgment in his words, just observation.

"She makes me long for things I've never truly missed before, James," Peter rushed on, confused. "The human pleasures that eluded me . . . touch, love, family, all the mundane blessings I chose to renounce without ever understanding their enormity. All I have willingly denied myself, I now long for. And I need to know why this should be so, as much as I need to know how to deal with the longing."

"Perhaps, she makes you human, Peter. Perhaps she brings the body into balance, where only the mind has held sway for a lifetime. One cannot really offer to God that which is unimportant to him, and consider it a worthy sacrifice. Perhaps, God has chosen to show you the value of your gift to Him, before asking you one last time if you choose to give it."

Peter, troubled, pondered what James had said, before speaking again. "I've lost my way . . . somehow. I find myself with desires and regrets . . . questioning everything . . . unable, or unwilling, to pull away from that which threatens me." He shrugged helplessly.

"I fear I'm seduced by my own humanity as much as by my feelings for Maggie. I'm not a boy to be led astray by hormones, James. I'm too old to be seduced merely by the expectation of mad raptures.

"It seems to me that in loving her, in striving to save Cody, I'm not turning from God, but toward him. I see my feelings for her, not as a descent into the carnal and material mire, but as the blithest expression of all that is best in God's creation. Oh James, *James,* I'm on dangerous ground here! When a man begins to think of potential sin as the expression of a paean to God, he's in very treacherous waters."

"But you're right in thinking love the best expression of God on earth, Peter. You must remember, however, that the test lies in how you navigate these waters, not in your mistaking the magnitude of the tide. And, when all is said and done, my friend, who among us is so firm he cannot be seduced?"

"Was I wrong in my battles with the Church, James? Was I deceived by the Adversary and my own pride? Am I deceived *now* in my perceptions of my place in the scheme of Maggie's dilemma? I keep remembering, the Devil himself can quote Scripture for his own purpose.

*"Am I not to be permitted one single sin of the flesh?* I ask myself that in the darkness." Peter confessed desperately. "Can I not sin like any other man and be forgiven? Am I never to know love—even for one infinitesimal moment—and if I do not, can I then truly love God? Are there some things you can learn *only* by risking sin?" The anguish in Peter's voice seemed to hover on the air between the two men for several moments.

"Only you can answer that question, Peter," James replied slowly, knowing full well the truth. "Some men eat apples with impunity . . . for Adam, a heavy price was exacted. And, perhaps, my friend, you must be careful to avoid Augustine's prayer, 'O Lord, give me chastity and continency, but not just now.' "

Peter stared at James for a long instant, then turned

away and let his gaze drift past the slate-gray river, toward infinity.

"Will you meet her, James?" he asked, without turning around.

"I would like that very much, Peter. Very much, indeed."

# CHAPTER 47

"Let me try this one out on you, Gino," Devlin said, putting his heels on the desk in a weary, contemplative posture. He was tired, but alert. Garibaldi had seen the look often enough to know it meant he had something on his mind that needed a sounding board.

"What if this Maa Kheru business is *not* just a local bunch of jerks, playing dress-up in Halloween costumes? What if we're dealing with an international cartel of some kind, that's using Vannier's banking network, and Sayles's media clout and armament connections, and the power of many other really prominent people, to run a scam so big, nobody would be willing to believe it's out there."

"Like BCCI?"

"Exactly like BCCI. What are the two hottest tickets in the contraband world?"

"Armaments and drugs."

"And we know Sayles's family is munitions dealer to the world . . . and it's beginning to look like Vannier's foundation is hip-deep in drug laundry. So, let's take a look at how it all might work." He pushed back his chair and took his feet off the desk.

"Dictators and drug lords need someplace to stash

the loot and someplace to launder it," Garibaldi offered. Devlin nodded, crossing his arms in front of his chest.

"And governments need someplace to keep sub rosa funds for black ops . . . you can't fund an Iran-contra deal out in the open, or topple some banana republic with overt taxpayer money—so maybe you go to a guy like Vannier, and you let him do the paperwork."

Garibaldi nodded, adding pieces to the puzzle. "And then those same governments, who need you for their own black ops, cover for you—so when anyone comes snooping too close, you just call in your CIA or MI5 buddies, and you let them take the heat off."

Devlin took up the recital. "And, meanwhile, you travel in very posh circles. The circles of corporate CEOs and rock stars, of Wall Street titans and megamillionaires. Big pocketbooks, big egos, big dreams of ruling the world . . .

"And what if, within the ranks of this very privileged enclave, there is a private and very elitist corps of heavy-hitters who have this quasi-religious nuttiness they subscribe to, where they've sold their souls to Satan, in order to achieve their goals."

Garibaldi shrugged. "Not so impossible to believe, Lieutenant . . . let's face it, anybody laundering Noriega's and Hussein's money has sold his soul to the Devil, whether he calls it that or not. So what's a little ceremony, and some nice Halloween outfits, if it puts you in the inner sanctum of the guys who are really pulling the world's strings?"

"And, *what if* there's the added attraction of sex and violence and blood and guts and high drama—and what if it all seems to *work*." Devlin pressed the point. "The money and the power increase, the women and drugs are there for the taking, and all you've betrayed to get this dream come true is something you probably didn't put much stock in anyway . . . like your soul."

"Holy shit, Malachy," Garibaldi said grimly. "You make this actually sound plausible."

"Right," Devlin said, with a rueful grunt. "Now all we have to do is prove it."

Devlin picked up the phone and dialed a number he reserved for special cases. Harry Fisk was a good guy, despite being in the Bureau. He and Harry went back a while, to better and worse times, but he wasn't a friend Devlin ever called in without good reason.

"Harry," he said, when he'd gotten through the various baffles. "I need the lowdown on a couple of high-powered slimes, who may or may not be protected by your guys."

Momentary silence greeted the statement, then, "I'm loose for lunch around 12:30. Does that place you used to take me to still make the best cheeseburgers in Manhattan?"

"Four stars in *Michelin*'s," Devlin replied, smiling to himself. Feds tended to be cautious on telephones; it was a good habit to get into. If you'd been a detective a long while, you'd crossed paths with the FBI enough for there to be a cautious exchange of information. The Bureau had computers that the cops did not; sometimes that alone saved a helluva lot of unnecessary legwork. And sometimes the Feds knew things that were not supposed to be known by local law enforcement. That, too, was a big time-saver. But Harry Fisk didn't fall into such a category. He was a friend.

Devlin glanced at the clock, and saw there'd be just enough time to get to McGovern's Bar and Grill.

Harry Fisk was a large man with thick wavy hair, the color of Phil Donahue's. Tall, muscular, and far more dangerous than he looked, Devlin knew; recruited after Vietnam, Harry'd brought a number of special skills to his job at the Bureau. And he was considerably smarter and cannier than a lot of the boys who'd come to the Bureau from the straight-out-of-college recruitment cookie cutter.

"So what do you need, Malachy?" Fisk asked after

a few preliminaries had been spoken. "And who do you think is protecting whoever you're after, from what?" He had the amused jadedness of a man who has seen most human foibles up close.

"That reminds me of an old Belfast song, Harry," Devlin said. " 'Whatever you say, say nothing, if you talk about you know what . . . for if you know who should hear you, you know what you'll get.' " Harry laughed.

"Eric Vannier and Nicholas Sayles ring any bells?" Devlin asked quietly, even though there was no one in earshot.

"A carillonful. Why are we listening for these particular ding-dongs?"

Devlin told him judiciously edited pieces of information. Professionals made judgments based on who was asking, not on the details of why. And Harry Fisk was the ultimate professional. He shook his head as he listened.

"A laundromat for dirty linens," he said finally. "If black ops uses them to any degree, they'll be beyond your reach, Malachy. A lot of pretty seedy things go down, worldwide, that have to be financed from somewhere. The way it usually works is this: Somebody rich and ugly owns a bank, whose assets are guaranteed by somebody even richer. Usually the bank gets incorporated in Luxembourg, and then opens a main branch someplace where nobody enforces rules much. Say Abu Dhabi or Karachi or Nigeria. Then the word goes out to dictators like Noriega and Marcos, and to the drug cartels like the Medellíns and to assorted groups like the PLO, and to hotbeds like Libya and Iraq, that not too many questions will be asked about how they came by their money, or where they wish to spend it.

"Next page in the banking manual, the word goes out to the CIA, MI5, the Mossad—and any other government agency with black ops potential—that the utmost secrecy will be maintained, that worldwide connections can be made, and that no regulatory agencies ever need apply."

"It's easy enough to see how the money rolls in, Harry," Malachy said, "but exactly how is it disseminated, and how come nobody in legitimate banking seems to know what's going on?"

Harry smiled a little. "Very Harvard Business School, Malachy—you diversify. You buy a big, fat shipping company here, and a fleet of planes there, and a chain of hotels somewhere else. You open up a branch in the Caymans, where anything goes, and you give a piss-pot full of money to legitimate charities—preferably those whose advocates have a lot of clout in government and banking circles. You purchase subsidiaries, even legitimate banks in several countries, so if anyone asks, you've got Clark Clifford on your board of directors.

"Last, but by no means least, you create your own black ops force, to deal with anybody who has second thoughts. You hire mercs—you call them bankers, but you train them for arms deals, bribery, espionage, extortion, drug trafficking, and interrogation.

"I'm not saying this is how *your* two boys are operating, Malachy, but given the givens . . . I'd say, there's a good chance I'm not far off. I'll see what I can find out for you, my friend, but if what you're doing is really unofficial, you could get your ass hung out to dry, if you piss off the wrong evil-doers. And let me tell you straight, you'll never bring them down. Not in seven million fucking years. You'll be like the flea on the ass of an elephant—the insignificant dead."

"It's good to know you're optimistic," Devlin answered with a crooked grin.

"You want me to look, I'll look."

Devlin nodded. "I don't need to topple the evil empire, here, Harry. I just need to dig up enough dirt to get the department involved, so I can give the bad guys enough *agita* to make them let go of one little kid."

Harry Fisk shrugged. "Even in Nam, Malachy . . . you've always been a pushover where kids are concerned."

"Ever know a cop who wasn't, Harry?" Devlin asked. "Guys like you and me see a lot of shit go down . . . and there's got to be someplace where we see the angels win."

The longtime FBI agent smiled sardonically. "It's always good to see a man of like mind, Malachy. I'll get back to you before the end of the week."

THE phone rang at Devlin's apartment; the clock said 11:30. He'd fallen asleep on the couch, reading a book.

"Malachy? Harry," the voice said. "Watch your back, kid. This may be bigger than I thought."

"What've you got, Harry?" Devlin was wide awake now.

"I don't know yet, but it looks like the Israelis are in on it, and maybe the Egyptians. There've been discreet inquiries inside and outside of channels. What's going down here, Malachy? Is this kid the illegitimate heir to the Kaliph of Baghdad, or something?"

"Or something," Malachy replied cryptically, and Fisk didn't press for answers.

"You'll hear from me when I know more." Then a dial tone.

The Mossad, and Mohabarat, yet. It made sense, of course. The Egyptians would know about the prophecy, and the Israelis would know about anything the Egyptians knew about. *Shit!* Devlin thought eloquently. These other players could only complicate his life.

He went to bed weighing whether it was getting to be time to rattle some chains. And if so, whose?

# CHAPTER 48

The doorbell's persistent ring dragged Maggie up from her basement. She was tired, and her sweats were soaked, but an hour of practicing kicks and kata had cleared her head and focused her intent. With April 30th looming nearer, and no sign of help from the authorities, Mr. Wong's teachings were beginning to look more practical than everybody else's combined.

Devlin was standing on the outside top step, waiting. For some reason, he always looked younger to her than she remembered.

"Oh, Lord," she said, breathless from the workout and the run up the stairs. "I look like nine miles of bad road. Was I expecting you?" She wiped the sweat from her face in a practiced gesture, and held the door open for him. Devlin thought she looked sexier than he'd ever seen her.

"No, you weren't," he said affably. "But I decided to use some of the information I'd unearthed as an excuse to see you. You've been on my mind."

"Hard to believe, considering the way I look at the moment," she said, wrinkling her nose. "Unless, of course, you're turned on by sweat, like all those men in the sneaker commercials."

"That all depends on who's sweating and under what circumstances," he answered with a grin.

"What's the news you found?"

"It's about Maa Kheru. There may be an expert out there . . . several people have remembered a reporter who made a career of following the thread of the supposed cartel for years. They say he was always trying

299

to interest legitimate newspapers and magazines in all the data he'd collected on those bozos, but nobody would ever chance running his stories, because they libeled so many prominent men and women. Seems he dropped out of sight a while back, and nobody's seen him for several years."

"Eric probably fed him to the rottweilers," Maggie said with a wry smile. "Do you think you can find out what the man knows?"

"First I have to find out who and where he is . . . then I can try," Dev said. "I can also take you out to dinner if you don't fight back too hard." He gestured to her sweatpants and belted gi. Her face was flushed from the heavy workout.

"I have a better idea," she countered. "I can make a decent omelet and salad, and since it's Maria's night off, we won't have to fight for the kitchen. If you're willing to go find a bottle of wine for yourself while I shower and pull myself together, you can tell me what you know about this reporter, without too many distractions. Okay?"

"Sounds nice," he responded. She could hear some emotion underlying the words, and felt a pang of concern that he might have thought she was being forward.

"Maggie," he said suddenly, "show me your dojo before you change . . . I'd like to see where you work out."

Surprised by the request, she led him down the cellar steps, and Devlin was startled by the size and quality of the room constructed there. A heavy bag hung from the ceiling, with a man-shaped punching bag next to it. A Wing Chun dummy dominated one corner and two well-pounded makiwara hung on the walls.

One side wall was covered in mirror, and a six-foot dancer's barre stood in front of it. There were assorted free weights on the floor, with a weight bench next to them.

"I know professional boxers who don't have setups

like this to train in," he said with a smile, and she nodded her head in acknowledgment.

"It's my sanctuary, in a way. Like my library. But down here the phone doesn't ring and I feel like a secret. You said you got a kick out of the martial arts you studied . . . you must know how it seduces."

"I liked it a lot . . . especially the practical maneuvers—techniques like disarming and take-downs are useful in my line of work. But you need a lot of commitment to be any good at this stuff . . . and there were always other priorities higher on the list. I did love the philosophy, though. *'Disperse in the face of superior force, as the mist before the dragon,'* " he quoted sonorously. " *'Coalesce in the center of weakness as freezing water splits a boulder.'* "

Maggie smiled at him, charmed by his quirks.

"I'd really like to kiss you, Maggie," he said, unexpectedly moving in so close she could feel his breath on her cheek, and the male warmth of his body. "But I think you'd disperse like the mist."

*Damn! He should have kissed me without asking,* she thought; now I have to decide. "I don't know if I could handle that . . ." she murmured, startled by her own response to him. "I don't have the strength for anything except trying to save Cody, and God knows, I may not have the strength for that. But I sure as hell can't fall . . ." She stopped, horribly embarrassed. Where had that slip come from?

"It's nice that you think you might," he said with an easy grin.

"Oh God! That's not what I meant at all!"

"It's okay. I could too."

"Now, you're teasing me!"

"Maybe a little. I like to see you laugh. In fact I like to see you do a lot of things." He smiled. "And I can think of a helluva lot more things I haven't seen you do, that I'd very much like to."

Maggie looked stricken.

"But not now," he finished swiftly, then he reached over and touched her cheek with his fingers so lightly she barely felt it.

"No?" Maggie felt a little bewildered by him. Devlin always caught her off guard.

"Not tonight. Tonight I'd just like an omelet."

She laughed aloud. He was very lovable when he was playful; it was hard not to be won over.

"I'm behaving like an idiot sixteen-year-old. Please forgive me, Dev. I've been out of the flirtation game for a very long time and I probably wasn't all that good at it back then. I guess I'm pretty off balance."

"Actually, you're behaving like someone who has a lot on her plate at the moment and doesn't need another course offered, just yet."

She nodded, gratefully, and turned to go upstairs. But he took her arm, and turned her around her to face him. "I intend to be your friend, Maggie," he said with quiet authority. "You're so beleaguered right now, you need another pressure like you need a migraine. So, that's not what I'm here for." She saw genuine concern in his expression. "But I *am* here. And I intend to stay here. In your life. You can take that to the bank."

They ate supper and cleaned up after, and he told her all he'd learned. He's so Irish in his complexities, she thought over dinner; brooding and melancholy, then merry in the face of the odds. "Oh, the Great Gaels of Ireland, are the men that God made mad," Chesterson had said. "For all their wars are merry and all their songs are sad." He was like that, but he was trustworthy, too, that lovely, overlooked word from the past. And he was more than that. Maybe quite a lot . . .

They took their coffee to the library and drank it by the fire, and he went home shortly before eleven o'clock, leaving Maggie confused by her own physical and emotional response to the man. Wanting to know him better . . . wanting him to *want*, too.

# CHAPTER 49

Father James sat quietly in a chintz armchair in Maggie's library, his huge frame filling the wingback ludicrously. Maggie had been trepidatious when Peter had said the younger priest would accompany him today. "He's a rare bird, Maggie," he'd told her, "and a good friend. He may see something we've overlooked."

She'd expected Father James Kebede to view her warily; he was Peter's friend, and she was Peter's complication. But instead, the charismatic priest greeted her with genuine warmth, his old-world manner charmingly at odds with the linebacker physique. He carried quiet within him, she saw; a unique serenity that extended its gentle comfort to all those in his immediate vicinity.

"Good and Evil, Maggie," Peter said, standing near the fireplace. "We will tell you what we know, or think we know—in hopes that this knowledge may prove to be a bulwark for you." She nodded expectantly.

"I think we should begin with an attempt at *defining* Evil," he said, always on sure ground when he was teaching. "Are nature's outrages evil? Famine, pestilence, hurricanes, volcanic eruptions . . . all these disasters harm innocent people—are we, then, to hold God responsible for their pain? In exorcisms, the Demonic Presence has been known to try to confound his enemies with stories of God's own wickedness, or at least His unwillingness to protect man from Nature's rages.

"Moral iniquity seems easier to identify. You don't need a theological definition to know that Central American death squads are heinous, or Nazi concentration camp atrocities, or Khmer Rouge genocide, or terrorism, no matter what its supposed ideology. As is depravity—we know that mass murderers and torturers and child molesters perpetrate terrible crimes against humanity. It is the subtler evils that sometimes sneak by our detection systems: the expediencies, the little lies, the good deeds left undone . . ."

James leaned forward and interjected a thought. "Evil *harms* people and it opposes life itself. It is opposed to civilization, and to order. It *lies* to accomplish its ends, for it is not bound by truth. Evil is mysterious and malignant. In its path, nothing grows, for it scorches the earth behind it."

"Yet, Evil can be charismatic, in its own way," Peter chimed in. "In Milton's *Paradise Lost*, Satan was more interesting than God. Rogues and scoundrels tend to be fascinating and seductive. And, of course, Evil is old and familiar—it has always been with us."

"So what exactly is God doing while all this is going on?" Maggie asked feistily. "Where does He stand on this subject?"

James smiled. " 'I am halfway through Genesis,' " a British writer named Ackerly once said, " 'and I am quite appalled by the disgraceful behavior of all the characters involved, including God.' "

I like this priest, Maggie thought; he looks on life with the indulgent affection of a longtime lover. She smiled back.

"Even Thomas Aquinas admitted that the existence of Evil is the best argument against the existence of God, Maggie," James said. "But remember, we've been given free will. It isn't God who chooses to let Evil loose in the world, it is *man* who does so.

"In truth, Maggie," James added gently, "I have always believed the mystery of *goodness* to be far greater than the mystery of Evil. It is so much easier to lie and cheat and steal, than to work honestly, conscientiously, and honorably. It is easier to give way to the grossest sins of the flesh, than to be moral, ethical, and self-restrained. It is easier to sink than to rise, to take the low road, not the high. And yet, Maggie, poor struggling humanity struggles to build, not destroy. To love, not hate. To nurture its children, not to harm them. To heal, and to help, and to strive to be better. And through all that enormous effort, it continues to love God in the face of the odds."

" 'Trust in God and do the right' as the poet says," Maggie mused. "I love the spirit of what you're saying, James, but, I still must ask the insoluble riddle: God is all Good. God is all powerful. Yet, Evil exists. You can reconcile any two of those statements, but not all three."

"A plausible answer to that riddle was posited by a psychiatrist named Peck, Maggie," James said. "An exorcist, in fact. He said God only *creates*, not destroys. And having forsaken destructive force, God is perhaps impotent to prevent the atrocities that we commit upon one another, because He *limited* himself when He gave us freedom. He can only continue to grieve with us. He will offer us Himself, and work to win us to the *good*, but He cannot make us choose to abide with Him, if we wish not to."

"Yet you've both performed exorcisms," Maggie countered, "in which God prevailed over the Satanic Presence. Wouldn't that alone suggest that Good is stronger than Evil, God is stronger than Satan?"

Peter nodded. "That's quite true, Maggie. But you must remember God uses us poor mortals to do His work, and we are woefully imperfect instruments."

"Yet for all that imperfection, Peter," she replied testily, "there is more order than chaos, more evidence of love than hate. We poor imperfect humans still spit in the face of tyrants, pick dying babies off dung heaps in Calcutta, race into burning buildings to save perfect strangers, and light one candle instead of cursing the darkness.

"You know, Peter, the more we talk about this, the more I realize, I don't need to know about heresies. I don't need homiletics or dialectics to know truth when

I trip over it. If God and the Good weren't stronger and better, we wouldn't be standing here, today. Because the bad guys don't *build* civilizations, they tear them down. They don't *nurture* children, they brutalize them—they're not capable of the feats of courage and daring we are, because they just don't *love* enough. And we do." She paused for breath. "I don't have to define Evil, Peter. I can spot it a mile away."

James caught Peter's eye with his own. The look said, *Now I understand.*

JAMES had offered to accompany Maggie to the store to buy groceries for dinner. Peter had extolled his friend's ability as a chef, and volunteered his services, to produce their evening meal; so Maggie had offered to supply the necessary ingredients. To her surprise, Maria Aparecida had taken an instant liking to the Ethiopian priest, proudly showing off her kitchen, when she heard he liked to cook.

"In the end of calculations, dona Maggie," she had said, bustling Maggie and Peter out of the kitchen, and taking James's arm in her own, "the padre and I will collaborate."

Maggie could see the delight James took in the abundance provided by the Jefferson Market and Balducci's. He handled each selection of fruit or vegetable as if it were both sacred obligation, and indescribable pleasure. It took quite some time for him to complete his selections, but she didn't want to hurry him, he seemed so enthralled in the joy of the task.

"You wanted to speak with me alone, James, didn't you?" she asked finally, on the way home.

"You have found me out," he answered amiably. "I must confess I simply wanted to get to know you, Maggie, at least a little, and one-to-one is always best for that, don't you think?"

"Do you disapprove of Peter's trying to help me so selflessly?" she asked.

"Not at all. I believe he is doing as he should. As he must, in fact. Peter Messenguer is a unique piece of God's handiwork, Maggie. He must follow where his unusual intellect leads him. And, in this case, his heart, as well."

Maggie looked up and saw James was smiling, just a little.

"I believe you and Cody have been placed in his path for a purpose, Maggie. At the moment only God knows precisely what that purpose is. Peter must find out."

They walked on silently for nearly a block. "What is it you wished to ask me, James?" she prompted finally. "I've been feeling the prickle of your question marks all afternoon."

He nodded. "If you cannot save the child, Maggie . . . how, then, will you feel about God?"

"I guess I haven't really let myself consider that possibility, James," she said slowly, a little taken aback by the question. She sensed that for some reason her answer was important to him.

"When my husband died," she began slowly, "I railed at God. I'd stormed heaven with my prayers and pleadings, for the three years of his illness, and I just couldn't believe God would allow such a good man to die—for no reason, and under such horrifying circumstances. The waste of it filled me with rage. And the loss I'd suffered . . . the terrible aloneness of widowhood . . . ate at me like a corrosive acid. Then, I was hit with the horror of Jenna's addiction and her disappearance. That, too, overwhelmed me . . . I felt like a modern-day Job. *I've tried so hard, God!* I ranted. *Why won't you help me? What is it You want from me?"* Her voice was electric with emotion.

"And then one day, after a very long while of asking for understanding, it occurred to me that perhaps all He wanted was my surrender to His will. There's so much soul's growth that comes from hardship and sorrow, James—not the kind you'd volunteer for, mind you. But it finally dawned on me that you can't *change* Fate, but maybe you can learn enough from it, to change *yourself* . . . and perhaps that, too, is what He requires of us. In a way, I guess, I decided I couldn't let my husband's death be the deciding issue between me and God.''

She smiled sadly. ''This is no easy battle we've been sent to wage, here, James—you have to be courageous just to survive, never mind grow. But, I do think God expects us to try our damnedest, whatever the obstacles.'' She paused to search a little further, then continued.

''All of which is just a roundabout way of saying this, I guess: I believe God wants me to fight like hell to save Cody. If I fail—or if for some reason, far beyond my ability to comprehend, He takes her home to Him, instead . . . I'll try very hard to surrender to that, too.'' She looked up at him with great vulnerability apparent in her face. ''She was His, before she was mine, James,'' she said softly.

James Kebede was deeply touched by what Maggie said, for he understood the magnitude of her declaration of faith, and what it would likely cost her to live up to it.

THE dream began softly, carrying Maggie on its billows out beyond the mists of time. She tossed and turned with its movement, rhythmically propelled by an unseen force that could not be denied.

*The time-mists dissipated; she was in a royal court. Pharaoh sat upon a golden throne made in the form of great winged lions; his dignitaries stood around him, and his warriors, archers, spearmen, fully armed, stood at attention, row upon row, along the limestone pillars of the great hall. Their oiled bodies gleamed, and scarlet feathers adorned their shields and helmets, for they were the elitist bodyguards of Pharaoh.*

*Beside the golden throne, a young man stood. He was tall as the Nile reeds that shade the sacred ibises, and he was obviously of Pharaoh's lineage. The finely chiseled nose and jaw, the stature far above the norm, the bearing of a king's son, marked him as the heir to the Crook and Flail of the Double Kingdom.*

*He was both foreign and familiar to the dream/Maggie. She watched and listened, straining to know why he filled her with such desperate longing.*

*The young man spoke and Pharaoh listened. The courtiers murmured among themselves at his wisdom, and the Ptah priests nodded knowingly to each other. The dreamer heard them say he would soon be ready to Cross the Abyss . . .*

Maggie stirred restlessly in her sleep. Fear lapped at her, somewhere in the dream world . . . She reached out again without knowing why.

Karaden. His royal name was Snefru, son of Zoser-Horus-Neteri-Khet, but he was called Karaden. He was speaking . . . pontificating really, as if he were much older than his years. And his manner, so formal, so imperial, was so familiar . . .

Peter. What was Peter doing in her dream? No, it couldn't be Peter at Pharaoh's court. That was so long ago . . .

So long . . .

So sad.

*So sad. So long . . .*

Maggie opened her eyes and tried to blink back the dream. Why did these strange dreams all fade so quickly, so elusively that only fragments of knowing remained.

She would give anything to remember. Except that they always made her feel so sad.

# CHAPTER 50

Jenna's body, seen through the nearly transparent black robe, was exquisite. High, full breasts with upturned nipples, waist narrow as a sigh, gently swelling hips, caught with an exquisite golden girdle of filigreed leaves and flowers. Her head was crowned with a gilded circlet, surmounted by a cobra's arching body; her pale blond hair beneath it gleamed nearly silver in the candlelight. Confidently, she took her place at the altar, and raised both arms skyward in salute to Sekhmet.

The malevolent cat-headed Goddess's statue was carved from black granite; around her neck and arms, huge precious gems reflected back the torchlight in a dazzling display. Looking every inch the priestess of an evil Goddess, Jenna took her place at the altar's foot. She had been looking forward to this new level of initiation into the rituals of Maa Kheru.

"Even you, Ghania, must admit she has done this in previous lifetimes," Eric said, watching the neophyte's performance with a critical eye, from the back of the chapel. "One doesn't learn this craft in a single incarnation."

"Had she never been a priestess, she would not have been chosen as the vessel, Eric, as you well know. By the same token, had she not failed her Goddess, she would not be quite so expendable."

"Touché, Ghania. You are right, as usual. You and I chose our Master long ago . . . Jenna arrived on his Left Hand Path by default. Nevertheless, she plays her role superbly well tonight. She is a pleasure to watch, is she not? The Gods have crafted her clay to perfection, if

310

not the spirit within." He glanced sideways at Ghania's scowl, then added with malicious amusement, "You are jealous of her body, Ghania . . . admit it to me. The perfect breasts, the loins so ripe for pleasure . . . you cannot tell me you do not envy her my bed."

"Age is an unrelenting master, Eric," Ghania replied, annoyed. "Someday, you, too, will envy youth."

"But I was your *favorite*, wasn't I, Ghania?" he prodded, like a petulant child. "And you *do* envy her. I insist that you tell me the truth."

Ghania smiled slyly. "In this century, perhaps you were the best, arrogant boy. But there have been other, *better* centuries." She turned and left him standing chagrined, at the mercy of Nicholas Sayles's knowing smirk.

"You may own the old witch, Eric," Nicky said, "but you will never best her."

"I could have her heart cut out and fried for supper," Eric replied harshly.

"True enough. But you will never best her." Nicky's laughter was very irritating, and reminded Eric that he might have let the man live too long, already.

# CHAPTER 51

Devlin and Maggie were already seated in her parlor, when Gino arrived. He was dressed in chinos and a navy sweater, that somehow accentuated his Mediterranean sensuality. He didn't look at all as Maggie had imagined him.

She shook his hand with a broad smile. "I've heard so much about you, Gino, I thought I'd recognize you

on sight, but Dev forgot to tell me you look like a movie
star.''

"You'd be surprised how few people he mentions
that to," Garibaldi laughed, caught off guard by her
openness.

"On second thought," Devlin interjected, "maybe
wanting you two to meet each other wasn't such a red-
hot idea."

"Nah," Gino countered, "we got too much to talk
about here to be distracted by just another pretty face.
Besides, you never looked lovelier yourself, Lieutenant."

It was obvious the two men were buddies, and that
made Maggie feel relieved; it was good to know Dev
wasn't entirely alone in his efforts.

"What've you got for us, Gino," Devlin prompted.

"A lot of not enough, Lieutenant. I called a guy who
called a guy, if you know what I mean, in the DEA, and
the story is they've been watching our pigeons for a long
time. We're talking big bucks here. Major pipeline out
of the Golden Triangle, through India and East Africa,
et cetera, et cetera. You know the drill.

"A lot of dirty money seems to go through the Vannier
family laundromat, but the word comes from on high
that nobody's supposed to pull the plug on their operation, because of Somebody's-Ongoing-Something-or-
Other, which makes it more important to keep these
creeps in business than to put them out of it. *Capische?*"

Maggie looked startled. "You mean to tell me that
the Drug Enforcement Agency knows that Vannier and
Sayles are in the heroin business, and doesn't do anything about it?"

The men exchanged glances and Gino answered her.
"What I'm saying is *sometimes*, for those guys in the
DEA, the devil you know is better than the devil you
don't know. And sometimes, they watch an operation a
long, long time before they pull the plug on it. Of course,
sometimes, they never pull the plug, because they're
told not to by somebody higher up."

"Who's higher up?"

"The Justice Department, the President, the FBI or CIA, maybe. A lot of people. Sometimes even a local DA, if he's got real clout. Face it, Maggie. A lot of scumbags never get nailed, because somebody needs them to roll over on some bigger scumbag . . . or just because the system sucks, about certain things. That's why a lot of the time we cops feel like we spend all our time rearranging the deck chairs on the *Titanic*."

Gino sat back, and looked at Maggie. "I been looking forward to meeting you," he said, with a genuine smile. "Believe it or not, the Lieutenant, here, is usually a very sane kinda guy. I wanted to see what kind of woman would make him take on Darth Vader and the Dark Side, all by his lonesome."

"I'm sorry to have involved either of you in anything so dangerous," Maggie said with concern. "I had absolutely no idea what I was getting you into, and I would understand completely if you ran like hell."

Gino scanned her face a moment, judging her sincerity, then said, "You're right, Lieutenant, she is a nice lady." Then he relaxed for the first time.

"Tell you what," he said leaning forward, his voice kindly. "Why don't you tell me some stuff about this little kid we all got on our minds . . . She must be real special . . ."

# CHAPTER 52

Ghania took the little mouse from the pocket of her djellabah and dangled it by its tail in front of Cody, before letting it crawl up her arm and perch on her shoulder. She was in rare good humor this morning;

Cody could see that Ghania was almost playful. This fact filled the child with apprehension, for it was a lie.

She felt a kind of numbness now, from the relentless succession of batterings and pleasantries that Ghania dished out, seemingly at random. In the beginning, she had tried to avoid provoking the fearsome attacks that brought pain—but the pain always came, anyway. The only escape was to go underground, hiding deep within herself, where there was safety in the Light. It was growing stronger . . . and sometimes, now, it seemed to her that someone lived there. Someone good.

"You may play with the mouse," the witch said, with an indulgent smile. "She is very soft, and very intelligent."

Cody reached out a tentative hand and picked up the tiny pinkish gray creature from Ghania's shoulder. It squiggled itself free of her grip, dropped to her lap, and scooted across the bench so speedily the child couldn't help but giggle.

"You can talk to the little creatures of the earth, like this mouse, you know. You have the gift," Ghania said, and Cody looked up in surprise. "You must listen carefully when they are near, child, and you must quiet your mind to listen, for they speak softly. You will hear their thoughts, if you do as I say."

Cody shook her head doubtfully.

"No?" Ghania queried. "You do not think so? Well, I know better!" She pursed her lips in a pensive expression.

"You do not remember your magic," she said finally, as if that fact filled her with sorrow.

Cody blinked. "What magic?"

"The magic that is in your soul, little one. It is very big, very powerful, but you have forgotten how to use it." She made a clucking sound of regret.

Cody looked puzzled. "I don't know any magic."

Ghania smiled expansively. "Ah, but you *do*, child! You do indeed. This is why Ghania is training you . . .

this is why Ghania is bothering with you at all! You have *much* magic . . . I do not bother with ordinary children."

"You don't?" Cody thought it would be very good if Ghania didn't bother with her, anymore.

"No, child," Ghania assured her in a most amiable way. "Ghania's skills are only for the *Special Ones*."

Cody frowned and said nothing; she had seen Ghania's skills in action. Even if Ghania was pretending to be nice today, it didn't mean she was a nice person.

"Would you like to learn about your magic?" Ghania wheedled, and Cody nodded, uncertainly.

"Here is what you must do then, little one. You must make your mind very still . . . then you must reach deep down inside yourself to the *secret* places. If you look hard enough, you will see things there that will make you remember."

"What kind of things?"

Ghania laughed and Cody shuddered. Ghania's laughter usually had ugly consequences.

"Everyone sees different things in the depths, child. Some see demons, some see angels. You have the rare power to see both! It is easiest to see them when you are hurt or frightened. That is why Ghania does things to you, sometimes. Ghania hurts you, to help you find your magic." Instinctively, Cody backed away.

"Not today, child. Do not fear," Ghania said with a knowing smile. "Today there will be no pain. But in the old days, in the time of the Old Gods, there was much suffering to be gone through, before the magic would come. I, myself, was buried for three days in an ant hill, before my magic was fully formed . . ." She shook her great head in disgust at the memory.

"Didn't the ants bite you?" Cody asked, fascinated, horrified.

"They bit me and they crawled into my eyes and my ears . . . I could not breathe or see. I could not scream, for I thought they would swarm into my mouth and kill me . . ." Ghania's face was haunted by remembered horror. "But the magic came," she said finally, her voice oddly hushed. "The magic came."

"I wouldn't want it to come that way," Cody exclaimed. "No magic!" she said vehemently, as if to ward it off.

"It will come to you, too, little one," Ghania said relentlessly, in a voice as close to compassion as Cody had ever heard her use. "You are trapped by the magic within you, as I was trapped by mine. To be chosen by the Gods is the most terrible fate of all."

# CHAPTER 53

Malachy Devlin watched the woman he was falling in love with, as she sat on the park bench next to him, eating a hot dog. He had found that asking her to dinner made her skittish, uncertain, but dropping by at odd hours, or calling and asking her to go for a brief walk so they could talk, kept her guard down. He would wear down her resistance, eventually. He had a cop's persistence, and he knew she needed him, even if she hadn't figured that out yet. The priest was the problem, that was apparent. There was something going on there— even if it was just some kind of affair of the spirit. But that would come to an end, one way or the other. Devlin also had a cop's pragmatism about reality.

"How did you learn about sex, Maggie?" he asked, catching her by surprise. He liked doing that; there was something about her spontaneous honesty in replying that gave him back his faith in the world.

"*The Rubáiyát of Omar Khayyám*," she answered, smiling between bites of hot dog. "I could show you the exact page that altered my carnal knowledge, forever."

Devlin's mouth turned down at the corners, in a crooked little smile.

" *'The Moving Finger writes,'* " she said, with an expansive gesture of the hand, " *'and, having writ, moves on: Nor all thy Piety nor Wit Shall lure it back to cancel half a line, nor all thy Tears wash out a word of it.'* I knew the instant I opened the book to that particular page, that it would change everything . . ." She grinned, and looked like a mischievous kid.

"It was the picture, as much as the words, Dev. The woman in the woodcut was draped across the giant Book of Fate, and the page was blotted by her sins. I could practically taste her desperation . . . hair streaming wildly, useless fingers clutching at the tainted page. I said to myself, *my God!* So this is what your Permanent Record looks like! No wonder Sister Benedict is so worried about it. I remember gripping the little book in sweaty hands, and hiding myself behind the XYZs, because nobody ever went there, so I could read on."

"How exactly did this teach you about sex?" he laughed, amused and puzzled.

"Well, you see, I longed to know about bodies, despite the fact that the people in my family didn't seem to have any. I mean, fathers and mothers were only seen and felt through clothing—you know, like those china dolls, whose heads and hands are made of a different material from what's in the middle? But, there in the *Rubáiyát,* lusty men with wine flasks in their hands were fondling women's breasts! Death with his sickle-scythe, was stalking young lovers in the grass. Naked men and women were *touching* each other, Dev. *Life* was on those pages. And I could tell that bodies were the key."

God, how he wanted to hold her. To touch her warm, soft parts and lie entangled in her sweetness. There was such an innocence about Maggie, despite her brain, her years, her experience, her current plight.

"You know something, Maggie?" he said, a tenderness in his voice she hadn't heard there before. "I'd like to give you things."

She finished the last bite of hot dog and asked, "What kind of things?"

"I don't know exactly. Crazy things. Sea dreams. Wild flowers in clay pots. Peace of spirit. Me."

She tilted her head and looked at him closely. There was something so lovable about him . . . no, that wasn't what she wanted to think. Was it?

She started to reply, but Devlin held up his hands to stop her. "I know. I know. No complications. Not now. But remember what I told you," he grinned suddenly, boyishly. "I intend to be your best friend, even if it's against your will."

She couldn't help but laugh. *If things were different* . . . no! That was ridiculous. She loved Peter—or something akin to love. You can't love two men at once. *Maybe she didn't love either one of them*. And besides, the very fact that she didn't have to be in love with Devlin took all the pressure off their relationship. No anxiety, no subterfuge, no longings that couldn't be fulfilled, just honest friendship. And she *needed* that. He was so easy to talk to, and he always made her smile. God, how she needed something joyful in her life, just to remember that such could be . . .

"Look, Maggie," he said, as if reading her thoughts, "I like Ellie a lot, and maybe the priest even has some good points, although I'll be damned if I can think what they are. But religion and metaphysics are not going to nail the sons of bitches who have Cody. Good old-fashioned police procedures might. So I intend to hang around for a while.

"But here's the bottom line, Maggie O'Connor, my elusive butterfly. The first thing I'm going to do is get those dirty bastards who destroy children to satisfy their own deluded lusts. Then, I'm going to get Cody back for you. And after all that's said and done . . ." He grinned suddenly, the dark eyes merry in the weathered face. "If you're such a damned fool you don't fall in love with me, I can't be held accountable for that."

There was moisture in Maggie's eyes when he finished, and she turned her head till she regained control; there was something about him that always gave her hope.

About an hour after he had walked her home, she found a piece of paper stuck under her front door. When she unfolded it, she read in Devlin's bold scrawl:

> Do me a favor and say what's on this paper
> ten times a day, until further notice:
> Nothing is too good to be true.
> Nothing is too good to happen to me.
> Nothing is too good to last forever.

# CHAPTER 54

There's renewal in sunshine, Maggie thought as she walked briskly down Sixth Avenue toward Bleecker in the early-morning sunlight. She'd gone to the 7:00 A.M. mass at St. Joseph's to ask for help in seeing through this maze. Now she needed a sounding board and Ellie was a good ear, so she'd stopped at the bakery for sweet rolls to bring with her, and the cozy bakery smells had buoyed her spirits. She remembered going with her father to morning Mass, and bringing back rolls in a paper bag from the bakery . . . warm buttery memories of joy and intimacy and love. *Oh God! what memories will Cody carry with her, after this?* If there is an *after this*? She hurried from the market to Ellie's building, needing to talk to a wise friend.

The rich dark scent of European coffee filled the apartment as she entered. She handed Ellie the sweet rolls, and was grateful to see there was a fire in the hearth.

"You and I are the only two people nutty enough to

be burning wood in April," she said with a smile, as Ellie handed her a steaming mug.

"Don't you believe it! The wood man told me March is his second busiest month, because all us diehards stock up for any cool nights or mornings we can still dredge out of the year."

They sat near the fire.

"Now what brings you here at an hour when the chickens are barely conscious?"

"I need to talk, Ellie," Maggie answered. "There's so much on my mind that needs sorting . . . I think I've got to try to *see* Cody, whatever it takes. I don't care if I have to stand on the Vannier lawn and throw rocks at the nursery window—every instinct tells me she needs to know I haven't forgotten her. I'm tired of feeling impotent, and waiting for somebody else to do something."

"I've been thinking along the same lines, Mags. But I have a hunch your best shot for getting her out may be on Walpurgisnacht, during the festival."

"Why *that* night? I'd imagine she'd be guarded then, better than ever."

Ellie shook her head noncommittally. "I don't know, Mags. It'll be a Grand Sabbat and that usually entails a helluva lot of revelry. Maybe even an orgy, to rev up the vibrations. Maybe a lot of things. I think they'll throw a huge party, and there are always people coming and going at a party . . . caterers, maybe . . . lots of servants. They'll need thirteen Adepts for the ritual . . . if they each have spouses, that's twenty-six, already. Plus, whoever else is a high-ranking member of the coven. Odds are they'll want to display their prize, and the power it gives them, to as many followers as possible. Besides, we might have the element of surprise on our side that night. If they've gotten that far without being thwarted, they may get cocky and think they're invulnerable."

Maggie thought for a minute, then shook her head. "I just can't wait for the thirtieth, Ellie. Maybe you're right, and we can't get her out till then, but I have to at least try to see her, *now*. It's driving me up the wall that I can't get through on the phone, and my nightmares are getting wilder. And you've said yourself that my dreams are accurate."

"Time and space don't constrain the soul in sleep, Mags. That's how precognitive dreams happen, especially to someone like you, who's brought the ability to travel outside the body into this lifetime." She caught Maggie's eyes with her own.

"You really need to get to the bottom of all this before the thirtieth, Maggie," she said very seriously. "You *need* to do a past-life regression to unlock the full story."

Maggie frowned, her distaste apparent.

"Look, Mags, I think it's imperative that we get more information than we have before we make our move. Eric, Jenna, Cody, you, me . . . we're none of us here by chance. It would help us to know what's really going on. And we're going to need every edge we can get," Ellie pursued. "A little clarity wouldn't be the worst thing. I know one or two people who specialize in regressions."

"Forgive me, Ellie, you know I'd trust you with my life, or Cody's, but I just can't take a chance on somebody planting any kind of debilitating thought in my head. Hypnosis scares me to death, and a 'past-life regressor' smacks too much of supermarket tabloids."

Ellie looked thoughtful. "Then don't go to a past-life regressor. Go to a bona fide psychiatrist-hypnotherapist. There's a whole psychiatric association full of them. I'll bet Amanda could find one, on her never-ending list of acquaintances."

"I'll think about it," Maggie said uncertainly. "I promise you I will."

"There's no time left for thinking, Mags," Ellie said relentlessly. "It's time to act."

Clarity was a seductive lure, Maggie thought as she left Ellie's apartment. If she knew more, maybe a solution would surface. She brooded about the possibilities for hours before calling Amanda for a recommendation. She almost hoped this would be the one time in history Amanda didn't know someone who knew someone.

ELLIE locked the door to her apartment, after Maggie left, shut off the phones and removed the clothes she'd been wearing. She prayed as she did so, quieting her mind and heart, asking for guidance and purification. It was time to get some answers of her own.

She deliberated before bathing, deciding which essence to add to the bathwater. Salt and soda would cleanse any negativity that might be clinging to her aura, as would vinegar. Ginger would ward off any malevolent energy that might be hovering around the apartment. She settled, finally, on cedar oil . . . an old Indian remedy to ward off the evil intentions of others. This task was too critical to risk invasion by unfriendly forces.

She debated her choice of garment with equal seriousness. There were robes of many colors in the armoire she always kept locked; each was suited to a different magical operation. She finally decided on purple, because it balanced the blue of Justice, with the red of Mercy, and it was apparent that both truths must be served in what she sought to learn today. She chose a long purple gown of soft linen, pulling it over her naked body, and belting it with the black ceremonial girdle, which she had merited, long, long ago, after many years of arduous training.

Ellie fingered the cord that was her magical girdle, reverently; the inner meaning of its complex symbology always warmed her. *"This magical cord forms the immediate Circle into which we are bound by our own wills,"* her Russian grandmother had intoned, as she tied it round her waist. *"The loop is the Ankh of eternity, and the free end connects you with all other human and Divine entities in the great chain of life. With it, we are pulled up by those Intelligences beyond us, just as we are bound to use our strength to pull up those below us who need our assistance. This magical girdle is the umbilicus which connects you to the Divine Mother, Illiana. Wear it only in Truth and Honor."*

Ellie belted the robe and arranged its pleats into an orderly line, remembering . . .

*"By robing properly for ceremony, child,"* her beloved Babooshka had said, *"you are assuming the mantle of the traveler in another world . . . the world of Spirit. With this mantle on your shoulders, you may seek admittance to the Inner Realms. With it you proclaim yourself a member, however humble, of the Holy Mysteries. With it, you may seek to be given the chance to make a contribution to the Great Work, on which the Company of Light is engaged. But do not forget for a single instant, that you will be observed by your Spiritual Superiors, and you will be judged by their exacting measure."*

Reverently, Ellie took a large abalone shell from its place in the armoire; she filled it with silver sage and cedar chips, before adding a braided snippet of sweet grass. She lit the mixture with a taper, and fanned it gently, with the eagle feathers her Cherokee grandmother had given her for the task, encouraging the small blaze, until the fire had spread sufficiently to catch all three substances. When she blew out the flames, a dense and fragrant smoke billowed from the shell.

"I salute thee, O Great Spirit, by the power of the Elements!" she chanted, lifting the smoking shell aloft. "Abalone shell for water; sage, cedar, and sweet grass from the earth; smoke to purify the air; and fire to fuse them into unity," she chanted the inventory with love. "I salute the Guardians of the Four Directions and ask their benevolent aid," she called out. "Be it known that through the Four Directions I seek the Way of Light! Be there peace between me and the East. Be there peace between me and the South. Be there peace between me and the West. Be there peace between me and the North."

She fanned the pungent, cleansing smoke in each direction, chanting as she did so. There were many magical systems she had been initiated into over the years, in diverse parts of the world, but the way of her grandmother, She Who Catches the Rainbow, still had special meaning.

"O Great Spirit," she cried out, "by the power of the Sacred Smoke, I entreat Thee to purify this place of worship. Father/Mother God, I ask thy blessing for the rites to be performed.

> *"Cleanse my soul and spirit*
> *Purify my heart*
> *Clear my vision, that I may see only Truth*
> *Make me wise in Thy ways of Honor*
> *On pain of death, do I pledge Thee*
> *To respect Thy teachings*
> *To serve beyond the self*
> *To give Thee thanks*
> *To keep silent what I learn."*

Ellie called upon the four mighty Archangels, who have been charged by God, to guard the Watchtowers of Creation. Raphael, Michael, Gabriel, Uriel. She addressed each by his litany of sacred names, and asked permission to leave her earth-body behind and travel safely in the Higher Realms.

As she made obeisance to each direction, Ellie lighted a tapered candle, at each of the cardinal points. Her consecrated objects lay on the altar before her. A centuries-old silver chalice, brought out of Russia before the Revolution. A horn-handled knife, in a braided deerskin sheath, that had been carried into battle by her grandfather, and his father before him. A wand carved by her own hand, from a lightning-struck hazel tree. A pentacle engraved with intricate sigils few on earth could decipher. A medicine pouch with objects gathered in the painstaking time of self-examination, before Vision

Quest. A crystal sphere that had been placed in her cradle at birth.

A Medicine woman of the Cherokee people, and a Magician of High Degree, Ellie was Rainbow Woman, Ellie was Illiana Petrovic—in this earth life. She had been many others, over the lifespan of her very old soul.

Tonight, she would seek to find her place in this Mystery of the Amulets. This was to be a battle of Goddesses; the counsel of the Gods would have little value, here. She would seek instead, communion with the Female Essence of the Universe, by means that had been secret since the dawn of time.

She had no way of knowing, as she entered the Silence, if she would survive the next twenty-four hours.

MAGGIE paced her library after leaving Ellie. She felt caged, trapped in impotence. Unable to help Cody, unable to even control her own mind. The Egypt dreams were impinging on the daytime now. Four separate times, she'd felt the ground shift under her, crashing her through the curtain of time into some bizarre bilocation.

First, she'd seen her hand become someone else's . . . then, those damned bells kept insinuating their eerie sound. Then, last night she'd been standing in her kitchen holding a jelly glass, and it had metamorphosed in her hand, becoming a golden goblet filled with some magical elixir. *That* was bad enough. But today's experience had really pushed her over the limit. Halfway home from Ellie's, she'd felt the reality shift coming . . . sweeping her into some kind of wrinkle in time. One minute she'd been passing the Ashby Studio on Cornelia Street, and the next minute, she was in an underground cavern, lit by torches. Even the temperature had changed to ice around her, and she had felt the weight of a golden girdle around her nearly naked hips.

She was in a labyrinth, in some ancient place, and she

was being tested . . . *by whom, for what purpose?* And why today? There was fear in her, and intense concentration, but there was confidence, too.

Then, the wrinkle had eased back into ordinary time; the cold had vanished, and she was back on Cornelia Street, nearly at the corner of Sixth Avenue. But she had brought something back with her . . . a different kind of *confidence*, for lack of a better word. She was scared, but empowered, as if she knew the test was a hard one, but she'd been trained for it. An Olympic athlete anxious for a shot at the gold, knowing it was not impossible . . .

Maybe she was losing her mind. All the stress and anxiety . . . all the fear for Cody. Maybe it had unhinged her. Maybe crazy people didn't realize they were crazy. *I've got to get a grip on myself.*

Maggie sat on the floor in the library, in a half lotus posture and closed her eyes. She needed to meditate, and she needed to do it, now. She pushed the worrying, frustrated cacophony of old thoughts away, as Mr. Wong had taught her to do, and battled back the surge of new ones that scurried in to fill the void.

*Okay.* A relatively blank screen. She forced her breathing to a meditative rhythm, and concentrated on the flow of air through her body. The ancients knew what they were doing . . . clear the mind to find *no-mind*. Let the Universal energies flow through you to heal and strengthen.

She was beginning to feel better. More harmonious, less frazzled.

Then she saw *her*. A living hologram in her mind's eye. *Cody*. Sitting on a bench in a garden. Never had she experienced a clearer vision. She saw the child's gaze turn slowly in her direction . . . self-contained, and sad beyond reckoning.

*"I'm here, sweetheart!"* Maggie's mind cried out to her excitedly. She saw the recognition spark for a moment, in the child's eyes, then die completely, as Cody

deliberately turned her head away from Mim, and returned to her own tormented world.

*Sweet Jesus!* Maggie breathed aloud, a new and more terrifying knowledge crashing in. *She's given up! They've taken even hope away from her!*

Rage pushed Maggie to her feet, more powerful than fear or sorrow. She picked up the phone and called Devlin, and something in her voice made him drop what he was doing with the sure knowledge that he had to get her.

"I've got to try to see her, Dev," Maggie said, the minute he charged through the door. "Everywhere I turn *I see her*. Every child on the street tears my heart out. I can't stand it anymore! It's been over two months since they took her and we don't even know if she's alive! We're just *assuming* Walpurgisnacht is the time they've got planned for this Materialization—we don't really know anything for a fact."

Devlin could see the toll taken in Maggie by the past few weeks. How many hours of sleep had there been for her since the child had been taken? he wondered. There were dark circles under her eyes, and the lines in her face that he'd found so winsome when they met were more pronounced now.

"We *do* know some things, Maggie," he said, trying to placate her. "All the experts pinpoint the *same* time—the astrologers, the Egyptologists, even Ellie. And we do know occultists attempt their specially evil magic on that night. That's all good circumstantial evidence. As to Cody's being alive . . . we know she's no good to them dead."

"Until after April 30th," she interjected. "That's two weeks away! *Two weeks.*"

"Until after April 30th," he agreed reluctantly, wondering what he could say to calm her perfectly sensible fears. The child could be dead already.

"I'm going up there, Dev. *Now.* Today. I'm going to knock on the damned door and demand to see my granddaughter. I don't care if I have to stand on the front lawn and scream my bloody head off, I have to let her know I still love her." She took a deep eloquent breath. "I was hoping you'd go with me."

Devlin had been around hardship long enough to know when emotions had outstripped arguments.

"I'll go with you," he answered evenly. "They'll be less likely to have you arrested for trespassing, if I'm there."

The drive to Greenwich was spent in pained silence; Maggie's head lay back against the seat of Devlin's car, her eyes were open but they didn't focus on the road. Dev reached over and took her hand in his own; she neither protested nor responded, but nonetheless, he held it tightly all the way to Greenwich, as if to impart his own robust strength to her depleted supply.

"You know, Dev," she said wistfully, "I keep asking myself, what if she dies, and she never knows I tried to save her?"

"I don't think that's the way it'll go down," he answered with a conviction he didn't really feel. Children died all the time at the hands of lunatics. "I think we'll get her out of there. We just won't do it today."

Maggie pounded on the Vannier door three separate times, before it was opened by a servant who told her no one was home. Exasperated, Maggie pushed past the woman into the house, and Devlin followed her, despite the maid's protests.

"Do not *tell me* they're not here," Maggie said tightly. "I want to see my granddaughter, and I know she's in this house." She was moving as she spoke, heading for the nursery wing; Devlin wondered just how far she intended to push this.

Vannier appeared in Maggie's path, before she'd made it past the library. "I'm afraid I'll have to ask you to leave my home," he said firmly, blocking her way with his own large form.

"I want to see Cody, Eric," Maggie snapped. "I'm

sick to death of being put off, when I call. I want to see her, *today!*"

"I'm afraid that isn't possible. The child is ill and not receiving visitors."

"I'll bet she's ill, you monster," Maggie spat, attempting to push past him, but he grabbed her arm painfully and jerked her to a halt.

"Don't do that!" Devlin ordered; there was enough quiet menace in the tone to startle Maggie and make Eric release his grip.

Eric's eyes met Devlin's evenly. "You are both intruders in my home," he said. "If I call the local authorities I think you know what will happen." Devlin began to reply, but Maggie, on impulse, started to run.

"Cody!" she screamed out, as loudly as she could. "Cody. I'm here! *Where are you?*"

An echoing cry sounded somewhere in the upper recesses of the house. "Mim!" a small voice shrieked out in absolute desperation. *"Help me!* Help . . ." The last scream was silenced abruptly. A door slammed somewhere on the second floor.

Maggie was already on the nursery stair, before Eric tackled her, bringing her down hard on the edge of the fifth step. Devlin landed, seconds later, atop the pile of arms and legs, pulling at Eric to keep his hands from Maggie's throat. As the two men grappled with each other, Maggie managed to extricate herself from the melee, and staggered up the stairs.

Ghania blocked her passage at the landing, like a human wall. "She has been removed from the house!" she hissed, as Maggie attempted to move around her. "See for yourself! The window!"

Maggie spun toward the huge window that flanked the landing, and saw two men carrying the flailing child between them, to a waiting car. Cody was screaming, and pounding uselessly against her captors; Maggie could hear her shrieks through the glass.

Frantic with frustration, and fury, Maggie picked up

the flower-filled vase from the table in front of the window and tearing the flowers out of it, flung them at Ghania. Before the huge woman recovered enough to move, Maggie smashed the heavy vase through the huge glass pane, sending shards crashing down to the patio below.

"Cody!" she screamed to the child, just as the men pushed her into the car. "I love you! *I'm coming back!*"

She saw Cody's stricken face turn wildly toward her, as the limo door slammed shut, and knew she'd heard the promise.

"She will die," Ghania croaked, picking the flowers from her ruined robe. "And you will watch!"

Maggie turned on the malevolent giant, a fury in her breast she could barely contain. "*You* will die!" she spat the words. "And *I* will watch!

Then, she turned on her heel and walked down the stairs, where Eric and Devlin now stood, like two small boys caught scrapping in the playground. They had obviously been separated by Eric's bodyguards.

"Get them out of my house!" Eric ordered hoarsely, and the guards reached out to hasten their departure. But Devlin's gun was suddenly in his hand, and both men stepped back again, uncertainly.

"We're leaving now," he said, steady as Gibraltar. "If everyone stays very calm and out of our way, there shouldn't be any trouble."

Devlin and Maggie backed cautiously from the house, and ran for their own car, but the limo, with Cody in it, was already out of sight.

Maggie made it only as far as the rest stop before she began to cry, softly at first, then, as the full impact of all that had happened hit, great gasping sobs wracked her body.

Devlin pulled the car to the side of the Merritt Parkway and took her into his arms, holding her, speaking comforting words to her, patting her like a child, until she finally subsided into an exhausted silence.

He drove directly to Ellie's without discussion. He had no intention of leaving her alone in such a state, and he needed to get back to the precinct because that was the place to get the goods on that arrogant, child-molesting son of a bitch. And that's just what he intended to do.

"THERE'S a Yiddish word for what's going on with you, right now, Mags," Ellie said caringly, after she'd settled her friend into a comfortable corner of the couch. Devlin had been right; she was in pretty bad shape.

Maggie looked at Ellie, hurt and angry; the weight of all that had happened was in her voice when she spoke. "Cody's in danger of death or worse, Jenna's sold her soul to the Devil, and I'm so worn out I don't remember how to tie shoelaces," she snapped. "How can there possibly be a word for all that?"

"Zerissenheit," Ellie answered softly.

"And what does that mean?"

"Torn-to-pieces-hood."

Maggie could think of no reply, quick tears filled her eyes.

"I've got the name of the hypnotherapist for you, Mags," Ellie prodded. "I called Amanda."

Maggie started to respond, but Ellie held up a hand to stop her. "I *know* certain things, now, Maggie," she said with authority. "You have no choice, but to know them, too!"

"Then tell me what they are, damnit!"

"If I tell you, you *will not* believe me—not deep down in your soul, where you must. For your own protection, you must call this number, Maggie. You are caught in a cosmic battle plan—I give you my word of honor, you and Cody cannot survive it if you don't have every possible weapon at your disposal. Call this doctor, Maggie . . . Amanda's already told him he'll hear from you."

Defeated by Ellie's determination, and by the harrowing vision of Cody's desperate face, Maggie agreed to call the number.

# CHAPTER 55

Dr. Heinrich Strater was Viennese, a fact for which Maggie felt mildly grateful, as she sat in his office, nervously wondering what regressive hypnosis would feel like. At least he looked the way psychiatrists were supposed to; bearded, middle-aged, round glasses on a fine Semitic nose. She found that a comforting spar in a sea of uncertainty.

"As I told you on the phone, Maggie," he was saying deliberately, "hypnosis is not a parlor game. It is an accepted medical tool, with which one can plumb the psyche, with a degree of clarity that is nearly impossible in ordinary consciousness."

"Why is that so, Doctor?"

"Because hypnosis accesses the part of the subconscious that is the 'tape recorder.' Everything you've ever seen, thought, spoken, heard, is recorded there indelibly. Sometimes, the material is quite linear and recognizable, sometimes it's couched in symbols—the mind speaking the mind's special language, you might say. But however it chooses to display itself to us, in regressive hypnosis, the mind permits us to 'rewind' to the experiences of other time slots, and replay their story—replete with sights, sounds, emotions—even memories as elusive as smell or taste."

"Have you ever attempted to regress anyone into a

past life, Doctor?'' Maggie asked earnestly. "Amanda has told me that's the request she made of you."

He chuckled. "I have not attempted to do so, because I do not have any knowledge that such lives exist! I have, of course, regressed people back as far as the womb, and occasionally their experiences during gestation are quite outstanding in their clarity. But beyond that . . ." He shrugged expressively.

"When Amanda told me of your desire to regress into a past life, Maggie, I explained that I thought this an unlikely goal. She is, however, most persuasive, as I expect you know, and she assured me you would be willing to simply regress back as far as we can go." He paused. "It would be helpful if you were to tell me why you find this journey such an urgent need."

"Dr. Strater," Maggie answered, liking his forthrightness, but not wanting to give him too much leading information, "I've been having a series of progressively more vivid dreams, all of which seem to take place in Ancient Egypt. They appear to be attempting to tell me a story that's of great consequence to my life, but they can't quite break through whatever barriers exist within me. At least that's how it feels to me. There are hundreds of fragments of these dreams running around inside me, now; but they're elusive, just beyond my grasp. I wake up filled with anxiety . . . frightened, sad . . . reaching for something . . ." She stopped for breath.

"A friend of mine who's involved in various occult disciplines suggested I go to a past-life reader, but frankly, that made me very wary. I don't want anyone who may be a charlatan, planting specious notions in my head about what these fragments mean. If they're *real*, and indicative of some ancient experience I've been through, I need to know that. But I don't want any New Age mumbo jumbo imposed on whatever I learn." She looked to him to see if he understood. "Does that make any sense to you, Doctor?"

"Indeed it does," he responded, obviously amused by her candor. "So you decided to try a legitimate psychiatric source, in hopes that whatever comes of it will, at least, be credible. Yes?"

"Exactly."

"Good. Then we are of like mind, here. So we will tape-record our sessions if you wish, that we may discuss whatever comes of our efforts, later in detail. Is this agreeable?" Maggie nodded.

"I find it best if you lie down on my couch, Maggie," he said, moving to the windows to draw the blinds. "Hypnosis requires a profound state of relaxation to be reached, which permits the access we spoke of earlier."

Maggie lay down on the couch; it was surprisingly comfortable, but she still felt inept and nervous. Dr. Strater sat down next to her and switched on the tape recorder.

"There are many methods of induction into the trance state that we call being hypnotized, Maggie. My preference is to guide you there with the sound of my voice. I will ask you to relax by taking several deep breaths, and then simply listening to my words, without demanding anything further of yourself."

Strater's voice was deep, kind, resonant—Maggie felt herself reluctantly letting go of her distrust, as he led her through a series of breathing exercises and step-by-step relaxation techniques, not unlike the ones she used in Yoga and martial arts.

Suddenly, she realized she was in a dual level of consciousness. She still knew exactly where she was, could sense the room around her, could feel the doctor's presence very clearly, yet as the voice directed her inward, she became cognizant of a second level of awareness—as if she had emerged into a profoundly tranquil landscape within herself. She heard the voice direct her to focus on an event that had happened in her life a year ago, and was surprised to find it recalled instantly, sharply delineated.

"We are moving backward in time now, Maggie," the

voice was saying. "We are flowing with the river of your memories, drifting back, gently back in time. There is a lovely sailboat on the river—you are sailing peacefully, back to the long ago. You are five years old, Maggie; tell me, what do you see?"

"I'm at my birthday party," she answered in a small voice. "My mommy baked a cake with a clown on it. When everybody goes home, I can have the clown part."

"That's very nice, Maggie," the voice congratulated. "Happy Birthday! How do you feel today?"

"I feel nice," she answered. "I got a dolly with red hair from my mommy, and a kitten from my daddy."

"Lovely presents, Maggie, lovely," the voice said encouragingly. "You must be a very good little girl. Now I'd like you to go back to the river with me and board the pretty boat again. You are drifting backward in time, and feeling very, very safe. You are two years old now, Maggie. Can you tell me where you are?"

"I'm in the kitchen," she replied, with a childish lisp. "The sink is high up. I want some water, but I can't climb up."

"Why not?"

"Not allowed. Mommy says I could hurt myself."

"That's true, Maggie. Your mommy is taking good care of you. Let's drift some more now, shall we? Let's go back to the day you were born and see how that feels, shall we?"

Dr. Strater watched the adult body on the couch curl up into a fetal position, twisting and turning as if in pain . . . Maggie's face screwed up suddenly and she started to cry like a newborn, tiny mewling sounds. The doctor hesitated for a moment, then plunged ahead. "It's all right, Maggie," he said gently. "Everything is just fine, now. We are going back to the river—we are going drifting again, and that will soothe your discomfort. This time we're looking for something very special, so you must help me. I want you to follow the river as far as you need to, until you can find the time most relevant to your current issues, Maggie. You may sail along very comfortably . . . and you may take as long as you need to find the time that keeps coming up in your dreams."

Maggie had ceased to cry and was lying very, very still now.

"Where are you, Maggie? Can you tell me where you are?"

"I'm in the temple." Her voice was clear and vibrantly youthful.

"What temple, Maggie?"

"The Temple of the Great Mother, of course. I am training to be her priestess."

Strater frowned and made a note on his pad.

"What have you learned in your training, Maggie?"

"Why do you call me by that name?"

"I beg your pardon?"

"My name is Mim. Why do you call me by another?"

Dr. Strater pursed his lips and jotted something hastily in his notebook.

"Forgive my error, Mim. I will call you by your proper name. I would like to learn of your training."

"Much is forbidden to a man. Of the Mother's Mysteries I may not speak."

"No, of course not. Is there anything you may tell me?"

"I have been a *Looking Girl*. That is not forbidden to reveal."

"A Looking Girl? What is a Looking Girl?"

"We are the scryers. We read events in the mirror pool, or in the crystal. I have been trained to Turn the Sands, as well."

"To Turn the Sands? What is that?"

Maggie's eyes narrowed, although they were shut.

"Are you a foreigner? You seem to know little of our ways."

Strater smiled. "I am a traveler, Mim. But I wish to understand your customs. Can you tell me of Turning the Sands?"

"I am not permitted to tell you the process, merely

that I can read the past and future, when I take my insect form."

"I see. Do you have other special gifts as well?"

"I am trained as a healer . . . I know the means of leading the Ka from the body during surgery, so there is no pain. Many people say this is a good gift."

"I should say it is," Strater responded genuinely. "Can you tell me how you do this?"

"Have you the Fourth Degree?"

"What is the Fourth Degree?"

"I must not speak of the process, unless you have been tested."

"I see. I see. Perhaps, it would be best if we speak of something else, then, Mim. My degrees are a bit different from yours, I believe."

She nodded approvingly, then brightened as if remembering something she could discuss.

"I am trained to walk the Astral and the Underworld," she offered. "To accompany the newly dead through their transformation. It is said that I have a special talent and that Anubis approves my efforts. But I must be careful to avoid pride. Mother Isis would be offended were I to boast to you."

"Mim, I have journeyed far to reach you here at the temple. I believe I have been brought here for a special purpose. Can you tell me what that purpose is?"

A look of confusion transformed Maggie's face. "I know not the purpose," she said hesitantly.

"Is it possible you could look into the mirrored pool and find out?"

"I will try," she answered and a great stillness suffused the body on the couch. Maggie lay breathing deeply and evenly, as if entranced, for nearly four minutes by the clock. Suddenly, her eyes snapped open in an expression of absolute terror. Maggie opened her mouth and screamed; there was despair and anguish in the sound. Her body trembled so violently she nearly fell from the couch.

Dr. Strater reached over and grasped Maggie's wrist

firmly for a moment, taking her pulse. His brows furrowed at the distress he read there. He leaned very close and spoke to her.

"Mim, dear, *do not be afraid,*" he instructed, with laser concentration. "I will help you. You are safe." The screams quieted to sobs. "You will be returning me to Maggie now, please." He waited a moment, watching her features rearrange themselves, then said, "Maggie, I want you to go back to the river, immediately. You will be safe there. When you reach the river, you will signal me by raising your right hand."

Maggie's hand began to elevate.

"Thank you, my dear. That's very good. You may lower your hand. You are now stepping onto your beautiful, swift sailboat and beginning to float toward me, on the river of time. You will follow it back toward where you began today's journey. You may take as long as you wish to return to the present day . . . my voice will guide you on the river, so you needn't worry about finding your way."

Maggie's body had begun to tremble violently again and Strater sat forward, a look of real concern on his face, as he took her hand in his own again. "Tell me what is happening now, Maggie. Where are you?" His voice was authoritative.

"Convent," she gasped. "They're coming for me. I have been denounced."

"Who's coming, Maggie."

"The Dominicans. They will take me to the Inquisitor."

"What year is it, now, Maggie?"

"Fourteen eighty-three!"

"Maggie, go to the river, *immediately!* You must do exactly as I say. Run swiftly to the river of time, and sail toward the sound of my voice. The Dominicans cannot touch you on the river." He waited a moment, watching her closely. "I am waiting for you in the year 1993, Maggie. You are coming closer now . . . you are very near me on the river. You are absolutely safe in the sound of my voice!"

The trembling ceased again, and Maggie's contorted face relaxed.

"I'm going to count from five to one, Maggie, to bring you back to ordinary consciousness. When I reach the number one, you will be fully awake, and aware of what has just happened. You will feel well and strong. Nod your head if you understand me, Maggie."

Her head moved slowly up and down.

"Five . . . four . . . three . . . you are back in 1993, now, in my office, Maggie. All is well. I will count backward from three to one—and when I reach it you will open your eyes. Three . . . two . . . *one,*" he said gently, encouragingly, worry under tight control.

Maggie opened her eyes and looked directly at Strater, her eyes wide and desperate. "I was there," she breathed tremulously. "Oh, God! We were *all* there!" Tears slid down her cheeks and glistened in her eyes, as she struggled to an upright position. She put her head in her hands and wept.

Dr. Heinrich Strater laid down his clipboard and pencil, reached over to shut off his tape recorder with a definitive .click. There was no sound in the room but Maggie's sobbing.

He stared at her for a while before speaking. "I don't know what to say," he murmured, handing her a box of tissues. "I simply don't know what we have here."

"What happened to me, Doctor?" Maggie asked hoarsely.

Strater shook his head slowly, thoughtfully. "In truth, Maggie, I don't know, I can only speculate . . .

"It would appear you became involved, somehow, in a parallel reality. Whether it has a basis in fact, or only in your own psyche, I cannot say."

"In other words, Doctor, there's a distinct possibility I may be cracked?" she said emphatically.

Strater smiled at her, great kindliness in his expression. "Someone once said that of William Blake, I believe, and Dame Edith Sitwell responded, 'That was where the Light came through.' "

She looked at him bleakly.

"Who is to say what is possible?" Strater went on, trying to soothe her. "There are those who believe that memory exists for us at a cellular, or even a DNA level . . . There are others in the psychoanalytic community who would be more likely to think of this in terms of Oedipal development, or any number of neuroses or psychoses. I would prefer to keep an open mind."

"I can't describe to you how *real* it all was to me," she said, distress making her voice unsteady. "I *was* that other woman—that priestess. I *felt* the youth and strength of her body, could *feel* her uncertainties . . . how can I possibly describe to you how vivid this all was for me, Dr. Strater?

"I knew *viscerally* the rites of the training she'd endured. Priestesses weren't just *servants* of the Gods or Goddesses . . . they were *conduits* for the Gods themselves! That's why they had to be pure; that's why they had to be celibate! They were actually *used* by the God or Goddess as lightning rods to bring down the energy! Changed on a cellular level, so the energy of the deity could come through . . . they were the receiving station for the transmission! That's why we speak of surrender to God . . . they surrendered their very being to the use of their God or Goddess. In my case, it was Isis."

"Wasn't Isis the Goddess of memory as well as all her other talents?" Dr. Strater probed. "According to the legend, didn't she search the length and breadth of Egypt to find Osiris's body, and then she *re*-membered him!"

Maggie sagged back against the couch, her mind on circuitry overload. "I've got to go back there," she said softly. "The answers are there, I know they are. I've got to go back for Cody's sake."

Dr. Strater pursed his lips and his bushy brows knitted together in a judicious frown. "The only place you need to go back to today, Maggie, is your home. If you wish to attempt another regression—after you've rested and had time to think this through—I would be willing to work with you. But you must accept that I am a doctor, and my first concern must be for your physical safety in *this* incarnation."

Maggie nodded, rising from the couch. "I'm very grateful to you, Dr. Strater. I think you may have given me the key to a greater mystery than you know of . . . if I can just find the courage to open the lock."

Strater put Maggie's coat about her shoulders, and held the door for her. After she'd stepped into the hallway, he called to her. "Just one thing, Maggie . . . before you go. Please. Do you know what happened to you, at the end of the regression? Do you know what it was that frightened you so?"

She turned to look at him again, an unreadable expression in her eyes.

"I earned the wrath of a Goddess," she said simply. "And the time has come to pay the price."

# CHAPTER 56

The Village streets appeared alien to Maggie as she made her way home from Strater's office. They seemed an unaccustomed gray, as if the desert sun that had seared her hypnotic memories had now been plucked from the world against her will, and all that was left was drab and eerie.

*Stop it Maggie!* It's dark, that's all, she chided herself, acidly. New York, *dusk*. With all its stone-gray filth and dreary, cranky-looking faces hurrying home from work. No more. No less.

She turned the key in the lock of home, and saw that her hand was trembling. She thought of calling Dev, or Peter, or Ellie, but even the effort of telephoning seemed beyond her.

*Weary*. She felt so weary it was an effort to climb the stairs to her bedroom. Maggie took off her eye makeup on auto-pilot, and splashed cool water on her face. Without undressing, she lay across the bed. There was a pounding in her head, as if something captive were trying to get out. And the dizziness was getting worse. There was something terribly wrong with her, but she was far too tired to care.

Maggie closed her eyes . . .

And awakened in Saqqara.

The temple garden was a colonnaded idyll of shade and sunlight. The royal gardeners had been consulted by the priestly ones long years ago in an effort to create an oasis worthy of Gods or pharaohs. Limestone from Sumeria, marble from Babylon. Irrigation conduits that could make even a desert into Paradise.

Mim loved the garden, with its tranquil pool and lacy, swaying shadows from the fruit trees that ringed it. But, she was restless today and rebellious. It was the time of the Nile's inundation; the time when all blood ran high to match the river's fecundity, or so Meri-Neyt, her tutor, had said.

She didn't like to fool Meri-Neyt, as she had today. The beautiful young priestess was friend as well as teacher, and she had a joyous disposition that made even the tedium of endless study, bearable. Mathematics, astronomy, architecture, philosophy, history, healing, religion. There was so much to learn and so much pressure to excel . . .

So, she had fibbed to Meri-Neyt and said she needed to rest in her cell today, instead of being tutored. The lie disturbed Mim's conscience, but the call of freedom was hard to deny.

The pool had been commissioned for the visits of highly placed dignitaries, and was seldom used at this time of year. Mim made her way to the garden carefully, excited by the mischief, and the prospect of her solitary swim.

But she was not alone. A young boy dove into the pool just as she emerged from the passageway door. His graceful young body cut the water like a dolphin, and he swam effortlessly the length of the pool and back again before he saw her watching.

"Wait!" he called out as she turned to go. "Don't leave."

There was ample time later to ponder what might have been her Fate had she not answered his summons on that afternoon so rife with destiny.

He left the water, shaking himself like a puppy, his long dark hair glistening in the sun. Mim was nine years old, and he seemed only a year or two more, but he was not as shy as she.

"You aren't supposed to be here," he said, imperiously for one so young, and she surprised them both by giggling.

"I live here," she replied, trying to contain her mirth. "I am training for initiation."

The boy eyed her appraisingly. "As am I," he said, in the same serious mode. But then a grin broke free, and he added in a conspiratorial tone, "I'm supposed to be doing my studies, but I tired of them. What's your name?

"Mim-Atet-Ra. But I am called Mim. And yours?"

"You may call me Karaden. It's a great privilege, you know, to call me by my secret name."

Mim giggled again. She had never known a boy before, except when she was very little, in her home at Mennofer. Here, at the temple, she had always been aware that her virginity was promised to Isis. Maybe all boys were pompous and overconfident, she thought, but she couldn't be sure. At least, he was interesting.

"Are you not afraid that they will find us together?" she asked. He dismissed the question with a gesture of the hand.

"I am Karaden," he said. "The servants must obey, when I speak. *All* must obey."

Karaden. The name seemed lovely and elegant, so she repeated it softly.

"Do you really *not* know who I am?" he asked, sounding miffed that she hadn't responded properly.

Mim shook her head.

"I am Snefru, the eldest son of Pharaoh. Heir to the Double Crown."

That startled Mim, but she had been emboldened by their conversation. "If you are truly heir to Pharaoh, why are you alone here?" she asked, uncertain if she could believe his boast.

A cloud passed over the boy's countenance, and when he spoke, he no longer sounded like a boy trying to be king, but rather, just a boy trying to be understood.

"It is difficult ever to be alone at the palace," he said. "I have many duties that I must perform daily, and my father expects me to sit beside him when he gives judgment, that I may learn to be just. Everyone watches me. The Vizier and the servants. Even the lowly food taster spies on me, lest some misstep of mine send poison to his gullet." The boy shook his head, seeming sadder and more vulnerable than before.

"It doesn't sound like people should envy you so . . ." Mim said judiciously. "Do you have any friends?"

Karaden shook his dark head. "It is difficult to have a friend, when everyone curries favor. There is much to gain by being close to Pharaoh's son, so it is hard to trust that anyone craves my company for myself, alone."

Mim cocked her head to one side and regarded him with curiosity. "I could be your friend," she said. "There is *nothing* I can gain from you or your father. I was promised to the Goddess at birth, and my life will be what the Goddess wills. No more, no less." She looked at the troubled boy with honest eyes. "I, too, am lonely," she said. "My tutor, Meri-Neyt, is a lovely person . . . very smart and very funny, sometimes. But she is many years older than I." She paused to think a moment, then said, "On my honor, I will never betray your trust, Karaden, if you wish me to be your friend."

He paused to consider the offer. She was only a girl, and appeared to be somewhat younger than himself. But she had a nice face; open and free of subterfuge. And, she was right that there was little influence she would ever need beg of Pharaoh. Priestesses of the Goddess were beyond worldly needs.

"I will be your friend," he pronounced as if bestowing the Crown Jewels, then he pulled a ring from his finger and held it out to her. "You may keep this as a token."

Mim giggled again, and moved toward the pool. "I need nothing of yours, Karaden," she called, as she waded into the refreshing water. "But I will race you to the other side, and *win!*" And she was off like a minnow beneath the silvered surface, with Karaden only lagging behind long enough to wonder why anyone would refuse a gift from Pharaoh's son.

MERI-NEYT sat on the stone bench, her cloak draped over the books beside her. She was very fond of her young charge; she understood the twenty-year tortuous journey the child would have to make in her company, before she could hope for initiation.

Meri-Neyt's humorous disposition lightened her lesson giving, and Mim sprawled now on the ground at her feet, listening diligently, as Meri outlined the rigors of the spiritual path ahead.

"The *Neophyte's* journey through the First Degree will teach you of the soul's descent into Hades, Mim," Meri-Neyt was saying. "This is symbolic of the soul's incarnation in a human body, of course, and is essential to your understanding of your destiny. After that, will come the *Initiate's* journey, in which you will learn the meaning of karma, and how to eventually escape the wheel of earthly rebirth. There will be many tests, of radically increasing difficulty, as you ascend the ladder of Enlightenment. Finally, you will reach the *Hierophant* phase, in which you will explore how a seeker after the Greater Mysteries may learn to unite her individual soul with the Divine Oversoul. Only after this, can you aspire to the Order of Melchizedek." Meri paused to see if Mim was listening.

"To join this Order you must survive the final initiation in Knut, the awesome House of Hidden Places, from which place of trial few ever return. This is why I teach you so relentlessly, Mim. Why I instruct you so strenuously in the mystery teachings of Thoth-Hermes, and feed you only the finest fruits, seeds, nuts, grains, vegetables, and plant proteins to enliven your brain and heart. You must be strong of body, mind, and spirit to survive the ordeal ahead."

"I understand your concern for me, Meri," Mim said, forcing herself to pay attention to her tutor. "And I am well content with my life, dear teacher. The temple studies give me pleasure as well as aggravation . . . and I love the Goddess beyond even what you know." Mim turned her face toward Meri earnestly.

"When I surrender myself to Her divine energy, I feel myself the luckiest of mortals." Truth was that Mim felt so deep a union with the Divine Mother that she often sought her out when she was troubled, just as if she were an earthly mother. With Her, she cried and laughed; to Her she offered a daily accounting of her life.

Meri observed her student closely. It was true that the girl had an uncommon devotion to Isis, that except for its exceptional innocence and piety, might have bordered on the profane. From the first, the child had seemed to feel almost a sense of camaraderie with the Divine Mother. It was a curiosity.

"Has it ever occurred to you, Mim," she asked the girl seriously, "that you might falter on the path of righteousness that leads to the foot of Her Eternal Throne?"

Mim looked genuinely shocked by the thought. "I am woefully imperfect, Meri-Neyt, as you well know. And I do worry sometimes, that I may fail Mother Isis through my ignorance. But she seems not to have withdrawn her favor from me because of my inadequacies."

"The way to her is long and arduous, Mim, dear," Meri said, the compassion of one who has already suffered in her tone. "Love alone will not be enough to protect you on the pilgrim's way."

Mim frowned at the thought.

"Whatever the Mother demands of me, I will give," she said.

Mim would have cause to recall these words in the fullness of time.

THE years of training sat well on Mim-Atet-Ra's shoulders, despite their rigors. She had a special gift for healing and spent many more hours in the healing temples than was required, as she possessed the skill to loose the Ka from the body during surgery, and was much in demand by the trepanners and surgeons.

She had a gift for games, as well, and was lithe and spirited as a young boy in her athletic skills. Meri-Neyt was heard to chuckle with another tutor that if her young charge were to fail the test of priesthood, she could always apply to Pharaoh's bodyguard as a warrior.

Mim studied all that was required of her willingly, and performed her duties without complaint. But, as she grew, it was not the time spent in training that filled her heart with joy, but rather the one sweet month per year, when she was heart-friend to Pharaoh's eldest son.

Karaden was pledged to Ra, and most of his training was conducted at On, the Temple of the Sun, at Heliopolis, but because his father was as much a mystic as a king, Karaden was also trained in the Great Mother's Mysteries, so that he might become a balanced ruler. Thus, for one month per year Karaden lived and studied at Saqqara.

Each year, in the time of inundation, he would come in a Royal Progress consisting of entourage, priests,

servants, couriers, and all the other endless retinue that
accompanies royalty. He would attend to the duties demanded of him, and then he would send for Mim. By
the lotus pool, they would renew their acquaintance, to
see how each had grown and changed . . . to share their
varied newfound knowledge . . . to tell the secrets
they'd been saving up for this precious moment of unburdening. They shared their aspirations and their
dreams; in her alone, he could confide his secret fears,
for she alone of all his subjects asked nothing of him but
his friendship.

To be Pharaoh was the greatest honor, he told her, but
it carried with it awesome responsibilities. The Double
Kingdom was the Great Work of civilization that the
Gods had given into mankind's care—but to follow in
the royal footsteps of one like Zoser was no easy task.
And, too, he had yet to face the Abyss, where not even
being Pharaoh's son would save him if he failed the test.

Mim lived for those blessed conversations. She, who
had no other true confidant; whose family, although kind
and loving, lived in Mennofer, while she dwelled apart
in the Temple of Isis; she, who would never in life be
free to choose as she wished, but only as she was destined, longed for these moments of intimacy.

She wondered later, when their time had run the glass,
if the elders of the temple allowed them such freedom
because they knew she was vowed to celibacy, and
could never be Karaden's seductress . . . or because
they knew full well the temptation they would undergo,
and considered it their karma.

IN the summer of her fifteenth year, Mim hastened to
the lotus pool, as usual, on the day of Karaden's arrival.
She was excited as a child at the prospect of seeing him,
and had to force herself to a dignified propriety, lest the
other priestesses murmur at her lack of dignity. But,

instead of the boy who had left the summer before, a man awaited her.

Karaden stood resplendent in the white linen toga of Kingship. He wore the golden girdle of Pharaoh's heir, and the uraeus crowned his head. Mim gazed transfixed from the doorway of the colonnade, suddenly shy as a fawn. Her heart caught in her throat as his eyes met hers and beckoned her forward, and she walked toward him never knowing where she placed her feet.

In the moment they touched, she knew that all had changed between them, irrevocably, and without their consent, for she saw in Karaden's eyes the same astonished love she felt in her own breast.

For the balance of the afternoon, the two young people sat, entranced by each other's existence until the golden sun had set behind the great step-pyramid. The servants came and went, wonderingly, for Karaden wouldn't heed their summons to his various duties, and when Meri-Neyt came to remind Mim of her obligations, the Prince commanded that Mim remain at his side. They talked for hours of what, she could never afterward be certain, yet the music of his voice remained. They drowned in each other's eyes; their souls touched, as they always had in childhood, but now all was more than it had been.

"You are so changed," she breathed, wanting to reach out and touch him, but fearing to.

"Nay, I am the same," he said. "You are the only one who knows who I am."

"But you are a *man*, my Karaden. For the first time you seem to me more Pharaoh's son, than the boy I raced with in the lotus pool."

He took her hand in his and clasped it to his lips. "*Never* say that, Mim. To everyone else I must be Pharaoh! . . . only to you am I Karaden. I've thought of you, night and day through this last year of dawning knowledge, Mim. I've sat in council and dreamed of asking your advice . . . I've sat in judgment, and known the goodness and wisdom of your heart would render fairer justice than mine . . . I've lain in my bed at night and longed to hold you in my arms. We are soul mates, Mim-Atet-Ra," he said. "Surely the Gods do not mean us to be separated . . ."

THE days that followed were a blur of unexpected emotion. Each morning he called for her to attend him; despite the murmurs of his retinue, and the disapproving looks of the elders, no one dared question Karaden's authority. Or perhaps, they simply better understood what was unfolding than the two young people who were in the eye of the rising storm.

There was a loneliness in Karaden, that touched Mim deeply.

"Do you love your father?" she asked one day, as they wandered beneath the acacia trees.

"He is wise and kind," Karaden answered hesitantly. "He has mastery of so much that I aspire to, Mim, that I sometimes tread the borderline of envy. I admire him, and I wish to learn from him, yet . . ." He walked a moment more, before continuing.

"When I was young I longed to be freed from the constraint of rulership. I saw the cobbler's son run to his father laughing, with a ball in his hand . . . I heard the fisherman speak with his father of unimportant things . . . and I envied them.

"Once, when I was small, I was hurt badly in a game and I ran to Pharaoh for comfort. He greeted me sternly, and said that kings must never allow their subjects to see them weak or vulnerable . . . that we owe our subjects courage beyond that of other mortals, because we are the seed of Gods." He smiled a little, but she could see there was moisture in his eyes. "I did not feel like a God, that day, my darling Mim. I felt like a little boy with a wounded leg, who needed comforting.

"Now that I've grown to manhood, I see that vulnerability is not an easy state for kings. Too often, it is their last . . ." He laughed shortly. "So I understand the value of the lesson he taught me . . . yet, I do sometimes wish that he could be my friend."

Mim took his hand tentatively in her own. "The son of Pharaoh has so much power and material treasure, and so little joy, my dear one. I wish I could change the balance for you."

It was then that he reached up and pulled her to him on the grass, and she let herself be drawn to the warm earth, and the young, virile strength of his body. And his lips sought hers hungrily, exploring the depths of her in a way she had never dreamed. She was carried on waves whose current was so strong it took her minutes to realize how far from shore and safety she had traveled on the tide.

Mim pulled herself from his arms, gasping, as the knowledge crashed through her that she *lusted*. Promised to the Lady Isis, the question of loving a man had never once been raised with Mim. She understood full well that she was to be celibate in order to be a pure vessel for the Mother's Essence. She knew, too, that at some point in the future it might be required that she mate and bring forth a child, but, if so, the man would be chosen by the Reverend Mother; he would be to her no more than a donor of the seed with which to quicken the sacrificial egg.

"Karaden, beloved," she breathed, exulting in the words, at the same moment they filled her with terror. "How can this be? I am promised to the Goddess."

"Others have been freed from their vows," he said, reaching for her once again. The touch of his flesh flooded her with desire, pulsing, urgent, not to be denied. And it was only the beginning . . .

KARADEN had come that summer in final preparation for the test of death and rebirth, that would take place

in one year's time. Three days would he lie in the stone
Sarcophagus, while his Ka traveled first beyond the
River Styx, then to the Crystal Temple of the Masters
on the Inner Plane, and finally, the length and breadth
of Egypt. If he survived the ordeals encountered at every turn, he would be Pharaoh.

Every morning he labored with the priests and priestesses to learn what he must in preparation; but late
every afternoon, he would come to the lotus pool and
command that Mim do the same. Meri-Neyt warned her
pupil of the terrible dangers of temptation, but she was
powerless to forbid her to heed the call of the heir to
Pharaoh's throne. And, indeed, Meri-Neyt was far too
wise to think she could keep the girl from her own destiny.

KARADEN lay on his back beside the still water and Mim
sat beside him, memorizing every detail of his face and
body.

"Do you never wonder why we exist on this earth?"
he asked suddenly, as it were the most important of
questions.

"To serve the Gods," she answered.

"But why, Mim? Why do they wish us to serve them?
And why have they made the game of life so unfair? The
good die young, the poor suffer illnesses they cannot
cure, the greedy often win, while the pure in heart are
left to suffer?"

"All will be fair in the end, my prince," she answered,
shocked by his question. "Poor in one life, wealthy in
another . . . king and slave, and all in between. When
we have lived enough lives so that we have found our
way back to God, we will see that all was fair."

Karaden propped himself up on an elbow, concentration etched on his brow. "But *why*, dear Mim, should
they require of us this hard journey? Why must we be

separated out from them in the first place, thrust from
Paradise, left to wander life after life, struggling to learn
what we once knew? Did you never wonder if it could
be merely a sadistic game for them to watch our struggles?"

"You are looking into a dark whirlpool, Karaden.
There are things we cannot, *must* not know."

"But I *wish* to know, Mim! I will be Pharaoh, and I
will be priest/hierophant and if it is possible for me to
know, I will find out."

"You dare the Gods when you speak thus, Karaden,"
she said uneasily.

"No," he answered with great seriousness. "I merely
challenge them to answer me. It is a fair question."

"Perhaps, because you are a king—"

"No!" he said quickly. "Because I am a man."

Karaden spoke of kingship, and Mim of prophecy,
and they shared their secret fears . . . but, when they
parted each night, Mim would hurry to her cell, ecstatic
and afraid. She would kneel before the Goddess and
pour forth her wonder and confusion. *What shall I do?
O Great Queen of Heaven*, she pleaded. *I never meant
for this to be!* She begged for guidance as was her custom, but the Goddess did not answer.

The days and nights became her torment and her exal-
tation; there was new meaning in every breath. Mim
prayed to the Goddess to understand and guide her;
Karaden, too, was a God, and she felt herself no match
for either of them. Her mind betrayed her, for she could
force no thought into its confines, but thought of him.
Her soul betrayed her, for she saw this not as sin, but
as the sweetest expression of the Goddess energy she
had been honed to channel.

*"Did not you love Osiris beyond all else in the Uni-
verse?"* she cried out in her prayers. *"Did you not move
Heaven and Earth by the power of your love for him?"*
But the Goddess was mute within her and made no
reply.

354 CATHY CASH SPELLMAN

As THE days wore on, Mim and Karaden bathed in the splendor of their growing love. They told each other nothing could come between them. Other priestess-designates had been freed from their vow of celibacy . . . other pharaohs had made their own choice of queen, in lieu of the court-planned alliance.

In her innocence, Mim thought their love as inevitable as the rising of the sun, or the phases of the moon. They were heart-friends, and in the great spiral dance of life, they knew each other's steps.

Karaden told her she was to be his queen, and was so certain they could marry that she almost believed. He was the earthly incarnation of a God, he reminded her; he could bargain with a Goddess, without desperate consequences.

"I will petition my father," he said, "and he will speak with the High Priestess. There have been priest and priestess on the throne of Khemu before. You have not yet taken your final vow of celibacy . . . the priestess will understand that you can serve your Goddess and the people best as my queen."

And, so she hoped with all her heart that the Goddess would relent.

But, Karaden's petition was denied.

KARADEN sent for Mim, and she found him pacing like a caged beast. His anger radiated, crackling from his clenched fists, as if he clutched a lightning bolt. She had never before seen his fury.

"Pharaoh has *spoken!*" Karaden said mockingly. She had never heard him other than respectful of his father and was troubled at the force of his anger. "We are admonished never to see each other again! I will face the Abyss *immediately* I am told—if I survive, my training will be deemed complete, and I will never return here, except on state occasions."

Mim stood, turned to stone, all hope extinguished in a breath. All life stretched out before her like the desert sands, barren and infinite; if hearts could break, hers did, in that instant. The pain would remain within her, when five thousand years had run the hourglass.

Karaden strode to Mim, and clasped her by the arms, forcing her tearful eyes to his. "I have thought about nothing but this, through the night, beloved," he said urgently. "We may yet prevail, but the road ahead is fraught with danger. You must hear my plan."

Mim nodded, too numb to wonder at his fierceness. Only a king could think to challenge both a pharaoh and a Goddess.

"If you are not a virgin they cannot consecrate you as they plan." She looked up, stricken to the soul— could he be suggesting that they steal from the Goddess?

"But, I have been *promised!*"

"But, not by *you*, beloved!" he said hurriedly. "Don't you see? Your parents dedicated you without your consent. You have the right to protest." He straightened, but kept her eyes riveted to his own. "As I have the right to refuse my father's choice of bride."

Karaden reached for Mim and clasped her in a wild embrace. He kissed her with all the pent-up passion of their long denial, holding, touching, probing. And she was inflamed with a lust beyond anything she had ever imagined. She *wanted* him. Desire raged in her, heightened by the desperate fear of loss. His hands caressed her breasts, her face, her very soul. She was mad with love, and in that moment might have let him have his way . . . but he drew back, flushed, struggling for control. "Not here," he said. "Tonight, beyond the temple, through the labyrinth. I will send my servant, Zeb, for you. He will lead you to me. Then we will make an offering of our love to both our Gods, and ask their blessing on it."

"But the Goddess will be angry . . ."

Karaden stood back and faced her, the power of his divine lineage apparent in his aspect. "I am of Pharaoh's seed," he said. "I, too, am sprung of Gods, and Ra is Greater than the Goddess. He will prevail."

"But I am *mortal*, Karaden!" Mim pleaded, terrified by what he suggested. "What will become of *me*, if Gods do battle for our souls?"

He did not answer her, for in his love and confidence he would not see clearly. But, Mim was suddenly in the grip of vision and saw a momentary flash of truth: *When Gods do battle over mortals, only the Gods prevail.*

There was a kind of madness upon her when she left him. She told Meri-Neyt she was ill, and must be left alone in her chamber, and Meri, knowing full well the cause of her illness, begged her to beware. But Mim was driven by the blindness of her love.

Beneath the temple city was a labyrinth of catacombs. Other temples had been built upon this site in ancient times, for Saqqara was a holy place on the energy grid of the Earth Mother, and sacred to her flame. The old ruins had always attracted the girl; she had felt *power* in this strange cavernous world below the temples, that was more comforting than anywhere else. Perhaps, it was the energy of the Earth Mother that pulsed from the ancient rock and sand, perhaps it was the inconceivable quiet that made her feel she had entered the silence of the Gods.

Mim hastened to this secret place of solace; her sorrow, fear, and confusion could be dealt with there. She wandered, mindlessly, through the ancient haunts of long-dead priestesses, and held strange, desperate conversations in her head, not knowing where she put her feet.

Perhaps, some unseen hand guided her way, for after a length of time that had no meaning to her, she found herself in a place she had not been before. A vast round chamber had been hewn from the primordial basalt and sandstone; twelve great arches made by man or nature formed a sanctuary.

Wonderingly, Mim approached the nearest arch; an incandescent glow was emanating from the interior. Unworldly, it was . . . as different from the light above, as the music of the celestial spheres would be from that of an earthly harpist.

She was drawn inexorably to the glow.

There, upon an altar cut from the largest crystal she had ever encountered, stood the Isis Amulet. But not as she had seen it in her father's house.

The Goddess energy pulsed within it now. Radiant, breathtaking, powerful, beyond mere mortal's capacity to contemplate . . . it had been consecrated by the Great Mother Herself. Awe filled the young priestess, for in that moment she knew that she blundered into the Holy of Holies. *This chamber was Her Womb.*

It was a sign. Surely the Goddess herself had led her here to this treasure, that Karaden and she might solve their terrible dilemma. Mim-Atet-Ra knelt and gave thanks that her prayer had been answered. It all seemed so clear to her, then . . . later, she wondered if she had gone mad for love. She touched the magic Amulet.

In that awesome instant, the power of the Goddess was drawn down through her as if she were a lightning rod! In that flash of unutterable power, she *understood* the mastery of priesthood. The Goddess energy swirled through her, electrifying every cell with brilliant light. She felt her pelvis expand into infinity, to *become* the Cauldron of the Mother. She was the essence of femaleness! Whirled out beyond her finite limits, she could *see* the eternal matrix—the blueprint for humanity itself. The male and female components of life revealed, with all their eternal vulnerability. She could see that while men felt they had strength in their pelvis, in fact it was their weakest part, for it led them into folly and wasted time. But to the female it was the Divine Center—the core of a strength so powerful it kept the world alive, for women are the cauldron from which life generates.

She was entranced . . . drunk with a power she was not yet schooled to channel.

Mim did a desperate thing. The kind of act that ever after seems inconceivable.

She took the Amulet from the altar. No one was near; no one would miss it for a few hours. Had not the Mother led her here to help her in her need? She would take it to Karaden. They would pray together to the Great Mother for deliverance, and she would see the purity of their love and hear their prayer.

Mim returned to her room to rest for a few hours before her scheduled rendezvous with Karaden, the Isis Amulet tucked inside her tunic, so near her heart. She drifted off to sleep.

And this is what she saw:

In a dream/vision the Goddess Isis came. She was robed in glory beyond what mortals ever know . . . She rode the crescent moon and the greatest stars of the firmament illumined her crown. She was wondrous and fierce, in the way of Immortals, and her voice was mightier than all the trumpets of the earth.

"Priestess, daughter, arise and hear me!" she demanded, and Mim felt her astral self lift from the boundaries of the physical body on the bed, held to it only by the silver etheric cord that nourishes the Ka.

She stood in the manner of priestesses, hands raised before her, and then made her obeisance, frightened and vulnerable, as if Tehuti held the final measurement of her life in his great scales. All hubris had dropped from her beneath the Eternal gaze, for it was Truth incarnate. Her soul trembled before the Mother, for the scales had fallen from her eyes and she knew, then, how gravely she had sinned.

"*Sin is in the heart-thought as well as in the act,*" the Goddess thundered. "You agreed to give to Karaden, what you had promised me. I will not be mocked!"

Mim might have argued with a human judge, for her rationalizations still held fast within her, but not with Her, for rationalization is not Truth.

"You have stolen my Amulet for personal gain . . ."

*By my life, Great Goddess, I had not thought of it*

*as that!* she wanted to cry out, and cringe before her awesome wrath and beg forgiveness, but she was a priestess, and to do so would have dishonored the Divine Mother.

The Goddess knew all that transpired in the girl's heart and tempered her wrath, a little.

"Yet, will I give you one last chance to redeem yourself," she said, "for the greater fault lies with the one who led you into folly. Despite your sin, Mim-Atet-Ra, there is purity and goodness in your heart, and Tehuti weighs the sins of the warm-hearted and those of the cold-blooded in different measures. As do I.

"There is a flaw in the design of mortals, which must be taken into account here. Free will, we gave them at Creation. It was Our one mistake."

She raised her hand and the heavens parted as if a veil had been drawn aside, taking with it stars and planets, galaxies and all beyond them . . .

*"Two futures . . ."* The words echoed down the corridors of time, as she faded from Mim's sight. And then a world unfolded before the stricken priestess:

In her vision she saw Karaden. He was a great and honorable pharaoh, beloved by the people of two kingdoms, for he had brought them naught but good. She watched his life unfold from youth to manhood to old age . . . she saw him wage war against the Ethiopians, and avert a devastating famine by his skillful manipulation of trade, and by opening the granaries of Pharaoh to the people. His was a long and fruitful reign, blessed by five sons and daughters, whom he loved, and by a peaceful and prosperous kingdom.

Beside him, through it all, was his queen—a good and loving woman, who brought order to his household and joy to his heart. Mim thought her own heart would strangle from the anguish of seeing another in the place she dared to dream of as her own.

The vision cleared. The night sky full of diamond stars again blanketed Mim's view, and the voice of the Great Mother filled the echoless space of eternity.

*"The future, too . . ."* she said, in a thunderous tone that could make mountains tremble into dust.

Again the veil of heaven was drawn back, to reveal the hour of her scheduled rendezvous with Karaden.

Aghast, and utterly fascinated, Mim saw herself lying wrapped in Karaden's arms. She watched as they made love as only those born to be together may, feeling each other's essence in cell and soul. She, who knew nothing of how to love a man, knew everything. He, who knew all, learned more from her trust. She watched, barely able to breathe, as their lifeforce left its accustomed place, and went to dwell in each other that they might be one. She felt his hands and mouth on her secret places, felt the moist swelling of desire, and the urgent pulse that pushes all beyond endurance to the place of bliss. In every lustful, exquisite detail, she lived her love for Karaden.

Before morning dawned, he left her, his kisses still warm upon her body, his seed already quickening in her womb. In the anguish of her heightened powers of vision, Mim saw that he was called to face the test of the Abyss.

Karaden was the greatest talent of any initiate the priests had ever trained, they said. But he entered the Ordeal, distracted by their love, and weakened by their ecstacy.

Mim watched him die.

In heartsickness beyond description, she watched the new Pharaoh take Karaden's place upon the Lotus Throne. He was a lesser man, of venal habits and flexible morality. She saw him lead Khemu into destruction, famine, war. A great pestilence swept the land in the wake of the carnage.

Mim saw, too, that a daughter had been conceived by her, with Karaden. She watched the unfoldment of the brilliant child, in a world made dangerous for the gifted, and knew that she had borne one chosen for a special destiny.

She fled with the child to the desert, to escape the

ravagement that came to Khemu-Amenti. They lived as fugitive ascetics, on the fringes of what had been her world, and she trained her daughter in the Mother's way.

The people cried out to the Gods in their despair, for evil priests seized control of the temples, and the Powers of Darkness overwhelmed the Light. Before the vision faded, Mim watched her daughter go to the Temple of Sekhmet to fight the priests there, for the Mother's sake . . . she saw not if she failed or triumphed.

The vision shimmered into nothingness and Mim was left staring into the Abyss of Eternity, as the Goddess filled the firmament again before her tear-blind eyes.

*"Choose!"* she demanded, relentless as death or birth.

And so Mim did.

*O Karaden, eternal beloved! Did you wait for me at the appointed rendezvous? Did you cry out in despair and think me cruel or fickle that I failed you? The Gods will not be mocked by mortals, dearest heart-friend. We had been called to serve or suffer. And the choice was theirs.*

*Sometimes in my sorrow I have thought—may Isis forgive me if I misjudge—that the Gods are far less just than men.*

Maggie felt herself drawn inexorably back to normal consciousness, the words of Mim still ringing in her head. Clear as truth. *Every word remembered.*

She sat up in bed, dazed and disoriented, then forced herself to rise unsteadily. She moved to the window and stared, unseeing, into the New York night that now seemed foreign to her. Images of Egypt lived within her cells, as surely as those of yesterday. Heart-mates tuned to a love five thousand years unfulfilled . . . *I know who we are to each other.*

There was an ending to this story, she knew that absolutely. But was it then and there . . . or here.

And *now.*

With faltering hands Maggie dialed Peter's number and told him to come, there was something he needed to know.

# CHAPTER 57

Maggie lay on the couch in Strater's office, hoping for the fortitude to go through with whatever was to happen. There were no choices now, she had to find the ending. Peter stood, his face furrowed with concern, near the bookshelves that lined the wall behind Strater's desk. It was his story, too.

Heinrich Strater closed the blinds, set the tape recorder on play, and sat down beside Maggie with the small sigh of a man about to undertake a demanding task. She had told him of the vision of the night before, and he had been alarmed by the state of mind it had produced in her. Today, he would try for a resolution of this continuing fantasy that would allow this woman to find peace.

He took Maggie's hand in his own and held it firmly, as he led her through the induction into the hypnotic state.

"My dear Maggie," he said gently, when he was certain she was under. "We are about to journey backward in time to find the answers you seek there. I will ask you to return to the time of the Priestess, Mim, after her confrontation with the Goddess Isis. When you have arrived at that moment safely, you will raise your right hand to let me know. Do you understand?"

Maggie's head moved somnambulantly back and forth. She seemed quite peaceful. A minute or two later, her hand elevated.

"Very good, Maggie. Thank you. Now, I would like you to tell us whatever you feel comfortable in revealing about this ancient experience. Do you understand?"

"I have paid a dear price for these memories," Maggie/Mim said distinctly. "They are mine to reveal. Not even the Goddess can deny me this."

Peter and Strater exchanged looks, and the psychiatrist put his finger to his lips to caution Peter to remain silent. *Mim* was with them now . . . she began to speak:

"I was awakened long before dawn by Meri-Neyt. She looked grave, and I was certain she knew full well what had transpired, but, in truth, I was too sorrowful and weary to care overmuch. What was earthly reprimand to me, who had been chastised by a Goddess?

"Wordlessly, she dressed me in a ceremonial gown, placed a golden girdle about my hips, and led me to the sanctuary of the High Priestess.

" 'You will be tested today, Mim-Atet-Ra,' the Reverend Mother said without emotion. But on Meri-Neyt's face I could see a stubborn compassion writ plainly, as she stood before the High Priestess's throne. I knew in that moment that my beloved tutor thought I would die during the Ordeal. I had a psychic flash that an argument had transpired between the two women (Could anyone argue with a High Priestess, I wondered? Would anyone dare?) but that the die had been cast and I, though unprepared, would face the great obstacle course that day. I, too, assumed I was meant to perish, but I cared not.

"Meri-Neyt stepped forward then to prepare me, as was allowed.

" 'These are the rules of the Ordeal,' she said in her ceremonial voice, and I knew I had left all innocence behind, and must stand to be counted, for good or ill. I was child and pupil no longer, but warrior on the battlefield of the Gods.

" 'View all temptations with suspicion. Many are the snares of mind and heart and spirit that will be set for you,' she warned. *'Trust no one, but your own heart.*

" 'Give wise counsel to any who seek it, but waste

not your substance on those who drain your resources, without willingness to change themselves.

" 'Even in the final extremity, purity and truth will overpower armies. Gird your loins with their armor.

" 'The ordeal is a microcosm. You are in mortal incarnation to build the soul. All life is but an initiation on your journey homeward. What you face today, all must face before returning. Life gives no quarter, so be brave.

" 'Remember the directive: To know. To will. To dare. To keep silent. Fail any of these admonitions and you fail the whole.'

"She smiled at me then, and I could see her love for me and her good will in that expression. 'I wait to welcome you in victory!' she cried out in ringing tones. I thought I saw her cast a defiant flicker in Reverend Mother's direction, but I might have been mistaken. Then she struck me sharply between the shoulder blades—this was the Thread Connecting Rite, which signified the passing on of power from teacher to student, and the thread that would connect us, always, for I carried within me the gift of her wisdom.

"She tied about me the apron of the Greater Mysteries; then I was blindfolded and led to a subterranean chamber where my testing would begin.

"Of the specifics of the Ordeal itself, I may not speak, on pain of death. But certain revelations I am permitted to share with you, for mankind needs the knowledge, now, as then:

"I saw the *Place of Torturers*—it was a dreadful world of infinite darkness where those who have brutalized others reap the harvest of their cruelty.

"I traversed the place where the *Speakers of Evil* suffer the ravages of their poisoned tongues.

"I saw the place where false priests and prophets dwell, damned to live their own lies for eternity.

"I saw the place where the rich and mighty dwelt, who had used their worldly goods on selfish ends. There do they hunger and thirst and wear the rags of those they might have saved by charity.

"Then did I see the *Place of Eternal Darkness*, where those who did evil in lifetime after lifetime are sent to reap the bitter harvest they have sowed, doomed to the company of their own kind, and the chaos they sought to perpetrate on others.

"And then I saw the Great Ones, who watch the earth and her children and aid those who work in conscience for the good of man. It is the place where all true prayers are answered.

"On I traveled to the *Place of Records*, where is writ the whole long history of mankind, and I read there the upward-moving spiral of man's climb from the mire to the Father/Mother's Kingdom.

"I heard the Music of the Spheres, and saw the *Place of Wisdom*, where all are judged, not by what they know, but by how generously they have shared it.

"Next I was brought to the *Seven Great Ordeals*, where I was forced to face my deepest, darkest fears. I waded the quicksand in the *Swamp of Lost Dreams* . . . I ran the *Plain of Archers*, where every arrow is a desperate fear . . . I swam the *River of Blood*, where the stream is fed by those who might have died had I not, in some incarnation, offered a helping hand . . . I survived the *Plain of Fires* that are stoked by pride and lust and jealousy and anger . . . I faced the *Pit of Vipers*, where delusions ensnare your feet like tendrils, and the poison of envy or covetousness sucks at every cell."

Dr. Strater glanced up at Peter, who seemed to be in some kind of distress; his face was furrowed, perhaps with concern for Maggie? Perhaps, something more than that . . . The psychiatrist returned his attention to his patient.

"I thought that all had ended then," Mim said, "for I saw a benevolent figure walking toward me carrying a giant Cobra, which was the sign of the upraised Kundalini and the opened Third Eye of illumination. So I approached the figure with relief, not wariness. As I drew abreast, the hideous snake reared up and coiled to strike, and the figure *flung* the serpent at my exhausted, unsuspecting body! The venomous head sped toward me and I very nearly perished in that instant. Yet, reflex supersedes thought, and I dashed the writhing reptile to the ground. I sought the Eye Ray, the magic wand of the mind; focused through the lens of the eye, it had the power to set the world aflame.

"I called on the last reserves of Power I possessed and turned the ray upon the snake. But just as I was about to kill it with this force, I knew that I must *not*. *For a far greater feat would be to conquer him with love.*

"I gathered the thought force, fighting back revulsion and fear, and replaced it with love for so beautiful, if deadly, an opponent. I hypnotized the snake with my eye-ray, and then beamed the love-ray from my heart. If it sensed our kinship, it would not seek to harm me. I backed away from its confusion and mustered my strength for the navel-ray, which was the Will, and the force needed for miracles."

Peter had risen from the chair he'd been sitting in; he looked agitated, as if some terrible internal upheaval were in progress. Strater frowned. It wouldn't do to disrupt Maggie's hypnotic state at this point. Damage could be done by too abrupt a return to present consciousness. He motioned Peter to be still.

"The viper pulled back its hood," Mim continued excitedly, "and I saw it lower its defenses. Its swaying eyes sought mine . . . I sent it love and friendship. Then, it simply disappeared—but with it went my last reserves of energy. If more were required of me, I knew I was surely doomed.

"Suddenly, two doors materialized beyond me on the ethers, and a voice said blaringly, *'Behind one, Victory . . . behind the other, Annihilation!'* So simple a test, after all I had endured? I reached out with my intuition and 'felt' beyond the portals—behind one I sensed safety, and beyond the other, only desolation.

"Then, did the strangest vision appear to me . . . quite clearly, I saw Meri-Neyt desperately gesturing for me to make the other choice! She had been my guide and advisor for a lifetime, so I stopped instantly, and reached out once more with my inner knowing. But once again, I perceived *Life* behind the left-hand portal, and *Death* beyond the right.

"I stood on that strange, barren plane, paralyzed by my perplexity. Meri would not ill advise . . . yet, did I feel with every fiber that the choice she pointed out was wrong. Desperately, I tried to remember the words of her admonitions—and it came to me . . . *Trust* . . ."

Maggie never finished the sentence, but Peter did.

"*Trust no one but your own heart!*" he cried out, as he rushed to Maggie's side.

"What are you doing?" Strater shouted, alarmed. But Peter had taken Maggie's limp body into his arms, and paid no heed to the psychiatrist.

"Naked and alone, beloved, you make your own choice!" Peter whispered urgently to her. "All else is but illusion. This was the test I failed, Mim. *This* was the test of the Abyss. You *must* not fail!"

Maggie continued to speak in Mim's voice, as it was apparent she either could not hear Peter's words, or did not choose to.

"I opened the left-hand door," she continued, as before. "A choir of angels greeted me beyond this portal . . . and I knew with certainty that the final test is this: At the moment of Truth, *naked and alone must you make your own choice*. All else is but illusion."

Peter laid his head on Maggie's breast, tears were running down his cheeks. To Strater, he seemed in as much of a trance state as she; he saw that Maggie/Mim had placed one arm about the man's shoulders in a strangely protective gesture, as she continued her story:

"Suddenly, I was back in the presence of the High Priestess, in her golden robes of office, and as I watched, entranced, she shimmered into nothingness, and where she had stood the Goddess rose, and her glory was greater than the world.

" 'You have faced the Abyss, Mim-Atet-Ra, daughter

of Isis. You have sinned and you have repented. You have been sorely tested and you have prevailed. Thus, shall you be punished and rewarded, for all that occurs in human incarnation is of the mortal's own forging.

" *'Guardian of the Isis Amulet, arise!* The child you would have borne to Karaden will be restored to you, somewhere in time.

" 'She will be my Messenger, and keeper of my Amulet throughout Eternity. You will be her Guardian. When mankind stumbles so gravely on the path that it endangers its own existence, then will I send you both forth. To the death and beyond, must you protect your sacred charges, my Messenger and my Amulet. Mankind is flawed, yet does it often please me, for it has the capacity to be greater than itself, in ways we did not envision at the first Creation. Thus, will I give it one last opportunity to rise above its flaws, though all the other Gods may turn away.

" 'But, know this, Guardian:

" 'There is another Amulet that has been forged. Sekhmet has invoked the Powers of Evil to challenge my gift to humanity. She has imbued a great onyx with the totality of all destructive forces that exist in this universe. Thus, may free will still prevail. For man will have to choose between our gifts. This only can I do to strengthen your hand: the Sekhmet Stone can never be Materialized *unless the Isis Messenger is already in the world*. Thus, when the Messenger Incarnates and Materializes the Amulet, she sets the game in play. Good or Evil will triumph. And man will choose his own destiny.

" 'Because this gift I give you is as cruel as it is great, Mim-Atet-Ra, I will allow you to sip an elixir that will ease your pain.' A golden goblet appeared before me, and numbly, I touched it to my lips, but something stayed my hand.

" 'What is this drink?' I asked, long past fear.

" 'It is the Water of Forgetfulness . . . that you will not remember your sin.'

"*Nor Karaden*, I thought. *Nor our child.* I handed

back the cup, for it is better to remember love, despite the anguish. Stubbornness or courage, call it what you will . . . I regret not my choice.

"And so my sorrow was wrought long ago, by my own hand. Many years did I live after that day, and longer still they seemed to me. I was High Priestess of the Goddess Isis at Saqqara, by the time I passed through the portals of earthly existence. I had healed many, and counseled many in my time, and I had served the Great Mother, faithfully. As I have done, in one way or another, through all the lifetimes since.

"While my soul has made its earthly sojourn, I have watched the Mother's Mysteries brought low. I have seen the balance shift for humanity—the Female Principle laid waste, and the Male Principle taking power, bringing with it male excesses. When will humanity understand, as I did on that fateful day of revelation, that only when male and female come into respectful balance, can life truly prosper? Excess of either principle brings distortion and dishonor.

"We stand now at the Great Crossroad. The Messenger and the Guardian have been sent forth for the final reckoning, and the players are assembled on the field. *O Isis, Ra, defend us and strengthen our frailties! We are too human for this task.*"

Dr. Heinrich Strater saw the stricken face of Peter Messenguer as he stared at Maggie. She opened her eyes and looked deeply into his, and said, in the voice of Mim:

*"Karaden, beloved twin-soul, had we been but simple fisher-folk, we could have lived our love, and left behind our seed. Instead we are unwilling players in the deadliest game of all, and the fate of the Universe hangs by the thread of our desires. Goddess help me, unworthiest of thy children! Let me not falter until the price be paid."*

Strater, stunned by the events of the previous few minutes, reached tentatively for Maggie's hand with his own.

"Mim, dear," he said tenderly, realizing with a pang

that Mim had become unutterably real to him, too. "We thank you for sharing your remarkable story with us . . . and we wish you well on your journey. We will pray for you." He glanced at Peter, who was now trying to collect himself. He seemed to have aged ten years in an hour.

"Please return Maggie to us now . . . it is time for her to come home to us. Will you raise your right hand when Maggie has returned?" The hand began to waver, upward. "Thank you," he said, then paused a moment. "It is time to reboard the sailboat on the river of time. Please instruct the pilot that under no circumstances are any stops to be made, until you have safely reached 1993, here in my office."

Minutes later, Maggie, Peter, and Dr. Strater sat staring at one another. Finally, the psychiatrist spoke.

"Quite frankly, I don't really understand what we've just experienced. But it appears there's a good deal of work to be done here . . ."

Maggie spoke decisively.

"Thank you, Dr. Strater," she said. "I appreciate what you've done to help me. But, I think I know now what it was I came here to learn. I'm afraid the resolution of this story is not within the province of psychiatry."

PETER watched Maggie very closely, as she seated herself at the small table; she looked injured by the memories that had struggled free. Burned out by an inner fire.

He had insisted they stop at the coffeehouse on the way back from Strater's office, because he knew the moment she entered her own home, the reality of Cody's absence would fold in around her like an ice mantle, and in the wake of these last revelations, she seemed too frail for that.

He ordered mulled cider for them both, and she sat staring into the mug, pushing the cinnamon stick from side to side, absently, as the steam rose from the crockery cup. She looked vulnerable, and exhausted.

"You were *there* with me, Peter," she said finally.

"Yes," he answered. "I saw the danger, clearly, in the labyrinth. It was the test I'd failed—I needed to save you from the same fate."

She nodded, understanding.

"It's real, isn't it, Maggie?" he asked, his voice hoarse with emotion. "Today was the first time I understood its reality."

"Yes, it's *real!* Peter. That's the problem," she snapped back at him, nearly upending the cider. "Christ! I can *feel* her youth, her vigor, her longing. You *are* Karaden. Ellie *is* Meri-Neyt. But what does that *mean*, Peter?" She looked haunted. "And, in God's name where is it going? There's some terrible ending to this story . . . I can feel it coming at me, and it scares me to death."

"I know, Maggie, dear," he soothed. "I know it does. It frightens me, too."

They finished their cider and Peter walked her home, but their pervasive sense of impending doom made any conversation they attempted seem superfluous. She didn't invite him in.

Maggie climbed the stairs to her room; she felt profoundly tired, as if she could sleep for a thousand years.

As she passed Cody's bedroom, she felt a terrible need to seek solace there. Maggie sat down on the edge of the frilly bed, carefully, fearing to dispel the remembered images that were secreted in this sanctuary. Of a little girl who was beautiful and fey in the manner of princesses in ancient bardic tales. With hair the color of sun-beaten flax, and mysterious gray eyes like the ocean before a summer storm. She heard again in the stillness of the empty room the quicksilver laughter that was full of old wisdom, and saw the shadow of this child who was shy in a Sphinxian way. Like a golden cloud in an imperfect firmament, or a seagull skimming the precarious wave, she was not entirely of this earth. *Why did I not see that you were not from here?* she breathed into the terrible silence. *Nothing as beautiful as you could be from here.*

Maggie let the wash of unbearable pain flood through her then, catching the wave, riding it, drowning in it. She lay back against the frilly pillow that still smelled of baby powder, and cried herself to sleep.

The dream sucked Maggie under and pulled her along in its inexorable tow. She felt herself scooped up by a cosmic whirlwind and cast far out into time/space . . . soaring through the firmament, past stars and planets, into the void.

*Oh God, they're taking me again*, she thought wildly, as a kaleidoscopic reprise of visions began to flash before her altered sight. She saw herself and Cody metamorphose into a dozen incarnations, in many different guises, sometimes male, sometimes female. Life after life dropped before her, like slides in an eternal viewer . . . Druid priestesses tending a sacred oak . . . devoted, but impoverished, husband and wife, in a Welsh fishing village . . . two nuns in a convent, during the Spanish Inquisition . . . pioneer mother and child in early America . . . warrior comrades fighting back to back on varied battlefields. Dozens of lives shimmered dizzyingly in and out of focus, until, finally, Maggie saw the Cody/essence as a Hopi Medicine Woman of high degree, the Maggie/essence as the Grandfather who had taught her medicine ways.

Abruptly, the hypnotic dream faded and Maggie woke up, drenched in sweat, every image alive within her, pulsating, radiating information. *The pattern.* Finally, she could see the pattern.

Always the bond between the two souls is absolute . . . always, one is present at the other's death.

# PART V
# THE
# ALLIES

Woe to him who is alone when he falleth, for he hath not another to help him up.

Ecclesiastes

# CHAPTER 58

Peter and Maggie sat in the Broome Street Bar, two days later, untouched hamburgers on their plates.

"I guess we really have to talk about this, Peter," she said finally. "Ever since the Regression, I feel afraid to be near you . . . and you obviously feel the same way." She hesitated. "I don't know what to do about any of this."

Peter pushed away the coffee cup he'd been toying with and looked into her face; his own was drawn from sleeplessness.

"I'm sorry, Maggie. I haven't been much use to you the last couple of days. I've been trying to regain my own equilibrium. Who are we to each other? I keep asking myself. Who have I been?" He looked as troubled as she felt.

"You know I went to Strater," Maggie said, a hint of bitterness in her voice, "thinking that 'knowing' Mim's story would make things clearer, better. But it's only made things much worse. How can we ever know what's real, now, Peter? I find myself struggling with feelings about you that *seem* like love. But what if that's really Mim loving Karaden, not you and me at all? Or what if

375

Mim and Karaden are just phantoms from my imagination, and I'm really just losing my mind?

"I never *wanted* to feel whatever it is I do for you, Peter. Look at me! I can't even *say* the word 'love' where you're concerned. But I damned well feel *something* out of the ordinary for you, and you feel it, too." Her voice was tightly controlled.

"I'm going to be painfully honest with you, Peter, because I don't know what else to be. Whenever we're together, I find myself wanting to *touch* you . . . to hold you, to be held . . . and to say things I have no right to say . . . and it all feels somehow inevitable. Now, I know it's tangled up with these *other* lives." She threw up her hands in a gesture of despair at trying to explain.

Peter's eyes caught hers and held them; tenderness had warmed the craggy features of his face, softening them.

"Maggie, Maggie, don't you see . . ." he said, reaching across the table for her hands, and holding them fast with his own. "I *do* love you! *Now*, and maybe then . . . who knows where it began? And, I do believe that you love me. That part is *pure*. Spotless. Nothing to be ashamed of, surely. What we choose to do about our love . . . *that*, I'm afraid, may be another matter, entirely. But for now—for this small moment in eternity, I think we must take care not to let that love weaken us in any way. If we can draw strength from what we feel for each other, then it's good. If not . . ." He ignored the stares from other tables.

"Right now, all you can think about is Cody. Nothing else is even remotely relevant. We have two weeks left in which to save her, so every minute has to count. You cannot be distracted by distrusting your own sanity, or by second-guessing whether or not we genuinely love each other. We simply do. Perhaps you must just let that be. Until April 30th everything is secondary to saving Cody. After that . . ." He sighed eloquently.

What he didn't say was that after April 30th he didn't

expect to be alive. There was no need for her to know that yet; he wasn't even certain why he felt it to be true, but there was an unshakable sense within him, that all time stopped for Peter Messenguer on April 30th.

Peter took Maggie home and handed her over to Maria with instructions to take good care of her, grateful that the housekeeper had answered the door. Grateful, too, that he hadn't been alone with Maggie any longer.

He started to walk the long way back to his borrowed apartment, then turned and headed for Thirteenth Street. He'd spend the night at the AIDS hospice and sublimate what he was feeling in good work. At least that way, if he didn't get any sleep again tonight, some poor needy soul would benefit from his insomnia.

# CHAPTER 59

"You know, Amanda," Maggie said, the next morning at the shop, pushing the papers emphatically into the desk drawer, too agitated to pay attention to them. "Ever since this regressive hypnosis business, I find myself looking under every crack in my life for ancient connections, like a cosmic Inspector Clouseau. I feel bi-located . . . like I'm living life in two time slots."

Amanda looked up and frowned. "Sounds like what happened to us all when everybody got into therapy. Remember? How we all started checking our motivations, as often as we checked our watches? Why am I doing this to myself? was supposed to be the key to every action of your life. If you walked down the street and a safe fell on your head, you must have placed yourself under there for some reason. If you got sick, you were trying to escape something. If you died, you probably had an old unresolved problem you couldn't deal with.'' She laughed at the foolishness.

"I remember," Maggie said, shaking her head. Amanda could make her chuckle at the foot of the gallows, she thought with a wry smile. "I remember thinking how confusing it must be for the Grim Reaper. Before Freud, he could just come get you on a simple time table: your grandparents all died at eighty-six, so he could put you on his receivables schedule for eighty-six. The country declared war, he could beef up his collection efforts. Famine? Pestilence? Get a bigger truck. Then all of a sudden, he had to watch everybody's motivations all the time to see what old garbage they were carrying around that might do them in."

Amanda laughed out loud. "The point I was making, dear heart, is that regression or not, you still have to get up in the morning and put one foot in front of the other. So, who cares what happened five thousand years ago, or whether your motivations are on straight—what matters is what Maggie does *today*. That's what's really making you crazy, anyway. You can't figure out how to help Cody, today."

Maggie stood up and turned off her desk lamp. "You couldn't be more right, Amanda. This inaction is killing me. She's there, I'm here, and all my efforts and anxiety and regressive hypnosis haven't changed a goddamned thing. And on top of that, now I'm wondering if I may be in love with Peter, and I can't see how it'll turn out one whit better in this century, than it did in three thousand B.C."

Amanda watched Maggie, worriedly, from the door of the shop before she locked up. A month ago, she would have thought anybody talking about past lives was three bricks short of a load, but now she wouldn't care which millennium help came from for Maggie, just as long as it came.

MAGGIE walked down Madison Avenue distractedly, trying to decide if she should tell Devlin about what she'd learned in hypnosis. During the sessions, it had all felt so real, now the whole thing was beginning to seem absurd. The whacked-out fantasy of a distraught brain. But it wasn't fair, somehow, *not* to let him know . . . and besides, she owed him a phone call. She didn't want to let herself think she was using him as a bulwark against her feelings for Peter, but there was a distinct possibility that was true. *Shit!* Who knew what truth was anymore.

"DEV," Maggie said uncertainly, when he arrived in answer to her call, "I really need to tell you some of what's happened to me the past couple of days, but it all sounds so nuts, I'm afraid you'll throw a net over me."

He'd been only a little surprised by the call that precipitated this late-night visit. Maggie'd dropped out of sight for a few days after the trip to Greenwich, and hadn't answered any of his phone calls. He'd intended to check up on her today anyway, but she'd beaten him to the punch.

He sat quietly in Maggie's living room, while she told him the story of Mim in Egypt. He asked no questions, but it was apparent he was listening intently; his eyes were lowered in concentration, and she couldn't see his face. By the time her recital was finished, Devlin had removed his jacket and tie, and poured himself a scotch.

"I've been trying to figure out if *you* were somewhere in the story, too, Dev," she said seriously, "and, if so, *who*."

"It's who I am *now* that matters, Maggie," he answered definitively. There was some unspoken emotion underlying the words. "I can see what a mind-fuck that whole experience must have been for you, but frankly I don't think any of it matters a tinker's dam. In the first place, there's no way to know if it's true. In the second, even if it is true, it doesn't get Cody back. And, in the third, and by far the most important place, if Malachy Devlin was not a major player in that story, the outcome here is going to be a helluva lot different."

"Dev, get serious!" she said, disappointed by his response. She wasn't sure how she'd expected him to react, but this wasn't it.

"I *am* serious, Maggie O'Connor. We're dealing with real live, flesh and blood villains, here and now, so who gives a rat's ass what happened five thousand years ago? *'Sufficient unto the day is the evil thereof,'* Maggie. What I need in order to get your kid back for you is hard evidence that ties Vannier into drugs and murder in 1993." He paused to regroup.

"The reporter who was an expert on Maa Kheru . . . *that's* real. The FBI links between Vannier, Sayles and drugs . . . *that's* real. The tattoo artist . . . *that's* real. These are things that can get Cody back for you, Maggie. Not past life readings, or tea leaves, or howling at the goddamned moon."

"But you *know* there's more to reality than what we can see, Dev," she protested, shocked by his anger. "You know all of this may be true!"

"I don't give a damn if it is true, Maggie. It doesn't matter if it's true or false or six shades of anything in between. What matters to me is that I find something big enough to blow the lid off Eric Vannier and his dirty little band. I can't let myself get distracted by irrelevancies. I have to keep my feet firmly planted in reality, because there's more than enough shit in this time slot to keep me busy, without worrying about shit from some other century."

"Malachy Devlin!" she said, reality suddenly dawning, "you're just angry because you weren't in the story. My God, you're jealous!"

"Damned right I am!" he exploded. "I don't want you fucking around with anybody, anywhere, in any millennium, Maggie, except me."

He took a deep breath and let it out hard.

"Look. I've got to go," he said in a husky voice. "I'm just acting like a horse's ass and I'd better get out of here before I make a complete fool of myself . . ." Devlin's moods could shift in an instant.

"I brought you something," he said, gruffly, reaching into his pocket. He pulled out a small leather-bound book with a ribbon bookmark in it.

"I thought someone who learned about sex from the *Rubáiyát* might have learned about courage from another poet."

Wonderingly, Maggie took the proffered gift from his hand. As she did so, Devlin reached over suddenly and pulled her into his arms, the book pressed between their two bodies. One hand was in her hair, and the other around her waist . . . and he was kissing her with all the explosive love and longing that had been driving him crazy. She felt the wildness, the desperation in the kiss. *Should we not all be loved desperately?* she thought madly, caught up in the frenzy. And she was kissing back because it seemed the only thing to do. And because she really *wanted* to. She could feel the love and the strength in him, that radiated like a current, energizing, electrifying. *Give all to love*, it said in the old poem. *Obey thy heart. Friends, kindred, days, estate, good fame, plans, credit and the muse—nothing refuse!* Oh sweet Jesus, it was good to *feel* and not to *think* anymore! If she could only give and take and not have to think about the consequences . . .

Devlin released his hold on her, abruptly, and they stood staring into each other's eyes, neither knowing what to say or do next.

Without a word, he reached for his coat, shrugged it

on, and headed for the door. When he got there, he spoke without looking back.

"I can love you *now*, Maggie," he said fiercely. "To hell with anything else."

Maggie's heart pounded out her confusions like a trip-hammer, after the door closed behind him. She saw that the little book had landed at her feet, and she picked it up. It had fallen open to the bookmarked page:

> *Out of the dark that covers me*
> *Black as the pit from pole to pole*
> *I thank whatever Gods may be*
> *For my unconquerable soul.*

How on earth did he know to choose Henley? Oh Lord, how did he know so many things? Memories flooded her, pried free by the tiny book of verse. She had never gone to bed one night in childhood, without memorizing a poem. Her father had given her that gift.

*Yours forever, Margaret, he had said. What you memorize is yours forever. How many other treasures are permanent in this life? How much else is there that cannot ever be taken from you?*

She was adrift in a sea of memories . . . her father so respectful of poetry he only recited it to those who loved it. Never using his great repertoire as others did, to bludgeon unsuspecting listeners with the weight of a classical education. For him it was a private grace, too cherished to be bandied with fools.

*In the fell clutch of circumstance*, she murmured the words of the poem to herself, grateful for their comfort, loving Dev for knowing her need . . . *I have not winced nor cried aloud. Under the bludgeoning of chance, my head is bloody but unbowed.*

The poem reminded her that she was not alone—*that's* what he'd meant her to know. Fate had not singled her out for punishment. *Why me, God? asks Job, in the old joke. I don't know, Job, says God. There's just something about you that pisses Me off.*

Maggie laughed a little, despite the moisture on her cheeks; he'd done it again; he'd made her feel alive and a little hopeful. For once, she decided not to try to figure out where Malachy Devlin fit into the complex puzzle of her life.

When she went upstairs to bed, Maggie put the small volume of poems on the night table, next to Jack's picture. It was absurd, of course, but she kept thinking if Jack were alive right now he would help her figure out the imponderables about these two strange men who had come into her life. He'd been her friend as well as her husband . . . she wondered if either Peter or Dev had the capacity to fill that most important of all loving roles.

# CHAPTER 60

Ghania gripped the child's hand in her own, so she could not flee. Cody blinked hard at the scene before her . . .

The little goat stood tethered to a pole in the center of the stone enclosure in the basement. The huge snake stalked it, watching, waiting, almost lazily, its forked tongue flicking in and out, in anticipation. It struck, a movement so fast it blurred; then it became languorous again, coiling its sinuous body around the bleating, helpless goat . . . tightening its coils inexorably, until all the fight for life had been spent and only terror remained.

Cody watched in wordless horror as the python's immense jaws unhinged themselves to accommodate the still living meal. It was swallowing the little goat *whole*— Cody could see the outline of its body, head and shoulders, even hooves protruding under the snake's skin, as it was pushed along inexorably toward the snake's belly.

"*Think*, my little one," Ghania said in a smooth, warm voice. "*Think* how dark it is for the goat inside the belly of the snake. It is screaming in there, you know, but no one can hear.

"Think on this, when next you refuse to do what Ghania tells you."

Cody pushed the scary words, and Ghania, and the snake away . . . far, far away, where they couldn't hurt her anymore. She turned her face toward the wall, and sought within herself for the comfort of the Light.

"*MIM! Mim! Mim!*" Cody's screams seared their way through Maggie's soul, in the dream. "*Don't let them hurt me. Mim! Help me . . .*"

"*I'm here, baby!*" she screamed back, arms and hands splayed white against some invisible glass wall that separated them from each other. Other arms and hands dragged her back and back into swirling blackness. Nightmare. Falling. Screaming. Help me, Mim! Echoes. Echoes. Darkness.

Black water rising all around her . . . where is Cody? She could hear her screams, but where were they coming from? Something slithered by her legs in the inky, swirling pit. Serpent! Snake . . . Horrible, writhing, lethal snake, under the water where it can't be seen. It was there to kill Cody. Frantically, Maggie swam against the murky nightmare tide, as thick as molasses, dark and rank.

"Mother, help me!" she heard a voice distinctly, and knew, even in the dream, that it was her own voice. Her mother had never let herself be called Mom, or Mommy, for these were too inelegant. *But, Mother is so distant, cold.* A designation, not a name of love. Help me, Mother, help me!

A stairway rose up from the deadly water and Maggie's mother, unperturbed, was on the stair.

"Don't shout, it's unladylike," she admonished her daughter. She was holding Cody's hand.

*"Cody is dying,"* Maggie thought in terror. *"My mother's come to get her."* The thought made her renew her useless struggles against the viscous water, but her arms were aching beyond endurance, and she felt herself dragged down beneath the surface, where the serpent lay. She saw her mother's hand reach down, to touch the coiling creature as it tensed to spring. The serpent shuddered once, then settled quietly to the bottom of the sea. She'd back her mother in a one-on-one with a sea serpent any day, but where had she come from? She had died so long ago . . .

The dream scene changed abruptly, and she was back on land. Maggie felt the world close in suffocatingly around her. A scorching sun, in a desert landscape. She felt powerless, weakened. A hideous sense of futility seemed to have drained all lifeforce from her body through a hidden spigot. *I cannot march against the dark much longer.*

"What will I do?" she cried into the hot desert wind, that seared the plain she stood on.

"You will fight against Fate and the Devil and the world and God and everybody, if you must!" a voice replied. Was it her own? "That's where the dignity lies, Maggie! You can't control what they do to you. Only what you do in return." Where was the voice coming from?

"This is no fair game we've been sent to play here, Margaret," said a woman's disembodied voice from somewhere. "Hateful things happen. People die. People suffer. People are born with no limbs, no sight, no hearing. Courage, Margaret. *That's all there is.*"

She couldn't tell who the woman was. Her Mother? Ellie? Could it have been the voice of God?

Maggie awoke, the dream still vivid, real, inside her. She lay very still. There had been truth in the dream, she had to sort it through, quickly, before it faded. *The snake!* That was it. There was a snake now in every nightmare. The snake had some kind of meaning. But what? Oh God, tell me what it is I'm supposed to know!

"THESE dreams are scaring me to death, Ellie," Maggie said, distraught, after she'd recounted the latest one.

"You know what Jung said about dreams, Mags?" Ellie answered. "He said, 'The dream is a small hidden door in the deepest most intricate sanctum of the soul . . .' These dreams are important pieces of the puzzle— even if they're hard to live with, your soul is telling you things you need to focus on."

"I don't know, Ellie," she said despairingly. "I'm getting crazy . . . even my prayers are crazy, now. Please don't do this, God, I say over and over. She's only a little girl and has done nothing bad. *I'm* the one You're after. If You'll save her, I'll give You anything You want. Do You hear me? Anything! Do anything. Be anything. Just name Your price."

Ellie looked at her friend with genuine compassion. "A teacher of mine . . ." she said, "a very wise man, he was . . . once said to me, 'The Gods laugh at us sometimes, Ellie. It's a tribute to our bravery.' I thought he was mad and said so. 'They do not pity us,' he told me. 'They must think us very courageous. Perhaps they give us great honor in this.' I was too young to understand."

"I don't understand either," Maggie said bitterly.

"You will, Mags," said Ellie, her voice inordinately tender. "I believe you will."

# CHAPTER 61

Rabbi Itzhak Levi was eighty-three years of age. His hair had thinned and whitened a quarter century before, and his beard, too, looked fragile as hoar frost, but his abundant white brows made up for any other hirsute deficiencies.

It was his eyes that startled Raphael Abraham, his eyes that riveted all of the man's considerable attention. He was used to observing men and assessing them by their eyes, but such eyes as these, he had never encountered.

Was it possible for eyes to be both benign and dangerous, at once? Would Moses' eyes have looked like these when they descended from the mountaintop? Abraham felt compelled to look away, as if he had glanced into the plutonium core of an atomic power plant without protective goggles . . . as if he might be blinded if he didn't avert his gaze.

The rabbi smiled a little, and benignity now drew the curtain closed on the rest, but Raphael Abraham had seen it, and would not forget.

"I bring greetings, Rebbe," he said, holding out the envelope that contained the Prime Minister's letter, as well as one from Rabbi Lutz in Tel Aviv.

The old man took them politely from his hand and motioned for Abraham to sit down. He didn't open the letters, or seem in any way curious about their contents.

"It would be good if you were to tell me what brings you to my door, with the sanction of such important men," the old man said, with a small smile that seemed to neutralize the concept that temporal power might have any importance whatsoever.

He sat quietly in a posture of waiting, and listened as Abraham told him the story of the Amulets. Something about the old rabbi's silent attentiveness made Abraham curb his usual acerbity in the telling of the ridiculous tale; something inside him said tread gently ... . in the presence of such a man, nothing is as it seems.

"So." Rabbi Levi said, when the tale was ended. "Such a story does not come to visit me every day." He closed his eyes—a gesture for which Abraham was profoundly grateful—and seemed to commune with himself, momentarily. Then he smiled.

"What is it, precisely, the Prime Minister wishes of me?" he asked, politely.

"He wants to know if such a thing is possible, Rebbe," Abraham said, unnerved by the tranquility of the old man. It engulfed him, and more than that, it made him feel weighed in the balance and found wanting. "Could an object, or two objects, embody such power?" *If you want to know the truth about war, ask a general,* the Prime Minister had said. *If you want to know the truth about magic, ask a mystic.* He almost repeated the story to the rabbi, but thought better of it.

"This is a complicated question you put before me," the Rebbe replied. "The simple answer is yes. The breastplate of Solomon possessed such power. The Ark of the Covenant . . . one or two other objects in all history. The more cogent answer is 'highly unlikely' that such could be. Not impossible, mind you . . . just not very likely."

"And if these two Amulets *did* embody such magic, could you control them?"

The Rebbe pursed his lips contemplatively and frowned. "Perhaps," he said. "Perhaps not. There would be mysteries involved, Major, of which one cannot speak freely. I would have to meet the child. It would be helpful to meet the woman, as well. It would be useful to know the specifics of the ancient writings on the subject. I assume you would be able to make such material available for study?''

"Whatever you require would be provided.''

The Rebbe's eyes smiled, although his lips did not. *Foolish boy*, the eyes said to Abraham's intuitive gaze. *What would be required by me, would be far beyond your skill, or that of any government.*

"Where is the child now, may I inquire?'' the old rabbi asked.

"She is with the addict mother, and the stepfather in Greenwich. We believe he heads a cult called Maa Kheru.''

The extraordinary eyes locked with Abraham's. "It would be best if you refrained from speaking such a name aloud, Major Abraham. These are Words of Power . . . the portals they open would be better left closed.'' He was silent a moment; a teacher who had reprimanded a usually bright student and wished him to reflect on his mistake.

"This stepfather . . .'' he began again. "He is an Adept of a mystery school of the Left Hand Path, I take it?'' Abraham nodded affirmation.

"He will not let her go willingly, then, we may assume.''

"If my orders are to take possession of the child, Rebbe, nothing will keep me from doing so.''

Rabbi Levi smiled again with his eyes. "To be so certain of things, Major . . . this must be a great comfort to you.''

Abraham, chagrined, stared at the old teacher. Why did this old man have the power to make him feel like an untried boy?

"I give you my word, Rebbe, I will not allow overconfidence to make me unduly careless. I meant only that my team is a good one—we have seen much of combat.''

"And of the Other World, my boy . . . what have you seen of that, hmm?'' He didn't wait for a reply.

"May I be privileged to know what, precisely, the State of Israel intends to do with this child and her

Amulets, after you and your fine team have so bravely secured them?''

"They are to be returned to Tel Aviv."

"Ah, I see. I see. You would forgive me, if I would say that Tel Aviv is not a place where the coolest heads prevail, perhaps. You would forgive me, maybe, if I were to wonder who in Tel Aviv would be so holy he would know what to do with this child and her magical Amulets." He chuckled a little and rose from his chair; only a slight tentativeness of movement betrayed his age. Abraham saw that the interview was at an end.

"Rebbe," he said, in a tone not at all like his usual professional one. "When I came in here I was sure of only one thing—that this story was ridiculous. Now . . . I ask you, what would happen to the world if this story is true?"

"Ah, so you look for something new to be sure of? So. What will happen? Only what God wishes, my boy," Rabbi Itzhak Levi said with a genuine twinkle. "You may be *sure* of that."

ABRAHAM drove from the Rebbe's house, thoughtful and serious. Automatically, he checked for any sign of surveillance, and satisfied that he was alone, he allowed himself the luxury of an internal dialogue. *Only when you talk to yourself can you be sure of the company you keep,* his grandmother would have said. He smiled at the memory and wondered what his grandma would think of the Rebbe.

For that matter, what did he, himself, think of the Rebbe? *If I were not such a confirmed agnostic, I would say I was in the presence of a holy man,* he answered himself. *Also smart. Also, not to be trifled with. The Rebbe will do what the Rebbe will do. And that's that.* He made an emphatic gesture of finality, by blowing the horn at the double-parked driver in front of him.

"To such a man, Major," the Prime Minister had said

to Abraham, a week ago in Tel Aviv, *"the Mossad, the government of Israel, the Prime Minister, the President of the United States . . . all these are insignificant. When you talk to God directly, who needs these piddling middlemen, eh?"*

Abraham had laughed aloud. The Prime Minister was a good man. Tough-minded, cunning. To be admired on all counts.

*"He sounds like my old Uncle Schlomo, the Kabbalist,"* Abraham had responded, *"who, I must confess, I thought was meshugge."*

The Prime Minister had looked at him thoughtfully, and replied, *"Someone wise once said, Major, 'Young men think old men are fools, but old men know young men are fools.' "*

Abraham returned his mind to his current work. He had placed intermittent surveillance on the grandmother and the child, and a team of Egyptian experts in Israel were trying to pin down the date when Vannier would do whatever it was he planned to secure the Amulets. The child was probably safe enough until that elusive date, so the sooner he knew the timing, the better. It was a pity the Egyptians seemed to have the ranking expert on the Amulet legend on their team. Abdul Hazred. The scholar, who was also very rich by virtue of coming from a long line of educated thieves.

Abraham pulled the car to a halt, checked right, left, and behind again, then closed and locked the car door. His group had a technique of surveillance using three cars in rotation, that made detection nearly impossible. Presumably, some other side could be equally clever. It was an interesting diversion to spot the real pros; a cat-and-mouse game with higher stakes than children played for.

Was Hazred as bad news as Vannier? Abraham asked himself, in the continuing dialogue, as he walked to the building where the meeting with his operative would take place. *Was Begin Jewish?*

# CHAPTER 62

"I've tracked down our missing reporter, Maggie," Devlin said as they walked in Washington Square Park. "Or rather, I know what happened to him. His name was Fellowes, and it seems he got killed on the Jersey Turnpike, a couple of years ago, in a car crash."

"Does that mean you can't find out if he had any real evidence about Maa Kheru?"

He shook his head. "I don't know yet. It seems there was a wife. I'm planning to see her tomorrow. Reporters can be closed-mouthed about their sources, but if he was really obsessed with this . . . some wives know pretty much everything about their husband's business, others aren't clued in worth a damn. It depends on what kind of marriage they had."

They walked on for a few minutes in silence, then Maggie spoke.

"Why didn't *you* ever remarry, Dev?" she asked quietly. The day was softer than the one before, and the promise of spring had lightened both their moods a little.

"I never met *you* before," he replied with a grin.

She laughed. "That's very flattering, but be serious. There must have been opportunities."

"I don't know, Maggie. A lot of things stopped me, I guess. The job . . . confusing memories. Women aren't all that easy to figure out, and I didn't want to screw up a second time." He walked on for a moment, then added, "We're very different . . . men and women. Different priorities, different needs. It's hard to know for sure if we can ever really fulfill each other's hopes or dreams. I think probably the worst thing you could say to a woman is 'I want a divorce'—but, may be the worst thing you could say to a guy is 'You're fired.' And that's a pretty tough emotional gap to bridge.''

She turned, curious to see his face; he looked troubled by the truth he'd just uttered.

"What do you suppose God had in mind, making us incompatible?" she asked, afraid it might be true.

"I don't know. But every time I've pondered Freud's old question, 'What do women want?' I've always wondered why nobody's ever made a list. You know, a crib sheet . . . 'Things I wish men knew about women.' It might not solve all the riddles for a guy, but it sure couldn't hurt.''

Maggie smiled mischievously. "Want me to do one for you?"

He looked to see if she were serious. "It'd have to be bedrock honest, Maggie," he answered. "No girlish demurs . . . no tell-him-what-he-wants-to-hear . . . no 'I can't say that to a guy.' Just the plain, unvarnished truth—or else you'll really mess with my head.''

"I'll see what I can do," she said, amused. If she'd been in love with this sweet man, she'd never have been willing to consider such a revealing task. But as it was . . .

After he left her, Maggie made a cup of tea and replayed their conversation in her mind. Then she picked up a notebook, and sat down at the kitchen table, near the sunniest window in the house. It really was an intriguing question to ask yourself, she thought; what *would* you like men to know that they didn't seem to? For a heartbeat, she wondered if maybe Ellie and Amanda should be asked to contribute to the list.

*No.* This is my list.

Almost without meaning to, Maggie began sifting through the years, and all the men she'd known—family, lovers, friends. What had she needed, dreamed, hoped about them? What would have made a difference had they known? She pondered for a long while, then wrote her list, trying very hard not to equivocate. She scratched out one thought, slightly embarrassed by it, then wrote it down a second time. *Bedrock honest or not at all.* She wondered if he'd understand.

Maggie read the page over twice before sealing it in an envelope, and writing Devlin's address on it. Then, on impulse, she decided to hand-deliver it. *Better do it quick, before I lose my nerve.* She wondered fleetingly what his apartment would be like . . . what would it say about who he really was? And what would he think about her, once he'd read this strange conglomeration of desires that cut so deep into who *she* was.

# CHAPTER 63

Devlin sat back and stared at the piece of paper in his hand—Mrs. Fellowes's address in New Jersey. Peapack. Now that was a surprise. Hunt country. Jackie O. country. Hardly the place you'd expect to find a reporter's widow. Of course, she could have come from money . . .

He glanced at his watch. With a little luck he could be there by 6:30. He pushed the never-ending pile of papers to a new corner of the desk and headed for the garage.

The house was large and rambling, newly built to simulate age and substance. Two cars sat low and over-indulged in the driveway; he jotted down both plate numbers before ringing the bell.

"Mrs. Fellowes?" he inquired of the tall zoftig brunette who answered the door in a silk dressing gown.

"Yes?"

He held up his shield. "Lieutenant Devlin, NYPD,"

he said. "I'd like to ask you a few questions about your late husband, if you don't mind."

She frowned. "Actually, Lieutenant, I do mind. As you can see, I'm dressing for a dinner party."

"Just ten minutes, Mrs. Fellowes," he cajoled with his best Irish smile. "Not a minute more, I give you my word. It would really be a big help to me if you'd reconsider. I'm up against a deadline here." A little charm tended to move recalcitrant mountains.

"Not a minute more," she said warily, opening the door enough to allow him entry.

The interior was as impressive as the facade. Good art, good furniture, good rugs. Plenty of money, and none of it old. These were not the tenderly worn heirlooms of the always rich.

"Sit down, Detective," she said, in an ice-water voice. "Tell me what it is I can do for you."

"Your husband's accident, Mrs. Fellowes. I hate to reopen old wounds, but if you could tell me a little about it?"

"There's nothing to tell, really. A crash on the Jersey Turnpike—the police said he might have had a heart attack or a stroke. He drove off the road, into a rockface, at eighty-five miles an hour. The car exploded and he was killed. End of story."

*Try to contain your grief, Mrs. Fellowes*, he thought wryly. No tears, or even pretense of tears.

"I see. And was there any suspicion of foul play at the time? Did your husband have any enemies who might have wanted him out of the way?"

"Foul play?" she responded incredulously. "Where'd you get that idea? Jim had no enemies. It was an accident. Pure and simple."

"No enemies, Mrs. Fellowes? In his line of work, wouldn't that be a little unusual?" It was Devlin's turn to be incredulous. "Good investigative reporting tends to ruffle feathers . . . he was looking into some kind of occult group wasn't he? Maa Kheru, I think it was called."

Mrs. Fellowes laughed; it was not a genuine sound. "That horseshit? Forgive me, Detective, but my husband had a loose screw where that particular garbage was concerned. He wasted a lot of valuable time on a total fantasy." She rose and tied her robe tighter.

"I'm sorry, Detective. I really am out of time, here." Devlin got to his feet instantly, with an ingratiating smile.

"You've been very helpful, Mrs. Fellowes. And I do apologize for the inopportune arrival. There's really only one other question I have for you, then I'll leave you to your party going. It's a little impertinent, I suppose, but my job doesn't allow me time for some of the more delicate social graces . . ."

"What is it, Detective?" she asked, the alert blue eyes looking vaguely amused.

"This house . . . the furnishings . . . I'm no expert, but they look expensive. Did your husband have a lot of insurance or something? Reporters usually don't."

Mrs. Fellowes smiled; she seemed to have more teeth than were strictly necessary.

"He had insurance, Detective, and I'm a whiz with the stock market. An absolute whiz."

Devlin nodded. She wasn't a good liar, just a cocky one.

"By the way, just to save me some time checking . . . did your husband have any other relatives?" he asked, as she let him out the door.

"No," she replied pleasantly. "Nary a one."

"Did he by any chance leave any papers that had to do with his research on Maa Kheru?"

"Out of luck there, too, Detective," she said amiably. "They all burned up with him, I'm afraid."

Devlin threw the car into gear and called in the license plate numbers of the cars in the driveway. Then he asked for Garibaldi.

"I need you to find me a relative, Gino," he said, when the detective answered.

"You can have one of mine," Garibaldi replied with a short laugh.

Devlin chuckled; Garibaldi usually had that effect on him. He was a good man to have around on a bad day. "Reporter named James Fellowes, died January 9, 1987, Jersey Turnpike accident. Worked for the *Times*, *Newsweek*, good publications . . . I need to find a living relative—not the grieving widow. Okay?"

"Gotcha. You coming back in?"

"Yeah. Maybe another two hours. And Gino . . . keep it under your ski mask, hmm?"

"Aye, aye, Lieutenant. Mum's the word. See ya."

Mrs. Fellowes was an interesting addition to the growing menagerie, Devlin thought as he drove. What exactly did she have to hide? She wasn't grief-stricken and she didn't seem scared. Maybe she was a bad guy, too. It was beginning to look like there were quite a few of them in the bushes.

The phone beeped.

"Devlin," he said, picking it up.

"Would you believe a nun?" Garibaldi's voice was amused by life, as usual.

"I'd believe the Pope, at this point."

"Fellowes had a sister, Janice. Now Sister Cecilia Concepta of the Blue Chapel, in Parsippany. Some kind of contemplative Carmelite thing . . . you know the kind that take vows of silence, which I always thought was a good thing in a woman."

Devlin grinned. "Got an address? I'm already in Jersey."

"Yeah, sure. Eighteen-oh-three Troy Hills Avenue, Parsippany, 201-555-6023. Mother Superior's name is Immaculata Stevens."

"How the hell did you get this so fast?"

"Superior police work, and my sister's husband has a niece in the next parish."

Devlin grinned. "Should have known it was dumb luck."

"Immaculata Stevens would probably prefer to think of it as an act of God," Garibaldi said archly. "Hey, Lieutenant, how's this, for interesting? Old Janice, who by the way is thirty-two, joined up only two weeks after her brother's fiery demise."

"Thanks, Gino. That's a big help." Devlin smiled as he put down the receiver. An act of God would be a welcome addition.

The Blue Chapel sat on a quiet knoll, in the small New Jersey township, far from the bustle of Manhattan. It even *looked* cloistered, Devlin thought, as he pulled up in front. Iron gates barred the door, and the austere architecture wasn't meant for garden parties. He dredged his memory banks for whatever fragments they contained about the cloistered Carmelites. He knew they took vows of poverty, chastity, obedience, and silence. He'd always wondered what could ever possess a young girl to join such a forbidding world. It occurred to him, that he'd never thought to ask what it was they were praying for, so devotedly. Maybe he'd ask Immaculata Stevens.

Devlin rang the bell and waited. A small peephole was opened and two eyes peered out curiously. He flashed his shield and asked for Sister Cecilia Concepta. The eyes looked shocked, then the peephole closed with a forbidding click, like a cell door in solitary.

New eyes appeared at the peephole—older, wiser eyes. "I am the Mother Superior of this convent," said the kind of nun voice he remembered from boyhood— the kind that could put the fear of God in an altar boy, if he picked up a cruet late for the Offertory. "We are a cloistered order and the hour is late."

Devlin was nine years old again. "You speak?" he said surprised.

"Very astute, Detective," the voice replied wryly. "I can see you're in the right line of work. Now kindly state your business, very briefly." Some things never change, he thought. This was a smart one.

"I'm investigating a possible murder, Mother, and a child abuse case that may involve satanism. There's a sister here named Janice Fellowes, who may be able to help us. I apologize for the intrusion, and the hour, but the case is urgent. I give you my word, Mother, I'm on God's side in this one."

"So was Lucifer, for a while, Detective," she said without skipping a beat. But he heard the bolt slide back, and the door opened slightly.

"Mother Immaculata," he said, assessing the aristocratic presence before him. Tall, confident, impenetrable. You either win her over, or you won't get through her with the Notre Dame offensive line. "I'm Detective Lieutenant Malachy Devlin. I wouldn't be here if it weren't urgent."

She nodded acknowledgment wordlessly, and led him down a dark corridor, into the convent's silence. "You may state for me your business with Sister Cecilia, Lieutenant," she said, when he was seated in what appeared to be her study. "Then I will decide if it is urgent enough to disturb Sister's peace of mind, or her vow of silence."

He did so and she listened.

"A most distressing story," she said judiciously, when he'd finished. "I will pray for the grandmother and for the child. More than that, I cannot guarantee. Sister Cecilia's welfare is in my hands, and I'm afraid, based on what you've just said, I can conceive of no way on this earth you could possibly convince me it's in her best interest to become involved in this ugliness."

Devlin looked directly into the imperturbable steel of the eyes. "Then don't do it for anything on this earth, Mother," he said. "Do it because it's right."

She stared at him blankly for a moment, then laughed outright. "May I assume a Jesuit education, Lieutenant? Ignatius would be proud of you." She rose; he felt he was in the presence of an empress, and did the same.

"I will dispense Sister from her vow of silence to speak with you . . . but only if it is her wish. I believe she would be a fool to do so." She turned to go.

"According to Francis of Assisi," he said quietly to the retreating back, "each of us must be God's fool, sometime, Mother." He couldn't see her face, but he felt her smile.

Devlin stared out the window of the Abbess's office into the peaceful darkened street below. Hard to believe evil could touch a tranquil, sleepy-headed town like this. He sighed. He'd been a cop too long to imagine anywhere was sacrosanct.

A short while later, Mother Immaculata returned, a small delicate young woman in a wimple following her soundlessly. She was soft and startled-looking as a fawn, and it was obvious, she'd been crying.

When she spoke, her voice was unsteady; Devlin wondered if disuse or the emotions she struggled against had constrained it.

"I loved my brother very much, Lieutenant," she began, her distress underscoring the simple words. "He was a wonderful man. A wonderful reporter. He cared so much . . ." Her voice cracked and she looked down at her lap, where she folded and unfolded her hands, then up at Mother Superior for encouragement.

"We were a very devout family. Jimmy always received the sacraments. He was a very good human being . . . very moral, forthright, honorable. All the good things . . ." Her voice broke and she took another breath . . . "Although his work often put him into strange and dangerous company. I used to worry about him because of that.

"Ten years ago, Jimmy covered a satanic murder for *Newsweek* . . . something about it overwhelmed him, and he just couldn't get it out of his head. It obsessed him. At first he wouldn't talk about it to me, but then, little by little, he began to let things slip. He told me he'd unearthed evidence of a group of very powerful men and women who had sold their souls to Satan, in return for unlimited power, wealth, and fame. He couldn't believe the names he was uncovering . . . their prominence staggered him. I can only remember some of the names now, but they were all terribly important people, Lieutenant. It just didn't seem possible, but Jimmy said he had real evidence that involved people like Senator James Trant, Iscariot the rock star, General John Pinkham, that TV talk show host, Nicholas Sayles . . ." She looked at Devlin despairingly. "The list was a veritable *Who's Who* of prominent men and women—if it were true, the implications for society were incalculably deadly. I think my brother began to feel he was on a kind of holy crusade, to unmask this horrible danger—but the media people turned a deaf ear to all his allegations."

The young nun stopped a moment to collect herself, and the Abbess handed her a glass of water, which she sipped gratefully. Devlin had decided not to interrupt, but to let her tell the tale in her own way; he could fill in the gaps later. Janice Fellowes seemed to have a methodical mind.

"Four years ago," she began again, "Jimmy came to visit me one night. He was horribly agitated, more distraught than I'd ever seen him. My brother'd been in Vietnam, Lieutenant . . . he'd covered riots and murders . . . my brother wasn't a man who spooked easily. But that night, Jimmy was a basket case. He told me he believed that his wife, Terry, had read his research and somehow sold him out to the satanists. If that was so, he said, and if they really were on to him, he had far too much evidence on them now, to be left alive." She bit her lip, and struggled for control, before continuing.

"He handed me a key and a signature card for a safety deposit box at Chase Manhattan Bank on Forty-third Street, and told me never, under any circumstances, to let it out of my possession, or let anyone know I had it. 'They're all around us, Jan,' he said in a desperate sort of voice. 'They're everywhere, sweetheart. You can't know who to trust, where to turn. You've got to hold this key for me till I figure out what to do—you're the only one I can count on now!'

"He said he had an appointment with an important

official at Quantico the following morning. The man was an old army buddy of Jimmy's from Vietnam, and he'd said he would help."

The young nun looked straight at Devlin. Tears shimmered in her eyes and on her pale cheeks. "My brother never made it to Quantico, Lieutenant. His car went out of control on the turnpike and he was trapped inside and burned to death." She had to stop again to regain control. "I took the key, and the day after my brother's funeral, I spent eight hours in the safety deposit vault at Chase Manhattan poring over his research. I was shocked beyond anything I could possibly convey to you. *Oh God*, I wish I'd never seen any of it! I wish my sweet Jimmy'd never heard of Maa Kheru! I locked it away again. It's still there.

"The next day, I applied to Mother Superior for admittance to the Carmelite Order. I was accepted as a novice and have never left here since." The young girl glanced at the older woman, and a knowing look passed between them; she had been given sanctuary.

"Not until you read Jimmy's notes, Lieutenant Devlin, will you understand why I'm here. There is no secular way to beat them. They're too strong, too powerful, too evil. Only here, with God, can I do my small part to fight them. I'm giving you the key, because Mother Superior says I should. May God have mercy on you, Lieutenant . . . and may God have mercy on me for placing you in such terrible danger."

"If any harm comes to Sister, Lieutenant Devlin," Mother Superior said authoritatively, "I shall hold you personally responsible." The old ruler-on-the-knuckles Voice of God, Devlin thought with an internalized smile.

"With you in her corner, Mother, I expect she's at least as safe as that bank vault at Chase," he said, meaning it.

Sister Cecilia was dismissed, and Mother Immaculata rose from her chair to see Devlin out. As she shot the bolt on the heavy front door, and moved aside to let him pass, she said, "Do you know what it is we do here, Lieutenant?"

"I know only that you pray, Mother, silently, before the Blessed Sacrament."

"From the moment that ornate iron gate clangs shut behind us, Lieutenant," she said with great seriousness, "separating us from home, family, friends, and the world—we, who enter the contemplative Carmelite Order, devote ourselves to one thing only: We fight on God's side for souls harassed by Satan and his legions.

"Twenty-four hours a day, seven days a week, three hundred sixty-five days a year, we maintain a vigil before the Blessed Sacrament. In eight-hour shifts, we pray for those tormented by the Evil One. You will find, Lieutenant, there are few priests who would perform an exorcism without first invoking our aid, or that of others like us."

She smiled, the glacial-but-genuine smile of a ruler who wishes to communicate with a recalcitrant subject, on a somewhat human level. "I do not tell you this out of pride, Lieutenant Devlin, but because I want you to know that you do not go into battle against this Adversary with no one at your back."

The woman's gesture touched him. He looked into the unwavering strength of her face. " *'Though Hell should bar the way, Mother . . .'* " he said with a crooked smile. "I'd fight beside you anytime."

She acknowledged the compliment with a small twitch of the mouth, that might have been mirth.

Then he was standing on the steps alone, looking into the New Jersey darkness, with quite a lot to think about.

Devlin arrived at his apartment building weary and troubled. He couldn't get into Chase until the A.M., but he could *feel* bad news coming his way, and the worse the news got, the more he worried about Maggie.

Automatically, he checked the mailbox before putting the key in the vestibule doorlock. Bills. Junk mail. Assorted garbage. What a crime it was to waste trees to produce such crap. There was a stampless envelope, written in a woman's hand, at the bottom of the pile.

Devlin glanced at the proper Palmer Method penmanship, and smiled. Catholic school . . . no mistaking that. The flap said Mrs. Margaret Cavan O'Connor. Maggie. He opened the envelope still standing in the hallway. There were two handwritten sheets inside the envelope. Hastily, he stuffed the rest of the mail into the grocery bag he was carrying from the deli on the corner, and hurried to his apartment. He dropped the bag on the table, turned on the light and concentrated on the letter that was still in his hand. She hadn't just mailed it. She'd hand-delivered it. There was no note. Just yellow-lined paper that read:

Things I wish men knew about women:

- Women need to be listened to.
- They do not encourage rapists.
- They crave romance and tenderness like drowning men crave life rafts.
- They follow their instincts and their hearts implicitly and are, therefore, immensely rational.
- They need to have birthdays and anniversaries remembered with the same enthusiasm as fight dates, hockey playoffs, and World Series.
- Their clitorises need to be fondled, not mauled.
- They do not get immense joy from cleaning ovens and bathrooms.
- They understand children intuitively, because the children grew under their hearts.
- They cry, not because they're weak, but because they're in touch with their feelings.
- Even if they are strong, they like to feel protected.
- They would sometimes like to make love at their convenience, not a man's.

- They are inordinately sexual, but not particularly promiscuous.
- To have husbands who are unfaithful is an injury to their souls.
- They don't want to be called "girls" at forty-five, or "gals" ever.
- Periods do not make them crazy, unclean, or prone to attacks by wild animals.
- They long to know that their husbands want to make love *before* they get into bed without their diaphragm.
- They suffer in their children's coming and in their going.
- Making love thirty seconds after a woman has put on makeup, fixed her hair, and gotten dressed to go out is not spontaneous and fun.
- They read Gothic novels because they still dream of someone loving them more than life itself.
- They need to be loved, desired, trusted and respected, not just during courtship, but forever.
- Certain things cannot be unsaid to them.

He sat down at the table and reread the list twice, wondering why it made him feel so sad.

DEVLIN met Sister Cecilia Concepta outside Chase Manhattan Bank when it opened at 8:00 A.M. the next day. After she'd signed him into the safety deposit box vault and left in the squad car he'd provided, he settled down, with a paper cup of coffee, and Jim Fellowes's exhaustive notes. In fifteen years on the New York City Police Force, Malachy Devlin thought he'd seen it all. He was wrong.

"Jesus Christ!" he whispered as he put down the last crumpled page, three hours later. *"Jesus fucking*

Christ." Devlin pushed the papers back into the box, as if they were contaminated, and sat for a long time, staring at the institutional-beige wall in front of him. Then he took out a handkerchief, wiped his eyes, and blew his nose in an attempt at composure, before handing the box back to the safety of the vault.

This was big. And far-reaching. And very, very bad.

# CHAPTER 64

Cody lay in bed feeling sad and sick from hunger. First, Ghania said she couldn't have any breakfast or lunch, and then she wouldn't give her dinner, either.

Now, her tummy hurt really bad. A burning kind of pain, that was hard to ignore. She tried not to think about it, but it was really hard because maybe she wouldn't get any breakfast tomorrow, either. Just because she wouldn't drink that awful stuff. *Couldn't drink it*. Even if she wanted to, something weird happened to her whenever the cup came near her lips.

Cody went to the bathroom and poured a glass of water, but it didn't help, so she got out her bear again and re-counted her treasures. There were six now, but the button was still her favorite.

She lay down on the bed next to the bear and put the button in her mouth. It was cool and nice. It made her think of ice cream. *That's what she wanted more than anything*. The Vanilla Crunch kind that Mim always got her at Häagen-Dazs on Eighth Street. That would put out the fire in her tummy.

Cody sucked on the button a long time before she fell into troubled sleep.

MAGGIE turned over in her bed and glanced at the clock on the table. She blinked. 3:48 A.M. It was *hunger* that had awakened her, but why on earth would she be hungry in the middle of the night?

Whatever reason, the insistent hollow feeling in her stomach urged her out of bed. She threw a robe around her shoulders, slid her feet into slippers and headed for the kitchen.

Half asleep, she opened the freezer door and pulled out a two-thirds empty carton of Häagen-Dazs. It wasn't until she was halfway through what remained of the Vanilla Almond Crunch, that she realized she was eating with Cody's spoon.

# CHAPTER 65

Ellie opened the door for Devlin and smiled when she saw the concern on his face. Obviously, he thought she'd called him because something was wrong with Maggie.

"Good of you to come, Dev," she said, leading him into the living room where Peter was already seated on the couch. The priest rose hastily and extended his hand to the newcomer, but it was easy to see that the natural antipathy between them made cordiality forced.

"I asked you both to come here for a very special reason," Ellie began. "I need to enlist your aid for Maggie, but I have to clear the air first." She took a deep breath and sat down.

"I'll come right to the point . . . there's no time left

for foolishness, and I've never seen any value in equivocation." She looked directly at Peter, then at Devlin.

"I know you both love Maggie," she said. "How much, or in what capacity, is none of my business. I also know you both want very much to help her. I have certain knowledge of what will transpire between now and the thirtieth, that makes the antagonism you both feel for each other dangerous." They both began to ask questions, and she held up a hand to halt the barrage.

"No. *No!* I don't know the final outcome, only a few scenes from the drama have been shown to me, but this much I do know: You each have a role to play that's crucial to a good outcome. So, you can't afford to let your antagonism for each other cloud your judgment, or your emotional stability. Wars have been lost because of jealousies.

"You're each strong, daring men—and you're each her champion, in a unique way. Had you met under different circumstances, the odds are you would have recognized each other's worth, and might even have been friends . . ."

She smiled suddenly, genuinely. "I'm well aware that you, Dev, think I'm slightly mad." She turned her smile on the priest. "And you, Peter, think I'm a trifle suspect, because I see the Gods in a different perspective from yours. Yet, I believe if the truth were told, you both instinctively *like* me, and being good judges of character, you both probably intuit the integrity of my friendship for Maggie.

"What I'm asking of you both, is that you give each other the same latitude you give me—and for pretty much the same reason."

She was amused to see the sheepish look on both men's faces. *A little boy sleeps in all men,* her Russian grandmother would have said, with consummate understanding. Ellie excused herself on the pretext of seeing to something in the kitchen. What they needed to thrash out, needed privacy.

Devlin stood up, tension radiating like a force field.

"Look, Peter," he said, deliberately not using the honorific Father, so as not to concede an edge. "I'm in love with her. I have no way of knowing if she'll have me, now or ever. But I love her, and I'm going to do my damnedest to help her save Cody." He paused, then plunged on.

"I don't know what there is between the two of you . . . and, I don't want to. Because I don't think anything can come of it. And, I sure as hell don't think anything should. As I see it, the only thing you can offer her is some kind of endless, mind-fucking soul search that'll tear her guts out, while it helps you carry your heavy conscience. She deserves better than that.

"I know you're smart, and I respect that. I'm even willing to believe you're well intentioned toward Maggie and Cody. But the bottom line is you're a priest, not a man." Peter frowned at the insult but said nothing. "And, even if you won her," Devlin rushed on, "you wouldn't know what to do with her. And I would. Because I've been there and back, where women are concerned. And, I'm old enough to know what counts in this life, and how to take care of it—because I've seen how careless men can be with the women they claim to love. Christ, I've been that careless, myself. And I know how easy it is to take them for granted, and figure there'll always be another one coming down the pike. But there aren't any other Maggies on the pike. And if she'll have me, I'll take damned good care of her." He looked Peter straight in the eye. "Can you say the same?" he asked, the huskiness of all the emotions he struggled with in his voice. "Because if you can, it's a different ballgame."

Ellie stood poised in the doorway with a tea pot in her hand, riveted to the spot.

Peter stood up, too agitated to remain seated, or perhaps it was an unconscious gesture of superiority. He towered over the detective, even though Devlin was not a small man. His eye caught Ellie's and she saw the cacophony of emotions that rampaged in him.

"Come in, Ellie," he said, his voice strained.

"There's no reason why you shouldn't hear what I have to say."

She nodded and entered the room, sitting quietly out of the line of fire.

"As a *man*, Devlin, I'd like nothing in this world so much as to knock your teeth out," Peter said in a tone that left no doubt about his sincerity. "Since you choose to make this a no-holds-barred contest, let's take an honest look at *your* qualifications for suitor. From what Maggie's told me, your track record with marriage and family is somewhat less than exemplary, and *your* profession seems to portend at least as much potential suffering for Maggie as mine does." He paused in his pacing to face Devlin.

"Do you think she has not seen enough loss and violence, so that sitting up nights waiting to hear if you're alive or dead, wouldn't 'tear her guts out' in your inelegant terminology, at least as much as sharing my conscience would? Has it occurred to you that perhaps she has not been as fortunate in her potential suitors, as you and I, in our arrogance, would like to believe?

"In answer to your unspoken question: Yes, I do love her. More, in fact, than I could have conceived possible. You're quite right in suggesting that I do not have the experience of women that you do—but I'm not at all certain that's such an indictment. Perhaps the love I could bring her would be less sullied than yours. And less selfish.

"But you are right, at least partially, Devlin, because beyond my love for her, I have nothing whatsoever to offer. I have no 'chick nor child,' as my Irish mother would have said. No home, no money, and no great prospects. My academic credentials would make me employable, I suspect, at some obscure college or university that would be willing to overlook my curiously circuitous route to them—and I could probably eke out a living from writing—but that's it. I've had my fifteen minutes of fame and I expect no more.

"Would I fight you for her? would seem to be the

question you're really asking me. You have thrown down the gauntlet and have every right to an answer, so here is the best I can do to give you one." His voice had lowered and he spoke almost reverently.

"For Maggie, I would fight you, or this world, or the next . . . if I truly believed that at the end of the battle, she would be well served by my victory. But you see, I do not think that's so. If all that was to be considered here were my own needs, my own selfish pleasures, my own frail hopes or dreams, I would give you a fight the likes of which you've never seen. But that is not all that's at stake here. *Maggie* is at stake, and Cody. Maggie's future, Maggie's heart, maybe even Maggie's soul. Does my loving her give me the right to jeopardize any part of her to satisfy my own needs? I think not.

"You've accused me of uncertainties. Well, you're right on about that, at least—I am tormented by them. But this one thing I can tell you with absolute certainty: I will do anything in my power to help Maggie save this child." He paused significantly. "Even if it means I must get along with you."

Devlin looked nonplussed by the momentum, the forthrightness, the love that was obvious in Peter's soliloquy. "Well, I'll be damned," he said, standing up, his face set in grim stone. He ran his fingers through his hair, agitatedly, and finally met Peter's eyes with his own. "I guess I take back my crack about your manhood, Peter," he said with grudging apology. "What do you say we call a truce until after this is over? If only so I don't have to feel like any more of a horse's ass than I already do. I guess the truth of the matter is, this choice is going to be Maggie's, not ours . . . and only if we keep her alive past April 30th."

Peter nodded. "Agreed," he said, accepting the hand Devlin offered him. *"Cras amet qui nunquam amavit,"* he murmured as he did so.

Devlin's head snapped up in recognition, and he smiled crookedly. *"Quique amavit, cras amet,"* he responded.

Peter looked genuinely surprised. "It seems we admire the same poets," he said, amused.

"My Latin's not up to yours," Ellie said, walking them both to the door. "What did you each just say?"

"It's a couplet from *Pervigilium Veneris*," Peter answered. "I quoted, 'May he love tomorrow who has never loved before' and Devlin answered me, 'And may he who has loved, love tomorrow as well.'"

Ellie shut the door and leaned against it with a small satisfied chuckle. It was hard to decide which of these two men she liked more.

# CHAPTER 66

Father James Kebede watched the interchange of ideas flow between Maggie and Peter. There was fluidity to it; a sort of reciprocal energy that enlivened each. He was returning to Rhinebeck today and had come to say goodbye to Maggie, surprised at how poignant this farewell seemed to him, as if he were parting from an old friend whom he might not meet again.

He'd grown strangely fond of her during the time he'd spent in New York, and he hadn't intended that. There was no guile in Maggie, and there was a great deal of goodness that touched him. Having been the oldest of fourteen children, in one of the poorest countries on earth, he respected strength of character, particularly in women. He could recollect with visceral intensity his mother's courage and kindness in the face of unrelenting poverty, and a new pregnancy every year. Against appalling odds, she had borne them, loved them, nurtured them . . . nursing their ills, burying the four she couldn't save; teaching them all the love of God, and a strict value system that still seemed to him the one the Almighty had in mind for humanity.

James watched the animated conversation intently, thinking he had never seen Peter so human. Maggie called forth in him a dimension that had not existed before, making him more than he had been. And, perhaps, less.

He'd pondered the metamorphosis throughout the course of the ten days he'd been here in New York, probing at Maggie, teaching her, pushing her, questioning her; trying to intuit what it was in her that had worked such potent alchemy in Peter.

Now, he thought he finally understood the chemistry—but, what was he to do with this knowledge? And what did this newfound intuition require of his conscience?

He watched the easy camaraderie of the man and woman, pondering as often before, the strange and terrible ways by which God worked His Mysteries.

He needed to go home to pray. There was a fragile balance, here, and he felt inept for the task of holding the scales. If only he were holier, and wiser, and more full of grace, perhaps he could more skillfully do whatever it was that God required of him . . .

A question Maggie had asked pulled him back from his reverie, into the conversation.

"Forgive me, Maggie," he said with a shy smile. "I fear I was wool-gathering. What was it you asked of me?"

She smiled and repeated the question. It was impossible not to love James, she'd told Peter; he was one of God's own. "I asked how it is you're able to believe that the soul of one who is Possessed is worth the risk of your own?" she said.

"Ah, Maggie . . ." he answered, full attention immediately back on center. "Let me try to explain this important point." He thought a moment before continuing.

"It is my belief that there are countless—perhaps even millions—of souls on this earth already Possessed by the Evil One, but they are content with the bargain they have made! Whether they sold their souls knowingly, or merely let them slip away through spiritual laziness, these people enjoy their evil and its spoils to the fullest. They are content to be legionnaires in the Devil's army—never would they dream of asking for exorcism. But the *others*, Maggie—the ones who come to us begging for help—it is because they *do* struggle so desperately with the Great Foe that they suffer! It is because they battle with all of their frail human strength against the Immortal Enemy of mankind that they are beset by demons.

"They cry out to God not to forsake them in their extremity, and, as priests, we have been given the great privilege of coming to their aid. If we did *not* go to their rescue, it would not be they, but we, who would be on the road to damnation."

"You're a lovely man, James," Maggie said, touched by the vehemence of his response. "I'll always be glad to have known you." She reached out to take his hand. "If I ever need an exorcism, I hope you'll be in the neighborhood."

His eyes softened. "That moment will never come, Maggie," he said gently. "The Adversary always knows who fights on the side of the angels. He might try to destroy you . . . but he would know he could never seduce you. 'He who abides in love,' Saint John tells us, 'abides in God, and God in him.' "

Maggie heard something in his voice—a kind of tender admiration—that made her wonder. "Thank you, James," she said, moved by his confidence. "I'd still like to know you were on my side."

The look in his eyes was so sad when she stood on tiptoe to kiss him good-bye, that she wondered if she might have inadvertently offended him.

Father James hung the purple chasuble on its hanger, and placed it carefully into the armoire that held the priestly vestments for the Mass. His moves were deliberate and reverent; the grace of the Holy Sacrifice he'd just performed still filled his heart.

He turned at a small sound behind him and was surprised to see Peter standing near the door.

"I didn't wish to disturb you, James," the older priest said, aware of the piety of the younger man. "But I received a message that you wished to see me."

James nodded; he seemed unwilling to speak.

"I could come back later . . ." Peter began.

"No, no, my friend," James responded, with a reassuring smile. "I have something I must say to you, Peter—it has been preying on my mind."

The two men left the sacristy behind and began the walk down the long marble corridor toward the kitchen.

"When we first spoke of your dilemma," James began, "you asked of me that I remain close to you in this upheaval of the soul. And I agreed."

Peter nodded acquiescence.

"This agreement has laid a great obligation upon my own conscience, Peter, for it demands of me honesty that goes beyond the dictates of friendship. Indeed, it demands an honesty that may ultimately undermine our friendship, which would be, for me, a most terrible loss." The large Ethiopian stopped speaking for a moment; his face was creased with the frown of one who must voice an unwanted truth. Peter, understanding, placed his hand on the other man's arm reassuringly.

"Let us hope our friendship is not so frail that truth can destroy it," he said with a sinking heart.

"I have prayed for the grace to be your mirror in this conflict, my friend," James said sadly. "Whatever I can tell you, you already know, of course . . . and yet, the obligation you have laid upon me demands that I be the one to speak the words aloud. When I saw you and Maggie together this last time, I knew there was no other course for me, but to say what is in my heart."

"Was I wrong in thinking you liked her, James? I distinctly felt a simpatico between the two of you, these past few days."

"Not only do I like her, Peter, but I care for her. The fact that I see her virtue so clearly is what forces me to speak."

"And what, old friend, is it you feel you must say?" James looked at Peter with immense compassion, but his words were stern.

"A priestly vocation is as monumental a work of God's, as any I can conceive . . . and you, Peter, are the most complex of men. Your intellect alone positions you within the circle in the spiral . . . and the convolutions of your emotions are surely no simpler.

"I do not believe that Maggie is your problem—but rather, that she is a symptom of a far greater ill. I believe you have collapsed into this woman's arms, Peter, when it is Christ's arms you seek, but have not found." He paused to let that potent thought sink in.

"You feel your Church has failed you, my friend, with its doublespeak, and its punitive attitude toward your work—and you think you have failed *yourself*, in not finding an acceptable answer to the anguished questions you have placed before the Throne of God. The gravity of these failures has put your priesthood into crisis, and the only place you have found comfort is in this woman, who has become, for you, the transcendental truth beyond reason.

"I believe, Peter, you have collapsed into the comfort of Maggie's absolute, unencumbered faith. It is not the *woman*, Peter . . . it is her understanding of God, which is greater than your own, that seduces you!" Peter stood still as stone, the magnitude of what James was saying reverberating through him, like a gong struck in his soul.

James's voice softened. "As a *man*, Peter, I understand your loneliness. As a *priest*, I understand your disillusionment with your Church, and your sense of abandonment. As your comrade, I understand your love for a woman worthy of it.

"But as your confessor, and the friend who is the mirror of your conscience—none of these understandings has ultimate relevancy." James's voice had become firm.

"When you entered the priesthood, Peter, you were already a man—as such, you made a solemn commitment to eternal chastity. You entered into a sacred trust with God, my friend. Now you may say, Ah! but in my youth I did not know the hardship my vow would bring! And I would ask you, does the man who takes a woman in marriage for better or worse, truly comprehend how bitter the hardships may be that are demanded by that vow? Certainly not.

"Because of your great and wondrous gifts from the Father, and because of your own extraordinary love for Him, you have always considered yourself the specially chosen of God, Peter. So, too, did Lucifer. Now, you seek to renegotiate your contract—and you must not presume you can do so, with impunity. You must not embrace the deadly illusion that you can have them both, Peter. *You* cannot. Perhaps, another man could . . . but *you* cannot.

"You are jousting with God and you are not His match! Brilliant, well meaning, pious, gifted beyond mere mortals—you are still no match for God.

"The Devil in the Sixth Circle, Peter! The cosmic paradox: to love Maggie is to destroy her and yourself."

Peter stood still as death, his head bent to his chest.

"God is pursuing you, Peter," James said with finality. "He must want you very badly. Do not flee Him at the crossroads."

PETER walked along the water's edge, the deserted river a gray comfort. He was lost in a morass of explosive emotions. Just a few days ago, he had brooded over his confrontation with Devlin, plumbing his conscience for absolutes, replaying the dialogue again and again, to sift for missed threads. But at the end of it, he'd felt relieved

. . . that their antagonism was out in the open and neutralized . . . that Ellie'd had the good sense and conscience to make them face each other, squarely . . . but most of all, that it had been a draw. Neither had vanquished the other, each had left with his dignity intact.

But the confrontation with James was a different story. There were no winners here, and there had been no draw. Maybe confrontation wasn't even the word for what had happened between them, yet some sort of clarion battle cry had been sounded. Could it be that James was only the courier, sent to announce the upcoming battle . . . and the confrontation must be with his own soul?

*Deus meus, Deus meus, ut quid dereliquisti me? My God, my God, why hast thou forsaken me?*

Peter picked up a handful of pebbles and skipped the first one out across the dirty gray-green water.

He felt rebellious. Just because James had said what he had, didn't make it true. Or at least, not the only truth.

What if it was merely time to go? What if Peter Messenguer's long struggle to remain in the Church had finally ground to an end. Not with a bang, but a whimper. *We don't receive wisdom*, Proust had said. *We must discover it for ourselves, after a journey that no one can take for us or spare us.* What if his own journey was meant to be at Maggie's side? Or what if he was blocked, like the man in Kafka's parable, by a door that could never open? Was the Church the block? Or was Maggie?

*Et clamor ad meus te veniat! And let my cry come unto thee . . .*

Peter skipped the last stone and rested his elbows on the iron fence, wearily.

*Domine, non sum dignus . . . Lord I am not worthy, but only say the word and my soul shall be healed.*

He was a better man since Maggie . . . he knew that in his soul. Maybe that in itself was a sign. He was less arrogant, less coldly Jesuitical, less sure of everything

. . . or of anything, really. More compassionate, more honest, more human.

What if she was, for him, the Christ in the stranger's guise? What if she was love, and love was all that mattered?

Or what if all this was just the tawdriest kind of rationalization, and she was merely mortal sin, disguised in angel's raiment?

What if the Demon had marked him, one last time, while his guard was down!

Father of Lies. Cosmic Lord of Death.

Watching.

Waiting.

Peter shook his head to clear it. Maggie was not an instrument of Evil. She was good. He knew that, if he knew nothing else. But what did he know of himself?

*Let my cry come unto thee, O Lord*, he prayed almost without intending to. *For if thou, O Lord, shall mark our iniquities, Lord who shall stand it?*

He turned from the river and walked resolutely back toward the book depository, but when he reached the door, he did not enter. He would return to New York and finish preparing Maggie for what was to come. Everything else could be tabled until after the thirtieth.

# CHAPTER 67

Devlin finished his recital of facts and wondered at the look on the Captain's face. It was the face of an old Irish pol, the kind the New York PD had once abounded in, but didn't anymore. Captain Francis X. O'Shaunessy had been around long enough for it to be said that he knew the location of every skeleton buried at City Hall since La Guardia left office.

At the moment, the face was a study in noncommittal blandness.

"And what exactly is your interest in this case, Lieutenant?" was the first question he asked. That in itself surprised Devlin. Ordinarily, there would have been astute probings during the recital of facts; the judicious inquiries of Irish intuition, and forty years of police experience. But not today.

Devlin flirted with the possibility of keeping his personal interest to himself, but thought better of it.

"I like the O'Connor woman," he said. "I think she's stumbled on to something very big and dirty. And, I'm convinced the child is in serious danger."

O'Shaunessy sat back, his barrel chest and buffalo shoulders making the move an emphatic gesture. "I see nothing in what you've told me to necessitate any action on our part," he said, and Devlin frowned. No give and take? No batting the possibilities around?

"But, Captain," he persisted, "the Fellowes material alone gives us plenty that falls into this jurisdiction. The club on Bleecker, the drug laundry—"

The Captain cut him off with a gesture. "All unsubstantiated, Lieutenant. All from a dead witness. If you think you've found something of current value, turn it over to the narcotics squad. The rest is unadulterated bullshit. Understood?"

Devlin rose to go. The dismissal in the Captain's manner was as apparent, as it was puzzling.

"Captain . . ." Devlin said, as he reached the door. "Do you know something I don't, about all this?" There was always the possibility he was inadvertently stepping on an ongoing investigation from some other jurisdiction.

O'Shaunessy's eyes were steady and unreadable. "What I know, Lieutenant, is when it's smart to drop something that's a dead end."

Devlin nodded and opened the door, when the Captain spoke again. "The papers from that reporter . . . what's his name . . . Fellowes. You can leave them with me for review."

Devlin turned, looking instinctively for something in the man's face to explain that request. "They're still in the vault, Captain," he answered evenly.

"Then get them out of the vault and onto my desk," the Captain said, dismissing him again, with a wave of the hand. Devlin made a mental note to get them the hell out of Chase, tonight. This was weird. This was very weird.

"What'd the Captain say?" Gino asked, already knowing the answer from the set of the Lieutenant's jaw.

"A very emphatic no," Devlin replied, the echoes of the conversation still resounding in his ears.

"Yeah, yeah, I can guess. Not our jurisdiction. No proof, only circumstantial. We got enough headaches already. Yada dada dada . . . Am I on the track, here."

"Like the A-train," Devlin replied thoughtfully. It wasn't what the Captain had said that was out of line, but everything about the way he said it.

"So what's that look on your face for? This wasn't exactly unexpected."

"I don't know, Gino. He acted strange, and he asked me for the Fellowes notes right after he said this was all bullshit and we should stay out of it."

Gino looked up sharply. "Hey, Lieutenant. What are we talkin' here?"

Devlin shook his head. "I don't know. But I'm moving the papers, just in case I turn out *not* to be paranoid."

Garibaldi nodded. He'd been around long enough to know that nothing was impossible where big bucks could change hands.

"So what do you want I should do?"

"Rattle some chains, I think; see what we shake

loose. I'll take Sayles, you see Vannier, since Eric already knows he doesn't like me. Let them think we've got more on them than we have.''

Garibaldi nodded, his mouth in a judicious twist. "Actually we know a lot, now, Lieutenant, we just don't have proof. How much of our hand do you want me to show this guy?''

"Am I being asked such a question by the department's best poker player?" Devlin responded, with a short laugh. "Show him nothing, and bring home the pot, just like always.''

The legendary card player grinned. "I don't like guys who beat on little kids and women, Lieutenant,'' he said. "I could really get a kick out of getting the goods on Tweedledum and Tweedledee.''

Devlin nodded. Garibaldi was a good man and a good friend. "Gino,'' he said before the door closed, "watch your back. Nothing feels right about this.''

Gino grinned. "What? A deviation in the Grand Design?" he said in mock disbelief. "Could be we ain't in Kansas anymore, Lieutenant.''

He closed the door behind him; Devlin took his jacket off the hook, and headed for Chase Manhattan.

# CHAPTER 68

Abdul Hazred waited in the Vannier library for the others to arrive. With less than two weeks until the Materialization, it was essential that each participant fully understood his role, but with a summit meeting of monumental egos, it was likely to be a difficult evening.

The thirteen most powerful magicians on the planet would gather in this room tonight; representatives of every major magical system that could command genuine power. Santería's evil Bantu sisters, Palo Monte and Palo Mayombe, would be represented, as would Haitian Voodoo, Candomblé, Obeah, two major satanic covens, the intellectually elite Crown of Choronzon, Gnosis of Xantha, and a strange Mithraic cult, that was barely heard of outside this circle.

He himself, Sayles, and Vannier would represent the Egyptian Mysteries, and Ghania . . . *ah, Ghania*, he thought, musingly. What could one say of her Malagasy magic, born in the last throes of Lemurian decadence, before it sank forever beneath the Pacific's southern waves? Only that it was the most malevolent of them all.

Each of the participants in tonight's meeting had survived the Abyss; each had dedicated his or her life to the accumulation of occult power over the material world. Some had earned their power in primitive shamanic cultures, others through an intellectual education so rigorous and advanced its scope could barely be catalogued by lesser minds. And, the only thing they had in common was their willingness to serve an Evil Master, in return for receiving their heart's desires. Some had come to their exalted knowledge through dynastic family commitments, some through personal avarice, some through intellectual pride. Of a certainty, none had come to this moment in a single lifetime.

All their stories were different from his own, Hazred thought, calculatingly, as he watched the newcomers' cars begin to fill the circular driveway outside the library window. He was here, not out of dedication to Evil, but out of love for a Goddess and her legend. Out of desperate, urgent need to possess the Amulets that had haunted his dreams since the moment in boyhood, when he'd learned of their existence. Evil was a necessary component of the equation for him—but it was not the whole equation—for what magician could consider himself a master, if he could not command both Left and Right Hand Magic?

He had been thirteen, the day he entered the Cairo Museum on a lark, and wandered through the cool, dim corridors aimlessly, until the statue of Sekhmet had called to him. *Attend me! Priest . . .* the riveting voice had demanded, and some long-buried energy had begun to resonate within him. He'd stood transfixed before the huge black granite statue and had known, in every corpuscle, the magnitude of the calling. Once a priest of the Goddess, always a priest of the Goddess. He had been called, and he had answered.

Standing before her statue, Hazred had seen her eyes open, and an aura of flames engulf them both. Information had begun to funnel into him—or perhaps it was merely reconstituted within him, from buried knowledge, once possessed, and long abandoned.

Skeletons had fed the flames in his vision, and legions had materialized to serve the fierce Goddess. They had led him with august ceremony to an altar where predatory hawk-headed figures guarded Sekhmet's mysteries. The walls of the museum had convulsed into nothingness, as vision after vision danced before Abdul Hazred's expanding consciousness, weaving themselves into his being, undulating through his cellular memories, until he was once again the High Priest of Sekhmet, born of a long-dead dynasty.

*I will instruct you!* The Goddess's voice had rung out to him. *The Messenger will be sent in thy lifetime. My Stone of destiny will be within the reach of humankind. The work shall be done. The way will be shown . . .*

Hazred was yanked back abruptly from his reverie by the arrival of the other guests.

"Number Three," a hearty voice expounded, in his direction. "We gather at last!" A tall distinguished man with an Oxford accent made an arcane sign of respectful greeting in the air, and smiled.

"Welcome, Number Eleven," Hazred responded with similarly feigned delight. "This dress rehearsal has been a long time coming."

A small Asian woman, who exuded malevolent

power, despite her diminutive size, had heard the exchange. "*Eons*, to put a fine point on it," she said with a dazzling smile, that despite her startling beauty, reminded Hazred of a shark's smile at feeding time.

"Number Five," he said to her in greeting, "you are as beautiful as ever, I see. Take care that the Goddess doesn't feel a twinge of envy."

The woman smiled her acknowledgment of the compliment, as a huge man with thick Negroid features swirled into the room in cloak and turban. "Number Six is as unobtrusive as ever," the woman said with a throaty laugh; as she turned to greet the newcomer, several more guests arrived at once. A stocky Caucasian with a jet black goatee, a bean stalk of a woman, dressed in black from head to toe, a smallish scholarly sort of man in the rumpled tweeds of academia.

Eric and Nicky entered the room in tandem, obviously still engaged in animated conversation. At the sight of the assemblage, they each moved into the room in a differing direction, dividing the chore of greeting neatly in half.

Ghania arrived behind the two men, dressed far more consequentially than usual, in a djellabah and turban of some extraordinary silver silk that gleamed in an almost incandescent manner, as if the fabric had an independent lifeforce.

"Speaking of unobtrusive entrances," Number Five chuckled, nodding at the witch, with a sort of grudging admiration. "Not bad for a girl of her age."

Ghania's gaze turned in the woman's direction, the moment the words were spoken, although ordinary human ears could never have overheard the remark. Number Five tilted her head toward Ghania in recognition of the feat, and Ghania smiled, her deadly smile.

"Let us all be seated, my dear colleagues," Eric began, positioning himself against an immensely ornate Jacobean desk that dominated the end of the room opposite the many scattered chairs and couches.

"We are assembled this evening for the final time

before the Great Feast. Whatever last-minute questions we have, should be laid to rest here, tonight, so there will be no dissension, to muddy the energies during the Materialization.''

A murmur of discordant voices greeted this opening gambit.

''Please, *please*, my Adepti,'' Eric calmed the storm with an imperial gesture. ''You all seek to learn who shall occupy which place in the Ceremony. Most understandable, of course, that you are curious. Number Two and Number Three?'' He turned his eyes to Sayles and Hazred. ''Perhaps you would delineate the role of each participant.'' The two men stepped forward.

''Look. Let's face it,'' Nicky began pointedly, ''anybody in this room tonight could perform any of the necessary rites, and everybody wants the best roles, so assignment has been a real pisser of a job. Screw trying to give everybody a fair shake, somebody just has to decide *who* does *what*. So, I've taken everybody's talents into account, where I could—for the rest, you'll just have to go with the flow.

''Eric Vannier will operate as High Priest, that goes without saying. Dr. Abdul Hazred, who holds the rank of Ipsissimus, and yours truly, a Magister Templi, will assist on the altar.

''Kazak Ra will set the Astral Defenses. His Mithraic Brotherhood of Arms gives him the edge in combat.

''Invocation of Elementals will be done by Varielli Le Res, because Elementals are meat and potatoes to Palo Mayombe.

''Proclamation of the Rite goes to our resident diva, Tanis Feyodorovna, the only one of us who can hit C above high C.

''Preliminary Conjuration of the Deities will be handled by Sir Reginald, since celestial protocol is his bag. Morrigan will be Administrator of Oaths. Madame Chan will man the North Gate. Professor Theopolis the South Gate. Giles Moreau the East Gate. Ghania the West Gate. Father Duchesne will distribute Communion.''

Vannier stepped forward. "Ghania will have a dual role, of course; as she has awakened the Messenger, she will conduct her on the Astral Journey." He cleared his throat. "One other important point should be made here. We seek to Materialize the Isis Amulet and the Sekhmet Stone through the Ancient Mysteries of my motherland, so needless to say, the Major Ritual and Materialization will be done according to the Egyptian formulae laid out at the Temple of Isis, millennia ago. However, in deference to the extraordinary assemblage of talent that the Master has brought together to achieve our end, we will salute the many denominations of Evil represented here by working the Enochian Keys, the Tunnels of Set, the Theban Formula, the Second Formula Clavis Rei, Primae and the Oranti Conjuration, as well."

A delighted murmuring broke out among the listeners and Kazak Ra stepped forward. "A most generous gesture," he said approvingly. "I speak for most here in saying we came to quarrel with your unilateral control of the proceedings, but perhaps that was a hasty conclusion. I salute your foresight."

"Hear, hear," said several voices.

"The goal is in sight," Madame Chan interjected frostily. "If *I* am content to be a doorkeeper at the North Gate, in order to secure the great prizes, who, here, has a right to quibble over ignominious accommodations? We've all signed our pacts . . . we'll each get what we most desire when the Amulet and Stone are in our grasp. Are we neophytes, to quarrel over trifles?"

Hazred smiled to himself at the tongue lashing; he saw Eric and Nicky exchange glances. Every man and woman in this room had a hidden agenda . . . any would kill the others without a pang of conscience if it served his or her own purpose. But for the moment, all were bound together by their greed. After that . . .

The tall cadaverous woman named Morrigan had begun to quiver like an inchworm in a windstorm, while Madame Chan was speaking. Quickly, two men stepped forward to hold her lanky body upright. They had all seen her in the throes of this energy before; it was the price of being an oracle.

"Beware the sacrificial offering!" she cried out in a high-pitched whine, as unnerving as the squeaking of chalk on a blackboard. "Beware the cloth where East and West are twain. Where Past and Present meet, the Future writes its own tale." She slumped suddenly and would have crumpled, but for the men who held her.

"What does that mean?" Theopolis demanded.

"That the gatekeepers of the Four Stations may have more to do than we'd imagined," Sayles interjected quickly. "East and West must be superbly guarded. Past and Present meet in the Amulet and Stone . . . whoever possesses them secures the future. The oracle foresees a benevolent end to our efforts."

Ghania smiled. It meant nothing of the kind, but it was a superb save by Nicholas.

A somewhat uneasy silence followed as all participants filed into the chapel for a last run-through of their respective roles.

Ghania closed the door on the final Adept with a smile frozen into place. She waited until the last car had rumbled out of the driveway before turning back toward the library. She made a mental note to visit several of the erstwhile visitors on the Astral tonight, while their individual plots were still foremost in their thoughts. Many would shield themselves before sleep, but she had added euphrasia to their wine at dinner and it might be sufficient to disrupt their psychic shields enough for penetration.

She returned to the library. Hazred had remained behind with Nicholas and Eric; as the third priest in the triumvirate who would Materialize, he had special privileges. She neither liked nor trusted the Egyptian, she thought with a sigh. Of course, she neither liked nor trusted any of the Adepti, although some she felt she knew well enough to understand their innermost motivations. Hazred was different. She had tried on numerous occasions to penetrate his mental armor, but either he was the most skilled magician of them all, or he was, indeed, as he claimed, shielded by his Goddess. Not that she trusted his Goddess either, come to think of it.

Sekhmet was an evil manifestation of the Goddess energy, not a genuine Goddess of Evil. Astaroth or Lilith, she would have trusted empirically, but Sekhmet was as unreliable toward Evil, as she was toward Good. She was too damned unpredictable. Some even claimed she was the malevolent side of the Isis coin.

As she entered the room, Hazred stood up to acknowledge her; neither of the other two ever did as much.

"Ghania," he greeted her. "How goes it with the child?" She glanced at Eric for leave to speak, and he nodded imperceptibly.

"I have used the old ways. She teeters on the brink of the Awakening. This week, I will push her to the edge of madness . . . her Guardians will not permit her destruction, so they will be forced to manifest. The key to our success is the timing of my efforts. No more than forty-eight hours can elapse between her Awakening and the Materialization. If I Awaken her too soon, she will have time to become proficient in the use of her power, and we will no longer control her. If I am too late, she will not have sufficient capability to withstand the astral journey and return. As it is, she may have to be drugged, or enchanted, until the moment of Materialization."

Hazred understood only too well the risks. "I commend you, Ghania. Only someone of your unique skills could undertake such a delicate labor with any hope of success," he said, the magnanimous praise of a king for a talented servant.

The nuance wasn't lost on the powerful woman. She inclined her head toward him ever so slightly in acknowledgment. "I serve my Master," she replied icily. She wondered if he could say the same.

# CHAPTER 69

Raphael Abraham looked around the anteroom of Rabbi Levi's office, and wondered why on earth he was there. He had already put in place all the surveillance teams necessary for his mission. He had sent his reports back to Tel Aviv in the standard Mossad double-coding system, in which each phonetic sound has a number, and each of these numbers has a "sleeve" letter or number equivalent. He had arranged for a Shicklut employee to secure listening equipment, for when it would be needed. And he had alerted the Sayonim network of loyal Jews in the area, who might be called on to render service to Israel. All exactly as was sensible and required.

All except this visit.

This was a whim. He smiled to himself, thinking no one, anywhere, at any time, had ever applied such a word to Raphael Abraham.

So why was he here?

The small, intense-looking rabbi, who seemed to be the guardian of the threshold, motioned to Abraham from the Rebbe's doorway, and he rose immediately to his feet to answer the summons, feeling like a small boy called to the headmaster's office for an unknown infringement.

"Rebbe," he said deferentially, as he entered the old man's presence. "Thank you for seeing me." There was no reply but a slight inclination of the head, and he felt compelled to explain his purpose, so he gestured with the folder in his hand.

"I've compiled as much information as we possess

on the Amulet legend, Rebbe," he said, "and some biographical material on all the people involved, particularly the woman and her grandchild." The Rebbe nodded again, but still did not speak. "If you need more, I'll be happy to supply whatever you require."

"I do not need even that which you hold in your hand," the Rebbe said matter-of-factly. "I have already seen the woman and the child."

Abraham frowned. "Forgive me, Rebbe," he said, "but that cannot be so . . . I have them both under surveillance and there has been no such visit."

The Rebbe pursed his lips, as if to say what point is there in explaining the obvious to a dimwit?

"Your surveillance cannot see as far as mine, perhaps?" he said, with a small measure of indulgence for the ignorant. "What I need to know of them, I know. When they come, I will know more."

Abraham looked puzzled. "Are you saying, Rebbe, that I am to bring them to you? My orders are unclear on this point."

"Your orders have nothing to do with the answer to this question," the old man said simply. "We will be brought together, if I am needed. Neither you, nor I, nor your order giver, whoever he may be, are involved with this decision."

Abraham's face was set in a frown of indecision; he was not in the least sure what he needed to ask, or say.

"Rebbe," he said finally. "When I come here, I am like a boy. Uncertain. The world I live in, I understand thoroughly. It's a hard world, full of realities best left undiscussed. I thought it was the only world. What I think I hear you telling me, is that there is more to this job I have been given . . . more that I may have to deal with, but I am ill-equipped . . ." He let the thought trail off, not knowing how to explain.

This time the Rebbe's eyes twinkled; encouraged, Abraham went on. "I begin to think I may be at a disadvantage because of some ignorance I was not even aware of . . . if this is so, perhaps, I cannot do my job as expected.''

"So." the Rebbe said. "The sands shift beneath your feet a little, and all may not be as you imagined." He was silent for a moment, contemplating the man before him, easy in the silence.

"What do you know of Kabbalah?" he asked finally. "Did your uncle teach you nothing?"

Abraham's eyes were instantly alert.

"My uncle? What do you know of my uncle?" he asked suspiciously.

The Rebbe moved his head back and forth a little, and shrugged. I know what I need to know, the gesture said.

"My uncle was a scholar," Abraham said, calculating his words carefully. "I respected his knowledge, but I did not understand him."

The Rebbe's great eyebrows rose in reproof. "Perhaps the truth is you did *not* respect his knowledge. Perhaps you thought he was *meshugge* because he knew of things you could not see, and tried to teach you things you could not substantiate by ordinary means."

Abraham realized he'd been caught again . . . what point was there in lying to this man whose surveillance saw farther than his own. "I stand reproved," he said quietly.

"Good boy," said the Rebbe. "Now we can begin. This matter of the Amulets . . . it involves Mysteries you have not imagined, and could not dream. Kabbalah is not something you can come and say, 'Tell me about this . . .' and learn. The Universe you know of, is a complex business, and it is only one of four such Universes. Too much to learn about in a day, or a year, or a lifetime. So go home. Read a book . . . maybe two. Gershom Scholem on Kabbalah would be good, to start. Then you will know how much you don't know. Then you will stop making conclusions you have no business making. And you will stop thinking you are in charge of anything. This will be a start."

"Now you are making fun of me," Abraham said, thoroughly bamboozled.

"A little. Maybe. God likes us to laugh."

"All I want, Rebbe, is to do the job I've been sent for. No more, no less."

"And what, exactly, do you imagine that job to be?"

"To secure the Amulets for Israel—if they exist, which seems to me impossible." There was more to his orders, that he didn't reveal.

"So. You want me to tell you if the impossible is possible. The answer is yes. But your job may turn out to be far different from what you imagine. Keep an open mind."

"Rebbe," Abraham said, in exasperation. "Why did I come here today?"

"You are a good boy, Rafi," the Rebbe said unexpectedly. Abraham looked up, startled by the familiarity. "But you think the answers to your questions will come from the world around you. This is not true. There you will find only illusion, for the logic you so prize is a limitation you place upon yourself."

Raphael Abraham leaped up from his chair, realization dawning. "My God!" he said, in shock.

He had been eleven years old when his Uncle Schlomo had said these exact words to him. The boys at school had laughed at the ragged old rabbi, who was a Kabbalist and therefore a fool. And Rafi had come home, angry, embarrassed, and said ugly, unkind things to his uncle. Uncalled-for things, that would have provoked a beating from his own father, had he known of the conversation. But no one knew . . . only Uncle Schlomo. And he had only smiled sadly, hurt by this favorite child's unkindness, but too good to hurt in return. How often after that had Abraham regretted the interchange, and not known how to heal the rift between them except perversely, by trying always to prove himself right and the old man wrong? How different might his life have been, had that day and all that sprang from it, never happened?

"What do you want of me?" he breathed, shocked and frightened in an unaccustomed way.

"I want nothing," the Rebbe said quietly. "But God . . ." He shrugged a little. "He may want more. He will let you know. He will let us *both* know."

The man who led Raphael Abraham from the Rebbe's office averted his gaze so as not to see tears in the eyes of one who had no business crying.

"MAA Kheru intends to perform the materialization on the night of April 30th," Hazred said to Colonel Hamid, in his office. "I will require military backup in two locations." He handed the man a slip of paper with the addresses.

"Mossad is involved now," the Colonel responded. "They are trouble."

"They are none of my affair," Hazred said. "Once the Amulets exist in material form, you must be able to secure them against all comers, if Egypt is to take its rightful place as a major world power. That's why you are involved."

"I do not need assistance from you, Doctor, to understand the scope of my orders, thank you," Hamid said, shortly. "We have engaged Mossad before." He glanced at the paper. "Why do we need to deploy men at two locations?"

"This is a most delicate operation," Hazred replied. "I must have a safe house, fully equipped, to which she can be brought after we have taken possession of the Amulets."

Hazred could see by the thinly disguised sneer, what Colonel Hamid thought of the probability of magical Amulets. No matter. If his plan worked out as he intended, it would soon matter very little what civil servants, or governments, or Maa Kheru, for that matter, thought about anything at all.

# CHAPTER 70

"Lieutenant Devlin, is it?" Nicholas Sayles's handsome face was set in just the right expression of perplexed hospitality as he greeted his unexpected visitor. "Is there something I can do for you?" He leaned back against his custom-made desk and looked amiable, but not patient. Like all in the public eye, he had long ago perfected the means of dealing with unwanted intrusions in a curt-but-civilized manner.

Devlin stood across the floor from him, his face unreadable. "Actually, Mr. Sayles, there's quite a bit you could do for me, but I suspect you may not want to."

Sayles raised a quizzical eyebrow.

"It has come to the attention of the police department that you are a member of an organization called Maa Kheru. Is that true?"

Sayles's handsome face was set in an arrogant smirk. "I belong to the University Club, the Metropolitan Club, and the New York A.C., Lieutenant. Not to an organization I've never heard of."

"And have you heard of heroin, Mr. Sayles?" Devlin pressed. "It appears the organization you've never heard of supports its many enterprises by running a very lucrative heroin trade."

Sayles's dark eyebrows knitted together in a frown. "You're fucking around with the wrong boy here, Lieutenant. Tossing around allegations like that could get your ass in a sling faster than you could zip your fly. Slander's a serious charge . . . so's false arrest. If you have anything further to say to me, say it through my lawyer. He's the one I have speak to the likes of you."

Devlin moved in closer, his voice deadly calm. "The likes of me can put the likes of you in Attica. I wonder how well it would sit with your loyal TV audience, and the banks who fund your television properties, if they knew you spend your nights dressed up in bedsheets, eating the bodies of children, Mr. Sayles. Or maybe they'd like to hear about your arms sales to Libya, or your heroin connections in the Golden Triangle, or the nice little porno flick sideline you and Eric Vannier have funded. Even if we couldn't prove all of it, some of the scum would stick to your shoes, before your lawyer could do jack shit."

"Get out of my office," Sayles said, his voice low and tightly controlled. "You haven't got enough proof of anything to give me a parking ticket."

"We know how your network functions. We have enough evidence, to put you where you won't have to worry about parking for a long time. Maybe, you and Eric Vannier are the ones who better watch your asses." Devlin waited only long enough to see the barb placed, then turned on his heel. He had come to find out how rattleable this media mogul might be in the clinches, and now he knew. Nicholas Sayles was used to power and the protection it offered; he couldn't be threatened, but he could be made nervous. That would have to do for the moment.

Sayles clenched his fists and released them several times to regain control of himself after Devlin left. It was high time they taught this detective something about power, and the meddlesome Maggie O'Connor something about fear.

Sayles didn't wait to be announced. He slammed past the servant who opened the door of the Vannier mansion, and didn't stop to remove his coat. He caught Eric lifting a coffee cup to his lips at the lunch table.

"We have to talk," he said peremptorily. "Now!"

Eric's irritation at the interruption was barely concealed. "Sit down, Nicky. And do take off your coat."

Sayles shrugged the outer garment into waiting hands, without even glancing at the servant. "I had a cop in my office this morning," he said, harshly. "A tough son of a bitch with a lot of attitude. Very cocky about what he knew."

Eric continued to eat, unperturbed.

"Which was what?"

"About Maa Kheru . . . about our relationship. About the bank's drug and arms deals. He said he had evidence and a witness. The son of a bitch was very careful not to step over the line, officially. No accusations, just a lot of saber rattling . . . but I don't like talk about guns and drugs in the same breath with my name."

"So, he had nothing, really," Eric said, patting his mouth with an exquisite linen napkin the size of a small tablecloth. "I'm used to dealing with governments, Nicky, local police are exceedingly small potatoes."

"He asked me if I was a member of Maa Kheru, Eric. No one except Fellowes has *ever* connected me to the group. Not even the stinking tabloids. I don't need this, Eric. Not now. Not *ever*."

Eric saw the tight jaw muscles in the handsome face; he despised whiners. It would be disagreeable if Nicky turned out to be one. "What precisely would you like me to do about this petty annoyance, Nicky? In another week, the Amulets will be in our possession, and we will hardly need worry about some trifling New York policeman and his unsubstantiated innuendos."

"The Materialization is the exact reason I don't want any assholes fucking around here, muddying the waters, Eric," Sayles insisted. "I'll bet any amount of money the O'Connor bitch is behind this. I told you the Sending wouldn't neutralize that cunt—she's on a fucking mission! I want her out of the picture and I want it done *my* way."

Eric's eyes narrowed slightly. There was more to this request than was obvious on the surface. He'd seen that malicious glint in Nicky's eyes too often to mistake the potency of its malice.

"What exactly *is* it you do want, Nicky? The policeman's ears on your belt? That shouldn't be hard to accomplish. We have friends downtown. And, Maggie's ears, too, for a matched set?"

"Nothing so mundane, Eric. I want a ritual sacrifice. One that'll scare the shit out of Maggie O'Connor."

"And that is?"

"Jenna."

Sayles's eyes engaged Eric's across the table. "She's surplus baggage now, Eric. And she's a royal pain in the ass for somebody so expendable. I want to use her to appease the Powers . . . and for my own fun and games. Then I want to make sure her mother knows exactly what happened to her fuck-up of a daughter, and will happen to her, too, if she sticks her nose where it doesn't belong."

Eric felt the blood rise to his temples; his fury at Nicky's insolence was only a flicker, compared to his fury at himself for having been outplayed. Sayles had always lusted after Jenna, from the first time he'd ever seen her naked. And Ghania! Obviously the witch had helped devise this trap. "Let me dispose of her in a way that will live in the mother's nightmares forever," she'd said in the garden. The seething anger beneath the surface of Eric's calm would not have been visible to anyone who didn't know him intimately. Nicky saw it clearly and smiled inwardly.

"When do you want to perform this ritual?" Eric asked tightly, unable to think of any reason to refute the validity of the request. Women were for the use of all the Adepti—it was only acknowledgment of his leadership, and the child's unique potential, that had kept Jenna sacrosanct.

"Tomorrow night will do just fine," Nicky replied offhandedly. "That'll give you time to say your goodbyes to your wife." He spoke the word with contempt.

Eric looked his companion in the eye, with as bland an expression as he could muster. "There are none to say. The girl means nothing to me."

"Then, be my guest," Nicky said casually. "Sacrifice her yourself."

"I'll take it under advisement, Nicky," Eric replied evenly. "I am already in psychic preparation for the Great Festival—but I will consider your suggestion."

Eric sat fuming at the table after Sayles had retrieved his coat and gone. He felt little for Jenna other than lust, but he had a proprietary instinct that balked at sharing her. It gave Nicky the aura of too much power before the thirteen Adepti—he would have to be certain to present this as if he'd chosen to sacrifice her for the common good.

# PART VI

# THE CRUCIBLE

I call saintliness not a state, but the moral procedure leading up to it.

**Jean Genet,**
*quoted by Sartre*

# CHAPTER 71

The fire in the hearth had dwindled, and neither occupant of Maggie's library had taken the time to fuss with it for the last half hour.

Maggie was seated behind her desk, weariness explicit in the sag of her shoulders, and the hair falling randomly from the clip that was supposed to be holding it back. She and Peter had been doing this work for endless hours. Or days . . . weeks . . . *years!* it seemed, she couldn't even remember how long it had been. Peter pacing and firing questions. She spewing out answers. Sometimes tangling up the esoteric details she'd learned from Ellie, with Peter's theology. Sometimes lost in the question of whether there was even a point to any of this monumental effort. And, Peter was acting so strange since he got back from Rhinebeck. Intense and remote.

With rising irritation, she watched him pacing back and forth in front of the fire, long legs striding to some rhythmic downbeat she could no longer hear through the thumping in her own head.

Peter fired a question at her and her mind was suddenly completely blank. Or rather it was so full of answers none could surface. Circuitry overload. Chronic

443

fatigue. Too much pressure . . . too much information . . . too little sleep . . . too dire consequence of failure.

"I don't *know!*" she snapped at him, pushing the papers she'd been fingering away from her, and rising from the desk in agitation.

"You *do* know!" She could hear the gritted teeth of his response. He, too, was under terrible pressure of a different kind . . . *the Church, choices, Maggie.* Peter repeated the question.

"I'm telling you, Peter, I *don't* know." Her voice had risen to a dangerous pitch. "I cannot remember a fucking thing! Don't you understand, I can't do this! It's just too much—too incredibly hopeless. There's so little time left, and I still don't know how to save Cody—and all you can do is stand there screaming useless questions at me that I don't have answers to!"

She saw the stricken response in his eyes, and suddenly, she wasn't crazy anymore . . . just frustrated and afraid.

"Oh, Peter," she breathed, horrified at how close to the edge she was, "I'm going to fail . . . and I *can't* fail . . . She's all alone with those monsters, and I don't know how to save her, and soon it will be *too late.*" Maggie's anger distilled into despair; she dropped her head to her chest, the momentary fury spent, and he could see her begin to sob, silently. It was the loneliest crying Peter had ever witnessed; as if there were so little help left in the world, even sound had become superfluous.

She looked up at him, beseeching him to understand her terrible hurt, and every cell of his wanted to do something to *help her* . . . Peter stood transfixed, sensing her terror empathically, gripped in the enormity of her pain. She was drowning in an ocean of the unknown, and he was the only spar. If he could just keep her afloat a little while longer . . .

Almost without conscious consent, Peter crossed the floor to Maggie's side, and took her into his arms.

Wasn't it only human to comfort one who was suffering so gravely? Wasn't it only . . .

"No, Peter!" she said, shocked by his unexpected response, guilty at having provoked it.

But she could feel the hard strength of him against her; feel the broken boundaries in his urgency. She knew she must not respond, yet some part of her *wanted* to . . . some part that seemed not to be Maggie.

"Please, Peter. Don't do this!" she gasped, struggling to pull away from his embrace. But how could she spurn this offering of self? she thought wildly: she loved him too much to reject him . . . And Peter was over the line now, where he had feared and longed to be. Out where nothing mattered but the need. The barriers so carefully erected . . . the taboos of the Church . . . the programming of a lifetime . . . the war for his soul's integrity. What did any of it mean in the face of such human need?

*I wished to be part of God*, he thought madly—*sought Him in His very sanctuary, made myself one with His Godhead . . . yet I am not God! I am only a man.*

He felt Maggie's ambivalence, clearly, but he also felt her trust and the love that flowed between them, like a stream of ions—negative drawn to positive—with an eternal inevitability that demanded fulfillment.

*How could this beauty be profane? How could such passionate communion be anything but sacrament?*

Maggie felt herself drawn in against her will. *I'm not in love with you, Peter*, she wanted to cry out, but if that was so, how did he know the things he knew of her? How to touch and how to kiss? How to understand the mutual craving that was older than everything but God? She felt disoriented, out of control.

He lifted her and she knew she shouldn't go with him . . . shouldn't let him awaken things in her that didn't belong to him. *Or did they?* Had they always . . . Something was driving her, too, distorting her boundaries . . .

Peter held her in his arms, lost in the newness of her. Did she have bones as well as flesh? She was soft and strong, fragile and mysterious. Her skin was a silken wonder he had never felt before. How had he found her naked breasts so soon? Where had her clothes gone . . . and his own?

Oh Maggie, *my Maggie* . . . how could I have not known? *You were the phantom in the sleepless nights . . . the silver mane of the Unicorn glimpsed for a heartbeat through the forest . . . you were the dream.*

Confusion wracked him, along with the certainties. I am a *man.* God forgive me. This is what I am!

"Peter, *please!* This isn't right," she breathed the words, afraid to the heart of hurting him. Not knowing any longer which would hurt him more—to surrender to his love, or to deny it. Because she wasn't separate from him any longer; maybe she had never been. Maybe she had never been whole without him, her former wholeness only an illusion. There were no certainties for Maggie, now—the demands of the past were growing stronger within her, the urgent cry of body needing body. Or was it soul needing soul? Was this moment of ecstacy owed to them, by a destiny not of their choosing? *Karaden and Mim,* fulfilled at last, after eons of waiting? The gift of a Goddess to those she had made to suffer?

Maggie's eyes were filled with tears, for there was no turning back now; she was caught in a cosmic tide, too far beyond the shore. She ceased to struggle, for he was no longer Peter and she was no longer Maggie, and all the need of an eternity of loving was suddenly within her. So, she reached for him . . .

Peter, too, felt his mind slipping away, fading into brilliance, like a star in nova . . . There were unaccustomed arms and legs wrapped around his own . . . there was hardened flesh that knew its cosmic destination, and unutterable warmth that longed to yield to its intrusion. In a moment she would be completely his, lost in forbidden love . . . forbidden . . . *forbidden* . . . Why, O sweet gentle Christ, why must this beauty be forbidden me?

*Because it must.*

Because this intensity would take precedence over everything. Because once tasted, the fruit of the apple brings not replenishment, but damnation.

With a groan of anguish as true as if his heart had been torn living from his body, Peter wrenched himself away from Maggie. Forcing his flesh away from hers, and his eyes, and his heart . . . panting, half mad with desire and unfulfilled dreams, he tore his body from her entangling one, and crouched like a great wounded lion, on the floor beside her.

Shocked beyond movement, Maggie lay absolutely still, almost fearing to breathe. She was mortally afraid. She watched Peter struggle to regain control of himself . . . of the moment . . . of a life coming undone. *Who am I? What have I done?*

There was no sound around them but the small hiss and crackle of the last log.

"I love you, Maggie," Peter whispered . . . his tortured voice, unfamiliar. "Please, *please* know that I love you . . ." She heard the defeat of it in his words. A lifetime vanquished in a moment.

"Forgive me for leading you to this, Maggie," he whispered. "It's my need, not yours, that's led us here."

She started to protest, but the look on his face stopped her.

"If we do this," he rushed on, urgently, needing to explain. "If I forswear my vows . . . it's the one sin that will put me in their reach, and I will not be able to protect you." He turned to look at her, naked and vulnerable in the last flickers of firelight . . . there was such sorrow in his gaze that she longed to touch him, to comfort him, but dared not.

"At this moment, my dearest Maggie," Peter said, in a voice that left no room for doubt, "for this one act . . . I think I would trade my own salvation." He stopped, for the barest heartbeat. "But I cannot trade yours."

She closed her eyes in terrible understanding. Tears broke free, and ran unnoticed down her face to the rug beneath her. *What have I done?* Her heart kept beating out the rhythm of the words. *What have I done?*

Maggie heard him gather his things, and let himself out the front door. "I love you, too, Peter," she whispered quietly, into the deafening silence. But she knew as she said it, that theirs was an old, old love . . . and not for now.

Peter stood on the top step outside Maggie's door and fought the violent desperation of his own heart.

What madness it had been on his part to have thought he knew life. Not until this hour had he ever been alive. What arrogance, to think he had known God, and could counsel others in that knowledge. How could anyone know God, without having known the love of another human being?

*You are as subtle and wily as Satan is, God!* he thought blasphemously. Leading your priests on . . . letting them believe in their superiority to meager humanity, when the reverse is true. No wonder you keep us from eating of this fruit of the Tree of Knowledge . . . who among us would have the strength to bear it and go on? What presumptuous pride to think that in our ignorance, we are the chosen ones.

He pulled the cold air forcefully into rebellious lungs and started down the limestone steps. Is this how Lucifer fell? he wondered heartbrokenly. Trying to be God-like and failing utterly. Did he, too, learn humility?

*"I will never regret you, Maggie,"* he said defiantly, and aloud, as he reached the corner of the deserted street. But before the words had faded, he already knew the sister truth. *I will regret—every moment of my life— what might have been.*

Maggie lay in a fetal position in her own bed, scarcely capable of breathing; how she had managed to get there she wasn't certain. She felt disoriented, confused and utterly alone.

*Love never dies*, a terrible internal voice cried out within her. Love never, never dies, and you, the mourner, are left with its forever agony. Prometheus on the rock . . . picked apart by carrion birds, and then restored to suffer the next day. *Alone*. *Alone*. Alone . . . Not even five thousand years are enough to expiate this pain.

Maggie drifted into the oblivion of sleep . . . and "awakened" in a dream:

The man was tall and fair; he moved easily in his lanky frame, like one who feels at peace with the world. The woman at his side was dark-haired and slender; she laughed as they walked, looking up into the man's face, love in her gaze.

Their hands were clasped, in the easy grace of those who know their love need not be hidden. Gold wedding bands were on the hands of each, and their joyous camaraderie was impossible to mistake.

They lay down on the soft, summer carpet of grass and wild flowers, smiling in the comforting radiance of the sun; the air was fragrant, and the sweet song of passing birds blessed the tranquility of the undisturbed meadow.

Their laughter quieted, and the man turned to trace a pattern with his fingers on the woman's lips. She smiled at the tingle the touch provoked, and moved nearer, closing her eyes to better sense the loving touch. His hand caressed her throat and shoulders, then slipped beneath the soft, sheer fabric of her dress. She moaned a little and drew the impeding fabric up over her head, tossing it carelessly behind her, reveling in the warmth of the sun on nakedness.

The man undressed with the controlled urgency of one who knows his lover's rhythm, better than his own; the woman lay lost in the dizzying beauty of sensual expectation. Maggie, the dreamer, felt one with the dream-woman, every cell alive, every nerve ending shared with her, in some cosmic symbiosis.

She *felt* the shadow of the man fall across the woman's face, cooling it. "You are so beautiful," he whispered, and the words seemed all the more important, because he was everything she had ever loved.

She lay wordlessly, on her belly, on the warm grass, weak with wanting, and her face turned so she could watch him as he reached for her, running his hand tenderly over her body, playing with her long loose hair, trailing strong fingers light as fireflies over shoulders, back, thighs, secret places. He spread her legs with consummate tenderness, and entered her suddenly, surprisingly, without another gesture.

She gasped at the quick intrusion, but the welcomed strength filled her utterly, and she felt exhilarated by the suddenness. He didn't move at all as she had expected him to, and sensing her surprise, he leaned his mouth close to her ear and whispered, "Lie very still . . ."

Maggie felt joy flood her own being, sharing the rapture of the woman in the grass. *To be loved.* To let go utterly. To surrender self. She felt she had been melted into a languorous puddle by her own mind, as much as by her body. How did he know so exactly how she wanted him? Needed him. Longed for him.

The man began to move with infinite care. He teased her hair and ears and neck, and moved within her carefully, knowingly. He was benevolently in control, and the knowledge that this was so was precisely what each one needed.

He moved his arms around and under her, moving his hands in rhythm to the movements of his manhood deep within. It was different from before; she felt crazily out of control, possessed, understood, found out. She never wanted this incredible feeling to cease, never this motion to end, never this fullness to subside.

She arched her back to meet the angle of his thrusts and he whispered, "Don't," softly, in her ear. "Let me do it all," And she was gone again, down the rabbit hole, into the cosmos, over the rainbow, deep within her own womanness.

"Not yet," she gasped, trying to stay the completion of such bliss, but the relentless motion increased, and she couldn't stop the tidal pulsations, cataclysms, reverberations, blissful circles of fulfillment until it was over.

But it wasn't . . . and she could feel him more forcefully than ever, pushing, touching, probing. "This time we'll do it together," he whispered and she knew there wasn't anything to do but what he'd said.

*Where were they in time?* Even in the dream, Maggie knew the two lovers were she and Peter, together as they were meant to be. Somewhere. *Somewhere in time.* Transcendent coupling of heart and soul. All words spoken, all needs fulfilled, all questions answered, all the emptiness of a thousand lifetimes filled to overflowing . . .

Maggie woke up.

She had dreaded having to face the morning, but now she was awake, replenished and redeemed. She lay back in bed, not wanting to let go of the beauty that had been. She replayed the dream in her mind, over and over and over again. And as she did so, the sure knowledge of its meaning filled her soul. This is all there would ever be for them . . . this was their bittersweet good-bye.

Peter Messenguer lay in his borrowed bed, replete and astonished. For he had dreamed the identical dream.

# CHAPTER 72

"I don't think it was a dream, Mags," Ellie said with authority. "You two were either on the Astral, where your bodies were freed from the constraints laid on them by this particular incarnation . . . or you were time traveling, to another reality, where the two of you were free to love each other. I think it was a gift you were given because you chose rightly.''

Maggie shook her head, uncertain if she had profaned the dream by recounting it to her friend. "It didn't feel like such a right decision at the time, Ellie. When Peter left me last night, it felt unbearably sad."

Ellie smiled a little at her friend; Maggie looked as if she'd been beaten. In a way, she had. " 'Thou art a priest forever, according to the Order of Melchizedek,' " she quoted unexpectedly. "That's how the words are spoken in ordination, Mags. There's no turning back from that—even the ones who've leaped over the wall know it in their hearts. That's why the Black Magicians are always on the prowl for priests who have forsworn their vows . . . they consider it their greatest victory. In fact, they can't really perform a Black Mass properly without one. To do the greatest conjuring, the Magician must be a defrocked priest, because he has already been consecrated to the unseen Universe. Maa Kheru must have one on tap for the shindig they're planning, or it'll never work.

"Maggie, my dear friend, you must know Peter made the only possible choice last night—and by God, you've got to give the man credit. After a lifetime of celibacy, to turn back at the crucial moment took some balls, you should forgive my saying. That's got to count for something with the Powers That Be."

"I don't know, Ellie. I'm so desperately disturbed by all that's happened. I realize now that I'm not *in love* with Peter, not in this lifetime anyway. Yet, I do *love* him . . . And despite what happened last night, I truly believe it's his destiny to be a priest. He was a priest then, and a priest *now*—I think that's his soul's purpose, somehow. But I'm afraid our relationship has confounded him, *harmed him*, and I don't know how to fix it."

Maggie looked so woebegone, Ellie tried another tack. "Look, Mags, you're loved by a spectacular human being—one who's risking everything he holds sacred in this world to save you. That's a helluva lot more than most people get in a given lifetime. I think it's a *good* thing you two touched each other in so intimate a way . . . a good thing you *saw* in him what you did. Last night resolved things for you . . . brought them to a genuine and loving conclusion. Hasn't it occurred to you that Peter's the past, Mags? And you must *release* the past, in order to let the future happen."

Maggie stared at Ellie, sudden knowledge seeping in.

Ellie took a critical look at her and sighed. "I'm not saying you've got an easy row to hoe here, my bedraggled friend. I'm just saying you're getting help with it. And who the hell said life was supposed to be easy anyway? Why don't you let it rest for today. I think you've had it with the books for the moment, too—you need a physical outlet, and no more brain fatigue. So, why don't you go see Mr. Wong and kick something around for a while, to get yourself back to center. You look like something that's been rained on."

Maggie sighed audibly and got up to go, but Ellie held her back. "I've decided to come with you for the battle, Mags," she said, entirely serious for a change. "It seems this is my fight, too, so you can count me in. I may be a little ditzy on the earth plane, but over there, on the Astral, I really have it together. So, why don't you go kick a bag or punch a post, or whatever it is you do with that cute little Chinaman, and then you and I will plan our strategy. Those fuckers don't hold all the aces, or it wouldn't be a fair fight . . . and the Universe loves a fair fight, Mags, especially when it looks absolutely hopeless. Just remember it was David who went home to supper, not Goliath."

Consoled by the love she felt from her friend, Maggie did as she'd been told, and went to Mr. Wong to find her center.

CODY sat hunched up at the head of her bed; tears were running down her cheeks, and her bottom lip was bitten till it bled. She was thinner now than she had been; every time she refused to drink the cocktail, Ghania made her go to bed without any food. But that wasn't the worst part anymore.

Ghania said that if she didn't drink it this time, she would leave her alone with the snake.

*Oh Mim! Why didn't you ever come back for me?* The little girl cried out, inside, angrily. *Why didn't you save me?* She held the tattered bear tightly in her arms. Sometimes she was very mad at Mim because she didn't care anymore. Sometimes she almost hated her. But then . . .

There wasn't anything to hold on to except the Mim-treasures.

One by one, Cody took them out, now, from the bear's torn place. The gold button, the string, the seashell, the picture from the storybook where the lady looked like Mim, the dead flower that smelled like Mim's perfume . . .

Maybe the snake would eat her tonight. She would be all alone inside him screaming to get out . . . she could almost touch the cramped, wet darkness that tormented her dreams. The child snuffled back her fear; she would take all her treasures with her. Cody held the gold button up to her cheek, and reached for the seashell.

Something made her look up—Ghania was watching her from the doorway.

And, she was smiling.

"Have you been keeping secrets from me?" the witch asked as she drew near the bed. Instinctively, Cody scrunched herself backward into the corner. She tried to hide the treasures beneath her, but Ghania was on her, swift as a cobra, tearing the precious tokens from her small hands. Cody's fingers closed on the button in desperation, but Ghania pried the little fingers back, one by one, until the child screamed in pain, and the button dropped into Ghania's waiting palm.

"No!" Cody shrieked, grabbing for it again. "No. *No! Give it to me.* It's mine!" Heedless of the consequences, she launched herself at Ghania, flailing, scratching, pounding; all the terror of her life, all the fear, all the hatred for her tormentor bubbled up and overflowed. Ghania held her like a struggling wildcat cub, at arm's length.

"It is *not* yours," she hissed, as she held the helpless child. "It is mine, now! As you are mine."

The Amah tossed her onto the bed like a bag of rumpled laundry. Then she crushed the fragile seashell under her heel, and tore the picture into shreds. She ripped off the head of the Teddy Bear with one violent wrench. The precious button, she dropped into the pouch she wore about her neck, and Cody knew she would never, ever see it again.

Cody sat on her bed, her face a marble mask, after Ghania had left the room. She didn't even cry.

There was nothing left now.

Nothing to love.

Nothing to hope for.

No secret place to hide from Ghania.

*And, Mim was never coming back.*

# CHAPTER 73

Raphael Abraham blinked back the uncomfortable memories from the past that had assailed him on his long walk home, and let himself into the house he currently occupied. He had been thinking about his Uncle Schlomo, ever since deciding to bone up on the Kabbalah. There had to be a great fund of knowledge stored within him, from his Orthodox childhood, but it had been long buried by choice. Now he must root it out, and add to its store, to fulfill this newest obligation to his profession—a profession he had chosen, in part, because it was so far afield from the religious nonsense of his boyhood. He almost smiled at the irony.

Without conscious thought, Abraham checked the security measures he'd put in place before leaving that morning. Satisfied that all was as he'd left it, he flipped on the light, shrugged off his jacket and locked the door behind him.

The pile of requested books, delivered the previous evening, sat neatly on the coffee table, along with a spiral-bound pad, two pens, and two colored highlighters. He glanced at them and sighed. There were so many irritating memories to be sorted here, along with the research data, and that was not a desirable state of affairs. Memories carried emotional baggage, and emotions could have deadly consequences in his line of work, so he allowed them scant entry into his world.

Abraham loosened his tie, rolled up his sleeves and made a cup of strong Turkish coffee. He had never developed a taste for the weak, watery kind preferred by Americans, and at home, he allowed himself this small indulgence. So much of his life had been lived apart from his family, he had become as proficient as any woman, with household chores. He was a decent cook, in fact, although he had no great desire for food this evening; and because of his personal orderliness of mind and body, there was never a hint of disarray in any dwelling he occupied.

Abraham started for the living room, but as he passed the refrigerator he paused . . . better to make a sandwich now and take it along, than to stop later on. He would need nourishment sometime between now and sunrise, if he was to complete all the reading he had in mind. To learn about Kabbalah before morning would be like trying to teach himself ancient Greek on a coffee break, but there were few choices.

*Kabbalah.* From the Hebrew root "KBL (Kibel)," *"to receive it"* . . . he remembered Uncle Schlomo saying reverently that all secret doctrine was received orally, and none was more secret than Kabbalah. Therefore, whatever could be found in books would be incomplete, an alphabet with half the letters missing; but perhaps it would be enough to jog his childhood memories, to fill in the blank spaces.

He knew that to outsiders, Kabbalah was always politely described as a philosophical and theosophical system originally created to answer man's questions about God and the Universe. They were told, too, that it was based on the numerical correspondences between human life and universal law. But that was as valid a definition as saying that nuclear fission lit light bulbs—it was true, as far as it went, but it didn't go very far.

Abraham set a place for himself at the table, poured the first cup of coffee of the night, and sat down to learn what it was that Uncle Schlomo knew that he did not.

He picked up the first volume, not at all certain what he was looking for. The Rebbe had said to read Scholem, so that was where he would start:

> "Kabbalah" is the traditional and most commonly used term for the esoteric teachings of Judaism and for Jewish mysticism, especially the forms which it assumed in the Middle Ages from the 12th century onward.
>
> There is no doubt that some kabbalistic circles (including those in Jerusalem up to modern times) preserved both elements (mystical and occult) in their secret doctrine, which would be acquired by means of revelation or by way of initiation rites.

Mystical and occult . . . these were the words that had repelled him as a boy. Even now, they made him bristle as he read on.

If his memory was correct, the Kabbalah spoke of a complex letter code based on the Hebrew alphabet, whose twenty-two *sounds* were supposed to be the foundation of all things. God somehow used these sounds to create, and those who were privy to His secret, could use the sounds to make things happen.

"Allegories and metaphors, Rafi!" Uncle Schlomo's words drifted back. "We must search for the hidden meanings in the Torah, based on the code. *Berashith Bera Elohim, Ath Ha Shamaim Va Ath Ha-Aretz.* 'In the beginning, God created the heavens and the earth.' Look to the letter code, Rafi, to understand what this *really* means. Interpret! Reach beyond yourself . . .' "

So the Torah said one thing but really meant another. *Sacred horseshit!* Complex gibberish, just as he remembered. No more no less. Poor Schlomo. A lifetime spent in the interpretation of sacred horseshit.

A chapter entitled "The Secret Names of God" caught his eye. They were important . . . he could remember his uncle's reverence whenever he spoke of this particular mystery. "The Names of God," he'd said, "contain the *power* of God, for their vibration is His Divine vibration." Many names were known by all— Jehovah, Elohim, Gebor, Jehovah Tzabaoth, Adonai ha-Aretz, but others were known only to the elect. These were the Secret Names that could work magic, potent enough to bring the Universe to annihilation. Few men in history had ever been privileged to know them. Who learns such a secret, Abraham wondered, and by what means? He thumbed the pages in search of what he needed to remember:

According to Eleazar of Worms, a famous Kabbalist of the 13th century, the Name is transmitted only to those specially chosen who are not prone to anger, who are humble and God-

fearing, and who carry out the commandments
of their Creator.

That should narrow the list, he thought with a wry smile.

The Name itself is invested with the power
to fulfill the desires of he who utters it. This
knowledge can only be imparted orally, from
Master to pupil, and there are very few Kabbalists in the world today who have attained the
knowledge of the Name.

Names. *Names*. There was something else about
names in one of these other books on Egyptian magic
. . . lower-right-hand corner of the page . . . Abraham
had the capacity to remember what he'd seen and where
he'd seen it, no matter how many sources he'd consulted. It was a useful gift in his profession. Ah! There
it was:

The Egyptians insisted the *names* of the
Gods—certainly Ra and Isis—were even more
powerful than the Gods themselves.

Interesting. The Kabbalists were not the only magicians to give credence to the idea that the names of
deities had power.
*Demons*, he thought, suddenly. Sekhmet was some
sort of demonic deity, and the satanic cult was embroiled
with demons, too. Better find out what the Kabbalah
has to say about them.
He frowned, as he scanned the indexes of the books;
there were pages and pages of information on demons
in each of the texts. And there was a similar abundance
of data on reincarnation, or the transmigration of souls,
both notions so at odds with rationality, it seemed inconceivable that so much space was wasted on them by
scholars. Abraham shook his head again, and looked up
some definitions.

*Transmigration.* In the Bahir it is stated that transmigration may continue for 1,000 generations . . . the righteous transmigrate endlessly for the benefit of the universe. . . .

*Ibbur.* The entry of another soul into a man, not during pregnancy nor at birth but during his life. In general, such an additional soul dwells in a man only for a limited time, for the purpose of performing certain acts or commandments.

*Dibbuk* (Dybbuk). An evil spirit or a doomed soul which enters into a living person, cleaves to his soul, causes mental illness, talks through his mouth, and represents a separate and alien personality.

Abraham rose, stretched his muscles, rotated his neck to counteract the stiffness caused by the hours of reading. He made himself another cup of coffee, picked the last book off the table and headed toward his favorite chair.

He opened to the chapter on Magical Ritual and was surprised to see that it started with a prayer. His uncle's words were again in his head.

"It would be best not to ask God for special favors, Rafi," the old man had once told him, then added with a twinkle, "but if you cannot resist doing so, this is what you may say: 'I would be immensely happy and grateful if you would illuminate me and show me how I may acquire this which I desire, in accordance with thy Holy Law.' Of course, first you must surrender your will to His, Rafi . . . and this, I am afraid, dear boy, is not something that comes to you naturally."

Despite himself, Abraham smiled at the memory. Then, as he looked back to the page, his eye fell on a quote from Abulafia on the practice of magic:

As a result of the activity of your concentration on the letters, your mind will become bound to them. The hairs on your head will stand on end and tremble . . . the blood within you will begin to vibrate because of the living permutations that loosen it . . . you will experience ecstacy and trembling, ecstacy for the soul and trembling for the body.

The preposterous idea annoyed him out of his mellowing mood. Poor old Schlomo, wasting his whole life, waiting for an apocryphal ecstacy that was only a bad joke. He put the book down . . . there was nothing useful in all this nonsense. Secret names of God, secret letter codes, magic formulas, magic children. *Garbage*. Pure and simple. There was no place for such garbage in his world of harsh realities. He was a man of action, not a man of the spirit.

Abraham washed the few dishes he had used, turned out the lights and went to bed.

# CHAPTER 74

"You wanted to see me, Nicky?" Jenna asked, in the same seductive purr she generally used with him. She'd always known that he wanted her, and it pleased her to imagine this arrogant son of a bitch lusting after what he couldn't attain. She liked the fact that as Eric's wife, she was the only woman in the coven who was unavailable to the others.

Nicky closed the door with a deliberate shove, and stood watching her. Jenna was wearing an apple green satin gown that left little to the imagination; beneath his insistent gaze, she felt suddenly naked and vulnerable.

"You enjoy teasing me, don't you, Jenna?" he said, in a husky voice that made her stop brushing her hair to pay closer attention. She turned from the dressing table mirror to face him, curiously.

"I don't know what you mean by that, Nicky," she replied uncertainly. "I never meant you any harm. Look . . . there are a lot of people coming tonight for some new ritual Eric's cooked up, and I've still got to finish dressing, so maybe you'd better go until he gets home."

Nicky took a step closer to the seated woman, and as he did, he slipped off his suit jacket, and dropped it soundlessly onto a boudoir chair, behind him. Jenna watched his movements as fascinated as a cobra with a mongoose. He began to loosen his tie and belt; there was something singularly threatening in the gestures. Self-protective instincts rose in her. She'd lived on the streets; she knew trouble when it was coming her way. Jenna smiled as disarmingly as her rising fear would allow, and turned away from Nicky, with what she hoped was nonchalance. If she could just make it to the dressing room behind her, the door there had a dead bolt . . .

"I was just about to get high, Nicky," she said off-handedly, as she stood up and began to move toward the door. "Want to join me? I keep a stash in my dressing room . . ."

Sayles's long legs crossed the room in two strides; the strength of his fingers on her wrist was stupefying. Jenna heard her bones crunch against each other with a sickening internal sound.

"Yes, I want to join you," he said, low and mean. "I think you've known that for a very long time—and you've had a great deal of fun at my expense thinking about it, haven't you?"

Jenna's sharp cry only made him squeeze her arm harder. "Please!" she gasped, as he twisted it upward behind her back, the pain forcing her to her knees. "You're hurting me. Are you crazy, Nicky. Eric will kill you!"

"Eric couldn't care less about you, bitch," he said,

holding her struggling helplessly, with one hand, while he used his other to tear the robe from her body.

"Ghania tells me you like to be naked," he breathed heavily, as he touched her flesh. His face flushed red with desire, and Jenna began to scream—piercing, ear-splitting sounds that should have brought the servants running. Nicky's laughter was the only response to her urgent cries.

She would have to save herself. The thought zinged through her, bringing everything into sharp focus. Nicky relaxed his grip enough to strip off his own clothes, and Jenna lurched away from him, scrambling to her feet, looking right and left for escape, like a fox in a snare. Why was nobody coming? The servants must have heard her! She threw herself at the dressing room door, but Nicky dragged her back, scraping her flesh hurtfully across the floor. She felt a splinter pierce her skin.

With the strength of genuine terror, Jenna wrenched her arm free of his grip once again, scratching at his eyes with her Mandarin nails. She aimed a kick at his jockey shorts, but Nicky parried it easily, and knocked her off her feet with a fierce blow to her head that dazed her. Then he was on top of her, and she was struggling against the risen flesh that pinned her, and the overwhelming male strength of his malevolent intent. And she was screaming again, loud enough to wake the dead.

Jenna felt Nicky force his way into her body, painfully, relentlessly, just as the bedroom door sprang open. *Thank God!* Someone had come to help her!

"Ghania!" she shrieked, outraged. "Help me! Get Eric. *Help me!*" Jenna's words were punctuated by the thrusting male force that was tearing her apart . . .

Other people were moving into the doorway, now, behind Ghania. Dinner guests, in evening gowns and tuxedos, were filing into the room past the witch, laughing and chatting, and pointing to the couple writhing on the floor. *Eric always has the best entertainment at his dinner parties*, was written on their leering faces. Jenna turned her head away and began to sob silently, hope-lessly, as Nicky rutted and fondled and spent himself, all the brutality of his nature finding freedom in the act.

A very long time later, the guests filed out again, and Nicky rose from on top of his victim, and stumbled away to the bathroom. Jenna lay hurt and bleeding, on the Aubusson carpet, too miserable and humiliated to move. Ghania surveyed the ruin with a practiced eye; there wasn't a lot of blood, but it was hard to get out of a good rug. She clucked her tongue in annoyance, and moved toward the sobbing girl, oblivious to her suffering.

"Why? Ghania, *why?*" Jenna rasped, as she felt the strong black hands begin to raise her from the floor.

"Because he wanted you," the woman responded simply. "Because you are unimportant, and are now more use to us dead."

Jenna's head jerked up. "Dead! What do you mean dead?" The unexpected threat made her pull way from her new captor, but she was no more match for Ghania's gargantuan strength, than she'd been for Nicky's.

"You will be the sacrifice at tonight's Mass," the Amah pronounced, as if discussing the inevitability of rain. "I will prepare you."

The full impact of betrayal rocked Jenna. "But I'm Eric's wife . . ." she blurted. "This is insane. He'd never allow such a thing."

"Fool!" Ghania spat contemptuously. "You were no more than a gift with purchase to Eric. It was the *child* we wanted. Only the child . . . whom you so willingly provided us. Even a hyena would be a better mother than you."

Jenna felt bile rise in her throat, reality seeping in as nauseatingly as the drug sickness. "He wanted Cody? That's why he married me?"

"He only married you, so he could adopt the child," Ghania gloated. "Had you been equipped with a less-lovely body, you would have been discarded long ago, you may be sure. And do not tell me you did not know the child would be sacrificed, for I know better." The Amah's eyes glinted with evil mischief.

"Sacrificed? What are you *talking* about?" Jenna's voice was shrill with fear. "No! I swear I didn't know that. Eric said she was special, but he never said anything about sacrifice . . ."

"Hypocrite! Do not play the innocent with me. You sold yourself and your daughter—there is no greater sin! You didn't even care enough to ask what would become of her. But I will tell you in detail, so you can carry the full magnitude of your guilt with you to your eternal torment.

"Do you know how carefully we stalked you, once the Prince knew that you had borne the Star-Child? Nurturing your need for drugs, luring you by your own weakness, into our snare. Do you know how easy it is to control an addict? How every fix opens your soul a little wider to the lower Astral where our minions wait impatiently? How every new drug you sample gives access to the demons, who have swarmed the fringes of humanity for eons, awaiting access. You and your generation of the damned have invited the Prince of Darkness within the Citadel . . . you have opened the floodgates to his Legions!" Ghania's voice had risen triumphantly. "And you are too stupid and selfish even to realize what you have done."

She shook her great head in disgust.

"I must say you gave us quite a turn when we found you'd left the baby with your mother. Of course, that wasn't by chance either—the other side, too, has its power to guide events . . .

"Oh, we did debate what to do about your little adventure into self-determination. But in the end, we knew there was no need to have possession of the child until a few weeks before the Ceremonial date. Long enough to Awaken her Powers, without having to cope with the results of them, too long."

"Powers? What *Powers?* What are you talking

about?'' Jenna demanded through the haze of memories Ghania's soliloquy was conjuring . . . Eric had never loved her. He had merely used her. They had *all* used her. Even the drugs had been a means to control her.

"You little fool," Ghania said disdainfully. "You bore mankind's only hope, and didn't even recognize her worth. Oh, you will suffer for your sins, you may be sure. Although, the Prince may choose to mitigate your agony somewhat because you made our job so easy. Your daughter is the Isis Messenger! The child who holds the key to Materializing the great Amulets of Good and Evil that have been stored on the Inner Planes these five thousand years! We have sought them down the corridors of the ages, and now, in one week's time, Cody will provide Maa Kheru with the means to control every horror on this planet. And all because you were too self-indulgent to question why a man like Eric Vannier would ever choose to be with a nothing like you."

"What will happen to Cody?" Jenna whispered in a daze. *Isis Messenger? Amulets of Good and Evil? What* lunacy was the old witch talking about?

"Her soul will be imprisoned by demons for all eternity . . . her body will become the immortal temple for the Goddess Sekhmet's flame."

Jenna barely struggled against the men who awaited Ghania's orders; she felt nausea, so rank and overwhelming, she could barely breath. Cody's soul would be damned because of her . . . her own life would be sacrificed! Remorse rushed through her like a flash flood, sweeping everything in its wake. Why had she not thought of this? Why had she not left the child with her mother? The drugs were quickly wearing off; reality was struggling to surface, puddling up in corrosive pools within her mind and body. She was almost tempted to pray to God for help, but she had been rebaptized to a different deity, and she knew in her heart that all was well and truly lost.

Ghania watched the dispirited girl led away to her

doom. She didn't pity her, but the waste of the body rankled.

The effects of her last high had dissipated hours ago. Jenna was dope-sick now. Her head pounded, she was vomiting, her flesh felt as if insects crawled inside it. An iron band of terror constricted her breathing—but that was a response to terrible reality, not drug-induced.

At first, she'd been too dazed by Nicky's attack and the devastation of Eric's betrayal, to even fight back. Her whole body hurt from being raped; she felt bruised and wounded, everywhere—it was not just her aching sexual parts that felt violated.

Eric had *never* loved her, *never* needed her, never wanted to share his world with her. He had used her— her body, her mind, even her child. *Oh Christ!* That bastard had made her sell out her kid! Jenna didn't know if dope deprivation, or that horrific knowledge, was the main cause of her nausea.

It had all been such a lark, when it began . . . an exciting, rich, and powerful man had wanted her. To the exclusion of all the others, he had chosen her to be his consort. When he'd finally shared with her the secret of his success—the whole Maa Kheru world of magic— some part of her had thrilled to the ceremony, the licentiousness, and the raw unbridled power of being so far beyond the law. She had loved dressing up and playing priestess . . . she hadn't wanted to kill anyone, of course, but even that conviction had been blunted by the dope. Eric knew more than any pharmacist about how to make everything work out the way he wanted. How to make you high, or bring you down, slow and easy. How to make you feel like queen of the world, smart and omnipotent, and free from the fucking rules that fettered lesser humanity. Eric knew how to make sex rage in you, so nothing else mattered—so you would kill for the chance to rut, or sell your soul to satisfy your desperate flesh. And then there wasn't any conscience anymore, or any need for one either . . . in the world of Maa Kheru *"Do what thou wilt shall be the whole of the Law"* was the only rule.

The thought of Cody floated into sharper focus in Jenna's mind, as the drugs continued to fade. She had loved Cody once . . . really loved her. Even leaving her with Maggie had been an act of love. Just like going on methadone had been, while she was pregnant. *Christ!* She had really meant to stay straight, all the time she was pregnant. She had meant *never* to stick another needle in her arm. How many times had she almost gone home? But then the baby got born, and it needed things. And it cried if it didn't get them. And it was a real pain in the ass to mind. And she needed money to take care of it, and patience to mind it, and the whole thing just looked hopeless again. So she'd dropped off Cody at her mom's. Her mother was a big pain in the ass, too, but she was so reliable . . . *that*, at least, had been the right thing to do. Then she'd gone back to the streets . . . and gotten the job at the club . . . and then Eric had come along, and everything had looked like maybe she'd done it all right, after all . . .

*How could I know it was all a fucking scam? How could I know it wasn't me he wanted?*

Jenna fought ferociously against the ropes that tied her hands and feet; rage and fear gave her renewed strength. But the restraints were hopelessly tight and her wrists were already bloody from the struggle. What the fuck did they intend to do with her tonight? She had seen people sacrificed. She had witnessed the convulsive agony of their dying. She had never thought they could do such brutal things to her!

Ghania was in the doorway, dressed for ritual; an inky black djellabah, embroidered with silver and gold sigils covered her body, a gold lamé turban adorned her head. Symbols of some obscure kind were written in red and yellow pigment on her face and arms.

The Amah motioned four large men to follow her into the room; they, too, were dressed for ceremony.

Jenna saw they weren't servants, but members of Maa Kheru.

"John!" she whispered urgently to the young Wall Street broker who had often made lustful overtures toward her in the past. "Help me! Don't let them hurt me, *John*, please!" She could see a flicker of doubt cloud his eyes, before he averted them.

"Do not be subverted from your task, John Menton!" Ghania thundered. "You, too, will be judged for your performance! You, too, have been bound by oath. Falter in your resolve and forfeit all you have gained."

Menton seized Jenna's arm with renewed vigor. There was a great deal at stake here—more than he cared to risk for a girl who'd never given him the time of day.

The Eric Vannier who entered the satanic chapel was very changed in appearance from the elegant international financier he was by day. Garbed in elaborate Egyptian robes, on which were embroidered cartouches and complex glyphs, he carried himself regally, as if awareness of his mission empowered every cell.

Ghania followed a few steps behind, resplendent in the full regalia of an Obeah priestess. She carried a large Madagascan smoky quartz crystal orb in her hands. It had been passed from High Priestess to High Priestess, since the Kingdom of Mu, and had been programmed with the evil gifts of each who'd owned it.

Eric motioned to the guards who restrained the struggling Jenna, and signaled them to begin the ceremony. Roughly, they dragged her to the center of the room, and up the marble altar steps. Eric frowned at her ragged condition; she looked strung out from drug deprivation, and ravaged by a fear so primal and palpable the chamber fairly hummed with its intensity. Even her usually perfect body was blemished by scratches and bruises from her long ordeal. Jenna cried out piteously to Eric as she passed him, begging him to remember all they'd been to each other, begging him for mercy. He found her cowardice distasteful in the extreme.

The sound of chanting rose around her; Jenna recognized the magical Enochian tongue, through the haze of terror that now possessed her. She fought her captors with every ebbing ounce of strength, but they dragged her inexorably to her final destination.

Other robed figures watched her frenzied struggles with a certain jaded excitement; there was such an intensive frequency to the energy of an unwilling sacrifice. All participants in the ritual were profoundly aware of the change in the room's vibratory rate, as Jenna's terror energized the chamber.

"She will make a superb altar, Number Four," said a cultivated voice, only slightly muffled by the cowled hood that shielded its face from view.

"I was frankly surprised by this summons, Number Seven," a Parisian male responded. "Delighted as I am by the opportunity to enjoy an unexpected sacramental meal before the Great Sabbath, I do hope this precipitously called gathering doesn't suggest that anything untoward has happened."

The larger cloaked figure shrugged. "I think it was inevitable that Eric rid himself of his bride, don't you? One can never entirely trust mothers, where children are concerned. She might have lost her nerve at an inopportune moment."

Another hooded figure joined them. It was apparent from the robe's topography that it housed a woman. "She was never a fitting consort for a High Priest," the newcomer said with authority.

"But, I'd wager she was a fitting bedmate," quipped Number Seven, to everyone's amusement. The woman started to respond, but the piercing sound of Tibetan tsingshas called the room's soft babble of voices to order. The bells were used to alter the chamber's vibrations, and to presage the beginning of ceremony.

Jenna lay stretched across the marble altar slab, now, chained at wrists and ankles; her head overhung the altar to the south, making it hard for her to breathe. Her feet were stretched to the north. She was sobbing in exhausted rasping breaths, her naked body straining convulsively against the inevitable. The full magnitude of her danger had finally stilled her pleas for mercy—she was in the wrong company to find compassion. The sounds of chanting flowed and ebbed in waves around her like an inland sea, as her mind flitted from terror to terror, seeking oblivion.

Jenna's life flashed by her in freeze-frames, stopping perversely at every crossroad where she'd taken a wrong turn. The thought of Cody pierced her heart . . . she would save her baby from this horror, if she could. She wanted to redeem herself, wanted one small righteous act to carry to eternity. *Wanted to rob Eric of his prize*.

The High Priest's knife gleamed eerily above her in the cavernous candlelit chapel. He raised the jewel-encrusted hilt of the ancient athame and made curious sweeping signs in the air above the sacrificial body. Jenna prayed silently he didn't intend the Death of Two Hundred Cuts, the longest and most excruciating possibility. She tried not to imagine what it would be like to be skinned alive.

Eric's arms were raised in the ancient salute to the Powers of Evil—he called upon the Prince of Darkness and the Goddess Sekhmet by their hidden names of power, and he asked them to accept the sacrifice of the vessel that had brought forth the Messenger.

The acolytes ceased swinging the censers of acrid incense, and handed two bowls to Ghania, who murmured over them before passing them to Eric. They were filled with blood and excrement, into which stolen Communion wafers had been dropped in desecration; he used the revolting substance to write arcane characters on Jenna's violently spasmed body.

The robed audience was attentive now. They were chanting softly, and the sounds blended sonorously with Jenna's pathetic sobs.

Eric lifted the sacred dagger above the girl's body once again, and intoned the ancient words to evoke the ferryman of Hades, who would carry the forfeit soul of the sacrifice to the Underworld. He removed a scroll from a tabernacle on the altar—it was the demonic pact which Jenna had signed in blood, at their marriage. He read the words sonorously, but she was far past understanding them.

Eric glanced at Jenna, no hint of caring in his face, nor even of genuine recognition. The girl had been a chosen vessel with which to bring forth the Isis Messenger. He had been kind to her when that was necessary, and cruel when that was more appropriate. At the moment, her sniveling was beginning to disturb his concentration—it interfered with the beautiful ritual words, which accompanied the sacrifice.

Jenna didn't mean to beg, but maybe some part of him would remember all they'd been to each other . . . maybe some memory would make him merciful. She shrieked out his name, an unforgivable affront . . .

When the knife found her tongue, her shrieks became gurgles. *I'm drowning!* she thought insanely. It seemed suddenly more important than the fear or the pain.

Jenna didn't think at all after that. She just suffered until she died. The last thing she saw on earth was Ghania's smiling face.

With her final lucid breath, Jenna O'Connor Vannier vowed revenge.

# CHAPTER 75

Nightmares filled with blood and pain plagued Maggie's sleep from the instant her head hit the pillow. She had tossed so fitfully, the covers lay in a tangled heap around her, when the shrill ringing of the telephone beside the bed awakened her at 3:00 A.M. "Is this Mrs. Margaret O'Connor?" a disembodied voice queried out of the darkness. She struggled to clear the sleep mist from her brain, and fumbled for the light. The voice said he was a police officer.

"There's been an accident near the Cloisters," the man said. "I'm sorry to have to tell you this, Mrs. O'Connor, but your daughter's car went out of control and plunged over the side of the Palisades. I'm afraid the body was burned beyond recognition, but her purse was thrown free by the fall. There was a business card from The Antiquarian Quest in it—that's how we found you so quickly."

"Oh, my God!" Maggie gasped, struggling for comprehension. "Officer, was there a child in the car with my daughter?"

"No. No child. She was alone. We're still investigating how it happened, ma'am. We'll have to check your daughter's dental records to make sure, of course . . . the body was pretty badly mangled by the explosion, as well as burned. Can you tell me her dentist's name?"

. . . This man was asking everyday questions, Maggie thought, as if she would be able to answer them. But that was insane. Didn't he know there were no answers left inside her? Maybe no answers left in the world . . .

She held the offending receiver a long while, before she could make her hand steady enough to replace it in the cradle. Maggie sat on the edge of the bed, paralyzed, clutching the phone, staring into space, trying to remember how to breathe.

Jenna was gone. Forever. Jenna would never be all right now. Never come home. Never be Cody's mommy, or Maggie's child. Never make up for lost time, or lost love, or lost hope. Eric had killed her, that was the simple truth, no matter what it looked like to the police. The heartless bastard who was Jenna's husband had killed Maggie's child.

And now Cody was absolutely alone with her

mother's murderer. A scream torn from some primitive place, far beneath the civilizing layers that have raised humanity above the other animal species, rent its way free. A secret reservoir of grief opened its floodgates and Maggie heard, with absolute horror, her own voice screaming.

Maria Aparecida raced down the hall from her bedroom at the sound. The plump, motherly woman ran to Maggie's side, and not knowing what tragedy had happened, or what to do about it, she simply wrapped her arms around Maggie and held her until she stopped thrashing and screaming. "Cry, my daughter," she crooned, as to a baby. "Cry out all the tears you have been hiding in the secret places . . . Maria understands the sorrows of your heart . . . Maria understands . . ."

Maggie opened her swollen eyes and squinted at the early-morning light. For one blessed moment she thought it had all been a hideous dream, but Maria Aparecida's face, looking anxious beside the bed, brought reality with it.

"Dona Maggie, forgive me. I would never have awakened you . . . you slept but an hour or two, God help you. The man, he said I must give this to you right away. He said it is to do with Jenna." She lowered her voice and made the sign of the cross, as she spoke the name of the newly dead.

Maggie nodded, uncomprehending. This made no more sense than any of the rest of it. How could any man know about Jenna . . . Her head pounded as she sat up. She couldn't remember falling asleep. Only crying. Only screaming. She could remember that. And the phone call.

Shakily, she got up and pushed her feet into the slippers next to the bed. There was a taste in her mouth like blood, and she felt sick everywhere.

Maggie tore the brown paper from the package. It revealed a videotape with no identification. She looked up at Maria, puzzled, then walked to the armoire facing her bed, and turned on the TV set, to see what it might be. She sat on the edge of her bed and motioned for Maria to sit on the little boudoir chair, to watch the cassette with her.

The videotape had the production value of a bad home movie; the picture was dark at first, the action barely discernible. Tiny points of light seemed to bob and weave across the blank screen, and then the sound came up—an eerie chanting, that made Maggie peer closer.

Suddenly, the focus cleared sharply, as if someone had turned on a klieg light, and Maggie recognized the tear-streaked, terrified face of her daughter, hanging over the edge of an altar, her glorious flaxen hair, heavy with sweat like a palomino's mane after a hard ride. Eric Vannier, in a bizarre outfit, was doing something . . . she couldn't quite see . . . *Oh Sweet Jesus!* He was slicing at her body with a jeweled knife! Like a butcher dressing a side of beef, deftly slicing, plunging his hands into the open wounds of her dying child! Maggie watched the screen, completely immobilized by shock.

Was that Maria Aparecida's voice among the chanters? No, no! This was some terrible mistake. *Hail Mary full of Grace* . . . she was saying the rosary! *Holy Mary, Mother of God, pray for us. Now and at the hour of our death* . . .

Maria Aparecida recited the prayers, assaulted into shock by what she'd seen. Blot out the butchery . . . *Now and at the hour* . . . Blot out the butchery . . . *The Lord is with thee.* She stared, paralyzed, at the now darkened TV screen ahead of her, but she did not see it. She saw, instead, a laughing baby girl named Jenna, on the day of her Baptism, pure, precious, close to God. And the young mother who held her so proudly outside the church, in love and hope and blessed ignorance of what the years would plunder and destroy.

Maggie barely made it to the bathroom before she vomited. She sat on the white tile floor, clinging to the toilet, tears of unutterable anguish rolling down her face. There was nothing on this earth that would ever erase the memory of what she had seen. *Sweet Jesus, have mercy on her*, she said over and over and over in her head, so no other merciless thought could break through. *Sweet Jesus, have mercy on her*.

Sweet Jesus have mercy on me.

Numb with grief, Maggie stumbled up the steps of the Sixth Precinct. She was barely coherent with the desk sergeant, but finally managed to get to Devlin. Sobbing uncontrollably, she blurted out the story of the video-tape she clutched in her hands. Devlin called in Garibaldi, who handed it to another detective to set it up in the VCR that sat in the corner of the interrogation room. He disappeared with it down the hall, while Gino and Devlin tried to calm Maggie down enough to understand what had happened.

"You let us take a look at this tape, Maggie," Garibaldi said, glancing significantly at Devlin. "You just wait for us in the Lieutenant's office here, while we see if this can help us in any way. It's bad enough you had to see it once."

Devlin took the sobbing woman into his arms, her head resting dispiritedly on his chest; Maggie was disturbingly limp, as if all lifeforce had been siphoned off. He sat her in a chair in his office, as gently as he could, and followed Garibaldi down the corridor to the interrogation room.

The two men sat down grimly, without speaking; they pushed the play button and waited. Only snow filled the screen. The two exchanged puzzled looks, and Garibaldi fast-forwarded, several times. The tape was completely blank.

"She's not so overwrought she could have imagined it, Lieutenant?" Garibaldi asked with real concern.

"Not a chance. Nobody makes up a story like that one. You know her, Gino. She's been run over by a train." He sat silently a moment, the image of Maggie's sobbing figure, in his office, vivid in his own mind.

"Send the dammed thing to the lab boys," he said

hoarsely, "and see if they can figure out what those sons of bitches did to erase the video. And tell them I'm not prepared to buy any stories about Black Magic."

Gino nodded, and left with the offending tape. Devlin took a very deep breath and wondered what in this sorry world he could do to convince Maggie she was not going insane.

She was sitting in the chair beside the desk, when Devlin returned to his office. She was folded over, like a rag doll, her knees drawn up protectively to her chest, arms around them, head despondently resting on her knees. He had seen the instinctive survival posture before. Kicked in the solar plexus by Fate, people folded in on themselves, escaping to a secret landscape. Sometimes they never come back.

He longed to reach out and touch her, comfort her, but he knew this was a desperate, private sorrow on which he must not intrude. "Come with me, Maggie," he said gently. "I'm getting you out of here."

She followed him on autopilot, all the way to his car, then balked at getting in. "I need to walk," she said, turning away, so he had to follow.

"Years ago," she said faintly, without looking at him, "when Jack and I were first married, we lived in the South for a year, so he could go to graduate school at Washington and Lee. We had this cleaning lady, who came in once a week—black, poverty-stricken—but a great beauty. She was tall and thin as a flute, I remember, but with high proud breasts, like a jungle princess . . ." her voice was hoarse and distant as a sleepwalker's.

Devlin wondered where on earth Maggie was headed with this strange train of thought; what had it to do with Jenna's death? Who could blame her for coming unhinged by what she'd witnessed? He took her arm, and she neither protested, nor responded, but continued in the strange rambling monotone.

"I was pregnant with Jenna," she said with a sigh,

answering his unspoken question, "and reveling in all the smug pride of early womanhood. I'd felt life move within me for the first time, and I was intoxicated with the splendor of my remarkable achievement." She laughed shortly, at her own expense, and Devlin saw how close to tears she was, and listened very carefully.

"The brokers used to pick up truckloads of poor blacks from the rural areas, and drop them off in the city to do day labor. They'd work dawn to dark for three dollars a day." Maggie sighed again. "I really liked this woman, I admired her courage . . ." This memory obviously had genuine pain in it and Devlin gripped her arm tighter, but she didn't notice. Tears slid down her cheeks and she ignored them.

"She had five children and there wasn't a moment of her life not filled with drudgery. Cook, clean, scrub, kowtow to her useless husband . . . he used to get drunk and beat her, unmercifully. Then she got pregnant again, so we'd talk about babies together, and we had a sort of tentative friendship going . . . Then one day, she missed coming to work, and of course she had no phone, so I didn't find out till the following week, that she'd given birth to her baby, and it had died a day later. Three dollars a day doesn't go a long way toward prenatal care when you're feeding five already.

"Anyway . . . in my twenty-one-year-old ignorance I said to her, 'I guess it's really for the best, isn't it, Emmy? Last thing you need is another mouth to feed.' " Maggie took a deep purgative breath, then looked at Devlin for the first time, tears streaming down her cheeks. "She didn't say a single word to me, Dev . . ." Her voice broke with the bitter sorrow of the memory.

"But I read it all in her eyes. Her anger at my incalculable stupidity in thinking it could ever be *better* to lose a child. Her resignation to the unfairness of life that had given me a good husband, money, and a healthy baby-to-be. And, a sort of lofty pity for me. As if to say, 'I know you don't mean to be so dumb, you're just a pampered fool and life hasn't ravaged you yet. One day it will and then you'll know what I know.' We never really spoke again. She'd written me off, and I deserved it." Maggie paused, wiped her eyes quickly, then plunged ahead.

"This morning Maria told my next-door neighbor about Jenna's death, and the woman said to me, 'Oh Maggie, I was so sorry to hear about your daughter . . . but I guess in some ways it frees you.' " She took a deep, convulsive breath. "I felt those *same* emotions flood me, Dev, the ones I saw in Emmy's face. It isn't freedom! It's the most monumental failure in the world. And it's forever." The confession had wrenched the plug from the bottleneck of sorrow, and Maggie began to sob, softly, convulsively, as if her heart would break.

A line from some Greek poet was suddenly in Devlin's mind, so clearly he could not escape its words, and so he spoke them softly. " '. . . In our sleep, pain, which cannot forget, falls drop by drop upon the heart, until, in our own despair, against our will, comes wisdom through the awful grace of God . . .' "

He pulled the suffering woman to a halt, turned and took her into his arms, unmindful of the stares of the passersby. "Oh, Maggie, Maggie, my Maggie," he breathed into her hair as he held her, patting her like a child, rocking her like a lost child. "I love you so."

After a while, she let him take her home. Listless, all lifeforce spent, she simply curled up on the couch in the parlor and fell asleep with her head on his lap.

Malachy Devlin sat beside her as she slept; he wouldn't move for fear of waking her. Sleep was the only respite she would find now. There was much yet to be faced . . . the body . . . the funeral . . . the emptiness in her heart where Jenna had resided. He remembered all of it, the waking nightmare of death and its macabre rituals.

*This could be taken away again.* The thought clawed at the edges of his mind. *I have found the one to love, and those sons of bitches are out to take her away from me. They've already beaten me to Jenna. I can't let them harm the child, or there'll be nothing left of Maggie's heart. It was my own failure that cost me Daniel and Jan*, he thought, fiercely self-honest. *But not this time. This time, I'll keep them safe.*

Three hours later, at the station house, Garibaldi handed the videotape back to Devlin with a grimace.

"The tech guys say this tape's never been used, Lieutenant."

Devlin looked up sharply.

"Impossible," he said.

"I guess that leaves us with a hallucination from all the stress, or an outright lie," Garibaldi said quietly.

Devlin shook his head slowly. "She isn't crazy and she doesn't lie. There's another explanation."

Both men stood staring at the offending tape; suddenly, their eyes met, knowledge dawning.

"It's not the same tape!" they said, almost in unison.

"Find out if Jackson let it out of his hand between my office and the VCR," Devlin ordered.

Garibaldi was gone and back in minutes. "He says he laid it on top of the machine, because a call came in while we were still talking to Maggie. There was plenty of time for somebody to switch the tape. But, Lieutenant, this means we got one of them here in the squad with us. That's pretty unbelievable, no?"

"Maybe not one of them, Gino. Maybe just somebody they've got on the occasional payroll. It's not impossible."

"Yeah . . . well, it means maybe we better watch our asses pretty damn good from here on in, Lieutenant. You think maybe we should take this to the Captain?"

"If the ME says Jenna's death was murder, I'll take it to the Captain."

The two men's eyes met again, the same sudden wariness in both. Now, not even the Captain was above suspicion.

* * *

The Medical Examiner pushed his half glasses a fraction of an inch higher on his large nose and looked up from the grisly work of attempting to ascertain the cause of Jenna Vannier's death. The body was charred and grotesque. Parts of it were missing.

He sought Devlin's eye, over the corpse. "What you have here, Lieutenant, is something very queer . . . something maybe you should keep under your hat until we know more . . ."

Devlin raised an eyebrow in lieu of asking the obvious question. Autopsies were not a favorite part of the job, and this one less than most.

"This woman didn't die in a car crash," the ME said definitively. "She was tortured to death. Her tongue and several vital organs are missing. And if they went up in smoke, you can bet your badge it wasn't in the fire from any car crash."

"Ever see anything like this before?" Devlin asked, trying not to look at the charred remains on the table. The lilting youngster in the picture on Maggie's desk kept swimming into focus in his mind.

"That case down in Texas a few years ago . . . all those satanic sacrifices they found in an old shed on the border . . . they all had their hearts removed, living," the ME said, thoughtfully. "The tongue's a new wrinkle, though. Maybe they just wanted to shut her up while they butchered her."

Devlin nodded, trying to think of some way to keep the worst of this from the newspapers. Any inkling of a ritual killing and they'd have a field day with the intimate pieces of Maggie O'Connor's life.

"Did you know her?" the Medical Examiner asked, seeing the haunted look in Devlin's eyes.

"No, never laid eyes on her. But the mother's a good friend of mine."

"Hmm. Worse yet, I guess. At least the kid's beyond pain now."

Devlin nodded a second time. There was nothing he could say.

"When the mother comes in to pick up the remains, I'll try not to give her all the grim details."

Devlin looked up sharply. "She already knows the details. Somebody sent her a video."

The Medical Examiner stared at him a moment, digesting that piece of information, then he removed his glasses in an expressive gesture, and pressed the bridge of his nose, as if to ward off a terminal headache, before speaking. "Nice world we've got here, Lieutenant, wouldn't you say? You think God is dead or He just doesn't give a rat's ass anymore?"

"'Homo homini lupus,'" Devlin murmured. The ME looked closer at the detective, surprised by the Latin.

"Man may be a wolf to man, Lieutenant," he said authoritatively, "but God damn well ought to know better."

# CHAPTER 76

Maggie felt the inexorable force of Jenna's death wash through her with nauseating intensity, as she stood beside the two-day-old grave. She had made it through the burial in a haze of numbness, Amanda and Ellie doing everything, leading her through the motions like a sleepwalker.

She had held back the heinous memory of the videotape by sheer force of will, till now; trying to stay alive, and in control of her faculties, long enough to do what she must. The fight for Cody was still ahead. Cody was alive. Cody *needed* her. But the floodgates hadn't held.

The horror kept seeping in. To her dreams, to her waking consciousness, inexorable and unstoppable. A living presence dripping blood through crevices, under doorways of the mind and heart. So Maggie had awakened this morning knowing she had to meet it face-to-face, in order to stay sane.

*You're trying to survive the cold, little flowers*, she thought, staring at the wilting daffodils on the ground at her feet. *So am I.* Silent and forlorn, she wondered how this tragedy could ever have engulfed their lives.

*Nobody knows, but you, what we were together in the good times, Jenna . . .* She breathed the thought to her daughter, wherever she was. *All they know is the end of love . . . but you and I shared the beginning.*

Maggie let the flood of ice-cold grief enfold her, rising within her like a drowning tide.

*How could it come to so bad an end, when there was so much love in it?* Did I nurse you too little, or love you too much? Did I leave you adrift too long, during your father's long dying? I never meant to, sweetheart. I would have fed you with my own heart's blood, if it could have saved you. Just as I will Cody. Do you understand that everything I do for her, I do for you, too?

*"I am not resigned to your going, Jenna,"* she whispered. *"I don't know how to say good-bye."*

It suddenly occurred to Maggie that the murdered girl who lay beneath the earth at her feet, wasn't Jenna at all. Jenna had died, long, long ago, when first she'd put a poisoned needle in her arm. *A poisoned spindle will prick your finger at sixteen, the wicked fairy had said at Sleeping Beauty's Christening. And so it had.*

She blessed herself and turned to go. As she left the silent cemetery plot behind, she wondered how long it would be before she slept beside her daughter on that quiet hill. And when that happened, would Cody share their endless rest?

# CHAPTER 77

Ghania stroked the body of her pet snake with a tolerant affection. "Oh, Malikali, my pet," she whispered seductively, "why did I ever choose you instead of a were-spider, or a cat, as my familiar?" She chuckled a little at her own question. "Either of them would be so easy to carry about, while you have become so plump and so long, it is a great bother to lift you." She patted the swaying head, taking a few moments to meet its placid reptilian gaze.

She had raised the snake from a hatchling, fed it on blood treats, and trained it meticulously for the tasks she expected of a witch's familiar. There'd been so many of them over the years; even Ghania's skill could not lengthen their lifespans more than two or three times nature's intended number. This one, at least, had the added virtue of being able to terrify merely by its appearance. Snakes were anathema to most humans; it was surprising how merely being threatened by the presence of one such as Malikali loosened most tongues.

The snake was a good-enough tool in some ways, she thought with a sigh, but singularly lacking in intelligence. At least with cats and dogs there was a responsive intellect to interact with the magician's whims. In Malikali and her kind, there was simple instinct to rely on, and a sort of plodding loyalty. And, of course, the snake was an unusually good channel for her mistress's psychic powers. If Malikali was present in a room, she was an excellent amplifier of energies, which made it easier to maintain surveillance on those Ghania chose to keep tabs on.

484

Ghania sighed again, patted the snake absently and stood up. She had decided to use this creature to awaken Cody's talents, fully. But the process would demand great care, for the child was just the right size to seem a perfect morsel to Malikali, whose obedience could be just as dull-witted as the rest of her. The witch shook her head at the imponderables; there was always so much to remember in these cases of awakening latent powers . . . and never had there been a reward like the one at the end of this rainbow.

Ghania opened the cage of rabbits and pulled out the two largest; the snake could use the exercise she'd get in running these two to ground. She dropped the protesting rabbits into the cement pit, which the snake used for feeding, and turned to go. There was no need to watch the spectacle. Malikali would have some fun torturing the two, and then, inevitably she would eat them. As familiars go, the snake might be boring, but she was really very little bother.

As she made the return trip to the nursery, Ghania pondered the precise methodology she would use on the child, now that the time had finally come. There was no question that Cody had made contact with the Guardians. The episode with the rabbit had been a perfect catalyst, the child's soft heart had made her particularly vulnerable to the animal's suffering, and she had been forced to the brink . . . where her Guardians hovered. She had made contact, all right. And she had been practicing communication with the animals, too; several of them had relayed that fact to Ghania, telepathically. She had even begun trying to communicate with the mineral and vegetable kingdoms, the Orishas had reported— although it seemed that Cody did not yet trust her own abilities.

At last, all the ingredients were in the cosmic beaker—all that was needed now was for Ghania to devise the perfect torment to complete the alchemical formula that would transmute child into Messenger.

The Infernal Names must be consulted, of course:

Sabazios of Phrygia, Astaroth, the Phoenician, Cimeries, ruler of all Africa, Nergal of Babylonia, Abaddam of the Hebrews . . . Ghania invoked their names reverently, as she stood before her altar, and awaited their response. All those arrogant fools of Adepti who had gathered for the dress rehearsal thought they knew true magic. But each was confined to his own system and his own demons, while Ghania was confined by no such artificial constraint. She belonged to the Prince of Darkness in all his manifestations; Babylon, Sumeria, Nineveh, Tyre, Greece, Rome, Egypt, wherever evil had ever prospered, Ghania held sway, for there was no limit to her Master's dominion. Only Eric, Nicky, and Hazred suspected her true powers, the others dismissed her as a glorified servant. The fools.

Ghania dropped her garment to the ground and stood clad only in the ibante loincloth that housed her potent magic; the ancient, blood-soaked rags had never left her body since the day of her initiation. She could cloud men's mind if need be, so they would not be repelled by its odious appearance, but she could never remove her Ju Ju.

Ghania raised her large arms in demonic salute, and entered into the company of true Evil. She would consult them on the Star-Child's final torment.

# CHAPTER 78

"You are like the caged lioness, tonight, dona Maggie," Maria said worriedly. She had watched Maggie push the food around her plate, then abandon it altogether—then she had seen her pick up a dozen projects, only to lay them down again, moments later. Now she watched her moving restlessly from place to place.

"It's Cody, Maria," Maggie answered her agitatedly. "I have this horrible foreboding about her tonight. Something *awful* is happening to her . . . something *strangling*. I can *feel* it. It's been growing worse all evening." She shook her head, frustrated by her apprehension. "I don't know how to explain it."

"The detective, dona Maggie," Maria offered tentatively. "Can he not make the police do something for us! He is a good man. Where is his posse to save this little one? Will he do nothing?"

Maggie shrugged expressively.

"And the priest? I have not seen him so much this week? Perhaps he has gone to visit my friend Padre James?" Maggie knew James had been elevated to near sainthood by his prowess in the kitchen, and his reverence for Maria's cooking.

"Perhaps he has," Maggie said noncommittally and Maria Aparecida raised her magnificent eyebrow, and pursed her lips at this unsatisfactory response.

"We are sorely tried," she said, including herself in the current purgatory. "But God will not abandon us."

"Why do you say that, Maria?"

"Our intention is only good for the little chicken, dona Maggie. When God sees into the heart and finds purity, He sends his angels. You will remember my words."

Maggie watched the huge retreating figure, wishing she could feel so assured. She glanced at the clock; it read 11:06. Eleven-oh-six on April 28th. Nearly Walpurgisnacht. The beginning or the end. She was suddenly afraid, in a new and internal way. It was a spiritual dampening, as if some alien force were lurking in the corners, spreading fear throughout the brownstone. *What other dungeon is as dark as one's own heart?*

She felt her life emptying . . . loved ones slipping away inexorably. Jenna, gone forever. Peter, too. There was an emptiness in her soul, where they had been; deep fathomless, inky, free-form—like a terrible hunger that couldn't be sated, or an essential task left undone. Who would be the next to go? *Not Cody, God!* Please not Cody.

Angry with herself, Maggie went to the kitchen to make tea, grateful for the small diversionary action and the whistling sound of the kettle in the still house. Maria was upstairs now, and even the cuckoo clock in the hall seemed quieter than usual.

Why did she suddenly feel so guilty at her aloneness? As if she'd failed some primal test of worthiness, and this was her just punishment. Perhaps, if she'd been a better person. Perhaps if she'd understood Jenna better. Perhaps, if Peter hadn't been a priest. Perhaps, if she'd known how to respond when Dev said "I love you." Perhaps, if Cody hadn't been kidnapped. Perhaps, if . . . perhaps, if . . .

She had to get through tonight; had to collect her thoughts enough to plan tomorrow. Time was running out. Why was it so hard to figure out how to do what she must? Why was she not bigger and smarter and more able to make everything turn out all right?

Was that creak a noise in the upstairs bedroom? Stop it! Now you're just letting yourself get spooked by the loneliness. Hating herself for needing to, Maggie tiptoed through the bedrooms and checked the closets for the source of the sound; finding no one, she turned on all the lights and pulled the shades, feeling vulnerable.

She tried to pass Cody's bedroom by, but couldn't, so she entered tentatively and stood staring at the child's stuffed toys that were so forlorn. "And I have come upon this place by lost ways . . ." she whispered aloud into the still room. "And by what way shall I go back?"

The room had been Jenna's, too. Oh, God! Don't let me think about that! Maggie walked to the bookcase and, on impulse, pulled out the little leather-bound book of poetry that had been hers, and Jenna's before it was Cody's; it opened to a well-worn place and she read the familiar words:

*Lord, behold our family here assembled*
*Give us peace, gaiety and the quiet mind*
*Soften us to our friends,*
*Strengthen us to our enemies,*
*That we may be brave in peril,*
*Constant in all changes of fortune,*
*And that down to the gates of death,*
*We may be loyal and love one another.*

Down to the gates of death . . . she repeated the words softly. Maybe that's where this all will lead, inevitably. Jack would be waiting. Maybe Jenna, too . . . She couldn't bring herself to leave the room, so with a sigh, Maggie lay down on Cody's bed, and pulling the child's favorite Love Bear into her arms, she drifted off to restless sleep.

THE room where Cody had been left by Ghania was windowless and very, very cold. There was no furniture, only a few boxes and an old cot mattress on the floor, that smelled of ancient sweat.

Cody huddled herself into the farthest corner, as close to the shelter of the walls as she could press her shivering body. She had no idea why Ghania was doing this terrible thing to her—she hadn't done anything that was against the rules. But suddenly with no warning at all, Ghania had pulled her from her own warm bed, and brought her to this cold, awful place with the snake. Then she had unlocked Malikali's cage and left them alone together in the icy darkness.

She had seen Ghania let him slither out into the room before she turned off the lights. Cody hunched down, making herself small as possible, listening with a terrible tension . . . the snake was somewhere close by; she was afraid to open her eyes for fear of seeing him.

Ghania had said she would die tonight. Malikali would

wrap himself around her, and squeeze and squeeze . . . then the snake would swallow her, like it had the goat, and she would be trapped inside it, screaming and screaming where nobody could hear . . . Cody whimpered in the darkness, her voice a tiny strangled sound. *"Mim . . . Please, Mim. Please don't let him eat me!"* She began to cry softly, afraid even to sniffle for fear the snake would come.

She could hear the sliding, slipping motion of the huge body, as it pulled itself along the concrete floor toward her. It was coming, now. Slithering closer. Cody pressed herself against the restraining wall and begged Mim to come for her. Why don't you come and save me? she had shrieked that terrible question so long, it had worn a hole in her heart that everything had fallen through.

"Mim!" she whispered urgently. Then she saw it clearly . . . its eyes, shining yellow slits in the darkness and all restraints broke loose at last. "Mim!" she shrieked in absolute terror. "Mim! Mim! Miiiiiiii . . ."

*"IIIIIM!"*

*The desperate scream pierced Maggie's consciousness in the dream. She was running toward the sound.*

*Cody was screaming her name. Over and over and over, the echoes reverberating all around her now.*

*But where was it coming from?*

*The dream/Maggie looked frantically right and left. Which way to run?*

*"Mim! Help me!"*

*Over there! Through the ink-black trees. Maggie started toward the sound.*

*"I'm coming!" she cried out. But the whipping wind blew the words back into her throat. "I'm coming, baby. Where are you?"*

*The tangling vines were reaching out to ensnare her feet. And the ground beneath was shifting . . .*

*"Mi i i i i i i i m m m m m . . ."* The long echoing
shriek was fading, *"M i i i i i i . . ."*

Maggie sat up in the frilly bed. She was soaked in
sweat and tears were running down her face.

Shakily she rose and turned on the bedside lamp. This
dream was real. Something terrible was happening to
Cody. *And, it was happening now.*

Maggie hurried to her own room, yanked off her dripping T-shirt and pulled on her sweatpants, hastily grabbing her keys from the bureau. She had to think . . . had
to move . . . had to figure it out. Tonight.

She pulled a hooded sweatshirt from the rack in the
front hall and let herself out the door. She needed to
run. Run to Cody. No. That was insane. The only way
to save her was to think it through.

Maggie started to run. Running was real. Running
would help her think. She rounded the darkened corner
of St. Luke's Place and calculated a route that wouldn't
take her into dangerous territory. Over to Sixth and up
toward Eighth—there would be streetlights there. And
people. No matter what the hour.

The cold damp air flooded her lungs, the oxygen infu-
sion pushed her brain to full wakefulness.

It was inventory time. All the mystical mumbo jumbo
in the world was not going to save Cody, if somebody
didn't get her out of that fucking house. All the police
work Dev had done was fine, as far as it went, without
him she wouldn't have known a fraction of the truth.
But if the department would not, or could not, get involved, then Dev's hands were tied, and there'd be no
point thinking the police would rescue her.

*And time was running out.*

There was only one possible course of action left—
she knew it as she hit the corner of Christopher Street
and turned right. She had to get Cody out of that house
herself. Okay! Then what? Then run like hell, if need
be. Run to somewhere, anywhere, that Cody would be
safe. Eric would have to give up eventually. The critical

date would be past, and what would be the point in pursuing Cody into infinity, if he didn't know where to look?

*But they can find you on the Astral*, the internal voice reminded her. If they can manifest a Sending, they can damned well find you wherever you're hiding!

Maggie's lungs were burning. She could feel her body straining against the demands of the run. She needed to stretch herself. Needed to force herself beyond the possible. There had to be a way out of this box.

Maggie pushed her run to the limit. *Fear and sorrow can deplete you*, Mr. Wong had said. The words were beating in her head to the rhythm of her feet on the pavement. *Some sorrows, too deep for tears*. Even too deep for laughter to root them out. They lodge in heart tissue, brain tissue, gut. They acid-etch the spirit and seep between the cracks of consciousness.

Some sorrows defeat you. *I cannot let that happen*.

She could feel heart, soul, mind, straining against the limits. Have to save her. *Have to save her*. Have to take control. *Have to take control*. The words beat in the rhythm of the flying feet. The streetlights seemed to dance before Maggie at the corner, tiny white lights buzzed past her vision like comets. The street seemed not solid anymore beneath her feet. I am lost . . . so far to go to find me. And in a strange neighborhood. Her thoughts were disjointed, muddled, yet crystal clear. As if she could see straight through herself. A crystal pane. A crystal pain. Help me, God! *Help me to save her*.

Suddenly she could feel Mim within her. Consciousness rising. A remembrance of power. Something was beginning to awaken. *Please God, let it be enough*.

You live and die alone, the thought was inside her suddenly, and irrefutable. But along the line your agonies come from the others. The mad ones, the sad ones, the sick ones, the needy ones. They all take suck from you. Lifeblood drunk randomly. Psychic vampires. Vampires of love.

But that's how it's supposed to be. Because love is all there is. All that matters. All that touches God.

*Cody is the Messenger and I am the Guardian.*

*I am the only one who can save her now.*

CODY'S terror drove her inward, now, away from the danger that was staring at her in the evil dark. Deep, deep, falling inward into emptiness . . . she pulled her mind in after her, fleeing toward safety. It was the place of fragmentation. The place where ordinary little children go, who have been pushed beyond endurance by their pain. The place of splitting off from the solid center, into self-protective "others." The Sybil place. Where personalities multiply to save their desperate host.

But Cody was no ordinary child.

And she was no longer alone in the dark. Giant golden wings whipped the air around her; they brushed the child's cheek, and settled in about her cowering form. Warmth and calm and light all radiated from the wings, a sheltering protection. Stunned and confused, Cody looked up. Great Beings made of Light more brilliant than the sun were moving in the room, and radiating far beyond it. Against such as these, the snake seemed suddenly small and insignificant. She knew they had come from the Place of Light to save her.

Wonderingly, she felt her body change and energize; she thought perhaps she'd died. Had she been old enough to understand molecular biology, she would have sensed the change in frequency, as every shimmering atom of her being was transformed. Light began to radiate from her tiny body, which now channeled energy from a celestial source. And she was growing larger . . .

Cody felt herself a child no more. Radiant beams of light spilled from the Guardians' hands and eyes—Cody recognized it as a vastly more powerful version of the energy that flowed from her own hands to the sick or hurt ones. Gratefully, she bathed herself in the incandescence they poured forth. Every thought had power, now. A wave of her hand would bring protection. She knew that, somehow. Just as she knew other unimaginable things . . . lifetimes collected in spirals of DNA . . . molecules replete with memory . . . humanity's frail and mighty history scribed in every cell.

*And love!* Sweet love, beyond anything and everything she had ever dreamed, poured forth from every pore. Love even for her tormentors . . . not for their wickedness, but for their fragile humanity that had allowed them, long ago, to choose Evil. Love for all humankind. Love for God/Goddess. Love, even for the deadly snake that quivered now before her dazzling form.

Cody turned her gaze upon the huge slithering beast, and saw, not the unremitting evil of its intent, but the intrinsic beauty and strength that were its birthright in nature. That it had been used for torment was not the python's fault, for Ghania's magic had bewitched it.

She remembered a test in a temple, long, long ago . . .

Now, the great snake drew back before the immense onslaught of love that poured from Cody's eyes. In many cultures, snakes were sacred to the Goddess, in others they were crushed beneath her feet . . . all this was communicated through Cody's eyes, and when the python slithered near her once again, it was to pay homage.

Ghania watched the child and the snake with intense concentration through the one-way mirror. The special optics incorporated into the glass gave her excellent clarity, despite the dark in the room beyond. It was a derivative of the technology used in night-vision glasses for combat—Eric and Nicky always had access to the best government equipment, especially if it could have use in wartime.

"She has Awakened to her powers!" she said triumphantly. Nicholas Sayles stood beside her in the small room, watching the drama being played next door. "Terror is always the fastest goad."

"Ten years of study, or two weeks of torture, eh, Ghania?" he responded. He enjoyed others' suffering, but loathed the snake. He'd had a run-in with Ghania's familiar once, and the memory lingered. "You could always be trusted to be expeditious. How dangerous will she be to have around, now that she's fully Awakened?"

"She is only a child in this incarnation, Nicholas. It would take time for her to learn the full use of the skills she now possesses . . . as yet she has no frame of reference for the use of her power. Each day she would remember something more, but there is only one day left to her. By the hour of the sacrifice, she will be a worthy Messenger. If she were older, the tale might have a different ending, but as it is . . ."

"Will you leave her alone with your precious pet all night, my cruel one?" he asked, fascinated, as always, by the unrelenting evil of the witch.

Ghania laughed a low, throaty sound. "I assure you, Nicholas, the only creature in danger, in that room tonight, is my python." She turned toward the door between the two rooms. "I must go to her now . . ." she said dismissively, and Nicholas Sayles allowed her the slight; she was very good at her work.

Ghania entered the room and saw the child standing quietly in its center. Cody O'Connor's three-year-old face looked serene as a Buddhist monk's, or at least as stubbornly composed. She was a different person now, and stared implacably at her jailer.

Ghania watched her every nuance, with calculation. The child had presence and fortitude, imperial stubbornness and grit . . . the Awakening was magnificent, as planned. It was gratifying to see that the old system worked so well—but the Materialization was still a day away.

Ghania saw that Malikali had returned, of her own volition, to her cage. She smiled at Cody and saw that another spirit had come to life within her. An old, wise, intractable spirit, honed by a thousand lifetimes for a single task.

She gazed at the child in fascination, and read the thoughts as clearly as if they'd been spoken. *Do not mistake me, witch,* they said to the Obeah priestess clearly. *Because I inhabit a child's body does not make me a neophyte.*

*Even Christ had to be taught by his mother to walk and speak his name. My Mother teaches me, too. Do not think you have caught me because I am in your snare. The game has not yet been played.*

Thank Darkness the body was still small and the earth years so few . . . even at that, she would have to be kept drugged until the Ceremony. There was no point in taking chances.

Ghania slid the needle deep into the child's arm and pushed the plunger.

MAGGIE rounded the corner of Cornelia and spotted Devlin's building, halfway down the block. She took the old limestone steps without pause, two at a time, opened the outer vestibule door and rang the bell insistently. The ancient intercom crackled out his sleepy voice. "Who is it?"

"It's me, Dev," she panted, still breathless. "Let me in. I have to see you."

The buzzer sounded, and then he was there beside her, a pair of gym shorts hastily pulled on, and shirtless, a puzzled, worried look on his face. His hair, uncombed, fell onto his forehead, making him look boyish.

"I'm going to get her out of there, Dev," Maggie said, without waiting for hello, as he led her into his apartment. "I'm going to find a way to kidnap her, before they do their ritual. Something happened to her tonight. I don't know what, but something *terrible* happened. I've been running . . . putting the pieces together . . ."

Devlin stared at her, still groggy from sleep. He held up a hand to stop the rush of words.

"For Christ's sake, Maggie," he said, "will you give me a minute to get up to speed here? It's 2:00 A.M."

"I don't care *what* time it is, Devlin!" she said fiercely. "They *hurt her* tonight. Don't ask me how I know. *I know.* Those bastards hurt her. And I'm going up there to get her."

"For Christ's sake, Maggie," Dev said again angrily. "Are you out of your mind? You'll get yourself killed or arrested. If I hadn't been there last time, you'd be chopped liver by now. Will you let me handle this my way? You are not equipped for this."

"*No*, I will *not* let you handle this your way!" she exploded. "Don't you get it? There's no time left for waiting for somebody *else* to do something. Cody's my grandchild and I'm the one who has to know I did everything that was humanly possible to save her."

"So you'll let your fucking ego get in the way of her safety and your own?"

Maggie's eyes widened. "You son of a bitch!" she blazed. "We're not talking egos, here! It's not my *ego* that's making me lay my life on the line—It's *love!*

"She's part of my heart, don't you understand that? I learned everything Ellie and Peter could throw at me, hoping against hope there'd be a magical formula somewhere that would make this whole fucking nightmare go away. But there isn't. And then I waited to see if your fabled policework could save her, but now we know it won't! Don't you think I'd be thrilled if somebody, *somewhere*, knew how to save her? Nobody knows better than I do how woefully inadequate I am for this job . . . I'm not equipped for this, by anything except love.

"But that one thing I have, Devlin. I do love her. Enough to face those maniacs—enough to die, if I have to. And that isn't ego talking. I am not a fool! Goddammit! If there were anyone else on this earth I could trust to get her out of that stinking house, I'd hand over the job in a heartbeat. But there isn't.

"Cody is three years old, Dev! And she's alone in a house full of monsters who kill children. And I told her I'd be back. So by God, *I will be back*. Even if I do nothing more than make sure she doesn't die alone, thinking nobody loved her enough to try to save her . . . *I will go back!*"

The intransigent frown that greeted her outburst infuriated her. Why did she want so much for him to understand?

"Oh, shit!" she said, frustrated beyond endurance. "I don't even know what I came here for . . ." She turned to go, but Devlin grabbed her arm and pulled her forcefully toward him. She started to protest, but then his mouth was on hers and one hand had tangled itself in her hair, and the other was holding her so tight she could barely breathe.

Maggie tried to wrench herself away, but he met her strength with strength of his own.

"Come with me!" he said, his face so close to hers she could feel him breathe. A demand, a request? To where? Come to where?

"Let me go!" she said, pushing his hand away. And then his arms were everywhere, and all the bottled-up emotion in her was there with them, too. The longing and the need. To love. To be loved. To explode outward and inward into someone who could receive the gift. She wrapped her arms around his hard body and buried the past in his kiss.

And then, they were on his bed; she had no idea how they'd gotten there. And there was flesh where there had been clothes and she suddenly knew the truth. That she *loved* this man. That she *wanted him* and had for a long time. Wanted him to touch and to probe and to love. Wanted to give back love, from the depths of her body and soul.

*"Come with me!"* he said again urgently, and this time it had all the meaning in the world.

The cool air raised goosebumps on her body and tightened her nipples; or was it anticipation? She felt the creak of bedsprings as he straddled her, saw him smiling as he touched her breasts, roughly, gently, fervently, for the first time. And the other places. She felt the heat of his loins pressing down on her, bringing strength to her own. His manhood loomed above her, an object to be touched and loved and tantalized, just as his hands and mouth tantalized her.

And he was bending low over her, his mouth on her lips, her throat, her cheek, her ear. And he was speaking in a voice that was only for lovemaking, soft words, encouraging words. Feel . . . want . . . come with me . . . so good. So beautiful.

And then it was he on the bed, and he was lifting her willing hips to sit astride him. Liquid, wildly soaring body, feeling only at the center. Exquisite, urgent fire.

"No!" she heard herself say, but she didn't know what it was she feared. Not *Dev* . . .

"Yes!" he said, suddenly thrusting into her, his whole body's strength in the thrust. She screamed, startled by the wildness of feeling. Primitive, out of control. Beyond the rational.

"Yes!" he said, holding her hips to him so she couldn't escape. The sudden thrust again, and again, like a stallion bucking. And she was lost, waves of pleasure spilling endlessly over each other. Lost in the undertow. She felt/heard/saw through a haze of drowning pleasure.

"No . . ." she heard herself gasp again through the distorted waves, a cry of negation to all the past that was set adrift forever by this act of love.

"Maggie!" he called out from afar, and she felt herself lifted again, all the strength of his body forcing its way into hers. Shattering, impossible thrust. Starburst. Madness. Life . . .

Hugging, holding, laughing perfection of love.

Maggie lay beside him on the bed, half covered by his body, every nerve, muscle, fiber, bone, liquid from lovemaking. All urgency dissolved into languid completion. What had just happened between them? she wondered. Ecstacy, comfort, a coda to the past, an affirmation of life in a deadeningly difficult world. And, oh, so very much more than that . . .

He moved to take her in his arms again. To touch and probe, and fondle and soar and plummet, different from before. Gentler now, touching each other's needs with tenderness and unhurried unity.

And then they were still; smiling into each other's skin, tired and replete.

"That's just the beginning for us, Maggie," he said pulling her body in close against his own, proprietarily. "On your hundredth birthday, I'm planning a surprise."

"Mmmmm?" she murmured wonderingly, touched by his need to connect their futures.

"I'm saving the best for last," he said sleepily. "I call it the Doomsday Fuck."

"That's nice," she answered, amused and filled to the brim. "It'll give me something to look forward to."

How sweet is laughter shared with one you love, she thought, suddenly, remembering that laughter is the last to die. There had been no sex for her and Jack for a very long time because of the illness. But every once in a while, something crazy would set off their laughter. And then the love would come flooding through. Washing over her in healing billows. Remembrance of the good times when there had been joy. And hope. And enough laughter to fill the galaxies.

"I love you, Maggie," Dev said, sensing the sudden quiet that had overtaken her.

"I love you, too," she answered, meaning it . . . wondering if there would be time for them to love. Glad for this one moment.

Both slept for an hour or two before the rising sunlight beaming through the curtainless windows brought reality and the coming day.

"I want you to stay put today, Maggie," Dev said, as he stood naked in the bathroom, still wet from the shower.

She looked up at him, startled, her sweatpants pulled halfway up her legs.

"I told you, Dev," she said evenly, "I have to go get Cody today."

He looked as shocked as if she'd struck him.

"What the hell are you talking about?" he asked testily. "I thought we settled all that last night."

It was Maggie's turn to look shocked. "You thought we *settled all that?*" she repeated incredulously. "How, Dev? By going to bed together? By making love? Oh, that's really *great.* The little woman's out of control here, maybe I'd better calm her down the old-fashioned way!"

Suddenly furious, and unutterably sad, she yanked her sweatshirt over her head and turned toward the door.

"The fact that I love you, Dev . . . or *made love to you*, doesn't change a goddamned thing, here. I'm still me . . . and I still have to get Cody out of that house."

She didn't wait for a reply, but slammed the door behind her. Devlin stood, a towel wrapped around his waist, fists clenched in frustration and impotent anger. She was so fucking brave and so fucking stupid! But he'd been stupid, too, thinking sex could distract her. *What an asshole I am*, he thought, disgusted, throwing the towel on the floor and pulling on his shorts. He went to the kitchen and poured a cup of coffee, took one sip, and threw the rest in the sink. If the department wouldn't back him up, he'd just have to go do it himself.

MAGGIE took inventory of her own condition after leaving Devlin; she regretted the way they'd parted, but there wasn't any way to change that. She felt depleted on every level. By sorrow, by fear, even by love. By more emotions than she could catalog, never mind control. And, she was dog-tired; not in shape for the kind of fight that was ahead. She'd have to ask for help.

She stood on the street corner, trying to breathe in enough oxygen to feel restored, but her breathing was constricted; she couldn't pull the breath down to her *dan tien*, as she'd been taught by Mr. Wong to do in times of great stress. And her eyesight was slightly blurry. A sure sign she'd drained her liver meridian with that burst of anger.

Sifu would know what to do, she thought, as she hurried in the direction of the apartment building where he lived. He wouldn't let her collapse at the starting gate.

Mr. Wong let her into his home with a small pleasant smile on his face; his expression did not in the least betray the fact that he'd read the severity of her depletion, the moment he opened the door. Voice, face, body language, skin color—every nuance of her being spoke to him eloquently of her condition. He had known since the beginning that this moment would come.

He had cast her horoscope, when she'd first applied to him as a teacher, so he'd known from the start that she would be tested in the Great Crucible of the Gods. Destiny had sent her to him for instruction, so he had accepted the challenge of preparing her for a battle she did not yet know she would fight.

Her combat skills were minimal, as was the case with all who had not trained from childhood on—five years training with him, and one before him, was barely time to learn the magnitude of what was yet to be learned. But Destiny had decided the timetable, not Master Wong, so he accepted the added challenge without acrimony. She had courage and endurance. Her spirit was old in the ways of combat; if her mind no longer remembered, her body would, when threatened with annihilation.

"I must face a great battle, Sifu," she said, too tired for lengthy explanations, and knowing he did not require them. "I've come to ask your help."

"It is difficult to ride the tiger, is it not?" he replied,

with a gentle inflection she had seldom heard in his voice.

He nodded. This was to be expected. He gestured to the small couch on which he treated those privileged few who understood his mastery of traditional Chinese medicine. *"Those who can kill must learn to heal,"* his own Master had told him, a lifetime ago. *"It is a matter of balance."*

He touched his fingers to her wrists with absolute concentration. The pulses beneath his knowing fingers told a complex, intelligent tale.

"Many channels are shut down," he said simply. "A strategy must be devised to restore the spirit, as well as the body."

"I need to understand what you'll do, Sifu," she answered him.

"Fear has depleted the kidneys," he said quietly. "Grief has attacked the lungs. Anger has drained the Liver channel. Gall Bladder and Small Intestine have been besieged by too many decisions, none with clear answers.

"The kidneys are the power source, Maggie. They must feed the whole. They have been ravaged by too many demands. The spirit has left, because the body cannot hold it.

"We must coax the physical, mental, and emotional energies back into the body, with great care. Only after that, can we coax the Spirit back."

He named the points for her as he needled them. *"Taichong, the Great Surge point . . . Hegu, the Union Valley.* The names were so poetic, more philosophic than medical. *Shen Men, the Spirit Gate, Bai Hui, the Hundred Convergences, Shen Ting, the Spirit Court . . .*

"If the body is too weakened, Maggie," he explained patiently, "the Spirit cannot remain there. Body and Spirit are magnetic forces, capable of attracting their polar complements—only once the body is able to hold it, can the Spirit return."

He stepped back to observe the changes in Maggie's condition. She knew he could see patterns of energy that were invisible to her, as could all Kung Fu Masters.

"More Yang energy is needed, Maggie," he said thoughtfully. "To do battle, the Yang must be very powerful.

"Your lifeforce must be empowered with energy of a specific warrior nature, that can survive great hardship. There is an ancient technique that can infuse such warrior energy, for a time. It is called *Fa Gong*. It is not done with needles." He paused, deciding how to explain.

"To do this I must extend the energy from my soul into the Universe, to grasp the *nature* of the ultimate fighting energy you require," he said, as if this were an ordinary task. "Then, I must transmit this warrior force directly into your body. I will do so by placing my hands above the Upper and Lower Sea of Qi. You know these centers well from your martial arts training." He didn't wait for her permission; he had offered a rare gift, knowing it would not be refused.

Maggie saw the small, powerful man ground himself, willing his sturdy body to connect solidly to the earth. She saw him extend his hands upward, to receive energy from the Universe, as if he were an antenna tuned to an invisible power source. As he lowered his hands to her abdomen and chest, Maggie felt the magnetic force surge through her, pulsating, energizing, strengthening . . . her body, her spirit, her resolve.

Maggie saw the Master smile, satisfied with his work.

She rose from the couch minutes later, wondering at her own renewed vigor. "How can I thank you, Sifu?" she asked. "I'm more grateful than I can say."

"Remember all I have taught you, Maggie. You do not go unarmed to this battle. Sun Tzu has said, 'If you know the enemy and you know yourself, you need not fear the result of a hundred battles! If you know yourself, but not the enemy, for every victory gained, you will also suffer a defeat. If you know neither the enemy nor yourself, you will succumb in every battle!'

"You have the spirit of a warrior, Maggie. In the end, this is more important than what skills you possess. 'In battle,' says Sun Tzu, 'a courageous spirit is everything. The value of a whole army is dependent on one man alone: such is the influence of spirit!'

"I have done my part . . . you will do yours. The outcome lies with the Gods. Whatever happens, is as it should be."

She looked at the kindly old man who had changed her life in so many extraordinary ways, and wondered if she would ever see him again.

"Thank you for being my friend, Sifu," she said, with emotion. She wanted to hug him, but she felt he might be offended; few dared even to shake his hand.

"Friendship, too, lies with the Gods," he murmured. Then in an unexpected gesture, he opened his arms to her and she stood a long moment in his embrace, feeling the power of his strength and wisdom, and wondering if he might have read her mind.

# CHAPTER 79

"I got us a witness, Lieutenant." Gino's grin reached both ears. "An honest-to-God witness."

"Witness to what?"

"To Eric Vannier, Esquire, that very elegant, blue-blooded fuck, officiating at a ritual sacrifice where a young lady was cut into dogmeat."

Devlin laid down the papers he'd been holding and paid strict attention . . . "How the hell did you pull that off?"

Garibaldi perched on the edge of Devlin's desk, one leg on the floor and smirked. "I went out to Greenwich to see Vannier, and while I was interviewing His Highness, where I have had more productive discourses with fence posts, one of the bodyguards looked a little familiar to me.

"So when that high-falutin scumbag pissed me off so much I could hardly stay on the road, I got to thinking, maybe I could place the guy.

"And sure enough, he turned out to be an alumnus of one of our finer institutions of correction. So, I dug a little deeper and found out that if he gets busted one more time, he goes back in the slammer forever . . . so, I had a little chat with him about the possibilities of rolling over on his boss, who it turns out, he didn't like all that much anyway . . ." Gino's smile was replete with satisfaction.

"Fantastic," Devlin said, meaning it. "The stars must be in the right place today, Gino. Jake, the Michelangelo of Tattoos, called to say he'd been summoned to the presence, for a little more artistry—seven, to be exact. And he heard them talking about some big ceremony to take place on April 30th, so it looks like Ellie was right on the money."

"To say nothing of having the best-looking tits it has ever been my privilege to see."

"You noticed."

"Stevie Wonder would have noticed."

Devlin grinned. "Things are looking up, Gino. Maybe we can pull this one out after all."

"It couldn't hurt to hope, Lieutenant."

"I'm going to run the drug angle by a friend on the narcotics task force and see if I can scare up some diversionary artillery for their shindig, and I think I might have a lead on the baby-breeding farm in Nyack. Then it's time to lay this on the Captain one more time."

"Sounds good," Gino replied, already moving toward the door. "I got a source who says he can give me the names of some uptown guys who frequent the Loopy Jupiter. I'm gonna see if that dredges anything out of the sludge."

"I'VE got the local tie-in you wanted on the O'Connor case, Captain," Devlin said as O'Shaunessy put down the telephone and turned his well-jowled face in his direction. "And a helluva lot more that begins to make this all make sense—"

"I thought I asked you for the material from that reporter, Lieutenant," O'Shaunessy interrupted, none too benevolently.

"I no longer have access to that file, Captain," Devlin said evenly. "It's been removed by the family from the vault." He didn't like lying to the Captain, but the switched videotape had made him warier than usual.

"What's the local angle?" O'Shaunessy asked, riveting his hard eyes on Devlin, as he listened to everything he had to say.

"You appear to have lost your way with this case, Lieutenant," he said inexplicably, when Devlin had finished. "I wouldn't like to think your judgment's been clouded by personal entanglements." He let the thought dangle.

"The child lives in Connecticut, that's not our jurisdiction. The only papers that might have relevancy, you can't seem to produce." He sat back in his chair, barrel chest expanding in displeasure like a pouter pigeon's. "This is a matter of no further interest to this precinct, Lieutenant. Do I make myself clear?"

"Very clear, sir," Devlin said wonderingly; there was obviously no room for negotiation. He stood up and headed for the door. As he reached the door the Captain spoke again.

"You're a good cop, Devlin," he said. "Because of that, I'll read those papers when you get them to me. Which, I'll expect to be no later than tonight. And that's an order. Is that understood?"

Devlin nodded, and left.

He was glad Mother Immaculata had grasped the urgency of his request to hide the Fellowes report somewhere far from Chase Manhattan Bank.

"You think the Captain could be one of them?" Gino asked after Devlin had relayed the story of his meeting with O'Shaunessy. They were on the street outside the precinct house.

Devlin shook his head no. "That seems pretty farfetched to me, Gino . . . but something's seriously out of whack here. Maybe it's political pressure from higher up. Maybe somebody's told him to stay clear of this one."

"So why's he want the file?"

"Maybe he doesn't, and somebody else does."

"How safe is it where you've got it stashed?"

"That depends on how badly they want it." Devlin thought of anybody short of the Devil himself brooking the wrath of Immaculata Stevens and almost smiled.

"I've decided to crash the Sabbat, Gino. Maggie's convinced they'll kill the child, and I can't let that happen without at least trying to intervene. If I go, maybe she'll stay home."

Gino took that in and nodded. "What about a little backup, Lieutenant?"

"This is strictly on my own, Gino. One career on the line is plenty."

"Forget that crap, Lieutenant," Garibaldi said. "You can't go in there without help, so don't even bother to argue with me, just tell me what exactly will this Sabbat consist of? Do we have to bring our bat wings and eye of newt?"

"According to Ellie, it's a real blowout. Feasting, maybe an orgy. Then around midnight, the Materialization. Eleven forty-three to be exact . . . they need some kind of astrological conjunction that's exact, in order to do their mumbo jumbo."

"I've never been to an orgy," Garibaldi said with a grin. "Might be worth the trip if any of these witches look halfway decent."

"Since when did they have to look decent?" Devlin replied with a smirk. They'd reached Gino's car; he turned the key in the lock.

"Can I drop you someplace, Lieutenant?" he asked, as he got in.

"I'm headed over to Maggie's to try to mend a fence. You could drop me at the corner of St. Luke's."

"Sure thing."

THE answering machine light was blinking on Maggie's desk. Amanda had called. She sounded urgent. Maggie dialed the number automatically.

"I think I know something you should know, darlin'," Amanda said. "There's going to be a major wing-ding on April 30th, at of all places, the Vannier mansion. A costume party, Maggie, with a very chichi guest list, a 'teddibly uppah' bunch of horse thieves all decked out for a May Day celebration, if you don't mind. My daddy used to say 'it ain't a trend till you see it twice,' and I've taken down six names from the bunch you told me about who are due to attend this high-class hoedown.

"It's all very hush-hush because they don't want the press to gate-crash, so it's being spoken of *sotto voce* by the social set . . . but it is being spoken of with considerable envy. This is top-drawer, darlin' . . . the 'A' list in spades."

God bless Amanda's connections, Maggie thought as she hung up the phone. Maybe the fact that it was a costume party would mean something to Ellie. There was also a message from Devlin. It said simply, "Please take care of yourself, Maggie. I don't want to have to live without you."

"COSTUME party, hmmm?" Ellie mused, when Maggie told her Amanda's findings. "Of course! It's a *Grand*

*Sabbat.* They'll probably each choose a Nom du Diable and take on the persona of some practitioner of the Black Arts in history. That's how they do it in Europe, Mags. I'll bet anything that's the plan.''

"Would they wear masks?" Maggie asked anxiously. "If so, it would make it a lot easier for me to get in there unnoticed.''

Ellie frowned. "Maybe masked, maybe not. The best bet is to find a getup for you that fits in with their theme, but still gives you maximum mobility. No long gowns or tight skirts that's for sure.''

"Wasn't there a cat burglar witch somewhere in history?" Maggie asked hopefully.

"Not exactly . . . but there were plenty of cats. Maybe you could go as the Goddess Bast. She had the body of a cat and the head of a lioness. You could wear a doctored-up leotard and make up your face like they do for the cast of *Cats.* That would make you pretty hard to spot.''

"Was Bast evil enough to pass muster?"

"Not particularly, but she does get named in the litany of a lot of magic spells, White or Black, so she'd do for the Sabbat. Remember, the Gods and Goddesses could do whatever they damn well pleased, good or bad . . . so I don't think anyone would quibble about Bast's curriculum vitae. Especially at a Grand Sabbat, where there's bound to be so much revelry going on—drinking, drugs, sex of every conceivable kind—more than enough to keep them busy. As a matter of fact, the fewer clothes you wear, the better they'll like it.

"I'll go as Tanith, the Carthaginian Moon Goddess," Ellie added, "that way I won't have to wear anything much, and maybe the bod will distract them from looking at our faces.''

"Wait a minute, Ellie," Maggie said adamantly. "I can't let you go with me. This is *my* fight.''

"Mine, too, Mags. You were sent to me for a purpose, so we're in this together, now. And, I may have to run verbal interference for you at the Sabbat—I know the jargon and you don't. Besides, nobody should have to walk into Hell alone."

What fool had spread the story that women were bitchy toward each other? Maggie wondered on the way home. The truth was, women friends were the ones who helped you with life. The honest evaluators who told you when you were full of shit and then held your hand in the hard times, and always came through in the clinches.

She hoped that with all her heart Ellie wouldn't pay for her friendship with her life.

# CHAPTER 80

Harry Fisk glanced right, left, and behind, as he spoke. Even when not doing that, it was easy to see the hair-trigger alertness with which he scanned the road ahead of him. He had chosen this place, far from the city, but he'd been in this game long enough to know that no place was safe, if you were a marked man. For today, he didn't think he fell into that category, but the habit of caution is not one you practice part-time.

Devlin walked beside him, hands plunged in his pockets. Harry hadn't called for a 6:00 A.M. meet in the woods, if there weren't dangerous topics to be discussed.

"Here's how it lays out," Fisk said, without the usual pleasantries. "Both your guys are protected by every intelligence service on the planet. They do big favors for all the big boys, and they're so fucking high up Washington's ass, you'd need a proctoscope to find them."

"So, you're telling me nobody'll care that they're eating kids for dinner, never mind the rest of the shit that's going down with these people?"

"I'm saying nobody'll care if they make kids into hors d'oeuvres for a White House lawn party, provided they're discreet about it, and nobody knows it's happening. And, provided Vannier and Sayles keep doing what they're doing for everybody's black ops. Hell, everybody's got some dark secret, is the way the rationalization goes—so what's a little Black Magic among friends?"

Devlin stopped walking. "I fucking well do not believe that *anybody* has that kind of underground power in this country, Harry."

"Grow up, Malachy!" Fisk said relentlessly. "Kennedy didn't kill himself, you know. And nobody's paid for that one, last time I looked."

Devlin took a deep breath and tried to handle his own anger. "What about the drug traffic? What about getting the DEA to raid the Sabbat?"

"And what'll they find? A bunch of naked rich guys smoking joints and snorting blow. Very embarrassing. For ten minutes, until the fix goes in, and a lot of important people make phone calls, and suddenly the story doesn't hit the papers 'in the interests of national security' and the police chief in the jurisdiction is told that 'other matters should be considered far more pressing on his attention.' And, maybe anybody who makes waves is told he'll be considered a traitor to his country, if he tells what he knows. Like all those doctors at Dallas Memorial Hospital who were so fucking intimidated by the Feds they're still scared shitless thirty years later." Harry kicked a rock out of the way.

"Whose money do you think is keeping the banks in business, these days, Malachy? It's *drug money* that's keeping the banks afloat—yank it and half the banks in America go down the tubes. Do you honestly think we couldn't keep drugs out of this country, if we really wanted to? Get a *grip!* Every Friday, suitcases of money go to senators and judges and police chiefs all over this great land of ours, just to make sure that doesn't happen."

Devlin needed to vent his fury, somewhere. "So what the fuck are you telling me, Harry? That we should lie down and play dead because you can't fight City Hall? And maybe we should stop chasing the bad guys because there's more of them than there are of us? Where exactly does that leave guys like you and me, Harry? With our thumbs up our asses?"

"With our fingers in the dike, Malachy, that's where. We hold back the tide where we can. Seal up the little cracks, so we can sleep nights, thinking we've done a good deed in a dirty world. And that's okay by me. If I fucking well get myself killed because I try to do the undoable, then all those little cracks I could have stuck my finger in, finally bring the dam down. You know the drill as well as I do, Malachy. You do what you can do, when you can do it—and you don't go off half cocked on a crusade that'll put your nuts in a vise, because then you're no good to anybody.

"You cannot bring these people down, Devlin," Harry said, evenly, "not in this lifetime. Their name is Legion, kid, just like it says in the Bible. So you gotta do what you can do, to keep the scorecard a little more even, and you gotta try to stay alive to fight another day."

"You know, Harry, that's such a self-serving crock of shit. Because where does it end?"

"That's just the way the rat race works, Malachy."

"Yeah. Well that's just fine if you want to be a rat, Harry, but it's not good enough if you give a damn.

"You know, I keep thinking, I had this ethics professor in college who used to say, 'I have this simple rule: Would Superman do it? Because everything he stands for makes the world a better place.' He wasn't so far off the mark, Harry."

Harry Fisk snorted sardonic laughter. "You are one crazy son of a bitch, Devlin, you know that? If you think you can play Superman, you better have a phone booth handy to duck into, because in the real world heros get shot first."

Devlin stopped walking and turned to face his friend. "There's this play called *All My Sons*, Harry," he said, deadly serious. "And in it, this father's been doing a lot of bad things and his kid is losing respect for him, so the father says to his boy, 'Son, I'm no worse than anyone else.' And the kid looks up at him and says, 'I know, Dad. But I thought you were better.' I remember you before you were a cynic, Harry. And, I'm asking you one last time . . . are you telling me there is not one fucking thing you can do for me on this one?"

Harry Fisk stood staring at Devlin for a long while before he spoke again. "There's a guy named Rafi Abraham," he said, finally, his voice charged with some emotion that hadn't been there before. "I'm pretty sure he's heading the Mossad team that's looking into this. He owes me, and he's a pretty good guy by the peculiar standards of my trade. I'll try to make sure his boys don't take you out, in the course of doing their job." He looked past Devlin to scan the road again.

"The Egyptian team is headed by a Colonel Hamid. He's a mean son of a bitch, and he doesn't like me any better than I like him, but he's not as smart as Abraham, so I'd put my money on Rafi to keep Hamid neutralized." He paused, then added, "That's all I got right now, but I'll keep my ear to the ground. Just like Jimmy Olson. Okay?"

"I owe you, Harry," Devlin said, without smiling.

"Damned straight, you do. And you can't do me any favors dead, so watch your idealistic Irish ass, will you, kid?"

The two men parted, and each drove back to the city by separate routes.

# CHAPTER 81

Maria Aparecida knocked diffidently on the door to the library, where Maggie was trying to meditate.

"Dona Maggie," she said, "the priest. He says he must see you."

Maggie looked up, startled; she had not seen or spoken to Peter since the night, a week ago . . .

"The cow has gone to the swamp," Maria said sonorously, "but a good man is still a good man."

*The cow has gone to the swamp.* The Brazilian proverb for "it's all over now." Maggie smiled wryly. Maria always knew everything that happened in the house, even when she wasn't there, by some servant osmosis.

"Please ask him to come in, Maria," she said, wondering how on earth to breach the embarrassment they each felt over their last encounter. She heard the familiar footfall on the stairs, and she wished fleetingly that she were in any room but this one.

Peter stood in the doorway, as if unwilling to cross the threshold. His face was careworn, dark circles framed his eyes, and his shoulders seemed heavily laden.

"I didn't have the courage to call you, Peter," she said, meeting his eyes. "Because I didn't know what to say."

"Maggie dear," he began . . . She could feel the love and the terrible tension in his voice. "Please say nothing until you've heard me out. I have so very much to say to you, and no idea if I shall have the courage to say half of it." He took a profound breath and entered the room. She saw him glance at his favorite chair, and

515

make a conscious decision not to sit in it. He would stand, it seemed.

"I can only pray, Maggie, that at the end of it, you will understand what I *mean* to tell you—if my words are hopelessly inadequate, you must listen with your heart."

She nodded and waited.

"When we met, Maggie, I was already in crisis—a crisis I never had the courage to explain to you . . . or perhaps, I just didn't know how. Now, I realize I must try to make you understand . . . or you will never know what's in my heart." He took another deep, pained breath and continued.

"The basic model for any priest is Christ, Maggie . . . that is the impossible benchmark he strives for. And he sees the institution of the Church as the larger expression of Christ's presence on earth. It's the Church that validates him throughout his ministry . . . the Church that provides the body of knowledge he draws upon, and the body of grace he taps into, for sustenance.

"We were taught that the Church is the *Mother*, Maggie, the eternal female nurturer, who succors or chastises, as needed . . . but of whose love he can always be assured."

Peter was moving now, not so much pacing, as moving restlessly from place to place, the momentum of memory carrying him. "When the crisis came for me, and my conscience led me into strange byways . . . I had big questions about just how nurturing that mother really was. 'Even when they're wrong, they're right,' you're taught in seminary . . . the Church may be wrong one season and right the next, so you'd better be there for the next season, for that is the ultimate act of faith. But I had been set adrift by my own hand, and could no longer make that act of faith.

"Am I following Christ by following my conscience, or am I merely being proud and inflexible in defying my superiors? Was I surrendering, or defying, in writing

*The Long Road from Calvary*? Was I on that famous road to Hell that's paved with good intentions? Or was I battling my way, against the disillusioning odds, to Heaven? I was going insane. And I was all alone." He paused significantly, visibly shaken. "It was in that fearsome aloneness that I floundered, when first you came to me, Maggie."

"Surely you're not telling me, Peter, that I was a momentary port in an ecclesiastical storm," she said icily. "That's demeaning and cruel."

Shock registered, and he stopped short in his pacing. "Dear God, no!" he blurted. "What I'm saying is that you were sent from Heaven, Maggie. Don't you see— I've thought all along that I was saving you, but it was you who was saving *me!*

"Your faith is absolutely pure. It does not spring from theology, or dialectics or two thousand years of Roman spiritual power. It springs from love of God! The essential female, Maggie! . . . the ultimate in every religion is the essential strength of the female. Every priest knows that, but we forget! You live in faith so unselfconsciously, Maggie . . . that's what you showed me! For all my intellectual convolutions—my chess game of Good and Evil, my Hamlet-like soul search that had entangled me in wheels within wheels, was useless. I was dying because I was trapped in a paradox. But you were not trapped!

"Oh, Maggie, my Maggie, don't you see? In essence, you said to me, 'Damnit, stop talking and do *something!* Let go of the paradox and save this child. This is not a debate, it's a life and death struggle to save Cody. Get moving! That alone is the ultimate act of faith.' You shocked me into understanding.

"You are not simple, Maggie, but your faith is. 'If I can live with my own conscience,' you said to me, in a thousand different ways, 'and do the best I can for everyone around me, I'm on God's side. I try to be a decent person, and to do good in the world, in small or large things. I try not to harm anyone, and to always love God. That's the best I can do, and I take full responsibility for doing it. But I cannot get lost in this bog of theology. I cannot let the Church do the thinking for me, because that's not what God wants of me. I don't care if this is intellectual pride, or that I am flying in the face of this two-thousand-year-old body of thinkers. I know right from wrong, and it's *right* to save this child, even if I die to do it.' That's what you said, in words and in deeds." He looked into her eyes, and she could see his soul so clearly in the gray depths of his own.

"You made me come to terms with life on *life's terms*, Maggie. Not *my* terms. And suddenly, I remembered . . . that Christ reveals *humanity*, not just divinity—and He bonds the two without compromising either. That's one of the great mysteries of faith . . . and that's what I saw in you.

"You have been the guardian of my *process*, not just Cody's. You were the compassionate witness and the catalyst.

"*Kairos!* Maggie. A moment in time when meaning comes at you from the *future*. When you must decide if you are up to accepting the risk of the unknown . . . of accepting the challenge of that which was *never* part of your agenda.

"Without you, Maggie, I could not have said *yes* to this kairos. I could not have said Let it be *now*, for me, Lord.

"In Christ's life there were women who moved the divine plan along when the men were screwed up, or in despair, or trying to cover their own asses . . . I don't know why it's so hard for us to remember that women have capabilities far different, and often far greater, than our own."

Maggie looked at him, suddenly understanding so many things. "You're in love with the God who called you, Peter," she said softly. "If I've helped you find your way back to Him, I'm gladder than you could possibly know."

"How could I not love you, Maggie?" Peter said so plaintively, it brought tears to her eyes. "You gave me back my priesthood . . . and myself."

She saw him struggle with his emotions. He lowered his head, and with a fathomless sigh, he said, "And in return, I asked of you, what you weren't prepared to give." She started to protest, but he silenced her with a gesture full of pain.

"I know now, Maggie, that you are not *in love* with me . . . not in *this* lifetime. Nor I with you. I also know that we do *love* each other, in very substantial ways. We are part of each other's spiritual unfoldment, that seems clear. And there are inexplicable threads from the past that seem to entangle us, confuse us . . .

"But this one thing bears no confusion. I'm your *friend*, Maggie. And you are mine. So, I ask you to let me help you, now. I am called to this battle, as surely as you and Cody are—and I need to fight it at your side."

Peter took a pained breath and then said, with great solemnity, "As for our 'other lifetime,' Maggie . . . who knows how God chooses to let us wend our way home? I only know I hope with all my heart, that *somewhere* in time we have been free to love each other."

He had come to a stop in front of Maggie's chair. She let her eyes search his. *Who are you to me?* they sought to know. *What lessons have there been that only you could teach me? To God you must be prepared to give everything and expect nothing.* Someone had said that . . . someone who knew.

She was seeing in a strangely detached perspective now . . . as if her world had focused in on Cody, and tomorrow night—and everything else had faded at the edges, like an old photograph. She thought it meant she was going to die.

"I believe we're caught up in a mystery far larger than ourselves," she answered him, taking care to find the right words. "Perhaps it's foolish arrogance on our part to imagine we could ever have comprehended what was expected of us, or why.

"You're my dear friend, Peter, and it seems you always have been. Whatever the battle that's in store for us, I'd be very grateful to have you share it with me."

She saw only goodness and generosity of spirit, in his eyes, and she was glad she had loved him, for however short or long a time, and for whatever reasons far beyond her understanding. What was left now, was to make things right between them.

"I have a favor to ask of you," she said, her voice low and calm.

"Anything in my power," he replied.

She smiled and reached out to touch his hand, love in the gesture. "Will you hear my confession, Father?" she asked softly.

Shocked by the request, Peter stood immobile for a long, irresolute moment, then he bent his knee beside her chair. He thought, as he listened to the unburdening of her heart on the eve of possible death, that it was a very uncertain question as to who should be granting absolution to whom.

PETER opened the book to Paul's Epistle to the Ephesians, Chapter 6, verses 12–13. Some of the words had been collecting unbidden in his consciousness, ever since leaving Maggie's house, and he needed to remember the rest.

> For we wrestle not against flesh and blood, but against Principalities, against Powers, against the Rulers of Darkness in this world, against spiritual wickedness in high places.
> Wherefore take unto you the whole armour of God, that ye may be able to withstand the evil day, and having done all, to stand.

It had come to that now, he knew; the moment to take a stand. This was the best way, the only way.

Ellie's words were somewhere in his head. "If a sacrifice has been promised to a deity," she'd reminded him, "a sacrifice must be made. That is Universal law, far older than Christianity."

Father Peter took the consecrated Host and sealed it in the case he carried when giving the Last Rites. If there was one substance on the face of the earth that had power against even the most potent Evil, it was the Blessed Sacrament. "With it you could walk unafraid into Hell, itself," his favorite theology professor had said in his student days. Peter smiled at the thought of the man . . . what would he think if he knew his words would soon be put to the acid test?

He had fasted since leaving Maggie, and was feeling a little light-headed—or perhaps it was the long hours he'd spent on his knees, that had made him unsteady. Or, the magnitude of what he intended to do.

He forced his mind to stillness, that he might take inventory of what lay ahead, and what tools he had to fight with.

Peter checked his pocket for the small leather-bound copy of the *Roman Ritual of Exorcism*. He knew most of it by heart, but the book comforted him.

Peter reverently kissed the purple stole of office, and placed it in his pocket, along with the vials of Holy Water and bottles of Holy Oil. The Chrism used at baptism was already tucked away; just in case they'd dared to rebaptize the child to Satan, he would retrieve her to the Faith of Christ.

He blessed himself and knelt at the prie-dieu, facing the large simple crucifix his mother had given him at ordination.

There would be a sacrifice made at the Walpurgisnacht Festival tonight, without question. But Peter didn't intend to let Cody or Maggie be the sacred offering.

MAGGIE knelt before the altar in the empty church, praying fervently for courage. She felt curiously at peace, for the first time since this madness had begun. Fear this profound forces you to root out the dross in your soul, to find out once and for all who you really are . . . she had done that, now. She wondered if this was how the early Christians felt on their way to the lions.

A lifetime had been lived in three months' time. *I am not the Maggie of "before." Who am I now?*

She stared hard at the statue of the Blessed Mother, trying to know her, as she really was . . . Queen of the Universe, like Isis, not the namby-pamby Virgin of her Catholic school childhood, bloodless and sexless and milk-white in her purity. But the *real* Mary, as she must have been. Strong, vital, *decisive*. Courageous beyond human measure. Capable of giving birth in a stable . . . of raising a boy who would change the world more than any king or army . . . and of standing at the foot of a cross to watch her child die in agony. Stronger and more fearless than the burly men friends who fled Him, at the last.

Was she Isis, too? she wondered, as she stared at the statue crowned with stars. Eternal Mother, Queen of Heaven. Did she simply wear different names and raiment in different epochs, yet still embody all that was the Universal female principle?

*If you exist, Dear Mother, anywhere in the cosmos . . . please hear my prayer!*

She was glad that the time had come for action. Glad that she could finally fight back. Maybe it was appropriate, somehow . . . maybe fighting for a child in peril was what women had been doing since the beginning of time.

Maggie stood up and blessed herself, then left the church.

RAPHAEL Abraham picked up the telephone with the private number; the voice on the other end was the Rebbe's.

"You will come to get me, *now*, Rafi," the old man said very clearly. "The time has come for us to do our work."

"What work is that, Rebbe?"

"Do not ask foolish questions, my boy," the Rebbe replied. "Just do as I say." A dial tone followed the interchange.

Abraham cursed silently beneath his breath. A second change of plans in one night was *two* too many.

Abraham checked the Desert Eagle he carried under his arm and headed resolutely for the door.

# CHAPTER 82

Devlin slipped the 9mm Glock into its holster, and dropped extra magazines into his pocket. There would be no assistance coming from headquarters on this one, and he had no illusions about Eric's willingness to resort to deadly force, so the seventeen rounds the Glock carried was a better bet than any revolver. Who could tell what kind of mercenary army Vannier might have in attendance. He and Garibaldi would be all the cavalry Maggie could count on.

The doorbell rang, just as he was about to open it to leave. Surprised, Devlin peered through the peephole to see two uniformed officers in the hall outside his door.

Nash and Schmidt, from the precinct; he didn't know either well, but he did know them.

"Message from Garibaldi, Lieutenant," Nash announced. "Says it's urgent." Devlin flipped back the lock, and the door burst in against him; both burly bodies behind it had weapons in their hands.

"Get his piece!" Nash ordered and Schmidt snapped the Glock out of its holster. "What else are you carrying, Lieutenant?" he asked, patting Devlin down to find the backup.

"What the fuck is this about?" Devlin spat.

"The Captain didn't want you getting into trouble tonight, Lieutenant. He says you got yourself screwed up over some bimbo, and he don't want you sticking your nose in where it don't belong."

"Son of a *bitch!*" Devlin said, disgusted with himself for not being more careful after the Captain's weird behavior.

"You going to kill me, Nash?" Devlin asked. "Or do you think maybe I won't mention this tomorrow, and you can just forget it ever happened?"

Nash smiled. "It won't matter after tonight, Lieutenant. The Captain says it'll all be history by morning. Even if you shoot off your mouth, who'll care? Your word against ours."

"That'll never fly and you know it," Devlin replied, glancing at the clock on the opposite wall.

"Yeah, well then, who's to say you won't meet with some fatal accident in the line of duty?"

Schmidt pushed Devlin back roughly, into a kitchen chair, and cuffed his hands behind him. Fuming at his own stupidity, and wondering if Gino was in the same predicament, Devlin watched the minutes tick by with growing anxiety.

Just before ten, sounds of disturbance in the hall outside the apartment roused the two uniforms. Nash gestured to Schmidt to check it out.

Schmidt grunted his assent, drew his revolver and unlocked the door, then he moved stealthily into the hallway, and Nash locked the door behind him.

Minutes elapsed with no further sounds. And no sign of Schmidt.

Twelve minutes by the clock. Then, fifteen. Devlin watched Nash grow more and more uneasy. Finally, too agitated to sit still, Nash cracked the door open a slit and called his partner's name.

Four heavily armed men were suddenly storming past him. Nash's body crashed backward with bone-crushing finality, and Devlin knew the man was dead before he reached the floor.

He upended his own chair and hit the floor hard; because of the handcuffs there was no way to protect himself, but instinct sent him sprawling out of the path of the gunmen.

A stocky, dark-complected man entered the room on the heels of the commando team, closing the door softly behind him. He stood just inside the room taking mental inventory, obviously in command, obviously a pro.

"We are on the same side, Lieutenant Devlin," he said in a heavily accented Israeli voice. "My name is Abraham. If you would care to join us, we are all going to the same party." He gestured to one of his men to unlock the handcuffs and Devlin stood up, rubbing his wrists to restore circulation.

"A man named Fisk put in a word for you," Abraham said shortly. "In my line of work, we respect each other's markers. We mean no harm to the woman and child, Lieutenant, and the woman trusts you. That fact may be useful to us." As if to underscore his intent, Abraham handed Devlin back his gun. "You may be needing this," he said.

Devlin rechecked the semi-automatic and slipped it into its holster. "We have a body here, and another I imagine, in the hall," he said evenly.

"Housekeeping deals with debris," Abraham replied with authority. "We are on a tight schedule, Lieutenant. I suggest we get moving."

A van outside the building swallowed up the Israelis and Devlin and headed for I-95.

"If you are concerned for your friend Garibaldi," Abraham said shortly, "we have him. He'll be kept out of harm's way for the remainder of the night."

A CAR and a convoy of several dissimilar vans raced along the New England Thruway on their way to Greenwich. They had already stopped to collect the Rebbe. When Devlin entered the car, he introduced himself to the old man, wondering how he fit into this convoluted puzzle.

It disturbed Abraham's sense of order that circumstances had added two civilians to his retinue. The detective could presumably handle himself under fire. But the Rebbe . . . who could tell what the Rebbe might do?

"We must discuss what will happen here," the old man said quietly in Hebrew, as if he'd been monitoring Abraham's thoughts.

"Since *you* called *me*, may I assume you know something that I do not?" Abraham responded, a sardonic edge to his voice.

"It appears the child's soul is held hostage by certain malevolent spirits," the Rebbe replied, unperturbed by the tone. "You might think of them as *dybbuks*, for the moment. I must work to free her by means you will not understand. Other allies for the child will be summoned. I will not work alone." Abraham accepted the statement; there was no point arguing with this man until he must.

"And what of the Amulets?"

"Tell me," the Rebbe asked, focusing his eyes on Abraham, in the car's darkness. "Do you think mankind, as you know it, is sufficiently evolved to cope with such power as is said to be embodied by these Amulets?"

Abraham avoided the disturbing eyes and looked down at his hands for a moment. "It is not my job to speculate on such questions, Rebbe. I'm a soldier. I obey orders."

"Ah." the Rebbe responded. "Such an answer you would give me? Like a good German, perhaps? I asked you a question!"

Abraham cleared his throat, but his voice remained husky. He glanced at Devlin, but it was apparent the man couldn't understand their conversation.

"Men are fools," he said. "No one could have such power and remain uncorrupted by it."

"So." said the Rebbe. "You have been ordered to ask me to destroy the Sekhmet Stone, and return the Isis Amulet to Israel." Abraham started to demand how the Rebbe knew this fact, but the old man cut him off.

"Now, I will tell you why that *cannot* be. We must presume that God permits Evil to exist because it allows man to choose for himself which way his soul shall go. Without Evil, how would man gauge his own exercise of free will? Without Evil to combat, how could his progress on the path to God be measured?

"The Universe—this one, and others you know not of—are held in a delicate balance of God's own design. We cannot presume to do better than He. We cannot delete from these Worlds, that which He has put in them." His tone left Abraham little space for argument.

"If you won't destroy the evil Amulet, Rebbe," he said, hedging, "I will take them both back to Israel with me. That will maintain the balance."

"Ah." said the Rebbe. "Let us consider this suggestion. Presumably, if the Amulets exist at all, they belong to the Isis Messenger. Will you steal them from her, to obey your orders? Will you kill the child and the grandmother, to possess them, perhaps? Or will you merely imprison them, to ensure the workings of the magical toys? And after you have secured these treasures, will you then hand them over to men in a government, and expect that government to adjudicate their use? I ask you, Rafi, the consequences of such an act.

Would that government, then, remain in power forever? Would Israel then use these Amulets to destroy her Arab neighbors, simply because she would now have the means? If so, what else might she destroy? Would you, Raphael Abraham, trust them to choose wisely, if the power formerly reserved to God was suddenly in the hands of the Knesset? And, if Israel no longer needed to fear for its existence, tell me this? Do you think its character would remain the same, in strength and courage and fortitude, or would it, perhaps, soften and deteriorate?''

Abraham, deeply troubled answered, "I do not know these answers, Rebbe.''

"You do not know these answers?'' The Rebbe exuded patriarchal power, when he asked, "Do you know *anyone* who knows these answers?''

"I have no response for such profound questions, Rebbe,'' Abraham replied, holding tight to the only thing he did know with certainty. "But I have been given a job to do. If it is in my power to do this job, I must do it. This is who I am. This is *what* I am.''

"Are you so certain, Rafi?'' the Rebbe added, fixing him with a stare that might even have incorporated a touch of compassion. "A man is what he is . . . *not what he has been.*''

Then he turned his attention to the road ahead. "We must hurry,'' he said commandingly. "Time becomes an issue here.''

With that he closed his eyes and remained lost in thought or prayer for the rest of the journey.

# CHAPTER 83

The lioness headdress from Brooke's costumers was more comfortable than Maggie had expected. The salesmen had handed her an instruction sheet for creating a lion face with theatrical makeup, and it proved surprisingly easy to conceal her features, without a mask. The costume itself consisted of a black leotard and a body-hugging, tabby-striped fur vest; black jazz shoes with painted-on paws completed the outfit. They were flat-heeled and good for both comfort and mobility.

Ellie's exotic regalia included a straight black Cleopatra wig, and plenty of upswept kohl around her eyes for camouflage; much of the rest of her was bare. Maggie glanced at her friend, certain that none at the Sabbat would even bother to look at Ellie's face.

The two women drove to Greenwich and parked their car at the home of Amanda's friends, the Randolphs, who were currently in Scottsdale. A groundskeeper led them to the boathouse, and gave them their pick of the rowboats and dinghies that sat like pilot fish around the large catamaran anchored there.

"Can you imagine what he's going to tell his wife tonight about the two dingbats in the dinghy," Ellie chuckled, as they settled into the small boat. Ellie rowed, and Maggie coached her on the floor plan of the Vannier house, one last time.

"There's a story I want you to hear, Mags," Ellie said, "before we hit the beach."

Maggie looked at her questioningly.

"The major male Deities of the Eastern Pantheon—Brahma, Shiva, Vishnu, and the like—left their village one day to go off into the mountains and do their thing, leaving Kali, Shakti, Lakshmi, and all the other female Deities alone to mind the kids and the village.

"The Demon saw their departure, and decided this was his great opportunity. He would conquer the female deities in short order, and the males would be so imbalanced, he could conquer them, too. So, he called up the demons from the Pit to overcome the women, who, he thought, would be a snap to defeat.

"All day the battle raged, and the women fought so valiantly to protect home and family—sometimes battling with children in their arms—that they held off the demons until nearly nightfall, when, in a last heroic moment, Durga, the Goddess of Battle, arrived back from her travels, riding her white tiger. With the help of her battle expertise, the demons were vanquished and thrown back into the Pit.

"Just about then, the male Gods arrived home, and saw the village in shambles, the women binding up wounds, and nursing the children's terrors.

" 'Did something happen here today?' Lord Brahma demanded, and Mother Kali stepped forward and said, 'Nothing we women couldn't handle, dear.' "

Maggie burst into laughter. "What a great story!"

Ellie shook her head. "Not just a story, Mags. A metaphysical allegory. It's been said that men must rely on ritual to defeat the Demon, but women are empowered by the Goddess to confront him face-to-face. You may need to remember that."

The light from the shore ahead began to grow larger and more defined. "The place is festooned like Versailles, before Le Déluge," Maggie said, peering over Ellie's shoulder at the house beyond the beach.

"So, where do we land?" Ellie asked, craning her neck to see behind her.

"Anyplace but near the dock, I guess. There's a stretch of beach, by the wooded end of the island. No decorations, or anything else that looks trafficked. I think we should try for there."

Ellie seemed remarkably calm and collected, Maggie thought, as she sat back and watched the land draw nearer. There was a taut, warrior energy about her friend tonight; strong, focused, and very spirited. Like Mr. Wong, before battle.

Maggie checked her own mind and body as they neared the shore. She'd made a new last will and testament, and put her affairs in order, as best she could; there wasn't much left undone she could think of, and that was freeing, somehow.

The small boat thudded and scrunched to a halt on the rough sand; Maggie and Ellie pulled it as far up the pebbly beach, toward the woods, as they could manage. Then, they hugged each other once for good luck, before scrambling up the embankment, and making their way through the wooded grove that skirted the large mansion.

The Vannier house was aglow with activity; lights were strung from tree to tree, and out along the elaborate balustrade. Hundreds of candles flickered in the breeze from the Long Island Sound, and elaborate floral decorations had transformed the early spring garden into the splendor of a bygone century.

Men and women in elaborate costumes wandered the grounds, entering and leaving the house at will. There appeared to be a hundred or more guests, and dozens of liveried servants scurrying back and forth, like ants in service to a demanding queen. Maggie spotted Ghania in animated conversation with a man in a cardinal's cummerbund, at the south end of the loggia.

"Look, Mags," Ellie whispered from the cover of trees at the edge of the garden. "That's Pope Honorius, the Anti-Christ! And over there—the plump one with the goatee—he's Dr. John Dee, Queen Elizabeth I's personal alchemist. I'd say we'd better hang out together until I identify a dozen or so of these costumes for you, just in case anybody wants to play Twenty Questions with you, after we split up."

"Twenty questions! I assure you, Ellie, I have no

intention of engaging any of these costumed creeps in conversation.''

"Look, Mags, part of the fun of dressing up like famous villains is to get other guests to identify you. It's a game they play. They've each chosen to emulate some diabolic creature they admire, tonight, so it flatters them when someone else guesses their identity.''

"Yuk!" Maggie replied eloquently and Ellie grinned.

"That tall distinguished-looking character with the opera cape . . . I'd peg him for Cagliostro. Of course, he could be Aleister Crowley, dressed up in his Cagliostro duds. No. I'll stick with my first impression. And, that woman in the black nun's habit—now, she could be any number of people . . . a sister from the Convent of Loudun, for instance, unless that's too plebeian for this crowd.'' She thought for a moment. "I've got it! She's the Abbess of the Convent of the Innocents, outside Paris, where five hundred babies were sacrificed, according to the tale. I can't recall her name at the moment.'' She looked to the right of the doorway. "That one, with the Marie Antoinette wig, is easy, Mags. She's Madame D'Urfé, the witch friend of Louis XV.''

Many of the revelers were masked, but others were quite distinguishable despite their costumes.

"My God, Ellie," Maggie said, as a new group moved into view. "Isn't that Dr. James Ambrose, the famous plastic surgeon, with Iscariot of the Apostle's Creed?''

The two women quickly catalogued a well-known anchorwoman, two senators, a half dozen film stars, and more industrialists than they could count.

"If all these heavy hitters are on Satan's payroll, Ellie," Maggie whispered, "even if there's no real magic involved, and it's only in their own sick minds that they've dedicated themselves to Evil—this is an incredibly potent force for destruction that's assembled here tonight.''

"Kind of makes you want to reconsider your stand on capital punishment, doesn't it?" Ellie sniffed. "But don't kid yourself, Mags. There's plenty of real magic afoot around here. My antenna is spinning from the forcefield their combined energies are producing."

*If Cody really is the Isis Messenger*, Maggie thought bleakly, *then before this night is over, the most powerful tool in the Universe could be in the hands of terrible men, and Cody could be lost forever.*

The two women moved out into the garden, and were relieved to see they could easily lose themselves among the costumed guests. The tall caped man they'd seen earlier engaged Ellie in conversation, giving Maggie a chance to slip away.

With her heart in her throat, Maggie-the-Cat-Goddess-Bast forced herself to walk at a normal pace through the throng of guests and servants on the patio, and on into the main house. She passed from room to room, smiling back pleasantly at those who smiled at her. The woman in the massive wig of an eighteenth-century French courtier caught Maggie's arm, just as she thought she'd cleared her way to the double-return stair, that led to the floor above.

"My dear," the woman gushed, "how droll of you to be another kitty on Sekhmet's home turf. Cats are notoriously territorial, you know. Aren't you afraid she won't want to share her litterbox?"

Maggie managed to find her voice, despite the terror constricting her throat. "Don't tell me," she said, with what she hoped was a diverting smile. "D'Urfé! Madame D'Urfé, right?"

The buxom little woman preened with pleasure at being recognized, and Maggie was able to escape.

Her heart was pounding so hard, she had to stand still a moment to center her breathing. *Calm, Maggie. You've got to stay calm.* She said the words over and over as she made her way toward the back stairs, hoping they'd be less populated.

"What are you doing back here?" a waiter called out to her, when she was halfway to the second floor; he stood at the foot of the pantry stair, frowning up at her.

"Shh!" she called back conspiratorially, putting her

finger to her lips. "There's a tomcat up there, waiting for me." She managed a slightly intoxicated wink, as she waved to him, and cleared the landing without further mishap.

PETER MESSENGUER drove by the Vannier estate once, before doubling back nearly a half mile, to the place he'd decided to leave his car.

He parked, and sat for a moment behind the wheel, collecting himself. Then, got out of the car and stretched his long limbs.

He slipped off his jacket and adjusted the hooded Dominican robe he'd borrowed from a friend—if anyone questioned his garb, he would call himself an Inquisitor. Peter adjusted his sandals, tied the cincture around his waist, and loaded the deep pockets of the borrowed habit with the tools he'd brought from home. *Holy Water, Holy Chrism, Blessed Sacrament* . . . he tucked the *Roman Ritual* inside the pocket of the slacks he wore under the robe, took inventory, then a deep breath, and started walking toward the Vannier estate. He was glad the strategy he'd worked out with Maggie and Ellie had split them all up, so there'd be a second team in place, if the women were discovered. He was glad, too, that it allowed him some moments of reflective solitude. Tonight, he felt he needed to be alone with God.

THE nursery wing was completely deserted, so Maggie was forced to do a systematic search of the house. *Fifty rooms, Jenna had said.* Her heart sank at the prospect of searching all of them. *Don't think of Jenna, now. You'll go crazy if you think of Jenna in this terrible place.*

The second and third floors yielded no sign of Cody; Maggie's anxiety was growing with every bedroom she checked to no avail. At least, there were fewer merry-makers on this floor, to distract her efforts. She was about to try a small door in an alcove, when she heard the sound of heavy footsteps behind it. Hastily, Maggie ducked into the nearest bedroom, leaving the door open a crack. She saw Ghania emerge from the alcove, smiling. Fearing to breathe, she stayed absolutely motionless as the Amah moved swiftly down the hallway, toward the main staircase, and descended to the floor below.

Her heart still hammering, Maggie doubled back and tried the door knob, gingerly. Inside, another stairway led upward, and she was surprised to see a sky full of stars above her head where the ceiling should have been.

An observatory! Of course. The perfect place to stash Cody on this star-crossed night. *Oh, please dear God,* she breathed as she tested the stair for creaks, *let her be up there! And don't let the entire coven be guarding her.*

Maggie climbed the stair, her heart in her throat; when she reached the top, she took a deep breath and peered over the edge of the landing. Cody lay on a leather couch, still as Sleeping Beauty on her bier. She was dressed in what looked like a miniature wedding gown. The exquisite white dress trailed a train of lace to the floor, clothing the child in ethereal splendor. Her pale blond hair was fanned out around her cherubic face, and there was a wreath of white flowers encircling her brow. She looked like she was lying in state.

Tears filled Maggie's eyes at the sight of her; Cody looked so frail, she was nearly see-through. She forced her thudding heart to quiet, and studied the woman, who sat beside the small captive in an armchair, studiously reading a book. Thank God the chair faced Cody, not the stairs.

Stealthy as a cat burglar, Maggie crept inch by inch toward Cody's guard. A single palm strike to the back of the head knocked the woman unconscious before she knew what had hit her; Maggie tied and gagged her, without a pang of conscience and turned to the child on the couch. Cody hadn't stirred a muscle.

Maggie picked up the beloved child, hugging her, kissing her sweet face, whispering to her urgently, but there was not the faintest flutter of response. Hastily, she pulled the wedding dress off Cody's comatose body. *Bride of what?* she wondered, glad not to know the answer. She couldn't be carried in that trailing dress, that was certain, but now there was nothing to clothe her in. Maggie slipped off the fur vest that was part of her costume, and wrapped it around the small body that looked so terrifyingly bloodless.

Trying to keep her wits about her, she examined the observatory windows for escape; the drop was precarious, and she'd have to carry Cody's weight. Her spirits flagged . . . to get this close and then have no way out was unthinkable. She'd have to get to the second floor and hide until there was a chance to steal down the servants' stair. Or, maybe the roof was flatter in another part of the house, and she could use that escape route. One thing was certain, she couldn't stay where she was.

Maggie tried to find a comfortable way to carry the sleeping child, but it was nearly impossible; Cody weighed thirty pounds, all deadweight. Doing the best she could with her burden, she made her way carefully down the observatory stair.

Anxiety escalating, she stole out of the stairwell and made her way toward the main staircase. She managed to reach the second floor without incident; once there, she ducked into an empty bedroom and laid Cody down on a chaise, grateful for the momentary respite. The child's weight was a serious problem.

Maggie glanced anxiously out the window, and saw that the roof below slanted downward at an impossible angle. *Damnation!* There would be no way out except through the guests or the kitchen help, either of which was hopeless.

Maggie touched the sleeping child's face, tenderly

brushing back a strand of golden hair. There was perspiration on the little brow, and her skin was clammy. *God damn these bastards to Hell for twice eternity, for whatever they'd done to her!* Maggie realized suddenly that she felt as much anger now, as she did fear. Maybe that was a good thing.

She kissed the soft pale cheek and lifted the child again into her arms . . . *"I'll do the best I can for you, sweetheart,"* she murmured resolutely. *"May God help us both."* Cody's head lolled on her shoulder, the small arms hung limp at her sides. Maggie crept out into the corridor, heading inexorably toward the stair.

If she could just get outside this horrible house and onto the grounds, the boat wasn't more than a hundred yards away.

GHANIA was talking to Senator Edmonds on the beach, when suddenly her head came up, and she began to sniff the air like a bloodhound on a scent.

The Messenger was being moved!

By all that was unholy! someone was trying to remove the child from the house.

She shouted to the guards to attend her, and hurried back toward the brightly lit mansion.

MAGGIE glanced down the back stairwell and saw a gaggle of servants at the bottom; one of them was a Vannier maid, who had seen her on two occasions and might recognize her. She ducked back, breathless, trying to decide what to do next. Every minute in that house brought them closer to 11:43.

Maggie made her way back to the central stair, and looked down trepidatiously; to her relief everyone seemed to have gathered in the garden or on the bench, and the room below was clear of guests. Clutching Cody, she started down the stairs, just as Ghania and two men entered the huge foyer from the opposite side of the house.

With no choices left, Maggie frantically cleared the bottom of the steps and made a desperate run through the French doors, sheltering Cody with her own body, as she sprinted across the lawn.

Ghania was shouting, people were running in all directions. A man lunged at Maggie, and she managed a fierce side kick to his ribs that sent him staggering, but there was another one, behind him. She couldn't fight with Cody in her arms, and she couldn't risk putting her down. Someone hit her from behind and she launched a lethal spinning back kick at him, that must have shattered his jaw. She found there was a bizarre calm that had engulfed her, and everything was happening in slow motion. There was no past or future . . . nothing but the moment and the battle and the child.

Maggie heard the sounds of broken bones, without knowing whose they were. Cody was lying on the ground at her feet, but she didn't remember putting her there. She crouched above her, on her feet and moving, and she was every woman, anywhere, who has ever fought for a child against the odds. There were people shouting all around her, and arms and legs moving, and blood spurting, and she was a warrior, waiting to die on her feet . . .

And then there was Peter. *Thank God!* In a Dominican's robe, grappling for something in his pocket.

"Stand back!" he was shouting, plucking the wafer from its silver case and thrusting it out before him. "This Host is sanctified!"

A horrified gasp escaped the crowd, and the blood mist cleared before Maggie's eyes, so she was back in ordinary time, panting, dripping blood and sweat, and still standing over Cody's body on the grass. She saw Ghania at the edge of the surrounding crowd, a thoughtful expression on the woman's hateful face, and maybe even a grudging admiration.

All motion seemed magically suspended; no one

moved toward them on the grass. With her last reserve of strength, Maggie picked up Cody, one last time; she and Peter began to back their way uneasily toward the water, as the circle of watchers parted like the Red Sea. This was too good; this was too *impossible . . . Where was Ellie?* They had nearly made it through the throng when a large man in the costume of a Renaissance cardinal broke from the crowd and lunged at Peter. To Maggie's astonishment, he plucked the Host from the priest's outstretched hand.

"A priest forever . . ." he hissed triumphantly, as he sent Peter sprawling, dumbfounded, to the ground. "Black or White, Father Messenguer, this wafer cannot hold a priest at bay—and a priest I most certainly am. You knew of course that we would have one in attendance for our little ceremony tonight? Permit me to introduce myself. I am Father Dominic Duchesne, currently defrocked by the quaint standards of this archdiocese, but in the eyes of the Assessors of men's vows, still and always, a priest."

Peter staggered to his feet, and the man grabbed his habit roughly, yanking him forward. "Allow me to dispose of your unpleasant little arsenal of sacramentals, Father . . . they make our host terribly uncomfortable." Two large bodyguards seized Peter's arms from behind, as the "Cardinal" removed the Holy Oil, Holy Water, and Chrism from Peter's robe.

Maggie stood with Cody pressed to her heart, in a last desperate embrace; she was totally spent, and finally, beaten. Ghania moved in close, and wrenched the child away with an atavistic smirk, like a hyena over its kill. Maggie turned her face away. She barely noticed that her arms were pinned behind her, and she and Peter were being bundled along in a flying wedge of guards. She didn't know where they were taking her and didn't really care much anymore.

ELLIE had watched the preparation for the orgy with mounting worry after Maggie left her. An immense circle, fifty feet across, had been staked out behind the cutting garden. Twelve giant black candles made of pitch and sulphur were planted at intervals and the stench of them was making her gag. Inside the circle, long refectory tables had been set with every manner of food and drink, in grotesque abundance. A huge ice sculpture dominated the center of each table—the first one was a giant phallus, the next a Mendes Goat with an immense erection, and so on and on. Intense cold was rising like swamp mist all around her; the satanic priests were obviously calling up all manner of evil emanations to attend them for the coming orgy.

She knew that everything would be done in direct opposition to the Christian ritual of the Mass. They would feast, not fast, gorging and drinking until satiated. Indiscriminate sexual excesses would be interspersed with the feasting, people breaking away in twos and threes and fours, to rut like animals on the grass, in full view of the other participants.

An imposing man in an ermine-trimmed papal cloak moved in beside her, and casually reached out to touch her breast with the back of his fingers. Ellie steeled herself to the intrusion, and to the evil she sensed in the toucher. It was quite acceptable to make such sexual overtures before an orgy. She smiled coolly at the man.

"Do you know who I am?" he asked, the arrogance of privilege in his inflection.

"Tonight you are Pope Honorius, the Anti-Christ," she replied in a tone to match his own. "At other times, you are Senator James Edmonds." She thawed enough to encourage him. "In a few moments, I expect you will be just another friend of Eros." She smiled disarmingly.

"I haven't seen you before," he said, "I'd remember you. You're Tanith, I take it. Are you as skilled as she, in the sexual arts?"

"Why else would I have chosen her image for this evening's pleasures?" Ellie asked archly. "Honorius was reputedly no slouch in these matters, either, as I recall. Perhaps we could pool our knowledge . . ." She smiled mysteriously and moved away before he could do more than acquiesce. "Till then . . ." she called out as she beat a hasty retreat, toward the noise that was mounting on the far side of the house.

She got there just in time to see the last of Maggie's battle and the advent of Peter. Ellie watched the spectacle, powerless to help against such immense odds; better to head for the boat and go for help. Surely Dev could do *something* if he had an eyewitness report that Maggie and Peter were held captive against their will. If not, the local police were a backup possibility.

Ellie dodged the other guests. Most were either chattering about the capture, or else they were already disporting themselves at the banquet tables. Many were coupling on the grass, as she headed toward the woods.

The boat was where she'd left it; Ellie breathed a relieved sigh as she reached it without being discovered. She tugged and pushed it down to the water's edge, then scrambled in, as it caught the tide; she was a strong rower and cleared the beach easily, heading out into the current.

The first wave came from nowhere, scooping the prow of the small craft high into the air, and dropping it shatteringly, back into the trough. Shaken by the unexpected assault, Ellie hung on to the oars, and brought the boat around just in time to keep from being hit broadside by the next wave.

*Damn!* Where were these waves coming from? The sea had been smooth as glass when she'd shoved off from the beach, now the wind was whipping up a frenzy of wave activity, and the face of the full moon that had lit their way over was covered by a huge black cloud. Ghania! It had to be Ghania who'd called up the sea elementals; Ellie glimpsed an ondine in the icy water just as the next wave smashed across the bow, and ripped the oars from her hands. Before she could recover, another wave lifted the tiny boat high off the water, and slammed it, bow-over-stern, back down onto the surface in a splintering crash landing.

Thrown clear of the capsizing boat, Ellie managed to break water, and gasp in a breath, before she was sucked down again, below the pitch black turbulence of the Sound.

Battling the icy waves, struggling to sense the direction of the shore, she cried out to her allies on the Inner Planes for help, before she went under one last time.

# CHAPTER 84

"Holy Mother of God!" Maggie breathed the exclamation, without meaning to. "We're in the fifteenth century." Peter's eyes took in the incredible scene below them in the basement's gloom, and he felt a visceral fear, born of knowledge. He murmured, more to himself than to her, "We're in the belly of the beast." Rough hands pushed them both down the steps to the stone chamber.

Three vast rooms had been hewn from the foundation rock of the huge mansion. The first, in which they now stood, was an alchemist's laboratory, replete with anvil and furnace, the heat from which contrasted spectacularly with the livid cold and damp of the ancient granite. Shelves filled with reagents, huge glass beakers and tubing, Bunsen burners, and coils of copper wire were clearly visible in the light of the torches carried by their captors.

Eric flipped a switch, and bathed the fifteenth-century room in twentieth-century incandescence. "You mustn't feel we've let time pass us by, my friends," he said genially. "We use modern conveniences when they make sense, and ancient techniques when they're preferable. Which is often, I might add, when one speaks of ritual magic. These pragmatic times don't lend themselves to High Ritual, I'm afraid."

His glance fell critically on Maggie and Peter; both were being trundled along, none too gently, by several men. "There's really no need for brutality, gentlemen," he said with authority. "Our guests have nowhere to run to, and damned little time left, so I daresay we can treat them with a bit more courtesy, for the moment. Let's head in the direction of that large lectern, my dear," he said to Maggie, taking hold of her arm. "As an antiquarian, I know you'll be interested in seeing my *Grimorium Verum*, Maggie."

"Is this the historic house tour, Eric," she snapped, yanking her elbow from his grip with difficulty.

"Feisty to the last, Maggie, eh? I must say I admire that in you. A pity your daughter didn't have the same fiber. She went to her death like a mewling infant. Begging for mercy, slobbering tears—but you already know that, of course. You'll do better, I think."

"You'll burn in Hell for your crimes, you vicious bastard," Father Peter said.

"Very astute," Eric replied with equanimity. "Hell is, of course, my final destination. As to burning . . . that really has been overdramatized by your boys, over the centuries, Peter. I expect I shall simply enjoy the company of my own kind . . ."

"That should be hell enough," Maggie said clearly.

"Very quick of you, Maggie. What a pity that wit of yours will so soon be extinguished. But do let us return to this lovely book we see before us."

The jewel-encrusted leather gleamed with four hundred years' patina, and the vellum pages gave off, not the musty damp of old books, but the scent of rare incense. The grimoire appeared to emanate a phosphorescent glow in the dim light. But, it was an unpleasant emanation, somehow . . . Maggie thought of swamp gas.

"This *Grimorium Verum* dates from the sixteenth

century, a first edition, of course. The later ones were corrupted with inaccuracies, I'm afraid. For example, this one calls for mole's blood and pimpernel juice to quench the steel of a magical sword at its firing. Later editions permitted magpie's blood and the juice of an herb called foirole, but I find that to be inferior." Maggie's eyes caught Peter's and read in them the same despairing realization—they were at the mercy of a madman.

Eric smiled his chilling, mirthless smile, and gestured them toward the next chamber. "Do permit me to introduce you to my *salon de vérité*," he said amiably, as the full impact of the room's purpose reached them. A rack and an iron maiden faced the entrance of the darkened chamber; the diabolical contrivances looked well and recently used, despite their obvious antiquity. There was dried blood everywhere.

"We're in Torquemada's country house," Maggie whispered to Peter. Barrels of pitch were lined up to her right—she remembered it was used for setting fire to the feet of victims who were "being put to the question."

"Are you both familiar with my favorite toy?" Eric asked, fingering an odd contrivance of weighted ropes and pulleys that ascended to the vaulted ceiling of the fortresslike room.

"Strappado," Peter answered quietly, and Maggie could hear the loathing in his voice.

Eric looked amused at his discomfort. "Strappado, indeed. Shall we explain its exquisite usefulness to the lady, who it seems, is unfamiliar with its nuances."

"During the Inquisition," Peter replied, his voice taut, "strappado was the favored torture device of Torquemada's death squad. When some poor wretch was being put to the question about consorting with the Devil, she would be attached to this grotesque device . . . arms bound behind her, wrists chained to pulleys— she would be drawn up toward the ceiling to hang with weights attached to her feet, while gravity dislocated her joints, one by one."

"Very informative, Peter," Eric applauded, "but

woefully incomplete. The beauty part was not just in the hanging, but every so often the pulleys would be raised . . ." He paused to crank them up toward the ceiling, forcing them all to look upward. "And then released . . . just *so!*" The weights plunged as Eric released the pulley, then snapped with a resounding crunch as he stopped their descent, abruptly. "The victim fell with them, of course.

"Such exquisite pain was incurred each time the victim plummeted and was wrenched back upward. Joints popping, bones rending . . . the shoulders always gave way first, then the elbows and the knees. Sometimes the entire pelvis would dislocate brilliantly. In the beginning, the screams would be deafening, piercing the brain like red-hot daggers with each new lurch. But by late afternoon or evening, there'd be only muffled moans of agony . . . not so much fun then, really. Nicky was the best of them. He could always keep them alive and screaming longer than anyone."

Peter shot Maggie a warning glance. Do not provoke him.

"Nicky?" she asked startled. "But this all happened five hundred years ago. Are you suggesting Nicholas Sayles was there?"

Eric looked at Maggie with a pained expression, as if she'd disappointed him with a stupid question.

"We were *all there*," he said. "Peter remembers, don't you, Father. You priests were such superb torturers. The Dominicans were the best, of course. Who did the Devil's work in those days, Peter? How many innocents did your boys murder in the name of your gentle Christ?"

"It was a brutal time," Peter replied. "The Church had much to answer for before the Throne of God."

"Don't flatter yourself, Peter. Those priests never saw the Throne of God—the Lords of Darkness waited just outside their Star Chambers to collect them for the Pit. There's a special place reserved in Hell for failed priests, Peter, did you know that? They are doomed to listening to each other's sermons and discussing Aquinas into eternity." Eric laughed at his little joke.

"Why are you treating us to this scholarly discourse, Eric?" Peter asked impatiently. "Surely there isn't time for you to use any of your little toys on us before the hour of the Materialization."

"True enough, I'm afraid, but fantasizing has its delights, too, don't you think?"

A vast stone archway led to the last of the great chambers. By far the largest, it was unmistakably the Satanic Chapel.

Maggie heard Peter's sharp intake of breath as they entered the huge space. She had felt it, too. A flash flood of icy-cold energy, and pure, unadulterated evil, so palpable she found it hard to breathe.

The floor of the altar room was painted with an immense circle, inscribed around an inverted Pentagram of mammoth proportion.

"The Grand Circle," Eric said proudly. "Do you see the strips of hide at the cardinal points, Peter? They are human flesh harvested from sacrifices. That strip at the south, Maggie, is your late lamented daughter. The nails are from the coffin of a parricide, of course."

Maggie felt suffocated by the visions of Jenna called up by Eric's words; she drew back, shocked and nauseated, and was pushed roughly upright by strong, hurtful hands.

"Courage, Maggie!" It was Peter's urgent voice she heard through the dark mist that suffused her; she fought her way back toward the sound, and tried to smile at him in reassurance, but her lips could only form a grimace.

A second circle had the altar at its center. Red velvet and black satin altar cloths, encrusted with precious gems, covered the intricately carved marble. Scenes of debauchery, murder, sexual perversion, were immortalized in the intricate carvings, and the same themes were echoed in tapestried hangings around the room. Hieronymous Bosch scenes of orgies, torture, and varied atrocities completed the thematic decor, and helped hide the stone walls of the cavernous space.

"Secure her to the pillar left of the altar," Eric ordered the acolytes, all pretense at charm now gone. "Hang the priest on the cross," he said with a dismissive nod toward the inverted cross above the altar. "You'll like that, Peter . . . so in keeping with your tradition. You'll be more of a traditionalist in death, than you were ever in life."

"No!" Maggie blurted. "This is *my* fight, Eric, not Peter's. You don't have any quarrel with him."

"No quarrel?" he said incredulously. "Are you mad? He is the Enemy . . . the Adversary. Do you think *you* have brought him here, Maggie? Don't delude yourself! He has been called to attendance by an old Foe, who will so much enjoy watching him finally die!"

"What will you do to Cody?" Maggie demanded.

"Quite a lot actually," Eric replied with equanimity. "She is, after all, the guest of honor. There will be a Black Mass celebrated, after the orgy. The Isis Amulet and the Sekhmet Stone will be Materialized for the final time. When they are both safely in my care, I shall destroy the Isis Amulet once and for all, so of course, Cody will no longer be needed to protect it. The child's Ka will be placed under suitable demonic guard for eternity, so that Sekhmet may have a human dwelling place. Cody has great powers, so she will require quite unpleasant entities to keep her neutralized. Two of the Crown Princes of Hell have offered their services, I'm told, but Sekhmet has her own agenda for guardianship. She will grant her host body immortality, of course, so there will be a certain consolation for you, I suppose . . ."

With intense effort Maggie wrenched her arm free and landed a right uppercut squarely on Eric's jaw. The shock and pain of it sent him reeling backward.

"No, Maggie!" Peter shouted, shocked as the rest.

"Oh, you'll pay dearly for that, bitch!" Eric spat, as followers helped him stand upright. He was holding his jaw, rubbing it to ease the obvious pain, then his hand shot out, closing on her throat, and he squeezed slowly until her eyes bulged in their sockets and the fight for breath dragged her to her knees. Then he released her, and she would have fallen had the acolytes not held up her sagging body.

"I don't want you dead until you see the child damned," he hissed. Then he signaled to the jailers to carry on, turned on his heel and left the chamber.

"*Augustine*, Maggie!" Peter called to her as they were dragged in separate directions. "When they sacked the city!" The words were urgent, meant to strengthen her. She tried to focus her mind through the pain in her throat and the disorientation of nearly suffocating. What did he mean? What had Augustine said?

Then suddenly she knew. When his priests had begged permission to flee the city before the conquering Vandal army could destroy them all, he had sent them each a message:

"*If we abandon our posts . . . who, then, will stand?*"

Tears filled her eyes and she let herself be dragged to the pillar, and bound there. They were not the first to suffer in a just cause . . . others had been brave in the face of death and torture. It was not beyond the power of the human spirit.

Maggie closed her eyes and began to pray.

# CHAPTER 85

Shortly before eleven, acolytes started to move among the bodies on the grass, encouraging them to end their revels, for the time of ceremony was approaching. Sated with food, drink, and sex of every conceivable permutation, the guests left their costumes behind, and donned the cowled robes being handed out by the servants.

All levity had ceased; it was apparent that the worshippers took the advent of the approaching ritual with utmost seriousness. They began to gather in an orderly fashion, to be lined up for the processional.

Within the house, the thirteen Adepti were already assembled in the library. For them, the evening had been one of preparation, not revelry. None had eaten, for fasting was essential to the conduction of the energies. None had indulged in sexual congress, for that would have squandered energies precious to the performance of their duties. The sexual activities of the revelers had been more than adequate to raise the energy field around the mansion to fever pitch, and the chanting of the congregation would add a vibrational boost as the ceremony progressed.

Maggie stood captive and helpless, to the left of the satanic altar. Peter hung on the inverted cross above it; he hadn't spoken for nearly half an hour, and she was uncertain if he were even conscious. His face was flushed with blood to the bursting point, and she hadn't seen him move for some time.

There was an ungodly chill in the great chamber and Maggie's legs felt numb and shaky beneath her; with mounting fear she saw the procession of silent, robed figures enter the chapel and file into the pews.

A ceremonial litter was visible behind the procession. Maggie strained at her bonds to see, and sucked in her breath sharply at the sight of Cody.

The child was deeply entranced or drugged, lying on an elaborate flower-strewn pallet. Clad in an Egyptian mist-linen gown, she had a garland of flowers encircling her brow. She was still and pale as death. Maggie called out her name, but there was no response, except a sharp blow to her face from a frowning acolyte. Disheartened, Maggie sank back into her bonds, dreading to watch whatever was to come.

Incense wafted from the gold censers, and the air

seemed thick with the heady fragrance and the eerie, continuous chanting.

From a doorway behind the altar, a new column of robed figures emerged. She counted thirteen in all, dressed in varied ceremonial costumes, some dazzlingly bejeweled, some starkly simple. At the tail of this procession, Maggie saw Eric and three priestly assistants, dressed in elaborate Egyptian ceremonial robes. Eric, Nicholas Sayles . . . she ticked them off in her mind as they stepped up to the altar. The priest who had overpowered Peter, and . . . Oh my *God!* she gasped audibly as Abdul Hazred moved into her line of sight. No wonder she had never liked that self-serving son of a bitch.

She could feel the atmosphere in the chamber begin to change, as if an electrical charge had begun to vibrate every molecule in the room in a rapidly escalating rhythm.

Maggie wanted to turn her face away as Eric and the other priests began the celebration of the Black Mass, but she dared not. *Our Father who art in Heaven, she breathed, hallowed be Thy name* . . . She would drown out the horror of the blasphemy, in her own mind at least. *And forgive us our trespasses as we forgive those* . . . she kept repeating the prayer over and over, a mantra against evil, until she heard the shuffle of sandal-clad feet returning to their pews, and saw that the travesty of Communion was done. *And lead me not into temptation* . . . she heard bells ring, and the congregation rise en masse, to its feet. *But deliver us from evil* . . .

Maggie watched in absolute terror, as Eric began to make strange signs over Cody's body, with what appeared to be a rod of some kind.

"I call on thee, Satan," he cried out, "by all the names wherewith thou mayest be adjured; blessed be our efforts on behalf of Darkness." There followed a litany of satanic names, most of which she had never heard before.

"Thou who imposeth evil and war and hatred and

desperation, keep thy great legions at the ready to crown our work tonight with victory.''

Eric raised his arms in salute to the unseen Power and cried out in a thunderous voice, ''I, Eric Vannier, Master of Masters, theurgist of theurgists, servant of the Old Gods, High Priest of Sekhmet, two hundred twenty-eighth in direct line from the first High Priest of the Dark Mother, hereby undertake to open the Covenant, the seals whereof were set before the Great One Herself.

''On this day shall the Isis Amulet be called forth from her Messenger. Behold, O Great Mother of Darkness and Pestilence, I set your rival's Messenger before thee, awakened to her task.''

There followed a tirade of ancient languages . . . Egyptian, Hebrew, Greek, Enochian, and others she couldn't recognize. As Eric intoned the words of power, Maggie saw the scene begin to alter—could there be a hallucinogenic in that incense? . . . *something* was affecting her mind . . . she struggled to keep control of her senses . . .

Out of Cody's sleeping body she saw a form emerge and take definite shape. It was the young priestess Maggie knew so achingly from her dreams, the daughter of Mim and Karaden. Around her neck gleamed a golden Amulet, shimmering with the radiance of the sun itself. With the sickening crash of a great tidal wave, the world of Mim engulfed her; she felt every cell awash in the power of the Amulet she had once profaned. She fought to maintain her own mind, as the bi-location swept her in its inescapable tide.

The etheric figure of the Isis Messenger stood at quiet attention above Cody's sleeping body, and Eric smiled with proud satisfaction.

Raising his arms once more, he called for Sekhmet's blessing. Addressing her by a lengthy litany of her names of power, first in English and then in her mother tongue, this second conjuration, too, produced its effect.

As Maggie watched, stunned and unwilling to believe her own senses, an etheric animation left Ghania's body.

This time it was a warrior, black and fierce beyond reckoning. Around its neck the Sekhmet Stone gleamed, with a cold leaden fire like that of a black opal. It seemed that Sekhmet, too, had chosen her champion.

A murmuring arose among the worshippers at the brilliant Manifestations, so clear they were nearly material.

Eric turned his attention to the congregation, a smile of unutterable satisfaction on his handsome face; this was an extraordinarily delicate magical Work he was attempting, and thus far it was a study in perfection.

"O great Mother of Evil," he cried out, "thy faithful children call on thee to order the events of this auspicious night. The Isis Amulet and the Sekhmet Stone have been called into etheric apparition, now must we conjure the Isis Amulet into material form, by the great formula set down in ancient days. I, who have commanded angels and devils to my bidding, adjure thee to come to our aid in this Great Work!" He motioned to the remaining twelve Adepti to move into a ring around the Amulets and their champions, and the solemn magi began to take their places around the child's litter.

Then, all hell broke loose.

A frenzied commotion shook the hall outside the chamber and rattled the bolted doors. Shots zinged through the chanting, screams reinforcing them. The unmistakable sounds of battle were followed by the splintering of wood, as the chapel door shattered inward, crashing onto the floor.

A camouflage-clad commando team poured through the doorway into the satanic service, stunning the assemblage into immobility, but Eric was the first to recover his equilibrium. He made a fierce, sweeping arcane gesture with his hands, and began to intone the words of a potent invocation of protection from Satan himself.

"Silence!" Hazred shouted, drawing an automatic pistol from under his robe. "Speak another syllable and you go to meet the two hundred and twenty-seven who preceded you!" Eric halted in mid-word.

Hazred turned to the child and hurriedly made certain

magical signs above her body, as he murmured something Maggie couldn't hear. The apparitions dispersed like mist before the sun, leaving her to wonder if they had ever really been there at all, or if some sort of mass hallucination had deceived her.

"Watch this one, carefully!" Hazred shouted to the soldiers, who were obviously at his command. "Watch the Twelve . . . if any speaks or moves a finger, kill him. Your own lives and sanity depend on it."

But, suddenly, the Mohabarat commandos had more to worry about than the thirteen Adepti on the altar. There was new gunfire at their backs, that spun their attention around toward the door of the chapel.

Abraham's team poured into the great chamber, as shots rang out in a dozen directions. A slug shattered Hazred's gun from his hand, and Eric saw his opportunity. He snatched up Cody from the litter, and used her body as cover to break through the gunfire; the general pandemonium protected his flight. Somehow, Ghania had already disappeared from the chapel.

Seconds later Devlin was at Maggie's side, cutting through the ropes that confined her. They hugged wildly for an instant, but there was no time.

"Get Peter!" she begged as he tried to pull her toward safety, but Abraham's men were already freeing the priest.

"Eric's got Cody!" she screamed above the din. There were bodies littering the floor, and soldiers with Uzis everywhere.

Abraham was shouting orders in Hebrew to his men, as they reached the door of the chapel with Peter close behind them, everything happening so fast, it was hard to comprehend it sequentially.

Maggie saw the old rabbi for the first time as he called to her urgently, "Mrs. O'Connor—you and the priest will come with me. I know which way he took the child!"

"Go!" Devlin urged from behind her. "I'll cover you. The Israelis are on our side!"

A barrage of gunfire urged her forward.

Shots could be heard in various parts of the house—who knew how many bodyguards there were, as well as the soldiers? The satanists might have their own army. Maggie took off at a run, following the rabbi down a hallway, marveling at how fast the old man could move.

"Who is he?" Maggie shouted over her shoulder to Peter, who seemed to have regained his equilibrium and was running behind her.

"God knows!" he shouted back, "but he seems to know where he's going."

Shots and shouts sounded close behind them, as they pursued the Rebbe deeper into the bowels of the old house. Maggie and Peter followed him down a winding stone stair into a cavernous subbasement; the walls were hewn of stone, weeping now with dampness.

Maggie heard another burst of gunfire, and Devlin's voice shouting, along with a deep Israeli voice that was barking commands. The submachine gun rat-a-tat-tat was too close for comfort and Devlin was in the middle of it, but she had to find Cody, so she kept on going.

They went through a doorway at the end of a winding corridor, and the Rebbe held up his hand to halt their passage. The old man leaned heavily against the wall, laboring to catch his breath, as Maggie bolted the door behind them, worried that Dev was on the other side.

The Rebbe spoke to Peter. "We have little time, Father. Too little for pleasantries. I am Rabbi Itzhak Levi, and I, too, have been called."

Peter looked into the Rebbe's eyes and saw clearly, this was a man with one foot in this world and another in the next, a condition that had very little to do with his advanced age. Something resonated within the priest beneath the Rebbe's piercing gaze. He knew of the man's extraordinary reputation as a scholar, but it was something more profound in him, that spoke to Peter, now—some camaraderie of the soul. The Rebbe was another who had touched the mystical ecstasy of God, and hungered after it enough to pursue Him into dangerous terrain, where there were no signposts and no boundaries.

The Rebbe nodded; his eyes never left the priest's for an instant, and Peter knew he was being weighed in the balance, like Nebuchadnezzar.

"I believe the child's soul has somehow been ensnared by demonic energies, called up for that purpose by evil men," Peter said. "With my own eyes, I saw the Amulet and the Stone in etheric form, close to Materialization, so I cannot discount their potential existence. Had not the conjuration been interrupted, I believe these objects would already be on the material plane."

There was acknowledgment in the Rebbe's expression. "The child's soul is under attack, as we speak. I have seen the Demon. I ask you now, what do you propose we do?"

"We must win it back, Rebbe," Peter answered firmly. "Cody is besieged through no fault of her own. I believe the only course open to us is an exorcism of some kind."

"The systems by which we deal with demons are vastly different," the Rebbe said judiciously. "This would not be an easy task. I know of no instance in which it has been done."

Maggie thought she would implode with anger. "You two won't have to wait for the people behind us to kill you, I'll damn well do it myself if you don't stop talking and start moving!"

The Rebbe smiled unexpectedly, and turned to move off down the darkened corridor. "What do you ask of God for this child, Mrs. O'Connor?" he called over his shoulder.

"That she be spared, if it's God's will," Maggie answered, hurrying after him. "That she be protected from all that is evil or profane."

"And for yourself?"

"That I have the courage to bear with whatever God decides."

The old man turned his head toward her, and the

intensity of his gaze seared deep into her soul; she had not the slightest doubt he could read what was written there.

"Do you trust us with this task that your priest friend suggests?"

Maggie nodded affirmatively.

"Because we are learned men?"

"No," she said steadily. "Because I believe you are good men."

"You know, of course, that my faith is vastly different from yours. If I attempt what Father Peter suggests, I must do so by the mysteries of Judaism. Does this trouble you?"

"No."

"And why not?"

"Truth is truth, Rebbe," she said unhesitantly. "The path you take to get there is surely irrelevant to God."

The old man nodded, the faintest trace of a smile on his lips.

"So." he said. "We will begin." He turned his attention to a great stone archway that was now visible, directly ahead of them. Then he moved forward like Joshua onto the plains of Jericho.

The spandrel of the arch that loomed before them was intricately carved with hideous gargoyles. The Rebbe came to a halt before it, and Maggie saw that the darkness beyond the arch was unlike any she had ever seen. It was viscous, somehow, and so inky-black she felt she was staring into infinity.

"It is a sealed portal between dimensions," the Rebbe said to Peter. "Feel the evil emanation." A bitter cold had arisen around them, and a nauseating evil seeped from the chamber, making it difficult to breathe.

"You will open this doorway to us!" the rabbi demanded, startling Maggie with his powerful voice.

A crackling sound like static electricity responded, and the air around them quivered. Seconds later, the candlelit interior beyond the arch swam into view; Cody lay within the chamber, Eric beside her.

"Welcome to the Devil's Portal," he called out to them coldly. "At the peril of your souls, you may enter the Doorway to Hell."

Peter and the Rebbe exchanged glances, then proceeded into the chamber, as Maggie stepped across the threshold with foreboding, thinking nothing, absolutely nothing in this world, but Cody, could make her enter this horrific place.

Eric raised his left hand and intoned some words she couldn't understand, and Maggie felt the archway seal itself behind her.

# CHAPTER 86

Ghania was breathless from her frenzied flight, by the time she made it back to her room. She slammed the door and leaned heavily against it, struggling for breath. *Curse Hazred*, for the traitor he was! She tore open the armoire and breathed easier at the sight of her untouched tools. Thank Darkness she'd been High Priestess to an evil Master long enough to know better than to ever leave anything to chance.

Eric had failed in his mission, but that did not mean the prize must be lost. There was no time to waste on regrets.

Ghania pulled the needed equipment for ritual from the shelf and hastily arranged the altar. She, too, possessed the ancient knowledge of how to imprison the child's Ka and snatch the dual prizes.

"Ah, little Isis Messenger," she murmured as she prepared her magic. "You wish to escape your destiny, but Ghania is old and wily and she thinks of everything.

Your nails, your hair, your blood, your sweat . . . I have them all. You, too, shall I have, when my spell is done!''

Ghania entered the Ritual Silence and circumambulated three times, in a counterclockwise circle. She poured her libation of blood and soaked the Cody doll in it, muttering incantations. Then she picked up a long and lethal-looking pin from its altar cushion. As she was about to pierce the doll's heart, a staggering blow from behind knocked the chalice from her grasp.

Ellie, wet, bedraggled and nearly naked, faced the priestess with a bloodied kris knife in one hand and a labrys in the other. She had plucked them from a display on the floor below; she, too, had a backup plan.

"Tried to drown me, witch?" she said, her voice low and deadly. "Did you think you were the only one who's known the Sea Gods in her time?"

Ghania grabbed her knife and unfastened her djellabah, letting it fall around her; she kicked it out of the way. The two women faced each other. Ghania was larger, heavier, but staring into Ellie's eyes she knew she faced her match.

"To the *death!*" she spat in challenge.

"You can bless your Gods, if I follow you no farther than *that*, witch!" Ellie retorted, her face fierce and grave.

They began to circle, taking each other's measure, weapons poised and eager. Ghania struck first, her knife slicing the air a hairsbreadth from Ellie's abdomen. Ellie feinted left and caught Ghania's great head with a ringing kick like a ballerina; she had spent one lifetime in the Cretan bullring and the knowledge gleaned there at death's elbow had never left her. Ghania's head snapped back with a grunt, but she kept on moving.

Each woman sought to engage the other's eyes in the way of magicians, but they were matched in skill and neither allowed entry. Ellie's teeth clamped shut as Ghania's knife scored her thigh; she whirled away from the blade and set her kris knife in the flesh of Ghania's arm.

They prowled around each other like tigresses; the

dual-headed axe blade carved the air in front of Ghania's breasts and would have opened her from gullet to navel, had it connected with its mark. Ghania threw back her head and laughed, but Ellie met the ugly sound with a Cherokee battle whoop, that had chilled the blood of enemy warriors since the Adoni People had taught it to the Tribe. The war whoop disrupted Ghania's energy field momentarily; Native American Magic was alien to her own. But, she managed to recover enough to lunge, knocking the axe from Ellie's hand with a shattering blow to the wrist.

Parrying, thrusting, feinting, the two women fought like Amazons, so evenly matched in combat skills that only exhaustion or Fate could tip the scales toward victory.

Ghania was chanting now, and Ellie tried to catch the drift of her spell. *Sweet Jesus!* she was calling up the elementals, opening the psychic door to allow entry from the spectral world. Christ! *anything* could enter through the Astral doorway . . . Ellie wracked her brain for a means of keeping out the Astral entities, but Something was already materializing before her, even as she fought. A female figure, gaunt bloodless, eyes so filled with bloodlust it was painful to focus on them. Ellie drew back in alarm. Her strength was too far gone to fight on both planes, simultaneously.

But the figure wasn't after her. It hurled itself at Ghania's immense body with a ferocity that pushed Ellie to the far side of the room.

Christ almighty, it was Jenna!

The entity attached itself like an etheric leech, strangling the witch with the strength of her own magic turned back upon itself.

Ellie, wounded and panting with exhaustion, fell against the armoire and watched in fascination as Ghania attempted to extricate herself from the entangling etheric stranglehold.

The old witch tried to curse her tormentor, spewing spells in a dozen different tongues, but every one was driven back before she could complete it, by the savagery of the Jenna/entity's attack. So fierce was its intent that Ellie felt compelled to look away, but as she did so, her eye fell on the sickle axe she'd dropped, and she reached for it instinctively as Ghania staggered toward her, once again.

"This is for *Cody!*" the Jenna/entity screamed, as it pounded the witch at every vital center.

"This is for *me!*" It grabbed her by the throat from behind and, with a mighty shove, sent her hurtling in Ellie's direction.

Ellie raised the labrys above her head and, with a single blow, split the witch from crown to collarbone. The falling body wrenched the crescent axe from her bloodied hands, as Ghania crumpled to the floor.

"*That* was for God," Ellie said evenly to the great corpse that lay at her feet.

She raised her head from the debacle, and saw the etheric entity already beginning to fade. The expression on its face was more victorious—and sadder—than any she had ever seen.

Ellie knelt down to pray.

DEVLIN crouched to the left of Abraham in the only cover available in that portion of the long stone corridor. The battle directly behind them had been bloody and swift; the Israelis were pros. Sounds of combat emanated from various areas of the house; the Vannier contingent had obviously employed both armed guards and booby traps for a contingency like this one.

Abraham's men had engaged the Mohabarat troops as well as the home team, who seemed more like mercs, than urban bodyguards, both in combat skills, and armament. It made sense, of course; with Vannier's international drug and arms connections, he would have access to the best soldiers of fortune money could buy.

Devlin spotted the sniper just as Abraham was about to move out into the corridor. It wasn't an easy shot in the semi-gloom—the man had better cover than theirs—but the detective dropped him with the first round.

Abraham touched Devlin's shoulder in acknowledgment, and moved out silently into the now empty corridor. By the time they reached the locked door at the end, all gunfire had ceased behind them.

"Housekeeping?" Dev said shortly.

Abraham nodded. "We must find the child and get out before the noise brings police."

"You've got twenty acres of privacy, here, plus the Long Island Sound," Devlin said. "That'll buy us some time."

Abraham grunted a noncommittal response and tried to force the door. When it didn't budge, he blew the lock with his automatic. Seconds later, they were on the other side, staring into the blackened maw of the portal straight ahead of them. Vaguely visible in the darkness were the occupants of the interior chamber. Rafi and Devlin exchanged glances, and Devlin headed into the archway that separated him from Maggie and Cody.

But he couldn't get through.

Shocked by the repulsion that hurled him backward, he threw his weight against the forcefield more vigorously. Only a slight electrical tremor betrayed the existence of the psychic seal.

Puzzled, Abraham lent his considerable strength to the effort, but with the same unsatisfactory result. Devlin shouted to Maggie, but it was obvious sound couldn't penetrate, either.

Devlin and Abraham exchanged confounded looks. How had the others entered? What kind of force was it that repelled them?

Abraham reached up to examine the edges of the spandrel for clues about what had produced the repulsion. "My men will be here shortly," he said. "We'll penetrate when reinforcements arrive."

MAGGIE had to struggle to keep her equilibrium within the freezing chamber. The Evil was so palpable in this place, so dense, it encroached on her lifeforce, sucking at her, leaching off energy like a black hole in space that swallows all in its path. She centered her breathing and prayed for protection, but it seemed in this place, even her prayers were thrown back at her, unable to find their way.

She moved toward Cody, who lay, pale as a lily, on the great stone altar in the chamber's center. The stone looked eons old, and emanated the temperature of an Arctic ice flow.

She reached out to touch the child, and Cody's eyes flicked open. Maggie drew back, shocked; it was not Cody who stared out from those alien eyes.

Peter, too, saw the Presence clearly. He made the sign of the Cross and opened the *Roman Ritual of Exorcism*, which had been blessedly overlooked by his captors, because it had been secreted in his pants pocket, not in the Dominican robe. *Oh, God*, he prayed, *let my frailties not tip the scales against us*.

Instinctively Maggie drew back from the eerie malevolence in the child's gaze, and did not touch her, as she'd intended. She turned shocked, questioning eyes to Peter, but the Rebbe spoke.

"They are here," he said. "The demons. There are many, but one is in authority." Peter glanced at the old man, whose eyes were shut. Obviously, he could see clairvoyantly.

"You bastard! What have you done to Cody?" Maggie demanded.

"What we've done, my dear Maggie," Eric responded, "is banish her soul to a place where it will be imprisoned for eternity.

"Cody is now no more than a nesting place for demons. Had we finished our conjuration, Sekhmet herself would have taken charge of her person, and granted her immortality. But since we were rather rudely interrupted, I had no choice but to bring her here. Now, of course, I intend to Materialize the Amulets, and I intend to kill you.''

Peter wasn't certain why he felt suddenly emboldened; perhaps it was the sense that he'd reached the final battleground. He stepped closer to Eric and spoke. ''The most propitious hour for Materialization has passed, Vannier,'' he said firmly. ''As to killing us . . . you have no weapon, and we outnumber you.''

''Then I shall simply call upon the Prince to kill you,'' Eric replied contemptuously.

''And why should he do that? Surely your Prince despises failure, at least as much as earthly princes do.''

''There has been no failure, here. Merely a change of plan.'' Eric turned away dismissively, but the air around them began to crackle ominously.

*''Failed mortal!''* The thunderous words came from no visible source. ''Thou hast chosen thy own fate.''

The walls began to quiver with the intensity of the sound. Eric suddenly clutched at his own throat, as if an unseen hand were strangling him. The three watchers saw him gasp and struggle for breath, like a man at the end of a hangman's rope.

*''There is a price to be paid!''* the awesome voice blasted the words, vibrating every nerve ending excruciatingly.

Eric's body was seized by creatures they could not see, but whose strength must have been beyond calculation. His large body was tossed about the chamber as effortlessly as if he were a beanbag, in the hands of demented children. It seemed to hang upside down from an invisible meat hook high above them for a time, then it crashed repeatedly into walls and ceiling, with bone-crushing violence.

And, then the laughter began, as the demons tore him limb from limb. Eric's shrieks nearly drowned out the ungodly sounds of rending flesh, as arms and legs were wrenched from the living torso. And there was flesh and bones, crushed and mangled, and the stench of burning, and the roar of some beast that had surely never left the Pit, but lived in a swamp of blood at the feet of its infernal Master.

Maggie, dumbstruck by the grotesque spectacle, tried to turn her head away, but the Rebbe said firmly, "It is no more than he has done to others, Mrs. O'Connor. It is *just.*"

The sounds of the debacle ceased; and Peter, Maggie, and the Rebbe stood stunned and uncertain in the wake of the carnage.

"Peter, Peter, *Peter!*" a male voice suddenly chided, startling their attention back to the altar. The voice seemed to emanate from Cody, but the child's lips hadn't moved. "I'm *so* glad you answered my call! Clever method I used this time, wouldn't you say?"

Peter frowned. He knew the voice; he had heard it last in an Indian village, twelve thousand miles from Greenwich.

He steeled himself against the sudden rush of fear the voice provoked in him; for an instant, he had almost forgotten the child on the altar. He took a deep breath and turned his attention to the *Roman Ritual* in his hand; with reverence, he started to read the text of the Rite of Exorcism that dated from the third or fourth century.

" '*Do not remember O Lord, our sins, or those of our forefathers . . .*' " He felt the strength of the ritual begin to fill him with a sense of renewal; all thought of self fell away, and only the powerful words remained.

" '*. . . lead us not into temptation, but deliver us from evil . . . Save this child, your servant, because she hopes in you, My God.*' "

"Fuck that, you pusillanimous dung heap!" The child spat the words, but the voice was not hers. "This one was given to us free and clear for all eternity . . . You will be, too, before we're through."

Peter felt the Presence engulf him, like a wall of icy

slime, oozing around him, looking for entry points. *I'm alone!* The thought was suddenly in his brain, and with it, an irrational terror. He felt as if an invisible hand clutched at his vocal chords and the unexpected force of the attack rocked him. These encounters usually started slowly and built up momentum, but this malevolence was already formidable.

"Alone. Alone. *Alone!*" the Presence mocked him, somewhere inside his own mind. "You will always be alone!"

"You are *not* alone!" the voice was the Rebbe's, clear as a trumpet. Forceful. In control. It jerked Peter back out, into reality.

"Don't fuck with me, pig priest!" the voice on the altar squealed sullenly; there was a chalk-on-blackboard screech to it, that raised goosebumps on all the flesh in the room. "I'll suck your wizened dick in Hell!" A demented laugh cackled out of the child's mouth, and the very air seemed to explode. Maggie watched the spectacle immobilized by shock; it was inconceivable that the *thing* on the altar was Cody. She bent her head and tried to pray.

Peter glanced at the Rebbe and saw his composure had not altered even slightly. It was apparent he had no intention of engaging the entity in conversation, as yet. Peter had the distinct feeling the old man was monitoring the confrontation, on some other inner level of clairvoyant consciousness.

" '*Unclean Spirit!*' " Peter intoned from the ritual. " '*Whoever you are, and all your companions who possess this servant of God . . .*' "

"You *know* who I am, Peter Messenguer!" the voice cried exultantly. "I've spent your whole life at your side. I'm the Prince of Pride! Your cosmic counterpart. I'm the one who led you down the garden path so neatly, you never even suspected me. *I* gave you the intellect . . . *I* made your seething, bloodsucking pride drown your faith in rationalizations. Oh, the singular horseshit of your puny efforts to know God! Peter the Great, Peter the Proud. Peter thinks he can fuck the bitch and God won't notice!''

*"Concentrate!"* The ferocity of the Rebbe's voice slashed through Peter's shock.

"And you, old hypocrite!" the demon roared, whipping his attention to the rabbi. "Do you think I'll leave *you* unmolested?"

The Rebbe felt the ground begin to shake under him, and a terrible stench rose all around him. It was a smell that never could be forgotten. Burning bodies, crematoria. *Devorah!*

The stench receded, but the iron band that had clutched his heart remained.

"Have patience, little man," the demon said, through Cody's mouth. "I'll have fun with you later."

The Rebbe felt the hair rise on the back of his neck; felt his stomach tighten. What madness, at my age, to fear anything, he admonished himself—but the stench of Auschwitz lingered in his nostrils and the memory of Devorah made him feel faint. He forced his concentration back to the sound of the priest's voice, and cast his mind out into the cosmos once again, seeking the Infinite.

Peter struggled to keep the words of the ritual in sharp focus. *Careful, Peter*, he admonished himself. *Don't lose control.*

"*The Long Road from Calvary*, indeed," the demon hissed at Peter before he'd finished the thought. "You pompous windbag! Did it never occur to you that the road was so *long* because you were headed in the wrong direction?" Demented laughter echoed through the room in nauseating shock waves that left everyone's nerves raw and bleeding. Maggie's eyes sought Peter's; she could see the livid hurt exposed there.

"How blithely you let me lead you right to Gehenna! A little turn here, a judicious twist there, and your superior intellect deftly came to all the wrong conclusions! You said yourself, it isn't the big decisions that sell you out, Peter, just the little expediencies, the small self-indulgences that open the door to the Enemy."

*Could it be true?* Peter's mind and heart slid inexorably toward the Abyss. *Dear Christ Almighty, what if it's true?* Confusion made him falter, momentarily unable to remember his place on the printed page.

*"He lies!"* the Rebbe rebuked, sternly. "He is not bound by Truth!"

The child's head swiveled toward the rabbi, a grotesquely lascivious smile on her small lips.

"Was Du erlebst, kann keine Macht der Welt Dir rauben," the voice said in perfect German. *What you have experienced, no power on earth can take from you.* All eyes were on the Rebbe.

"She was so soft and pure, wasn't she, *Liebchen?"* the demon whispered, intimately. "Her hair, her skin, the way she used to say your name in bed at night. Why didn't you save her? *Coward.* Self-serving worm! They raped her, you know. All six of them. They thought she was soft and pretty, too. They made her suck them, did you know that, Itzhak? They told her if she didn't drink every drop, they would torture you to death. She thought she was saving you, poor terrified innocent that she was. All she saved was a poor old fake who tells people he's holy, while he let his wife be tortured in his place. She died in *agony*, Itzhak . . . she was quite mad by then, of course. Did you know she watched them kill the children?"

Anguish etched itself in the old man's face, and tears ran unchecked down his cheeks, but he held his ground.

*Devorah . . . Devorah. Set me like a seal upon your heart . . . love is as strong as death.* He had waited a lifetime to find her again. Death could only bring him peace . . .

The old man wrenched his consciousness back to the present, with supreme effort, the words of the Torah burning in his ears . . . *for the L-rd your G-d puts you to proof, to know whether ye do love the L-rd your G-d with all your heart and with all your soul.*

Peter could see how well the poisoned barb had been set in the old man's heart by the malevolent Intelligence; he turned on the Demon, furious at its wanton malice.

"I exorcise you, Most Unclean Spirit!" he thundered. " 'Invading Enemy! All Spirits! Everyone of you! In the Name of . . .' "

"Speak to me, gentlemen!" the voice shrieked, drowning Peter out. "Speak to *me!* This will not do at all! Hiding behind the printed page. This is a *wrestling* match I've called you to, not a chess game! You'll sweat with me, or I'll kill the child before you ever finish reading from your stupid little book!"

To underscore the threat, the body on the altar began to bloat, its arms and legs filling up like balloons. Maggie stood transfixed, watching the horror happen, not knowing what to do. Cody's face was contorted with pain and an agonized groan issued from her lips.

"I order you to leave this child without harming her in any way!" the Rebbe commanded. "You have no power here!"

"No power!" The demon's shriek of outrage rattled the walls around them. "*I destroyed the Temple!*" The laughter echoed and reechoed, peal after peal, as if all the asylums in the world had loosed their most deranged inmates.

"I will use the Words of Power to dislodge . . ." the Rebbe began.

"Words of Power!" the demon cut him off, exultantly. "Oh, do let's talk of Words of Power. *Coward.* Craven. Recreant. Cur. Deserter. All they wanted from you was a *Name.* Don't you remember, *Liebchen?* Here . . . Let me help you . . ."

The Rebbe staggered backward, as a crashing blow seemed to strike his solar plexus; before he could recover his balance, he felt himself transported backward in time . . . *There were dead and dying all around him. They had taken him to the edge of a communal grave. Made him watch the men digging their final humiliation.*

*Made him watch the pathetic, skeletal humans, hardly
plumper than the shovels in their hands, as they were
clubbed or shot from behind by the laughing soldiers.
Made him listen to the sobs for mercy from those who,
not quite dead yet, felt the earth shoveled in on top of
them.*

*"You can save them!" they had told him. "Tell us the
Name." But his lips had been sealed and the men had
died, although their agony had lodged within him, forever.*

*Then they had shown him the women and children in
the hospital; the starved and the gangrenous and the
dying. "You can save them," they had told him. "Tell
us the Name!" But he had remained steadfast, although
his heart was shredded and bleeding in his breast.*

*Then they had shown him his beloved. Devorah of the
gentle eyes and gentler heart. Mother of his children,
companion of his soul. The one true love there would
ever be.*

*She was naked in the room, trying to cover her hun-
ger-shrunken breasts with her hands, as they fondled
her. She had not begged for mercy, where none could
be, but tears from her beautiful desperate eyes had glistened in the harsh glow of the naked light bulb on the
ceiling. And, they had pushed him into the room to
watch. She had died then, he knew, in her soul. He had
caught her eyes with his own and seen the horror and
humiliation that was more terrible than death.*

*"You can save her!" they had said. "Tell us the
Name!"*

"Rebbe. *Rebbe!*" Peter was shouting and shaking the
Rebbe by the shoulders. "Listen to me! The demon is
doing this to you! You *must* listen to me!"

"I couldn't tell them," the old man whispered,
trapped in his own undoing. Peter knew the demon could
do that, leeching on to your inmost horror and exploiting
it from within, so you felt defenseless, ravaged, undone.
And the Rebbe was old . . . it took great physical

strength to withstand an assault of this magnitude. "The hidden Name of God, they wanted," he murmured. "Not even to save her, could I speak it . . ."

"No. No! Of course not," Peter soothed, holding the fierce old man, made frail by anguish. "They were the People of the Lie, Rebbe! They would not have kept their bargain. You did what you had to do."

Peter turned to face the demon, fury raging in him at this unspeakable evil that crushed whatever stood in its path. Just as it would all humanity, unless it could be stopped.

"You issued this invitation for *me*, demon!" he shouted, trying to master his own wrath. "Let us find out why?" It was dangerous to depart from the prescribed ritual. *"Never engage the Entity, my boy!"* It was the one admonition no one must ever transgress. But he needed to provoke it out into the open.

Cody turned her unseeing eyes toward Peter, her mouth in a hideous sneer. "An egotist to the end," the demon laughed with satisfaction. "Certain as always, that *you're* the star attraction. But that's all right, Peter, dear. We'll have some fun. You have more faults to play with than the old man."

Peter forced his eyes back to the book. *I must not let this creature bait me, or we are lost.* He began to recite again: " *'He who commands you is He who ordered you to be thrown down from the Highest Heaven into the depths of Hell. He who commands you is He who dominated the sea, the wind, and the stars. Hear therefore, and fear, Satan! Enemy of Faith. Enemy of the human race!'* "

"Oh, the human race!" the voiced hissed. "The dunghill race! *Cadaver race!* Don't you fucking well know you've already *lost* the race! We've got all the cards in our hands, Peter the Cheater! Do you really think the human race wants *God* to win, you ecclesiastical asshole? Have you ever seen any indication whatsoever that the world *isn't on our side?* Take a look around you!

"Your beloved humans rape and torture and maim and kill. For greed and avarice, and even for their trumped-up sanctimonious ideals. Men wage war on each other to extinction! Why, they even wage war on their own planet, now that technology allows that. Your lovely human race is so greedy it'll suck up the ozone, until every living thing is dead of cancer. It'll destroy the forests, so there's no more air to breathe, and poison the streams and rivers, until nothing can live that isn't mutant.

"And let us not forget man's inhumanity to man, Peter my holy-go-pious fool!" Peter could feel his mind sliding, slipping away . . . He struggled to pull it back, when the Rebbe's voice broke through to him, intoning a prayer.

"Hofked alav rasha v' Satan al y' min . . ." Peter tried desperately to concentrate on the Hebrew words, as the Rebbe began the verse, again, this time backward. There were certain Kabbalistic formulae, Peter remembered, that could call up angelic forces . . .

He forced his eyes back to the page, grateful for the Rebbe's reinforcement, and relentlessly began again: " *'God, creator and defender of the Human Race, look on this your servant . . .'* "

"Creator and defender of the human race, indeed!" the demon mocked. "Peter the soiled priest, trying to debate with your betters . . . But I won't hold that against you. Instead, I might even offer you a sporting chance to *win!* Of course you'll have to accept my challenge to do so."

The voice took on a seductive tone. "I can give you each your heart's desires, you know . . ." it cajoled. "Every man has his price. Behold, what I offer . . ."

Again, visions rose within them. This time, of their most secret dreams . . . and oh, it was hard to push them away, for to each he showed the one thing needed more than life itself. The one desperate vulnerability of the heart and soul . . . And what were these foolish Amulets, after all, compared to such compelling needs?

And why should such a burden fall on the shoulders of the merely human . . .

ELLIE rounded the last corner of the basement labyrinth and hit the stairway, just as two of Abraham's men did.

One seized her left arm as she attempted to run past him. The bloodied sickle axe in her right hand whizzed through the air so fast, the man was down before his companion could cover him.

"*Let her go!*" Abraham's voice rang out in the echoing dark of the corridor. "Let the woman through!"

She was down the stairs and at their side in seconds, staring at the arch before them, with a deep frown of concentration on her face.

Warrior. Abraham noted. He knew her from the dossier, but this he hadn't known. This one gives no quarter. She had most likely just killed his man, but there were no girlish protestations of remorse on her lips, just concentration on the objective.

"They're in there, Ellie," Devlin said quickly. "We can't get through."

Ellie nodded, moved forward to touch the forcefield with her hand, then stepped back to examine the carvings on the spandrel. There were sigils and figures, as well as the carved writings to be deciphered.

"It's called the *Devil's Doorway*," she said finally. "It says, 'Who enters here, enters Hell.' The words 'Maa Kheru' open the Gates of Hell . . . this must be one of them. Probably an energy vortex of some kind that allows easy passage back and forth from the demonic dimensions."

"Look, Ellie," Devlin interjected. "I'll believe it's Club Med for Demons, if you can just get me in there."

Ellie shook her head. "Eric's sealed the sanctuary with the help of powerful forces, Dev. I can't undo that alone . . . I'll have to ask help from my ancestors, and the Angelic Plane. But I'll see what I can do."

She turned to Abraham. "I assume the soldiers are yours?" He nodded yes.

"Keep them, and everything else, away from me, while I'm in trance. My nervous system will be vulnerable to sound and impact."

She turned toward Devlin. "We're deep within the earth here—I'll ask the spirits of my Cherokee ancestors to entreat the Earth Mother to aid us. Indian magic has purer roots than Eric's—there's no Black Magic for a Cherokee. All magic, like all life, belongs to the Great Spirit. That may give us an edge."

With that, she turned her face to the portal, raised her arms in a Shaman's salute to the Powers of the Four Directions, and asked entry to the Shadow World. Minutes passed before she began to chant, a low moaning sound at first, then a rising resonance that filled the cavernous space like the roar of a waterfall in a box canyon.

The air vibrated around them in an escalating frequency that made the hair on the men's necks stand on end. The blackness of the portal began to shimmer under the archway, like an iridescent curtain rippled by the wind.

"Go when the shimmer fades!" Ellie rasped hoarsely; it was easy to see it was taking all her power to battle back the forces protecting the sanctuary. "I can't break the seal, but I can weaken it enough to get us through."

Both men poised themselves to wait for the moment they could charge . . .

MAGGIE dragged herself back from the brink of acceptance of the demon's offer, shocked at her own weakness. She caught Peter's eyes with her own, and saw in him the same terror that pounded in her own breast. She wondered what it was he'd dreamed . . . She saw him pull himself together again with desperate concentration, to face down the enemy. The Presence saw it, too.

"So our sacerdotal excrescence girds for the fray, does he?" it baited. "Does this mean you have realized this is not your average garden-variety exorcism, pious Peter?"

"It means that I accept your challenge," Peter replied evenly. "Name it!"

*Never engage the demon in conversation, my boy. Only your pride makes you think you can win.*

"How delicious," the demon voice crackled. "The sinner-in-priest's-clothing steps out from behind his little book, does he? Well, my challenge is very simple, really. All you need do is *prove* to me that Good is stronger than Evil. Of course, you'll never pull *that* off because your world is now, and ever shall be, the true crucible of Evil. *Behold!*"

Perversions rose in the minds of each person in the room; against their wills they saw the Holocaust . . . the Killing Fields . . . Caligula's court. Children molested, old women murdered in their beds. The oil fires of Kuwait, cadaverous bodies behind barbed-wire fences. Torturers at their trade, grinning over the mutilated bodies of their victims. Armies clashing, and sirens shattering eardrums . . . pain beyond endurance rose in each of them, pummeling them, assaulting every sensibility. Man's inhumanity to man, too fearsome for the soul to contemplate . . .

Maggie groaned despite herself, but Peter and the Rebbe held their ground against the onslaught, and quickly as it had come, the wall of thought subsided.

Peter drew himself up to his full stature with immense effort. "*That* isn't *all* we are!" he shouted fiercely. "We are so much *more!* We humans are capable of loving one another, without thought of self. No greed. No avarice. No self-aggrandizement. Only love. Mothers sacrifice a kidney to save a dying child . . . fathers slave in coal mines, knowing they'll spit up their lungs piecemeal, to provide a better life for their children. Christian families saved Jewish children from the Nazis at the cost of their own lives. Men have allowed themselves to be tortured to save a comrade. They don't do these things for profit, or for fame . . . they do it out of *goodness*. There are a million unsung acts of selfless heroism every hour of every day, that counterbalance any horror you could possibly conjure up."

"It is not enough!" the demon rasped. "At best it would only be a draw."

And suddenly, Peter knew what he'd been called to do. All his life, every moment of seeking God, had been in preparation for this moment. *When a sacrifice has been promised, a sacrifice must be made.*

"I know how to defeat you, demon!" he cried out in a clear, ringing voice. "I will trade you my life for the child's!"

Maggie gasped aloud and the Rebbe stepped toward Peter. The demon roared with laughter and the air shook around them like half-done Jell-O.

"I don't want *you*, you arrogant *nothing*," it spat. "I want it all! The child. The Amulets. All the power in the world! What are *you* compared to that? An intellectually pretentious failure of a priest? Why, you even failed at being a heretic!

"I don't want *you* . . . you're *nothing*. Do you understand me? Nothing. Nothing. *Nothing!*"

The contempt in the demon's voice breached Peter's last defenses. The words reverberated somewhere deep inside, flaying him, laying him bare and bleeding. He had offered the ultimate sacrifice of self, so certain it would be *enough*. The absolute rejection shocked him, humiliated him. He felt he could see his soul, its flaws displayed like open wounds. He had *used* Maggie to tease his self-identity into being . . . he had loathed his superiors' frailties, but not his own . . . he had sought God through the mind, when only the heart was real . . .

All meaning in his life was obliterated in an anguished instant of annihilation . . . all he had been, all he could *never be*, burst across his brain like a cosmic hailstorm. *Eli! Eli! Lama sabachthani! My God! My God! Why hast Thou forsaken me?*

Desolation of the soul . . . no place left to go . . . *no place left to hide* . . .

The Seal crackled behind them. Ellie shouted a triumphant "Ho!" and collapsed to her knees before the opening of the portal, as Devlin raced through the archway toward Maggie. Rafi, try as he might, could not force his way through the barrier . . .

"You're not permitted in!" Ellie shouted to him. "Only those who believe . . ." Then she followed where Dev had led, and Rafi, confounded by his inability to follow, stood in the shadow of the ancient arch, staring inward. At least, he now could see quite clearly what was happening within the chamber.

The interior was littered like a charnel house with the remains of Eric's last encounter with the demons. And the body of the child, now bloated and grotesque, seemed almost to float above the stone altar.

Cody's contorted face whipped around to greet the entry of the new arrivals, its demonic eyes focusing on Devlin.

"*Help me, Daddy!*" it cried out, in the voice of a dying little boy. "It *hurts* me, Daddy!"

Devlin stopped dead in his tracks. The child on the altar wasn't Cody anymore. *Daniel's* fragile face was turned to his, blood trickling from his nose and mouth, a ragged bloody hole where his chest should have been. The child opened his lips to speak again, but it was his *eyes* that riveted everyone in the room. Helpless terror and pleading were in those eyes. *Help me, Daddy*, they begged. *Don't let me die!*

"No!" Devlin cried out, wildly. "No!" He ran toward the dying child, as a shock wave hit him like a wall of buckshot. And suddenly, the pain of dying was within his own body. Pain. Fear. Life being sucked from him through the hole in his own chest. Draining. Fading. Dying with his son.

Devlin battled back the agony with every ounce of strength he possessed. He forced the illusion from his brain, rooting it out mercilessly. *This was not Daniel!*

This beleaguered child was *Cody*, only Cody. And he would save her, no matter what it cost him. This time he would not fail.

With a shout wrenched from a place beyond pain, he forced his way forward, and lunged for the body on the altar.

A sound hurtful as clenched fists to the eardrums rent the space. An electrical ion storm crashed in around Devlin, skewering him with its white-hot lightning, seizing him in its explosive power, thrusting and tearing him simultaneously, as if he'd touched a high-tension wire. The force of it lifted his body, arcing it off the ground with a thunderous crack, until seconds later, it dropped in a crumpled heap on the floor at Maggie's feet. She could see the wounds, smell the burning flesh; she felt she had endured it all with him empathically, just as now she felt his encroaching death. She dropped to her knees beside his body, but Devlin was far beyond her help.

The *thing* on the altar was laughing, the self-satisfied cackle of conscienceless evil. *It* wasn't her grandchild anymore, it was the Enemy, and Cody was completely at its mercy. As were they all. Suddenly, Maggie was filled with a righteous rage beyond anything she had ever known. *This* was not just about Cody anymore. This was about every vile act that had ever been perpetrated on suffering humanity by the forces of Evil.

She sprang to her feet, shouting "Coward!" to the Presence that engulfed the small body. "Using children to play your filthy games. Don't hide behind a three-year-old! Come out and fight with the *grown-ups!*" Her voice was fierce, derisive.

"Don't engage it! Maggie," Peter cried out. "You can't possibly win!"

"So, the mother of a drug addict has the audacity to fight for a child, does she?" the voice mocked her contemptuously. "And where were you when your daughter put that needle in her arm? *Mother?* Why didn't you save that one? You could have, if you'd cared enough."

"Don't listen!" the Rebbe commanded. "He is the Prince of Lies. He wounds you to weaken you!" He moved in closer to the child on the altar, his lips moving in some prayer or incantation.

"Don't get caught up in it, Maggie!" Peter begged. "Don't speak to it directly."

"That's right, protect your paramour!" the evil thing shrieked gleefully. Cody's body was discoloring into large splotches of blue and purple, as if it had been hideously beaten. The bloated head turned to Maggie, and the soul that mocked her through its opened eyes was not Cody's.

"You think you can fight me, do you, cunt?" it hissed through the child's bleeding lips. *"Failed mother.* Mother of the Damned! So fucking willing to fight for this one you let us carve up the other one for fun! Listen to your friends. You can't fight me!"

But something was happening to Maggie, and she wasn't afraid anymore.

"Oh, yes I can!" she shouted back. "You cowardly son of a bitch—women have been fighting you since the dawn of time!"

"The *Abyss, Mim!"* Ellie shouted. She slapped Maggie violently between the shoulder blades. "The lesson of the Abyss!"

And it all came flooding back. *"At the moment of truth, trust only your heart. All else is illusion."*

And suddenly she knew. She *did* have the power! Of every good deed that had ever been done since time began. Of every selfless act of love and courage in the whole, long history of humanity. Of every woman who had ever fought for a child against the odds.

"You can *kill* me, demon," she shouted at the *thing* on the altar, "but you can't *win*, because *I own my own soul. That's my power*, and it comes from God!

"So you can take your threats and your bribes . . . I reject them, as I reject you. You can take these Amulets and all the riches and power they could ever provide— take them back with you to Hell, for all we care. Mankind doesn't need them or want them. We'll muddle along just the way we are in our imperfection, because it's our imperfection that makes us great.

"We struggle against the odds that are meant to break us and we *prevail. Do you hear me? We prevail!* We light one candle instead of cursing the darkness . . . and then we light a thousand more of them, or a million, until the likes of you are blinded by their brilliance. If we were perfect, there'd be no heroism in our goodness. As it is, we reach for God with clumsy hands, but still *we reach!* We *love*, and you *cannot* . . . and because we love you can *never* win. Because there will *always* be goodness and mercy and heroism, as long as imperfect humanity is capable of love. And love is as much part of us as our blood and bone. It is our one glorious *perfection*.

"And one day, maybe eons from now, we'll no longer be imperfect, because we've made that steady climb, *despite* you. And when that day dawns, you and all your evil Kingdom will cease to be. So, don't talk to me of power! *Coward*. Yours is temporary and ours is eternal, because it comes from God."

The demon hissed with fury. "You have no weapon to use against me!" it roared.

"You don't know much about *grandmothers!*" Maggie spat back. "But how could you? We're on the *other side!*" She was feeling her own Power, *knowing* finally where it came from.

"I know your Achilles heel, demon!" she shouted. "You can't *take* me, without my permission. You can only *seduce*. And I'm not *buying*. I *reject you*, with all the power of my immortal soul. You can't have me and you can't have Cody. *She didn't choose you*. And neither did I. *And we never will!*"

A thunderous rending sound was heard before her words had died away, and a rushing of winds rattled through the space, as if the chamber had been plucked up by a tornado and cast out into the heavens.

So many things happened simultaneously she could

never afterward be certain in what order they had manifested. She saw the Presence blink out in Cody, like an extinguished light bulb . . . saw an unearthly radiance illuminate the primordial dark.

Some part of Cody rose from the altar, and stood with Maggie, but the ethereal form was no longer that of a child. The young priestess raised her hand in ritual salutation and spoke in a voice of unimaginable sweetness.

"Hail Guardian. The Mother sends you greetings."

Maggie touched her hand to that of the luminous apparition.

"Hail Messenger," she replied steadily. "Thank you for showing me the Way."

Ellie smiled in the darkness; she had waited a very long time for this moment, and she had kept the faith.

The Isis Messenger knelt beside Devlin's body and touched the glowing Amulet to his injured face, and Maggie knew in her soul that his life had been returned to him. Then the celestial apparition stood again, and smiled at Maggie one last time, before she shimmered into nothingness, and only the child remained.

Cody sat up, and looked around the room.

"You came back to get me, Mim?" she whispered softly, joyously. "I knew you'd come."

"Yes, sweetheart," Maggie murmured, taking the child in her arms. "I came back to get you."

"I love you, Mim," the little girl said, smiling. "I want to go home."

Raphael Abraham stood riveted on the other side of the doorway, although the seal had vanished. What had he seen here? What had he heard? What manner of battle had been fought in this place? Profoundly shaken, he waited for the Rebbe to emerge from the chamber.

"What has happened here, Rebbe?" he demanded. "I *must* know. You must tell me."

"We have seen why God has made woman the heart of our faith," the Rebbe replied, with an infinitesimal smile.

"But the Light, the Voices . . . never have I seen anything like that in my life."

"Then you must be sure to say a prayer of thanks for the great gift you have been given."

"But the *Amulets*, Rebbe. What of the Amulets?"

"If I told you we could not save the child *and* the Amulets, what would you say then?"

"I would say what is the life of one child, Rebbe, if the good of the many are at stake? We have made a foolish choice."

"And, if I told you the Amulets had been banished back to Eternity by the woman's deeds, because mankind has not yet developed the strength of character required to possess such potent weapons?"

Abraham smiled sardonically. "That, too, would seem to me a foolish choice."

The Rebbe smiled. "So," he said. "Now you have learned for yourself why mankind cannot be trusted to choose wisely enough to possess such weapons."

"And of these choices that have been made here, Rebbe?" Abraham asked, "When I answer for my mission to the Prime Minister, what exactly do you expect me to tell him?"

The Rebbe's expression was stern, but his eyes were merry. "You may tell him there are Higher Powers than he, who have been served today."

Abraham left the old rabbi, to return to his men; he was shaken, awed, bewildered. He would have to decide what to tell them . . . what to tell his superiors. What to tell *himself*.

He shook his head to clear it, and walked outside the Vannier house to stare at the sea. The night air refreshed him. He looked up at the moon and the pinprick stars that blanketed the heavens, and for the first time since he was a boy, he asked the God of his Uncle Schlomo to hear his prayers.

# CHAPTER 87

There was an air of unreality for Maggie in the days that followed. The world of ordinary, everyday events seemed almost alien in the wake of the bizarre experiences of the past three months.

Devlin had suffered the burns and internal injuries usually associated with electrocution, the doctors said, and they'd kept him in intensive care for forty-eight hours, before he began a steady recovery. Gino assured her the Lieutenant was far too much of a pain in the ass for Heaven to want to deal with him. He also told her that the Screamers had been freed and hospitalized, that Ghania was dead, and that the bodies found at the Vannier estate had been attributed, in the media, to the work of a political terrorist organization out of Libya. She already knew from Ellie the truth of Ghania's death.

They managed to keep Dev in the hospital for nearly two weeks, and Maggie spent a great deal of time at his bedside trying to come to terms with what she felt for him, and with the aftermath of all they'd endured. He was an impossible patient, once he was well enough to break the rules, and she felt a profound sense of relief when he finally grew cranky enough to complain about being cooped up; his complaints seemed so human, and so alive.

She went to Mass at St. Joseph's every morning, for Peter, as well as for Dev. Peter had said extraordinary things to her, after their ordeal was over; words that still played and replayed in her mind.

"It was stripped away, Maggie!" he'd told her, the

582

metamorphosis still animating his eyes, as they'd stood in the hospital lobby awaiting news of Devlin. "All of it. The pride, the intellectual gifts, the hubris, the paradox . . . all stripped away so I could see my soul laid bare.

"When the demon rejected my offer of sacrifice, I was utterly undone . . . For the first time in my entire life, I was *nothing*. It humbled me into the Truth—that God didn't love me *because* of my great gifts, but *despite* them! That all my life I'd sought Him through intellect, when He can only be reached through love! I finally understood where I'd been trying to go, when I turned that corner and lost my way. In that blinding darkness, Maggie, I found my way home."

And she'd nodded, too overwhelmed by all that had happened, to reply.

"There's a term used when the theology of the Reign of God is taught, Maggie," he went on, the emotion of what he'd undergone in his voice. "*Prolepsis*. It's a forehappening . . . a precursor to the final future. I believe Cody is a *prolepsis* of the future of mankind . . . We've been promised by God that the time will come when men and women will live beyond the anomalies, and the conflicts, and the savaging—when we will live fully in the grace of God. I think she's been sent to remind us of that. *Bless her!* I say, Maggie. Bless the child and all she means for humanity."

He had a great deal of work to do, he'd said, and the renewed vigor with which to do it.

It occurred to her, on the walk home from church on the fifteenth of May, that it was only a little more than two weeks since all their lives had nearly come to an end; and in some ways, it felt an eternity. She had a sudden, overwhelming impulse to gather all those who had given so much—to say thank you from the heart, and to celebrate life.

MARIA APARECIDA was playing jacks with Cody on the kitchen floor, as she waited, with the precise timing of a surgeon, for the roast to turn the proper shade of pink. Maria, too, had changed with all that had happened; Maggie had not heard a single grumble about anything large or small, since Cody came home.

"God sorts the sheep from the goats, dona Maggie," she had pronounced, when Maggie had placed the child in her waiting arms. "The Good Shepherd always leaves the flock to find the lost lamb."

Now the sounds of their mingled laughter heartened Maggie, as she sat on the big chintz couch in her living room, a cushion away from Devlin.

He looked thinner, she thought as she watched him, and he moved carefully, but his mood was good, if pensive.

"There's a lot I've been needing to say to you, Maggie," he began, reaching for her hand across the cushion. "And I'd like to say it before everybody arrives, tonight." He stopped, obviously juggling thoughts and emotions.

"I love you, Maggie O'Connor. More than I ever thought I could love anybody . . . and I'd like the chance to find out if we can have a future together. I figure I can't ask you to live the life of a cop's wife—I think the fear that goes along with that would curdle your soul— but I've been thinking, there must be something I could do with that law degree, besides decorate my apartment. I can't see myself on Wall Street or anything like that, but maybe I could find a way to use what I know to do some good in the world. If there's one thing all this has taught me, it's that whatever each of us can do for the good, we better do it, now." He took a deep breath, and caught her eyes with his own.

"Give me a chance not to lose you and Cody, Maggie. I love you more than you know."

Maggie touched her fingers to his lips, as if she could hold back these words that demanded decisions.

"I love you, too, Dev," she said slowly, carefully.

"But I'm too battered right now, to know much more than that. I think I need some time to understand all that's happened to me. Where I've been . . . *where I'm going*. In the space of the last three months, the world as I knew it has come to an end. Nothing is exactly as I thought . . ." She bit her underlip, a young girl's gesture. How could she possibly express all the ways in which life had forced her to expand, exponentially. She wasn't even sure she knew yet who she had become.

"Love's been a little bit hard on me, lately, Dev. If you'll just give me some time to put my heart back together before I ask anything of it, I promise not to take the love you've offered me lightly."

Devlin brushed a strand of dark hair back from her cheek. "You'll see, Maggie," he said, relieved that she hadn't said no. "One of these days the light will hit me in a certain way and you won't be able to resist . . ." They laughed together, and it felt right.

"Dev," she said musingly, "what do you think really happened to us that incredible night? How much of what we think we saw was real? I keep going over and over it all in my head—one minute I'm certain, and the next, my rational mind rebels."

He shrugged. "I don't know, Maggie. The Coast Guard said there were no heavy seas in the Sound except for the exact few minutes it took to swamp Ellie's boat. You *saw* those entities emerge from Cody and Ghania. You *saw* the Amulet and the Stone materialize. I saw Daniel in that infernal portal . . . hell, I even died with him . . . and yet I'm sitting here tonight. Who could possibly explain all that?"

Maggie nodded. "Ellie swears that Jenna helped her put an end to that beast, Ghania, and I *want* to believe that, because in a way it redeems her . . ." She let the thought drift off, confused and uncertain. "But what does all this mean for Cody and me, if it's real . . . what does it mean for the rest of our lives, and the rest of humanity, for that matter?"

" 'Do not seek to know more than is appropriate . . .' "

Devlin replied quietly; in his world, knowledge always seemed to bring pain. "Saint Augustine said that of man's struggle to understand the notion of Good and Evil, Maggie. He was a smart guy."

"But do *you* think we had supernatural help in saving Cody, Dev?" she persisted. "Just your opinion, not Saint Augustine's. I think it's important that I know for sure, what you believe about all this. Did Sekhmet and those satanists really try to steal Cody's Ka? Or was that some crazy mass hallucination, provoked by that ghastly place and the emotional horror of all we went through? Was a battle really fought in some other dimension for Cody's soul, or was that just a figment of Peter's, and the Rebbe's, and my own overpowering belief in God? Is it really *possible* that we were all joined by a bond of love that endured for millennia . . . or did we all just need to believe that, so we could live with what's happened to us?

"I feel as if I need to know so *many* things . . ." She shook her head, still lost in the enormity of all they experienced.

Devlin grinned suddenly. "I'd like to be able to tell you it was all superior police work that saved the day," he said, "but that'd be a bigger stretch for your imagination than all the rest put together."

Maggie laughed out loud; it was apparent he no longer thoroughly *dis*-believed, and that was important to her. Maybe they could figure it all out together.

"I guess the biggest question left is what happens next?" she said, pushing the imponderables back a little. "Do you think any members of Maa Kheru will be prosecuted? For Jenna's murder, or the kidnapping? Or, for anything at all?"

Devlin shook his head, too knowledgeable for optimism. "It looks to me like the fix is already in, Maggie. Too many prominent names . . . too much money changing hands . . . too many people calling William Kunstler and F. Lee Bailey on the hot line, I imagine. Besides, Eric, Nicky, and Ghania are dead, so who's to get blamed for the Screamers, and Jenna, and everything else that went on down in that hell house? I think we just have to content ourselves with the fact that God seems to have provided His own justice, rather than waiting for ours." He paused for inventory.

"At least the bastards didn't get the Amulet or the Stone. Imagine what those sons of bitches could have done to the world with tools like that in their hands? Anyway, after what happened to Eric, it seems Satan's pissed off at them, for getting trounced . . . And you have to admit it was a nice touch that the demon himself did in that son of a bitch."

Maggie nodded. "You know, Ellie told me a funny thing . . . she could have tipped us off earlier about Hazred being on the wrong team, if I'd ever mentioned his name. It seems *Abdul Hazred* is the name of one of the gatekeepers of Hell—but I just kept calling him 'the Egyptian . . .'."

Devlin laughed. "It does look as if we were being manipulated by unseen hands, doesn't it?" he said, leaning back with a sigh. "My mother would have gotten some kick out of seeing me tangled up in the world of spooks and spirits." He smiled at her memory, then looked at Maggie and said, "I just keep thinking I'm glad it's over and you're safe."

"And, I keep wanting there to be a more tangible justice, Dev," Maggie replied, ruefully. "There were a lot of powerful, influential people at that Sabbat, who are still out there doing their dirty work. If nobody gets punished, and the world never knows what really happened to us, maybe Camus was right, and 'The reign of the Beast has begun.'"

"Maybe. Or maybe we've just been reminded that here on earth, God's work must surely be our own."

Maggie smiled. "I think we did get a chance to help Him out, at least a little, and his friend Isis, too, come to think of it. Didn't we, Dev? And whatever it was that happened to us, Cody's safe now. The child psychologist I took her to says she's astonishingly healthy, considering all they did to her. And now, she's free to be just a regular little girl again. She doesn't have to fend off demons, or save the world, or do anything except love us and be loved. And she never has to hear the word 'Amulet' again! From here on in, she can just have a plain old ordinary childhood, like every other three-year-old in America.''

The doorbell rang and Maggie ran to greet Ellie and Amanda, who had arrived simultaneously. Peter and Gino would be along any minute. Everyone laughed and hugged and made a fuss over Cody, until it was her bedtime, when Maggie lifted the child she loved so much into her arms, and carried her happily up the stairs to tuck her in.

CODY smiled at Mim from underneath the pink-and-white-checkered coverlet; it was so good to be home. So good to be loved so completely.

Mim blew her a last kiss from the doorway, and closed the bedroom door behind her. Cody listened for the old familiar football on the stair. She knew everyone they loved had come to their house for a special dinner party, tonight; Cody could hear the soft music playing on the stereo, and knew that tomorrow Maria Aparecida would have saved the best goodies from dessert, for her lunch.

Cody waited until she was certain Mim was downstairs, then she slipped out of bed, and walked to the window. It was a beautiful, clear night; the stars twinkled brilliantly as fireflies, and a gentle breeze billowed the organdy curtains, where Mim had left the window open a crack for fresh air.

The child stood for a long moment, staring up at the crescent moon outside, seemingly lost in reverie. She had quite a lot to think about.

Finally, she held out her hand, so that a moonbeam fell across the open palm. She murmured a few words in an ancient tongue; there was no longer the lisp of childhood in her speech, but rather, the authority of one who knows her mission.

The Isis Amulet materialized solidly in her little palm; the fire of its rich gold and precious gem exterior gleamed with a most unearthly radiance.

Cody smiled. It was a sweet, well-satisfied smile, thousands of years older than her small body.

"These humans have great potential, Mother," she murmured proudly. "You did well to believe in them."

Then, with a gesture only she had ever known, the Isis Messenger tucked the Amulet away, somewhere in the Cosmos, for safekeeping.

The time of Choice would one day come again.

She would be ready.

# AUTHOR'S ENDNOTE

Mysticism lives in the genes of the Celts, as Malachy
Devlin would say. Because my family is Irish, volatile,
literate, and psychic, researching *Bless the Child* became for me, in turns, a lark, a spiritual challenge, an
intellectual odyssey, and a crash course in hands-on
mysticism. It led me to a great deal of esoteric knowledge, only a fraction of which could be contained within
the framework of my story, without running longer than
the Harvard Shelf of Books. So . . . in the event that
any of the fertile subjects I've touched upon in *Bless the
Child* may intrigue you enough to want to pursue them,
I'd like to offer the following partial bibliography.

# BIBLIOGRAPHY

### EXORCISM

*Hostage to the Devil*, Malachi Martin, Reader's Digest
Press
*People of the Lie*, M. Scott Peck, Simon & Schuster

591

## REINCARNATION

*The World Within*, Gina Cerminara, Sloane
*The Search for Omm Sety*, Jonathan Cott, Doubleday
*Many Lives, Many Masters*, Barry Weiss, MD, Simon &
Schuster

## KABBALAH

*Kabbalah*, Gershom Scholem, Meridian
*On the Mystical Shape of the Godhead*, Gershom Scholem,
Schocken
*Kabbalah for the Layman, Volumes I, II, III*, Dr. Phillip
S. Berg
*A Kabbalah for the Modern World*, Migene Gonzales-Wip-
pler, Llewellyn
*The Mystical Kabbalah*, Dion Fortune, Ben Publishing Re-
search Center for the Kabbalah

## CHRISTIAN MYSTICISM

*The Phenomenon of Man*, Pierre Teilhard de Chardin,
Harper
*The Seven Storey Mountain*, Thomas Merton, Harcourt
Brace Jovanovich

## METAPHYSICS, PHYSICS, AND THE UNSEEN
UNIVERSE

*The Secret Teachings of the Ages*, Manly P. Hall, Philo-
sophical Research Society
*The Tao of Physics*, Fritjof Capra, Bantam
*Uncommon Wisdom*, Fritjof Capra, Bantam
*The Dancing Wu Li Masters*, Gary Zukav, Bantam
*Quantum Reality*, Nick Herbert, Anchor

## MAGIC

*The Training and Work of an Initiate*, Dion Fortune, Weiser
*The Cosmic Doctrine*, Dion Fortune, Helios
*Enochian Physics*, Gerald J. Schueler, Llewellyn

## HEALING

*Quantum Healing*, Deepak Chopra, MD, Bantam
*Unconditional Life*, Deepak Chopra, MD, Bantam
*Hands of Light*, Barbara Brennan, Bantam
*Vibrational Medicine*, Richard Gerber, MD, Bear & Co.
*The Body Electric*, Robert O. Becker, MD, Morrow

## ANCIENT EGYPTIAN MAGIC

*Egyptian Magic*, E.A. Wallace Budge, Dover
*Egyptian Magic*, Florence Farr, Aquarian
*Egypt—The Syrius Connection*, Hope Murray, Element
*The Secret Teachings of the Temple of Isis*, Ishbel, Llewellyn
*Initiation in the Great Pyramid*, Earlyne Chaney, Astara

## CHINESE MEDICINE

*The Web That Has No Weaver*, Ted J. Kaptchuk, OMD, Congdon and Weed
*Acupuncture for Everyone*, Dr. Ruth Lever, Penguin
*The Energy Within*, Richard Chin, MD, OMD, Paragon
*The Foundations of Chinese Medicine*, Giovani Maciocia, Churchill Livingstone

## INDIAN WISDOM

*Black Elk, The Sacred Ways of a Lakota*, Wallace Black Elk, Harper and Row
*Lame Deer, Seeker of Visions*, John Lame Deer and Richard Erdoes, Washington Square
*Fools Crow*, Thomas E. Mails, University of Nebraska

*Buffalo Woman Comes Singing*, Brooke Medicine Eagle, Ballantine
*The Wisdomkeepers*, Steve Wall, Beyond Words

## PERSONAL JOURNEYS TOWARD ENLIGHTENMENT

*Medicine Woman*, Lynn V. Andrews
*The Way of the Peaceful Warrior*, Hillman, HJ Kramer
*Ecstacy Is a New Frequency*, Chris Griscom, Bear & Co.
*Dancing in the Light*, Shirley MacLaine, Bantam
*Hidden Journey*, Andrew Harvey, Holt
*Journey to Ladakh*, Andrew Harvey, Houghton Mifflin

## GRANDPARENTS-AS-PARENTS SUPPORT GROUPS

*Grandparents as Parents*, Sylvie de Toledo, 2801 Atlantic Avenue, Long Beach, CA 90801
*Grandparents Raising Children*, Barbara Kirkland, P.O. Box 104, Cloyeville, TX 76034
*Second Time Around Parents*, Michele Daily, Family and Community Service of Delaware County, 100 W. Front Street, Media, PA 19063

# By the year 2000, 2 out of 3 Americans could be illiterate.

It's true.

Today, 75 million adults... about one American in three, can't read adequately. And by the year 2000, U.S. News & World Report envisions an America with a literacy rate of only 30%.

Before that America comes to be, you can stop it... by joining the fight against illiteracy today.

Call the Coalition for Literacy at toll-free **1-800-228-8813** and volunteer.

## Volunteer Against Illiteracy. The only degree you need is a degree of caring.

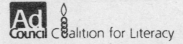

Ad Council  Coalition for Literacy

Warner Books is proud to be an active supporter of the Coalition for Literacy.